BEAR ISLAND

A film unit sets sail for a deserted island north of the Arctic Circle. But what begins as a routine trip for the charter ship *Morning Rose* turns into a whirlpool of murderous intrigue.

Bear Island is lonely, desolate and bathed in Arctic darkness most of the year—an eerie setting for the men and women who become caught in a web of violence. Is there a pathological killer in their midst? Does Bear Island guard a secret more valuable than five lives?

ALISTAIR MACLEAN

Bear Island

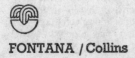

FONTANA / Collins

First published by Wm. Collins 1971
First issued in Fontana Books 1973

© Alistair MacLean 1971

Printed in Great Britain
Collins Clear-Type Press London and Glasgow

TO IAN AND MARJORY

CONDITIONS OF SALE:
This book is sold subject to the condition that
it shall not, by way of trade or otherwise, be lent,
re-sold, hired out or otherwise circulated without
the publisher's prior consent in any form of
binding or cover other than that in which it is
published and without a similar condition
including this condition being imposed on the
subsequent purchaser

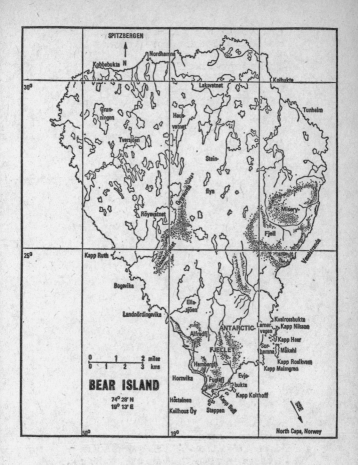

SPITZBERGEN

Nordhamna

Kobbebukta   N

Kolhukta

30°   Lakavatnet

Grun-
ningen   Haus-
vatnet   Tunheim

Tversjøen

Stein-
flya

Røyevatnet   Misery-
Fjell

25°   Kapp Ruth

Bogavika

Landnørdingsvika   Ella-
sjøen

Kvalrossbukta
Lerner-   Kapp Nilsson
vegen
Alfredfj   ANTARCTIC-   Kapp Haer
Sør-   Måkehl
hamna
FJELLET   Kapp Roalkvam
Kapp Malmgren
Hamberfj
Evje-
Hornvika   Fuglefj   bukta
Kapp Kolthoff
Høstelnen
Keilhous Øy   Stappen

0   1   2 miles
0   1   2   3 kms

BEAR ISLAND
74° 28' N
19° 13' E

SSE

50°   19°   North Cape, Norway

CHAPTER ONE

To even the least sensitive and perceptive beholder the *Morning Rose,* at this stage of her long and highly chequered career, must have seemed ill-named, for if ever a vessel could fairly have been said to be approaching, if not actually arrived at, the sunset of her days it was this one. Officially designated an Arctic Steam Trawler, the *Morning Rose,* 560 gross tons, 173 feet in length, 30 in beam and with a draught, unladen but fully provisioned with fuel and water, of 14.3 feet, had, in fact, been launched from the Jarrow slipways as far back as 1926, the year of the General Strike.

The *Morning Rose,* then, was far gone beyond the superannuation watershed, she was slow, creaking, unstable and coming apart at the seams. So were Captain Imrie and Mr Stokes. The *Morning Rose* consumed a great deal of fuel in relation to the foot-pounds of energy produced. So did Captain Imrie and Mr Stokes, malt whisky for Captain Imrie, Jamaican rum for Mr Stokes. And that was what they were doing now, stoking up on their respective fuels with the steadfast dedication of those who haven't attained septuagenarian status through sheer happenstance.

As far as I could see, none of the sparse number of diners at the two long fore-and-aft tables was stoking up very much on anything. There was a reason for this, of course, the same reason that accounted for the poor attendance at dinner that night. It was not because of the food which, while it wouldn't cause any sleepless nights in the kitchens of the Savoy, was adequate enough, nor was it because of any aesthetic objections our cargo of creative artists might have entertained towards the dining saloon's decor, which was, by any standards, quite superb: it was a symphony in teak furniture and wine-coloured carpets and curtains, not, admittedly, what one would look to find on the average trawler, but then, the average trawler, when its fishing days are over—as the *Morning Rose*'s were deemed to be in 1956—doesn't have the good fortune to be re-engined and converted to a luxury yacht by, of all people, a shipping millionaire whose enthusiasm for the sea was matched only by his massive ignorance of all things nautical.

The trouble tonight lay elsewhere, not within the ship but without. Three hundred miles north of the Arctic Circle, where we at the present moment had the debatable fortune to be, the weather conditions can be as beautifully peaceful as any on earth, with mirror-smooth, milky-white seas stretching from horizon to horizon under a canopy of either washed-out blue or stars that are less stars than little chips of frozen fire in a black, black sky. But those days are rare and, usually, to be found only in that brief period that passes for summer in those high latitudes. And whatever summer there had been was long gone. We were deep into late October now, the period of the classical equinoctial gales, and there was a real classical equinoctial beauty blowing up right then. Moxen and Scott, the two stewards, had prudently drawn the dining saloon curtains so that we couldn't see quite how classical it was.

We didn't have to see it. We could hear it and we could feel it. We could hear the wild threnody of the gale in the rigging, a high-pitched, ululating, atonic sound, as lonely, lost and eerie as a witch's lament. We could hear, at monotonously regular intervals, the flat explosive clap of sound as the bluff bows of the trawler crashed into the troughs of the steep-sided waves marching steadily eastwards under the goad of that bitter wind born on the immensity of the Greenland ice-cap, all of seven hundred miles away. We could hear the constantly altering variation in the depth of the engine note as the propeller surged upwards, almost clearing water level, then plunged deep down into the sea again.

And we could feel the storm, a fact that most of those present clearly found a great deal more distressing than just listening to it. One moment, depending upon which side of the fore-and-aft tables we were sitting, we would be leaning sharply to our left or right as the bows lurched and staggered up the side of a wave: the next, we would be leaning as sharply in the other direction as the stern, in turn, rode high on the crest of the same wave. To compound the steadily increasing level of misery and discomfort the serried ranks of waves beyond the damask drapes were slowly but ominously beginning to break down into confused seas which violently accentuated the *Morning Rose*'s typical fishing-boat propensity for rolling continuously in anything short of mill-pond conditions. The two different motions, lateral and transverse, were now combining to produce an extremely unpleasant corkscrewing effect indeed.

Because I'd spent most of the past eight years at sea, I wasn't experiencing any distressing symptoms myself, but I didn't have to be a doctor—which my paper qualifications declared me to be—to diagnose the symptoms of *mal de mer*. The wan smile, the gaze studiously averted from anything that resembled food, the air of rapt communication with the inner self, all the signs were there in plenty. A very mirth-provoking subject, sea-sickness, until one suffers from it oneself: then it ceases to be funny any more. I'd dispensed enough sea-sickness pills to turn them all buttercup-yellow, but these are about as effective against an Arctic gale as aspirin is against cholera.

I looked round and wondered who would be the first to go. Antonio, I thought, that tall, willowy, exquisite, rather precious but oddly likeable Roman with the shock of ludicrously blond and curling hair. It is a fact that when a person reaches that nadir of nausea which is the inevitable prelude to violent sickness the complexion does assume a hue which can only be described as greenish: in Antonio's case it was more a tinge of apple-green chartreuse, an odd coloration that I'd never seen before, but I put it down to his naturally sallow complexion. Anyway, no question but that it was the genuine symptom of the genuine illness: another particularly wild lurch and Antonio was on his feet and out of the saloon at a dead run—or as near a dead run as his land-lubber legs could achieve on that swaying deck—without either farewell or apology.

Such is the power of suggestion that within a very few seconds and on the very next lurch three other passengers, two men and a girl, hurriedly rose and left. And such is the power of suggestion compounded that within two minutes more there were, apart from Captain Imrie, Mr Stokes and myself, only two others left: Mr Gerran and Mr Heissman.

Captain Imrie and Mr Stokes, seated at the heads of their respective and now virtually deserted tables, observed the hurried departure of the last of the sufferers, looked at each other in mild astonishment, shook their heads and got on with

9

the business of replenishing their fuel reserves. Captain Imrie, a large and splendidly patriarchal figure with piercing blue eyes that weren't much good for seeing with, had a mane of thick white hair that was brushed straight back to his shoulders, and, totally obscuring the dinner tie he affected for dinner wear, an even more impressively flowing beard that would have been the envy of many a biblical prophet: as always, he wore a gold-buttoned, double-breasted jacket with the thick white ring of a commodore of the Royal Navy, to which he wasn't entitled, and, partly concealed by the grandeur of his beard, four rows of medal ribbons, to which he was. Now, still shaking his head, he lifted his bottle of malt scotch from its container—not until that evening had I understood the purpose of that two-foot-high wrought-iron contraption bolted to the saloon deck by the side of his chair —filled his glass almost to the top and added the negligible amount of water required to make it brimming full. It was at this precise moment that the *Morning Rose* reared unusually high on the crest of a wave, hovered for what appeared to be an unconscionably long time, then fell both forwards and sideways to plunge with a resounding, shuddering crash into the shoulder of the next sea. Captain Imrie didn't spill a drop: for any indication he gave to the contrary he might have been in the tap-room of the Mainbrace in Hull, which was where I'd first met him. He quaffed half the contents of his glass in one gulp and reached for his pipe. Captain Imrie had long mastered the art of dining gracefully at sea.

Mr Gerran, clearly, hadn't. He gazed down at his lamb chops, brussels sprouts, potatoes, and glass of hock which weren't where they ought to have been—they were on his napkin and his napkin was on his lap—with a vexed frown on his face. This was, in its small way, a crisis, and Otto Gerran could hardly be said to be at his ineffectual best when faced with crisis of any kind. But for young Moxon, the steward, this was routine: his own napkin at the ready and bearing a small plastic bucket he'd apparently conjured from nowhere, he set about effecting running repairs while Gerran gazed downwards with an expression of perplexed distaste.

Seated, Otto Gerran, apart from his curiously narrow, pointed cranium that widened out to broad, fleshy jowls, looked as if he might have been cast in one of the standard moulds which produce the vast majority of human shapes and forms: it was not until he stood up, a feat he performed with great difficulty and as infrequently as possible, that one appreciated how preposterous this misconception was. Gerran stood five feet two inches in his elevator shoes, weighed two hundred and forty-five pounds and, were it not for his extremely ill-fitting clothes—one would assume that the tailor just gave up—was the nearest thing to a perfect human sphere I'd ever clapped eyes on. He had no neck, long slender sensitive hands and the smallest feet I've ever seen for a man of his size. The salvage operation over, Gerran looked up and at Imrie. His complexion was puce in colour, with the purple much more in evidence than the brown. This did not mean that he was angry, for Gerran never showed anger and was widely believed to be incapable of it: puce was as standard for him as the peaches and cream of the mythical English rose. His coronary was at least fifteen years overdue.

'Really, Captain Imrie, this is preposterous.' For a man of his vast bulk, Gerran had a surprisingly high-pitched voice: surprisingly, that is, if you weren't a medical practitioner. 'Must we keep heading into this dreadful storm?'

'Storm?' Captain Imrie lowered his glass and looked at Gerran in genuine disbelief. 'Did you say "storm"? A little blow like this?' He looked across to the table where I was sitting with Mr Stokes. 'Force Seven, you would say, Mr Stokes? A touch of Eight, perhaps?'

Mr Stokes helped himself to some more rum, leaned back and deliberated. He was as bereft of cranial and facial hair as Captain Imrie was over-endowed with it. With his gleaming pate, tightly-drawn brown face seamed and wrinkled into a thousand fissures, and a long, thin, scrawny neck, he looked as aged and as ageless as a Galapagos turtle. He also moved at about the same speed. Both he and Captain Imrie had gone to sea together—in mine-sweepers, as incredibly far back as World War I—and had remained together until they had officially retired ten years previously. Nobody, the legend went, had ever heard them refer to each other except as Captain Imrie and Mr Stokes. Some said that, in private, they used the terms Skipper and Chief (Mr Stokes was the Chief Engineer) but this was discounted as an unsubstantiated and unworthy rumour which did justice to neither man.

Moments passed, then Mr Stokes, having arrived at a

measured opinion, delivered himself of it. 'Seven,' he said.

'Seven.' Captain Imrie accepted the judgement as unhesitatingly as if an oracle had spoken and poured himself another drink: I thanked whatever gods there be for the infinitely reassuring presence of Smithy, the mate, on the bridge. 'You see, Mr Gerran? Nothing.' As Gerran was at that moment clinging frantically to a table that was inclined at an angle of 30 degrees, he made no reply. 'A storm? Dearie me, dearie me. Why, I remember the very first time that Mr Stokes and I took the *Morning Rose* up to the Bear Island fishing grounds, the very first trawler ever to fish those waters and come back with full holds, 1928, I think it was—'

'1929,' Mr Stokes said.

'1929.' Captain Imrie fixed his bright blue eyes on Gerran and Johann Heissman, a small, lean, pale man with a permanently apprehensive expression: Heissman's hands were never still. 'Now, that was a storm! We were with a trawler out of Aberdeen, I forget its name—'

'The *Silver Harvest*,' Mr Stokes said.

'The *Silver Harvest*. Engine failure in a Force Ten. Two hours she was broadside to the seas, two hours before we could get a line aboard. Her skipper—her skipper—'

'MacAndrew. John MacAndrew.'

'Thank you, Mr Stokes. Broke his neck. Towed his boat—and him with his broken neck in splints—for thirty hours in a Force Ten, four of them in a Force Eleven. Man, you should have seen yon seas. I tell you, they were mountains, just mountains. The bows thirty feet up and down, up and down, rolling over on our beam ends, hour after hour, every man except Mr Stokes and myself coughing his insides up—' He broke off as Heissman rose hurriedly to his feet and ran from the saloon. 'Is your friend upset, Mr Gerran?'

'Couldn't we heave to or whatever it is you do?' Gerran pleaded. 'Or run for shelter?'

'Shelter? Shelter from what? Why, I remember—'

'Mr Gerran and his company haven't spent their lives at sea, Captain,' I said.

'True, true. Heave to? Heaving to won't stop the waves. And the nearest shelter is Jan Mayen—and that's three hundred miles to the west—into the weather.'

'We could run before the weather. Surely that would help?'

'Aye, we could do that. She'd steady up then, no doubt

about it. If that's what you want, Mr Gerran. You know what the contract says—captain to obey all orders other than those that will endanger the vessel.'

'Good, good. Right away, then.'

'You appreciate, of course, Mr Gerran, that this blow might last another day or so?'

With amelioration of the present sufferings practically at hand Gerran permitted himself a slight smile. 'We cannot control the caprices of Mother Nature, Captain.'

'And that we'll have to turn almost ninety east?'

'In your safe hands, Captain.'

'I don't think you are quite understanding. It will cost us two, perhaps three days. And if we run east, the weather north of North Cape is usually worse than it is here. Might have to put into Hammerfest for shelter. Might lose a week, maybe more. I don't know how many hundred pounds a day it costs you to hire the ship and crew and pay your own camera crew and all those actors and actresses—I hear tell that some of those people you call stars can earn a fortune in just no time at all—' Captain Imrie broke off and pushed back his chair. 'What am I talking about? Money will mean nothing to a man like you. You will excuse me while I call the bridge.'

'Wait.' Gerran looked stricken. His parsimony was legendary throughout the film world and Captain Imrie had touched, not inadvertently, I thought, upon his tenderest nerve. 'A week! Lose a whole week?'

'If we're lucky.' Captain Imrie pulled his chair back up to the table and reached for the malt.

'But I've already lost three days. The Orkney cliffs, the sea, the *Morning Rose*—not a foot of background yet.' Gerran's hands were out of sight but I wouldn't have been surprised if he'd been wringing them.

'And your director and camera crew on their backs for the past four days,' Captain Imrie said sympathetically. It was impossible to say whether a smile lay behind the obfuscatory luxuriance of moustache and beard. 'The caprices of nature, Mr Gerran.'

'Three days,' Gerran said again. 'Maybe another week. A thirty-three day location budget, Kirkwall to Kirkwall.' Otto Gerran looked ill, clearly both the state of his stomach and his film finances were making very heavy demands upon him. 'How far to Bear Island, Captain Imrie?'

'Three hundred miles, give or take the usual. Twenty-eight hours, if we can keep up our best speed.'

'You *can* keep it up?'

'I wasn't thinking about the *Morning Rose*. It can stand anything. It's your people, Mr Gerran. Nothing against them, of course, but I'm thinking they'd be more at home with those pedal boats in the paddling ponds.'

'Yes, of course, of course.' You could see that this aspect of the business had just occurred to him. 'Dr Marlowe, you must have treated a great deal of sea-sickness during your years in the Navy.' He paused, but as I didn't deny it, he went on: 'How long do people take to recover from sickness of this kind?'

'Depends how sick they are.' I'd never given the matter any thought, but it seemed a logical enough answer. 'How long they've been ill and how badly. Ninety rough minutes on a cross-Channel trip and you're as right as rain in ten minutes. Four days in an Atlantic gale and you'll be as long again before you're back on even keel.'

'But people don't actually *die* of sea-sickness, do they?'

'I've never known of a case.' For all his usual indecisiveness and more than occasional bumbling ineptitude which tended to make people laugh at him—discreetly and behind his back, of course—Otto, I realized for the first time and with some vague feeling of surprise, was capable of determination that might verge on the ruthless. Something to do with money, I suppose. 'Not by itself, that is. But with a person already suffering from a heart condition, severe asthma, bronchitis, ulcerated stomach—well, yes, it could see him off.'

He was silent for a few moments, probably carrying out a rapid mental survey of the physical condition of cast and crew, then he said: 'I must admit that I'm a bit worried about our people. I wonder if you'd mind having a look over them, just a quick check? Health's a damn sight more important than any profit—hah! profit, in these days!— that we might make from the wretched film. As a doctor I'm sure you whole-heartedly agree.'

'Of course,' I said. 'Right away.' Otto had to have something that had made him the household name that he had become in the past twenty years and one had to admire this massive and wholly inadmirable hypocrisy that was clearly part of it. He had me all ways. I had said that sea-sickness alone did not kill so that if I were to state categorically that some member or members of his cast or crew were in no condition to withstand any further punishment from the sea he would insist on proof of the existence of some disease which, in conjunction with sea-sickness, might be potentially lethal, a proof that, in the first place, would have been very difficult for me to adduce in light of the limited examination facilities available to me aboard ship and, in the second place, would have been impossible anyhow, for every single member of cast and crew had been subjected to a rigorous insurance medical before leaving Britain: if I gave a clean bill of health to all, then Otto would press on with all speed for Bear Island, regardless of the sufferings of 'our people' about whom he professed to be so worried, thereby effecting a considerable saving in time and money: and, in the remote event of any of them inconsiderately dying upon our hands, why, then, as the man who had given the green light, I was the one in the dock.

I drained my glass of inferior brandy that Otto had laid on in such meagre quantities and rose. 'You'll be here?'

'Yes. Most co-operative of you, Doctor, most.'

'We never close,' I said.

I was beginning to like Smithy though I hardly knew him or anything about him: I was never to get to know him, not well. That I should ever get to know him in my professional capacity was unthinkable: six feet two in his carpet slippers and certainly nothing short of two hundred pounds, Smithy was as unlikely a candidate for a doctor's surgery as had ever come my way.

'In the first-aid cabinet there.' Smithy nodded towards a cupboard in a corner of the dimly-lit wheel-house. 'Captain Imrie's own private elixir. For emergency use only.'

I extracted one of half a dozen bottles held in place by felt-lined spring clamps and examined it under the chart-table lamp. My regard for Smithy went up another notch. In latitude 70° something north and aboard a superannuated trawler, however converted, one does not look to find Otard-Dupuy VSOP.

'What constitutes an emergency?' I asked.

'Thirst.'

I poured some of the Otard-Dupuy into a small glass and offered it to Smithy, who shook his head and watched me as I sampled the brandy, then lowered the glass with suitable reverence.

'To waste this on a thirst,' I said, 'is a crime against nature. Captain Imrie isn't going to be too happy when he comes up here and finds me knocking back his special reserve.'

'Captain Imrie is a man who lives by fixed rules. The most fixed of the lot is that he never appears on the bridge between 8 p.m. and 8 a.m. Oakley—he's the bo'sun—and I take turns during the night. Believe me, that way it's safer for everyone all round. What brings you to the bridge, Doctor —apart from this sure instinct for locating VSOP?'

'Duty. I'm checking on the weather prior to checking on the health of Mr Gerran's paid slaves. He fears they may start dying off like flies if we continue on this course in these conditions.' The conditions, I'd noted, appeared to be deteriorating, for the behaviour of the *Morning Rose,* especially its degree of roll, was now distinctly more uncomfortable than it had been: perhaps it was just a function of the height of the bridge but I didn't think so.

'Mr Gerran should have left you at home and brought along his palm-reader or fortune-teller.' A very contained man, educated and clearly intelligent, Smithy always seemed to be slightly amused. 'As for the weather, the 6 p.m. forecast was as it usually is for these parts, vague and not very encouraging. They haven't,' he added superfluously, 'a great number of weather stations in those parts.'

'What do you think?'

'It's not going to improve.' He dismissed the weather and smiled. 'I'm not a great man for the small-talk, but with the Otard-Dupuy who needs it? Take the weight off your feet for an hour, then go tell Mr Gerran that all his paid slaves, as you call them, are holding a square dance on the poop.'

'I suspect Mr Gerran of having a suspicious checking mind. However, if I may—?'

'My guest.'

I helped myself again and replaced the bottle in the cabinet. Smithy, as he'd warned, wasn't very talkative, but the silence was companionable enough. Presently he said: 'Navy, aren't you, Doc?'

'Past tense.'

'And now this?'

'A shameful come-down. Don't you find it so?'

'Touché.' I could dimly see the white teeth as he smiled in the half-dark. 'Medical malpractice, flogging penicillin to the wogs or just drunk in charge of a surgery?'

'Nothing so glamorous. "Insubordination" is the word they used.'

'Snap. Me too.' A pause. 'This Mr Gerran of yours. Is he all right?'

'So the insurance doctors say.'

'I didn't mean that.'

'You can't expect me to speak ill of my employer.' Again there was that dimly-seen glimpse of white teeth.

'Well, that's one way of answering my question. But, well, look, the bloke must be loony—or is that an offensive term?'

'Only to psychiatrists. I don't speak to them. Loony's fine by me. But I'd remind you that Mr Gerran has a very distinguished record.'

'As a loony?'

'That, too. But also as a film-maker, a producer.'

'What kind of producer would take a film unit up to Bear Island with winter coming on?'

'Mr Gerran wants realism.'

'Mr Gerran wants his head examined. Has he any idea what it's like up there at this time of year?'

'He's also a man with a dream.'

'No place for dreamers in the Barents Sea. How the Americans ever managed to put a man on the moon—'

'Our friend Otto isn't an American. He's a central European. If you want the makers of dreams or the peddlers of dreams, there's the place to find them—among the headwaters of the Danube.'

'And the biggest rogues and confidence men in Europe?'

'You can't have everything.'

'He's a long way from the Danube.'

'Otto had to leave in a great hurry at a time when a large number of people had to leave in a great hurry. Year before the war, that was. Found his way to America—where else?—then to Hollywood—again, where else? Say what you like about Otto—and I'm afraid a lot of people do just that—you have to admire his recuperative powers. He'd left a thriving film business behind him in Vienna and arrived in California 'with what he stood up in.'

'That's not so little.'

'It was then. I've seen pictures. No greyhound, but still about a hundred pounds short of what he is today. Anyway, inside just a few years—chiefly, I'm told, by switching at the psychologically correct moment from anti-Nazism to anti-Communism—Otto prospered mightily in the American film industry on the strength of a handful of nauseatingly super-patriotic pictures, which had the critics in despair and the audiences in raptures. In the mid-fifties, sensing that the cinematic sun was setting over Hollywood—you can't see it but he carries his own built-in radar system with him—Otto's devotion to his adopted country evaporated along with his bank balance and he transferred himself to London, where he made a number of avant-garde films that had the critics in rapture, the audiences in despair and Otto in the red.'

'You seem to know your Otto,' Smithy said.

'Anybody who has read the first five pages of the prospectus for his last film would know his Otto. I'll let you have a copy. Never mentions the film, just Otto. Misses out words like "nauseating" and "despair" of course and you have to read between the lines a bit. But it's all there.'

'I'd like a copy.' Smithy thought some, then said: 'If he's in the red where's the money coming from? To make this film, I mean.'

'Your sheltered life. A producer is always at his most affluent when the bailiffs are camped outside the studio gates —rented studio, of course. Who, when the banks are foreclosing on him and the insurance companies drafting their ultimatums, is throwing the party of the year at the Savoy? Our friend the big-time producer. It's kind of like the law of nature. You'd better stick to ships, Mr Smith,' I added kindly.

'Smithy,' he said absently. 'So who's bank-rolling your friend?'

'My employer. I've no idea. Very secretive about money matters is Otto.'

'But someone is. Backing him, I mean.'

'Must be.' I put down my glass and stood up. 'Thanks for the hospitality.'

'Even after he's produced a string of losers? Seems barmy to me. Fishy, at least.'

'The film world, Smithy, is full of barmy and fishy people.'
I didn't, in fact, know whether it was or not but if this ship-load was in any way representative of the cinema industry it seemed a pretty fair extrapolation.

'Or perhaps he's just got hold of the story to end all stories.'

'The screenplay. There, now, you may have a point—but it's one you would have to raise with Mr Gerran personally. Apart from Heissman, who wrote it, Gerran is the only one who's seen it.'

It hadn't been a factor of the height of the bridge. As I stepped out on to the starboard ladder on the lee side—there were no internal communications between bridge and deck level on those elderly steam trawlers—I was left in no doubt that the weather had indeed deteriorated and deteriorated sharply, a fact that should have probably been readily apparent to anyone whose concern for the prevailing meteoro-logical conditions hadn't been confronted with the unfair challenge of Otard-Dupuy. Even on this, what should have been the sheltered side of the ship, the power of the wind, bitter cold, was such that I had to cling with both hands to the handrails: and with the *Morning Rose* now rolling, erratically and violently, through almost fifty degrees of arc —which was wicked enough but I'd once been on a cruiser that had gone through a hundred degrees of arc and still survived—I could have used another pair of arms.

Even on the blackest night, and this was incontestably one of the blackest, it is never wholly dark at sea: it may never be possible precisely to delineate the horizon line where sea and sky meet, but one can usually look several vertical degrees above or below the horizon line and say with certainty that here is sky or here is sea: for the sea is always darker than the sky. Tonight, it was impossible to say any such thing and this was not because the violently rolling *Morning Rose* made for a very unstable observation platform nor because the big uneven seas bearing down from the east made for a tumbling amorphous horizon: because tonight, for the first time, not yet dense but enough to obscure vision beyond two miles, smoke frost lay on the surface of the sea, that peculiar phenomenon which one finds in Norway where the glacial land winds pass over the warm fjord waters or, as here, where the warm Atlantic air passed over the Arctic waters. All I could see, and it was enough to see, was that the tops were now being torn off the waves, white-veined on their leeward sides, and that the seas were breaking clear across the foredeck of the *Morning Rose,* the white and icy spume hissing into the sea on the starboard. A night for carpet slippers and the fireside.

I turned for'ard towards the accommodation door and bumped into someone who was standing behind the ladder and holding on to it for support. I couldn't see the person's face for it was totally obscured by wind-blown hair but I didn't have to, there was only one person aboard with those long straw-coloured tresses and that was Mary dear: given my choice of people to bump into on the *Morning Rose* I'd have picked Mary dear any time. 'Mary dear', not 'Mary Dear': I'd given her that name to distinguish her from Gerran's continuity girl whose given name was Mary Darling. Mary dear was really Mary Stuart but that wasn't her true name either: Ilona Wisniowecki she'd been christened but had prudently decided that it wasn't the biggest possible asset she had for making her way in the film world. Why she'd chosen a Scots name I didn't know: maybe she just liked the sound of it.

'Mary dear,' I said. 'Aboard at this late hour and on such a night.' I reached up and touched her cheek, we doctors can get away with murder. The skin was icily cold. 'You can carry this fresh air fanatic bit too far. Come on, inside.' I took her arm—I was hardly surprised to find she was shivering quite violently—and she came along docilely enough.

The accommodation door led straight into the passenger lounge which, though fairly narrow, ran the full width of the ship. At the far end was a built-in bar with the liquor kept behind two glassed-in iron-grilled doors: the doors were kept permanently locked and the key was in Otto Gerran's pocket.

'No need to frog-march me, Doctor.' She habitually spoke in a low-pitched quiet voice. 'Enough is enough and I was coming in anyway.'

'Why were you out there in the first place?'

'Can't doctors always tell?' She touched the middle button of her black leather coat and from this I understood that her internal economy wasn't taking too kindly to the roller-coaster antics of the *Morning Rose*. But I also understood that even had the sea been mirror-smooth she'd still have been out on that freezing upper deck: she didn't talk much to the others nor the others to her.

She pushed the tangled hair back from her face and I could see she was very pale and the skin beneath the brown eyes tinged with the beginnings of exhaustion. In her high-cheek-boned Slavonic way—she was a Latvian but, I supposed, no less a Slav for that—she was very lovely, a fact that was freely admitted and slightingly commented upon as being her only asset: her last two pictures—her only two pictures—were said to have been disasters of the first magnitude. She was a silent girl, cool and aloofly remote and I liked her, which made me a lonely minority of one.

'Doctors aren't infallible,' I said. 'At least, not this one.' I peered at her in my best clinical fashion. 'What's a girl like you doing in these parts on this floating museum?'

She hesitated. 'That's a personal question.'

'The medical profession are a very personal lot. How's your headache? Your ulcer? Your bursitis? We don't know where to stop.'

'I need the money.'

'You and me both.' I smiled at her and she didn't smile back so I left her and went down the companionway to the main deck.

Here was located the *Morning Rose*'s main passenger accommodation, two rows of cabins lining the fore-and-aft central passage-way. This had been the area of the former fish-holds and although the place had been steam-washed, fumigated and disinfected at the time of conversion it still stank most powerfully and evilly of cod liver oil that has lain too long in the sun. In ordinary circumstances, the atmosphere was nauseating enough: in those extraordinary ones it was hardly calculated to assist sufferers in a rapid recovery from the effects of sea-sickness. I knocked on the first door on the starboard side and went in.

Johann Heissman, horizontally immobile on his bunk, looked like a cross between a warrior taking his rest and a medieval bishop modelling for the stone effigy which in the fullness of time would adorn the top of his sarcophagus. Indeed, with his thin waxy fingers steepled on his narrow chest, his thin waxy nose pointing to the ceiling and his curiously transparent eyelids closed, the image of the tomb seemed particularly opposite in this case: but it was a deceptive image for a man does not survive twenty years in a Soviet hard-labour camp in Eastern Siberia just to turn in his cards from *mal de mer*.

'How do you feel, Mr Heissman?'

'Oh, God!' He opened his eyes without looking at me, moaned and closed them again. 'How do I feel?'

'I'm sorry. But Mr Gerran is concerned—'

'Otto Gerran is a raving madman.' I didn't take it as any indication of some sudden upsurge in his physical condition but, no question, this time his voice was a great deal stronger. 'A crackpot! A lunatic!'

While privately conceding that Heissman's diagnosis lay somewhere along the right lines, I refrained from comment and not out of some suitably due deference to my employer. Otto Gerran and Johann Heissman had been friends much too long for me to risk treading upon the delicate ground that well might lie between them. They had known each other, as far as I had been able to discover, since they had been students together at some obscure Danubian gymnasium close on forty years ago and had, at the time of the Anschluss in 1938, been the joint owners of a relatively prosperous film studio in Vienna. It was at this point in space and time that they had parted company suddenly, drastically and, it seemed at the time, permanently, for while Gerran's sure instinct had guided his fleeing footsteps to Hollywood, Heissman had unfortunately taken off in the wrong direction altogether and, only three years previously, to the total disbelief of all who had known him and believed him dead for a quarter of a century, had incredibly surfaced from the bitter depths of his long Siberian winter. He had sought out Gerran and now it appeared that their friendship was as close as ever it had been. It was assumed that Gerran knew about the hows and whys of Heissman's lost years and if this were indeed the case then he was the only man who did so for Heissman, understandably enough, never discussed his past. Only two things about the men were known for certain —that it was Heissman, who had a dozen pre-war screenplays to his credit, who was the moving spirit behind this venture to the Arctic, and that Gerran had taken him into full partnership in his company, Olympus Productions. In light of this, it behooved me to step warily and keep my comments on Heissman's comments strictly to myself.

'If there's anything you require, Mr Heissman—'

'I require nothing.' He opened his transparent eyelids again and this time looked—or glared—at me, eyes of washed-out grey streaked with blood. 'Save your treatment for that cretin Gerran.'

'Treatment?'

'Brain surgery.' He lowered his eyelids wearily and went back to being a medieval bishop again, so I left him and went next door.

There were two men in this cabin, one clearly suffering quite badly, the other equally clearly not suffering in the slightest. Neal Divine, the unit director, had adopted a death's door resignation attitude that was strikingly similar to that favoured by Heissman and although he wasn't even within hailing distance of death's door he was plainly very sea-sick indeed. He looked at me, forced a pale smile that was half apology, half recognition, then looked away again. I felt sorry for him as he lay there, but then I'd felt sorry for him ever since he'd stepped aboard the *Morning Rose*. A man dedicated to his craft, lean, hollow-cheeked, nervous and perpetually balanced on what seemed to be the knife-edge of agonizing decisions, he walked softly and talked softly as if he were perpetually afraid that the gods might hear him. It could have been a meaningless mannerism but I didn't think so: no question, he walked in perpetual fear of Gerran, who was at no pains to conceal the fact that he despised him as a man just as much as he admired him as an artist. Why Gerran, a man of indisputably high intelligence, should behave in this way, I didn't know. Perhaps he was one of that far from small group of people who harbour such an inexhaustible fund of ill-will towards mankind in general that they lose no opportunity to vent some of it on the weak, the pliant or those who are in no position to retaliate. Perhaps it was a personal matter. I didn't know either man or their respective backgrounds well enough to form a valid judgement.

'Ah, 'tis the good healer,' a gravelly voice said behind me. I turned round without haste and looked at the pyjama-clad figure sitting up in his bunk, holding fast with his left hand to a bulkhead strap while with the other he clung equally firmly to the neck of a scotch bottle, three parts empty. 'Up the ship comes and down the ship goes but naught will come between the kindly shepherd and his mission of mercy to his

23

queasy flock. You will join me in a post-prandial snifter, my good man?'

'Later, Lonnie, later.' Lonnie Gilbert knew and I knew and we both knew that the other knew that later would be too late, three inches of scotch in Lonnie's hands had as much hope as the last meringue at the vicar's tea-party, but the conventions had been observed, honour satisfied. 'You weren't at dinner, so I thought—'

'Dinner!' He paused, examined the word he'd just said for inflexion and intonation, decided his delivery had been lacking in a proper contempt and repeated himself. 'Dinner! Not the hogswash itself, which I suppose is palatable enough for those who lack my esoteric tastes. It's the hour at which it's served. Barbaric. Even Attila the Hun—'

'You mean you no sooner pour your apéritif than the bell goes?'

'Exactly. What does a man do?'

Coming from our elderly production manager, the question was purely rhetorical. Despite the baby-clear blue eyes and faultless enunciation, Lonnie hadn't been sober since he'd stepped aboard the *Morning Rose*: it was widely questioned whether he'd been sober for years. Nobody—least of all Lonnie—seemed to care about this, but this was not because nobody cared about Lonnie. Nearly all people did, in greater or lesser degrees, dependent on their own natures. Lonnie, growing old now, with all his life in films, was possessed of a rare talent that had never bloomed and never would now, for he was cursed—or blessed—with insufficient drive and ruthlessness to take him to the top, and mankind, for a not always laudable diversity of reasons, tends to cherish its failures: and Lonnie, it was said, never spoke ill of others and this, too, deepened the affection in which he was held except by the minority who habitually spoke ill of everyone.

'It's not a problem I'd care to be faced with myself,' I said. 'How are you feeling?'

'Me?' He inclined his bald pate 45 degrees backwards, tilted the bottle, lowered it and wiped a few drops of the elixir from his grey beard. 'Never been ill in my life. Who ever heard of a pickled onion going sour?' He cocked his head sideways. 'Ah!'

'Ah, what?' He was listening, that I could see, but I couldn't hear a damned thing except the crash of bows against seas and the metallic drumming vibration of the ancient steel hull which accompanied each downwards plunge.

' "The horns of Elfland faintly blowing," ' Lonnie said. ' "Hark! The Herald Angels." '

I harked and this time I heard. I'd heard it many times, and with steadily increasing horror, since boarding the *Morning Rose,* a screechingly cacophonous racket that was fit for heralding nothing short of Armageddon. The three perpetrators of this boiler-house bedlam of sound, Josh Hendriks's young sound crew assistants, might not have been tone stone deaf but their classical musical education could hardly be regarded as complete, as not one of them could read a note of music. John, Luke and Mark were all cast in the same contemporary mould, with flowing shoulder-length hair and wearing clothes that gave rise to the suspicion that they must have broken into a gurus' laundry. All their spare time was spent with recording equipment, guitar, drums and xylophone in the for'ard recreation room where they rehearsed, apparently night and day, against the moment of their big break-through into the pop-record world where they intended, appropriately enough, to bill themselves as 'The Three Apostles'.

'They might have spared the passengers on a night like this,' I said.

'You underestimate our immortal trio, my dear boy. The fact that you may be one of the most excruciating musicians in existence does not prevent you from having a heart of gold. They have *invited* the passengers along to hear them perform in the hope that this might alleviate their sufferings.' He closed his eyes as a raucous bellow overlaid with a high-pitched scream as of some animal in pain echoed down the passageway outside. 'The concert seems to have begun.'

'You can't fault their psychology,' I said. 'After that, an Arctic gale is going to seem like a summer afternoon on the Thames.'

'You do them an injustice.' Lonnie lowered the level in the bottle by another inch then slid down into his bunk to show that the audience was over. 'Go and see for yourself.'

So I went and saw for myself and I had been doing them an injustice. The Three Apostles, surrounded by that plethora of microphones, amplifiers, speakers and arcane electronic equipment without which the latter-day troubadours will not —and, more importantly, cannot—operate, were performing on a low platform in one corner of the recreation room and maintaining their balance with remarkable ease largely, it seemed, because their bodily gyrations and contortions, as inseparable a part of their art as the electronic aids, seemed to synchronize rather well with the pitching and rolling of the *Morning Rose*. Rather conservatively, if oddly, clad in blue jeans and psychedelic caftans, and bent over their microphones in an attitude of almost acolytic fervour, the three young sound assistants were giving of their uninhibited best and from what little could be seen of the ecstatic expressions on faces eighty per cent concealed at any given moment by wildly swinging manes of hair, it was plain that they thought that their best approximated very closely to the sublime. I wondered, briefly, how angels would look with ear-plugs, then turned my attention to the audience.

There were fifteen in all, ten members of the production crew and five of the cast. A round dozen of them were very clearly the worse for the wear, but their sufferings were being temporarily held in abeyance by the fascination, which stopped a long way short of rapture, induced by the Three Apostles who had now reached a musical crescendo accompanied by what seemed to be some advanced form of St Vitus' Dance. A hand touched me on the shoulder and I looked sideways at Charles Conrad.

Conrad was thirty years old and was to be the male lead in the film, not yet a big-name star but building up an impressive international reputation. He was cheerful, ruggedly handsome, with a thatch of thick brown hair that kept falling over his eyes: he had eyes of the bluest blue and most gleamingly white perfect teeth—like his name, his own—that would have transported a dentist into ecstasies or the depths of despair, depending upon whether he was primarily interested in the aesthetic or economic aspects of his profession. He was invariably friendly, courteous and considerate, whether by instinct or calculated design it was impossible to say. He cupped his hand to my ear, nodded towards the performers.

'Your contract specifies hairshirts?'

'No. Why? Does yours?'

'Solidarity of the working classes.' He smiled, looking at me with an oddly speculative glint in his eyes. 'Letting the opera buffs down, aren't you?'

'They'll recover. Anyway, I always tell my patients that a change is as good as a rest.' The music ceased abruptly and I lowered my voice about fifty decibels. 'Mind you, this is carrying it too far. Fact is, I'm on duty. Mr Gerran is a bit concerned about you all.'

'He wants his herd delivered to the cattle market in prime condition?'

'Well, I suppose you all represent a pretty considerable investment to him.'

'Investment? Ha! Do you know that that twisted old skinflint of a beer-barrel has not only got us at fire-sale prices but also won't pay us a penny until shooting's over?'

'No, I didn't.' I paused. 'We live in a democracy, Mr Conrad, the land of the free. You don't have to sell yourselves in the slave market.'

'Don't we just! What do you know about the film industry?'

'Nothing.'

'Obviously. It's in the most depressed state in its history. Eighty per cent of the technicians and actors unemployed. I'd rather work for pennies than starve.' He scowled, then his natural good humour reasserted itself. 'Tell him that his prop and stay, that indomitable leading man Charles Conrad, is fit and well. Not happy, mind you, just fit and well. To be happy I'd have to see him fall over the side.'

'I'll tell him all of that.' I looked around the room. The Three Apostles, mercifully, were refreshing themselves, though clearly in need of something stronger than ginger ale. I said to Conrad: 'This little lot will get to market.'

'Instant mass diagnosis?'

'It takes practice. It also saves time. Who's missing?'

'Well.' He glanced around. 'There's Heissman—'

'I've seen him. And Neal Divine. And Lonnie. And Mary Stuart—not that I'd expect her to be here anyway.'

'Our beautiful but snooty young Slav, eh?'

'I'll go half-way with that. You don't have to be snooty to avoid people.'

'I like her too.' I looked at him. I'd only spoken to him twice, briefly. I could see he meant what he said. He sighed. 'I wish she were my leading lady instead of our resident Mata Hari.'

'You can't be referring to the delectable Miss Haynes?'

'I can and I am,' he said moodily. 'Femmes fatales wear

27

me out. You'll observe she's not among those present. I'll bet she's in bed with those two damned floppy-eared hounds of hers, all of them having the vapours and high on smelling salts.'

'Who else is missing?'

'Antonio.' He was smiling again. 'According to the Count —he's his cabin-mate—Antonio is *in extremis* and unlikely to see the night out.'

'He did leave the dining-room in rather a hurry.' I left Conrad and joined the Count at his table. The Count, with a lean aquiline face, black pencil moustache, bar-straight black eyebrows and greying hair brushed straight back from his forehead, appeared to be in more than tolerable health. He held a very large measure of brandy in his hand and I did not have to ask to know that it would be the very best cognac obtainable, for the Count was a renowned connoisseur of everything from blondes to caviare, as precisely demanding a perfectionist in the pursuit of the luxuries of life as he was in the performance of his duties, which may have helped to make him what he was, the best lighting cameraman in the country and probably in Europe. Nor did I have to wonder where he had obtained the cognac from: rumour had it that he had known Otto Gerran a very long time indeed, or at least long enough to bring his own private supplies along with him whenever Otto went on safari. Count Tadeusz Leszczynski—which nobody ever called him because they couldn't pronounce it—had learned a great deal about life since he had parted with his huge Polish estates, precipitately and for ever, in mid-September, 1939.

'Evening, Count,' I said. 'At least, you look fit enough.'

'Tadeusz to my peers. In robust health, I'm glad to say. I take the properly prophylactic precautions.' He touched the barely perceptible bulge in his jacket. 'You will join me in some prophylaxis? Your penicillins and aureomycins are but witches' brews for the credulous.'

I shook my head. 'Duty rounds, I'm afraid. Mr Gerran wants to know just how ill this weather is making people.'

'Ah! Our Otto himself is fit?'

'Reasonably.'

'One can't have everything.'

'Conrad tells me that your room-mate Antonio may require a visit.'

'What Antonio requires is a gag, a straight-jacket and a nursemaid, in that order. Rolling around, sick all over the floor, groaning like some miscreant stretched out on the rack.' The Count wrinkled a fastidious nose. 'Most upsetting, most.'

'I can well imagine it.'

'For a man of delicate sensibilities, you understand.'

'Of course.'

'I simply *had* to leave.'

'Yes. I'll have a look at him.' I'd just pushed my chair back to the limit of its securing chain when Michael Stryker sat down in a chair beside me. Stryker, a full partner in Olympus Productions, combined the two jobs, normally separate, of production designer and construction manager—Gerran never lost the opportunity to economize. He was a tall, dark and undeniably handsome man with a clipped moustache and could readily have been mistaken for a matinee idol of the mid-thirties were it not for the fashionably long and untidy hair that obscured about ninety per cent of the polo-necked silk sweater which he habitually affected. He looked tough, was unquestionably cynical and, from what little I had heard of him, totally amoral. He was also possessed of the dubious distinction of being Gerran's son-in-law.

'Seldom we see you abroad at this late hour, Doctor,' he said. He screwed a long black Russian cigarette into an onyx holder with all the care of a precision engineer fitting the tappets on a Rolls-Royce engine, then held it up to the light to inspect the results. 'Kind of you to join the masses, *esprit de corps* and what have you.' He lit his cigarette, blew a cloud of noxious smoke across the table and looked at me consideringly. 'On second thoughts, no. You're not the *esprit de corps* type. We more or less have to be. You don't. I don't think you could. Too cool, too detached, too clinical. too observant—and a loner. Right?'

'It's a pretty fair description of a doctor.'

'Here in an official capacity, eh?'

'I suppose so.'

'I'll wager that old goat sent you.'

'Mr Gerran sent me.' It was becoming increasingly apparent to me that Otto Gerran's senior associates were unlikely ever to clamour for the privilege of voting him into the Hall of Fame.

'That's the old goat I mean.' Stryker looked thoughtfully

at the Count. 'A strange and unwonted solicitude on the part of our Otto, wouldn't they say, Tadeusz? I wonder what lies behind it?'

The Count produced a chased silver flask, poured himself another generous measure of cognac, smiled and said nothing. I said nothing either because I'd already decided that I knew the answer to that one: even later on, in retrospect, I could not and did not blame myself, for I had arrived at a conclusion on the basis of the only facts then available to me. I said to Stryker: 'Miss Haynes is not here. Is she all right?'

'No, I'm afraid she's no sailor. She's pretty much under the weather but what's a man to do? She's pleading for sedatives or sleeping drugs and asking that I send for you, but of course I had to say no.'

'Why?'

'My dear chap, she's been living on drugs ever since we came aboard this damned hell-ship.' It was as well for his health, I thought, that Captain Imrie and Mr Stokes weren't sitting at the same table. 'Her own sea-sick tablets one moment, the ones you doled out the next, pep pills in between and barbiturates for dessert. Well, you know what would happen if she took sedatives or more drugs on top of that lot.'

'No, I don't. Tell me.'

'Eh?'

'Does she drink? Heavily, I mean?'

'Drink? No. I mean, she never touches the stuff.'

I sighed. 'Why don't cobblers stick to their own lasts? I'll leave films to you, you leave medicine to me. Any first-year medical student could tell you—well, never mind. Does she know what kind of tablets she's taken today and how many —not that it could have been all that many or she'd have been unconscious by now?'

'I should imagine so.'

I pushed back my chair. 'She'll be asleep in fifteen minutes.'

'Are you sure? I mean—'

'Which is her room?'

'First on the right in the passageway.'

'And yours?' I asked the Count.

'First left.'

I nodded, rose, left, knocked on the first door on the right and went inside in response to a barely-heard murmur. Judith Haynes was sitting propped up in her bed with, as Conrad had predicted, a dog on either side of her—two rather beautiful and beautifully groomed cocker spaniels: I could not, however, catch any trace of smelling salts. She blinked at me with her rather splendid eyes and gave me a wan smile, at once tremulous and brave. My heart stayed where it was.

'It was kind of you to come, Doctor.' She had one of those dark molasses voices, as effective at close personal quarters as it was in a darkened cinema. She was wearing a pink quilted bed-jacket which clashed violently with the colour of her hair and, high round her neck, a green chiffon scarf, which didn't. Her face was alabaster white. 'Michael said you couldn't help.'

'Mr Stryker was being over-cautious.' I sat down on the edge of the mattress and took her wrist. The cocker spaniel next me growled deep in its throat and bared its teeth. 'If that dog bites me, I'll clobber it.'

'Rufus wouldn't harm a fly, would you, Rufus darling?'

It wasn't flies I was worried about but I kept silence and she went on with a sad smile: 'Are you allergic to dogs, Doctor Marlowe?'

'I'm allergic to dog bites.'

The smile faded until her face was just sad. I knew nothing about Judith Haynes except what I'd heard at second hand, and as all I'd heard had been from her colleagues in the industry I heavily discounted about ninety per cent of what had been told me: the only thing I had so far learned with any certainty about the film world was that back-biting, hypocrisy, double-dealing, innuendo and character assassination formed so integral a part of its conversational fabric that it was quite impossible to know where the truth ended and falsehood began. The only safe guide, I'd discovered, was to assume that the truth ended almost immediately.

Miss Haynes, it was said, claimed to be twenty-four and had been, on the best authority, for the past fourteen years. This, it was said darkly, explained her predilection for chiffon scarves, for it was there that the missing years showed: equally, she may just have liked chiffon scarves. With equal authority it was stated that she was a complete bitch, her only redeeming quality being her total devotion to her two cocker spaniels and even this back-handed compliment was qualified by the observation that as a human being she had to have something or somebody to love, something or somebody to return her affection. She had tried cats, it was said, but that hadn't worked: the cats, apparently, didn't love her back. But one thing was indisputable. Tall, slender, with wonderful titian hair and classically beautiful in the sculptured Greek fashion, Miss Haynes, it was universally conceded, couldn't act for toffee. Nonetheless, she was a very hot box office attraction indeed: the combination of the wistfully regal expression, which was her trade-mark, and the startling contrast of her lurid private life saw to that. Nor was her career in any way noticeably hindered by the facts that she was the daughter of Otto Gerran, whom she was said to despise, the wife of Michael Stryker, whom she was said to hate, and a full partner in the Olympus Productions company.

There was nothing much wrong with her physical condition that I could see. I asked her how many tablets of various kinds she had consumed in the course of the day and after dithering about helplessly for a bit and totting up the score with the shapely and tapering forefinger of her right hand on the shapely and tapering fingers of her left—she was alleged to be able to add up pounds and dollars with the speed and accuracy of an IBM computer—she gave me some approximate figures and in return I gave her some tablets with instructions as to how many and when to take them, then left. I didn't prescribe any sedatives for the dogs—they looked OK to me.

The cabin occupied by the Count and Antonio was directly opposite across the passageway. I knocked twice, without reply, went inside and saw why there had been no reply: Antonio was there all right, but I could have knocked until doomsday and Antonio would not have heard me, for Antonio would never hear anything again. From the Via Veneto via Mayfair to die so squalidly in the Barents Sea: for the gay and laughing Antonio there could never have been a right or proper or suitable place to die, for if ever I'd met a man in love with life it had been Antonio: and for this cosseted creature of the sybaritic salons of the capitals of Europe to die in those bleak and indescribably bitter surroundings was so incongruous as to be shocking, so unreal as to momentarily suspend both belief and comprehension. But there he was, just there, lying there at my feet, very real, very dead.

The cabin was full of the sour-sweet smell of sickness and

there was physical evidence of that sickness everywhere. Antonio lay not on his bunk but on the carpeted deck beside it, his head arched impossibly far back until it was at right angles to his body. There was blood, a great deal of blood, not yet congealed, on his mouth and on the floor by his mouth. The body was contorted into an almost impossible position, arms and legs outflung at grotesque angles, the knuckles showing ivory. Rolling around, the Count had said, sick, a man on the rack, and he hadn't been so far out at that, for Antonio had died as a man on the rack dies, in agony. Surely to God he must have cried out, even although his throat would have been blocked most of the time, he must have screamed, he *must* have, he would have been unable to prevent himself: but with the Three Apostles in full cry, his cries would have gone unheeded. And then I remembered the scream I had heard when I'd been talking to Lonnie Gilbert in his cabin and I could feel the hairs prickling on the back of my neck: I should have known the difference between the high-pitched yowling of a rock singer and the scream of a man dying in torment.

I knelt, made a cursory examination, finding out no more in the process than any layman would have done, closed the staring eyes and then, with the advent of *rigor mortis* in mind, straightened out the contorted limbs with an ease that I found vaguely surprising. Then I left the cabin, locked the door and hesitated for only a moment before dropping the key in my pocket: if the Count were possessed of the delicate sensibilities he claimed, he'd be glad I'd taken the key with me.

'Dead?' Otto Gerran's puce complexion had deepened to a shade where I could have sworn it was overlaid with indigo. 'Dead, did you say?'

'That's what I said.' Otto and I were alone in the dining saloon: it was ten o'clock now and at nine-thirty sharp Captain Imrie and Mr Stokes invariably left for their cabins, where they would remain incommunicado for the next ten hours. I lifted from Otto's table a bottle of raw fire-water on which someone had unblushingly stuck a label claiming that the contents were brandy, took it to the stewards' pantry, returned with a bottle of Hine and sat down. It said much for Otto's unquestioned state of shock that not only had he not appeared to note my brief absence, he even stared directly at me, unblinkingly and I'm sure unseeingly, as I poured out two fingers for myself: he registered no reaction whatsoever. Only something pretty close to a state of total shock could have held Otto's parsimonious nature in check and I wondered what the source of this shock might be. True, the news of the death of anyone you knew can come as a shock, but it comes as a numbing shock only when the nearest and dearest are involved, and if Otto had even a measurable amount of affection for anyone, far less for the unfortunate Antonio, he concealed it with great skill. Perhaps he was, as many are, superstitious about death at sea, perhaps he was concerned with the adverse effect it might have on cast and crew, maybe he was bleakly wondering where, in the immensity of the Barents Sea, he could lay hands on a make-up artist, hairdresser and wardrobe man, for Otto, in the sacred name of economy, had combined all three normally separate jobs in the person of one man, the late Antonio. With a visibly conscious effort of will-power he looked away from the Hine bottle and focused his eyes on me.

'How can he be dead?'

'His heart's stopped. His breathing's stopped. That's how he can be dead. That's how anyone can be dead.'

Otto reached out for the bottle of Hine and splashed some brandy into a glass. He didn't pour it, he literally splashed it, the spreading stain on the white tablecloth as big as my hand: his own hand was shaking as badly as that. He poured out three fingers as compared to my two, which may not sound so very much more but then Otto was using a balloon glass whereas mine was a tulip. Tremblingly, he lifted the glass to his mouth and half of its contents disappeared in one gulp, most of it down his throat but a fair proportion on his shirt-front. It occurred to me, not for the first time, that if ever I found myself in a situation where all seemed lost, and the only faint hope of life depended on having one good man and true standing by my right shoulder, the name of Otto Gerran was not one that would leap automatically to my mind.

'How did he die?' The brandy had done some good, Otto's voice was low, just above a whisper, but it was steady.

'In agony, I would say. If you mean why did he die, I don't know.'

'You don't know? You—you're supposed to be a doctor.' Otto was having the greatest difficulty in remaining in his seat: with one hand clutching the brandy glass, the other was barely sufficient to anchor his massive weight against the wild plunging of the *Morning Rose*. I said nothing so he went on: 'Was it sea-sickness? Could that have done it?'

'He was sea-sick, all right.'

'But you said a man doesn't die just from that.'

'He didn't die just from that.'

'An ulcerated stomach, you said. Or heart. Or asthma—'

'He was poisoned.'

Otto stared at me for a moment, his face registering no comprehension, then he set his glass on the table and pushed himself abruptly to his feet, no mean accomplishment for a man of his bulk. The trawler rolled wickedly. I leaned quickly forward, snatched up Otto's glass just as it began to topple and at the same moment Otto lurched to one side and staggered across to the starboard—the lee—door of the saloon leading to the upper deck. He flung this open and even above the shrieking of the wind and the crash of the seas I could hear him being violently sick. Presently he re-entered, closed the door, staggered across the deck and collapsed into his chair. His face was ashen. I handed him his glass and he drained the contents, reached out for the bottle and re-filled his glass. He drank some more and stared at me.

'Poison?'

'Looked like strychnine. Had all—'

'Strychnine? Strychnine! Great God! Strychnine! You—you'll have to carry out a post-mortem, an—an autopsy.'

'Don't talk rubbish. I'll carry out no such thing, and for a number of excellent reasons. For one thing, have you any idea what an autopsy is like? It's a very messy business indeed, I can assure you. I haven't the facilities. I'm not a specialist in pathology—and you require one for an autopsy. You require the consent of the next of kin—and how are you going to get that in the middle of the Barents Sea? You require a coroner's order—no coroner. Besides, a coroner only issues an order where there's a suspicion of foul play. No such suspicion exists here.'

'No—no foul play? But you said—'

'I said it looked like strychnine. I didn't say it was strychnine. I'm sure it's not. He seemed to show the classical symptoms of having had tetanic spasms and opisthotonos—that's when the back arches so violently that the body rests on the head and the heels only—and his face showed pure terror: there's nearly always this conviction of impending death at the onset of strychnine poisoning. But when I straightened him out there were no signs of tetanic contractions. Besides, the timing is all wrong. Strychnine usually shows its first effects within ten minutes and half an hour after taking the stuff you're gone. Antonio was at least twenty minutes here with us at dinner and there was nothing wrong with him then—well, sea-sickness, that's all. And he died only minutes ago—far too long. Besides, who on earth would want to do away with a harmless boy like Antonio? Do you have in your employ a raving psycho who kills just for the kicks of it? Does it make any kind of sense to you?'

'No. No, it doesn't. But—but poison. You said—'

'Food poisoning.'

'Food poisoning! But people don't die of food poisoning. You mean ptomaine poisoning?'

'I mean no such thing for there is no such thing. You can eat ptomaines to your heart's content and you'll come to no harm. But you can get all sorts of food poisoning—chemically contaminated—mercury in fish, for instance—edible mushrooms that aren't edible mushrooms, edible mussels that aren't edible mussels—but the nasty one is *salmonella*. And that can kill, believe me. Just at the end of the war one variety of it, *salmonella enteritidis*, laid low about thirty people in Stoke-on-Trent. Six of them died. And there's an even nastier one called *clostridium botulinum*—a kind of half-cousin of botulinus, a charming substance that is guaranteed to wipe out a city in a night—the Ministry of Health makes it. This *clostidium* secretes an exotoxin—a poison—which is probably the most powerful occurring in nature. Between the wars a party of tourists at Loch Maree in Scotland had a picnic lunch—sandwiches filled with potted duck paste. Eight of them had this. All eight died. There was no cure then, there is no cure now. Must have been this or something like this that Antonio ate.'

'I see, I see.' He had some more brandy, then looked up at me, his eyes round. 'Good God! Don't you see what this means, man! We're all at risk, all of us. This *clostridium* or whatever you call it could spread like wildfire—'

'Rest easy. It's neither infectious nor contagious.'

'But the galley—'

'You think that hadn't occurred to me? The source of infection can't be there. If it were, we'd all be gone—I assume that Antonio—before his appetite deserted him, that was—had the same as all of us. I didn't pay any particular attention but I can find out probably from the people on either side of him—I'm sure they were the Count and Cecil.'

'Cecil?'

'Cecil Golightly—your camera focus assistant or something like that.'

'Ah! The Duke.' For some odd reason Cecil, a diminutive, shrewd and chirpy little Cockney sparrow was invariably known as the Duke, probably because it was so wildly unsuitable. 'That little pig see anything! He never lifts his eyes from the table. But Tadeusz—well, now, he doesn't miss much.'

'I'll ask. I'll also check the galley, the food store and the cold room. Not a chance in ten thousand—I think we'll find that Antonio had his own little supply of tinned delicacies —but I'll check anyway. Do you want me to see Captain Imrie for you?'

'Captain Imrie?'

I was patient. 'The master must be notified. The death must be logged. A death certificate must be issued—normally, he'd do it himself but not with a doctor aboard—but I'll have to be authorized. And he'll have to make preparations for the funeral. Burial at sea. Tomorrow morning, I should imagine.'

He shuddered. 'Yes, please. Please do that. Of course, of course, burial at sea. I must go and see John at once and tell him about this awful thing.' By 'John' I assumed he meant John Cummings Goin, production accountant, company accountant, senior partner in Olympus Production and widely recognized as being the financial controller—and so in many ways the virtual controller—of the company. 'And then I'm going to bed. Yes, yes, to bed. Sounds terrible, I know, poor Antonio lying down there, but I'm dreadfully upset, really dreadfully upset.' I couldn't fault him on that one, I'd rarely seen a man look so unhappy.

'I can bring a sedative to your cabin.'

'No, no, I'll be all right.' Unthinkingly, almost, he picked up the bottle of Hine, thrust it into one of the capacious pockets of his tent-like jacket and staggered from the saloon. As far as insomnia was concerned, Otto clearly preferred home-made remedies to even the most modern pharmaceutical products.

I went to the starboard door, opened it and looked out. When Smithy had said that the weather wasn't going to improve, he'd clearly been hedging his bets: conditions were deteriorating and, if I were any judge, deteriorating quite rapidly. The air temperature was now well below freezing and the first thin flakes of snow were driving by overhead, almost parallel to the surface of the sea. The waves were now no longer waves, just moving masses of water, capriciously tending, it seemed, in any and all directions, but in the main still bearing mainly easterly. The *Morning Rose* was no longer just cork-screwing, she was beginning to stagger, falling into a bridge-high trough with an explosive impact more than vaguely reminiscent of the flat, whip-like crack of a not so distant naval gun, then struggling and straining to right herself only to be struck by a following wall of water that smashed her over on her beam ends again. I leaned farther outwards, looking upwards and was vaguely puzzled by the dimly seen outline of the madly flapping flag on the foremast: puzzled, because it wasn't streaming out over the starboard side, as it should have been, but towards the starboard quarter. This meant that the wind was moving round to the north-east and what this could portend I could not even guess: I vaguely suspected that it wasn't anything good. I went inside, yanked the door closed with some effort, made a silent prayer for the infinitely reassuring and competent presence of Smithy on the bridge, made my way to the stewards' pantry again and helped myself to a bottle of Black Label, Otto having made off with the last of the brandy —the drinkable brandy, that is. I took it across to the captain's table, sat in the captain's chair, poured myself a small measure and stuck the bottle in Captain Imrie's convenient wrought-iron stand.

I wondered why I hadn't told Otto the truth. I was a convincing liar, I thought, but not a compulsive one: probably because Otto struck me as being far from a stable character and with several more pegs of brandy inside him, in addition to what he had already consumed, he seemed less than the ideal confidant.

Antonio hadn't died because he'd taken or been given strychnine. Of that I was quite certain. I was equally certain that he hadn't died from *clostridium botulinum* either. The exotoxin from this particular anaerobe was quite as deadly as I had said but, fortunately, Otto had been unaware that the incubation period was seldom less than four hours and, in extreme cases, had been known to be as long as forty-eight—not that the period of incubation delay made the final results any less fatal. It was faintly possible that Antonio might have scoffed, say, a tin of infected truffles or suchlike from his homeland in the course of the afternoon, but in that case the symptoms would have been showing at the dinner table, and apart from the odd chartreuse hue I'd observed nothing untoward. It had to be some form of systematic poison, but there were so many of them and I was a long way from being an expert on the subject. Nor was there any necessary question of foul play: more people die from accidental poisoning than from the machinations of the ill-disposed.

The lee door opened and two people came staggering into the room, both young, both bespectacled, both with faces all but obscured by wind-blown hair. They saw me, hesitated, looked at each other and made to leave, but I waved them in and they came, closing the door behind them. They staggered across to my table, sat down, pushed the hair from their faces and I identified them as Mary Darling, our continuity girl, and Allen—nobody knew whether he had another name or whether that was his first or second one—the clapper/loader. He was a very earnest youth who had recently been asked to leave his university. He was an intelligent lad but easily bored. Intelligent but a bit short on wisdom—he regarded film-making as the most glamorous job on earth.

'Sorry to break in on you like this, Dr Marlowe.' Allen was very apologetic, very respectful. 'We had no idea—to tell you the truth we were both looking for a place to sit down.'

'And now you've found a place. I'm just leaving. Try some of Mr Gerran's excellent scotch—you both look as if you could do with a little.' They did, indeed, look very pale indeed.

'No, thank you, Dr Marlow. We don't drink.' Mary Darling—everyone called her Mary darling—was cast in an even more earnest mould than Allen and had a very prim voice to go with it. She had very long, straight, almost platinum hair that fell any old how down her back and that clearly hadn't been submitted to the attentions of a hairdresser for years: she must have broken Antonio's heart. She wore a habitually severe expression, enormous horn-rimmed glasses, no make-up —not even lipstick—and had about her a businesslike, competent, no-nonsense, I can-take-care-of-myself-thank-you attitude that was so transparently false that no one had the heart to call her bluff.

'No room at the inn?' I asked.

'Well,' Mary darling said, 'it's not very private down in the recreation room, is it? As for those three young—young—'

'The Three Apostles do their best,' I said mildly. 'Surely the lounge was empty?'

'It was not.' Allen tried to look disapproving but I thought his eyes crinkled. 'There was a man there. In his pyjamas. Mr Gilbert.'

'He had a big bunch of keys in his hands.' Mary darling paused, pressed her lips together, and went on: 'He was trying to open the doors where Mr Gerran keeps all his bottles.'

'That sounds like Lonnie,' I agreed. It was none of my business. If Lonnie found the world so sad and so wanting there was nothing much I or anybody could do about it: I just hoped that Otto didn't catch him at it. I said to Mary: 'You could always try your cabin.'

'Oh, no! We couldn't do *that*.'

'No, I suppose not.' I tried to think why not, but I was too old. I took my leave and passed through the stewards' pantry into the galley. It was small, compact, immaculately clean, a minor culinary symphony in stainless steel and white tile. At this late hour I had expected it to be deserted, but it wasn't: Haggerty, the chief cook, with his regulation chef's hat four-square on his greying clipped hair, was bent over some pots on a stove. He turned round, looked at me in mild surprise.

'Evening, Dr Marlowe.' He smiled. 'Carrying out a medical inspection of my kitchen?'

'With your permission, yes.'

He stopped smiling. 'I'm afraid I do not understand, sir.' He could be very stiff, could Haggerty, twenty-odd years in the Royal Navy had left their mark.

'I'm sorry. Just a formality. We seem to have a case of food poisoning aboard. I'm just looking around.'

'Food poisoning! Not from this galley, I can assure you. Never had a case in my life.' Haggerty's injured professional pride quite overcame any humanitarian concern he might have had about the identity of the victim or how severe his case was. 'Twenty-seven years as a cook in the *Andrew*, Dr Marlowe, last six as Chief on a carrier, and if I'm to be told I don't run a hygienic galley—'

'Nobody's telling you anything of the sort.' I used to him the tone he used to me. 'Anyone can see the place is spotless. If the contamination came from this galley, it won't be your fault.'

'It didn't come from this galley.' Haggerty had a square ruddy face and periwinkle blue eyes: the complexion, suffused with anger, was now two shades deeper and the eyes hostile. 'Excuse me, I'm busy.' He turned his back and started rattling his pots about. I do not like people turning their backs on me when I am talking to them and my instinctive reaction was to make him face me again, but I reflected that his pride had been wounded, justifiably so from his point of view, so I contented myself with the use of words.

'Working very late, Mr Haggerty?'

'Dinner for the bridge,' he said stiffly. 'Mr Smith and the bo'sun. They change watches at eleven and eat together then.'

'Let's hope they're both fit and well by twelve.'

He turned very slowly. 'What's that supposed to mean?'

'I mean that what's happened once can happen again. You know you haven't expressed the slightest interest in the identity of the person who's been poisoned or how ill that person is?'

'I don't know what you mean, sir.'

'I find it very peculiar. Especially as the person became violently ill just after eating food prepared in this galley.'

'I take orders from Captain Imrie,' he said obliquely. 'Not from passengers.'

'You know where the captain is at this time of night. In bed and very, very sound. It's no secret. Wouldn't you like to come with me and see what you've done? To look at this poisoned person.' It wasn't very nice of me but I didn't see what else I could do.

'To see what *I've* done!' He turned away again, deliberately placed his pots to one side and removed his chef's hat. 'This had better be good, Doctor.'

I led the way below to Antonio's cabin and unlocked the door. The smell was revolting. Antonio lay as I had left him, except that he looked a great deal more dead now than he had done before: the blood had drained from face and hands leaving them a transparent white. I turned to Haggerty.

'Good enough?'

Haggerty's face didn't turn white because ruddy faces with a mass of broken red veins don't turn that way, but it did become a peculiar muddy brick colour. He stared down at the dead man for perhaps ten seconds, then turned away and walked quickly up the passage. I locked the door and followed, staggering from side to side of the passage as the *Morning Rose* rolled wickedly in the great troughs. I made my erratic way through the dining saloon, picked up the Black Label from Captain Imrie's wrought-iron stand, smiled pleasantly at Mary darling and Allen—God knows what thoughts were in their minds as I passed through—and returned to the galley. Haggerty joined me after thirty seconds. He was looking ill and I knew he had been ill. I had no doubt that he had seen a great deal during his lifetime at sea but there is something peculiarly horrifying about the

42

sight of a man who has died violently from poisoning. I poured him three fingers of scotch and he downed it at a gulp. He coughed, and either the coughing or the scotch brought some colour back to his face.

'What was it?' His voice was husky. 'What—what kind of poison could kill a man like that? God, I've never seen anything so awful.'

'I don't know. That's what I want to find out. May I look round now?'

'Christ, yes. Don't rub it in, Doctor—well, I didn't know, did I? What do you want to see first?'

'It's ten past eleven,' I said.

'Ten past—my God, I'd forgotten all about the bridge.' He prepared the bridge dinner with remarkable speed and efficiency—two cans of orange juice, a tin opener, a flask of soup, and then the main course in snap-lidded metal canteens. Those he dumped in a wicker basket along with cutlery and two bottles of beer and the whole preparation took just over a minute.

While he was away—which wasn't for more than two minutes—I examined what little open food supplies Haggerty carried in his galley, both on shelves and in a large refrigerator. Even had I been capable of it, which I wasn't, I'd no facilities aboard for analysing food, so I had to reply on sight, taste and smell. There was nothing amiss that I could see. As Haggerty had said, he ran a hygienic galley, immaculate food in immaculate containers.

Haggerty returned. I said, 'Tonight's menu, again.'

'Orange juice or pineapple juice, oxtail—'

'All tinned?' He nodded. 'Let's see some.' I opened two tins of each, six in all, and sampled them under Haggerty's now very apprehensive eye. They tasted the way those tinned products usually taste, which is to say that they didn't taste of anything very much at all, but all perfectly innocuous in their pallid fashion.

'Main course?' I said. 'Lamb chops, brussels, horseradish, boiled potatoes?'

'Right. But these things aren't kept here.' He took me to the adjacent cool room, where the fruits and vegetables were stored, thence below to the cold room, where sides of beef and pork and mutton swung eerily from steel hooks in the harsh light of naked bulbs. I found precisely what I had

43

expected to find, nothing, told Haggerty that whatever had happened was clearly no fault of his, then made my way to the upper deck and along an interior passage till I came to Captain Imrie's cabin. I tried the handle, but it was locked. I knocked several times, without result. I hammered it until my knuckles rebelled, then kicked it, all with the same result: Captain Imrie had still about nine hours' sleep coming up and the relatively feeble noises I was producing had no hope of penetrating to the profound depths of unconsciousness he had now reached. I desisted. Smithy would know what to do.

I went to the galley, now deserted by Haggerty, and passed through the pantry into the dining saloon. Mary darling and Allen were sitting on a bulkhead settee, all four hands clasped together, pale—very pale—faces about three inches apart, gazing into each other's eyes in a kind of mystically miserable enchantment. It was axiomatic, I knew, that shipboard romances flourished more swiftly than those on land, but I had thought those phenomena were confined to the Bahamas and suchlike balmy climes: aboard a trawler in a full gale in the Arctic I should have thought that some of the romantically essential prerequisites were wholly absent or at least present in only minimal quantities. I took Captain Imrie's chair, poured myself a small drink and said 'Cheers!'

They straightened and jumped apart as if they'd been connected to electrodes and I'd just made the switch. Mary darling said reproachfully: 'You did give us a fright, Dr Marlowe.'

'I'm sorry.'

'Anyway, we were just leaving.'

'Now I'm really sorry.' I looked at Allen. 'Quite a change from university, isn't it?'

He smiled wanly. 'There is a difference.'

'What were you studying there?'

'Chemistry.'

'Long?'

'Three years. Well, almost three years.' Again the wan smile. 'It took me all that time to find out I wasn't much good at it.'

'And you're now?'

'Twenty-one.'

'All the time in the world to find out what you are good

at. I was thirty-three before I qualified as a doctor.'

'Thirty-three.' He didn't say it but his face said it for him: if he was that old when he qualified what unimaginable burden of years is he carrying now? 'What did you do before then?'

'Nothing I'd care to talk about. Tell me, you two were at the captain's table for dinner tonight, weren't you?' They nodded. 'Seated more or less opposite Antonio, weren't you?'

'I think so,' Allen said. That was a good start. He just thought so.

'He's not well. I'm trying to find out if he ate something that disagreed with him, something he may have been allergic to. Either of you see what he had to eat?'

They looked at each other uncertainly.

'Chicken?' I said encouragingly. 'Perhaps some French fries?'

'I'm sorry, Dr Marlowe,' Mary darling said. 'I'm afraid —well, we're not very observant.' No help from this quarter, obviously they were so lost in each other that they couldn't even remember what they had eaten. Or perhaps they just hadn't eaten anything. I hadn't noticed. I hadn't been very observant myself. But then, I hadn't been expecting a murder to happen along.

They were on their feet now, clinging to each other for support as the deck tried to vanish from beneath their feet. I said: 'If you're going below I wonder if you'd ask Tadeusz if he'd be kind enough to come up and see me here. He'll be in the recreation room.'

'He might be in bed,' Allen said. 'Asleep.'

'Wherever he is,' I said with certainty, 'he's not in bed.'

Tadeusz appeared within a minute, reeking powerfully of brandy, a vexed expression on his aristocratic features. He said without preamble: 'Damned annoying. Most damned annoying. Do you know where I can find a master key? That idiot Antonio has gone and locked our cabin door from the inside and he must be hopped to the eyebrows with sedatives. Simply can't waken him. Cretin!'

I produced his cabin key. 'He didn't lock the door from the inside. I did from the outside.' The Count looked at me for an uncomprehending moment, then mechanically reached for his flask as shocked understanding showed in his face. Not too much shock, just a little, but I was sure that what little there was was genuine. He tilted the flask and two or three drops trickled into his glass. He reached for the Black Label, helped himself with a steady but generous hand and drank deeply.

'He couldn't hear me? He—he is beyond hearing?'

'I'm sorry. Something he ate, I can't think what else, some killer toxin, some powerful, quick-acting and deadly poison.'

'Quite dead?' I nodded. 'Quite dead,' he repeated. 'And I told him to stop making such a grand opera Latin fuss and walked away and left a dying man.' He drank some more scotch and grimaced, an expression that was no reflection on Johnnie Walker. 'There are advantages in being a lapsed Catholic, Dr Marlowe.'

'Rubbish. Sackcloth and ashes not only don't help, they're simply just not called for here. All right, so you didn't suspect there was anything wrong with him. I saw him at table and I wasn't any cleverer and I'm supposed to be a doctor. And when you left him in the cabin it was too late anyway: he was dying then.' I helped him to some more scotch but left my own glass untouched: even one relatively sober mind around might prove to be of some help, although just how I couldn't quite see at that moment. 'You sat beside him at dinner. Can you remember what you ate?'

'The usual.' The Count, it was clear, was more shaken than his aristocratic nature would allow him to admit. 'Rather, he didn't eat the usual.'

'I'm not in the right frame of mind for riddles, Tadeusz.'

'Grapefruit and sunflower seeds. That was about what he lived on. One of those vegetarian nuts.'

'Walk softly, Tadeusz. Those nuts may yet be your pall-bearers.'

The Count grimaced again. 'A singularly ill-chosen remark. Antonio never ate meat. And he'd a thing against potatoes. So all he had were the sprouts and horseradish. I remember particularly well because Cecil and I gave him our horseradish, to which, it seems, he was particularly partial.' The Count shuddered. 'A barbarian food, fit only for ignorant Anglo-Saxon palates. Even young Cecil has the grace to detest that offal.' It was noteworthy that the Count was the only person in the film unit who did not refer to Cecil Golightly as the Duke: perhaps he thought he was being upstaged in the title stakes but, more probably, as a dyed-in-the-wool aristocrat himself, he objected to people taking frivolous liberties with titles.

'He had fruit juice?'

'Antonio had his own homemade barley water.' The Count smiled faintly. 'It was his contention that everything that came out of a can had been adulterated before it went into that can. Very strict on those matters, was Antonio.'

'Soup? Any of that?'

'*Ox*-tail?'

'Of course. Anything else? That he ate, I mean?'

'He didn't even finish his main course—well, his sprouts and radish. You may recall that he left very hurriedly.'

'I recall. Was he liable to sea-sickness?'

'I don't know. Don't forget, I've known him no longer than yourself. He's been a bit off-colour for the past two days. But then, who hasn't?'

I was trying to think up another penetrating question when John Cummings Goin entered. His unusual surname he'd inherited from a French grandfather in the High Savoy, where, apparently, this was not an altogether uncommon name. The film crew, inevitably, referred to him as Comin' and Goin', but Goin was probably wholly unaware of this: he was not the sort of man with whom one took liberties.

Any other person entering the dining saloon from the main deck on a night like that would have presented an appearance that would have varied from the wind-blown to the dishevelled. Not one hair of Goin's black, smooth, centre-parted, brushed-back hair was out of place: had I been told that he eschewed the standard proprietary hairdressing creams in favour of cow-hide glue, I would have seen no reason to doubt it. And the hairstyle was typical of the man—everything smooth, calm, unruffled and totally under control. In one area only did the comparison fall down. The hairstyle was slick, but Goin wasn't: he was just plain clever. He was of medium height, plump without being fat, with a smooth, unlined face. He was the only man I'd ever seen wearing *pince-nez*, and that only for the finest of fine print which, in Goin's line of business, came his way quite often: the *pince-nez* looked so inevitable that it was unthinkable that he should ever wear any other type of reading aid. He was, above all, a civilized man and urbane in the best sense of the word.

He picked up a glass from a rack, timed the wild staggering of the *Morning Rose* to walk quickly and surely to the seat on my right, picked up the Black Label and said: 'May I?'

'Easy come, easy go,' I said. 'I've just stolen it from Mr Gerran's private supply.'

'Confession noted.' He helped himself. 'This makes me an accessory. Cheers.'

'I assume you've just come from Mr Gerran,' I said.

'Yes. He's most upset. Sad, sad, about that poor young boy. An unfortunate business.' That was something else about Goin, he always got his priorities right: the average company accountant, confronted with the news of the death of a member of a team, would immediately have wondered how the death would affect the project as a whole: Goin saw the human side of it first. Or, I thought, he spoke of it first: I knew I was being unfair to him. He went on: 'I understand you've so far been unable to establish the cause of death.' Diplomacy, inevitably, was second nature to Goin: he could so easily and truthfully have said that I just hadn't a clue.

So I said it for him. 'I haven't a clue.'

'You'll never get to Harley Street talking that way.'

'Poison, that's certain. But that's all that's certain. I carry the usual sea-going medical library around with me, but that isn't much help. To identify a poison you must be able either to carry out a chemical analysis or observe the poison at work on the victim—most of the major poisons have symptoms peculiar to themselves and follow their own highly idiosyncratic courses. But Antonio was dead before I got to him and I lack the facilities to do any pathological work, assuming I could do it in the first place.'

'You're destroying all my faith in the medical profession. Cyanide?'

'Impossible. Antonio took time to die. A couple of drops of hydrocyanic—prussic acid—or even a tiny quantity of pharmacopoeial acid, and that's only two per cent of anhydrous prussic acid—and you're dead before your glass hits the floor. And cyanide makes it murder, it always makes it murder. There's no way I know of it can be administered by accident. Antonio's death, I'm certain, was an accident.'

Goin helped himself to some more scotch. 'What makes you so certain it was an accident?'

'What makes me so certain?' That was a difficult one to answer off the cuff owing to the fact that I was convinced it was no accident at all. 'First, there was no opportunity for the administering of poison. We know that Antonio was alone in his cabin all afternoon right until dinner-time.' I looked at the Count. 'Did Antonio have any private food supplies with him in his cabin?'

'How did you guess?' the Count looked surprised.

'I'm not guessing. I'm eliminating. He had?'

'Two hampers. Full of glass jars—I think I mentioned that Antonio would never eat anything out of a tin—with all sorts of weird vegetable products inside, including dozens of baby food jars with all sorts of purées in them. A very finicky eater, was poor Antonio.'

'So I'm beginning to gather. I think our answer will lie there. I'll have Captain Imrie impound his supplies and have them analysed on our return. To get back to the opportunity factor. Antonio came up to the dining saloon here, had the same as the rest of us—'

'No fruit juices, no soup, no lamb chops, no potatoes,' the Count said.

'None of those. But what he did have we all had. Then straight back to his cabin. In the second place, who would want to kill a harmless person like that—especially as Antonio was a total stranger to all of us and only joined us at Wick for the first time? And who but a madman would administer a deadly poison in a closed community like this, knowing that he couldn't escape and that Scotland Yard would be leaning over the quay walls in Wick, just waiting for our return?'

'Maybe that's the way a madman would figure a sane person would figure,' Goin said.

'What English king was it who died of a surfeit of lampreys?' the Count said. 'If you ask me, our unfortunate Antonio may well have perished from a surfeit of horseradish.'

'Like enough.' I pushed back my chair and made to rise. But I didn't get up immediately. Way back in the dim and lost recesses of my mind the Count had triggered off a tiny bell, an infinitesimal tinkle so distant and remote that if I hadn't been listening with all my ears I'd have missed it completely: but I had been listening, the way people always listen when they know, without knowing why, that the old man with the scythe is standing there in the wings, winding up for the back stroke. I knew both men were watching me. I sighed. 'Decisions, decisions. Antonio has to be attended to—'

'With canvas?' Goin said.

'With canvas. Count's cabin cleaned up. Death has to be logged. Death certificate. And Mr Smith will have to make the funeral arrangements.'

'Mr Smith?' The Count was vaguely surprised. 'Not our worthy commanding officer.'

'Captain Imrie is in the arms of Morpheus,' I said. 'I've tried.'

'You have your deities mixed up,' Goin said. 'Bacchus is the one you're after.'

'I suppose it is. Excuse me, gentlemen.'

I went directly to my cabin but not to write out any death certificate. As I'd told Goin, I did carry a medical library of sorts around with me and it was of a fair size. I selected several books, including Glaister's *Medical Jurisprudence and Toxicology*, 9th edition (Edinburgh 1950), Dewar's *Textbook of Forensic Pharmacy* (London 1946) and Gonzales, Vance and Helpern's *Legal Medicine and Toxicology*, which seemed to be a pre-war book. I started consulting indices and within five minutes I had it.

The entry was listed under 'Systematic Poisons' and was headed '*Aconite*. Bot. A poisonous plant of the order *Ranunculaceae*. Particular reference *Monkshood* and *Wolfsbane*. Phar. *Aconitum napellus*. This, and *aconitine*, an alkaloid extract of the former, is commonly regarded as the most lethal of all poisons yet identified: a dose of not more than 0.004 gm is deadly to man. Aconite and its alkaloid produce a burning and peculiar tingling and numbing effect where applied. Later, especially with larger doses, violent vomiting results, followed by paralysis of motion, paralysis of sensation and great depression of the heart, followed by death from syncope.

'Treatment. To be successful must be immediate as possible. Gastric lavage, 12 gm of tannic acid in two gallons of warm water, followed by 1.2 gm tannic acid in 180 ml tepid water: this should be followed by animal charcoal suspended in water. Cardiac and respiratory stimulants, artificial respiration and oxygen will be necessary as indicated.

'N.B. The root of aconite has frequently been eaten in mistake for that of horseradish.'

CHAPTER THREE

I was still looking at, but no longer reading the article on *Aconite* when it was gradually borne in upon my preoccupation that there was something very far amiss with the *Morning Rose*. She was still under way, her elderly oil-fired steam engines throbbing along as dependably as ever, but her motion had changed. Her rolling factor had increased till she was swinging wickedly and dismayingly through an angle of close on 70 degrees: the pitching factor had correspondingly decreased and the thudding jarring vibration of the bluff bows smashing into the quartering seas had fallen away to a fraction of what it had previously been.

I marked the article, closed the book, then lurched and stumbled—I could not be said to have run for it was physically impossible—along the passageway, up the companionway, through the lounge and out on to the upper deck. It was dark but not so dark as to prevent me from gauging direction by the feel of the gale wind, by the spume blowing off the top of the confused seas. I shrank back and tightened my grip on a convenient handrail as a great wall of water, black and veined and evil, reared up on the port side, just for'ard of the beam: it was at least ten feet higher than my head. I was certain that the wave, with the hundreds of tons of water it contained, was going to crash down square on the fore-deck of the trawler, I couldn't see how it could fail to, but but fail it did: as the wave bore down on us, the trough to starboard deepened and the *Morning Rose*, rolling over to almost forty degrees, simple fell into it, pressed down by the great weight of water on its exposed port side. There came the familiar flat explosive thunderclap of sound, the *Morning Rose* vibrated and groaned as over-stressed plates and rivets adjusted to cope with the sudden shearing strain, white, icily-cold water foamed over the starboard side and swirled around my ankles, and then it was gone, gurgling through the scuppers as the *Morning Rose* righted itself and rolled far over on its other side. There was no worry about any of this, no threat to safety and life, this was what Arctic trawlers had been built for and the *Morning Rose* could continue to absorb this punishment indefinitely. But there *was* cause for worry, if such a word can be used to express a desperately acute anxiety: that massive wave which had caught the trawler on her port bow, had knocked her almost 20 degrees off course. She was still 20 degrees off course, and 20 degrees off course she remained: nobody was making any attempt to bring her round. Another, and a smaller sea, and then she was lying five more degrees over to the east and here, too, she remained. I ran for the bridge ladder.

I bumped into and almost knocked down a person at the precise spot where I'd bumped into Mary dear an hour ago. Contact this time was much more solid and the person said 'Oof!' or something of that sort. The kind of gasp a winded lady makes is quite different from a man's and instinct and a kind of instantaneous reasoning told me that I had bumped into the same person again: Judith Haynes would be in bed with her spaniels and Mary darling was either with Allen or in bed dreaming about him: neither, anyway, was the outdoor type.

I said something that might have been misconstrued as a brusque apology, side-stepped and had my foot on the first rung when she caught my arm with both hands.

'Something's wrong. I know it is. What?' Her voice was calm, just loud enough to make itself heard over the high-pitched obbligato of the wind in the rigging. Sure she knew something was wrong, the sight of Dr Marlowe moving at anything above his customary saunter was as good as a police or air raid siren any day. I was about to say something to this effect when she added: 'That's why I came on deck,' which effectively rendered stillborn any cutting remarks I'd been about to make, because she'd been aware of trouble before I'd been: but, then, she hadn't had her thoughts taken up with *Aconitum napellus*.

'The ship's not under command. There's nobody in charge on the bridge, nobody trying to keep a course.'

'Can I do anything?'

She was wonderful. 'Yes. There's a hot-water electric geyser on the galley bulkhead by the stove. Bring up a jug of hot water, not too hot to drink, a mug and salt. Lots of salt.'

I sensed as much as saw her nod and then she was gone. Four seconds later I was inside the wheel-house. I could dimly see one figure crumpled against the chart-table, another apparently sitting straight by the wheel, but that was all I could see. The two overhead lights were dull yellow glows. It took me almost fifteen frantic seconds to locate the instrument panel just for'ard of the wheel, but only a couple of seconds thereafter to locate the rheostat and twist it to its clockwise maximum. I blinked in the hurtfully sudden wash of white light.

Smithy was by the chart-table, Oakley by the wheel, the former on his side, the latter upright, but that, I could see, didn't mean that Oakley was in any better state of health than the first mate, it was just that neither appeared capable of moving from the positions they had adopted. Both had their heads arched towards their knees, both had their hands clasped tightly to their midriffs. Neither of them was making any sound. Possibly neither was suffering pain and the contracted positions they had assumed resulted from some wholly involuntary motor mechanism: it was equally possible that their vocal cords were paralysed.

I looked at Smithy first. One life is as important as the next, or so any one of a group of sufferers will think, but in this case I was concerned with the greatest good of all concerned and the fact that the 'all' here just coincidentally included me had no bearing on my choice: if the *Morning Rose* was running into trouble, and I had a strange fey conviction that it was, Smithy was the man I wanted around.

Smithy's eyes were open and the look in them intelligent. Among other things the aconite article had stated that full intelligence is maintained to the very end. Could this be the end? Paralysis of motion, the article had said and paralysis of motion we undoubtedly had here. Then paralysis of sensation—maybe that's why they weren't crying out in agony, it could have been that they had been screaming their heads off up on the bridge here with no one around to hear them, but now they weren't feeling anything any more. I saw and vaguely recorded the fact that there were two metal canteens lying close together on the floor, both of them very nearly emptied of food. Both of them, I would have thought, were *in extremis* but for one very odd factor: there was no sign of the violent vomiting of which the article had spoken. I wished to God that somewhere, sometime, I had taken the trouble to learn something about poisons, their causes, their effects, their symptoms and aberrant symptoms—which we seemed to have here—if any.

Mary Stuart came in. Her clothes were soaking and her hair was in a terrible mess, but she'd been very quick and she'd got what I'd asked her to—including a spoon, which I'd forgotten. I said: 'A mug of hot water, six spoons of salt. Quick. Stir it well.' Gastric lavage, the book had said, but as far as the availability of tannic acid and animal charcoal was concerned I might as well have been on the moon. The best and indeed the only hope lay in a powerful and quick-acting emetic. Alum and zinc sulphate was what the old boy in my medical school had preferred but I'd never come across anything better than sodium chloride—common salt. I hoped desperately that aconitine absorption into the bloodstream hadn't progressed too far—and that it was aconitine I didn't for a moment doubt. Coincidence is coincidence but to introduce some such fancy concoction as curare at this stage would be stretching things a bit. I levered Smithy into a sitting position and was just getting my hands under his armpits when a dark-haired young seaman, clad—in that bitter weather—in only jersey and jeans came hurrying into the wheel-house. It was Allison, the senior of the two quarter-masters. He looked—not stared—at the two men on the deck: he was very much a seaman cast in Smithy's mould.

'What's wrong, Doctor?'

'Food poisoning.'

'Had to be something like that. I was asleep. Something woke me. I knew something was wrong, that we weren't under command.' I believed him, all experienced seamen have this in-built capacity to sense trouble. Even in their sleep. I'd come across it before. He moved quickly to the chart-table then glanced at the compass. 'Fifty degrees off course, to the east.'

'We've got all the Barents Sea to rattle about in,' I said. 'Give me a hand with Mr Smith, will you?'

We took an arm each and dragged him towards the port door. Mary dear stopped stirring the contents of the metal mug she held in her hand and looked at us in some perplexity.

'Where are you going with Mr Smith?'

'Taking him out on the wing.' What did she think we were going to do with him, throw him over the side? 'All that fresh air. It's very therapeutic.'

'But it's snowing out there! And bitterly cold.'

'He's also—I hope—going to be very, very sick. Better outside than in. How does that concoction taste?'

She sipped a little salt and water from her spoon and screwed up her face. 'It's awful!'

'Can you swallow it?'

She tried and shuddered. 'Just.'

'Another three spoons.' We dragged Smithy outside and propped him in a sitting position. The canvas wind-dodger gave him some protection but not much. His eyes were open and following our actions and he seemed aware of what was going on. I put the emetic to his lips and tilted the mug but the fluid just trickled down his chin. I forced his head back and poured some of the emetic into his mouth. Clearly, all sensation wasn't lost, for his face contorted into an involuntary grimace of distaste: more importantly, his Adam's apple bobbed up and down and I knew he'd swallowed some of it. Encouraged, I poured in twice as much, and this time he swallowed it all. Not ten seconds later he was as violently ill as ever I've seen a man be. Over Mary's protests and in spite of Allison's very evident apprehension I forced some more of the salt and water on him: when he started coughing blood I turned my attention to Oakley.

Within fifteen minutes we had two still very ill men on our hands, clearly suffering violent abdominal pains and weak to the point of exhaustion, but, more importantly, we had two men who weren't going to go the same way as the unfortunate Antonio had gone. Allison was at the wheel, with the *Morning Rose* back on course: Mary dear, her straw-coloured hair now matted with snow, crouched beside a very groggy Oakley: Smithy was now sufficiently recovered to sit on the storm-sill of the wheel-house, though he still required my arm to brace him against the staggering of the *Morning Rose*. He was beginning to recover the use of his voice although only to a minimal extent.

'Brandy,' he croaked.

I shook my head. 'Contra-indicated. That's what the textbooks say.'

'Otard-Dupuy,' he insisted. At least his mind was clear enough. I rose and got him a bottle from Captain Imrie's private reserve. After what his stomach had just been through, nothing short of carbolic acid was going to damage it any more. He put the bottle to his head, swallowed and was immediately sick again.

'Maybe I should have given you cognac in the first place,' I said. 'Salt water comes cheaper, though.'

He tried to smile, a brief and painful effort, and tilted the bottle again. This time the cognac stayed down, he must have had a stomach lined with steel or asbestos. I took the bottle from him and offered it to Oakley, who winced and shook his head.

'Who's got the wheel?' Smithy's voice was a hoarse and strained whisper as if it hurt him to speak, which it almost certainly did.

'Allison.'

He nodded, satisfied. 'Damn boat,' he said. 'Damn sea. I'm sea-sick. Me. Sea-sick.'

'You're sick, all right. Nothing to do with the sea. This damn boat wallowing about in this damn sea was all that saved you: a flat calm and Smithy was among the immortals.' I tried to think why anyone who was not completely unhinged should want Smithy and Oakley among the immortals but the idea was so preposterous that I abandoned it almost the moment it occurred to me. 'Food poisoning and I was lucky. I got here in time.'

He nodded but kept quiet. It probably hurt him too much to talk. Mary dear said: 'Mr Oakley's hands and face are freezing and he's shaking with the cold. So am I, for that matter.'

And so, I realized, was I. I helped Smithy to a bolted chair beyond the wheel, then went to assist Mary dear who was trying to get a jelly-kneed Oakley to his feet. We'd just got Oakley approximately upright, no easy task, for he was practically a dead weight and we required one hand for him and one for ourselves, when Goin and the Count appeared at the top of the ladder.

'Thank God, at last!' Goin was slightly out of breath but not one hair was out of place. 'We've been looking for you every—what on earth! Is that man drunk?'

'He's sick. The same sickness as Antonio had, only he's been lucky. What's the panic?'

'The same sickness—you must come at once, Marlowe. My God, this is turning into a regular epidemic.'

'A moment.' I helped Oakley inside and lowered him into as comfortable a position as possible atop some kapok life-jackets. 'Another casualty, I take it?'

'Yes, Otto Gerran.' Maybe I lifted an eyebrow, I forget, I do know I felt no particular surprise, it seemed to me that anyone who had been within sniffing distance of that damned aconite was liable to keel over at any moment. 'I called at his cabin ten minutes ago, there was no reply and I went in and there he was, rolling about the carpet—'

The irreverent thought came to me that, with his almost perfectly spherical shape, no one had ever been better equipped for rolling about a carpet than Otto was: it seemed unlikely that Otto was seeing the humorous side of it at that moment. I said to Allison: 'Can you get anyone up here to help you?'

'No trouble.' The quartermaster nodded at the small exchange in the corner. 'I've only to phone the mess-deck.'

'No need.' It was the Count. 'I'll stay.'

'That's very kind.' I nodded at Smithy and Oakley in turn. 'They're not fit to go below yet. If they try to, they'll like as not end up over the side. Could you get them some blankets?'

'Of course.' He hesitated. 'My cabin—'

'Is locked. Mine's not. There are blankets on the bed and extra ones at the foot of the hanging locker.' The Count left and I turned to Allison. 'Short of dynamiting his door open, how do I attract the captain's attention? He seems to be a sound sleeper.'

Allison smiled and again indicated the corner exchange. 'The bridge phone hangs just above his head. There's a resistance in the circuit. I can make the call-up sound like the QE 2's fog-horn.'

'Tell him to come along to Mr Gerran's room and tell him it's urgent.'

'Well.' Allison was uncertain. 'Captain Imrie doesn't much like being woken up in the middle of the night. Not without an awfully good reason, that is, and now that the mate and bo'sun are all right again, like—'

'Tell him Antonio is dead.'

CHAPTER FOUR

At least Otto wasn't dead. Even above the sound of the wind and the sound of the sea, the creakings and groanings as the elderly trawler slammed her way into the Arctic gale, Otto's voice could be distinctly heard at least a dozen feet from his cabin door. What he was saying, however, was far from distinct, the tearing gasps and agonized moans boded ill for what we would see when we opened the door.

Otto Gerran looked as he sounded, not quite *in extremis* but rapidly heading that way. As Goin had said, he was indeed rolling about the floor, both hands clutching his throat as if he was trying to throttle himself: his normally puce complexion had deepened to a dark and dangerous-looking purple, his eyes were bloodshot and a purplish foam at his mouth had stained his lips to almost the same colour as his face: or maybe his lips were purplish anyway, like a man with cyanosis. As far as I could see he hadn't a single symptom in common with Smithy and Oakley: so much for the toxicological experts and their learned text-books.

I said to Goin: 'Let's get him on his feet and along to the bathroom.' As a statement of intent it was clear and simple enough, but its execution was far from simple: it was impossible. The task of hoisting 245 lbs of unco-operative jelly-fish to the vertical proved to be quite beyond us. I was just about to abandon the attempt and administer what would certainly be a very messy first aid on the spot when Captain Imrie and Mr Stokes entered the cabin. My surprise at the remarkable promptness with which they had put in an appearance was as nothing compared to my initial astonishment at observing that both men were fully dressed: it was not until I noticed the horizontal creases in their trousers that I realized that they had gone to sleep with all their clothes on. I made a brief prayer for Smithy's swift and complete recovery.

'What in the name of God goes on?' Whatever condition Captain Imrie had been in an hour or so ago, he was completely sober now. 'Allison says that Italian fellow's dead and—' He stopped abruptly as Goin and I moved sufficiently apart to let him have his first glimpse of the prostrate, moaning Gerran. 'Jesus wept!' He moved forward and stared down. 'What the devil—an epileptic fit?'

'Poison. The same poison that killed Antonio and nearly killed the mate and Oakley. Come on, give us a hand to get him along to the bathroom.'

'Poison!' He looked at Mr Stokes as if to hear from him confirmation that it couldn't possibly be poison, but Mr Stokes wasn't in the mood for confirming anything, he just stared with a kind of numbed fascination at the writhing man on the floor. 'Poison! On *my* ship. What poison? Where did they get it? Who gave it to them. Why should—'

'I'm a doctor, not a detective. I don't know anything about who, where, when, why, what. All I know is that a man's dying while we're talking.'

It took the four of us less than thirty seconds to get Otto Gerran along to the bathroom. It was a pretty rough piece of manhandling but it was a fair assumption that he would rather be Otto Gerran, bruised but alive, than Otto Gerran, unmarked but dead. The emetic worked just as swiftly and effectively as it had with Smithy and Oakley and within three minutes we had him back in his bunk under a mound of blankets. He was still moaning incoherently and shivering so violently that his teeth chattered uncontrollably, but the deep purple had begun to recede from his cheeks and the foam had dried on his lips.

'I think he's OK now but please keep an eye on him, will you?' I said to Goin. 'I'll be back in five minutes.'

Captain Imrie stopped me at the door. 'If you please, Dr Marlowe, a word with you.'

'Later.'

'Now. As master of this vessel—' I put a hand on his shoulder and he became silent. I felt like saying that as master of this vessel he'd been awash in scotch and snoring in his bunk when people were all around dropping like flies but it would have been less than fair: I was irritable because unpleasant things were happening that should not have been happening and I didn't know why, or who was responsible.

'Otto Gerran will live,' I said. 'He'll live because he was lucky enough to have Mr Goin here stop by his cabin. How many other people are lying on their cabin floors who haven't been lucky enough to have someone stop by, people so far gone that they can't even reach their doors? Four casualties so far: who's to say there isn't a dozen?'

'A dozen? Aye. Aye, of course.' If I was out of my depth, Captain Imrie was submerged. 'We'll come with you.'

'I can manage.'

'Like you managed with Mr Gerran here?'

We made our way directly to the recreation room. There were ten people there, all men, mostly silent, mostly unhappy: it is not easy to be talkative and cheerful when you're hanging on to your seat with one hand and your drink with the other. The Three Apostles, whether because of exhaustion or popular demand, had laid the tools of their trade aside and were having a drink with their boss Josh Hendriks, a small, thin, stern and middle-aged Anglo-Dutchman with a perpetual worried frown. Even when off-duty, he was festooned with a mass of strap-hung electronic and recording equipment: word had it that he slept so accoutred. Stryker, who appeared far from overcome by concern for his ailing wife, sat at a table in a corner, talking to Conrad and two other actors, Gunther Jungbeck and Jon Heyter. At a third table John Halliday, the stills photographer and Sandy, the props man, made up the company. No one, as far as I could judge, was suffering from anything that couldn't be accounted for by the big dipper antics of the *Morning Rose*. One or two glances of mildly speculative curiosity came our way, but I volunteered no explanation for our unaccustomed visit there: explanations take time but the effects of *aconitine*, as was being relentlessly borne in upon me, waited for no man.

Allen and Mary darling we found in the otherwise deserted lounge, more green-faced than ever but clasping hands and gazing at each other with the rapt intensity of those who know there will be no tomorrow: their noses were so close together that they must have been cross-eyed from their attempts to focus. For the first time since I'd met her Mary darling had removed her enormous spectacles—misted lenses due to Allen's heavy breathing, I had no doubt—and without them she really was a very pretty young girl with none of that rather naked and defenceless look that so often characterizes the habitual wearer of glasses when those are removed. One thing was for sure, there was nothing wrong with Allen's eyesight.

I glanced at the liquor cupboard in the corner. The glass-fronted doors were intact from which I assumed that Lonnie Gilbert's bunch of keys were capable of opening most things: had they failed here I would have looked for signs of the use of some other instrument, not, perhaps, the berserk wielding of a fire-axe but at least the discreet employment of a wood chisel: but there were no such signs.

Heissman was asleep in his cabin, uneasily, restlessly asleep, but clearly not ill. Next door Neal Divine, his bed-board raised so high that he was barely visible, looked more like a medieval bishop than ever, but a happily unconscious one this time. Lonnie was sitting upright in his bunk, his arms folded across his ample midriff, and from the fact that his right hand was out of sight under the coverlet, almost certainly and lovingly wrapped round the neck of a bottle of purloined scotch, and the further fact that he wore a beatific smile, it was clear that his plethora of keys could be put to a very catholic variety of uses.

I passed up Judith Haynes's cabin—she'd had no dinner—and went into what I knew to be, at that moment, the last occupied cabin. The unit's chief electrician, a large, fat, red-faced and chubby-cheeked individual rejoicing in the name of Frederick Crispin Harbottle, was propped on an elbow and moodily eating an apple: appearances to the contrary, he was an invincibly morose and wholly pessimistic man. For reasons I had been unable to discover, he was known to all as Eddie: rumour had it that he had been heard to speak, in the same breath, of himself and that other rather better-known electrician, Thomas Edison.

'Sorry,' I said. 'We've got some cases of food poisoning. You're not one of them, obviously.' I nodded towards the recumbent occupant of the other bed, who was lying curled up with his back to us. 'How's the Duke?'

'Alive.' Eddie spoke in a tone of philosophical resignation. 'Moaning and groaning about his bellyache before he dropped off. Moans and groans nearly every night, come to that. You know what the Duke's like, he just can't help himself.'

We all knew what he was like. If it is possible for a person to become a legend within the space of four days then Cecil

Golightly had become just that. His unbridled gluttony lay just within the bounds of credibility and when Otto, less than an hour previously, had referred to him as a little pig who never lifted his eyes from the table he had spoken no more than the truth. The Duke's voracious capacity for food was as abnormal as his obviously practically defunct metabolic system, for he resembled nothing so much as a man newly emerged from a long stay in a concentration camp.

More out of habit than anything I bent over to give him a cursory glance and I was glad I did, for what I saw were wide-open, pain-dulled eyes moving wildly and purposelessly from side to side, ashen lips working soundlessly in an ashen face and the hooked fingers of both hands digging deep into his stomach as if he were trying to tear it open.

I'd told Goin that I'd be back in Otto's cabin in five minutes: I was back in forty-five. The Duke, because he had been so very much longer without treatment than Smithy, Oakley or Gerran, had gone very, very close to the edge indeed, to the extent that I had on one occasion almost given up his case as being intractably hopeless, but the Duke was a great deal more stubborn than I was and that skeletal frame harboured an iron constitution: even so, without almost continuous artificial respiration, a heart stimulant injection and the copious use of oxygen, he would surely have died: now he would as surely live.

'Is this the end of it, then? Is this the end?' Otto Gerran spoke in a weakly querulous voice and, on the face of it, I had to admit that he had every right to sound both weak and querulous. He hadn't as yet regained his normal colour, he looked as haggard as a heavily-jowled man ever can and it was clear that his recent experience had left him pretty exhausted: and with this outbreak of poisoning coming on top of the continuously hostile weather that had prevented him from shooting even a foot of background film, Otto had reason to believe that the fates were not on his side.

'I should think so,' I said. In view of the fact that he had aboard some ill-disposed person who was clearly a dab hand with some of the more esoteric poisons this was as unwarrantedly optimistic a statement as I could remember making, but I had to say something. 'Any other victims would have shown the symptoms before now: and I've checked every-one.'

'Have you now?' Captain Imrie asked. 'How about my crew? They eat the same food as you do.'

'I hadn't thought of that.' And I hadn't. Because of some mental block or simply because of lack of thought, I'd assumed, wholly without reason, that the effects would be confined to the film unit people: Captain Imrie was probably thinking that I regarded his men as second-rate citizens who, when measured against Otto's valuable and expensive cast and crew, hardly merited serious consideration. I went on: 'What I mean is, I didn't know that. That they ate the same food. Should have been obvious. If you'll just show me—'

With Mr Stokes in lugubrious attendance, Captain Imrie led me round the crew quarters. Those consisted of five separate cabins—two for the deck staff, one for the engine-room staff, one for the two cooks and the last for the two stewards. It was the last one that we visited first.

We opened the door and just stood there for what then seemed like an unconscionably long time but was probably only a few seconds, mindless creatures bereft of will and speech and power of motion. I was the first to recover and stepped inside.

The stench was so nauseating that I came close to being sick for the first time that night and the cabin itself was in a state of indescribable confusion, chairs knocked over, clothes strewn everywhere and both bunks completely denuded of sheets and blankets which were scattered in a torn and tangled mess over the deck. The first and overwhelming im-pression was that there had been a fight to the death, but both Moxen and Scott, the latter almost covered in a shredded sheet, looked curiously peaceful as they lay there, and neither bore any marks of violence.

'I say we go back. I say we return now.' Captain Imrie wedged himself more deeply into his chair as if establishing both a physically and argumentatively commanding position. 'You gentlemen will bear in mind that I am the master of this vessel, that I have responsibilities towards both passengers and crew.' He lifted his bottle from the wrought-iron stand and helped himself lavishly and I observed, automatically and with little surprise, that his hand was not quite steady. 'If I'd typhoid or cholera aboard I'd sail at once for quarantine in the nearest port where medical assistance is available. Three dead and four seriously ill, I don't see that cholera or typhoid could be any worse than we have here on the *Morning Rose*. Who's going to be the next to die?' He looked at me almost accusingly. Imrie seemed to be adopting the understandable attitude that, as a doctor, it was my duty to preserve life and that as I wasn't making a very good job of it what was happening was largely my fault. 'Dr Marlowe here admits that he is at a loss to understand the reasons for this—this lethal outbreak. Surely to God that itself is reason enough to call this off?'

'It's a long, long way back to Wick,' Smithy said. Like Goin, seated beside him, Smithy was swathed in a couple of blankets and, like Otto, he still looked very much under the weather. 'A lot can happen in that time.'

'Wick, Mr Smith? I wasn't thinking of Wick. I can be in Hammerfest in twenty-four hours.'

'Less,' said Mr Stokes. He sipped his rum, deliberated and made his pronouncement. 'With the wind and the sea on the port quarter and a little assistance from me in the engine-room? Twenty hours.' He went over his homework and found it faultless. 'Yes, twenty hours.'

'You see?' Imrie transferred his piercing blue gaze from myself to Otto. 'Twenty hours.'

When we'd established that there had been no more casualties among the crew Captain Imrie, in what was for him a very peremptory fashion, had summoned Otto to the saloon and Otto in turn had sent for his three fellow directors, Goin, Heissman and Stryker. The other director, Miss Haynes, was, Stryker had reported, very deeply asleep, which was less than surprising in view of the sedatives I'd prescribed for her. The Count had joined the meeting without invitation but everyone appeared to accept his presence there as natural.

To say that there was an air of panic in the saloon would have been exaggeration, albeit a forgivable one, but to say that there was a marked degree of apprehension, concern and uncertainty would have erred on the side of understatement. Otto Gerran, perhaps, was more upset than any other person present, and understandably so, for Otto had a great deal more to lose than any other person present.

'I appreciate the reasons for your anxiety,' Otto said, 'and your concern for us all does you the greatest credit. But I think this concern is making you over-cautious. Dr Marlowe says that this—ah—epidemic is definitely over. We are going to look very foolish indeed if we turn and run now and then nothing more happens.'

Captain Imrie said: 'I'm too old, Mr Gerran, to care what I look like. If it's a choice between looking a fool and having another dead man on my hands, then I'd rather look a fool any time.'

'I agree with Mr Gerran,' Heissman said. He still looked sick and he sounded sick. 'To throw it all away when we're so near—just over a day to Bear Island. Drop us off there and then go to Hammerfest—just as in the original plan. That means—well, you'd be in Hammerfest in say sixty hours instead of twenty-four. What's going to happen in that extra thirty-six hours that's not going to happen in the next twenty-four? Lose everything for thirty-six hours just because you're running scared?'

'I am not running scared, as you say.' There was something impressive about Imrie's quiet dignity. 'My first—'

'I wasn't referring to you personally,' Heissman said.

'My first concern is for the people under my charge. And they are under *my* charge. *I* am the person responsible. *I* must make the decision.'

'Granted, Captain, granted.' Goin was his usual imperturbable self, a calm and reasonable man. 'But one has to strike a balance in these matters, don't you think. Against what Dr Marlow now regards as being a very remote possibility of another outbreak of food poisoning occurring, there's the near certainty—no, I would go further and say that there's the inevitability—that if we go directly to Hammerfest we'll be put in quarantine for God knows how long. A week, maybe two weeks, before the port medical authorities give us clearance. And then it'll be too late, we'd just have to abandon all ideas about making the film at all and go home.' Less than a couple of hours previously, I recalled, Heissman had been making most disparaging remarks about Otto's mental capacities, but he'd backed him up against Captain Imrie and now here was Goin doing the same thing: both men knew which side of their bread required butter. 'The losses to Olympus Productions will be enormous.'

'Don't be telling me that, Mr Goin,' Imrie said. 'What you

mean is that the losses to the insurance company—or companies—will be enormous.'

'Wrong,' Stryker said and from his tone and attitude it was clear that directorial solidarity on the board of Olympus Productions was complete. 'Severally and personally, all members of the cast and crew are insured. The film project—a guarantee as to its successful conclusion—was uninsurable, at least in terms of the premiums demanded. We, and we alone, bear the loss—and I would add that for Mr Gerran, who is by far and away the biggest shareholder, the effects would be ruinous.'

'I am very sorry about that.' Captain Imrie seemed genuinely sympathetic but he didn't for a moment sound like a man who was preparing to abandon his position. 'But that's your concern, I'm afraid. And I would remind you, Mr Gerran, of what you yourself said earlier on this evening. "Health," you said, "is a damned sight more important than any profit we might make from this film." Wouldn't you say this is a case in point?'

'That's nonsense to say that,' Goin said equably. He had the rare gift of being able to make potentially offensive statements in a quietly rational voice that somehow robbed them of all offence. ' "Profit", you say was the word Mr Gerran used. Certainly, Mr Gerran would willingly pass up any potential profit if the need arose, and that need wouldn't have to be very pressing or demanding. He's done it before.' This was at variance with the impression I'd formed of Otto, but then Goin had known him many more years than I had days. 'Even without profit we could still make our way by breaking even, which is as much as most film companies can hope for these days. But you're not talking—*we're* not talking —about lack of profit, we're talking about a total and non-recoverable loss, a loss that would run into six figures and break us entirely. We've put our collective shirt on this one, Captain Imrie, yet you're talking airily of liquidating our company, putting dozens of technicians—and their families —on the breadline and damaging, very likely beyond repair, the careers of some very promising actors and actresses. And all of this for what? The remote chance—according to Dr Marlowe, the very remote chance—that someone may fall ill again. Haven't you got things just a little bit out of proportion, Captain Imrie?'

If he had, Captain Imrie wasn't saying so. He wasn't saying anything. He didn't exactly have the look of a man who was thinking and thinking hard.

'Mr Goin puts it very succinctly,' Otto said. 'Very succinctly indeed. And there's a major point that seems to have escaped you, Captain Imrie. You have reminded me of something I said earlier. May I remind you of something *you* said earlier. May I remind you—'

'And may I interrupt, Mr Gerran,' I said. I knew damn well what he was going to say and the last thing I wanted was to hear him say it. 'Please. A peace formula, if you wish. You want to continue. So does Mr Goin, so does Mr Heissman. So do I—if only because my reputation as a doctor seems to depend on it. Tadeusz?'

'No question,' said the Count. 'Bear Island.'

'And, of course, it would be unfair to ask either Mr Smith or Mr Stokes. So I propose—'

'This isn't Parliament, Dr Marlowe,' Imrie said. 'Not even a local town council. Decisions aboard a vessel at sea are not arrived at by popular vote.'

'I've no intention that they should be. I suggest we draw up a document. I suggest we note Captain Imrie's proposals and considered opinions. I suggest if more illness occurs we run immediately for Hammerfest, even although we are at the time only one hour distant from Bear Island. I suggest it be recorded that Captain Imrie be protected and absolved from any accusation of hazarding the health of his crew and passengers in light of the medical officer's affidavit—which I will write out and sign—that no such hazard exists: the only charge the captain has to worry about at any time is the physical hazarding of his vessel and that doesn't exist here. Then we will state that the captain is absolved from all blame and responsibility for any consequences arising from our decision: the navigation and handling of the vessel remain, of course, his sole responsibility. Then all five of us sign it. Captain Imrie?'

'Agreed.' There is a time to be prompt and Captain Imrie clearly regarded this as such a time. At best, the proposal was a lame compromise, but one he was glad to accept. 'Now, if you gentlemen will excuse me. I have to be up betimes —4 a.m. to be precise.' I wondered when he had last risen at that unearthly hour—not, probably, since his fishing days

68

had ended: but the illness of mate and bo'sun made for exceptional circumstances. He looked at me. 'I will have that document at breakfast?'

'At breakfast. I wonder, Captain, if on your way to bed you could ask Haggerty to come to see me. I'd ask him personally, but he's a bit touchy about civilians like myself.'

'A lifetime in the Royal Navy is not forgotten overnight. Now?'

'Say ten minutes? In the galley.'

'Still pursuing your inquiries, is that it? It's not your fault, Dr Marlowe.'

If it wasn't my fault, I thought, I wished they'd all stop making me feel it was. Instead I thanked him and said good night and he said good night to us and left accompanied by Smithy and Mr Stokes. Otto steepled his fingers and regarded me in his best chairman of the board fashion.

'We owe you our thanks, Dr Marlowe. That was well done, an excellent face-saving proposal.' He smiled. 'I am not accustomed to suffering interruption lightly but in this case it was justified.'

'If I hadn't interrupted we'd all be on our way to Hammerfest now. You were about to remind him of that part of your contract with him which states that he will obey all your orders other than those that actually endanger the vessel. You were about to point out that, as no such physical danger exists, he was technically in breach of contract and so would be legally liable to the forfeiture of the entire contract fee, which would certainly have ruined him. But for a man like that money ranks a long, long way behind pride and Captain Imrie is a very proud man. He'd have told you to go to hell and turned his ship for Hammerfest.'

'I'd say that our worthy physician's assessment is a hundred per cent accurate.' The Count had found some brandy and now helped himself freely. 'You came close there, Otto, my boy.'

If the company chairman felt annoyance at being thus familiarly addressed by his cameraman, he showed no evidence of it. He said: 'I agree. We are in your debt, Dr Marlowe.'

'A free seat at the première,' I said, 'and all debts discharged.' I left the board to its deliberations and weaved my unsteady way down to the passenger accommodation. Allen and Mary darling were still in the same place in the lounge, only now she had her head on his shoulder and seemed to be asleep. I gave him a casually acknowledging wave of my hand and he answered in kind: he seemed to be becoming accustomed to my peripatetic presence.

I entered the Duke's cabin without knocking, lest there was someone there asleep. There was. Eddie, the electrician, was very sound indeed and snoring heavily, the sight of his cabin mate's close brush with the reaper hadn't unnerved him any that I could see. Cecil Golightly was awake and looking understandably very pale and drawn but not noticeably suffering, largely, it seemed very likely, because Mary Stuart, who was just as pale as he was, was sitting by his bedside and holding his far from reluctant hand. I was beginning to think that perhaps she had more friends than either she or I thought she had.

'Good lord!' I said. 'You still here?'

'Didn't you expect me to be? You asked me to stay and keep an eye on him. Or had you forgotten?'

'Certainly not,' I lied. 'Didn't expect you to remain so long, that's all. You've been very kind.' I looked down upon the recumbent Duke. 'Feeling a bit better?'

'Lots, Doctor. Lots better.' With his voice not much more than a strained whisper he didn't sound it, but then, after what he'd been through in the past hour I didn't expect him to.

'I'd like to have a little talk with you,' I said. 'Just a couple of minutes. Feel up to it?'

He nodded. Mary dear said: 'I'll leave you then,' and made to rise but I put a restraining hand on her shoulder.

'No need. The Duke and I share no secrets.' I gave him what I hoped would be translated as a thoughtful look. 'It's just possible, though, that the Duke might be concealing a secret from me.'

'Me? A—a secret?' Cecil was genuinely puzzled.

'Tell me. When did the pains start?'

'The pains? Half-past nine. Ten. Something like that, I can't be sure.' Temporarily bereft of his quick wit and chirpy humour, the Duke was a very woebegone Cockney sparrow indeed. 'When this thing hit me I wasn't feeling much like looking at watches.'

'I'm sure you weren't,' I said sympathetically. 'And dinner was the last bite you had tonight?'

'The last bite.' His voice even sounded firm.

'Not even another teeny-weeny snack? You see, Cecil, I'm puzzled. Miss Stuart has told you that others have been ill, too?' He nodded. 'Well, the odd thing is that the others began to be ill almost at once after eating. But it took well over an hour in your case. I find it very strange. You're absolutely sure? You'd nothing?'

'Doctor!' He wheezed a bit. 'You know me.'

'Yes. That's why I'm asking.' Mary dear was looking at me with coolly appraising and rather reproachful brown eyes, any moment now she was going to say didn't I know Cecil was a sick man. 'You see, I know that the others who were sick were suffering from some kind of food poisoning that they picked up at dinner and I know how to treat them. But your illness must have had another cause, I've no idea what it was or how to treat it and until I can make some sort of diagnosis I can't afford to take chances. You're going to be very hungry tomorrow morning and for some time after that but I have to give your system time to settle down: I don't want you to eat *anything* that might provoke a reaction so violent that I mightn't be able to cope with it this time. Time will give the all clear.'

'I don't understand, Doctor.'

'Tea and toast for the next three days.'

The Duke didn't turn any paler than he was because that was impossible: he just looked stricken.

'Tea and toast?' His voice was a weak croak. 'For three days!'

'For your own good, Cecil.' I patted him sympathetically on the shoulder and straightened, preparing to leave. 'We just want to see you on your feet again.'

'I was feeling peckish, like,' the Duke explained with some pathos.

'When?'

'Just before nine.'

'Just before—half an hour after dinner?'

'That's when I feel the most peckish. I nipped up into the galley, see, and there was this casserole on a hot plate but I'd only time for one spoonful when I heard two people coming so I jumped into the cool room.'

'And waited?'

'I had to wait.' The Duke sounded almost virtuous. 'If I'd opened the door even a crack they'd have seen me.'

'So they didn't see you. Which means they left. Then?'
'They'd scoffed the bleedin' lot,' the Duke said bitterly.
'Lucky you.'
'Lucky?'
'Moxen and Scott, wasn't it? The stewards?'
'How—how did you know?'
'They saved your life, Duke.'
'They what?'
'They ate what you were going to eat. So you're alive.
They're both dead.'

Allen and Mary darling had obviously given up their midnight vigil for the lounge was deserted. I'd five minutes before I met Haggerty in the galley, five minutes in which to collect my thoughts: the trouble was that I had to find them first before I could collect them. And then I realized I was not even going to have the time to find them for there were footsteps on the companionway. Trying with very little success to cope with the wild staggering of the *Morning Rose*, Mary Stuart made her unsteady way towards an armchair opposite me and collapsed into rather than sat in it. Insofar as it was possible for such an extraordinarily good-looking young woman to look haggard, then she looked haggard: her face was grey. I should have felt annoyed with her for interrupting my train of thought, assuming, that was, that I ever managed to get the train under way, but I could feel no such emotion: I was beginning to realize, though only vaguely, that I was incapable of entertaining towards this Latvian girl any feeling that remotely bordered on the hostile. Besides, she had clearly come to talk to me, and if she did she wanted some help, or reassuring or understanding and it would come very hardly indeed for so proud, so remote, so aloof a girl to ask for any of those. In all conscience, I couldn't make things difficult for her.

'Been sick?' I asked. As a conversational gambit it lacked something but doctors aren't supposed to have manners. She nodded. She was clasping her hands so tightly that I could see the faint ivory gleam of knuckles.

'I thought you were a good sailor?' The light touch.

'It is not the sea that makes me ill.'

I abandoned the light touch. 'Mary dear, why don't you lie down and try to sleep?'

'I see. You tell me that two more men have been poisoned and died and then I am supposed to drop off to sleep and have happy dreams. Is that it?' I said nothing and she went on wryly: 'You're not very good at breaking bad news, are you?'

'Professional callousness. You didn't come here just to reproach me with my tactlessness. What is it, Mary dear?'

'Why do you call me "Mary dear"?'

'It offends you?'

'Oh, no. Not when you say it.' From any other woman the words would have carried coquettish overtones, but there were none such here. It was meant as a statement of fact, no more.

'Very well, then.' I don't know what I meant by 'Very well, then,' it just made me feel obscurely clever. 'Tell me.'

'I'm afraid,' she said simply.

So she was afraid. She was tired, overwrought, she'd tended four very, very sick men who'd been poisoned, she'd learnt that three others whom she knew had died of poison and the violence of the Arctic gale raging outside was sufficient to give pause to even the most intrepid. But I said none of those things to her.

'We're all afraid at times, Mary.'

'You too?'

'Me too.'

'Are you afraid now?'

'No. What's there to be afraid of?'

'Death. Sickness and death.'

'I have to live with death, Mary. I detest it, of course I do, but I don't fear it. If I did, I'd be no good as a doctor. Would I now?'

'I do not express myself well. Death I can accept. But not when it strikes out blindly and you know that it is not blind. As it is here. It strikes out carelessly, recklessly, without cause or reason, but you know there is cause and reason. Do you —do you know what I mean?'

I knew perfectly well what she meant. I said: 'Even at my brightest and best, metaphysics are hardly my forte. Maybe the old man with the scythe does show discrimination in his indiscrimination, but I'm too tired—'

'I'm not talking about metaphysics.' She made an almost angry little gesture with her clasped hands. 'There's something terribly far wrong aboard this ship, Dr Marlowe.'

'Terribly far wrong?' Heaven only knew that I couldn't have agreed with her more. 'What should be wrong, Mary dear?'

She said gravely: 'You would not patronize me, Dr Marlowe? You would not humour a silly female?'

I had to answer at once so I said obliquely but deliberately: 'I would not insult you, Mary dear. I like you too much for that.'

'Do you really?' She smiled faintly, whether amused by me or pleased at what I'd said I couldn't guess. 'Do you like all the others, too?'

'Do I—I'm sorry.'

'Don't you find something odd, something very strange about the people, about the atmosphere they create?'

I was on safer ground here. I said frankly: 'I'd have to have been born deaf and blind not to notice it. One is warding off barely-expressed hostilities, elbowing aside tensions, wading through undercurrents the whole of the livelong day, and at the same time, if you'll forgive the mixing of the metaphors, trying to shield one's eyes from the constant shower of sparks given off by everyone trying to grind their own axes at the same time. Everyone is so frighteningly friendly to everyone else until the moment comes, of course, when everyone else is so misguided as to turn his or her back. Our esteemed employer, Otto Gerran, cannot speak too highly of his fellow directors, Heissman, Stryker, Goin and his dear daughter, all of whom he vilifies most fearfully the moment they are out of earshot, all of which would be wholly unforgivable were it not for the fact that Heissman, Stryker and his dear daughter each behave in the same fashion to Otto and *their* co-directors. You get the same petty jealousies, the same patently false sincerities, the same smilers with the knives beneath the cloaks on the lower film unit crew level —not that they, and probably rightly, would regard themselves as being any lower than Otto and his chums—I use the word 'chums', you understand, without regard to the strict meaning of the word. And, just to complicate matters, we have this charming interplay between the first and second divisions. The Duke, Eddie Harbottle, Halliday, the stills man, Hendriks and Sandy all cordially detest what we might call the management, a sentiment that is strongly reciprocated by the management themselves. And everybody seems to have a down on the unfortunate director, Neal Divine. Sure, I've noticed all of this, I'd have to be a zombie not to have, but I disregard ninety-odd per cent and just put it down to the normally healthy backbiting bitchery inseparable from the cinema world. You get fakes, cheats, liars, mountebanks, sycophants, hypocrites the world over, it's just that the movie-making milieu appears to act as a grossly distorting magnifying-glass that selects and highlights all the more undesirable qualities while ignoring or at best diminishing the more desirable ones—one has to assume that there are some.'

'You don't think a great deal of us, do you?'

'Whatever gave you that impression?'

She ignored that. 'And we're all bad?'

'Not all. Not you. Not the other Mary or young Allen— but maybe that's because they're too young yet or too new in this business to have come to terms with the standard norms of behaviour. And I'm pretty sure that Charlie Conrad is on the side of the angels.'

Again the little smile. 'You mean he thinks along the same lines as you?'

'Yes. Do you know him at all?'

'We say good morning.'

'You should get to know him better. He'd like to know you better. He likes you—he said so. And, no, we weren't discussing you—your name cropped up among a dozen others.'

'Flatterer.' Her tone was neutral, I didn't know whether she was referring with pleasure to Conrad or with irony to myself. 'So you agree with me? There is something very strange in the atmosphere here?'

'By normal standards, yes.'

'By any standards.' There was a curious certainty about her. 'Distrust, suspicion, jealousy, one looks to find those things in our unpleasant little world, but one does not look to find them on the scale that we have here. Do not forget that I know about those things. I was born in a Communist country, I was brought up in a Communist country. You understand?'

'Yes. When did you get away?'

'Two years ago. Just two years.'

'How?'

'Please. Others may wish to use the same way.'

'And I'm in the pay of the Kremlin. As you wish.'

'You are offended?' I shook my head. 'Distrust, sus-picion, jealousy, Dr Marlowe. But there is more here, much more. There is hate and there is fear. I—I can smell it. Can't you?'

'You have a point to make, Mary dear, and you're leading up to it in a very tortuous fashion. I wish you would come to it.' I looked at my watch. 'I do not wish to be rude to you but neither do I wish to be rude to the person who is waiting to see me.'

'If people hate and fear each other enough, terrible things can happen.' This didn't seem to require even an affirmative, so I kept silent and she went on: 'You say that those illnesses, those deaths, are the result of accidental food poisoning. Are they, Dr Marlowe? *Are* they?'

'So this is what has taken you all this long time to lead up to? You think—you think it may have been deliberate, have been engineered by someone. *That's* what you think?' I hoped it was clear to her that the idea had just occurred to me for the first time.

'I don't know what to think. But yes—yes, that's what I think.'

'Who?'

'Who?' She looked at me in what appeared to be genuine astonishment. 'How should I know who? Anybody, I sup-pose.'

'You'd be a sensation as a prosecuting counsel. Then if not who, why?'

She hesitated, looked away, glanced briefly back at me, then looked at the deck. 'I don't know why, either.'

'So you've no basis for this incredible suggestion other than your Communist-trained instincts.'

'I've put it very badly, haven't I?'

'You'd nothing to put, Mary. Just examine the facts and see how ridiculous your suggestion is. Seven disparate people affected and all struck down completely at random—or can you give me a reason why so wildly diverse a group as a film producer, a hairdresser, a camera focus assistant, a mate, a bo'sun and two stewards should be the victims? Can you tell me why some lived, why some died? Can you tell me why two of the victims assimilated this poison from food served at the saloon table, two from food consumed in the galley and one, the Duke, who may have been poisoned in either the galley or the saloon? Can you, Mary?'

She shook her head, the straw-coloured hair fell over her eyes and she let it stay there. Maybe she didn't want to look at me, maybe she didn't want me to look at her.

'After today,' I said, 'I've been left standing, I've been widely given to understand, among the ruins of my professional reputation but I'll wager what's left of it, together with anything else you care to name, that this whole-sale poisoning is completely accidental and that no person aboard the *Morning Rose* wished to, hoped to or intended to poison those seven men.' Which was a different thing entirely from claiming that there was no one aboard the *Morning Rose* who was responsible for the tragedy. 'Not unless we have a madman aboard, and you can say what you like—you've already said it—about our highly—ah—individualistic shipboard companions, none of them is unhinged. Not, that is, criminally unhinged.'

She hadn't looked at me once when I was speaking, and even when I'd finished, continued to present me with a view of the crown of her head. I rose, lurched across to the armchair where she was sitting, braced myself with one hand on the back of her chair and placed a finger of the other under her chin. She straightened and brushed back the hair from her eyes, brown eyes, large and still and full of fear. I smiled at her and she smiled back and the smile didn't touch her eyes. I turned and left the lounge.

I was quite ten minutes late for my appointment in the galley and as Haggerty had already made abundantly clear to me that he was a stickler for the proprieties, I expected to find him in a mood anywhere between stiff outrage and cool disapproval. Haggerty's attention, however, was occupied with more immediate and pressing matters, for as I approached the galley through the stewards' pantry I could hear the sound of a loud and very angry altercation. At least, Haggerty was being loud and angry.

It wasn't so much an altercation as a monologue and it was Haggerty, his red face crimson now with anger and his periwinkle blue eyes popping, who was conducting it: Sandy, our props man, was the unfortunate party on the other side of this very one-sided argument and his silent acceptance of the abuse that was being heaped upon him stemmed less from the want of something to say than from the want of air. I thought at first that Haggerty had his very large red hand clamped round Sandy's scrawny neck but then realized that he had the two lapels of Sandy's jacket crushed together in one hand: the effect, however, was about the same, and as Sandy was only about half the cook's size there was very little he could do about it. I tapped Haggerty on the shoulder.

'You're choking this man,' I said mildly. Haggerty glanced at me briefly and got back to his choking. I went on, just as mildly: 'This isn't a naval vessel and I'm not a Master-At-Arms so I can't order you about. But I am what the courts would accept as an expert witness and I don't think they'd question my testimony when you're being sued for assault and battery. Could cost you your life's savings, you know.'

Haggerty looked at me again and this time he didn't look away. Reluctantly, he removed his hand from the little man's collar and just stood there, glaring and breathing heavily, momentarily, it seemed, at a loss for words.

Sandy wasn't. After he'd massaged his throat a bit to see if it were still intact, he addressed a considerable amount of unprintable invective to Haggerty, then continued, shouting: 'You see? You heard, you great big ugly baboon. It's the courts for you. Assault and battery, mate, and it'll cost you—'

'Shut up,' I said wearily. 'I didn't see a thing and he didn't lay a finger on you. Be happy you're still breathing.' I looked at Sandy consideringly. I didn't really know him, I knew next to nothing about him, I wasn't even sure whether I liked him or not. Like Allen and the late Antonio, if Sandy had another name no one seemed to know what it was. He claimed to be a Scot but had a powerful Liverpool accent. He was a strange, undersized, wizened leprechaun of a man, with a wrinkled walnut-brown face and head—his pate was gleamingly bald—and stringy white hair that started about earlobe level and cascaded in uncombed disarray over his thin shoulders. He had quick-moving and almost weasel-like eyes but maybe that was unfair to him, it may have been the effect of the steel-legged rimless glasses that he affected. He was given to claiming, when under the influence of gin, which was as often as not, that he not only didn't know his birthday, he didn't even know the year in which he had been born, but put it around 1919 or 1920. The consensus of informed shipboard opinion put the date, not cruelly, at 1900 or slightly earlier.

I noticed for the first time that there were some tins of sardines and pilchards on the deck, and a larger one of corned beef. 'Aha!' I said. 'The midnight skulker strikes again.'

'What was that?' Haggerty said suspiciously.

'You couldn't have given our friend here a big enough helping for dinner,' I said.

'It wasn't for myself.' Sandy, under stress, had a high-pitched squeak of a voice. 'I swear it wasn't. You see—'

'I ought to throw the little runt over the side. Little sneaking robbing bastard that he is. Down here, up to his thieves' tricks, the minute any back's turned. And who's blamed for the theft, eh, tell me that, who's blamed for the theft? Who's got to account to the captain for the missing supplies? Who's got to make the loss good from his own pocket? And who's going to get his pay docked for not locking the galley door?' Haggerty's blood pressure, as he contemplated the injustices of life, was clearly rising again. 'To think,' he said bitterly, 'that I've always trusted my fellow men. I ought to break his bloody neck.'

'Well, you can't do that now,' I said reasonably. 'You can't expect me, as a professional man, to perjure myself in the witness box. Besides, there's no harm done, nothing stolen. You've no losses to pay for, so why get in bad with Captain Imrie?' I looked at Sandy, then at the tins on the floor; 'Was that all you stole?'

'I swear to God—'

'Oh, do be quiet.' I said to Haggerty: 'Where was he, what was he doing when you came in?'

'He'd his bloody great long nose stuck in the big fridge there, that was what he was doing. Caught him red-handed, I did.'

I opened the refrigerator door. Inside it was packed with a large number of items of very restricted variety—butter, cheeses, long-life milk, bacon and tinned meats. That was all. I said to Sandy: 'Come here. I want to look through your clothes.'

'*You* want to look through my clothes?' Sandy had taken heart from his providential deliverance from the threat of physical violence and the knowledge that he would not now be reported to those in authority. 'And who do you think *you* are then? A bleedin' cop? The CID, eh?'

'Just a doctor. A doctor who's trying to find out why three people died tonight.' Sandy stared at me, his eyes widening behind his rimless glasses, and his lower jaw fell down. 'Didn't you know that Moxen and Scott were dead? The two stewards?'

'Aye, I'd heard.' He ran his tongue over his lips. 'What's that got to do with me?'

'I'm not sure. Not yet.'

'You can't pin that on me. What are you talking about?' Sandy's brief moment of truculence was vanished as if it had never been. 'I've nothing to do—'

'Three men died and four almost did. They died or nearly died from food poisoning. Food comes from the galley. I'm interested in people who make unauthorized visits to the galley.' I looked at Haggerty. 'I think we'd better have Captain Imrie along here.'

'No! Christ, no!' Sandy was close to panic. 'Mr Gerran would kill me—'

'Come here.' He came to me, the last resistance gone. I went through his pockets but there was no trace of the only instrument he could have used to infect foodstuffs in the refrigerator, a hypodermic syringe. I said: 'What were you going to do with those tins?'

'They weren't for me. I told you. What would I want with them? I don't eat enough to keep a mouse alive. Ask anyone. They'll tell you.'

I didn't have to ask anyone. What he said was perfectly true: Sandy, like Lonnie Gilbert, depended almost exclusively upon the Distillers Co., Ltd to maintain his calorific quota. But he could still have been using those tins of meat as an insurance, as a red herring, if he'd been caught out as he had been.

'Who were the tins for, then?'

'The Duke. Cecil. I've just been to his cabin. He said he was hungry. No, he didn't. He said he was *going* to be hungry 'cos you'd put him on tea and toast for three days.' I thought back to my interview with the Duke. I'd only used the tea and toast threat to extract information from him and it wasn't until now that I recalled that I had forgotten to withdraw the threat. This much of Sandy's story had to be true.

'The Duke asked you to get some supplies for him?'

'No.'

'You told him you were going to get them?'

'No. I wanted to surprise him. I wanted to see his face when I turned up with the tins.'

Impasse. He could be telling the truth. He could equally well be using the story as a cloak for other and more sinister activities. I couldn't tell and probably would never know. I said: 'You better go and tell your friend the Duke that he'll be back on a normal diet as from breakfast.'

'You mean—I can go?'

'If Mr Haggerty doesn't wish to press a charge.'

'I wouldn't lower myself.' Haggerty clamped his big hand round the back of Sandy's neck with a grip tight enough to make the little man squeal in pain. 'If I ever catch you within sniffing distance of my galley again I won't just squeeze your neck, I'll break the bloody thing.' Haggerty marched him to the door, literally threw him out and returned. 'Got off far too easy if you ask me, sir.'

'He's not worth your ire, Mr Haggerty. He's probably telling the truth—not that makes him any less a sneak-thief. Moxen and Scott ate here tonight after the passengers had dinner?'

'Every night. Waiting staff usually eat before the guests —they preferred it the other way round.' With the departure of Sandy, Haggerty was looking a very troubled and upset man, the loss of the two stewards had clearly shaken him badly and was almost certainly responsible for the violence of his reaction towards Sandy.

'I think I've traced the source of the poison. I believe the horseradish was contaminated with a very unpleasant organism called *clostridium botulinum*, a sporing anaerobe found most commonly in garden soil.' I'd never heard of such a case of contamination but that didn't make it impossible. 'No possible reflection on you—it's totally undetectable before, during and after cooking. Were there any leftovers tonight?'

'Some. I made a casserole for Moxen and Scott and put the rest away.'

'Away?'

'For throwing. There wasn't enough to re-use for anything.'

'So it's gone.' Another door locked.

'On a night like this? No fear. The gash is sealed in poly-thene bags, then they're punctured and go over the side—in the morning.'

The door had opened again. 'You mean it's still here?'

'Of course.' He nodded towards a rectangular plastic box secured to the bulkhead by butterfly nuts. 'There.'

I crossed to the box and lifted the lid. Haggerty said: 'You'll be going to analyse it, is that it?'

'That's what I intended. Rather, to keep it for analysis.' I dropped the lid. 'That won't be possible now. The bin's empty.'

'Empty? Over the side—in this weather?' Haggerty came and unnecessarily checked the bin for himself. 'Bloody funny. And against regulations.'

'Perhaps your assistant—'

'Charlie? That bone-idle layabout. Not him. Besides, he's off-duty tonight.' Haggerty scratched the grey bristle of his hair. 'Lord knows why they did it but it must have been Moxen or Scott.'

'Yes,' I said. 'It must have been.'

I was so tired that I could think of nothing other than my cabin and my bunk. I was so tired that it wasn't until I had arrived at my cabin and looked on the bare bunk that I recalled that all my blankets had been taken away for Smithy and Oakley. I glanced idly at the small table where I'd left the toxicological books that I had been consulting and my tiredness very suddenly left me.

The volume on Medical Jurisprudence that had provided me with the information on *aconitine* was lying with its base pressed hard against the far fiddle of the table, thrown there, of course, by one of the violent lurches of the *Morning Rose*. The silken bookmark ribbon attached to the head of the book stretched out most of its length on the table, which was an unremarkable thing in itself were it not for my dear and distinct recollection that I'd carefully used the bookmark to mark the passage I'd been reading.

I wondered who it was who knew I'd been reading the article on *aconitine*.

CHAPTER FIVE

I suddenly didn't fancy my cabin very much any more. Not, that was, as a place to sleep in. The eccentric shipping millionaire who'd had the *Morning Rose* completely stripped and fitted for passenger accommodation had had a powerful aversion to locks on cabin doors and, having had the means and the opportunity to do so, had translated his theories into practice. It may have been just a phobia or it may have stemmed from his assertion that many people had unnecessarily lost their lives at sea through being trapped in locked cabins as their ships went down—which, in fact, I knew to be true. However it was, it was impossible to lock a cabin door in the *Morning Rose* from the inside: it didn't even have a sliding bolt.

The saloon, I decided, was the place for me. It had, as I recalled, a very comfortable corner bulkhead settee where I could wedge myself and, more importantly, protect my back. The lockers below the settee seats had a splendid assortment of fleecy steamer rugs, another legacy, like the lockless doors, from the previous owner. Best of all, it was a brightly lit and public place, a place where people were liable to come and go even at that late hour, a place where no one could sneak up on you unawares. Not that any of this would offer any bar to anyone so ill-disposed as to take a potshot at me through the saloon's plate glass windows. It was, I supposed, some little consolation that the person or persons bent on mayhem had not so far chosen to resort to overt violence, but that hardly constituted a guarantee that they wouldn't: why the hell couldn't the publishers of reference books emulate the prestigious *Encyclopædia Britannica* and do away with book-marks altogether?

It was then that I recalled that I'd left the board of Olympus Productions in full plenary session up in the saloon. How long ago was that? Twenty minutes, not more. Another twenty minutes, perhaps, and the coast would be clear. It wasn't that I harboured any particular suspicion towards any of the four: they might just consider it very odd if I were to elect to sleep up there for the night when I'd a perfectly comfortable cabin down below.

Partly on impulse, partly to kill some of the intervening time, I decided to have a look at the Duke, to check on his condition, to ensure him a restful night by promising he'd be back on full rations come breakfast time and to find out if Sandy had been telling the truth. His was the third door to the left: the second to the right was wide open, the door stayed back at 90 degrees. It was Mary Stuart's cabin and she was inside but not asleep: she sat in a chair wedged between table and bunk, her eyes wide open, her hands in her lap.

'What's this, then?' I said. 'You look like someone taking part in a wake.'

'I'm not sleepy.'

'And the door open. Expecting company?'

'I hope not. I can't lock the door.'

'You haven't been able to lock the door since you came aboard. It doesn't have a lock.'

'I know. It didn't matter. Not till tonight.'

'You—you're not thinking that someone might sneak up and do you in while you're sleeping?' I said in a tone of a person who could never conceive of such a thing happening to himself.

'I don't know what to think. I'm all right. Please.'

'Afraid? Still?' I shook my head. 'Fie on you. Think of your namesake, young Mary Darling. She's not scared to sleep alone.'

'She's not sleeping alone.'

'She isn't? Ah, well, we live in a permissive age.'

'She's with Allen. In the recreation room.'

'Ah! Then why don't you join them? If it's safety you wrongly imagine you need, why then, there's safety in numbers.'

'I do not like to play—what you say—gooseberry.'

'Oh, fiddlesticks!' I said and went to see the Duke. He had colour, not much but enough, in his cheeks and was plainly on the mend. I asked him how he was.

'Rotten,' said the Duke. He rubbed his stomach.

'Still pretty sore?'

'Hunger pains,' he said.

'Nothing tonight. Tomorrow, you're back on the strength—

forget the tea and toast. By the way, that wasn't very clever of you to send Sandy up to raid the galley. Haggerty nabbed him in the act.'

'Sandy? In the galley?' The surprise was genuine. '*I* didn't send him up.'

'Surely he told you he was going there?'

'Not a word. Look, Doc, you can't pin—'

'Nobody's pinning anything on anybody. I must have taken him up wrong. Maybe he just wanted to surprise you— he said something about you feeling peckish.'

'I said that all right. But honest to God—'

'It's all right. No harm done. Good night.'

I retraced my steps, passing Mary Stuart's open door again. She looked at me but said nothing so I did the same. Back in my cabin I looked at my watch. Five minutes only had elapsed, fifteen to go. I was damned if I was going to wait so long, I was feeling tired again, tired enough to drop off to sleep at any moment, but I had to have a reason to go up there. For the first time I devoted some of my rapidly waning powers of thought to the problem and I had the answer in seconds. I opened my medical bag and extracted three of the most essential items it contained—death certificates. For some odd reason I checked the number that was left—ten. All told, thirteen. I was glad I wasn't superstitious. I stuffed the certificates and a few sheets of rather splendidly headed ship's notepaper—the previous owner hadn't been a man to do things by half—into my briefcase.

I opened the cabin door wide so as to have some light to see by, checked that the passage was empty and swiftly unscrewed the deck-head lamp. This I dropped on the deck from gradually increasing heights starting with about a foot or so until a shake of the lamp close my ear let me hear the unmistakable tinkle of a broken filament. I screwed the now useless lamp back into its holder, took up my briefcase, closed the door and made for the bridge.

The weather, I observed during my very hurried passage across the upper deck and up the bridge ladder, hadn't improved in the slightest. I had the vague impression that the seas were moderating slightly but that may have been because of the fact that I was feeling so tired that I was no longer capable of registering impressions accurately. But one aspect of the weather was beyond question: the almost horizontally driving snow had increased to the extent that the masthead light was no more than an intermittent glow in the gloom above.

Allison was at the wheel, spending more time looking at the radarscope than at the compass, and visibility being what it was, I could see his point. I said: 'Do you know where the captain keeps his crew lists? In his cabin?'

'No.' He glanced over his shoulder. 'In the chart-house there.' He hesitated. 'Why would you want those, Dr Marlowe?'

I pulled a death certificate from the briefcase and held it close to the binnacle light. Allison compressed his lips.

'Top drawer, port locker.'

I found the lists, entered up the name, address, age, place of birth, religion and next of kin of each of the two dead men, replaced the book and made my way down to the saloon. Half an hour had elapsed since I'd left Gerran, his three co-directors and the Count sitting there, and there all five still were, seated round a table and studying cardboard-covered folders spread on the table before them. A pile of those lay on the table, some more were scattered on the floor where the rolling of the ship had obviously precipitated them. The Count looked at me over the rim of his glass: his capacity for brandy was phenomenal.

'Still abroad, my dear fellow? You do labour on our behalf. Much more of this and I suggest that you be co-opted as one of our directors.'

'Here's one cobbler that sticks to his last.' I looked at Gerran. 'Sorry to interrupt, but I've some forms to fill up. If I'm interrupting some private session—'

'Nothing private going on here, I assure you.' It was Goin who answered. 'Mainly studying our shooting script for the next fortnight. All the cast and crew will have one tomorrow. Like a copy?'

'Thank you. After I've finished this. Afraid my cabin light has gone on the blink and I'm not much good at writing by the light of matches.'

'We're just leaving.' Otto was still looking grey and very tired but he was mentally tough enough to keep going long after his body had told him to stop. 'I think we could all do with a good night's sleep.'

'It's what I would prescribe. You could postpone your

departure for five minutes?'

'If necessary, of course.'

'We've promised Captain Imrie a guarantee or affidavit or what will you exonerating him from all blame if we have any further outbreaks of mysterious illness. He wants it on his breakfast table, and he wants it signed. And as Captain Imrie will be up at 4 a.m. and I suspect his breakfast will be correspondingly early, I suggest it would be more convenient if you all signed it now.'

They nodded agreement. I sat at a nearby table and in my best handwriting, which was pretty bad, and best legal jargon, which was awful, I drafted a statement of responsibility which I thought would meet the case. The others apparently thought so too or were too tired to care, for they signed with only a cursory glance at what I had written. The Count signed too and I didn't as much as raise an eyebrow. It had never even crossed my mind that the Count belonged to those elevated directorial ranks, I had thought that the more highly regarded cameramen, of which the Count was undoubtedly one, were invariably freelance and therefore ineligible for election to any film company board. But at least it helped to explain his lack of proper respect for Otto.

'And now, to bed.' Goin eased back his chair. 'You, too, Doctor?'

'After I've filled out the death certificates.'

'An unpleasant duty.' Goin handed me a folder. 'This might help amuse you afterwards.'

I took it from him and Gerran heaved himself upright with the usual massive effort. 'Those funerals, Dr Marlowe. The burials at sea. What time do they take place?'

'First light is customary.' Otto closed his eyes in suffering. 'After what you've been through, Mr Gerran, I'd advise you to give it a miss. Rest as long as possible tomorrow.'

'You really think so?' I nodded and Otto removed his mask of suffering. 'You will stand in for me, John?'

'Of course,' Goin said. 'Good night, Doctor. Thank you for your co-operation.'

'Yes, yes, thank you, thank you,' Otto said.

They trooped off unsteadily and I fished out my death certificate forms and filled them out. I put those in one sealed envelope, the signed affidavit—I just in time remembered to add my own signature—in another, addressed them to Captain

Imrie and took them up to the bridge to ask Allison to hand them over to the captain when he came on watch at four in the morning. Allison wasn't there. Instead, Smithy, heavily clad and muffled almost to the eyebrows, was sitting on a high stool before the wheel. He wasn't touching the wheel, which periodically spun clockwise and counter-clockwise as of its own accord, and he'd turned up the rheostat. He looked pale and had dark circles under his eyes but he didn't have a sick look about him any more. His recuperative powers were quite remarkable.

'Automatic pilot,' he explained, almost cheerfully, 'and all the lights of home. Who needs night-sight in zero visibility?'

'You ought to be in bed,' I said shortly.

'I've just come from there and I'm just going there. First Officer Smith is not yet his old self and he knows it. Just come up to check position and give Allison a break for coffee. Also, I thought I might find you here. You weren't in your cabin.'

'I'm here now. What did you want to see me about?'

'Otard-Dupuy,' he said. 'How does that sound?'

'It sounds fine.' Smithy slid off his stool and headed for the cupboard where Captain Imrie kept his private store of restoratives. 'But you weren't hunting the ship to offer me a brandy.'

'No. Tell you the truth, I've been trying to figure out some things. No dice with the figuring, if I was bright enough for that I'd be too bright to be where I am now. Thought you could help me.' He handed me a glass.

'We should make a great team,' I said.

He smiled briefly. 'Three dead and four half dead. Food poisoning. What poisoning?'

I told him the story about the sporing anaerobes, the one I'd given Haggerty. But Smithy wasn't Haggerty.

'Mighty selective poison, isn't it? Clobbers A and kills him, passes up B, clobbers C and doesn't kill him, passes up D and so on. And we all had the same food to eat.'

'Poisons are notoriously unpredictable. Six people at a picnic can eat the same infected food: three can land in hospital while the others don't feel a twinge.'

'So, some people get tummy-aches and some don't. But that's a bit different from saying that a poison that is deadly enough to kill, and to kill violently and quickly, is going to leave others entirely unaffected. I'm no doctor but I flat out don't believe it,'

'I find it a bit odd myself. You have something in mind?'

'Yes. The poisoning was deliberate.'

'Deliberate?' I sipped some more of the Otard-Dupuy while I wondered how far to go with Smithy. Not too far, I thought, not yet. I said: 'Of course it was deliberate. And so easily done. Take our poisoner. He has this little bag of poison. Also, he has this little magic wand. He waves it and turns himself invisible and then flits around the dining tables. A pinch for Otto, none for me, a pinch for you, a pinch for Oakley, no pinches for, say, Heissman and Stryker, a double pinch for Antonio, none for the girls, a pinch for the Duke, two each for Moxen and Scott, and so on. A wayward and capricious lad, our invisible friend: or would you call it being selective?'

'I don't know what I'd call it,' Smithy said soberly. 'But I know what I'd call you—devious, off-putting, side-tracking and altogether protesting too much. Without offence, of course.'

'Of course.'

'I wouldn't rate you as anybody's fool. You can't tell me that you haven't had some thoughts along those lines.'

'I had. But because I've been thinking about it a lot longer than you, I've dismissed them. Motive, opportunity, means— impossible to find any. Don't you know that the first thing a doctor does when he's called in to a case of accidental poisoning is to suspect that it's not accidental?'

'So you're satisfied?'

'As can be.'

'I see.' He paused. 'Do you know we have a transmitter in the radio office that can reach just about any place in the northern hemisphere? I've got a feeling we're going to have to use it soon.'

'What on earth for?'

'Help.'

'Help?'

'Yes. You know. The thing you require when you're in trouble. I think we need help now. Any more funny little accidents and I'll be damn certain we need help.'

'I'm sorry,' I said. 'You're way beyond me. Besides, Britain's a long long way away from us now.'

'The NATO Atlantic forces aren't. They're carrying out fleet exercise somewhere off the North Cape.'

'You're well informed,' I said.

'It pays to be well informed when I'm talking to someone who claims to be as satisfied as can be over three very mysterious deaths when I'm certain that someone would never rest and could never be satisfied until he knew exactly how those three people had died. I've admitted I'm not very bright but don't completely under-estimate what little intelligence I have.'

'I don't. And don't overestimate mine. Thanks for the Otard-Dupuy.'

I went to the starboard screen door. The *Morning Rose* was still rolling and pitching and shaking and shuddering as she battered her way northwards through the wild seas but it was no longer possible to see the wind-torn waters below: we were in a world now that was almost completely opaque, a blind and bitter world of driving white, a world of snowy darkness that began and ended at scarcely an arm length's distance. I looked down at the wing bridge deck and in the pale light of wash from the wheel-house I could see footprints in the snow. There was only one set of them, sharp and clearly limned as if they had been made only seconds previously. Somebody had been there, for a moment I was certain that someone had been there, listening to Smith and myself talking. Then I realized there was *only* one set, the set I had made myself, and they hadn't been filled in or even blurred because the blizzard driving horizontally across the wind-dodger was clearing the deck at my feet. Sleep, I thought, and sleep now: for with that lack of sleep, the tiring events of the past few hours, the sheer physical exhaustion induced by the violent weather and Smithy's dark forebodings, I was beginning to imagine things. I realized that Smithy was at my shoulder.

'You levelling with me, Dr Marlowe?'

'Of course. Or do you think *I'm* the invisible Borgia who's flitting around, a little pinch here, a little pinch there?'

'No, I don't. I don't think you're levelling with me, either.' His voice was sombre. 'Maybe some day you are going to wish you were.'

Some day I was going to wish I had, for then I wouldn't have had to leave Smithy behind in Bear Island.

Back in the saloon, I picked up the booklet Goin had given me, went to the corner settee, found myself a steamer blanket, decided I didn't require it yet and wedged myself into the corner, my feet comfortably on a swivel chair belonging to the nearest table. I picked up, without much interest, the cardboard file and was debating whether to open it when the lee door opened and Mary Stuart came in. There was snow on the tangled corn-coloured hair and she was wearing a heavy tweed coat.

'So this is where you are.' She banged the door shut and looked at me almost accusingly.

'This,' I acknowledged, 'is where I am.'

'You weren't in your cabin. And your light's gone. Do you know that?'

'I know that. I'd some writing to do. That's why I came here. Is there something wrong?'

She lurched across the saloon and sat heavily on the settee opposite me. 'Nothing more than has been wrong.' She and Smithy should meet up, they'd get on famously. 'Do you mind if I stay here?'

I could have said that it didn't matter whether I minded or not, that the saloon was as much hers as mine, but as she seemed to be a touchy sort of creature I just smiled and said: 'I would take it as an insult if you left.' She smiled back at me, just an acknowledging flicker, and settled as best she could in her seat, drawing the tweed coat around her and bracing herself against the violent movements of the *Morning Rose*. She closed her eyes and with the long dark lashes lying along pale wet cheeks her high cheek-bones were more pronounced than ever, her Slavonic ancestry unmistakable.

It was no great hardship to look upon Mary Stuart but I still felt an increasing irritation as I watched her. It wasn't so much her fey imaginings and need for company that made me uneasy, it was the obvious discomfort she was experiencing in trying to keep her seated balance while I was wedged so very comfortably in my own place: there is nothing more uncomfortable than being comfortable oneself and watching another in acute discomfort, not unless, of course, one has a feeling of very powerful antagonism towards the other party, in which case a very comfortable feeling can be induced: but I had no such antagonism towards the girl opposite. To compound my feeling of guilt she began to shiver involuntarily.

'Here,' I said. 'You'd be more comfortable in my seat. And there's a rug here you can have.'

She opened her eyes. 'No, thank you.'

'There are plenty more rugs,' I said in something like exasperation. Nothing brings out the worst in me more quickly than sweetly-smiling suffering. I picked up the rug, did my customary two-step across the heaving deck and draped the rug over her. She looked at me gravely and said nothing.

Back in my corner I picked up the booklet again but instead of reading it got to wondering about my cabin and those who might visit it during my absence. Mary Stuart had visited it, but then she'd told me she had and the fact that she was here now confirmed the reason for her visit. At least, it seemed to confirm it. She was scared, she said, she was lonely and so she naturally wanted company. Why my company? Why not that of, say, Charles Conrad who was a whole lot younger, nicer, and better-looking than I was? Or even his other two fellow actors, Gunther Jungbeck and Jon Heyter, both very personable characters indeed? Maybe she wanted to be with me for all the wrong reasons. Maybe she was watching me, maybe she was virtually guarding me, maybe she was giving someone the opportunity to visit my cabin while—I was suddenly very acutely aware that there were things in my cabin that I'd rather not be seen by others.

I put the book down and headed for the lee door. She opened her eyes and lifted her head.

'Where are you going?'

'Out.'

'I'm sorry. I just—are you coming back?'

'I'm sorry, too. I'm not rude,' I lied, 'just tired. Below. Back in a minute.'

She nodded, her eyes following me until I closed the door behind me. Once outside I remained still for twenty seconds or so, ignoring the vagrant flurries of snow that even here, on the lee side, seemed bent on getting down my collar and up the trouser cuffs, then walked quickly for'ard. I peered through the plate glass window and she was sitting as I'd left her, only now she had her elbows on her knees and her face in her hands, shaking her head slowly from side to side. Ten years ago I'd have been back in that saloon pretty rapidly, arms round her and telling her that all her troubles were over. That was ten years ago. Now I just looked at her, wondered if she had been expecting me to take a peek at her, then made my way for'ard and down to the passenger accommodation.

It was after midnight but not yet closing hours in the lounge bar, for Lonnie Gilbert, with a heroically foolhardy disregard for what would surely be Otto's fearful wrath when the crime was discovered, had both glass doors swung open and latched in position, while he himself was ensconced in some state behind the bar itself, a bottle of malt whisky in one hand, a soda-siphon in the other. He beamed paternally at me as I passed through and as it seemed late in the day to point out to Lonnie that the better-class malts stood in no need of the anaemic assistance of soda I just nodded and went below.

If anybody had been in my cabin and gone through my belongings, he'd done it in a very circumspect way. As far as I could recall everything was as I had left it and nothing had been disturbed, but then, a practised searcher rarely left any trace of his passing. Both my cases had elasticized linen pockets in the lids and in each pocket in each lid, holding the lids as nearly horizontal as possible, I placed a small coin just at the entrance to the pocket. Then I locked the cases. In spite of the trawler's wildly erratic behaviour those coins would remain where they were, held in place by the pressure of the clothes inside but as soon as the lid was opened, the pressure released, and the lid then lifted even part way towards the vertical, the coins would slide down to the feet of the pockets. I then locked my medical bag—it was considerably large and heavier than the average medical bag but then it held a considerably greater amount of equipment— and put it out in the passage. I closed the door behind me, carefully wedging a spent book match between the front of the door and the sill: that door would have to open only a crack and the match would drop clear.

Lonnie, unsurprisingly, was still at his station in the lounge when I reached there.

'Aha!' He regarded his empty glass with an air of surprise, then reached out with an unerring hand. 'The kindly healer with his bag of tricks. Hotfoot to the succour of suffering mankind? A new and dreadful epidemic, is it? Your old Uncle Lonnie is proud of you, boy, proud of you. This Hippocratic spirit—' He broke off, only to resume almost at once. 'Now that we have touched, inadvertently chanced upon, as one might say, this topic—spirit, the blushful Hippocrene—I wonder if by any chance you would care to join me in a thimbleful of the elixir I have here—'

'Thank you, Lonnie, no. Why don't you get to bed? If you keep it up like this, you won't be able to get up tomorrow.'

'And that, my dear boy, is the whole point of the exercise. I don't want to get up tomorrow. The day after tomorrow? Well, yes, if I must, I'll face the day after tomorrow. I don't want to, mind you, for tomorrows, I've found, are always distressingly similar to todays. The only good thing you can say about a today is that at any given moment such and such a portion of it is already irrevocably past—' he paused to admire his speech control—'irrevocably past, as I say, and, with the passing of every moment, so much less of it to come. But *all* of tomorrow is still to come. Think of it. *All* of it—the livelong day.' He lifted his recharged glass. 'Others drink to forget the past. But some of us—very, very few and it would not be right of me to say that we're gifted with a prescience and understanding and intelligence far beyond the normal ken, so I'll just say we're different—some of us, I say, drink to forget the future. How, you will ask, can one forget the future? Well, for one thing, it takes practice. And, of course, a little assistance.' He drank half his malt in one gulp and intoned: ' "Tomorrow and tomorrow and tomorrow creeps in this petty pace from day to day to the last syllable—" '

'Lonnie,' I said, 'I don't think you're the least little bit like Macbeth.'

'And there you have it in a nutshell. I'm not. A tragic figure, a sad man, fated and laden with doom. Now, me, I'm not like that at all. We Gilberts have the indomitable spirit, the unconquerable soul. Your Shakespeares are all very well, but Walter de la Mare is my boy.' He lifted his glass and squinted myopically at it against the light. ' "Look your last on all things lovely every hour." '

'I don't think he quite meant it in that way, Lonnie. Anyway, doctor's orders and do me a favour—get to hell out of here. Otto will have you drawn and quartered if he finds you here.'

'Otto? Do you know something?' Lonnie leaned forward confidentially. 'Otto's really a very kindly man. I like Otto. He's always been good to me, Otto has. Most people are good, my dear chap, don't you know that? Most people are kind.

Lots of them very kind. But none so kind as Otto. Why, I remember—'

He broke off as I went round the back of the bar, replaced the bottles, locked the doors, placed the keys in his dressing-gown pocket and took his arm.

'I'm not trying to deprive you of the necessities of life,' I explained. 'Neither am I being heavy-handed and moralistic. But I have a sensitive nature and I don't want to be around when you find out that your assessment of Otto is a hundred per cent wrong.' Lonnie came without a single murmur of protest. Clearly, he had his emergency supplies cached in his cabin. On our stumbling descent of the companionway he said: 'You think I'm headed for the next world with my gas pedal flat on the floor, don't you?'

'As long as you don't hit anybody it's none of my business how you drive, Lonnie.'

He stumbled into his cabin, sat heavily on his bed, then moved with remarkable swiftness to one side: I could only conclude that he'd inadvertently sat on a bottle of scotch. He looked at me, pondering, then said: 'Tell me, my boy, do you think they have bars in heaven?'

'I'm afraid I have no information on that one, Lonnie.'

'Quite, quite. It makes a gratifying change to find a doctor who is not the source of all wisdom. You may leave me now, my good fellow.'

I looked at Neal Divine, now quietly asleep, and at Lonnie, impatiently and for obvious reasons awaiting my departure, and left them both.

Mary Stuart was sitting where I'd left her, arms straight out on either side and fingers splayed to counteract the now noticeably heavier pitching of the *Morning Rose*: the rolling effect, on the other hand, was considerably less, so I assumed that the wind was still veering in a northerly direction. She looked at me with the normally big brown eyes now preternaturally huge in a dreadfully tired face, then looked away again.

'I'm sorry,' I found myself apologizing. 'I've been discussing classics and theology with our production manager.' I made for my corner seat and sat down gratefully. 'Do you know him at all?'

'Everybody knows Lonnie.' She tried to smile. 'We worked

together in the last picture I made.' Again she essayed a smile. 'Did you see it?'

'No.' I'd heard about it though, enough to make me walk five miles out of my way to avoid it.

'It was awful. I was awful. I can't imagine why they gave me another chance.'

'You're a very beautiful girl,' I said. 'You don't have to be able to act. Performance detracts from appearance. Anyway, you may be an excellent actress. I wouldn't know. About Lonnie?'

'Yes. He was there. So were Mr Gerran and Mr Heissman.' I said nothing so she went on: 'This is the third picture we've all made together. The third since Mr Heissman—well, since he—'

'I know. Mr Heissman was away for quite a bit.'

'Lonnie's such a nice man. He's so helpful and kind and I think he's a very wise man. But he's a funny man. You know that Lonnie likes to take a drink. One day, after twelve hours on the set and all of us dead tired, when we got back to the hotel I asked for a double gin and he became very angry with me. Why should he be like that?'

'Because he's a funny man. So you like him?'

'How could I not like him? He likes everybody so everybody just likes him back. Even Mr Gerran likes him—they're very close. But then, they've known each other for years and years.'

'I didn't know that. Has Lonnie a family? Is he married?'

'I don't know. I think he was. Maybe he's divorced. Why do you ask so many questions about him?'

'Because I'm a typically knowing, prying sawbones and I like to know as much as possible about people who are or may be my patients. For instance, I know enough about Lonnie now never to give him a brandy if he were in need of a restorative for it wouldn't have the slightest effect.'

She smiled and closed her eyes. Conversation over. I took another steamer rug from under my seat, wrapped it around me—the temperature in the saloon was noticeably dropping —and picked up the folder that Goin had given me. I turned to Page 1, which, apart from being titled 'Bear Island', started off without any preamble.

'It is widely maintained,' it read, 'that Olympus Productions is approaching the making of this, its latest production, in conditions so restrictive as to amount to an aura of almost total secrecy. Allegations to this effect have subsequently made their appearance in popular and trade presses and in light of the absence of production office denials in the contrary those uncorroborated assertions have achieved a considerable degree of substance and credence which one might regard, in the circumstances, as being a psychological inevitability.' I read through this rubbish again, a travesty of the Queen's English fit only for the columns of the more learned Sunday papers, and then I got it: they were making a hush-hush picture and didn't care who knew. And very good publicity it was for the film, too, I thought, but, no, I was doing the boys an injustice. Or so the boys said. The article continued:

'Other cinematic productions'—I assumed he meant films —'have been approached and, on occasion, even executed under conditions of similar secrecy but those other and, one is afraid spurious *sub rosa* ventures have had for their calculated aim nothing less, regrettably, than the extraction of the maximum free publicity. This, we insist, and with some pride, is not the objective of Olympus Productions.' Good old Olympus, this I had to see, a cinema company who didn't want free publicity: next thing we'd have the Bank of England turning its nose up at the sound of the word 'money'. 'Our frankly cabbalistic approach to this production, which has given rise to so much intrigued and largely ill-informed speculation, has, in fact, been imposed upon us by considerations of the highest importance: the handling of this, a story which in the wrong hands might well generate potentially and dangerously explosive international repercussions, calls for the utmost in delicacy and finesse, essential qualities for the creation of what we confidently expect will be hailed as a cinematic masterpiece, but qualities which even we feel —nay, are certain—would not be able to overcome the immense damage done by—and we are certain of this—the world-wide furore that would immediately and automatically follow the premature leaking of the story we intend to film.

'We are confident, however, that when—there is no "if"—this production is made in our own way, in our own time, and under the very strictest security conditions—this is why we have gone to the quite extraordinary lengths of obtaining notarized oaths of secrecy from every member of the cast and crew of the film project under discussion, including the managing director and his co-directors—we will have upon our hands, when this production is presented to a public, which will have been geared by that time to the highest degree of expectancy, a *tour de force* of so unparalleled an order that the justification for—'

Mary Stuart sneezed and I blessed her, twice, once for her health and once for the heaven-sent interruption of the reading of this modestly phrased manifesto. I glanced at her again just as she sneezed again. She was sitting in a curiously huddled fashion, hands clasped tightly together, her face white and pinched. I laid down the Olympus manifesto, unwrapped my rug, crossed the saloon in a zigzag totter which resulted from the now very pronounced pitching of the *Morning Rose,* sat beside her and took her hands in mine. They were icily cold.

'You're freezing,' I said somewhat unnecessarily.

'I'm all right. I'm just a bit tired.'

'Why don't you go below to your cabin? It's at least twenty degrees warmer down there and you'll never sleep up here if you have to keep bracing yourself all the time from falling off your seat.'

'No. I don't sleep down there either. I've hardly slept since—' She broke off. 'And I don't feel nearly so—so queasy up here. Please.'

I don't give up easily. I said: 'Then at least take my corner seat, you'll be much more comfortable there.'

She took her hands away. 'Please. Just leave me.'

I gave up. I left her. I took three wavering steps in the direction of my seat, halted in irritation, turned back to her and hauled her none too gently to her feet. She looked at me, not speaking, in tired surprise, and continued to say nothing, and to offer no resistance, as I led her across to my corner, brought out another two steamer rugs, cocooned her in those, lifted her feet on to the settee and sat beside her. She looked up at me for a few seconds, her gaze transferring itself from my right eye to my left and back again, then she turned her face to me, closed her eyes and slid one of her icy hands under my jacket. During all this performance she didn't speak once or permit any expression to appear on her face and I would have been deeply moved by this touching trust in me were it not for the reflection that if it were her

98

purpose or instructions to keep as close an eye as possible on me she could hardly, even in her most optimistic moments, have hoped to arrive at a situation where she could keep an eye within half an inch of my shirt-front. I couldn't even take a deep breath without her knowing all about it. On the other hand, if she were as innocent as the driven snow that had now completely obscured the plate glass not six inches from my head, then it was less than likely that any ill-disposed citizen or citizens would contemplate taking action of a violent and permanent nature against me as long as I had Mary Stuart practically sitting on my lap. It was, I thought, a pretty even trade. I looked down at the half-hidden lovely face and reflected that I was possibly having a shade the better of the deal.

I reached for my own rug, draped it round my shoulders in Navaho style, picked up the Olympus manifesto again and continued to read. The next two pages were largely a hyperbolic expansion of what had gone before, with the writer—I assumed it was Heissman—harping on at nauseating length on the twin themes of the supreme artistic merit of the production and the necessity for absolute secrecy. After this self-adulatory exercise, the writer got down to facts.

'After long consideration, and the close examination and subsequent rejection of a very considerable number of possible alternatives, we finally decided upon Bear Island as the location for this project. We are aware that all of you, and this includes the entire crew of the *Morning Rose* from Captain Imrie downwards, believed that we were heading for a destination in the neighbourhood of the Lofoten Islands off Northern Norway and it was not exactly, shall we say, through fortuitous circumstances, that this rumour was gaining some currency in certain quarters in London immediately prior to our departure. We make no apologies for what may superficially appear to be an unwarranted deception, for it was essential to our purposes and the maintenance of secrecy that this subterfuge be adopted.

'For the following brief description of Bear Island we are indebted to the Royal Geographical Society of Oslo, who have also furnished us with a translation.' That was a relief, just as long as the translator wasn't Heissman I might be able to get it on the first reading. 'This information, it is perhaps superfluous to add, was obtained for us through the good offices of a third party entirely unconnected with Olympus Productions, a noted ornithologist who must remain entirely incognito. It may be mentioned in the passing that the Norwegian government has given us permission to film on the island. We understand that it is their understanding that we propose to make a wild life documentary: such an understanding, far less a commitment, was not obtained from us.'

I wondered about that last bit—not the cleverer-than-thou smugness of it, that was clearly inseparable from everything Heissman wrote—but the fact that he should say it at all. Heissman, clearly, was not a man much given to hiding his own brilliance—the phrase 'low cunning' would not have occurred to him—under a bushel but equally he wasn't a man who would permit this particular type of self-gratification to lead him into danger. Almost certainly if the Norwegians did find out they had been deluded there would be nothing in international law they could do about it—Olympus wouldn't have overlooked anything so obvious—other than ban the completed film from their country, and as Norway could hardly be regarded as a major market this would cause few sleepless nights. On the other hand, it would be effective in stilling any qualms of conscience—true, this was the world of the cinema but Heissman would be unlikely to overlook even the most remote possibility—that might have arisen had the project been denied even this superficial official blessing, and the very fact that they were being made privy to the secret inner workings of Olympus would tend to bind both cast and crew closer to the company, for it is an almost universal law of nature that mankind, which is still in the painful process of growing up, dearly loves its little closed and/or secret societies, whether those be the most remote Masonic Lodge in Saskatchewan or White's of St James's, and tends to form an intense personal attachment and loyalty to other members of that group while presenting a united front to the world of the unfortunates beyond their doors. I did not overlook the possibility that there might be another, and conceivably sinister, interpretation of Heissman's confidential frankness but as it was now into the early hours of the morning I didn't particularly feel like seeking it out.

'Bear Island,' the résumé began. 'One of the Svalbard group, of which Spitzbergen is much the largest. This group remained neutral and unclaimed until the beginning of the twentieth century when, because of its very considerable investments in the exploitation of mineral resources and the establishment of whaling operations, Norway requested sovereignty of the area, placing her petition before the Conference'—they didn't specify what conference—'at Christiania (Oslo) in 1910, 1912 and again in 1914. On each occasion Russian objections prevented ratification of the proposals. However, in 1919 the Allied Supreme Council granted Norway sovereignty, formal possession being taken on August 14th, 1925.'

Having established the ownership beyond all doubt the report proceeded: 'The (Bear) island, 74° 28'N., 19° 13'E., lies some 260 miles N.N.W. of North Cape, Norway, and some 140 miles south of Spitzbergen and may be regarded as the meeting point of the Norwegian, Greenland and Barents Seas. In terms of distance from its nearest neighbours, this is the most isolated island in the Arctic.'

There followed a long and for me highly uninteresting account of the island's history which seemed to consist mainly of interminable squabbles between Norwegians, Germans and Russians over whaling and mining rights—although I was mildly intrigued to learn that as recently as the twenties there had been as many as a hundred and eighty Norwegians working the coal mines at Tunheim in the north-east of the island—I would have imagined that even the polar bears, after whom the island was named, would have given this desolation as wide a berth as possible. The mines, it seemed, had been closed down following a geological survey which showed that the purity and thickness of the seams were not sufficient to make it a profitable proposition. The island, however, was not entirely uninhabited even today: it appeared that the Norwegian Government maintained a meteorological and radio station at Tunheim.

Then came articles on the natural resources, vegetation and animal life, all of which I took as read. The references to the climate, however, which might be expected to concern us all, I found much more intriguing and highly discouraging. 'The meeting of the Gulf Stream and the Polar Drift,' it read, 'makes for extremely poor weather conditions, with large rainfall and dense fogs. The average summer temperature rises to not more than five degrees above freezing. Not until mid-July do the lakes become ice-free and the snow melts. The midnight sun lasts for 106 days from April 30th to

101

August 13th: the sun remains below the horizon from November 7th to February 4th.' This last item made our presence there, this late in the year, very odd indeed as Otto couldn't expect more than a few hours of daylight at the most: perhaps the script called for the whole story to be shot in darkness.

'Physically and geologically,' it went on, 'Bear Island is triangular in shape with its apex to the south, being approximately twelve miles long on its north-south axis in width varying from ten miles in the north to two miles in the south at the point where the southernmost peninsula begins. Generally speaking the north and west consist of a fairly flat plateau at an elevation of about a hundred feet, while the south and east are mountainous, the two main complexes being the Misery Fell group in the east and the Antarcticfjell and its associated mountains, the Alfredfjell, Harbergfjell and Fuglefjell in the extreme south-east.

'There are no glaciers. The entire area is covered with a network of shallow lakes, none more than a few yards in depth: those account for about one-tenth of the total area of the island: the remainder of the interior of the island consists largely of icy swamps and loose scree which makes it extremely difficult to traverse.

'The coastline of Bear Island is regarded as perhaps the most inhospitably bleak in the world. This is especially true in the south where the island ends in vertical cliffs, the streams entering the sea by waterfalls. A characteristic feature of this area is the detached pillars of rock that stand in the sea close to the foot of the cliffs, remnants from that distant period when the island was considerably larger than it is now. The melting of the snows and ice in June/July, the powerful tidal streams and the massive erosion undermine those coastal hills so that large masses of rock are constantly falling into the sea. The great polomite cliffs of Hambergfjell drop sheer for over 1400 feet: at their base, projecting from the seas are sharp needles of rock as much as 250 feet high, while the Fuglefjell (Bird Fell) cliffs are almost as high and have at their most southerly point a remarkable series of high stacks, pinnacles and arches. To the east of this point, between Kapp Bull and Kapp Kolthoff, is a bay surrounded on three sides by vertical cliffs which are nowhere less than 1000 feet high.

'Those cliffs are the finest bird breeding grounds in the Northern Hemisphere.'

It was all very fine for the birds, I supposed. That was the end of the Geographical Society's report—or as much of it as the writer had chosen to include—and I was bracing myself for a return to Heissman's limpid prose when the lee door opened and John Halliday staggered in. Halliday, the unit's highly competent stills photographer, was a dark, swarthy, taciturn and unsmiling American. Even by his normal cheerless standards Halliday looked uncommonly glum. He caught sight of us and stood there uncertainly, holding the door open.

'I'm sorry.' He made as if to go. 'I didn't know—'

'Enter, enter,' I said. 'Things are not as they seem. What you see before you is a strictly doctor-patient relationship.' He closed the door and sat down morosely on the settee that Mary Stuart had so lately occupied. 'Insomnia?' I asked. 'A touch of the *mal de mer*?'

'Insomnia.' He chewed dispiritedly on the wad of black tobacco that never seemed to leave his mouth. 'The *mal de mer*'s all Sandy's.' Sandy, I knew, was his cabin-mate. True, Sandy hadn't been looking very bright when last I'd seen him in the galley but I'd attributed this to Haggerty's yearning to eviscerate him: at least it explained why he hadn't called in to see the Duke after he'd left us.

'Bit under the weather, is he?'

'Very much under the weather. Kind of a funny green colour and sick all over the damned carpet.' Halliday wrinkled his nose. 'The smell—'

'Mary.' I shook her gently and she opened sleep-dulled eyes. 'Sorry, I've got to go for a moment.' She said nothing as I half helped her to a sitting position, just glanced incuriously at Halliday and closed her eyes again.

'I don't think he's all that bad,' Halliday said. 'Not poisoning or anything like that, I mean. I'm sure of it.'

'No harm to take a look,' I said. Halliday was probably right: on the other hand Sandy had had the freedom of the galley before Haggerty had caught him and with Sandy's prehensile and sticky fingers anything was conceivable, including the possibility that his appetite was not quite as bird-like as he claimed. I picked up my medical bag and left.

As Halliday had said, Sandy was of a rather peculiar green-

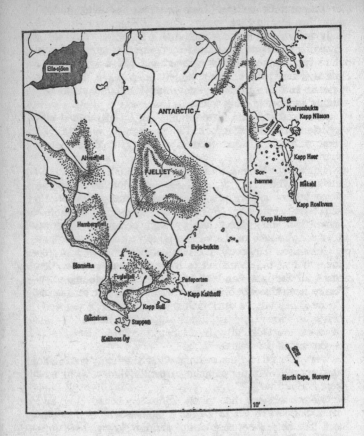

ish shade and he'd obviously been very sick indeed. He was
sitting propped up in his bunk, with both forearms wrapped
round his middle: he glared at me balefully as I entered.

'Christ, I'm dying,' he wheezed. He swore briefly, pun-
gently and indiscriminately at life in general and Otto in particular. 'Why that crazy bastard wants to drag us aboard
this bloody old stinking hell-ship—'

I gave him some sleeping-sedatives and left. I was beginning to find Sandy a rather less than sympathetic character:

more importantly, sufferers from *aconitine* poisoning couldn't speak, far less indulge in the fluent Billingsgate in which Sandy was clearly so proficient.

Swaying from side to side and again with her arms stretched out to support herself, Mary Stuart still had her eyes shut: Halliday, dejectedly chewing his wad of tobacco, looked up at me in lackadaisical half-inquiry as if he didn't much care whether Sandy was alive or dead.

'You're right,' I said. 'Just the weather.' I sat down a little way from Mary Stuart and not as much as by a flicker of a closed eyelid did she acknowledge my presence. I shivered involuntarily and drew the steamer rug around me. I said: 'It's getting a bit nippy in this saloon. Why don't you take one of these and kip down here?'

'No thanks. I'd no idea it would be so damn cold here. My blankets and pillow and it's me for the lounge.' He smiled faintly. 'Just as long as Lonnie doesn't trample all over me with his hob-nailed boots in the middle watch.' It was apparently common knowledge that the liquor in the lounge drew Lonnie like a lodestone. Halliday chewed some more, then nodded at the bottle in Captain Imrie's wrought-iron stand. 'You're a whisky man, Doc. That's the stuff to warm you up.'

'Agreed. But I'm a very choosy whisky man. What is it?' Halliday peered. 'Black Label.'

'None better. But I'm a malt man myself. You're cold, you try some. It's on the house. Stole it from Otto.'

'I'm not much of a one for scotch. Now bourbon—'

'Corrodes the digestive tract. I speak as a medical man. Now, one sip of that stuff there and you'll swear off those lethal Kentucky brews for ever. Go on. Try it.'

Halliday looked at the bottle, as if uncertainly. I said to Mary Stuart: 'How about you? Just a little? You've no idea how it warms the cockles.'

She opened her eyes and gave me that oddly expressionless look. 'No thank you. I hardly ever drink.' She closed her eyes again.

'The flaw that makes for perfection,' I said absently, because my mind was on other things. Halliday wouldn't drink from that bottle, Mary Stuart wouldn't drink from that bottle, but Halliday seemed to think it was a good idea that I should. Had they both remained in their seats during my absence or had they been busy little bees, one keeping guard against my premature return while the other altered the character of the Black Label with ingredients not necessarily made in Scotland? Why else had Halliday come up to the saloon if not to lure me away? Why hadn't he gone direct to the lounge with blankets and pillow instead of wandering aimlessly up here to the saloon where he must have known from meal-times that the temperature was considerably colder than it was down below? Because, of course, before Mary Stuart had made her presence known to me here, she'd seen me through the outer windows and had reported to Halliday that a certain problem had arisen that could only be solved by bringing about my temporary absence from the saloon. Sandy's sickness had been a convenient coincidence—if it had been a coincidence, I suddenly thought: if Halliday was the person, or was in cahoots with the person who was so handy with poisons, then the introduction of some mildly emetic potion into Sandy's drink would have involved no more problem than that of opportunity. It all added up.

I became aware that Halliday was on his feet and was lurching unsteadily in my direction, bottle in one hand and glass in the other: the bottle, I noticed almost mechanically, was about one-third full. He halted, swaying, in front of me and poured a generous measure into the glass, bowed lightly, offered me the glass and smiled. 'Maybe we're both on the hide-bound and conservative side, Doc. In the words of the song, I will if you will so will I.'

I smiled back. 'Your willingness to experiment does you credit. But no thanks. I told you, I just don't like the stuff. I've tried it. Have you?'

'No, but I—'

'Well, how can you tell, then?'

'I don't think—'

'You were going to try it anyway. Go on. Drink it.'

Mary Stuart opened her eyes. 'Do you always make people drink against their will? Is this what doctors do—force alcohol on those who don't want it?'

I felt like scowling and saying, 'Why don't you shut up?' but instead I smiled and said: 'Teetotal objections overruled.'

'So what's the harm?' Halliday said. He had the glass to his lips. I stared at him until I remembered I shouldn't be staring, which was all of a fraction of a second, smiled indulgently, glanced at Mary Stuart whose ever so slightly compressed lips

106

registered no more than a trace of prudish disapproval, then looked back in time to see Halliday lowering his half empty glass.

'Not bad,' he pronounced. 'Not bad at all. Kind of a funny taste, though.'

'You could be arrested in Scotland for saying that,' I said mechanically. The villain had nonchalantly quaffed the hemlock while his accomplice had looked on with indifference. I felt very considerably diminished, a complete and utter idiot: as a detective, my inductive and deductive powers added up to zero. I even felt like apologizing to them except that they wouldn't know what I was talking about.

'You may in fact be right, Doc, one could even get to like this stuff.' Halliday topped up his glass, drunk again, took the bottle across to its wrought-iron rest and resumed his former seat. He sat there silently for perhaps half a minute, finished off the scotch with a couple of swallows and rose abruptly to his feet. 'With that lot inside me I can even ignore Lonnie's hob-nails. Good night.' He hurried from the saloon.

I looked at the doorway through which he had vanished, my mind thoughtful, my face not. I still didn't understand why he had come to the saloon in the first place: and what thought had so suddenly occurred to him to precipitate so abruptly a departure? An unprofitable line of thinking to pursue, I couldn't even find a starting-point to begin theorizing. I looked at Mary Stuart and felt very guilty indeed: murderesses, I knew, came in all shapes, sizes and guises but if they came in this particular guise then I could never trust my judgement again. I wondered what on earth could have led me to entertain so ludicrous a suspicion: I must be even more tired than I thought.

As if conscious of my gaze she opened her eyes and looked at me. She had this extraordinary ability to assume this still and wholly expressionless face, but beneath this remoteness, this distance, this aloofness lay, I thought, a marked degree of vulnerability. Wishful thinking on my part, it was possible: but I was oddly certain it wasn't. Still without speaking, still without altering her expression or lack of it, she half-rose, hobbled awkwardly in her cocoon of steamer rugs and sat close beside me. In my best avuncular fashion I put my arm round her shoulders, but it didn't stay there for long for she took hold of my wrist and deliberately and without haste lifted my arm over the top of her head and pushed it clear of her. Just to show that doctors are suprahuman and incapable of being offended by patients who aren't really responsible for their own behaviour, I smiled at her. She smiled back at me and her eyes, I saw with an astonishment that I knew was not reflected in my face, were filled with unshed tears: almost as if she were aware of those tears and wished to hide them, she suddenly swung her legs up on the settee, turned towards me and got back to the short-range examination of my shirt-front, only this time she put both her arms around me. As far as freedom of mobility was concerned I was as good as handcuffed, which was doubtless what she wanted anyway. That she harboured no lethal intent towards me I was sure: I was equally sure that she was determined not to let me out of her sight and that this was the most effective way she knew of doing just that. How much it cost that proud and lonely person to behave like this I couldn't guess: even less could I imagine what made her do it at all.

I sat there and tried to mull things over in my now thoroughly befogged mind and, predictably, made no progress whatsoever. Besides, my tired eyes were being almost hypnotized by the behaviour of the scotch inside the Black Label bottle, with the almost metronomic regularity with which the liquid ascended and descended the opposite sides of the bottle in response to the regular pitching of the *Morning Rose*. One thing led to another and I said: 'Mary dear?'

'Yes?' She didn't turn her face up to look at me and I didn't have to be told why: the area around the level of my fourth shirt-button was becoming noticably damp.

'I don't want to disturb you but it's time for my nightcap.'

'Whisky?'

'Ah! Two hearts that beat as one.'

'No.' She tightened her arms.

'No?'

'I hate the smell of whisky.'

'I'm glad,' I said *sotto voce*, 'I'm not married to you.'

'What was that?'

'I said "Yes, Mary dear".'

Five more minutes passed and I realized that my mind had closed down for the night. Idly I picked up the Olympus manifesto, read some rubbish about the sole completed copy of the screen-play being deposited in the vaults of a London bank, and put it down again. Mary Stuart was breathing quietly and evenly and seemed to be asleep. I bent and blew lightly on the left eyelid which was about the only part of her face that I could see. It didn't quiver. She was asleep. I shifted my position experimentally, not much, and her arms automatically tightened round me, she'd clearly left a note to her subconscious before turning in for the night. I resigned myself to remaining where I was, it wasn't a form of imprisonment that was likely to scar me permanently: I wondered vaguely whether the idea behind this silken incarceration was to prevent me from doing things or from chancing upon some other devilry that might well be afoot. I was too tired to care. I made up my mind just to sit there and keep a sleepless vigil until the morning came: I was asleep within not more than two minutes.

Mary Stuart was not and didn't look as if she was built along the lines of a coal-heaver but she wasn't stuffed with swansdown either, for when I woke my left arm was asleep, wholly numb and almost useless, a realization that was brought home to me when I had to reach across my right hand to lift up my left wrist to see what time the luminous hands of my watch said it was. They said it was 4.15.

It says much for my mental acuity that at least ten seconds elapsed before it occurred to me why it had been necessary for me to consult the luminous hands. Because it was dark, of course, but why was the saloon dark? Every light had been on when I'd gone to sleep. And what had wakened me? Something had, I knew without knowing why that I hadn't wakened naturally but that there had been some external cause. What and where was the cause? A sound or a physical contact, it couldn't be anything else, and whoever was responsible for whatever it had been was still with me. He had to be, insufficient time had elapsed since I'd worked for him to have left the saloon: more importantly the hairs on the back of my neck told me there was another and inimical presence in the saloon with me.

Gently I took hold of Mary Stuart's wrists to ease her arms away. Again the resistance was automatic, hers was not a subconscious to go to sleep on the job, but I was in no mood to be balked by any subconscious. I prised her arms free, slid along the settee, lowered her carefully to the horizontal, rose and moved out towards the middle of the saloon.

I stood quite still, my hands grasping the edge of a table to brace myself, my breathing almost stopped as I listened intently. I could have spared myself the trouble. I was sure that the weather had moderated, not a great deal but enough to be just noticeable, since I'd gone to sleep, but it hadn't moderated to the extent where any stealthy movements—and I could expect none other—could possibly be heard above the sound of the wind and the seas, the metallic creakings and groanings of the ancient plates and rivets of the *Morning Rose*.

The nearest set of light switches—there was a duplicate set by the stewards' pantry—was by the lee door. I took one step in the remembered direction then stopped. Did the presence in the room know that I was awake and on my feet? Were his eyes more attuned to the darkness than my newly opened ones? Could he dimly discern my figure? Would he guess that my first move would be towards the switches and was he preparing to block my way? If he were, how would he block my way? Would he be carrying a weapon and what kind of weapon—I was acutely aware that all I had were two hands, the left one still a fairly useless lump of tingling pins and needles. I stopped, irresolute.

I heard the metallic click of a door handle and a gust of icy air struck me: the presence was leaving by the lee door. I reached the door in four steps, stepped outside on to the deck, flung up an instinctively protective right forearm as a bright light abruptly struck my eyes and immediately wished I had used my left forearm instead for then it might have offered me some measure of protection against something hard, heavy and very solid that connected forcibly and painfully with the left side of my neck. I clung to the outside edge of the door to support myself but I didn't seem to have much strength left in my hands: and I seemed to have none at all in my legs for although I remained quite conscious I sank to the deck as if my legs had been filleted: by the time the momentary paralysis had passed and I was able to use the support of the door to drag myself shakily to my feet, I was alone on the deck. I had no idea where my assailant had gone and the matter was one of only academic interest, my legs could barely cope with supporting my weight in a static position: even the thought of running or negotiating ladders and companionways at speed was preposterous.

Still clinging to whatever support was to hand I stepped back into the saloon, fumbled the lights on and pulled the lee door closed behind me. Mary Stuart was propped on an elbow, the heel of one palm rubbing an eye while the lid of the other was half open in the fashion of a person just rousing from a very deep or drugged sleep. I looked away, stumbled towards Captain Imrie's table and sat down heavily in his chair. I lifted the bottle of Black Label from its stand. It was half full. For what seemed quite a long time but could have been no more than seconds I stared at this bottle, not seeing it, then looked away to locate the glass that Halliday had been using. It was nowhere to be seen, it could have fallen and rolled out of sight in a dozen different directions. I selected another glass from the table rack, splashed some scotch into it, drank it and made my way back to my seat. My neck felt awful. One good shake of my head and it would fall off.

'Don't breathe through your nose,' I said, 'and you'll hardly smell the demon drink at all.' I propped her up to a sitting position, rearranged her rugs and forestalled her by, for a change, putting my arms around her. I said: 'There now.'

'What was it? What happened?' Her voice was low and had a shake to it.

'Just the door. Wind blew it open. Had to close it, that's all.'

'But the lights were off.'

'I put them off. Just after you'd gone to sleep.'

She wriggled an arm free from the blankets and gently touched the side of my neck.

'It's colouring already,' she whispered. 'It's going to be a huge ugly bruise. And it's bleeding.' I reached up with my handkerchief and she wasn't making any mistake: I stuffed my handkerchief into my collar and left it there. She went on in the same little voice: 'How did it happen?'

'One of those stupid things. I slipped on the snow and struck my neck on the storm-sill of the door. Does ache a bit, I must say.'

She didn't answer. She freed her other arm, caught me by both lapels, stared at me with a face full of misery and put her forehead on my shoulder. Now it was my collar's turn to become damp. It was the most extraordinary behaviour for a wardress—that her function was to keep tabs on and effectively immobilize me I was increasingly sure—but then, she was the most extraordinary wardress I'd ever come across. And the nicest. Dr Marlowe, I said, the lady is in distress and you are but human. I let my suspicions take five and stroked the tangled yellow hair. I'd been led to believe, I forget by what or by whom, that nothing was as conducive to the calming of upset feminine feelings as that soothing gesture: only seconds later I was wondering where I'd picked up this piece of obviously blatant misinformation for she suddenly pushed herself upright and struck me twice on the shoulder with the base of her clenched left fist. I was more than ever convinced that she wasn't made of swansdown.

'Don't do that,' she said. 'Don't *do* that.'

'All right,' I said agreeably. 'I won't do that. I'm sorry.'

'No, no, please! *I'm* sorry. I don't know what made me—I really—' She stopped speaking, although her lips kept on moving, and stared at me with tear-filled eyes, the no longer beautiful face defenceless and defeated and full of despair: it made me feel acutely uncomfortable for I do not like to see proud and self-contained people thus reduced. There was a quick indrawing of breath, then, astonishingly, she had her arms wound round my neck and so tightly that it would appear that she was bent upon my instant asphyxiation. She wept in silence, her shoulders shaking.

Splendidly done, I thought approvingly, quite splendidly done. Irrespective of for whose benefit it might be—and then I despised myself for my cynicism. Quite apart from the fact that her acknowledged limitations as an actress put such a performance out of the question I was convinced, without knowing why I was convinced, that what I was seeing was genuine uninhibited emotion. And what on earth had she to gain by pretending to lower her defences in front of me?

For whom, then, the tears? Not for me, of that I was certain, why in the world for me? I scarcely knew her, she scarcely knew me, I was only a shoulder to cry on, likely enough I was only a doctor's shoulder to cry on, people have the oddest misconceptions about doctors and maybe their

112

shoulders are regarded as being more reliable and comforting than the average. Or more absorbent. Nor were the tears for herself, I was equally certain of that, to survive, intact, the kind of upbringing she'd hinted she'd had, one had to be possessed of an unusual degree of self-reliance and mental toughness that almost automatically excluded considerations of self-pity. So for whom, then, the tears?

I didn't know and, at that moment, I hardly cared. In normal circumstances and with no other matter so significantly important as to engage my attention, so lovely a girl in such obvious distress would have had my complete and undivided concern, but the circumstances were abnormal and my thoughts were elsewhere engaged with an intensity that made Mary Stuart's odd behaviour seem relatively unimportant.

I couldn't keep my eyes from the bottle of scotch by the captain's table. When Halliday had had, at my insistence as I now bitterly recalled, his first drink, the bottle had been about a third full: after his second drink it had been about a quarter full: and now it was half full. The quiet and violent man who had so recently switched off the lights and moved through the saloon had switched bottles and, for good measure, had removed the glass that Halliday had used.

Mary Stuart said something, her voice so muffled and indistinct that I couldn't make it out: what with salt tears and salt blood this night's work was going to cost me a new shirt. I said: 'What?'

She moved her head, enough to enable her to speak more clearly, but not enough to let me see her face.

'I'm sorry. I'm sorry I was such a fool. Will you forgive me?'

I squeezed her shoulder in what was more or less an automatic gesture, my eyes and my thoughts were still on that bottle, but she seemed to take it as sufficient answer. She said hesitantly: 'Are you going to sleep again?' She hadn't stopped being as foolish as she thought: or perhaps she wasn't being foolish at all.

'No, Mary dear, I'm not going to sleep again.' Whatever tone of firm resolution my tone carried, it was superfluous: the throbbing pain in my neck was sufficient guarantee of my wakefulness.

'Well, that's all right then.' I didn't ask what this cryptic remark was intended to convey. Physically, we couldn't have been closer but mentally I was no longer with her. I was with Halliday, the man whom I had thought had come to kill me, the man I'd practically forced to have a drink, the man who'd drunk what had been intended for me.

I knew I would never see him again. Not alive.

CHAPTER SIX

Dawn, in those high latitudes and at that time of year, did not come until half-past ten in the morning, and it was then that we buried the three dead men, Antonio and Moxen and Scott, and surely their shades would have forgiven us for the almost indecent dispatch with which their funerals were carried out, for that driving blizzard was still at its height, the wind was full of razored knives and struck through both clothes and flesh and laid its icy fingers on the marrow. Captain Imrie, a large and brass-bound Bible in his mittened hands, read swiftly through the burial service, or at least I assumed he did, he could have been reading the Sermon on the Mount for all I could tell, the wind just plucked the inaudible words from his mouth and carried them out over the grey-white desolation of waters. Three times a canvas-wrapped bundle slid smoothly out from beneath the *Morning Rose*'s only Union Flag, three times a bundle vanished soundlessly beneath the surface of the sea: we could see the splashes but not hear them for our ears were full of the high and lonely lament of the wind's requiem in the frozen rigging.

On land, mourners customarily find it difficult to tear themselves away from a newly-filled grave, but here there was no grave, there was nothing to look at and the bitter cold was sufficient to drive from every mind any thought other than that of immediate shelter and warmth: besides, Captain Imrie had said that it was an old fisherman's custom to drink a toast to the dead. Whether it was or not I had no idea, it could well have been a custom that Imrie had invented himself, and certainly the deceased had been no fishermen: but whatever its origin I'm sure that it made its contributory effect towards the extremely rapid clearing of the decks.

I remained where I was. I felt inhibited from joining the others not because I found Captain Imrie's proposal distasteful or ethically objectionable—only the most hypocritical could find in the Christian ethic a bar to wishing *bon voyage* to the departed—but because, in crowded surroundings, it could be very difficult to see who was filling my glass and what he was filling it with. Moreover, I'd had no more than three hours' sleep the previous night, my mind was tired and a bit fuzzy round the edges and it was my hope that the admittedly heroic treatment of exposure to an Arctic blizzard might help to blow some of the cobwebs away. I took a firm hold on one of the numerous lifelines that were rigged on deck, edged my way out to the largest of one of the numerous deck cargoes we were carrying, took what illusory shelter was offered in its lee and waited for the cobwebs to fly away.

Halliday was dead. I hadn't found his body, I'd searched, casually and unobtrusively, every likely and most of the unlikely places of concealment on the *Morning Rose*: he had vanished and left no trace. Halliday, I knew, was lying in the black depths of the Barents Sea. How he'd got there I didn't know and it didn't seem to be important: it could be that someone had helped him over the side but it was even more probable that he had required no assistance. He'd left the saloon as abruptly as he had because the poison in his scotch—my scotch—had been as fast acting as it had been deadly. He had felt the urgent need to be sick and the obvious place to be sick was over the side: a slip on the snow or ice, one of the hundreds of trough-seeking lurches that the trawler had experienced during the night and in what must have been by that time his ill, weakened and dazed state, and he would have been quite unable to prevent himself from pitching over the low guard-rails. The only consolation, if consolation it was, was that he had probably succumbed to poison before his lungs had filled with water. I did not subscribe to the popular belief that death from drowning was a relatively easy and painless way to go, if for no other reason than that it was a theory that in the nature of things lacked positive documentation.

I was as certain as could be that Halliday's absence had so far gone unnoticed by everyone except myself and the person responsible for his death, and there was not even certainty about that last point, it was quite possible that he knew nothing of Halliday's brief visit to the saloon. True, Halliday had not appeared for breakfast but as a few others had done the same and those who had come had done so intermittently over the best part of a couple of hours, his absence had gone unremarked. His cabin-mate, Sandy, was still feeling under the weather to the extent that Halliday's presence or absence was a matter of total indifference to him: and as Halliday had been very much a solitary there was no one who would be sufficiently concerned to inquire anxiously as to his whereabouts. I hoped that his absence remained undiscovered as long as possible: although the signed guarantee given to Captain Imrie that morning had contained no specific reference as to the action to be taken in the event of someone going missing, he was quite capable of seizing upon this as a pretext to abandon the trip and make with all speed for Hammerfest.

The match I'd left jammed between the foot of my cabin door and the sill had no longer been in position when I'd returned to my cabin early in the morning. The coins I'd left in the linen pockets of the lids of my suitcases had shifted position from the front to the back of the pockets, sure evidence that my cases had been opened in my absence. It says much for my frame of mind that the discovery occasioned me no particular surprise—which was in itself surprising, for although someone aboard was aware that the good doctor had been boning up on *aconitine* and so had more than a fair idea that the poisoning had not been accidental, that in itself was hardly reason to start examining the doctor's hand luggage. More than ever, it behooved me to watch my back.

I heard a sound behind my back. My instinctive reaction was to take a couple of rapid steps forward, who knew what hard or sharp implement might be coming at my occiput or shoulder-blades, then whirl round, but a simultaneous reasoning told me that it was unlikely that anyone would propose to do me in on the upper deck in daylight under the interested gaze of watchers on the bridge, so I turned round leisurely and saw Charles Conrad moving into what little shelter was offered in the lee of the bulk deck cargo.

'What's this, then?' I said. 'The morning constitutional at all costs? Or don't you fancy Captain Imrie's scotch?'

'Neither.' He smiled. 'Curiosity is all.' He tapped the tarpaulin-covered bulk beside us. It was close on ten feet in height, semi-cylindrical—the base was flat—and was lashed in position by at least a dozen steel cables. 'Do you know what this is?'

'Is this a clever question?'

'Yes.'

'Prefabricated Articized huts. Or so the word went in Wick. Six of them, designed to fit one inside the other for ease of transportation.'

'That's it. Made of bonded ply, kapok insulation, asbestos and aluminium.' He pointed to another bulky item of deck cargo immediately for'ard of the one behind which we were sheltering. This peculiarly shaped object appeared to be roughly oval along its length, perhaps six feet high. 'And this?'

'Another clever question?'

'Of course.'

'And my answer will be wrong? Again?'

'If you still believe what you were told in Wick, yes. Those aren't huts because we don't need huts. We're heading for an area called the Sor-hamna—the South Haven—where there already *are* huts, and perfectly usable ones. Bloke called Lerner came there seventy years ago, prospecting for coal— which he found, by the way: a bit of an odd-ball who painted the rocks on the shore in the German colours to indicate that this was private property. He built huts— he even built a road across the headland to the nearest bay, the Kvalross Bukta or Walrus Bay. After him a German fishing company based themselves here—and *they* built huts. More importantly, a Norwegian scientific expedition spent nine months here during the most recent International Geophysical Year—and *they* built huts. Whatever else is lacking at South Haven it's not accommodation.'

'You're very well informed.'

'I don't forget something that I finished reading only half an hour ago. Comin' and Goin's been making the rounds this morning handing out copies of the prospectus of what's going to be the greatest film ever made. Didn't you get one from him?'

'Yes. He forgot to give me a dictionary, though.'

'A dictionary would have helped.' He tapped the tarpaulin beside us. 'This is a mock-up of the central section of a submarine—just a shell, nothing inside it. When I say it's a mock-up, I don't mean it's made of cardboard—it's made of steel and weighs ten tons, including four tons of cast-iron ballast. That other item in front is a conning-tower which is to be bolted on to this once it's in the water.'

'Ah!' I said because I couldn't think of any other comment. 'And those alleged tractors and drums of fuel on the after deck—they'll be tanks and anti-aircraft guns?'

'Tractors and fuel, as stated.' He paused. 'Do you know there's only one copy of the screen-play for this film and that's locked up in the Bank of England or some such?'

'I went to sleep about that bit.'

'They haven't even got a shooting script for the scenes to be shot on the island. Just a series of unrelated incidents which, taken together, make no sense at all. Sure, there must be connecting links to make sense of it all: but they're all in the vaults in Threadneedle Street or whatever this damned bank is. No part of it makes sense.'

'Maybe it's not meant to make sense.' I was conscious that my feet were slowly turning into blocks of ice. 'Not at this stage. There may be excellent reasons for the secretiveness. Besides, don't some producers encourage directors who play it off the cuff, who improvise as they go along and as the mood takes them?'

'Not Neal Divine. He's never shot an off-the-cuff scene in his life.' Not much of Conrad's forehead was to be seen beneath the thick brown hair that the snow and wind had brought down almost to eyebrow level, but what little was visible was very heavily corrugated indeed. 'If a Divine shooting script calls for you to be wearing a bowler hat and doing the can-can in Scene 289, then you're doing a bowler-hatted can-can in 289. As for Otto, he never moves until everything's calculated out to the last matchstick and the last penny. Especially the last penny.

'He has the reputation for being careful.'

'Careful!' Conrad shivered. 'Doesn't the whole set-up strike you as being crazy.'

'The entire film world,' I said candidly, 'strikes me as being crazy, but as an ordinary human being exposed to it for the first time I wouldn't know whether this current particular brand of craziness differs from the norm or not. What do your fellow actors think of it?'

'What fellow actors?' Conrad said glumly. 'Judith Haynes is still closeted with those two pooches of hers. Mary Stuart is writing letters in her cabin, at least she says it's letters, it's probably her last will and testament. And if Gunther Jungbeck and Jon Heyter have any opinion on everything they're carefully keeping it to themselves. Anyway, *they* are a couple of odd-balls themselves.'

'Even for actors?'

'Touché.' He smiled, but he wasn't trying too hard. 'Sea burials bring out the misanthrope in me. No, it's just that they know so little about the film world, at least the British film world, understandable enough I suppose, Heyter's done all his acting in California, Jungbeck in Germany. They're not odd, really, it's just that we have nothing in common to talk about, no points of reference.'

'But you must know of them?'

'Not even that, but that's not surprising. I like acting but the film world bores me to tears and I don't mix socially. That makes me an odd-ball too. But Otto vouches for them —in fact, he speaks pretty highly of them, and that's good enough for me. They'll both probably act me off the screen when it comes to the bit.' He shivered again. 'Conrad's curiosity remains unsatisfied, but Conrad has had enough. As a doctor, wouldn't you prescribe some of this scotch which old Imrie is supposed to be dispensing so liberally?'

We found Captain Imrie dispensing the scotch with so heavy a hand that plainly it came from his own private supplies and not from Otto's, for Otto, heavily wrapped in a coloured blanket and with his puce complexion still a pale shadow of its former self, was sitting in his accustomed dining chair and raising no objections that I could see. There must have been at least twenty people present, ship's crew and passengers, and they were very far indeed from being a merry throng. I was surprised to see Judith Haynes there, with her husband, Michael Stryker, hovering attentively over her. I was surprised to see Mary darling there, her sense of duty or what was the done thing must have been greater than her aversion to alcohol, and was even more surprised to note that she had so abandoned all sense of the proprieties as to be holding young Allen by the arm in a positively proprietorial fashion: I was not surprised to see that Mary Stuart was absent. So were Heissman and Sandy. The two actors with whom Conrad claimed to have so little in common, Jungbeck and Heyter, were together in one corner and for the first time I looked at them with some degree of real interest. They *looked* like actors, no question of that, or, more accurately, they looked like what I thought actors ought to look like. Heyter was tall, fair, good-looking, young and twenty years ago would have been referred to as clean-cut: he had a mobile, expressive, animated face. Jungbeck was at least fifteen years his senior, a thick-set man with heavy shoulders, a five o'clock shadow and dark, curling hair just beginning to grey: he had a ready, engaging smile. He was cast, I knew, as the villain in the forthcoming production and despite the appropriate build and blue jowls didn't look the least bit like one.

The almost complete silence in the saloon, I soon realized, didn't stem entirely from the solemnity of the occasion, although that element must have been there: Captain Imrie had been holding the floor and had only broken off to acknowledge our entrance and to take the opportunity of dispensing some more liquor, which I refused. And now, it was clear, Captain Imrie was taking up where he had left off.

'Aye,' he said heavily, ''tis fitting, 'tis fitting. They have gone today, sadly, tragically gone, three of Britain's sons—' I was almost glad, for the moment, that Antonio was no longer around—'but it comes to us all, sooner or later the hour strikes, and if they must rest where better to lie than in those honoured waters of Bear Island where ten thousand of their countrymen sleep?' I wondered, uncharitably, what hour struck when Captain Imrie poured himself his first restorative of the morning but then recalled that as he had been up since 4 a.m. he was no doubt now rightly regarding the day as being pretty far advanced, a supposition which he proceeded to prove correct by replenishing his glass without, however, interrupting the smooth flow of his monologue. His audience, I noted with regret, had about them the look of men and women who wished themselves elsewhere.

'I wonder what Bear Island means to you people,' he went on. 'Nothing, I suppose, why should it? It's just a name, Bear Island, just a name. Like the Isle of Wight or what's yon place in America, Coney Island: just a name. But for people like Mr Stokes here and myself and thousands of others it's a wee bit more than that. It was a kind of turning-point, a dividing point in our lives, what those geography or geology fellows would call a watershed: when we came to know the name we knew that no name had ever meant so much to us before—and no name would ever mean so

121

much again. And we knew that nothing would ever be the same again. Bear Island was the place where boys grew up, just over the night, as it were: Bear Island was the place where middle-aged men like myself grew old.' This was a different Captain Imrie speaking now, quietly reminiscent, sad without bitterness, and the captive audience was now voluntarily so, no longer glancing longingly at the saloon exits.

'We called it "the Gate",' he went on. 'The gate to the Barents Sea and the White Sea and those places in Russia where we took those convoys through all the long years of the war, all those long years ago. If you passed the Gate and came back again, you were a lucky man: if you did it half-a-dozen times you'd used up all your luck for a lifetime. How many times did we pass the Gate, Mr Stokes?'

'Twenty-two times.' For once, Mr Stokes had no need for deliberation.

'Twenty-two times. I am not saying it because I was there but people on those convoys to Murmansk suffered more terribly than people have ever suffered in war before or will ever suffer in war again, and it was here, in those waters, at the Gate, that they suffered most of all, for it was here that the enemy waited by night and by day and it was here that the enemy struck us down. The fine ships and the fine boys, our boys and the German boys, more of them lie in those waters than anywhere in the world, but the waters run clean now and the blood is washed away. But not in our minds, not in our minds: thirty years have passed now and I cannot hear the words "Bear Island", not even when I say them myself, but my blood runs cold. The graveyard of the Arctic and we hope they are at peace now, but still my blood runs cold.' He shivered, as if he felt a physical chill, then smiled slightly. 'The old talk too much, a blether talks too much, so you know now how terrible it is to have an old blether stand before you. All I'd really meant to say is that our shipmates are in good company.' He raised his glass. '*Bon voyage.*'

Bon voyage. But not the last goodbye, not the last time we would be saying goodbye, I felt it deep in my bones and I knew that Captain Imrie felt it also. I knew that it was some sort of fore-knowledge or premonition that had made him talk as he had done, that had been responsible for a rambling reminiscence as uncalled for as it was irrelevant—or appeared to be. I wondered if Captain Imrie was even dimly aware of this thought transference process, of the substitution of the fearful things, the dreadful things of long ago for the unrealized awareness that such things were not confined to the actions of overt warfare, that violent death acknowledged no restrictions in time and space, that the bleak and barren waters of the Barents Sea were its habitat and its home.

I wondered how many others of those present felt this atavistic fear, this oddly nameless dread so often encountered in the loneliest and most desolate places on earth, a dread that reaches back over the aeons to primitive man who as yet knew not fire, to those unthinkably distant ancestors who crouched in terror in their lightless caves while the forces of evil and darkness walked abroad in the night: a fear that, here and now, was all too readily reinforced and compounded by the sudden, violent and inexplicable deaths of three of their company the previous night.

It was hard to tell, I thought, just who was feeling affected by such primeval stirrings of foreboding, for mankind does not readily acknowledge even to itself, far less show or discuss, the existence of such irrationally childlike superstitions. Captain Imrie and Mr Stokes, without a doubt: they had gone into a corner by themselves and were staring down, unseeingly, I was sure, and certainly without speaking, at the glasses in their hands, and as the two of them rarely if ever sat together without discussing, at great length, matters of the gravest import, this was highly significant in itself. Neal Divine, more hollow-cheeked than ever but apparently slightly recovered from his very low state of the previous evening, sat by himself, continuously twirling the empty glass in his hand, his usual nervous preoccupied self, but whether he was preoccupied with *mal de mer,* the thought that he was about to begin his directorial duties and so consequently be exposed to the lash of Gerran's tongue or whether he, too, was feeling fingers from the dead past reach deep into him was impossible to say.

Comin' and Goin' was seated by Otto at the head of the table and they, too, were silent. I wondered just what the relationship between the two men was. They seemed to be on cordial enough terms but they only sought each other out, I had observed, when questions of business were to be discussed. It could well have been that, personally, they had little in common, but the fact that Comin' and Goin' had recently been made Vice-President and heir-apparent to Olympus Productions seemed to speak highly enough of Otto's regard for him. And as they were together now and not talking I assumed that they were pondering over matters similar to those that were engaging the attention of Imrie and myself.

The Three Apostles weren't talking, but that meant nothing, when they were deprived of their instruments, their music magazines and their garishly primary-coloured comics, the presence of all of which they had probably deemed as being inappropriate in the present circumstances, they were habitually bereft of speech. Stryker, still in solicitously close attendance upon his wife, was talking quietly to the Count, while the Duke was conspicuously not talking to his cabin-mate Eddie, but as they were rarely on speaking terms anyway, this was hardly significant. I became aware that Lonnie Gilbert was at my elbow and I wondered what degree, if any, of the underlying significance of Captain Imrie's words had penetrated his befuddled mind. Lonnie was clutching a glass of scotch, both container and contents of genuine family size, a marked contrast to the relatively small portions he'd been pouring himself in the lounge bar about midnight: I could only assume that somewhere in the remoter recesses of Lonnie's mind there lurked some vestigial traces of conscience which permitted him only modest amounts of hooch not honestly come by.

' "Envy and calumny and hate and pain, and that unrest which men miscall delight shall touch them not and torture not again," ' Lonnie intoned. He tilted his glass, lowered the liquid level by two fingers and smacked his lips. ' "From the contagion—" '

'Lonnie.' I nodded at the glass. 'When did you start this morning?'

'Start? My dear fellow, I never stopped. A sleepless night. "From the contagion of the world's slow stain they are secure, and now can never mourn the heart grown cold, the head grown grey—" '

Aware that he had lost his audience, Lonnie broke off and followed my line of sight. Mary darling and Allen, proprieties observed, were leaving. Mary hesitated, stopped in front of Judith Haynes's chair, smiled and said: 'Good morning, Miss Haynes. I hope you're feeling better today?'

Judith Haynes smiled, a fractionally glimpsed set of perfect teeth, then looked away: a false smile meant to be seen and understood as a false smile, followed by a complete and contemptuous dismissal. I saw colour stain Mary darling's cheeks and she made as if to speak, but Allen, his lips tight, took her arm and urged her gently towards the lee door.

'Well, well,' I said. 'I wonder what all that was about. A clearly offended Miss Haynes but I can't conceive of our little Mary giving offence to anybody.'

'But she has done, my boy, she has done. Our Judith is one of those sad and unfortunate females who can't abide any other female who is younger, better-looking or more intelligent than she is. Our little Mary offends on at least two of those counts.'

'You disappoint me,' I said. 'Here I was, manfully trying to discount—or at least ignore—what appears to be the universally held opinion that Judith Haynes is a complete and utter bitch and now—'

'And you were right.' Lonnie regarded his empty glass with an expression of faint astonishment. 'She isn't a bitch, at least she doesn't make a career out of it, except inadvertently. To those who offer no threat or competition, little children or pets, she is capable of generous impulses, even affection. But that apart, a poor, poor creature, incapable of loving or inspiring love in others, to wit and in short, a loveless soul, perverse but pitiable, a person who having once seen herself and not liking what she has seen, turns away from reality and takes refuge in misanthropic fantasy.' Lonnie executed a swift sideways scuttle in the direction of an unattended scotch bottle, replenished his glass with the speed and expertise born of a lifetime of practice, returned happily and warmed to his theme.

'Sick, sick, sick, and it is the sick, not the whole, who require our help and sympathy.' Lonnie could, on occasion, sound very pontifical indeed. 'She's one of the hapless band of the world's willing walking wounded—how's that, four w's and never a stutter—who takes a positive delight in being hurt, in being affronted, and if the hurt is not really there, why, then, all the better, they can imagine one even closer to the heart's desire. For those unfortunates who love only themselves the loving embrace of self-pity, close hugged like an old and dear friend, is the supreme, the most precious luxury in life. I can assure you, my dear fellow, that no hippo ever wallowed in his African mud-bath with half the relish—'

'I'm sure you're right, Lonnie,' I said, 'and a very apt analogy that is, too.' I wasn't listening to him any more, my attention had been caught and held by the fleeting glimpse I'd had of a figure hurrying by on the deck outside. Heissman, I was almost sure it was Heissman, and if it were I'd three immediate questions that asked for equally immediate answers. Heissman was rarely observed to move at any but the most deliberate and leisurely speed so why the uncharacteristic haste? Why, if he were moving aft, did he choose the weather instead of the lee side of the superstructure unless he hoped to avoid being observed through the large snow-obscured windows on the weather side of the saloon? And what, in view of his well-known and almost pathological aversion to cold— an inevitable legacy, one supposed, of his long years in Siberia—was he doing on the upper deck anyway? I clapped Lonnie on the shoulder. 'Back, as the saying goes, in a trice. I have to visit the sick.'

I left, not hurriedly, through the lee door, then paused to see if anyone was interested enough in my departure to follow me out. And someone did follow me, almost immediately, but if he had any interest in my movements he wasn't letting me see it. Gunther Jungbeck smiled at me briefly, indifferently, and hurried forward to the entrance to the passenger accommodation. I waited a few more seconds, then climbed up the vertical steel ladder to the boat deck, immediately abaft the bridge and radio office.

I circled the funnel and engine intake fans casing and found no one there. I hadn't expected to, even a polar bear wouldn't have hung around that bitter and totally exposed boat deck without a very compelling reason. I moved aft by one of our two motorized lifeboats, took what illusory shelter I could find beside a ventilator and peered out over the after-deck.

For the first few moments I could see nothing, nothing, that was, that was likely to be of any interest to me, not so much because of the driving snow as the fact that all objects crowding the after-deck—and there were well over a score of them, ranging from fuel drums to a sixteen-foot work-boat on a special cradle—were so deeply shrouded in their shapeless cocoons of snow that, in most cases, it was virtually impossible to decide upon not only their identity but whether they were inanimate or not. Not until any of them might move.

One of the cocoons stirred, a slender ghostly form detaching itself from the shelter of a square bulky object which I knew to be the cabin for a Sno-Cat. The figure half-turned in my direction and although the face was almost entirely hidden by a hand that held both sides of the parka hood closed against the snow, enough of straw-coloured hair showed to let me identify the only person aboard with that colour of hair. Almost at once she was joined by a person moving into my line of vision from behind the break of the boat deck and I didn't even have to see the thin ascetic face to know that this was Heissman.

He approached the girl directly, took her arm without, as far as I could see, any kind of opposition being offered, and said something to her. I sank to my knees, partly to reduce the risk of detection if either chanced to look up, partly to try and make out what was being said. The concealment part worked but the eavesdropping failed, partly because the wind was in the wrong direction but chiefly because they had their heads very close together either because they regarded suitably low and conspiratorial conversation as being appropriate to the occasion or because they were affording each other's faces protection from the snow. I inched forward to the very end of the boat deck and squatted back on my heels with my head bent forward but this was of no help either.

Heissman now had an arm around Mary Stuart's shoulders and this time the gesture of intimacy did produce a reaction although scarcely the expected one for she reached up an arm around his neck and put her head on his shoulder. At least another two minutes were spent in this highly confidential tête-à-tête, then they walked slowly away towards the living accommodation, Heissman still with his arm around the girl's shoulders. I made no move to follow them, for such a move would not only have almost certainly resulted in quick detection but it would have been pointless: whatever personal they'd had to say had already been said.

'Yoga in the Barents Sea,' a voice said behind me. 'That's

dedication for you.'

'Fanatics always carry everything to excess,' I said. I rose awkwardly but without too much haste before turning round for I knew I had nothing to fear from Smithy. Clad in a hooded duffel-coat and looking a great deal fitter than he had been doing just before midnight, he was looking at me with what might have been an expression of quizzical amusement except that his eyes didn't seem to find anything humorous in what they saw. 'You have to be regular in these things,' I explained.

'Of course.' He walked past me, looked over the boat deck guard-rail and examined the deep tracks left in the snow by Mary and Heissman. 'Bird-watching?'

'The haunts of coot and hern.'

'Yes, indeed. But an oddly assorted pair of love-birds, wouldn't you say?'

'It's this film world, Smithy. It seems to be full of very oddly assorted birds.'

'Odd birds, period.' He nodded for'ard, towards the chart-house. 'Warmth and cheer, Doc, just the place for some more ornithological research.'

There wasn't a great deal of warmth owing to the fact that Smithy had left the side door open after he'd looked out through the window and observed me moving cautiously along the boat deck but there was a certain amount of cheer in the shape of a bottle he produced from a cupboard. He said: 'Shall we send for the king's taster?'

I looked at the unbroken lead seal. 'Not unless you think someone has brought his own bottling plant aboard.'

'I've checked.' Smithy broke the seal. 'We talked last night. At least, I did. You may or may not have listened. I was worried last night. I thought you might not be levelling with me. I'm worried stiff now. Because I know you're not.'

'Because I've taken up ornithology?' I said mildly.

'That among other things. This wholesome poisoning, now. I've had time to think, just a bit. Of course you couldn't have had any idea who the poisoner was—it's hardly conceivable that if you knew the person who had done in that Italian boy that you'd have let him do the same to six others, two of whom were to die. In fact you couldn't even have been sure that the whole thing wasn't accidental, the poisoning was on so apparently haphazard a basis.'

'Thank you kindly,' I said. My opinion of Smithy had fallen sharply. 'Except that it wasn't on an apparently haphazard basis. It *was* haphazard.'

'That was last night.' It was as if he hadn't heard me. 'Then you couldn't have had any idea. Now you can. Things have happened, haven't they?'

'What things?' My opinion of Smithy had risen sharply. He was sure that there was mayhem afoot, but why? Was he making a mental short list, guessing as to who might be the handy lad with the aconite—not that he could possibly know the poison used was aconite—wondering where he had got it, where he kept it now, where he had learned to prepare it so skilfully that it could indetectably be introduced into food? And not only who was the poisoner but *why* was the poisoner acting as he did? And why the random nature of the poisoning? Was he basing his guesses just on my stealthy behaviour?

'Lots of things, not all of which have necessarily lately happened, just things that have come to light or seem odd in view of what we might call recent developments. For instance, why have Captain Imrie and Mr Stokes been chosen for the job instead of any two young and efficient yacht and charter skippers and engineers who usually find themselves unemployed at this time of year? Because they're so old and so soaked in scotch and rum that they can't tell the time of day twenty hours out of the twenty-four. They just don't see what goes on and even if they were to they'd probably attach no significance to it anyway.'

I didn't put down my glass, look keenly at Smithy or in any other way indicate that I was listening with undivided attention. But I was. This thought had never occurred to me.

Smithy continued. 'I said last night that I thought the presence of Mr Gerran and his company up here at this time in the year was a bit odd. I don't think so any more. I think it's damned peculiar and calls for some sort of rational explanation from your friend Otto, which we're not likely to get.'

'He's not my friend,' I said.

'And this.' He pulled out a copy of the Olympus Productions manifesto. 'A load of meaningless rubbish that old smoothie Goin has been inflicting on everybody in sight. Have you—'

'Goin? A smoothie?'

'An untrustworthy, time-serving, money-grubbing smoothie

with his two hands never on speaking terms, and I'd say that even if he weren't a professional accountant.'

'Maybe he'd better not be my friend either,' I said.

'All this ridiculous secrecy they harp on in this clap-trap. To protect the importance of their damned screen-play. A hundred gets one it's a screen to protect something an awful lot more important than their screen-play. Another hundred gets one that there's no screen-play in the bank vaults they speak of for the reason that there is no screen-play. And their shooting schedule for Bear Island. Have you read that? It's not even comic. Just a lot of unrelated incidents about caves, and mysterious motor-boats and shooting dummy submarines and climbing cliffs and falling into the sea and dying in Arctic snows that any five-year-old could have dreamed up.'

'You've got a very suspicious mind, Smithy,' I said.

'Have I not? And this young Polish actress, the blonde one—'

'Latvian. Mary Stuart. What of her?'

'A strange one. Aloof and alone. Never mixes. But when there's illness on the bridge, or in Otto's cabin or in the cabin of that young lad they call the Duke, who's there? Who but our friend Mary Stuart.'

'She's a kind of Samaritan. Would you be so conspicuous if you wanted to avoid attention?'

'Might be the very best way to achieve it. But if that's not the case, why make a point of being so damned inconspicuous just now when meeting Heissman in a blizzard on the after-deck?'

I would very much rather, I thought, have Smith for me than against me. I said: 'A romantic assignation, perhaps?'

'With *Heissman*?'

'You're not a girl, Smithy.'

'No.' He grinned briefly. 'But I've met 'em. Why are all the big nobs on the management side so pally with Otto in public and so critical in private? Why is a cameraman a director? Why—'

'How did you know that?'

'Uh-huh. So you knew too. Because Captain Imrie showed me this guarantee thing that you and the directors of Olympus had signed: the Count had signed as one of them. Why is the director, this Divine fellow who is supposed to be so good at his job, so scared of Otto, while Lonnie, who is not only a permanent alcoholic layabout but latches on to Otto's private hooch supplies with impunity, doesn't give a damn about him?'

'Tell me, Smithy,' I said, 'just how much time have you been devoting lately to steering and navigating this boat?'

'Hard to say. Just about as much time, I would say, as you have been to the practice of medicine.'

I didn't say 'Touché' or anything like that, I just let Smithy pour some more of the aconite-free drink into my glass and looked out of the window at the grey swirling icy world beyond. So many whys, Smithy, so many whys. Why had Mary been foregathering clandestinely with Heissman when the Heissman I'd observed last night had been so clearly unwell as to be unable to indulge in any skullduggery—not that this ruled out the chilling possibility that Heissman might be one of two or more who held life so lightly and might easily be either a principal or a go-between. Why had Otto, though himself a poisoning victim, reacted so violently—including having been violently ill—when he'd heard that Antonio had been a poisoning victim? Had Cecil's larder raid been as innocuous as he had claimed? Had Sandy's? Who had checked on the *aconitine* article, disposed of the leftovers in the galley, been in my cabin during the night and searched my baggage? Why had he searched my baggage—this extremely active poisoner, the same man, perhaps, who had doctored the scotch bottle, clobbered me and been responsible for Halliday's death? Again, was there more than one of them? And if Halliday had died accidentally, as I was sure he had, then why had he come to the saloon, where his visit, I was equally sure, had not been accidental?

It was all so full of 'ifs' and 'buts' that I was beginning to clutch at ridiculous straws rather than fight my way through the impenetrable fog. What accounted for Lonnie's diatribe— for it had amounted to no less—against Judith Haynes to the effect that she detested all mankind, especially when they were womankind? No doubt Miss Haynes was as capable of being catty and jealous as many other otherwise likeable females are, but one would have thought that she had too much going for her in the way of wealth, success, fame, position and looks to have to bother too much about despising every woman she met. But if that were so, why had she cold-shouldered Mary darling?

But what could that have to do with murder? I didn't know, but nothing the slightest bit odd, I thought gloomily, could be dismissed out of hand as having nothing to do with the very odd goings-on aboard the *Morning Rose*. Were Jungbeck and Heyter, for instance, to be considered as being possibly under suspicion because one had recently followed me from the saloon—especially as Conrad had earlier thrown a degree of suspicion on them by disclaiming all knowledge of them as actors? Or did this factor of apparently throwing suspicion bring Conrad himself under just the tiniest cloud? Dammit to hell, I thought wearily, if I keep on thinking like this I'll be casting young Allen as the master poisoner just because he'd told me that he'd once studied chemistry, briefly, at university.

'A penny for your thoughts, Dr Marlowe.' Smithy wasn't very much of a one for letting his face act as a front man for his mind.

'Don't throw your money away. What thoughts?'

'Two thoughts. Two kinds of thoughts. All the thoughts you're having about all the things you're not telling me and all the guilty thoughts you're having about not telling me them.'

'It's like a rule of nature,' I said. 'Some people are always more liable to have injustices done to them than others.'

'So you've told me all your thoughts?'

'No. But the ones I haven't told aren't worth the telling. Now, if I had some facts—'

'So you admit something is pretty far wrong?'

'Of course.'

'And you've told me everything you know, just not everything you think?'

'Of course.'

'I speak in sorrow,' Smithy said, 'for my lost illusions about the medical profession.' He reached up under the hood of my parka, pulled down the scarf around my neck and stared at what was by now the great multi-coloured and blood-encrusted weal on my neck. 'Jesus! That is something. What happened to you?'

'I fell.'

'The Marlowes of this world don't fall. They're pushed. Where did you fall?' I didn't much care for the all but imperceptible accent on the word 'fall'.

'Upper deck. Port side. I struck my neck on the storm-sill of the saloon door.'

'Did you now? I would say that this was caused by what the criminologists call a solid object. A very solid object about half-an-inch wide and sharp-edged. The saloon door sill is three inches wide and made of sorbo-rubber. All the storm doors on the *Morning Rose* are—it's to make them totally windproof and waterproof. Or perhaps you hadn't noticed? The way you perhaps haven't noticed that John Halliday, the unit's still photographer, is missing?'

'How do you know?' He'd shaken me this time, not just a little, or my face would have shown it, but so much that I knew my features stayed rigidly fixed in the same expression.

'You don't deny it?'

'I don't know. How do you?'

'I went down to see the props man, this elderly lad they call Sandy. I'd heard he was sick and—'

'Why did you go?'

'If it matters, because he's not the sort of person that people visit very much. He doesn't seem liked. Seems a bit hard to be sick *and* unpopular at the same time.' I nodded, this would be in character with Smithy. 'I asked him where his room-mate Halliday was as I hadn't seen him at breakfast. Sandy said he'd gone for breakfast. I didn't say anything to Sandy but this made me a bit curious so I had a look in the recreation room. He wasn't there either, so I got curiouser until I'd searched the *Morning Rose* twice from end to end. I think I covered every nook and cranny in the vessel where even a stray seagull could be hiding and you can take my word for it. Halliday's not in the *Morning Rose*.'

'Reported this to the captain?'

'Well, well, what an awful lot of reaction. No, I haven't reported it to the captain.'

'Why not?'

'Same reason as you haven't. If I know my Captain Imrie, he'd at once declare that there was no clause in that agreement you signed that was binding on this particular case, that saying that foul play wasn't involved in this case also would be altogether too much of a good thing, and turn the *Morning Rose* straight for Hammerfest.' Smithy looked at me dead-pan over the rim of his glass. 'I'm rather curious to see what does happen when we get to Bear Island.'

'It might be interesting.'

'Very non-committal. It might, says he thoughtfully, be equally interesting to provoke some kind of reaction in Dr Marlowe. Just once. Just for the record—my own private record. I wonder if I could do it. Do you remember I said on the bridge in the very early hours of this morning that we might just possibly have to call for help and that if we had to we had a transmitter here that could reach almost anywhere in the northern hemisphere. Not, perhaps, my exact words, but the gist is accurate?'

'The gist is accurate.' Even to myself the repetition of the words sounded mechanical and I had to make a conscious effort not to shiver as an ice-shod centipede started up a fandango between my shoulder-blades.

'Well, we can call for help till we're blue in the face, this transmitter here can no longer reach as far as the galley.' For once, almost unbelievably, Smithy's face was registering an emotion other than amusement. His face tight with anger, he produced a screwdriver from his pocket and turned to the big steel-blue receiver-transmitter on the inner bulkhead.

'Do you always carry a screwdriver about with you?' The sheer banality of the question made it apposite in the circumstances.

'Only when I call up the radio station at Tunheim in north-east Bear Island and get no reply. And that's no ordinary radio station, it's an official Norwegian Government base.' Smithy set to work on the face-plate screws. 'I've already had this damned thing off about an hour ago. You'll see in a jiffy why I put it back on again.'

While I was waiting for this jiffy to pass I recalled our conversation on the bridge in the very early hours of the morning, the time he'd referred to the radio and the relative closeness—and, by inference, the availability—of the NATO Atlantic forces. It had been immediately afterwards that I'd looked through the starboard screen door and seen the sharp fresh footprints in the snow, footprints, I'd been immediately certain, that had been made by an eavesdropper, a preposterous idea I'd almost as quickly put out of my mind when I'd appreciated that there had been only one set of footprints there, those which I made myself. For some now inexplicable reason it had never occurred to me that any person clever enough to have been responsible for the series of undetected crimes that had taken place aboard the *Morning Rose* would have been far too clever to have overlooked the blinding obviousness of the advantage that lay in using footsteps already there. The footsteps had, indeed, been newly made, our ubiquitous friend had been abroad again.

Smithy removed the last of the screws and, not without some effort, removed the face-plate. I looked at the revealed interior for about ten seconds, then said: 'I see now why you put the face-plate back on. The only thing that puzzles me is that that cabinet looks a bit small for a man to get inside it with a fourteen pound sledge-hammer.'

'Looks just like it, doesn't it?' The tangled mess of wreckage inside was, literally, indescribable. The vandal who had been at work had seen to it that, irrespective of how vast a range of spares were carried, the receiver-transmitter could never be made operable again. 'You've seen enough?'

'I think so.' He started to replace the cover and I said: 'You've radios in the lifeboats?'

'Yes. Hand-cranked. They'll reach farther than the galley but a megaphone would be about as good.'

'You'll have to report this to the captain, of course.'

'Of course.'

'Then it's heigh-ho for Hammerfest?'

'Twenty-four hours from now and he can heigh-ho for Tahiti as far as I'm concerned.' Smithy tightened the last screw. 'That's when I'm going to tell him. Twenty-four hours from now. Maybe twenty-six.'

'Your outside limit for dropping anchor in Sor-hamna?'

'Tying up. Yes.'

'You're a very deceitful man, Smithy.'

'It's the company I keep. And the life I lead.'

'You're not to blame yourself, Smithy,' I said kindly. 'We live in vexed and troubled times.'

CHAPTER SEVEN

When the Norwegian compilers of the report on Bear Island had spoken of it as possessing perhaps the most inhospitably bleak coastline in the world, they had been speaking with the measured understatement of true professional geographers. As we approached it in the first light of dawn—which in those latitudes, at that time of year, and under grey and lowering skies which were not only full of snow but getting rid of it as fast as they could, was as near mid forenoon as made no difference—it presented the most awesome, awe-inspiring and, in the true sense of the word, awful spectacle of nature it had ever been my misfortune to behold. A frightening desolation, it was a weird combination of the wickedly repellent and unwillingly fascinating, an evil and dreadful and sinister place, a place full of the terrifying intimation of mortality, the culmination of all the terrors for our long-lost Nordic ancestors, for whom hell was the land of eternal cold and for whom this would be the eternally frozen purgatory to be visited only in their dying nightmares.

Bear Island was black. That was the shocking, the almost frightful thing about it. Bear Island was black, black as a widow's weeds. Here in the regions of year-long snow and ice, where, in winter, even the waters of the Barents Sea ran a milky white, to find this ebony mass towering 1500 vertical feet up into the grey overcast evoked the same feeling of total disbelief, the same numbing impact, although here magnified a hundredfold, as does the first glimpse of the black cliff of the north face of the Eiger rearing up its appalling grandeur among the snows of the Bernese Oberland: this benumbment of the senses stemmed from a dichotomous struggle to accept the evidence before the eyes, for while reason said that it had to be so, that primeval part of the mind that existed long before man knew what reason was just flatly refused to accept it.

We were just south-west of the most southerly tip of Bear Island, steaming due east through the calmest seas that we had encountered since leaving Wick, but even that term was only relative, it was still necessary to hang on to something if one wished to maintain the perpendicular. Overall, the weather hadn't changed any for the better, the comparative moderating of the seas was due entirely to the fact that the wind blew now directly from the north and we were in the lee of whatever little shelter was afforded by those giant cliffs. We were making this particular approach to our destination at Otto's request for he was understandably anxious to build up a library of background shots which, so far, was completely non-existent, and those bleak precipices would have made a cameraman's or director's dream: but Otto's luck was running true to form, those driving gusts of snow, which would in any event have driven straight into the camera lens and completely obscured it, more often than not obscured the cliffs themselves.

Due north lay the highest cliffs of the island, the polomite battlements of the Hambergfjell dropping like a stone into the spume-topped waves that lashed its base, with, standing out to sea, an imposing rock needle thrusting up at least 250 feet: to the north-east, and less than a mile distant, stood the equally magnificent Bird Fell cliffs with, clustered at their foot, an incredible series of high stacks, pinnacles and arches that could only have been the handiwork of some Herculean sculptor, at once both blind and mad.

All this we—about ten others and myself—could see purely by courtesy of the fact that we were on the bridge which had its for'ard screen windows equipped with a high-speed Kent clear-view screen directly in front of the helmsman—which at this particular moment was Smithy—while on either side were two very large windscreen-wipers which coped rather less effectively with the gusting snow.

I was standing with Conrad, Lonnie and Mary Stuart in front of the port wiper. Conrad, who was by no means as dashing in real life as he was on the screen, appeared to have struck up some kind of diffident friendship with Mary, which, I reflected, was as well for her social life as she'd barely spoken to me since the morning of the previous day, which might have been interpreted as being a bit graceless of her considering I'd incurred a large variety of aches and cramps in preventing her from falling to the floor during most of the preceding night. She hadn't exactly avoided me in the past twenty-four hours but neither had she sought me out, maybe she had certain things on her mind, such as her conscience and her unforgiveable treatment of me: nor had I exactly sought her out for I, too, had a couple of things on my mind, the first of which was herself.

I had developed towards her a markedly ambivalent feeling: while I had to be grateful to her for having, however unwittingly, saved my life because her aversion to scotch had prevented me from having the last nightcap I'd ever have had in this world, at the same time she'd prevented me from moving around and, just possibly, stumbling upon the lad who had been wandering about in the middle watches with ill-intent in his heart and a sledge-hammer in his hand. That she, and for whomsoever she worked, knew beyond question that I was a person who might have reason to be abroad at inconvenient hours I no longer doubted. And the second thing in my mind was the 'whomsoever': I no longer doubted that it was Heissman and perhaps he didn't even stand in need of an accomplice: doctors, by the nature of their profession, are even more fallible and liable to error than the average run of mankind and I might well have been in error when I'd seen him on his bed in pain and judged him unfit to move around. Moreover, Goin apart, he was the only man with a cabin to himself and so able to sally out and return undetected by a room-mate. And, of course, there was always this mysterious Siberian background of his. None of which, not even his secret meeting with Mary Stuart, was enough to hang a cat on.

Lonnie touched my arm and I turned. He smelt like a distillery. He said: 'Remember what we were talking about? Two nights ago.'

'We talked about a lot of things.'

'Bars.'

'Don't you ever think of anything else, Lonnie? Bars? What bars?'

'In the great hereafter,' Lonnie said solemnly. 'Do you think there are any there? In heaven, I mean. I mean, you couldn't very well call it heaven if there are no bars there, now could you? I mean, I wouldn't call it an act of kindness to send an old man like me to a prohibition heaven, now would you? It wouldn't be kind.'

'I don't know, Lonnie. On biblical evidence I should expect there would be some wine around. And lots of milk and honey.' Lonnie looked pained. 'What leads you to expect that you're ever going to be faced with the problem?'

'I was but posing a hypothetic question.' The old man spoke with dignity. 'It would be positively _un_Christian to send me there. God, I'm thirsty. Unkind is what I mean. I mean, charity is the greatest of Christian virtues.' He shook his head sadly. 'An act of the greatest uncharity, my dear boy, the very negation of the spirit of kindness.' Lonnie gazed out through a side window at the fantastically shaped islets of Keilhous Oy, Hosteinen and Stappen, now directly off our port beam and less than half a mile distant. His face was set in lines of tranquil sacrifice. He was as drunk as an owl.

'You do believe in this kindness, Lonnie?' I said curiously. After a lifetime in the cinema business I didn't see how he possibly could.

'What else is there, my dear boy?'

'Even to those who don't deserve it?'

'Ah! Now. There is the point. Those are the ones who deserve it most.'

'Even Judith Haynes?'

He looked as if I had struck him and when I saw the expression on his face I felt as if I had struck him, even although I felt his to be a mysteriously exaggerated reaction. I reached out a hand even as I was about to apologize for I knew not what, but he turned away, a curious sadness on his face, and left the bridge.

'Now I've seen the impossible,' Conrad said. He wasn't smiling but he wasn't being censorious either. 'Someone has at last given offence to Lonnie Gilbert.'

'One has to work at it,' I said. 'I've transgressed against Lonnie's creed. He thinks that I'm unkind.'

'Unkind?' Mary Stuart laid a hand on the arm I was using to steady myself. The skin under the brown eyes was perceptibly darker than it had been thirty-six hours ago and was even beginning to look puffy and the whites of the eyes themselves were dulled and slightly tinged with red. She hesitated, as if about to say something, then her gaze shifted to a point over my left shoulder. I turned.

Captain Imrie closed the starboard wheel-house door behind him. Insofar as it was possible to detect the shift and play of expression on that splendidly bewhiskered and bearded face, it seemed that the captain was upset, even agitated. He crossed directly to Smithy and spoke to him in a low and urgent voice. Smithy registered surprise, then shook his head. Captain Imrie spoke again, briefly. Smithy shrugged his shoulders, then said something in return. Both men looked at me and I knew there was more trouble coming, if not actually arrived, if for no reason other than that so far nothing untowards had happened with which I hadn't been directly or indirectly concerned. Captain Imrie fixed me with his piercing blue eyes, jerked his head with most uncharacteristic peremptoriness towards the chart-room door and headed for it himself. I shrugged my own shoulders in apology to Mary and Conrad and followed. Captain Imrie closed the door behind me.

'More trouble, mister.' I didn't much care for the way he called me 'mister'. 'One of the film crew, John Halliday, has disappeared.'

'Disappeared where?' It wasn't a very intelligent question but then it wasn't meant to be.

'That's what I'd like to know.' I didn't much care for the way he looked at me either.

'He can't just have disappeared. I mean, you've searched for him?'

'We've searched for him, all right.' The voice was harsh with strain. 'From anchor locker to stern-post. He's not aboard the *Morning Rose*.'

'My God,' I said. 'This is awful.' I looked at him in what I hoped registered as puzzlement. 'But why tell me all this?'

'Because I thought you might be able to help us.'

'Help you? I'd like to, but how? I assume that you can only be approaching me in my medical capacity and I can assure you that there's absolutely nothing in what I've seen of him or read in his medical history—'

'I wasn't approaching you in your bloody medical capacity!' Captain Imrie had started to breathe very heavily. 'I just thought you might help me in other ways. Bloody strange, isn't it, mister, that you've been in the thick of everything that's been happening?' I'd nothing to say to this, I'd just been thinking the same thing myself. 'How it was you who just "happened" to find Antonio dead. How it was you who just "happened" to go to the bridge when Smith and Oakley were ill. How was it you who went straight to the stewards' cabin in the crew quarters. Next thing, I suppose, you'd have gone straight to Mr Gerran's cabin and found him dead also, if Mr Goin hadn't had the good luck to go there first. And isn't it bloody strange, mister, that a doctor, the one person who could have helped those people and seemingly couldn't is the one person aboard with enough medical knowledge to make them sick in the first place?'

No question—looking at it from his angle—Captain Imrie was developing quite a reasonable point of view. I was more than vaguely surprised to find that he was capable of developing a point of view in the first place. Clearly, I'd been underestimating him: just how much I was immediately to realize.

'And just why were you spending so much time in the galley late the night before last—when I was in my bed, damn you? The place where all the poison came from. Haggerty told me. He told me you were poking around—*and* got him out of the galley for a spell. You didn't find what you wanted. But you came back later, didn't you? Wanted to find out where the food left-overs were, didn't you? Pretended you were surprised when they were gone. That would look good in court.'

'Oh, for heaven's sake, you silly old—'

'And you were very, very late abroad that night, weren't you? Oh, yes, I've been making inquiries. Up in the saloon— Mr Goin told me: up on the bridge—Oakley told me: down in the lounge—Gilbert told me: and—' he paused dramatically —'in Halliday's cabin—his cabin-mate told me. And, most of all, who was the man who stopped me from going to Hammerfest when I wanted to and persuaded the others to sign this worthless guarantee of yours absolving me from all blame? Tell me that, eh, mister?'

His trump card played, Captain Imrie rested his case. I had to stop the old coot, he was working himself up to having me clapped in irons. I sympathized with him, I was sorry for what I would have to say to him, but clearly this wasn't my morning for making friends anyway. I looked at him coldly and without expression for about ten seconds then said: 'My name's "Doctor" not "mister". I'm not your damned mate.'

'What? What was that?'

I opened the door to the wheel-house and invited him to pass through.

'You just mentioned the word "court". Just step out there and repeat those slanderous allegations in the presence of witnesses and you'll find yourself standing in a part of a court you never expected to be in. Can you imagine the extent of the damages?'

From his face and the perceptible shrinking of his burly frame it was apparent that Captain Imrie immediately could. I was a long, long way from being proud of myself, he was a worried old man saying honestly what he thought had to be said, but he'd left me with no option. I closed the door and wondered how best to begin.

I wasn't given the time to begin. The knock on the door and the opening of the door came on the same instant. Oakley had an urgent and rather apprehensive look about him.

'I think you'd better come down to the saloon right away, sir,' he said to Imrie. He looked at me. 'You, too, I'm afraid, Dr Marlowe. There's been a fight down there, a bad one.'

'Great God Almighty!' If Captain Imrie still had had any lingering hopes that he was running a happy ship, the last of them was gone. For a man of his years and bulk he made a remarkably rapid exit: I followed more leisurely.

Oakley's description had been reasonably accurate. There had been a fight and a very unpleasant affair it must have been too during the period it had lasted—obviously, the very brief period it had lasted. There were only half a dozen people in the saloon altogether—one or two were still suffering sufficiently from the rigours of the Barents Sea to prefer the solitude of their cabins to forbidding beauties of Bear Island, while the Three Apostles, as ever, were down in the recreation room, still cacophonously searching for the bottom rung on the ladder to musical immortality. Three of the six were standing, one sitting, one kneeling and the last stretched out on the deck of the saloon. The three on their feet were Lonnie and Eddie and Hendriks, all with the air of concerned but hesitant helplessness that afflicts uncommitted bystanders on such occasions. Michael Stryker was sitting in a chair at the captain's table, using a very bloodstained handkerchief to dab a deep cut on the right cheekbone: it was noticeable that the knuckles of the hand that held the handkerchief were quite badly skinned. The kneeling figure was Mary Darling. All I could see was her back, the long blonde tresses falling to the deck and her big horn-rimmed spectacles lying about two feet away. She was crying, but crying silently, the thin shoulders shaking convulsively in incipient hysteria. I knelt and raised her, still kneeling, to an upright position. She stared at me, ashen-faced, no tears in her eyes, not recognizing me: without her glasses she was as good as blind.

'It's all right, Mary,' I said. 'Only me. Dr Marlowe.' I looked at the figure on the floor and recognized him, not without some difficulty, as young Allen. 'Come on, now, be a good girl. Let me have a look at him.'

'He's terribly hurt, Dr Marlowe, terribly hurt!' She had difficulty in getting her words out during long and almost soundless gasps. 'Oh, look at him, look at him, it's awful!' Then she started crying in earnest, not quietly this time. Her whole body shook. I looked up.

'Mr Hendriks, will you please go to the galley and ask Mr Haggerty for some brandy? Tell him I want it. If he's not there, take it anyway.' Hendriks nodded and hurried away. I said to Captain Imrie: 'Sorry, I should have asked permission.'

'That's all right, Doctor.' We were back on professional terms again, however briefly: perhaps it was because his reply was largely automatic for the bulk of his interest, and all that clearly hostile, was for the moment centred on Michael Stryker. I turned back to Mary.

'Go and sit on the settee, there. And take some of that brandy. You hear?'

'No! No! I—'

'Doctor's orders.' I looked at Eddie and Lonnie and without a word from me they took her across to the nearest settee. I didn't wait to see whether she followed doctor's orders or not: a now stirring Allen had more pressing claims on my attention. Stryker had done a hatchet job on him: he had a cut forehead, a bruised cheek, an eye that was going to be closed by night, blood coming from both nostrils, a split lip, one tooth missing and another so loose that it was going to be missing very soon also. I said to Stryker: 'You do this to him?'

'Obvious, isn't it?'

'You have to savage him like this? Christ, man, he's only a kid. Why don't you pick on someone your own size next time?'

'Like you, for instance?'

'Oh, my God!' I said wearily. Beneath Stryker's tissue-thin veneer of civilization lay something very crude indeed. I ignored him, asked Lonnie to get water from the galley and cleaned up Allen as best I could. As was invariable in such cases the removal of surface blood improved his appearance about eighty per cent. A plaster on his forehead, two cotton-wool plugs for his nose, and two stitches in a frozen lip and I'd done all I could for him. I straightened as an indignant Captain Imrie started questioning Stryker.

'What happened, Mr Stryker?'

'A quarrel.'

'A quarrel, was it now?' Captain Imrie was being heavily ironic. 'And what started the quarrel?'

'An insult. From him.'

'From that—from that child?' The captain's feelings clearly matched my own. 'What kind of insult to do that to a boy?'

'A private insult.' Stryker dabbed the cut on his cheek and, Hippocrates in temporary abeyance, I felt sorry that it wasn't deeper, even although it looked quite unpleasant enough as it was. 'He just got what anyone gets who insults me, that's all.'

'I shall endeavour to keep a still tongue in my head,' Captain Imrie said drily. 'However, as captain of this ship—'

'I'm not a member of your damned crew. If that young fool there doesn't lodge a complaint—and he won't—I'd be obliged if you'd mind your own business.' Stryker rose and left the saloon. Captain Imrie made as if to follow, changed his mind, sat down wearily at the head of his own table and reached for his own private bottle. He said to the three men now clustered round Mary: 'Any of you see what happened?'

'No, sir.' It was Hendriks. 'Mr Stryker was standing alone over by the window there when Stuart went up to speak to him, I don't know what, and next moment they were rolling about the floor. It didn't last more than seconds.'

Captain Imrie nodded wearily and poured a considerable measure into his glass, he was obviously and rightly depending on Smithy to make the approach to anchorage. I got Allen, now quite conscious, to his feet and led him towards the saloon door. Captain Imrie said: 'Taking him below?'

I nodded. 'And when I come back I'll tell you all about how I started it.' He scowled at me and returned to his scotch. Mary, I noticed, was sipping at the brandy and shud-

144

dering at every sip. Lonnie held her glasses in his hand and I escaped with Allen before he gave them back to her.

I got Allen into his bunk and covered him up. He had a little colour in his battered cheeks now but still hadn't spoken.

I said: 'What was all that about?'

He hesitated. 'I'm sorry. I'd rather not say.'

'Why ever not?'

'I'm sorry again. It's a bit private.'

'Someone could be hurt?'

'Yes, I—' He stopped.

'It's all right. You must be very fond of her.' He looked at me for a few silent moments, then nodded. I went on: 'Shall I bring her down?'

'No, Doctor, no! I don't want—I mean, with my face like this. No, no, I couldn't!'

'Your face was an awful sight worse just five minutes ago. She was doing a fair job of breaking her heart even then.'

'Was she?' He tried to smile and winced. 'Well, all right.'

I left and went to Stryker's cabin. He answered my knock and his face didn't have welcome written all over it. I looked at the still bleeding cut.

'Want me to have a look at that?' Judith Haynes, clad in a fur parka and trousers and looking rather like a red-haired Eskimo, was sitting on the cabin's only chair, her two cocker spaniels in her lap. Her dazzling smile was in momentary abeyance.

'No.'

'It might scar.' I didn't give a damn whether it scarred or not.

'Oh.' The factor of his appearance, it hadn't been too hard to guess, was of importance to Stryker. I entered, closed the door, examined and dabbed the cut, put on astringent and applied a plaster. I said: 'Look, I'm not Captain Imrie. Did you have to bang that boy like that? You could have flattened him with a tap.'

'You were there when I told Captain Imrie that it was a purely personal matter.' I'd have to revise my psychological thinking, clearly neither my freely offered medical assistance nor my reasonableness of approach nor the implied flattery had had the slightest mollifying effect. 'Having MD hung round your neck doesn't give you the right to ask impertinent prying questions. Remember what else I said to Imrie?'

'You'd be obliged if I minded my own damned business?'

'Exactly.'

'I'll bet young Allen feels that way too.'

'That young Allen deserves all he got,' Judith Haynes said. Her tone wasn't any more friendly than Stryker's. I found what she said interesting for two reasons. She was widely supposed to loathe her husband but there was no evidence of it here: and here might lie a more fruitful source for inquiry for, clearly, she wasn't as good at keeping her emotions and tongue under wraps as her husband was.

'How do you know, Miss Haynes? You weren't there.'

'I didn't have to be. I—'

'Darling!' Stryker's voice was abrupt, warning.

'Can't trust your wife to speak for herself, is that it?' I said. His big fists balled but I ignored him and looked again at Judith Haynes. 'Do you know there's a little girl up in the saloon crying her eyes out over what your big tough husband did to that kid? Does that mean nothing to you?'

'If you're talking about that little bitch of a continuity girl, she deserves all that comes her way too.'

'Darling!' Stryker's voice was urgent. I stared at Judith Haynes in disbelief but I could see she meant what she said. Her red slash of a mouth was contorted into a line as straight and as thin as the edge of a ruler, the once beautiful green eyes were venomous and the face ugly in its contorted attempts to conceal some hatred or viciousness or poison in the mind. It was an almost frightening display of what must have been a very, very rare public exhibition of what powerful rumour in the film world—to which I now partially apologized for my former mental strictures—maintained to be a fairly constant private amalgam of the peasant shrew and the screaming fishwife.

'That—harmless—child?' I spaced the words in slow incredulity. 'A bitch?'

'A tramp, a little tramp! A slut! A little gutter—'

'Stop it!' Stryker's voice was a lash, but it had strained overtones. I had the feeling that only desperation would make him talk to his wife in this fashion.

'Yes, stop it,' I said. 'I don't know what the hell you're talking about, Miss Haynes, and I'm damned sure you don't either. All I know is you're sick.'

I turned to go. Stryker barred my way. He'd lost a little colour from his cheeks.

'Nobody talks to my wife that way.' His lips hardly moved as he spoke.

I was suddenly sick of the Strykers. I said: 'I've insulted your wife?'

'Unforgivably.'

'And so I've insulted you?'

'You're getting the point, Marlowe.'

'And anyone who insults you gets what's coming to them. That's what you said to Captain Imrie.'

'That's what I said.'

'I see.'

'I thought you might.' He still barred my way.

'And if I apologize?'

'An apology?' He smiled coldly. 'Let's try one out for size, shall we?'

I turned to Judith Haynes. I said: 'I don't know what the hell you're talking about, Miss Haynes, and I'm damned sure you don't either. All I know is you're sick.'

Her face looked as if invisible claws had sunk deep into both cheeks all the way from temple to chin and dragged back the skin until it was stretched drumtight over the bones. I turned to face Stryker. His facial skin didn't look tight at all. The strikingly handsome face wasn't handsome any more, the contours seemed to have sagged and jellied and the cheeks were bereft of colour. I brushed by him, opened the door and stopped.

'You poor bastard,' I said. 'Don't worry. Doctors never tell.'

I was glad to make my way up to the clean biting cold of the upper deck. I'd left something sick and unhealthy and more than vaguely unclean down there behind me and I didn't have to be a doctor to know what the sickness was. The snow had eased now and as I looked out over the weather side—the port side—I could see that we were leaving one promontory about a half-mile behind on the port quarter while another was coming up about the same distance ahead on the port bow. Kapp Kolthoff and Kapp Malmgrem, I knew from the chart, so we had to be steaming north-east across the Evjebukta. The cliffs here were less high, but we were even more deeply into their lee than twenty minutes previously and the sea had moderated even more. We had less than three miles to go.

I looked up at the bridge. The weather, obviously, was improving considerably or interest and curiosity had been stimulated by the close proximity of our destination, for there was now a small knot of people on either wing of the bridge but with hoods so closely drawn as to make features indistinguishable. I became aware that there was a figure standing close by me huddled up against the fore superstructure of the bridge. It was Mary Darling with the long tangled blonde tresses blowing in every direction of the compass. I went towards her, put my arm round her with the ease born of recent intensive practice, and tilted her face. Red eyes, tear-splotched cheeks, a little woebegone face half-hidden behind the enormous spectacles: the slut, the bitch, the little tramp.

'Mary Darling,' I said. 'What are you doing here? It's far too cold. You should be inside or below.'

'I wanted to be alone.' There was still the catch of a dying sob in her voice. 'And Mr Gilbert kept wanting to give me brandy—and, well—' she shuddered.

'So you've left Lonnie alone with the restorative. That'll be an eminently satisfactory all-round conclusion as far as Lonnie—'

'Dr Marlowe!' She became aware of the arm round her and made a half-hearted attempt to break away. 'People will see us!'

'I don't care,' I said. 'I want the whole world to know of our love.'

'You want the whole—' She looked at me in consternation, her normally big eyes huge behind her glasses, then came the first tremulous beginnings of a smile. 'Oh, Dr Marlowe!'

'There's a young man below who wants to see you immediately,' I said.

'Oh!' The smile vanished, heaven knows what gravity of import she found in my words. 'Is he—I mean, he'll have to go to hospital, won't he?'

'He'll be up and around this afternoon.'

'Really? Really and truly?'

'If you're calling my professional competence into question—'

'Oh, Dr Marlowe! Then what—why does he—'

'I should imagine he wants you to hold his hand. I'm putting myself in his shoes, of course.'

'Oh, Dr Marlowe! Will it—I mean in his cabin—'

'Do I have to drag you down there?'

'No.' She smiled. 'I don't think that will be necessary.' She hesitated. 'Dr Marlowe?'

'Yes?'

'I think you're wonderful. I really do.'

'Hoppit.'

She smiled, almost happily now, and hopped it. I wished I even fractionally shared her opinion of me, for if I was in a position to do so there would be a good number fewer of dead and sick and injured around. But I was glad of one thing, I hadn't had to hurt Mary Darling as I'd feared I might, there had been no need to ask her any of the questions that had half-formed in my mind even as I had left the Strykers' cabin. If she were even remotely capable of being any of those things that Judith Haynes had, for God knew what misbegotten reasons, accused her of being, then she had no right to be in the film industry as a continuity girl, she was in more than a fair way to making her fame and fortune as one of the great actresses of our time. Besides, I didn't have to ask any questions now, not where she and Allen and the Strykers were concerned: it was hard to say whether my contempt for Michael Stryker was greater than my pity.

I remained where I was for a few minutes watching some crew members who had just come on to the foredeck begin to remove the no longer necessary lashings from the deck cargo, strip off tarpaulins and set slings in places, while another two set about clearing away the big fore derrick and testing the winch. Clearly, Captain Imrie had no intention of wasting any time whatsoever upon our arrival: he wanted, and understandably, to be gone with all dispatch. I went aft to the saloon.

Lonnie was the sole occupant, alone but not lonely, not as long as he had that bottle of Hine happily clutched in his fist. He lowered his glass as I sat down beside him.

'Ah! You have assuaged the sufferings of the walking wounded? There is a preoccupied air about you, my dear fellow.' He tapped the bottle. 'For the instant alleviation of workaday cares—'

'That bottle belongs to the pantry, Lonnie.'

'The fruits of nature belong to all mankind. A soupçon?'

'If only to stop you from drinking it all. I have an apology to make to you, Lonnie. About our delectable leading lady. I don't think there's enough kindness around to waste any in throwing it in her direction.'

'Barren ground, you would say? Stony soil?'

'I would say.'

'Redemption and salvation are not for our fair Judith?'

'I don't know about that. All I know is that I wouldn't like to be the one to try and that, looking at her, I can only conclude that there's an awful lot of unkindness around.'

'Amen to that.' Lonnie swallowed some more brandy. 'But we must not forget the parables of the lost sheep and the prodigal son. Nothing and nobody is ever entirely lost.'

'I dare say. Luck to leading her back to the paths of the righteous—you shouldn't have to fight off too much competition for the job. How is it, do you think, that a person like that should be so different from the other two?'

'Mary dear and Mary darling? Dear, dear girls. Even in my dotage I love them dearly. Such sweet children.'

'They could do no wrong?'

'Never!'

'Ha! That's easy to say. But what if, perhaps, they were deeply under the influence of alcohol?'

'What?' Lonnie appeared genuinely shocked. 'What are you talking about? Inconceivable, my dear boy, inconceivable!'

'Not even, say, if they were to have a double gin?'

'What piffling nonsense is this? We are speaking of the influence of alcohol, not about apéritifs for swaddling babes.'

'You would see no harm in either of them asking for, say, just one drink?'

'Of course not.' Lonnie looked genuinely puzzled. 'You do harp on so, my dear fellow.'

'Yes, I do rather. I just wondered why once, after a long day on the set, when Mary Stuart had asked you for just that one drink you flew completely off the handle.'

In curiously slow-motion fashion Lonnie put bottle and glass on the table and rose unsteadily to his feet. He looked old and tired and terribly vulnerable.

'Ever since you came in—now I can see it.' He spoke in a kind of sad whisper. 'Ever since you came in you've been leading up to this one question.'

He shook his head and his eyes were not seeing me. 'I thought you were my friend,' he said quietly, and walked uncertainly from the saloon.

CHAPTER EIGHT

The north-west corner of the Sor-hamna bight, where the *Morning Rose* had finally come to rest, was just under three miles due north-east, as the crow flies, from the most southerly tip of Bear Island. The Sor-hamna itself, U-shaped and open to the south, was just over a thousand yards in width on its east-west axis and close on a mile in length from north to south. The eastern arm of the harbour was discontinuous, beginning with a small peninsula perhaps three hundred yards in length, followed by a two hundred-yard gap of water interspersed with small islands of various sizes then by the much larger island of Makehl, very narrow from east to west, stretching almost half a mile to its most southerly point of Kapp Roalkvam. The land to the north and east was low-lying, that to the west, or true island side, rising fairly steeply from a shallow escarpment but nowhere higher than a small hill about 400 feet high about halfway down the side of the bight. Here were none of the towering precipices of the Hambergfjell or Bird Fell ranges to the south: but, on the other hand, here the entire land was covered in snow, deep on the north-facing slopes and their valleys where the pale low summer sun and the scouring winds had passed them by.

The Sor-hamna was not only the best, it was virtually the only reasonable anchorage in Bear Island. When the wind blew from the west it offered perfect protection for vessels sheltering there, and for a northerly wind it was only slightly less good. From an easterly wind, dependent upon its strength and precise direction, it afforded a reasonable amount of cover—the gap between Kapp Heer and Makehl was the deciding factor here and, when the wind stood in this quarter and if the worst came to the worst, a vessel could always up anchor and shelter under the lee of Makehl Island: but when the wind blew from the south a vessel was wide open to everything the Barents Sea cared to throw at it.

And this was why the degree of unloading activity aboard the *Morning Rose* was increasing from the merely hectic to the nearly panic-stricken. Even as we had approached the

Sor-hamna the wind, which had been slowly veering the past thirty-six hours, now began rapidly to increase its speed of movement round the compass at disconcerting speed so that by the time we had made fast it was blowing directly from the east. It was now a few degrees south of east, and strengthening, and the *Morning Rose* was beginning to feel its effects: it only had to increase another few knots or veer another few degrees and the trawler's position would become untenable.

At anchor, the *Morning Rose* could comfortably have ridden out the threatened blow, but the trouble was that the *Morning Rose* was not at anchor. She was tied up alongside a crumbling limestone jetty—neither iron nor wooden structures would have lasted for any time in those stormy and bitter waters—that had first been constructed by Lerner and the *Deutsche Seefischerei-Verein* about the turn of the century and then improved upon—if that were the term—by the International Geophysical Year expedition that had summered there. The jetty, which would have been condemned out of hand and forbidden for public use almost anywhere else in the northern hemisphere, had originally been T-shaped, but the left arm of the T was now all but gone while the central section leading to the shore was badly eaten away on its southward side. It was against this dangerously dilapidated structure that the *Morning Rose* was beginning to pound with increasing force as the south-easterly seas caught her under the starboard quarter and the cushioning effect as the trawler struck heavily and repeatedly against the jetty was sufficient to make those working on deck stagger and clutch on to the nearest support. It was difficult to say what effect this was having on the *Morning Rose,* for apart from the scratching and slight indentations of the plates none was visible, but trawlers are legendarily tough and it was unlikely that she was coming to any great harm: but what was coming to harm, and very visibly so, was the jetty itself, for increasingly large chunks of masonry were beginning to fall into the Sor-hamna with dismaying frequency, and as most of our fuel, provisions and equipment still stood there, the seemingly imminent collapse of the pier into the sea was not a moment to be viewed with anything like equanimity.

When we'd first come alongside shortly before noon, the unloading had gone ahead very briskly and smoothly indeed, except for the unloading of Miss Haynes's snarling pooches.

153

Even before we'd tied up, the after derrick had the sixteen-foot work-boat in the water and three minutes later an only slightly smaller fourteen-footer with an outboard had followed it: those boats were to remain with us. Within ten minutes the specially strengthened for'ard derrick had lifted the weirdly-shaped—laterally truncated so as to have a flat bottom—mock-up of the central section of a submarine over the side and lowered it gently into the water, where it floated with what appeared to be perfect stability, no doubt because of its four tons of cast-iron ballast. It was when the mock-up conning-tower was swung into position to be bolted on to the central section of the submarine that the trouble began.

It just wouldn't bolt on. Goin and Heissman and Stryker, the only three who had observed the original tests, said that in practice it had operated perfectly: clearly, it wasn't operating perfectly now. The conning-tower section, elliptical in shape, was designed to settle precisely over a four-inch vertical flange in the centre of the mid-section, but settle it just wouldn't do: it turned out that one of the shallow curves at the foot of the conning-tower was at least a quarter-inch out of true, a fact that was almost certainly due to the pounding that we'd taken on the way up from Wick: just one lashing not sufficiently bar-taut would have permitted that microscopic freedom of vertical movement that would have allowed the tiny distortion to develop.

The solution was simple—just to hammer the offending curve back into shape—and in a dockyard with skilled plate-layers available this would probably have been no more than a matter of minutes. But we'd neither technical facilities nor skilled labour available and the minutes had now stretched into hours. A score of times now the for'ard derrick had offered up the offending conning-tower piece to the flange: a score of times it had had to be lifted again and painstakingly assaulted by hammers. Several times a perfect fit had been achieved where it had been previously lacking only to find the distortion had mysteriously and mischievously transferred itself a few inches farther along the metal. Nor, now, despite the fact that the submarine section was in the considerable lee afforded by both pier and vessel, were matters being made any easier by the little waves that were beginning to creep around the bows of the *Morning Rose* and rock it, gently at first but with increasing force, to the extent that the ultimate

154

good fit was clearly going to depend as much on the luck of timing as the persuasion of the hammers.

Captain Imrie wasn't frantic with worry for the sound reason that it wasn't in his nature to become frantic about anything, but the depth of his concern was evident enough from the fact that he had not only skipped lunch but hadn't as much as fortified himself with anything stronger than coffee since our arrival in the Sor-hamna. His main concern, apart from the well-being of the *Morning Rose*—he clearly didn't give a damn about his passengers—was to get the fore-deck cleared of its remaining deck cargo because, as I'd heard Otto rather unnecessarily and unpleasantly reminding him, it was part of his contractual obligations to land all passengers and cargo before departure for Hammerfest. And, of course, what was exercising Captain Imrie's mind so power-fully was that, with darkness coming on and the weather blow-ing up, the for'ard deck cargo had not yet been unloaded and would not be until the fore derrick was freed from its present full-time occupation of holding the conning-tower suspended over the mid-section.

The one plus factor about Captain Imrie's concentration was that it gave him little time to worry about Halliday's dis-appearance. More precisely, it gave him little time to try to do anything constructive about it, for I knew it was still very much on his mind from the fact that he had taken time off to tell me that upon his arrival in Hammerfest his first intention would be to contact the law. There were two things I could have said at this stage, but I didn't. The first was that I failed to see what earthly purpose this could serve—it was just, I suppose, that he felt that he had to do something, anything, however ineffectual that might be: the second was that I felt quite certain that he would never get the length of Hammerfest in the first place, although just then hardly seemed the time to tell him why I thought so. He wasn't then in the properly receptive mood: I had hopes that he would be shortly after he had left Bear Island.

I went down the screeching metal gangway—its rusty iron wheels, apparently permanently locked in position, rubbed to and fro with every lurch of the *Morning Rose*—and made my way along the ancient jetty. A small tractor and a small Sno-Cat—they had been the third and fourth items to be unloaded from the trawler's after-deck—were both equipped with towing sledges and everybody from Heissman downwards was helping to load equipment aboard those sledges for haulage up to the huts that lay on the slight escarpment not more than twenty yards from the end of the jetty. Everybody was not only helping, they were helping with a will: when the temperature is fifteen degrees below freezing the temptation to dawdle is not marked. I followed one consignment up to the huts.

Unlike the jetty, the huts were of comparatively recent construction and in good condition, relics from the latest IGY—there could have been no possible economic justification in dismantling them and taking them back to Norway. They were not built of the modern kapok, asbestos and aluminium construction so favoured by modern expeditions in Arctic regions as base headquarters: they were built—although admittedly pre-sectioned—in the low-slung chalet design fairly universally found in the higher Alpine regions of Europe. They had about them that four-square hunch-shouldered look, the appearance of lowering their heads against the storm, that made it seem quite likely that they would still be there in a hundred years' time. Provided they are not exposed to prevailing high winds and the constant fluctuation of temperature above and below the freezing point, man-made structures can last almost indefinitely in the deep-freeze of the high Arctic.

There were five structures here altogether, all of them set a considerable distance apart—as far as the shoulder of the hill beyond the escarpment would permit. Little as I knew of the Arctic, I knew enough to understand the reason for this spacing: here, where exposure to cold is the permanent and dominating factor of life, it is fire which is the greatest enemy, for unless there are chemical fire-fighting appliances to hand, and there nearly always are not, a fire, once it has taken hold, will not stop until everything combustible has been destroyed: blocks of ice are scarcely at a premium when it comes to extinguishing flames.

Four small huts were set at the corners of a much larger central block. According to the rather splendid diagram Heissman had drawn up in his manifesto, those were to be given over, respectively, to transport, fuels, provisions and equipment: I was not quite sure what he meant by equipment. Those were all square and windowless. The central and very much larger building was of a peculiar starfish shape with a pentagonal centrepiece and five triangular annexes all forming an integral whole: the purpose of this design was difficult to guess, I would have thought it one conducive to maximum heat-loss. The centrepiece was the living, dining and cooking area: each arm held two tiny bare rooms for sleeping quarters. Heating was by electric oil-filled black heaters bolted to the walls, but until we got our own portable generator going we were dependent on simple oil stoves: lighting was by pressurized Coleman kerosene lamps. Cooking, which was apparently to consist of the endless opening and heating of contents of tins, was to be done on a simple oil stove. Otto, needless to say, hadn't brought a cook along: cooks cost money.

With the notable exception of Judith Haynes everyone, even the still groggy Allen, worked willingly and as quickly as the unfamiliar and freezing conditions would permit: they also worked silently and joylessly, for although no one had been on anything approaching terms of close friendship with Halliday, the news of his disappearance had added fresh gloom and apprehension to a company who believed themselves to be evilly jinxed before even the first day of shooting. Stryker and Lonnie, who never spoke to each other except when essential, checked all the stores, fuel, oil, food, clothing, arctizing equipment—Otto, whatever his faults, insisted on thoroughness: Sandy, considerably recovered now that he was on dry land, checked his props, Hendriks his sound equipment, the Count his camera equipment, Eddie his electrical gear, and I myself what little medical kit I had along. By three o'clock, when it was already dusk, we had everything stowed away, cubicles allocated and camp-beds and sleeping-bags placed in those: the jetty was now quite empty of all the gear that had been unloaded there.

We lit the oil stoves, left a morose and muttering Eddie— with the doleful assistance of the Three Apostles—to get the diesel generator working and made our way back to the *Morning Rose*, myself because it was essential that I speak to Smithy, the others because the hut was still miserably bleak and freezing whereas even the much-maligned *Morning Rose* still offered a comparative haven of warmth and comfort. Very shortly after our return a variety of incidents occurred in short and eventually disconcerting succession.

At ten past three, totally unexpectedly and against all indications, the conning-tower fitted snugly over the flange of the midship section. Six bolts were immediately fitted to hold it in position—there were twenty-four altogether—and the work-boat at once set about the task of towing the unwieldy structure into the almost total shelter offered by the right angle formed by the main body of the jetty and its north-facing arm.

At three-fifteen the unloading of the foredeck cargo began and, with Smithy in charge, this was undertaken with efficiency and dispatch. Partly because I didn't want to disturb him in his work, partly because it was at that moment impossible to speak to Smithy privately, I went below to my cabin, removed a small rectangular cloth-bound package from the base of my medical bag, put it in a small purse-string duffel bag and went back on top.

This was at three-twenty. The unloading was still less than twenty per cent completed but Smithy wasn't there. It was almost as though he had awaited my momentary absence to betake himself elsewhere. And that he had betaken himself elsewhere there was no doubt. I asked the winchman where he had gone, but the winchman, exclusively preoccupied with a job that had to be executed with all dispatch, was understandably vague about Smithy's whereabouts. He had either gone below or ashore, he said, which I found a very helpful remark. I looked in his cabin, on the bridge, in the chart-house, the saloon and all the other likely places. No Smithy. I questioned passengers and crew with the same result. No one had seen him, no one had any idea whether he was aboard or had gone ashore, which was very understandable because the darkness was now pretty well complete and the harsh light of the arc lamp now rigged up to aid unloading threw the gangway into very heavy shadow so that anyone could be virtually certain of boarding or leaving the *Morning Rose* unnoticed.

Nor was there any sign of Captain Imrie. True, I wasn't looking for him, but I would have expected him to be making his presence very much known. The wind was almost round to the south-south-east now and still freshening, the *Morning Rose* was beginning to pound regularly against the jetty wall with a succession of jarring impacts and a sound of screeching metal that would normally have had Imrie very much in evidence indeed in his anxiety to get rid of all his damned passengers and their equipment in order to get his ship out to the safety of the open sea with all speed. But he wasn't around, not any place I could see him.

At three-thirty I went ashore and hurried up the jetty to the huts. They were deserted except for the equipment hut where Eddie was blasphemously trying to start up the diesel. He looked up as he saw me.

'Nobody could ever call me one for complaining, Dr Marlowe, but this bloody—'

'Have you seen Mr Smith? The mate?'

'Not ten minutes ago. Looked in to see how we were getting on. Why? Is there something—'

'Did he say anything?'

'What kind of thing?'

'About where he was going? What he was doing?'

'No.' Eddie looked at the shivering Three Apostles, whose blank expressions were of no help to anyone. 'Just stood there for a couple of minutes with his hands in his pockets, looking at what we were doing and asking a few questions, then he strolls off.'

'See where he went?'

'No.' He looked at the Three Apostles, who shook their heads as one. 'Anything up, then?'

'Nothing urgent. Ship's about to sail and the skipper's looking for him.' If that wasn't quite an accurate assessment of how matters stood at that moment, I'd no doubt it would be in a very few minutes. I didn't waste time looking for Smithy. If he had been hanging around with apparent aimlessness at the camp instead of closely supervising the urgent clearing of the foredeck, which one would have expected of him and would normally have been completely in character, then Smithy had a very good reason for doing so: he just wanted, however temporarily, to become lost.

At three-thirty-five I returned to the *Morning Rose*. This time Captain Imrie was very much in evidence. I had thought him incapable of becoming frantic about anything, but as I looked at him as he stood in the wash of light at the door of the saloon I could see that I could have been wrong about that. Perhaps 'frantic' was the wrong term, but there was no doubt that he was in a highly excitable condition and was mad clear through. His fists were balled, what could be seen of his face was mottled red and white, and his bright blue eyes were snapping. With commendable if lurid brevity he repeated to me what he'd clearly told a number of people in the past few minutes. Worried about the deteriorating weather—that wasn't quite the way he'd put it—he'd had Allison try to contact Tunheim for a forecast. This Allison had been unable to do. Then he and Allison had made the discovery that the transceiver was smashed beyond repair. And just over an hour or so previously the receiver had been in order—or Smith had said it was, for he had then written down the latest weather forecast. Or what he *said* was the latest weather forecast. And now there was no sign of Smith. Where the hell was Smith?

'He's gone ashore,' I said.

'Ashore? Ashore? How the hell do you know he's gone ashore?' Captain Imrie didn't sound very friendly, but then, he was hardly in a friendly mood.

'Because I've just been up in the camp talking to Mr Harbottle, the electrician. Mr Smith had just been up there.'

'Up there? He should have been unloading cargo. What the hell was he doing up there?'

'I didn't see Mr Smith,' I explained patiently. 'So I couldn't ask him.'

'What the hell were *you* doing up there?'

'You're forgetting yourself, Captain Imrie. I am not responsible to you. I merely wished to have a word with him before he left. We've become quite friendly, you know.'

'Yes you have, haven't you?' Imrie said significantly. It didn't mean anything, he was just in a mood for talking significantly. 'Allison!'

'Sir?'

'The bo'sun. Search-party ashore. Quickly now, I'll lead you myself.' If there had ever been any doubt as to the depth of Captain Imrie's concern there was none now. He turned back to me but as Otto Gerran and Goin were now standing beside me I wasn't sure whether he was addressing me or not. 'And we're leaving within the half-hour, with Smith or without him.'

'Is that fair, Captain?' Otto asked. 'He may just have gone for a walk or got a little lost—you see how dark it is—'

'Don't you think it bloody funny that Mr Smith should vanish just as I discover that a radio over which he's been claiming to receive messages is smashed beyond repair?'

Otto fell silent but Goin, ever the diplomat, stepped in smoothly.

'I think Mr Gerran is right, Captain. You could be acting a little bit unfairly. I agree that the destruction of your radio is a serious and worrisome affair and one that is more than possibly, in light of all the mysterious things that have happened recently, a very sinister affair. But I think you are wrong immediately to assume that Mr Smith has any connection with it. For one thing, he strikes me as much too intelligent a man to incriminate himself in so extremely obvious a fashion. In the second place, as your senior officer who knows how vitally important a piece of equipment your radio is, why should he do such a wanton thing? In the third place, if he were trying to escape the consequences of his actions, where on earth could he escape to on Bear Island? I do not suggest anything as simple as an accident or amnesia: I'm merely suggesting that he may have got lost. You could at least wait until the morning.'

I could see Captain Imrie's fists unballing, not much, just a slight relaxation, and I knew that if he weren't wavering he was at least on the point of considering, a state of approaching uncertainty that lasted just as long as it took Otto to undo whatever Goin might have been on the point of achieving.

'That's it, of course,' he said. 'He just went to have a look around.'

'What? In the pitch bloody dark?' It was an exaggeration but a pardonable one. 'Allison! Oakley! All of you. Come on!' He lowered his voice a few decibels and said to us: 'I'm leaving within the half-hour, Smith or no Smith. Hammerfest, gentlemen, Hammerfest and the law.'

He hurried down the gangway, half a dozen men close behind. Goin sighed. 'I suppose we'd better lend a hand.' He left and Otto, after hesitating for a moment, followed.

I didn't, I'd no intention of lending a hand, if Smithy didn't want to be found then he wouldn't be. Instead I went down to my cabin, wrote a brief note, took the small duffel bag with me and went in search of Haggerty. I had to trust somebody, Smithy's most damned inconvenient disappearing trick had left me with no option, and I thought Haggerty was my best bet. He was stiff-necked and suspicious and, since Imrie's questioning of him that morning, he must have become even more suspicious of me: but he was no fool, he struck me as being incorruptible, he was, I thought, amenable to an authoritative display of discipline and, above all, he'd spent twenty-seven years of his life in taking orders.

It was fifteen minutes' touch and go, but at last he grudgingly agreed to do what I asked him to.

'You wouldn't be making a fool out of me, Dr Marlowe?' he asked.

'You'd be a fool if you even thought that. What would I have to gain?'

'There's that, there's that.' He took the small duffel bag reluctantly. 'As soon as we're safely clear of the island—'

'Yes. That, and the letter. To the captain. Not before.'

'Those are deep waters, Dr Marlowe.' He didn't know how deep, I was close to drowning in them. 'Can't you tell me what it is all about?'

'If I knew that, Haggerty, do you think I'd be remaining behind on this godforsaken island?'

For the first time he smiled. 'No, sir, I don't really think you would.'

Captain Imrie and his search-party returned only a minute or two after I'd gone back up to the upper deck. They returned without Smithy. I was surprised neither by their failure to find him nor the brevity of their search—an elapsed time of only twenty minutes. Bear Island, on the map, may be only the veriest speck in the high Arctic, but it does cover an area of 73 square miles and it must have occurred to Captain Imrie very early on indeed that to attempt to search even a fraction of one per cent of that icily mountainous terrain in darkness was to embark upon a monumental folly. His fervour for the search had diminished to vanishing point: but his failure to find Smithy had, if anything, increased his determination to depart immediately. Having ensured that the last of the foredeck cargo had been unloaded and that all of the film company's equipment and personal effects were ashore, he and Mr Stokes courteously but swiftly shook hands with us all as we were ushered ashore. The derricks were already stayed in position and the mooring ropes singled up: Captain Imrie was not about to stand upon the order of his going.

Otto, properly enough, was the last to leave. At the head of the gangway, he said: 'Twenty-two days it is, then, Captain Imrie? You'll be back in twenty-two days?'

'I won't leave you here the winter, Mr Gerran, never fear.' With both the mystery and his much-unloved Bear Island about to be left behind, Captain Imrie apparently felt that he could permit himself a slight relaxation of attitude. 'Twenty-two days? At the very outset. Why, man, I can be in Hammerfest and back in seventy-two hours. I wish you all well.'

With this Captain Imrie ordered the gangway to be raised and went up to the bridge without explaining his cryptic remark about the seventy-two hours. It was more likely than not that what he had in mind at that very moment was, indeed, to be back inside seventy-two hours with, his manner seemed to convey, a small regiment of heavily-armed Norwegian police. I wasn't concerned: I was as certain as I could be that, if that were indeed what he had in mind, he would change his mind before the night was out.

The navigation lights came on and the *Morning Rose* moved off slowly northwards from the jetty, slewed round in a half-circle and headed down the Sor-hamna, her engine note deepening as she picked up speed. Opposite the jetty again Captain Imrie sounded his hooter—only the captain could have called it a siren—twice, a high and lonely sound almost immediately swallowed up in the muffling blanket of snow: within seconds, it seemed, both the throb of the engine and the pale glow of the navigation lights were lost in the snow and the darkness.

For what seemed quite some time we all stood there, huddled against the bitter cold and peering into the driving snow, as if by willing it we could bring the lights back into view again, the engine throb back into earshot. The atmosphere was not one of voyagers happily arrived at their hoped-for destination but of castaways marooned on an Arctic desert island.

The atmosphere inside the big living cabin was not much of an improvement. The oil heaters were functioning well enough and Eddie had the diesel generator running so that the black heaters on the walls were just beginning to warm up, but the effects of a decade of deep-freeze were not to be overcome in the space of an hour: the inside temperature was still below freezing. Nobody went to their allocated cubicles for the excellent reason that they were considerably colder than the central living space. Nobody appeared to want to talk to anybody else. Heissman embarked upon a pedantic and what promised to be lengthy lecture about Arctic survival, a subject concerning which his long and intimate acquaintance with Siberia presumably made him uniquely qualified to speak, but there were no takers, it was questionable whether he was even listening to himself. Then he, Otto and Neal Divine began a rather desultory discussion of their plans for—weather permitting—the following day's shooting, but obviously they hadn't their hearts even in that. It was, eventually, Conrad who put his finger on the cause of the general malaise, or, more accurately, expressed the thought that was in the mind of everybody with the possible exception of myself.

He said to Heissman: 'In the Arctic, in winter, you require torches. Right?'

'Right?'

'We have them?'

'Plenty, of course. Why?'

'Because I want one. I want to go out. We've been in here now, all of us, how long, I don't know, twenty minutes at least, and for all we know there may be a man out there sick or hurt or frostbitten or maybe fallen and broken a leg.'

'Oh, come now, come now, that's pitching it a bit strongly, Charles,' Otto said. 'Mr Smith has always struck me as a man eminently able to take care of himself.' Otto would probably have said the same thing if he'd been watching Smithy being mangled by a polar bear: because of both nature and build Otto was not a man to become unnecessarily involved in anything even remotely physical.

'If you don't really care, why don't you come out and say so?' This was a new side of Conrad to me and he continued to develop his theme at my expense. 'I'd have thought you'd have been the first to suggest this, Dr Marlowe.' I might have been, too, had I not known considerably more about Smithy than he did.

'I don't mind being the second,' I said agreeably.

In the event, we all went, with the exception of Otto, who complained of feeling unwell, and Judith Haynes who roundly maintained that it was all nonsense and that Mr Smith would come back when he felt like it, an opinion which I held myself but for reasons entirely different from hers. We were all provided with torches and agreed to keep as closely together as possible or, if separated, to be back inside thirty minutes at the latest.

The party set off in a wide sweep up the escarpment fronting the Sor-hamna to the north. At least, the others did. I headed straight for the equipment hut where the diesel generator was thudding away reassuringly, for it was unlikely that any one of us would be missed—no one would probably be aware of the presence of any other than his immediate neighbours—and the best place to sit out a wild goose chase was the warmest and most sheltered spot I could find. With my torch switched off so as not to betray my presence I opened the door of the hut, passed inside, closed the door, took a step forward and swore out loud as I stumbled over something comparatively yielding and almost measured my length on the planked floor. I recovered, turned and switched on my torch.

A man was lying stretched out on the floor and to my total lack of surprise it proved to be Smithy. He stirred and groaned, half-turned, raised a feeble arm to protect his eyes from the bright glare of the torch, then slumped back again, his arm falling limply by his side, his eyes closed. There was blood smeared over his left cheek. He stirred uneasily, moving from side to side and moaning in that soft fashion a man does when he is close to the borderline of consciousness.

'Does it hurt much, Smithy?' I asked.

He moaned some more.

'Where you scratched your cheek with a handful of frozen snow,' I said.

He stopped moving and he stopped moaning.

'The comedy act we'll keep for later in the programme,' I said coldly. 'In the meantime, will you kindly get up and explain to me why you've behaved like an irresponsible idiot?'

I placed the torch on the generator casing so that the beam shone upwards. It didn't give much light, just enough to show Smithy's carefully expressionless face as he got to his feet.

'What do you mean?' he said.

'PQS 182131, James R. Huntingdon, Golden Green and Beirut, currently and wrongly known as Joseph Rank Smith, is who I mean.'

165

'I guess I'm the irresponsible idiot you mean,' Smithy said. 'It would be nice to have introductions all round.'

'Dr Marlowe,' I said. He kept the same carefully expressionless face. 'Four years and four months ago when we took you from your nice cosy job as Chief Officer in that broken-down Lebanese tanker we thought you had a future with us. A bright one. Even four months ago we thought the same thing. But here, now, I'm very far from sure.'

Smithy smiled but his heart wasn't in it. 'You can't very well fire me on Bear Island.'

'I can fire you in Timbuctoo if I want to,' I said matter-of-factly. 'Well, come on.'

'You might have made yourself known to me.' Smithy sounded aggrieved and I supposed I would have been also in his position. 'I was beginning to guess. I didn't know there was anyone else aboard apart from me.'

'You weren't supposed to know. You weren't supposed to guess. You were supposed to do exactly what you were told. Just that and no more. You remember the last line in your written instructions? They were underlined. A quotation from Milton. *I* underlined it.'

' "They also serve who only stand and wait",' Smithy said. 'Corny, I thought it at the time.'

'I've had a limited education,' I said. 'Point is, did you stand and wait? Did you hell! Your orders were as simple and explicit as orders could ever be. Remain constantly aboard the *Morning Rose* until contacted. Do not, under any circumstances, leave the vessel even to step ashore. Do not, repeat not, attempt to conduct any investigations upon your own, do not seek to discover anything, at all times behave like a stereotype merchant navy officer. This you failed to do. I wanted you aboard that ship, Smithy. I *needed* you aboard —now. And where are you—stuck in a godforsaken hut on Bear Island. Why in God's name couldn't you follow out simple instructions?'

'OK. My fault. But I thought I was alone. Circumstances alter cases, don't they? With four men mysteriously dead and four others pretty close to death—well, damn it all, am I supposed to stand by and do *nothing*? Am I supposed to have *no* initiative, nor to think for myself even once?'

'Not till you're told to. And now look where you've left me—one hand behind my back. The *Morning Rose* was my other hand and now you've deprived me of it. I wanted it on call and close to hand every hour of the day and night. I might need it at any time—and now I haven't got it. Is there anybody aboard that blasted trawler who could maintain position just off-shore in the darkest night or bring her up the Sor-hamna in a full blizzard? You know damn well there's not. Captain Imrie couldn't bring her up the Clyde on a midsummer's afternoon.'

'You have a radio with you then? To communicate with the trawler?'

'Of course. Built into my medical case—no more than a police job, but range enough.'

'Be rather difficult to communicate with the *Morning Rose*'s transceiver lying in bits and pieces.'

'How very true,' I said. 'And why is it in bits and pieces? Because on the bridge you started talking freely and at length about shouting for help over that self-same radio and whistling up the NATO Atlantic forces if need be, while all the time some clever-cuts was taking his ease out on the bridge wing drinking in every word you said. I know, there were fresh tracks in the snow—well, my tracks, but re-used, if you follow me. So, of course, our clever-cuts hies himself off and gets himself a heavy hammer.'

'I could have been more circumspect at that, I suppose. You can have my apologies if you want them but I don't see them being all that useful at this stage.'

'I'm hardly in line myself for a citation for distinguished services, so we'll leave the apologies be. Now that you're here—well, I won't have to watch my back so closely.'

'So they're on to you—whoever *they* are?'

'Whoever *they* are are unquestionably on to me.' I told him briefly all I knew, not all I thought I knew or suspected I knew, for I saw no point in making Smithy as confused as myself. I went on: 'Just so we don't act at cross-purposes, let me initiate any action that I—or we—may think may have to be taken. I need hardly say that that doesn't deprive you of initiative if and when you find yourself or think you find yourself physically threatened. In that event, you have my advance permission to flatten anybody.'

'That's nice to know.' Smithy smiled briefly for the first time. 'It would be even nicer to know who it is that I'm likely to have to flatten. It would be even nicer still to know what you who are, I gather, a fairly senior Treasury official, and I, whom I know to be a junior one, are doing on this god-damned island anyway.'

'The Treasury's basic concern is money, always money, in one shape or other, and that's why we're here. Not our money, not British money, but what we call international dirty money, and all the members of the Central Banks co-operate very closely on this issue.'

'When you're as poor as I am,' Smithy said, 'there's no such thing as dirty money.'

'Even an underpaid civil servant like yourself wouldn't touch this lot. This is all ill-gotten gains, illegal loot from the days of World War II. This money has all been earned in blood and what has been recovered of it—and that's only a fraction of the total—has almost invariably been recovered in blood. Even as late as the spring of 1945 Germany was still a land of priceless treasures: by the summer of that year the cupboard was almost entirely bare. Both the victors and the vanquished laid their sticky fingers on every imaginable object of value they could clap eyes on—gold, precious stones, old masters, securities—German bank securities issued forty years ago are still perfectly valid—and took off in every conceivable direction. I need hardly say that none of those involved saw fit to declare their latest acquisitions to the proper authorities.' I looked at my watch. 'Your worried friends are scouring Bear Island for you—or a very small part of it, anyway. A half-hour search. I'll have to bring in your unconscious form in about fifteen minutes.'

'It all sounds pretty dull to me,' Smith said. 'All this loot, I mean. Was there much of it?'

'It all depends what you call much. It's estimated that the Allies—and when I say "Allies" I mean Britain and America as well as the much-maligned Russians—managed to get hold of about two-thirds of the total. That left the Nazis and their sympathizers with about a paltry one-third, and the conservative estimate of that one-third—conservative, Smithy—is that it amounts to approximately £350 million. Pounds sterling, you understand.'

'A thousand million all told?'

'Give or take a hundred million.'

'That childish remark about this being a dull subject. Strike it off the record.'

'Granted. Now this loot has found its way into some very odd places indeed. Some of it, inevitably, lies in secret numbered bank-accounts. Some of it—there is no question about this—lies in the form of specie in some of the very deepest Austrian Alpine lakes and has so far proved irrecoverable. I know of two Raphaels in the cellar gallery of a Buenos Aires millionaire, a Michaelangelo in Rio, several Halses and Rubenses in the same illegal collection in New York, and a Rembrandt in London. Their owners are either people who have been in, were in, or are closely connected to the governments or armed forces of the countries concerned: there's nothing the governments concerned can do about it and there are no signs that they're particularly keen to do anything about it anyway, they themselves might be the ultimate beneficiaries. As lately as the end of 1970 an international cartel went on to the market with £30 millions' worth of perfectly valid German securities issued in the 'thirties, approaching in turn the London, New York and Zürich markets, but the Federal Bank of Germany refused to cash those until proper owner identification was established: the point is that it's an open secret that those securities were taken from the vaults of the Reichsbank in 1945 by a special Red Army unit who were constituted as the only legalized military burglars in history.

'But that's only the tip of the iceberg, so to speak; the vast bulk of this immense fortune is hidden because the war is still too recent and people—the illegal owners—still too scared to convert their treasures into currency. There's a special Italian Government Recovery Office that deals exclusively with this matter, and its boss, one Professor Siviero, estimates that there are at least seven hundred old masters, many of them virtually priceless, still untraced, while another expert, a Simon Wiesenthal of the Austrian Jewish Documentation Service, says virtually the same thing—he, incidentally, maintains that there are countless highly-wanted characters, such as top-ranking officers in the SS, who are living in great comfort from hundreds of numbered bank accounts scattered throughout Europe.

'Siviero and Wiesenthal are the acknowledged legal experts in this form of recovery Unfortunately, there are known to be a handful of people—they amount to certainly not more than three or four—who are possessed of an equal or even

169

greater expertise in this matter, but who unfortunately are lacking in the high principles of their colleagues, if that is the word, who operate on the right side of the law. Their names are known but they are untouchable because they have never committed any known crimes, not even fraudulent conversion of stocks, because the stocks are always good, the claimants always proven. They are, nevertheless, criminals operating on an international level. We have the most skilful and successful of the lot with us here on Bear Island. His name is Johann Heissman.'

'Heissman!'

'None other. He's a very gifted lad is our Johann.'

'But Heissman! How can that be? Heissman? What kind of sense can that make? Why it's only two years—'

'I know. It's only two years since Heissman made his spectacular escape from Siberia and arrived in London to the accompaniment of lots of noise and TV cameras and yards of newspaper space and enough red carpet to go from Tilbury to Tomsk, since which time he has occupied himself exclusively with his old love of film-making, so how can it possibly be Heissman?

'Well, it can be Heissman and it is Heissman for our Johann is a very downy bird indeed. We have checked, in fact, that he was a movie studio partner of Otto in Vienna just before the war and that they did, in fact, attend the same gymnasium in St Polten, which is not all that far away. We do know that Heissman ran the wrong way while Otto ran the right way at the time of the Anschluss, and we do know that Heissman, because of his then Communist sympathies, was a very welcome guest of the Third Reich. What followed was one of those incredibly involved double and treble dealing spy switches that occurred so frequently in central Europe during the war. Heissman was apparently allowed to escape to Russia, where his sympathies were well known, and then sent back to Germany where he was ordered to transmit all possible misleading but still acceptable military information back to the Russians.'

'Why? Why did he do it?'

'Because his wife and two children were captured at the same time as he was. A good enough reason?' Smithy nodded. 'Then when the war was over and the Russians overran Berlin and turned up their espionage records, they found out what

170

Heissman had really been doing and shipped him to Siberia.'

'I would have thought they would have shot him out of hand.'

'They would have, too, but for one small point. I told you that Heissman was a very downy bird and that this was a treble deal. Heissman was, in effect and actually, working throughout the war for the Russians. For four years he faithfully sent back his misleading reports to his masters and even though he had the help of the German Intelligence in the preparation of his coded messages, they never once latched on to the fact that Heissman was using his own overlaid code throughout. The Russians simply spirited him away at the end of the war for his own safety and allegedly sent him to Siberia. Our information is that he's never been to Siberia: we believe that his wife and two married daughters are still living very comfortably in Moscow.'

'And he has been working for the Russians ever since?' Smithy was looking just faintly baffled and I had some fellow-feeling for him, Heissman's masterful duplicity was not for ready comprehension.

'In his present capacity. During his last eight years in his Siberian prison, Heissman, in a variety of disguises, has been traced in North and South America, South Africa, Israel and, believe it or not, in the Savoy Hotel in London. We know but we cannot prove that all those trips were in some way concerned with the recovery of Nazi treasure for his Russian masters—you have to remember that Heissman had built up the highest connections in the Party, the SS and the Intelligence: he was almost uniquely qualified for the task. Since his "escape" from Siberia he has made two pictures in Europe, one in Piedmont, where an old widow complained that some tattered old paintings had been stolen from the loft of her barn, the other in Provence, where an old country lawyer called in the police about some deed boxes that had been removed from his office. Whether either pictures or deed boxes were of any value we do not know: still less can we connect either disappearance with Heissman.'

'This is an awful lot to take in all at once,' Smithy complained.

'It is, isn't it?'

'OK if I smoke?'

'Five minutes. Then I've got to drag you back by the heels.'

'By the shoulders, if it's all the same to you.' Smithy lit his cigarette and thought a bit. 'So what you've got to find out is what Heissman is doing on Bear Island.'

'That's why we're here.'

'You've no idea?'

'None. Money, it's got to be money. This would be the last place on earth I'd associate with money and maybe that association would be wrong anyway. Maybe it's only a means to the money. Johann, as I trust you've gathered by this time, is a very devious character indeed.'

'Would there be a tie-up with the film company? With his old friend Gerran? Or would he just be making use of them?'

'I've simply no idea.'

'And Mary Stuart? The secret rendezvous girl? What could the possible connection be there?'

'Same answer. We know very little of her. We know her real name—she's never made any attempt to conceal that—age, birthplace and that she's a Latvian—or comes from what used to be Latvia before the Russians took it over. We also know—and this information she hasn't volunteered—that it was only her mother who was Latvian. Her father was German.'

'Ah! In the Army perhaps? Intelligence? SS?'

'That's the obvious connection to seek. But we don't know. Her immigration forms say that her parents are dead.'

'So the department has been checking on her too?'

'We've had a rundown on everyone here connected with Olympus Productions. We may as well have saved ourselves the trouble.'

'So no facts. Any hunches, feelings?'

'Hunches aren't my stock in trade.'

'I somehow didn't feel they would be.' Smithy ground out his cigarette. 'Before we go, I'd like to mention two very uncomfortable thoughts that have just occurred to me. Number one. Johann Heissman is a very big-time very successful international operative? True?'

'He's an international criminal.

'A rose by any other name. The point is that those boys avoid violence wherever possible, isn't that true?'

'Perfectly true. Apart from anything else, it's beneath them.'

'And have you ever heard Heissman's name being associated with violence?'

'There's no record of it.'

'But there's been a considerable amount of violence, one way or the other, in the past day or two. So if it isn't Heissman, who's behind the strong-arm behaviour?'

'I don't say it isn't Heissman. The leopard can change his spots. He may be finding himself, for God knows what reason, in so highly unusual a situation that he has no option other than to have recourse to violence. He may, for all we know, have violent associates who don't necessarily represent his attitude. Or it may be someone entirely unconnected with him.'

'That's what I like,' Smithy said. 'Simple straightforward answers. And there's the second point that may have escaped your attention. If our friends are on to you the chances are that they're on to me too. That eavesdropper on the bridge.'

'The point had not escaped my attention. And not because of the bridge, although that may have given pause for thought, but because you deliberately skipped ship. It doesn't matter what most of them think, one person or possibly more is going to be convinced that you did it on purpose. You're a marked man, Smithy.'

'So that when you drag me back there not everyone is going to feel genuine pangs of sorrow for poor old Smithy? Some may question the *bona fides* of my injuries?'

'They won't question. They'll damn well know. But we have to act as if.'

'Maybe you'll watch my back too? Now and again?'

'I have a lot on my mind, but I'll try.'

I had Smithy by the armpits, head lolling, heels and hands trailing in the snow, where two flashlights picked us up less than five yards from the door of the main cabin.

'You've found him then?' It was Goin, Harbottle by his side. 'Good man!' Even to my by now hypersensitive ear Goin's reaction sounded genuine.

'Yes. About quarter of a mile away.' I breathed very quickly and deeply to give them some idea as to what it must have been like to drag a two-hundred-pound dead-weight over uneven snow-covered terrain for such a distance. 'Found him in the bottom of a gully. Give me a hand, will you?'

They gave me a hand. We hauled him inside, fetched a camp-cot and stretched him out on this.

'Good God, good God, good God!' Otto wrung his hands, the anguished expression on his face testimony to the fresh burden now added to the crippling weight of the cross he was already carrying. 'What's happened to the poor fellow?' The only other occupant of the cabin, Judith Haynes, had made no move to leave the oil stove she was monopolizing, unconscious men being borne into her presence might have been so routine an affair as not even to merit the raising of an eyebrow.

'I'm not sure,' I said between gasps. 'Heavy fall, I think, banged his head on a boulder. Looked like.'

'Concussion?'

'Maybe.' I probed through his hair with my fingertips, found a spot on the scalp that felt no different from anywhere else, and said: 'Ah!'

They looked at me in anxious expectancy.

'Brandy,' I said to Otto. I fetched my stethoscope, went through the necessary charade, and managed to revive the coughing, moaning Smithy with a mouthful or two of brandy. For one not trained to the boards, he put up a remarkable performance, high-lighted, at its end, with a muted series of oaths and an expression of mingled shock and chagrin when I gently informed him that the *Morning Rose* had sailed without him.

During the course of the histrionics most of the other searchers wandered in in twos or threes. I watched them all carefully without seeming to, looking for an expression that was other than surprise or relief, but I might have spared myself the trouble: if there was one or more who was neither surprised nor relieved he had his emotions and facial muscles too well schooled to show anything. I would have expected nothing else.

After about ten minutes our concern shifted from a now obviously recovering Smithy to the fact that two members of the searching party, Allen and Stryker, were still missing. After the events of that morning I felt the absence of those two, of all of us, to be rather coincidental; after fifteen minutes I felt it odd, and after twenty minutes I felt it downright ominous, a feeling that was clearly shared by nearly everyone there. Judith Haynes had abandoned her squatter's rights by her oil stove and was walking up and down in

174

short, nervous steps, squeezing her hands together. She stopped in front of me.

'I don't like it, I don't like it!' Her voice was strained and anxious, it could have been acting but I didn't think so. 'What's keeping him? Why is he so long? He's out there with that Allen fellow. Something's wrong. I know it is, I *know* it.' When I didn't answer she said: 'Well, aren't you going out to look for him?'

'Just as you went out to look for Mr Smith here,' I said. It wasn't very nice, but then I didn't always feel so very kind to other people as Lonnie did. 'Maybe your husband will come back when *he* feels like it.'

She looked at me without speaking, her lips moving but not speaking, no real hostility in her face, and I realized for the second time that day that her rumoured hatred for her husband was, in fact, only a rumour and that, buried no matter how deep, there did exist some form of concern for him. She turned away and I reached for my torch.

'Once more into the breach,' I said. 'Any takers?'

Conrad, Jungbeck, Heyter and Hendriks accompanied me. Volunteers there were in plenty but I reasoned that not only would increased numbers get in one another's way, but the chances of someone else becoming lost would be all the greater. Immediately after leaving the hut the five of us fanned out at intervals of not more than fifteen feet and moved off to the north.

We found Allen inside the first thirty seconds: more accurately, he found us, for he saw our torches—he'd lost his own—and came stumbling towards us out of the snow and the darkness. 'Stumbled' was the operative word, he was weaving and swaying like one far gone in alcohol or exhaustion, and when he tried to speak his voice was thick and slurred. He was shivering like a man with the ague. It seemed not only pointless but cruel to question him in that condition so we hurried him inside.

I had a look at him as we sat him on a stool by an oil stove and I didn't have to look twice or very closely to see that this hadn't exactly been Allen's day. Allen had been in the wars again and the damage that had been inflicted on him this time at least matched up to the injuries he'd received that morning. He had two nasty cuts above what had been up till then his undamaged eye, a bruised and scratched right

175

cheek, and blood came from both his mouth and nose, blood already congealed in the cold but his worst injury was a very deep gash on the back of the head, the scalp laid open clear to the bone. Someone had given young Allen a very thorough going over indeed.

'And what happened to you this time?' I asked. He winced as I started to clean up his face. 'Or should I say, do you know what happened to you?'

'I don't know,' he said thickly. He shook his head and drew his breath in sharply as some pain struck through either head or neck. 'I don't remember. I don't remember.'

'You've been in a fight, laddie,' I said. 'Again. Someone's cut you up, and quite badly.'

'I know. I can feel it. I don't remember. Honest to God, I don't remember. I—I just don't know what happened.'

'But you must have seen him,' Goin said reasonably. 'Whoever it was, you must have been face to face with him. God's sake, boy, your shirt's torn and there's at least a couple of buttons missing from your coat. And he *had* to be standing in front of you when he did this to you. Surely you must have caught a glimpse of him at least.'

'It was dark,' Allen mumbled. 'I didn't see anything. I didn't feel anything, all I knew was that I woke up kind of groggy like in the snow with the back of my head hurting. I knew I was bleeding and—*please,* I don't know *what* happened.'

'Yes you do, yes you do!' Judith Haynes had pushed her way to the front. The transformation that had taken place in her face was as astonishing as it was ugly, and although her morning performance had partially prepared me for something of this kind, and though this expression was different from the one that had disfigured her face that time, it was still an almost frightening thing to watch. The red gash of the mouth had vanished, the lips drawn in and back over bared teeth, the green eyes were no more than slits and, as had happened that morning, the skin was stretched back over her cheekbones until it appeared far too tight for her face. She screamed at him: 'You damned liar! Wanted your own back, didn't you? You dirty little bastard, what have you done with my husband? Do you hear me? Do you hear me? What have you done with him, damn you? Where is he? Where did you leave him?'

Allen looked up at her in a half-scared astonishment, then

176

shook his head wearily. 'I'm sorry, Miss Haynes, I don't know what—'

She hooked her long-nailed fingers into talons and lunged for him, but I'd been waiting for it. So had both Goin and Conrad. She struggled like a trapped wild-cat, screaming invective at Allen, then suddenly relaxed, her breath coming in harsh, rasping sobs.

'Now then, now then, Judith,' Otto said. 'That's no—'

'Don't you "now then" me, you silly old bastard!' she screamed. Filial respect was clearly not Judith Haynes's strong point, but Otto, though clearly nervous, accepted his daughter's abuse as if it were a matter of course. 'Why don't you find out instead what this young swine's done to my husband? Why don't you? Why don't you!' She struggled to free her arms and as she was trying to move away we let her go. She picked up a torch and ran for the door.

'Stop her,' I said.

Heyter and Jungbeck, big men both, blocked her flight.

'Let me go, let me out!' she shouted. Neither Heyter nor Jungbeck moved and she whirled round on me. 'Who the hell are you to—I want to go out and find Michael!'

'I'm sorry, Miss Haynes,' I said. 'You're in no condition to go to look for anyone. You'd just run wild, no trace of where you'd been, and in five minutes' time you'd be lost too and perhaps lost for good. We're leaving in just a moment.'

She took three quick steps towards Otto, her fists clenched, her teeth showing again.

'You let him push me around like this?' This with an incinerating glare in my direction. 'Spineless, that's you, absolutely spineless! Anybody can walk over you!' Otto blinked nervously at this latest tirade but said nothing. 'Aren't I supposed to be your bloody daughter? Aren't you supposed to be the bloody boss? God's sake, who gives the orders about here? You or Marlowe?'

'Your father does,' Goin said. 'Naturally. But, without any disrespect to Dr Marlowe, we don't hire a dog just to bark ourselves. He's a medical man and we'd be fools not to defer to him in medical matters.'

'Are you suggesting I'm a medical case?' All the colour had drained from her cheeks and she looked uglier than ever. 'Are you? Are you, then? A mental case, perhaps?'

Heaven knows I wouldn't have blamed Goin if he'd said

'yes' straight out and left it at that, but Goin was far too balanced and diplomatic to say any such thing, and besides, he'd clearly been through this sort of crisis before. He said, quietly but not condescendingly: 'I'm suggesting no such thing. Of course you're distressed, of course you're over-wrought, after all it is your husband that's missing. But I agree with Dr Marlowe that you're not the person to go looking for him. We'll have him back here all the quicker if you co-operate with us, Judith.'

She hesitated, still halfway between hysteria and rage, then swung away. I taped the gash on Allen's head and said: 'That'll do till I come back. Afraid I'll have to shave off a few locks and stitch it.' On the way to the door I stopped and said quietly to Goin: 'Keep her away from Allen, will you?'

Goin nodded.

'And for heaven's sake keep her away from Mary darling.'

He looked at me in what was as close to astonishment as he was capable of achieving. 'That kid?'

'That kid. She's next on the list for Miss Haynes's attentions. When Miss Haynes gets around to thinking about it, that is.'

I left with the same four as previously. Conrad, the last out, closed the door behind him and said: 'Jesus! My charming leading lady. What a virago she is!'

'She's a little upset,' I said mildly.

'A little upset! Heaven send I'm in the next county if she ever gets really mad. What the hell do you think can have happened to Stryker?'

'I have no idea,' I said, and because it was dark I didn't have to assume an honest expression to go with the words. I moved closer to him so that the others, already fanned out in line of search, couldn't hear me. 'Seeing we're such a bunch of odd-balls anyway, I hope an odd request from another odd-ball won't come amiss.'

'You disappoint me, Doctor. I thought you and I were two of the very few halfway normal people around here.'

'By the prevailing standards, any moderate odd-ball is normal. You know anything of Lonnie's past?'

He was silent for a moment, then said: 'He has a past?'

'We all have a past. If you think I mean a criminal past, no. Lonnie hasn't got one. I just want to find out if he was married or had any family. That's all.'

'Why don't you ask him yourself?'

'If I felt free to ask him myself, would I be asking you?' Another silence. 'Your name really Marlowe, Doc?'

'Marlowe, as ever was. Christopher Marlowe. Passport, birth certificate, driving licence—they're all agreed on it.'

'Christopher Marlowe? Just like the playwright, eh?'

'My parents had literary inclinations.'

'Uh-huh.' He paused again. 'Remember what happened to your namesake—stabbed in the back by a friend before his thirtieth birthday?'

'Rest easy. My thirtieth birthday is lost in the mists of time.'

'And you're really a doctor?'

'Yes.'

'And you're really something else too?'

'Yes.'

'Lonnie. Marital status. Children or no. You may rely on Conrad's discretion.'

'Thanks,' I said. We moved apart. We were walking to the north for two reasons—the wind, and hence the snow, were to our backs and so progress was easier in that direction, and Allen had come stumbling from that direction. In spite of Allen's professed total lack of recall of what had happened, it seemed likely to me that we might find Stryker also somewhere in that direction. And so it proved.

'Over here! Over here!' In spite of the muffling effects of the snow Hendriks's shout sounded curiously high-pitched and cracked. 'I've found him, I've found him!'

He'd found him all right. Michael Stryker was lying face down in the snow, arms and legs outspread in an almost perfectly symmetrical fashion. Both fists were clenched tight. On the snow, beside his left shoulder, lay a smooth elliptical stone which from its size—it must have weighed between sixty and seventy pounds—better qualified for the name of boulder. I stooped low over this boulder, bringing the torch close, and at once saw the few dark hairs embedded in the dark and encrusted stain. Proof if proof were required, but I hadn't doubted anyway that this was what had been used to smash in the back of Stryker's skull. Death would have been instantaneous.

'He's dead!' Jungbeck said incredulously.

'He's all that,' I said.

'And murdered!'

'That too.' I tried to turn him over on his back but Conrad and Jungbeck had to lend their not inconsiderable weights before this was done. His upper lip was viciously split all the way down from the nostril, a tooth was missing and he had a peculiar red and raw-looking mark on his right temple.

'By God, there must have been a fight,' Jungbeck said huskily. 'I wouldn't have thought that kid Allen had had it in him.'

'I wouldn't have thought so either,' I said.

'Allen?' Conrad said. 'I'd have sworn he was telling the truth. Could he—well, do you think it could have happened when he was suffering from amnesia?'

'All sorts of funny thing can happen when you've had a bump on the head,' I said. I looked at the ground around the dead man, there were footprints there, not many, already faint and blurred from the driving snow: there was no help to be gained from that quarter. I said: 'Let's get him back.'

So we carried the dead man back to the camp and it wasn't, in spite of the uneven terrain and the snow in our faces, as difficult a task as it might have been for the same reason that I'd found it so difficult to turn him over—the limbs had already begun to stiffen, not from the onset of rigor mortis, for it was too soon for that yet, but from the effects of the intense cold. We laid him in the snow outside the main cabin. I said to Hendriks: 'Go inside and ask Goin for a bottle of brandy—say that I sent you back for it, that we need it to keep us going.' It was the last thing I would ever have recommended to keep anyone warm in bitter outdoor cold, but it was all I could think of on the spur of the moment. 'Tell Goin—quietly—to come here.'

Goin, clearly aware that there was something far amiss, walked out casually and casually shut the door behind him, but there was nothing casual about his reaction when he saw Stryker lying there, his gashed and marble-white face a death's head in the harsh light of several torches. Goin's own face was clear enough in the backwash of light reflected from the snow. The shocked expression on his face he could have arranged for: the draining of blood that left it almost as white as Stryker's he couldn't.

'Jesus Christ!' he whispered. 'Dead?'

I said nothing, just turned the dead man over with Conrad's

and Jungbeck's help again. This time it was more difficult. Goin made a strange noise in his throat but otherwise didn't react at all, I suppose he'd nothing left to react with, he just stood there and stared as the driving snow whitened the dead man's anorak and, mercifully, the fearful wound in the occiput. For what seemed quite a long time we stood there in silence, gazing down at the dead man: I was aware, almost subconsciously, that the wind, now veering beyond south, was strengthening, for the thickening snow was driving along now almost parallel to the ground: I do not know what the temperature was, but it must have been close on thirty degrees below freezing. I was dimly aware that I was shaking with the cold: looking around, I could see that the others were also. Our breaths froze as they struck the icy air, but the wind whipped them away before the vapour had time to form.

'Accident?' Goin said hoarsely. 'It could have been an accident?'

'No,' I said. 'I saw the boulder that was used to crush his skull in.' Goin made the same curious noise in his throat again, and I went on: 'We can't leave him here and we can't take him inside. I suggest we leave him in the tractor shed.'

'Yes, yes, the tractor shed,' Goin said. He really didn't know what he was saying.

'And who's going to break the news to Miss Haynes?' I went on. God alone knew that I didn't fancy doing it.

'What?' He was still shocked. 'What was that?'

'His wife. She'll have to be told.' As a doctor, I supposed I was the one to do it, but the decision was taken from my hands. The cabin door was jerked abruptly open and Judith Haynes, her two dogs by her ankles, stood there framed against the light from the interior, with Otto and the Count just vaguely discernible behind her. She stood there for some little time, a hand on either door jamb, quite immobile and without any expression that I could see, then walked forward in a curiously dreamlike fashion and stooped over her husband. After a few moments she straightened, looked around as if puzzled, then turned questioning eyes on me, but only for a moment, for the questioning eyes turned up in her head and she crumpled and fell heavily across Stryker's body before I or anyone could get to her.

Conrad and I, with Goin following, brought her inside

and laid her on the camp-cot so lately occupied by Smithy. The cocker spaniels had to be forcibly restrained from joining her. Her face was alabaster white and her breathing very shallow. I lifted up her right eyelid and there was no resistance to my thumb: it was only an automatic reaction on my part, it hadn't even occurred to me that the faint wasn't genuine. I became aware that Otto was standing close by, his eyes wide, his mouth slightly open, his hands clenched together until the ivory knuckles showed.

'Is she all right?' he asked hoarsely. 'Will she—'

'She'll come to,' I said.

'Smelling salts,' he said. 'Perhaps—'

'No.' Smelling salts, to hasten her recovery to the bitter reality she would have to face.

'And Michael? My son-in-law? He's—I mean—'

'You saw him,' I said almost irritably. 'He's dead, of course he's dead.'

'But how—but how—'

'He was murdered.' There were one or two involuntary exclamations, the shocked indrawing of breath, then a silence that became intensified with the passing of seconds by the hissing of the Coleman lamps. I didn't even bother to look up to see what the individual reactions might be for I knew by now that I'd learn nothing that way. I just looked at the unconscious woman and didn't know what to think. Stryker, the tough, urbane, cynical Stryker had, in his own way, been terrified of this woman. Had it been because of the power she had wielded as Otto's daughter, his knowledge that his livelihood was entirely dependent on her most wayward whim—and I could imagine few more gifted exponents of the wayward whim than Judith Haynes? Had it been because of her pathological jealousy which I knew beyond all question to exist, because of the instant bitchiness which could allegedly range from the irrational to the insane, or had she held over his head the threat of some nameless blackmail which could bring him at once to his knees? Had he, in his own way, even loved his wife and hoped against hopeless hope that she might reciprocate some of this and been prepared to suffer any humiliation, any insult, in the hope that he might achieve this or part of it? I'd never know, but the questions were academic anyway, Stryker no longer concerned me, I was only turning them over in my mind wondering in what way they could throw any light on Judith Haynes's totally unexpected reaction to Stryker's death. She had despised him, she must have despised him for his dependence upon her, his weakness, his meek acceptance of insult, the fear he had displayed before me, for the emptiness and nothingness that had lain concealed behind so impressively masculine a façade. But had she loved him at the same time, loved him for what he had been or might have been, or was she just desolated at the loss of her most cherished whipping-boy, the one sure person in the world upon whom she knew she could with impunity vent her wayward spleen whenever the fancy took her? Even without her awareness of it, he might have become an integral, an indispensable part of her existence, an insidiously woven warp in the weft of her being, always dependable, always there, always ready to hand when she most needed him even when that need was no more than to absorb the grey corrosive poison eating away steadily at the edges of her mind. Even the most tarnished cornerstone can support the most crumbling edifice: take that away and the house comes tumbling down. The traumatic reaction to Stryker's death could, paradoxically, be the clinching manifestation of a complete and irredeemable selfishness: the as yet unrealized realization that she was the most pitiful of all creatures, a person totally alone.

Judith Haynes stirred and her eyes fluttered open. Memory came back and she shuddered. I eased her to a sitting position and she looked dully around her.

'Where is he?' I had to strain to hear the words.

'It's all right, Miss Haynes,' I said, and, just to compound that fatuous statement, added: 'We'll look after him.'

'Where is he?' she moaned. 'He's my husband, my husband. I want to see him.'

'Better not, Miss Haynes.' Goin could be surprisingly gentle. 'As Dr Marlowe says, we'll take care of things. You've seen him already and no good can come—'

'Bring him in. Bring him in.' A voice devoid of life but the will absolute. 'I must see him again.'

I rose and went to the door. The Count barred my way. His aquiline, aristocratic features held a mixture of revulsion and horror. 'You can't do that. It's too ghastly—it's—it's macabre.'

'What do you think that I think it is?' I felt savage but

I know I didn't sound that way, I think I only sounded tired. 'If I don't bring him in, she'll just go outside again. It's not much of a night for being outside.'

So we brought him in, the same three of us, Jungbeck and Conrad and myself, and we laid him on his back so that the fearful wound in the occiput didn't show. Judith Haynes rose from her camp-cot, moved slowly towards him like a person in a dream and sank to her knees. Without moving, she looked at him for some moments then reached out and gently touched the gashed face. No one spoke, no one moved. Not without effort, she pulled his right arm close in to his side, made to do the same with his left, noticed that the fist was still clenched and carefully prised it open.

A brown circular object lay in the palm of his hand. She took it, placed it in the palm of her own hand, straightened —still on her knees—and swung in a slow semi-circle showing us what she held. Then, her hand outstretched towards him, she looked at Allen. We all looked at Allen.

The brown leather button in her hand matched the still remaining buttons on Allen's torn coat.

CHAPTER NINE

I'm not sure how long the silence went on, a silence that the almost intolerable hiss of the lamps and the ululating moan of the south wind served only to deepen. It must have lasted at least ten seconds, although it seemed many times as long, a seemingly interminable period of time during which nobody moved and nothing moved, not even eyes, for Allen's eyes were fixed on the button in Judith Haynes's hand in fascinated uncomprehension, while every other eye in the room was on Allen. That one small leather-covered button held us all in thrall.

Judith Haynes was the first to move. She rose, very slowly, as if it called for a tremendous effort of both mind and muscle, and stood there for a moment, as if irresolute. She seemed quiet now and very resigned and because this was the wrong reaction altogether I looked past her towards Conrad and Smithy and caught the eyes of both. Conrad lowered his eyes briefly as if in acknowledgment of a signal, Smithy shifted his gaze towards Judith Haynes and when she began to move away from the body of her husband both of them moved casually towards each other to block off her clearly intended approach to Allen. Judith Haynes stopped, looked at them and smiled.

'That won't be necessary at all,' she said. She tossed the button to Allen who caught it in involuntary reaction. He held it in his hand, staring at it, then looked up in perplexity at Judith Haynes, who smiled again. 'You'll be needing that, won't you?' she said, and walked in the direction of her allocated room.

I relaxed and was aware that others were doing so also, for I could hear the slow exhalation of breaths of those standing closest to me. I looked away from Judith Haynes to Allen, and that was a mistake because I had relaxed too soon, I'd been instinctively aware that the seemingly quiet and sad resignation had been wholly out of character but had put it down to the effects of the shattering shock she had just received.

'You killed him, you killed him!' Her voice was an insane scream, but no more insane than the demented fury with which she was attacking Mary Darling who had already stumbled over backwards, the other woman falling on top of her, clawing viciously with hooked fingers. 'You bitch, you whore, you filthy slut, you—you murderess! You're the person who killed him! You killed my husband! You! You!' Sobbing and shrieking maniacal invective at the terrified and momentarily paralysed Mary Darling who had already lost her big hornrimmed spectacles, Judith Haynes wound one hand round the unfortunate Mary's hair and was reaching for her eyes with the other when Smithy and Conrad got to her. Both were big strong men but she fought with such crazed and tigerish ferocity—and they had at the same time to cope with two equally hysterical dogs—that it took them quite some seconds to pull her clear, and even then she clung with the strength of madness to Mary's hair, a grip that Smithy ruthlessly and without hesitation broke by squeezing her wrist until she shrieked with pain. They dragged her upright and she continued to scream hysterically with all the strength of her lungs, no longer attempting even to mouth words, just that horrible nerve-drilling shrieking like some animal in its dying agony, then the sound abruptly ceased, her legs buckled and Smithy and Conrad eased her to the floor.

Conrad looked at me. 'Act two?' He was breathing heavily and looked pale.

'No. This is real. Will you please take her to her cubicle?' I looked at the shocked and sobbing Mary but she didn't need any immediate assistance from me, for Allen, his own injuries forgotten, had dropped to his knees beside her, raised her to a sitting position and was using a none too clean handkerchief to dab at the three deep and ugly scratches that had been torn down the length of her left cheek. I left them, went into my cubicle, prepared a hypodermic and entered the cubicle where Judith Haynes had been taken. Smithy and Conrad were standing watchfully by and had been joined by Otto, the Count and Goin. Otto looked at the syringe and caught my arm.

'Is that—is that for my daughter? What are you going to do to her? It's all over now, man—good God, you can see she's unconscious.'

'And I'm going to see that she bloody well stays that way,' I said. 'For hours and hours and hours. That way it's best for her and best for all of us. All right, I'm sorry for your daughter, she's had a tremendous shock, but medically I'm not concerned with that, I'm just concerned with how best to treat her for the condition she's in now, which is frankly unbalanced, unstable and highly dangerous. Or do you want to have a look at Mary Darling again?'

Otto hesitated but Goin, calmly reasonable as always, came to my help. 'Dr Marlowe is perfectly right, Otto—and it's for Judith's own good, after such a shock a long rest can only help. This is the best thing for her.'

I wasn't so sure about that, I'd have preferred a strait-jacket, but I nodded my thanks to Goin, administered the injection, helped bundle her into a zipped sleeping-bag, saw that she was covered over and above that with a sufficiency of blankets and left her. I took the dogs with me and put them in my own cubicle—I don't much like having animals, especially highly-strung ones, in the company of a person under sedation.

Allen had Mary Darling seated on a bench now but was still dabbing her cheek. She'd stopped sobbing now, was just breathing with long quivering in-drawn gasps and, scratches apart, didn't seem much the worse for an experience that must have been as harrowing as it was brief. Lonnie was standing a few feet away, looking sorrowfully at the girl and shaking his head.

'Poor, poor lassie,' he said quietly. 'Poor little girl.'

'She'll be all right,' I said. 'If I do a halfway job the scratches won't even scar.' I looked at Stryker's body and decided that its removal to the tractor shed was clearly the first priority: apart from Lonnie and Allen, no one had eyes for anything else, and even although out of sight would not necessarily be out of mind, the absence of that mutilated body could hardly fail to improve morale.

'I wasn't talking about young Mary.' Lonnie had my attention again. 'I was thinking about Judith Haynes. Poor, lonely lassie.' I looked at him closely but I should have known him well enough by then to realize that he was incapable of either dissimulation or duplicity: he looked as sad as he sounded.

'Lonnie,' I said, 'you never cease to astonish me.' I lit the oil stove, put some water on to heat, then turned to Stryker. Both Smithy and Conrad were waiting and words were unnecessary. Lonnie insisted on coming with us, to open doors and hold a flash-light: we left Stryker in the tractor shed and went back to the main cabin. Smithy and Conrad went inside but Lonnie showed no intentions of following them. He stood there as if deep in thought, seemingly oblivious of a wind now strong enough to have to lean against, of a thickening driving snow now approaching the proportions of a blizzard, of the intense and steadily deepening cold.

'I think I'll stay out here a bit,' he said. 'Nothing like a little fresh air to clear the head.'

'No, indeed,' I said. I took the torch from him and directed its beam at the nearest hut. 'In there. On the left.' Wherever else Olympus Productions may have fallen short in the commissariat department, it hadn't been in the line of alcoholic stimulants.

'My dear fellow.' He retrieved his torch with a firm grasp. 'I personally supervised its storage.'

'And not even a lock to contend with,' I said.

'And what if there was? Otto would give me the key.'

'Otto would give you a key?' I said carefully.

'Of course. Do you think I'm a professional safe-cracker who goes around festooned with strings of skeleton keys? Who do you think gave me the keys to the lounge locker on the *Morning Rose*?'

'Otto did?' I said brightly.

'Of course.'

'What kind of blackmail are you using, Lonnie?'

'Otto is a very, very kind man,' Lonnie said seriously. 'I thought I'd told you that?'

'I'd just forgotten.' I watched him thoughtfully as he plodded purposefully through the deep snow towards the provisions hut, then went inside the main cabin. Most of the people inside, now that Stryker had gone, had transferred their attention to Allen, who was clearly self-consciously aware of this, for he no longer had his arm around Mary, although he still dabbed at her cheek with a handkerchief. Conrad, who had clearly become more than a little smitten by Mary Stuart for he'd sought out her company whenever possible in the past two days, was sitting beside her chafing one of her hands—I assumed she'd been complaining of the temperature which was still barely above freezing—and although she seemed half-reluctant and was smiling in some embarrassment, she wasn't objecting to the extent of making a song and dance about it. Otto, Goin, the Count and Divine were talking in low voice near one of the oil stoves: Divine, not surprisingly, was there not in the capacity of a contributor to the conversation, but as a bar-tender for he was laying out glasses and bottles under Otto's fussy direction. Otto beckoned me across.

'After what we've just been through,' he said, 'I think we're all badly in need of a restorative.' That Otto should be lashing out so recklessly with his private supplies was sufficient indication of the extent to which he had been shaken. 'It will also give us time to decide what to do with him.'

'Who?'

'Allen, of course.'

'Ah. Well, I'm sorry, I'm afraid you gentlemen will have to count me out for both drink and deliberations.' I nodded to Allen and Mary Darling, both of whom were watching us with some degree of apprehension. 'A little patching up to do there. Excuse me.'

I took the now hot water from the oil stove, brought it into my cubicle, put a white cloth on the rickety table that was there, laid out a basin, instruments and what medicaments I thought I'd require, then returned to where Conrad and Mary Stuart were sitting in the main body of the cabin. Like all the other little groups in the cabin they were talking in voices so low as to be virtually whispering, whether from a desire for privacy or because they still felt themselves to be in the presence of death I didn't know. Conrad, to my complete lack of surprise, was now industriously massaging her other hand, and as that was her left or faraway one I assumed that he hadn't had to fight for it.

I said: 'I'm sorry to interrupt the first-aid but I want to patch up young Allen a bit. I wonder if Mary dear will look after Mary darling for a bit?'

'Mary dear?' Conrad raised an inquiring eyebrow.

'To distinguish her from Mary darling,' I explained. 'It's what I call her when we're alone in the long watches of the night.' She smiled slightly but that was her only reaction.

'Mary dear,' Conrad said appreciatively. 'I like it. May I call you that?'

'I don't know,' she said mock-seriously. 'Perhaps it's copyright.'

189

'He can have the patent under licence,' I said. 'I can always rescind it. What were you two being so conspiratorial about?'

'Ah, yes,' Conrad said. 'Your opinion, Doc. That stone out there, I mean the lump of rock Stryker was clobbered with. I'd guess the weight about seventy pounds. Would you?'

'The same.'

'I asked Mary here if she could lift a rock like that above her head and she said don't be ridiculous.'

'Unless she's an Olympic weight-lifter in disguise, well, yes, you are ridiculous. She couldn't. Why?'

'Well, just look at her.' He nodded across at the other Mary. 'Skin and bone, just skin and bone. Now how—'

'I wouldn't let Allen hear you.'

'You know what I mean. A rock that size. "Murderess", Judith Haynes called her. Well, so OK, she was out there looking with the others, but how on earth—'

'I think Miss Haynes had something else in mind,' I said. I left them, beckoned to Allen, then turned to Smithy who was sitting close by. 'I require a surgery assistant. Feeling up to it now?'

'Sure.' He rose. 'Anything to take my mind off Captain Imrie and the report he must be writing out about me right now.'

There was nothing I could do to Allen's face that nature couldn't do better so I concentrated on the gash on the back of his head. I froze it, shaved the area around it, and jerked my head to Smithy to have a look. He did this and his eyes widened a little but he said nothing. I put eight stitches in the wound and covered it with plaster. During all of this we hadn't exchanged a word and Allen was obviously very conscious of this.

He said: 'You haven't got much to say to me, have you, Dr Marlowe?'

'A good tradesman doesn't talk on the job.'

'You're just thinking what all the others are thinking, aren't you?'

'I don't know. I don't know what all the others are thinking. Well, that's it. Just comb your hair straight back and no one will know you're prematurely bald.'

'Yes. Thank you.' He turned and faced me, hesitated and said: 'It does look pretty black against me, doesn't it?'

'Not to a doctor.'

'You—you mean you *don't* think I did it?'

'It's not a matter of thinking. It's a matter of knowing. Look, all in all you've had a pretty rough day, you're more shaken up than you realize, and when that anaesthetic wears off you're going to hurt a bit. Your cubicle's next to mine, isn't it?'

'Yes, but—'

'Go and lie down for a couple of hours.'

'Yes, but—'

'And I'll send Mary through when I've finished with her.'

He made to speak, then nodded wearily and left. Smithy said: 'That was nasty. The back of his head, I mean. It must have been one helluva clout.'

'He's been lucky that his skull isn't fractured. Doubly lucky in that he's not even concussed.'

'Uh-huh.' Smithy thought for a moment. 'Look, I'm not a doctor and I'm not very good at coining phrases, but doesn't this put a rather different complexion upon matters?'

'I am a doctor and it does.'

He thought some more. 'Especially when you have a close look at Stryker?'

'Especially that.'

I brought Mary Darling in. She was very pale, still apprehensive and had a little-girl-lost look about her, but she had herself under control. She looked at Smithy, made as if to speak, hesitated, changed her mind and let me get on with doing what I could. I cleaned and disinfected the scratches, taped them up carefully and said: 'It'll itch like fury for a bit, but if you can resist the temptation to haul the plasters off then you'll have no scars.'

'Thank you, Doctor. I'll try.' She looked very wan. 'Can I speak to you, please?'

'Of course.' She looked at Smithy and I said: 'You can speak freely. I promise you it will go no farther.'

'Yes, yes, I know, but—'

'Mr Gerran is dispensing free scotch out there,' Smithy said, and made for the door. 'I'd never forgive myself if I passed up an experience that can happen only once in a lifetime.'

She had me by the lapels even before Smithy had the door fully closed behind him. There was a frantic worry in her face, a sick misery in the eyes that made me realize just how much it had cost her to maintain her composure while Smithy had been there.

'Allen didn't do it, Dr Marlowe! He didn't, I know he didn't, I swear he didn't. I know things look awful for him, the fight they had this morning, and now this other fight and that button in—in Mr Stryker's hand and everything. But I know he didn't, he told me he didn't, Allen couldn't tell a lie, he wouldn't tell me a lie! And he couldn't hurt anything, I mean just not kill anybody, I mean hurt anybody, he just couldn't do it! And *I* didn't do it.' Her fists clenched until the knuckles showed she was even, for some odd reason, trying to shake me now, and tears were rolling down her face; whatever she'd known in her short life hadn't prepared her for times and situations like those. She shook her head in despair. 'I didn't, I didn't! A murderess, that's what she called me! In front of everybody, she called me a murderess! I couldn't kill anybody, Dr Marlowe, I—'

'Mary.' I stopped the hysterical flow by the simple process of putting my fingers across her lips. 'I seriously doubt whether you could dispose of a fly without worrying yourself sick afterwards. You and Allen together—well, if it were a particularly obnoxious fly you just might manage it. I wouldn't bet on it, though.'

She took my hand away and stared at me: 'Dr Marlowe, do you mean—'

'I mean you're a silly young goose. Together, you make a fine pair of silly young geese. It's not that I just don't believe that Allen or you had anything to do with Stryker's death. I *know* you hadn't.'

She sniffed a bit and then she said: 'You're an awfully kind person, Dr Marlowe. I know you're trying to help us—'

'Oh, do shut up,' I said. 'I can prove it.'

'Prove it? Prove it?' There was some hope in the sick eyes, she didn't know whether to believe me or not, and then it seemed that she decided not to, for she shook her head again and said numbly: 'She said I killed him.'

'Miss Haynes was speaking figuratively,' I said, 'which is not the same thing at all, and even then she was wrong. What she meant was that you were the precipitating factor in her husband's death, which of course you weren't.'

'Precipitating factor?'

'Yes.' I took her hands from my now badly crushed lapels, held them in mine and looked at her in my best avuncular fashion. 'Tell me, Mary darling, have you ever dallied in the moonlight with Michael Stryker?'

'Me? Have I—'

'Mary?'

'Yes,' she said miserably. 'I mean no, no, I didn't.'

'That's very clear,' I said. 'Let's put it this way. Did you ever give Miss Haynes reason to suspect that you had been? Dallying, I mean.'

'Yes.' She sniffed again. 'No. I mean he did.' I kept my baffled expression in cold storage and looked at her encouragingly. 'He called me into his cabin, just the day we left Wick, that was. He was alone there. He said that he wanted to discuss some things about the film with me.'

'A change from etchings,' I said.

She looked at me uncomprehendingly and went on: 'But it wasn't about the film he wanted to talk. You must believe me, Dr Marlowe. You must!'

'I believe you.'

'He closed the door and grabbed me and then—'

'Spare my unsullied mind the grisly details. When the villain was forcing his unwelcome attentions upon you there came the pit-a-pat of feminine footsteps in the corridor outside, whereupon the villain rapidly assumed a position where you appeared to be forcing your unwelcome attentions upon him and when the door opened—to reveal, of course, none other than his better half—there he was, fending off the licentious young continuity girl and crying, "No, no, Nanette, control yourself, this can never be," or words to that effect.'

'More or less.' She looked more miserable than ever, then her eyes widened. 'How did you know?'

'The Strykers of this world are pretty thick upon the ground. The ensuing scene must have been pretty painful.'

'There were two scenes,' she said dully. 'Something like it happened on the upper deck the following night. She said she was going to report me to her father—Mr Gerran. He said—not when she was there, of course—that if I tried to make trouble he'd have me fired. He was a director, you know. Later, when I got, well, friendly with Allen, he said he'd get us both fired if need be and make sure that neither of us

B.I. G   193 would ever again get a job in films. Allen said that this was all wrong, why should we accept this when neither of us had done anything, so—'

'So he tried to make him see the error of his ways this morning and got clobbered for his pains. Don't worry, you've neither of you anything to worry about. You'll find your wounded knight-errant next door, Mary.' I smiled and gently touched the swollen cheek. 'This should be something to see. Love's young dream in sticking-plaster. You do love him, don't you, Mary?'

'Of course.' She looked at me solemnly. 'Dr Marlowe.'

'I'm wonderful?'

She smiled, almost happily, and left. Smithy, who must have been watching for her departure, came in almost at once and I told him what had been said.

'Had to be that, of course,' he said. 'The truth's always obvious when it's hung up in front of you and you're beaten over the head with a two-by-four to make you take notice. And now?'

'And now, I think, three things. The first, to clear the names of the two love-birds next door: that's not important at this stage, but they're sensitive souls and I think they'd like to be on speaking terms with the rest of the company again. Second thing is, I've no intention of being stranded here for the next twenty-two days—two days is a lot more like it: who knows, I might be able to pressure unknown or unknowns into precipitate action.'

'I should have thought there had been enough of that already,' Smithy said.

'You may have a point. Third thing is, I could make life a great deal easier and safer for both of us if we had every person so busy watching every other person that it would make it a great deal more difficult for the disaffected to creep up upon our backs unawares.'

'You touch upon a very sympathetic nerve,' Smithy said. 'Your plan into action and at once, I say. A small chat with the assembled company?'

'A small chat with the assembled company. I suggested a couple of hours' lie-down to Allen but I think he and Mary should be there. Would you?'

Smithy left and I went into the living area. Goin, Otto and the Count, all armed with glasses as was almost every other person there, were still in solemn and low-voiced conclave. Otto beckoned me across.

'One moment,' I said. I went outside, coughed and caught my breath as the bitter air cut into my lungs, then trudged against that snow-filled gale across to the provisions hut. Lonnie was seated on a packing case, lovingly examining the amber contents of a glass against the light from his torch.

'Ha!' he said. 'Our peripatetic healer. You know, when one consumes a noble wine like this—'

'Wine?'

'A figure of speech. When one consumes a noble scotch like this, half the pleasure lies in the visual satisfaction. Ever tried it in the darkness? Flat, stale, strangely lacking in bouquet. There's a worthwhile monograph here, I'm sure.' He waved his glass in the direction of the crates of bottles by one wall. 'Harking back to my earlier allusions to the hereafter, if they can have bars in Bear Island then surely—'

'Lonnie,' I said, 'you're missing out on the largesse stakes. Otto is dispensing noble wine at this very moment. He's using very large glasses.'

'I was on the very point of leaving.' He tilted his head and swallowed rapidly. 'I have a dread of being thought a misanthrope.'

I took this friend of the human race back to the main cabin and counted those there. Twenty-one, myself included, as it should have been: the twenty-second and last, Judith Haynes, was deeply unconscious and would be so for hours. Otto beckoned me a second time and I went across.

'We've been having what you might call a council of war,' Otto said importantly. 'We've arrived at a conclusion and would like to have your opinion.'

'Why mine? I'm just an employee, like everyone else here, apart, of course, from the three of you—and Miss Haynes.'

'Consider yourself a co-opted director,' the Count said generously. 'Temporary and unpaid, of course.'

'Your opinion would be valued,' Goin said precisely.

'Opinion about what?'

'Our proposed measures for dealing with Allen,' Otto said. 'I know that in law every man is presumed innocent until proved otherwise. Nor do we have any wish to be inhumane. But simply in order to protect ourselves—'

'I wanted to talk to you about that,' I said. 'About protect-

195

ing ourselves. I wanted to talk to everybody about that. In fact, that's what I propose to do this very moment.'

'You propose to do what?' Otto could arrange his eyebrows in a very forbidding fashion when he put his mind to it.

'A brief address only,' I said. 'I'll take up hardly any of your time.'

'I can't permit that,' Otto said loftily. 'At least, not until you give us some idea what you have in mind and then we may or may not give our consent.'

'Your permission or lack of it is irrelevant,' I said indifferently. 'I don't require permission when I'm talking about something that may affect lives—you know, the difference between living and dying.'

'I forbid it. I would remind you of what you have just reminded me.' Otto had forgotten about the need for conducting delicate matters in conspiratorial murmurs and we had the undivided attention of everyone in the cabin. 'You are an employee of mine, sir!'

'And I'll now perform my last act as a dutiful employee.' I poured myself a measure of Otto's scotch which, as he and several others were drinking it, I presumed to be safe to drink. 'Health to one and all,' I said, 'and I don't mean that lightly or in the conventional sense. We're going to need it all before we leave this island, and let each one of us hope that he or she is not the one who is going to be abandoned by fortune. As for being your employee, Gerran, you can consider my resignation as being effective as from this moment. I do not care to work for fools. More importantly, I do not care to work for those who may be both fools and knaves.'

This, at least, had the effect of reducing Otto to silence for, to judge by the indigo hue his complexion was assuming, he appeared to be having some little difficulty in his breathing. The Count, I observed, had a mildly speculative expression on his face, while Goin's face held the impassivity of one withholding judgement. I looked round the cabin.

I said: 'It is, I know, belabouring the obvious to say that this trip of ours, so far, has been singularly luckless and ill-starred. We have been plagued by a series of tragic and extraordinarily strange events. We had Antonio die. This might have been the merest mischance: it might equally well

196

be that he was the victim of a premeditated murder or the hapless victim of a misplaced murder attempt that was aimed at someone else. Exactly the same can be said of the two stewards, Moxen and Scott. Similar attempts may or may not have been aimed at Mr Gerran, Mr Smith, Oakley and young Cecil here: all I can say with certainty is that if I hadn't been so lucky as to be in the vicinity when they were struck down at least three of those might have died. You may wonder why I make such a fuss about what could have been a simple, if deadly, outbreak of food poisoning: it is because I have reason to believe, without being able to prove it, that a deadly poison called *aconitine,* which is indistinguishable in appearance from horseradish, was introduced at specific points into the evening meal we had on the occasion when those people were struck down.'

I checked to see if I had the attention of those present and I've never made a more superfluous check. They were so stunned that they hadn't even got to the lengths of looking at each other: Otto's liquid largesse wholly forgotten, they had eyes only for me, ears only for what I was saying, the average university lecturer would have found it a dream of paradise: but then the average university lecturer rarely had the doubtful fortune to chance upon such wholly absorbing subject-matter as I had to hand.

'And then we have the mysterious disappearance of Halliday. I have no doubt that the cause of his death could be established beyond doubt if an autopsy could be carried out, but as I've equally no doubt that the unfortunate Halliday lies on the floor of the Barents Sea this can never be possible. But it is my belief—and this, again, is but conjecture—that he died not from any form of food poisoning but because he had a nightcap from a poisoned whisky bottle that was intended for me.' I looked at Mary Stuart: huge eyes and parted lips in a white shocked face, but I was the only one who saw it.

I pulled down the collar of my duffel-coat and showed them the impressively large and impressively multi-coloured bruise on the left-hand side of my neck

'This, of course, could have been self-inflicted. Or maybe I just slipped somewhere and banged myself. Or take this odd business of the smashed radio. Somebody with an aversion to radios, perhaps, and suchlike outward manifestations of what

197

we choose to call progress, or someone who found the Arctic just too much for him and had to take it out on something —you know, the equivalent of going cafard in the desert.

'So far, nothing but conjecture. An extraordinary and even more extraordinarily unconnected series of violent and tragic mishaps, one might claim, coincidence is an accepted part of life. But not, surely, coincidence multiplied up to the nth degree like this; that would have to lie at the very farthest bounds of possibility. I think you would admit that if we could prove the existence, beyond any doubt, of a carefully premeditated and carefully executed crime, then the other violent happenings must cease to be regarded as conjectural coincidences and considered as being what they then would be, deliberately executed murders in pursuit of some goal that can't yet even be guessed at but must be of overwhelming importance.'

They weren't admitting anything, or, at least, if they were admitting anything to themselves they weren't saying it out loud, but I think it was really a case of their minds having stopped working, not all their minds, there had to be one exception, probably more.

'And we have this one proven crime,' I went on. 'The rather clumsily executed murder of Michael Stryker which was at the same time an attempt, and not a very clever attempt, to frame young Allen here for something he never did. I don't think the murderer had any special ill-will towards Allen, well, no more than he seems to have for the general run of mankind: he just wanted to divert any possible suspicion from himself. I think if you'd all had time enough to think about it you'd have come to the eventual conclusion that Allen couldn't possibly have had anything to do with it: with a doctor in the house, if you'll excuse the phrase, he hadn't a hope in hell.

'Allen says he has no recollection at all about what happened. I believe him absolutely. He's sustained a severe blow on the back of the head—the scalp is open to the bone. How he escaped a fractured skull, far less concussion, I can't imagine. It certainly must have rendered him unconscious for a considerable period. Which leads one to assume that this assailant was still in excellent shape after what was clearly his *coup de grâce*. Are we to assume then that Allen, after having been knocked senseless, immediately leapt up and smote his assailant hip and thigh? That doesn't make any kind of sense at all. What does make sense, what is the only answer, is that the unknown crept up behind Allen and laid him out, not with his hands but with some heavy and solid object—probably a stone, there's more than enough lying around. Having done this, he proceeded to cut the unconscious Allen up about the face, ripped his coat and tore off a couple of buttons—all to give the very convincing impression that he'd been in a fight.

'The same thing, but this time on a lethal scale, happened to Stryker. I'm convinced that it was no accident that Allen was merely knocked unconscious while Stryker was killed— our friend, who must be a bit of an expert in such matters, knew just how much weight to bring to bear in each case, by no means as easy a matter as you might think. Then this ghoul, in a stupid attempt to create the impression that Stryker had been the other party to the fight, proceeded to rough up Stryker's face as he had done Allen's: I leave it to you to form your own estimate of just how evil must be the mind of a man who will deliberately set about mutilating the face of a dead man.'

I left them for a little to form their own estimates. For the most part they looked neither sick nor revolted: their reactions were mainly of shock and minds still consciously fighting against comprehension. No glances were exchanged, no eyes moved: their eyes were only for me.

'Stryker had a split upper lip, a tooth missing and a reddish rough mark on his temple which I think must have been caused by another stone—very probably all the injuries were inflicted in this fashion to avoid any tell-tale marking of the hands or knuckles. Had those injuries been sustained in the course of a fight there would have been extensive bleeding and fairly massive bruising: there were no signs of either because Stryker was dead and circulation had ceased before those wounds were caused. To complete what he thought would be a most convincing effect, the murderer then closed the dead man's hand round one of the buttons torn from Allen's coat. Incidentally, there were no signs whatever of the churned-up snow one would have expected to find at the scene of a fight: there were two sets of tracks leading to the place where Stryker lay, one set leading away. No fuss, no commotion, just a quick if not particularly clean dispatch.'

I sipped some more of Otto's scotch—it must have come from his own private supply for it was excellent stuff—then asked in my best lecturer's fashion: 'Are there any questions?'

Predictably, there were none. They were all clearly far too busy asking themselves questions to have any time to put any to me.

I went on: 'I think you'd agree, then, that it now seems extremely improbable that any of the four previous deaths were the results of innocent coincidence. I think that only the most gullible and the most naïve would now be prepared to believe that those deaths were unconnected and not the work of the same agent. So what we have is, in effect, a mass murderer. A man who is either mad, a pathological killer, or a vicious and evil monster who finds it essential to murder with what can be only an apparent indiscrimination in order to achieve God knows what murky ends. He may, it is possible, be all three of those at once. Whatever he is or whoever he is, he's in this cabin now. I wonder which one of you it is?'

For the first time their eyes left me as they looked quickly and furtively at one another as if in the ludicrous hope that they might by this means discover the identity of the killer. None of them examined one another as closely as I observed them all over the rim of my glass; if one pair of eyes remained fixed on mine it could only be because its owner knew who the murderer was and didn't have to bother to look around: but I knew, even as I watched them, that I had no real foundation for any such hope, the murderer may have been no great shakes at physiology, but he was far too clever to walk into what, for an intelligent man with five deaths on his conscience, must have been a very obvious trap indeed. I was certain that there wasn't a pair of eyes before me that didn't flicker surreptitiously around the cabin. I waited patiently until I had their combined attention again.

'I have no idea who this murderous fiend may be,' I said, 'but I think I can with certainty say who it isn't. Counting the absent Miss Haynes, there are twenty-two of us in this cabin: to nine of those I cannot see that any suspicion can possibly attach.'

'Merciful God!' Goin muttered. 'Merciful God! This is monstrous, Dr Marlowe, unbelievable. One of us here, one of the people we know, one of our friends has the blood of five people on his hands? It can't be! It just can't be!'

'Except that you know that it must be,' I said. Goin made no reply. 'To begin with, I myself am in the clear, not because I know I am—we could all claim that—but because two hostile acts have been committed against my person, one of which was intended to be lethal. Further, I was bringing in Mr Smith here when Stryker was killed and Allen injured.' This last was the truth but not the whole truth, but only the killer himself would know that and as he was already on to me his opinion was unimportant because he couldn't possibly voice it. 'Mr Smith is in the clear because not only was he unconscious at the time, he was a nearly fatal victim of the poisoner's activities and it's hardly likely that he would go around poisoning himself.'

'Then that let's me out, Dr Marlowe!' The Duke's voice was a cracked falsetto, hoarse with strain. 'It wasn't me, it couldn't—'

'Agreed, Cecil, it wasn't you. Apart from the fact that you were another poisoning victim, I don't think—well, I'm not being physically disparaging but I'd think it very unlikely that you could have hoisted that rock that was used to kill Stryker. Mr Gerran, too, is above suspicion: not only was he poisoned but he was in the cabin here at the time of Stryker's death. Allen, obviously, could have had nothing to do with it and neither did Mr Goin here, although you'll have to take my word for that.'

'What does that mean, Dr Marlowe?' Goin's voice was steady.

'Because when you first saw Stryker's body you turned as white as the proverbial sheet. People can do lots of things with their bodies, but they can't switch on and off the epidermal blood supply at will. Had you been prepared for the sight you saw you wouldn't have changed colour. You did. So you weren't prepared. Our two Marys here we'll have to leave out of the reckoning for it would have been a physical impossibility for either of them to have attacked Stryker with that rock. And Miss Haynes, of course, doesn't come into the reckoning at all. Which, by my count, leaves thirteen potential suspects in all.' I looked round the cabin and counted. 'That's right. Thirteen. Let's hope it's going to be a very unlucky number for one of you.'

'Dr Marlowe,' Goin said. 'I think you should consider

withdrawing your resignation.'

'Consider it withdrawn. I was beginning to wonder what I'd do for food anyway.' I looked at my now empty glass, then at Otto. 'Seeing that I'm now back on the strength, as it were, would it be in order—'

'Of course, of course.' Otto, looking stricken, sunk heavily on to a providentially sturdy stool and insofar as it was possible for over two hundredweights of lard to look like a punctured balloon, he looked like a punctured balloon. 'Dear God, this is ghastly. One of us here is a murderer. One of us here has killed five people!' He shivered violently although the temperature had by this time risen well above freezing point. 'Five people. Dead. And the man who did it is here!'

I lit a cigarette, sipped a little more of Otto's scotch and waited for some further contributions to the conversation. Outside, the wind had strengthened until it was now a high and lonesome moaning sound that set the teeth on edge, a moan that regularly climbed up the register into a weird and eldritch whistling as the wind gusted and fell away, everyone appeared to be listening to it and listening intently, a weirdly appropriate litany for the fear and the horror that was closing in on their minds, a fit requiem for the dead Stryker. A whole minute dragged by and no one spoke so I took up the conversational burden again.

'The implications will not have escaped you,' I said. 'At least, when you have had as much time to think about them as I've had, they won't. Stryker is dead—and so are four others. Who should want them dead? Why should they have died? Is there a reason, a purpose behind those slayings? Have we a psychopathic murderer amongst us? If there is a purpose, has it been achieved? If it hasn't—or if the killer is a psychopath —which one of us is going to be next? Who is going to die tonight? Who is going to go to his cubicle tonight knowing that anyone, a crazed killer, it may be, is going to enter at any time—or even, possibly, one's own room-mate may be waiting his turn with a knife or a suffocating pillow? In fact, I should think that the room-mate possibility might be by far the more likely—for who would do anything so crazily obvious as that? Except, of course, a crazy man. So, before us, we have what you might call a sleepless vigil. Perhaps we can all keep it up for one night. But for twenty-two nights— can we keep it up for twenty-two nights? Is there any of us here who can be sure of still being alive when the *Morning Rose* returns?'

From their expressions and the profound silence that greeted this last question it was apparent that no one was prepared to express any such certainty. When I came to consider it myself, instead of just asking them to do so, I realized that the question of continued existence applied more particularly and more strongly to myself than to any of the others, for if the killer were no wayward psycho who struck out as the fancy took him but was an ice-cold and calculating murderer with a definite objective in view, then I was convinced that I was first on his calling list. I didn't for a moment think that any attempt to dispose of me would be because that was any part of the killer's preconceived plans but solely because I represented a threat to those plans.

'And how are we going to comport ourselves from now on?' I said. 'Do we now polarize into two groups, the nine acknowledged innocent giving a very wide berth and a leery eye to the thirteen potentially guilty even although this is going to be a mite hard on, say, twelve of the latter? Shall we be like oil and water and resolutely refuse to mix? Or about your shooting plans for tomorrow. Mr Gerran and the Count, I believe, are heading for the fells tomorrow, a goodie and a potential baddie—Mr Gerran is going to make sure that he has at least another goodie along with him to watch his back? Heissman is taking the work-boat to reconnoitre possible locations along the Sor-hamna and perhaps a bit farther south. I believe Jungbeck and Heyter here have volunteered to go along with him. Three of those, you note, whose innocence is not proved. Any white sheep going to go along with black wolf or wolves who may come back and sorrowfully explain that the poor sheep fell over the side and that in spite of their heroic efforts the poor fellow perished miserably? And those splendid precipices at the south of the island—one little well-timed nudge, a deft clicking together of the ankles—well, sixteen hundred feet is a considerable drop, especially when you bear in mind that it's straight down all the way. A perplexing and difficult problem, isn't it, gentlemen?'

'This is preposterous,' Otto said loudly. 'Absolutely preposterous.'

'Isn't it?' I said. 'A pity we can't ask Stryker his opinion about that. Or the opinions of Antonio and Halliday and

Moxen and Scott. When your pale ghost looks down from Limbo, Mr Gerran, and watches you being lowered into a hole in the frozen snow—do you think it will still look preposterous?'

Otto shuddered and reached for the bottle. 'What in God's name are we going to do?'

'I've no idea,' I said. 'You heard what I just said to Mr Goin. I have reverted to the position of employee. I haven't got my shirt on this film as I heard Mr Goin say to Captain Imrie that you had, I'm afraid this is a decision to arrive at at directorial level—well, the three directors that are still capable of making decisions.'

'Would our employee mind telling us what he means?' Goin tried to smile but it didn't come off, his heart wasn't in it.

'Do you want to go ahead with shooting all your scenes up here or don't you? It's up to you. If we all stay here in the cabin permanently, at least half a dozen awake at any given time, looking with all their eyes and listening with all their ears, then the chances are high that we'll all still be in relatively mint condition by the time the twenty-two days are up. On the other hand, of course, that means that you won't get any of your film shot and you'll lose all your investment. It's a problem I wouldn't like to have to face. That's excellent scotch you have there, Mr Gerran.'

'I can see that you appreciate it.' Otto would have liked a touch of asperity in his voice, but all he managed to do was to sound worried.

'Don't be so mean.' I helped myself. 'These are times that try men's souls.' I wasn't really listening to Otto, I was barely listening to myself. Once before, since leaving Wick, on the occasion when the Count had said something about a surfeit of horseradish, certain words had had the effect of a touch-paper being applied to a trail of gun-powder, triggering off a succession of thoughts that came tumbling in one after the other almost faster than my mind could register them, and now the same thing had happened again, only this time the words had been triggered off by something I'd said myself. I became aware that the Count was speaking, presumably to me. I said: 'Sorry, mind on other things, you know.'

'I can see that.' The Count was looking at me in a thoughtful fashion. 'All very well to opt out of responsibility, but what would *you* do?' He smiled. 'If I were to co-opt you again as a temporary unpaid director?'

'Easy,' I said, and the answer did come easily—as the result of the past thirty seconds' thinking. 'I'd watch my back and get on with the ruddy film.'

'So.' Otto nodded, and he, the Count and Goin looked at one another in apparent satisfaction. 'But now, this moment, what would you do?'

'When do we have supper?'

'Supper?' Otto blinked. 'Oh, about eight, say.'

'And it's now five. About to have three hours' kip, that's what I'm going to do. And I wouldn't advise anyone to come near me, either for an aspirin or with a knife in their hand, for I'm feeling very nervous indeed.'

Smithy cleared his throat. 'Would I get clobbered if I asked for an aspirin now? Or something a bit more powerful to make a man sleep? I feel as if my head has been on a butcher's block.'

'I can have you asleep in ten minutes. Mind you, you'll probably feel a damn sight worse when you wake up.'

'Impossible. Lead me to the knock-out drops.'

Inside my cubicle I gripped the handle of the small square double-plate-glazed window and opened it with some difficulty. 'Can you do that with yours?'

'You do have things on your mind. No mangers allocated for uninvited guests.'

'All the better. Bring a cot in here. You can borrow one from Judith Haynes's room.'

'Of course,' he said. 'There's a spare one there.'

CHAPTER TEN

Five minutes later, wrapped to the eyes against the bitter cold, the driving snow and that wind that was now howling, not moaning, across the frozen face of the island, Smithy and I stood in the lee of the cabin, by my window which I'd wedged shut against a wad of paper: there was no handle on the outside to pull it open again, but I had with me a multi-tooled Swiss army knife that could pry open just about anything. We looked at the vaguely seen bulk of the cabin, at the bright light—Coleman lamps have an intensely white flame—streaming from one of the windows in the central section and the pale glimmer of smaller lights from a few of the cubicles.

'No night for an honest citizen to be taking a constitutional,' Smithy said in my ear. 'But how about bumping into one of the less honest ones?'

'Too soon for him or them to be stirring abroad,' I said. 'For the moment the flame of suspicion burns too high for anyone even to clear his throat at the wrong moment. Later, perhaps. But not now.'

We went directly to the provisions store, closed the door behind us and, since the hut was windowless, switched on both our torches. We searched through all the bags, crates, cartons and packages of food and found nothing untoward.

'What are we supposed to be looking for?' Smithy asked.

'I've no idea. Anything, shall we say, that shouldn't be here.'

'A gun? A big black ribbed bottle marked "Deadly Poison"?'

'Something like that.' I lifted a bottle of Haig from a crate and stuck it in my parka pocket. 'Medicinal use only,' I explained.

'Of course.' Smithy made a farewell sweep of his torch beam round the walls of the hut: the beam steadied on three small highly varnished boxes on an upper shelf.

'Must be very high grade food in those,' Smithy said. 'Caviar for Otto, maybe?'

'Spares medical equipment for me. Mainly instruments. No

poisons. Guaranteed.' I made for the door. 'Come on.'

'Not checking?'

'No point. Be a bit difficult to hide a sub-machine-gun in one of those.' The boxes were about ten inches by eight.

'OK to have a look, all the same?'

'All right.' I was a bit impatient. 'Hurry it up, though.'

Smithy opened the lids of the first two boxes, glanced cursorily at the contents and closed them again. He opened the third box and said: 'Broken into your reserves already, I see.'

'I have not.'

'Then somebody has.' He handed over the box and I saw the two vacant moulds in the blue felt.

'Somebody has indeed,' I said. 'A hypodermic and a tube of needles.'

Smithy looked at me in silence, took the box, closed the lid and replaced it. He said: 'I don't think I like this very much.'

'Twenty-two days could be a very long time,' I said. 'Now, if we could only find the stuff that's going to go inside this syringe.'

'If. You don't think somebody may have borrowed it for his own private use? Somebody on the hard stuff who's bent his own plunger? One of the Three Apostles, for instance? Right background, after all—pop world, film world, just kids?'

'No, I don't think that.'

'I don't think so either. I wish I did.'

We went from there to the fuel hut. Two minutes was sufficient to discover that the fuel hut had nothing to offer us. Neither had the equipment hut although it afforded me two items I wanted, a screwdriver from the tool-box Eddie had used when he was connecting up the generator, and a packet of screws. Smithy said: 'What do you want those for?'

'For the screwing up of windows,' I said. 'A door is not the only way you can enter the cubicle of a sleeping man.'

'You don't trust an awful lot of people, do you?'

'I weep for my lost innocence.'

There was no temptation to linger in the tractor shed, not with Stryker lying there, his face ghastly in the reflected wash from the torches, his glazed eyes staring unseeingly at the ceiling. We rummaged through tool-boxes, examined metal panniers, even went to the length of probing fuel tanks, oil tanks and radiators: we found nothing.

We made our way down to the jetty. From the main cabin it was a distance of just over twenty yards and it took us five minutes to find it. We did not dare use our torches, and with that heavy and driving snow reducing visibility to virtually arm's length, we were blind people moving in a blind world. We edged our way very gingerly out to the end of the jetty—the snow had covered up the gaps in the crumbling limestone and, heavily clad as we were, the chances of surviving a tumble into the freezing waters of the Sor-hamna were not high—located the work-boat in the sheltered north-west angle of the jetty and climbed down into it by means of a vertical iron ladder that was so ancient and rusty that the outboard ends of some of the rungs were scarcely more than a quarter of an inch in diameter.

On a dark night the glow from a torch can be seen from a considerable distance even through the most heavily falling snow but now that we were below the level of the jetty wall we switched our torches on again, though still careful to keep them hooded. A quick search of the work-boat revealed nothing. We clambered into the fourteen-footer lying alongside and had the same lack of success. From here we transferred ourselves to the mock-up submarine—an iron ladder had been welded both to its side and the conning-tower.

The conning-tower had a platform welded across its circumference at a distance of about four feet from the top. A hatch in this led to a semi-circular platform about eighteen inches below the flange to which the conning-tower was secured: from here a short ladder led to the deck of the submarine. We went down and shone our torches around.

'Give me subs any time,' Smithy said. 'At least they keep the snow out. That apart, I don't think I'd care to settle down here.'

The narrow and cramped interior was indeed a bleak and cheerless place. The deck consisted of transverse spaced wooden planks held in position at either side by large butterfly nuts. Beneath the planks we could see, firmly held in position, rows of long narrow grey-painted bars—the four tons of cast-iron that served as ballast. Four square ballast tanks were arranged along either side of the shell—those could be filled to give negative buoyancy—and at one end of the shell stood a small diesel, its exhaust passing through the deck-head as far as the top of the conning-tower, to which it was bolted: this engine was coupled to a compressor unit for emptying the ballast tanks. And that, structurally, was all that there was to it: I had been told that the entire mock-up had cost fifteen thousand pounds and could only conclude that Otto had been engaged in the producers' favourite pastime of cooking the books.

There were several other disparate items of equipment. In a locker in what I took to be the after end of this central mock-up were four small mushroom anchors with chains, together with a small portable windlass: immediately above these was a hatch in the deck-head which gave access to the upper deck: the anchors could only be for mooring the model securely in any desired position. Opposite this locker, securely lashed against a bulkhead, was a lightweight plastic reconstruction of a periscope that appeared to be capable of operating in a sufficiently realistic fashion. Close by were three other plastic models, a dummy three-inch gun, presumably for mounting on the deck, and two model machine-guns which would be fitted, I imagined, somewhere in the conning-tower. In the for'ard end of the craft were two more lockers: one held a number of cork life-jackets, the other six cans of paint and some paint-brushes. The cans were marked 'Instant Grey'.

'And what does that mean?' Smithy asked.

'Some sort of quick-drying paint, I should imagine.'

'Everything shipshape and Bristol fashion,' Smithy said. 'I wouldn't have given Otto the credit.' He shivered. 'Maybe it isn't snowing in here, but I'd have you know that I'm very cold indeed. This place reminds me of an iron tomb.'

'It isn't very cosy. Up and away.'

'A fruitless search, you might say?'

'You might. I didn't have many hopes anyway.'

'Is that why you changed your mind about their getting on with the making of the film? One minute indifference, the next advising them to press on? So that you could, perhaps, examine their quarters and their possessions when they're out?'

'Whatever put such a thought in your mind, Smithy?'

'There are a thousand snowdrifts where a person could hide anything.'

'That's a thought that's also in my mind.'

We made the trip from the jetty to the main cabin with much greater ease than we had the other way for this time we had the faint and diffuse glow of light from the Colemans to guide us. We scrambled back inside our cubicle without too much difficulty, brushed the snow from our boots and upper clothing and hung the latter up: compared to the interior of the submarine shell the warmth inside the cubicle was positively genial. I took screwdriver and screws and started to secure the window, while Smithy, after some references to the low state of his health, retrieved the bottle I'd taken from the provisions shed and took two small beakers from my medical box. He watched me until I had finished.

'Well,' he said, 'that's us safe for the night. How about the others?'

'I don't think most of the others are in any danger because they don't offer any danger to the plans of our friend or friends.'

'Most of the others?'

'I think I'll screw up Judith Haynes's window too.'

'Judith Haynes?'

'I have a feeling that she is in danger. Whether it's grave danger or imminent danger I have no idea. Maybe I'm just fey.'

'I shouldn't wonder,' Smithy said ambiguously. He drank some scotch absently. 'I've just been thinking myself, but along rather different lines. When, do you think, is it going to occur to our directorial board to call some law in or some outside help or, at least, to let the world know that the employees of Olympus Productions are dying off like flies and not from natural causes either?'

'That's the decision you would arrive at?'

'If I wasn't a criminal, or, in this case, the criminal and had very powerful reasons for not wanting the law around, yes, I would.'

'I'm not a criminal but I've very powerful reasons for not wanting the law around either. The moment the law officially steps into the picture every criminal thought, intent and potential action will go into deep freeze and we'll be left with five unresolved deaths on our hands and that'll be the end of it, for there's nothing surer than that we haven't got a thing to hang on anyone yet. There's only one way and that's by giving out enough rope for a hanging job.'

'What if you give out too much rope and our friend, instead of hanging himself, hangs one of us instead? What if there's murder?'

'In that case we'd have to call in the law. I'm here to do a job in the best way I can but that doesn't mean by any means I can: I can't use the innocent as sacrificial pawns.'

'Well, that's some relief. But if the thought does occur to them?'

'Then obviously we'll have to try to contact Tunheim—there's a Meteorological Office radio there that should just about reach the moon. Or we'll have to offer to try to contact Tunheim. It's less than ten miles away but in weather conditions like these it might as well be on the far side of Siberia. If the weather eases, it might be possible. The wind's veering round to the west now and if it stayed in that quarter a trip by boat up the coast might be possible—pretty unpleasant, but just possible. If it goes much north of west, it wouldn't —those are only open work-boats and would be swamped in any kind of sea. By land—if the snow stopped—well, I just don't know. In the first place, the terrain is so broken and mountainous that you couldn't possibly use the little Sno-Cat—you'd have to make it on foot. You'd have to go well inland, to the west, to avoid the Misery Fell complex for that ends in cliffs on the east coast. There are hundreds of little lakes lying in that region and I've no idea how heavily they may be frozen over, maybe some of them not very much, maybe just enough to support a covering of snow and not a man—and I believe some of those lakes are over a hundred feet deep. You might be ankle-deep, knee-deep, thigh-deep, waist-deep in snow. And apart from being bogged-down or drowned, we're not equipped for winter travel, we haven't even got a tent for an overnight stop—there isn't a hope of you making it in one day—and if the snow started falling again and kept on falling I bet Olympus Productions haven't even as much as a hand compass to prevent you from walking in circles until you drop dead from cold or hunger or just plain old exhaustion.'

' "You, you, you",' Smithy said. 'You're always talking about me. How about you going instead?' He grinned. 'Of course, I could always set off for there, search around till

211

I found some convenient cave or shelter, hole up there for the night, and return the next day announcing mission impossible.'

'We'll see how the cards fall.' I finished my drink and picked up screwdriver and screws. 'Let's go and see how Miss Haynes is.'

Miss Haynes seemed to be in reasonable health. No fever, normal pulse, breathing deeply and evenly: how she would feel when she woke was another matter altogether. I screwed up her window until nobody could have entered her room from the outside without smashing their way in—and breaking through two sheets of plate glass would cause enough racket to wake up half the occupants of the cabin. Then we went into the living area of the cabin.

It was surprisingly emptly. At least ten people I would have expected to be there were absent, but a quick mental count of the missing heads convinced me that there was no likely cause for alarm in this. Otto, the Count, Heissman and Goin, conspicuously absent, were probably in secret conclave in one of their cubicles discussing weighty matters which they didn't wish their underlings to hear. Lonnie had almost certainly betaken himself again in his quest for fresh air and I hoped that he hadn't managed to lose himself between the cabin and the provisions hut. Allen, almost certainly, had gone to lie down again, and I presumed that Mary darling, who appeared to have overcome a great number of her earlier inhibitions, had returned to her dutiful hand-holding. I couldn't imagine where the Three Apostles had got to nor was I particularly worried: I was sure that there was nothing to fear from them other than permanent damage to the eardrums.

I crossed to where Conrad was presiding over a three-burner oil cooker mounted on top of a stove. He had two large pans and a large pot all bubbling away at once, stew, beans and coffee, and he seemed to be enjoying his role of chef not least, I guessed, because he had Mary Stuart as his assistant. In another man I would have looked for a less than altruistic motive in this cheerful willingness, the hail-fellow-well-met leading man playing the democrat to an admiring gallery, but I knew enough of Conrad now to realize that this formed no part of his nature at all: he was just a naturally helpful character who never thought to place himself above his fellow-actors. Conrad, I thought, must be a very *rara avis* indeed in the cinema world.

'What's all this, then?' I said. 'You qualified for this sort of thing? I thought Otto had appointed the Three Apostles as alternate chefs?'

'The Three Apostles had it in mind to start improving their musical technique in this very spot,' Conrad said. 'I did a self-defence trade with them. They're practising across in the equipment hut—you know, where the generator is.'

I tried to imagine the total degree of cacophony produced by their atonal voices, their amplified instruments and the diesel engine in a confined space of eight by eight, but my imagination wasn't up to it. I said: 'You deserve a medal. You too, Mary dear.'

'Me?' She smiled. 'Why?'

'Remember what I said about the goodies pairing off with the baddies? Delighted to see you keeping a close eye on our suspect here. Haven't seen his hand hovering suspiciously long over one of the pots, have you?'

She stopped smiling. 'I don't think that's funny, Dr Marlowe.'

'I don't think it is either. A clumsy attempt to lighten the atmosphere.' I looked at Conrad. 'Can I have a word with the chef?'

Conrad looked at me briefly, speculatively, nodded and turned away. Mary Stuart said: 'That's nice. For me, I mean. Why can't you have a word with him here?'

'I'm going to tell him some funny stories. You don't seem to care much for my humour.' I walked away a few paces with Conrad and said: 'Had a chance of a word with Lonnie yet?'

'No. I mean, I haven't had an opportunity yet. Is it that urgent?'

'I'm beginning to think it may be. Look, I haven't seen him there but I'm certain as can be that Lonnie is across in the provisions hut.'

'Where Otto keeps all those elixirs of life?'

'You wouldn't expect to find Lonnie in the fuel shed? Diesel and petrol aren't his tipples. I wonder if you could go across there, seeking liquid solace from this harsh and weary world, from Bear Island, from Olympus Productions, from whatever you like, and engage him in crafty conversation. Touch upon the theme of how you're missing your family. Anything. Just get him to tell you about his.'

He hesitated. 'I like Lonnie. I don't like this job.'

'I'm past caring now about people's feelings. I'm just concerned with people's lives—that they should keep on living, I mean.'

'Right.' He nodded and looked at me soberly. 'Taking a bit of a chance, aren't you? Enlisting the aid of one of your suspects, I mean.'

'You're not on my list of suspects,' I said. 'You never were.'

He looked at me for some moments then said: 'Tell that to Mary dear, will you?' He turned and made for the outer door. I returned to the oil cooker. Mary Stuart looked at me with her usual grave and remote lack of expression.

I said: 'Conrad tells me to tell you that I've just told him —you're following me?—that he's not on my list of suspects and never was.'

'That's nice.' She gave me a little smile but there was a touch of winter in it.

'Mary,' I said, 'you are displeased with me.'

'Well.'

'Well what?'

'Are you a friend of mine?'

'Of course.'

'Of course, of course.' She mimicked my tone very creditably. 'Dr Marlowe is a friend of all mankind.'

'Dr Marlowe doesn't hold all mankind in his arms all night long.'

Another smile. This time there was a touch of spring in it. She said: 'And Charles Conrad?'

'I like him. I don't know what he thinks about me.'

'And I like him and I know he likes me and so we're all friends together.' I thought better of saying 'of course' again and just nodded. 'So why don't we all share secrets together?'

'Women are the most curious creatures,' I said. 'In every sense of the word "curious".'

'Please don't be clever with me.'

'Do you always share secrets?' She frowned a little, as if perplexed, and I went on: 'Let's play kiddies' games, shall we? You tell me a secret and I'll tell you one.'

'What on earth do you mean?'

'This secret assignation you had yesterday morning. In the snow and on the upper deck. When you were being so very affectionate with Heissman.'

I'd expected some very positive reaction from this and was correspondingly disappointed when there was none. She looked at me, silently thoughtful, then said: 'So you were spying on us.'

'I just happened to chance by.'

'I didn't see you chancing by.' She bit her lip, but not in any particularly discernible anguish. 'I wish you hadn't seen that.'

'Why?' It had been briefly in my mind to be heavily ironic but I could hear a little warning bell tinkling in the distance.

'Because I don't want people to know.'

'That's obvious,' I said patiently. 'Why?'

'Because I'm not very proud of it. I have to make a living, Dr Marlowe. I came to this country only two years ago and I haven't got any qualifications for anything. I haven't even got any qualifications for what I'm doing now. I'm a hopeless actress. I know I am. I've just got no talent at all. The last two films I was in—well, they were just awful. Are you surprised that people give me the cold shoulder, why they're wondering out loud why I'm making my third film with Olympus Productions? Well, you can guess now: Johann Heissman is the why.' She smiled, just a very small smile. 'You are surprised, Dr Marlowe? Shocked, perhaps?'

'No.'

The little smile went away. Some of the life went from her face and when she spoke her voice was dull. 'It is so easy, then, to believe this of me?'

'Well, no. The point is that I just don't believe you at all.'

She looked at me, her face a little sad and quite uncomprehending. 'You don't believe—you don't believe this of me?'

'Not of Mary Stuart. Not of Mary dear.'

Some of the life came back and she said almost wonderingly: 'That's the nicest thing anybody's ever said to me.' She looked down at her hands, as if hesitating, then said, without looking up: 'Johann Heissman is my uncle. My mother's brother.'

'Your uncle?' I'd been mentally shuffling all sorts of possibilities through my mind, but this one hadn't even begun to occur to me.

'Uncle Johann.' Again the little, almost secret smile, this time with what could have been an imagined trace of mischief: I wondered what her smile would be like if she ever smiled in pure delight or happiness. 'You don't have to believe me. Just go and ask him yourself. But privately, if you please.'

Dinner that night wasn't much of a social success. The atmosphere of cheerful good fellowship which is required to make such communal get-togethers go with a swing was noticeably lacking. This may have been due, partially, to the fact that most people either ate by their solitary selves or, both sitting and standing, in scattered small groups around the cabin, their attention almost exclusively devoted to the unappetizing goulash in the bowls held in their hands: but it was mainly due to the fact that everybody was clearly and painfully aware that we were experiencing the secular equivalent of our own last supper. For the interest in the food was not all-absorbing: frequently, but very very briefly, a pair of eyes would break off their rapt communion with the stew and beans, glance swiftly around the cabin, then return in an oddly guilty defensiveness to the food as if the person had hoped in that one lightning ocular sortie to discover some unmistakable tell-tale signs that would infallibly identify the traitor in our midst. There were, needless to say, no such overt indications of self-betrayal on display, and the problem of identification was deepened and confused by the fact that most of those present exhibited a measure of abnormality in their behaviour that would ordinarily have given rise to more than a modicum of suspicion anyway: for it is an odd characteristic of human nature that even the most innocent person who knows himself or herself to be under suspicion tends to over-react with an unnatural degree of casual indifference and insouciant concern that serves only to heighten the original suspicion.

Otto, clearly, was not one of those thus afflicted. Whether it was because he knew himself to be one of those who was regarded as being completely in the clear or because, as chairman of the company and producer of the film, he regarded himself as being above and apart from the problems that afflicted the common run of mankind, Otto was remarkably composed and, astonishingly, even forceful and assertive. Unlikely though it had appeared up to that moment, Otto, normally so dithering and indecisive, might well be one of those who only showed of their best in the moments of crisis. There was certainly nothing dithering or indecisive about him when he rose to speak at the end of the meal.

'We are all aware,' said Otto briskly, 'of the dreadful happenings of the past day or two, and I think that we have no alternative to accepting Dr Marlowe's interpretation of the events. Further, I fear we have to accept as very real the doctor's warnings as to what may happen in the near future.

'Those are inescapable facts and entirely conceivable possibilities so please don't for a moment imagine that I'm trying to minimize the seriousness of the situation. On the contrary, it would be impossible to exaggerate it, impossible to exaggerate an impossible situation. Here we are, marooned in the high Arctic and beyond any reach of help, with the knowledge that there are those of us who have come to a violent end and that this violence may not yet be over.' He looked unhurriedly around the company and I did the same: I could see that there were quite a number who were as impressed by Otto's calm assessment of the situation as I was. He went on: 'It is precisely because the state of affairs in which we find ourselves is so unbelievable and so abnormal that I suggest we comport ourselves in the most rational and normal fashion possible. A descent into hysteria will achieve no reversal of the awful things that have just occurred and can only harm all of us.

'Accordingly, my colleagues and I have decided that, subject, of course, to taking every possible precaution, we should proceed with the business in hand—the reason why we came to this island at all—in as normal a fashion as possible. I am sure you will all agree with me that it is much better to have our time and attention taken up—I will not say gainfully employed—by working steadily at something purposive and constructive rather than sit idly by and have those awful things prey upon our minds. I do not suggest that we can pretend that those things never happened: I do suggest that it will benefit all of us if we act as if they hadn't.

'Weather permitting, we will have three crews in the field tomorrow.' Otto wasn't consulting, he was telling: I'd have done the same in his place. 'The main group, under Mr

Divine here, will go north up Lerner's Way—a road built through to the next bay about the turn of the century, although I don't suppose there are many traces left of it now. The Count, Allen and Cecil here will, of course, accompany him. I intend to go along myself and I'll want you there too, Charles.' This to Conrad.

'You'll require me along, Mr Gerran?' This from Mary Darling, her hand upraised like a little girl in class.

'Well, it'll be nearly all background—' He broke off, glanced at Allen's battered face, then looked again at Mary with what I took to be a roguish smile. 'If you wish to, certainly. Mr Hendriks, with Luke, Mark and John here, will try to capture for us all the sounds of the island—the winds on the fells, the birds on the cliffs, the waves breaking against the shore. Mr Heissman here is taking a hand-camera out in the boat to seek out some suitable seaward locations—Mr Jungbeck and Mr Heyter, who have nothing on tomorrow, have kindly volunteered to accompany him.

'These, then, are our decisions for tomorrow's programme. But the most important decision of all, which I have left to the last, is in no way connected with our work. We have decided that it is essential that we seek help with all possible speed. By help I mean the law, police or some such recognized authority. It is not only our duty, it may well be essential for our own self-preservation, to have a thorough and expert investigation made as quickly as is humanly possible. To call for help we need a radio and the nearest is at the Norwegian Meteorological Station in Tunheim.' I carefully refrained from looking at Smithy and was confident that he would reciprocate. 'Mr Smith, your presence here may prove to be a blessing—you are the only professional seaman amongst us. What would be the chances of reaching Tunheim by boat?'

Smithy was silent for a few seconds to lend weight to his observations, then said: 'In the present conditions so poor that I wouldn't even consider trying it, not even in these desperate circumstances. We've had very heavy weather recently, Mr Gerran, and the seas won't subside for quite some time. The drawback with those work-boats is that if one does encounter rough seas ahead you can't do what you would normally do, that is, turn and run before the sea: those boats are completely open at the back and would almost certainly be pooped—that is, they'd fill up with water and sink. So you'd have to be pretty certain of your weather before you set out.'

'I see. Too dangerous for the moment. When the sea moderates, Mr Smith?'

'Depends upon the wind. It's backing to the west right now and if it were to stay in that quarter—well, it's feasible. If it moves round to the north-west or beyond, no. Not on.' Smithy smiled. 'I wouldn't say that an overland trip would be all that easier, but at least you wouldn't be swamped in heavy seas.'

'Ah! So you think that it is at least possible to reach Tunheim on foot?'

'Well, I don't know. I'm no expert on Arctic travel, I'm sure Mr Heissman here—I'm told he's been giving a lecture about this already—is much more qualified to speak about it than I am.'

'No, no.' Heissman waved a deprecating hand. 'Let's hear what you think, Mr Smith.'

So Smithy let them hear what he thought, which was more or less a verbatim repetition of what I'd said to him in our cubicle earlier. When he'd finished, Heissman, who probably knew as much about winter travel in Arctic regions as I did about the back side of the moon, nodded sagely and said: 'Succinctly and admirably put. I agree entirely with Mr Smith.'

There was a thoughtful silence eventually broken by Smithy who said diffidently: 'I'm the supernumerary here. If the weather eases, I don't mind trying.'

'And now I have to disagree with you,' Heissman said promptly. 'Suicidal, just suicidal, my boy.'

'Not to be thought of for an instant,' Otto said firmly. 'For safety—for mutual safety—nothing short of an expedition would do.'

'I wouldn't want an expedition,' Smithy said mildly. 'I don't see that the blind leading the blind would help much.'

'Mr Gerran.' It was Jon Heyter speaking. 'Perhaps I could be of help here.'

'You?' Otto looked at him in momentary perplexity, then his face cleared. 'Of course. I'd forgotten about that.' He said in explanation: 'Jon here was my stuntman in *The High Sierra*. A climbing picture. He doubled for the actors who were terrified or too valuable for the climbing sequences. A really first-class alpinist, I assure you. How about that then, eh, Mr Smith?'

I was about to wonder how Smithy would field that one when he answered immediately. 'That's about the size of the expedition I'd have in mind. I'd be very glad to have Mr Heyter along—he'd probably have to carry me most of the way there.'

'Well, that's settled then,' Otto said. 'Very grateful to you both. But only, of course, if the weather improves. Well, I think that covers everything.' He smiled at me. 'As co-opted board member, wouldn't you agree?'

'Well, yes,' I said. 'Except with your assumption that everyone will be here in the morning to play the parts you have assigned to them.'

'Ah!' Otto said.

'Precisely,' I said. 'You weren't seriously contemplating that we should *all* retire for the night, were you? For certain people with certain purposes in mind there is no time like the still small hours. When I say "people", I'm not going out-with the bounds of this cabin: when I say "purposes", I refer to homicidal ones.'

'My colleagues and I have, in fact, discussed this,' Otto said. 'You propose we set watches?'

'It might help some of us to live a little longer,' I said. I moved two or three steps until I was in the centre of the cabin. 'From here I can see into all five corridors. It would be impossible for any person to leave or enter any of the cubicles without being observed by a person standing here.'

'Going to call for a rather special type of person, isn't it?' Conrad said. 'Someone with his neck mounted on swivels.'

'Not if we have two on watch at the same time,' I said. 'And as the time's long gone when anybody's hurt feelings are a matter of any importance, two people on watch who are not only watching the corridors but watching each other. A suspect, shall we say, and a non-suspect. Among the non-suspects, I think we might gallantly exclude the two Marys. And I think that Allen too could do with a full night's sleep. That would leave Mr Gerran, Mr Goin, Mr Smith, Cecil and myself. Five of us, which would work out rather well for two-hour watches between, say, 10 p.m. and 8 a.m.'

'An excellent suggestion,' Otto said. 'Well, then, five volunteers.'

There were thirteen potential volunteers and all thirteen immediately offered their services. Eventually it was agreed that Goin and Hendriks should share the ten to midnight watch, Smith and Conrad the midnight to two, myself and Luke the two to four, Otto and Jungbeck the four to six, and Cecil and Eddie the six to eight. Some of the others, notably the Count and Heissman, protested, not too strongly, that they were being discriminated against: the reminder that there would be still another twenty-one nights after this one was sufficient to ensure that the protest was no more than a token one.

The decision not to linger around in small talk and socializing was reached with a far from surprising unanimity. There was, really, only one thing to talk about and nobody wished to talk about it in case he had picked the wrong person to talk to. In ones and twos, and within a very few minutes, almost everybody had moved off to their cubicles. Apart from Smithy and myself, only Conrad remained and I knew that he wished to talk to me. Smithy glanced briefly at me, then left for our cubicle.

'How did you know?' Conrad said. 'About Lonnie and his family?'

'I didn't. I guessed. He's talked to you?'

'A little. Not much. He had a family.'

'Had?'

'Had. Wife and two daughters. Two grown-up girls. A car crash. I don't know if they hit another car, I don't know who was driving. Lonnie just clammed up as if he had already said too much. He wouldn't even say whether he had been in the car himself, whether anyone else had been present, not even when it had taken place.'

And that was all that Conrad had learnt. We talked in a desultory fashion for some little time, and when Goin and Hendriks appeared to begin the first watch I left for my cubicle. Smithy was not in his camp-bed. Fully clothed, he was just removing the last of the screws I'd used to secure the window frame: he'd the flame of the little oil lamp turned so low that the cubicle was in semi-darkness.

'Leaving?' I said.

'Somebody out there.' Smithy reached for his anorak and I did the same. 'I thought maybe we shouldn't use the front door.'

'Who is it?'

'No idea. He looked in here but his face was just a white blur. He doesn't know I saw him, I'm sure of that, for he went from here and shone a torch through Judith Haynes's window, and he wouldn't have done that if he thought anyone was watching.' Smithy was already clambering through the window. 'He put his torch out but not before I saw where he was heading. Down to the jetty, I'm sure.'

I followed Smithy and jammed the window shut as I had done before. The weather was very much as it had been earlier, still that driving snow, the deepening cold, the darkness and that bitter wind which was still boxing the compass and had moved around to the south-west. We moved across to Judith Haynes's window, hooded our torches to give thin pencil beams of light, picked up tracks in the snow that led off in the direction of the jetty, and were about to follow them when it occurred to me that it might be instructive to see where they came from. But we couldn't find where they came from: whoever the unknown was he'd walked, keeping very close to the walls, at least twice round the cabin, obviously dragging his feet as he had gone, so that it was quite impossible to discover which cubicle window he'd used as an exit route from the cabin. That he should have so effectively covered his tracks was annoying: that he should have thought to do it at all was disconcerting for it plainly demonstrated at least the awareness that such late-night sorties might be expected.

We made our way quickly but cautiously down to the jetty, giving the unknown's tracks a prudently wide berth. At the head of the jetty I risked a quick flash with the narrowed beam of my torch: a single line of tracks led outwards.

'Well, now,' Smithy said softly. 'Our lad's down at the boats or the sub. If we go to investigate we might bump into him. If we go down to the end of the jetty for a quick look-see and don't bump into him he's still bound to see our tracks on his return trip. We want to make our presence known?'

'No. No law against a man taking a stroll when he feels like it, even though it is in a blizzard. And if we declare ourselves you can be damn sure he'll never put another foot wrong as long as we remain on Bear Island.'

We withdrew to the shelter of some rocks only a few yards distant along the beach, an almost wholly superfluous precaution in that close to zero visibility.

'What do you think he's up to?' Smithy said.

'Specifically, no idea. Generally, anything between the felonious and the villainous. We'll check down there when he's gone.'

Whatever purpose he'd had in mind, it hadn't taken him long to achieve it for he was gone within two minutes. The snow was so thick, the darkness so nearly absolute, that he might well have passed by both unseen and unheard had it not been for the erratic movement of the small torch he held in his hand. We waited for some seconds then straightened.

'Was he carrying anything?' I said.

'Same thought here,' Smithy said. 'He could have been. But I couldn't swear to it.'

We followed the double tracks in the snow down to the end of the jetty, where they ended at the head of the iron ladder leading down to the submarine mock-up. No question but this was where he'd gone, for apart from the fact that there was nowhere else where he could have been his footprints were all over the hull and, when we'd climbed into it, the platform in the conning-tower. We dropped down into the hull of the submarine.

Nothing was changed, nothing appeared to be missing from our earlier visit. Smithy said: 'I've taken a sudden dislike to this place. Last time we were here I called it an iron tomb. I wouldn't want it to be our tomb.'

'You feel it might?'

'Our friend seemingly didn't take anything away. But he must have had some purpose in coming here so I assume he brought something. On the track record to date that purpose wouldn't be anything I'd like and neither would be that something he brought. How would it be if he'd planted something to blow the damn thing up?'

'Why would he want to do a crazy thing like that?' I didn't feel as disbelieving as I sounded.

'Why has he done any of the crazy things he's done? Right now, I don't want a reason. I just want to know whether, as of now, and here and now, he's just done another crazy thing. What I mean is, I'm nervous.'

He wasn't the only one. I said: 'Assuming you're right, he couldn't blow this thing up with a little itsy-bitsy piece of plastic explosive. It would have to be something big enough to make a big bang. So, a delayed-action fuse.'

'To give him time to be asleep in his innocent bed when the explosion goes off? I'm more nervous than ever. I wonder how long he figured it would take him to get back to his bed.'

'He could do it in a minute.'

'God's sake, why are we standing here talking?' Smithy flashed his torch around. 'Where the hell would a man put a device like that?'

'Against a bulkhead, I'd say. Or on the bottom.'

We examined the deck first but all the bars of iron ballast and their securing wooden battens appeared to be undisturbed and firmly in place. There was just no room there for even the smallest explosive device. We turned to the rest of the hull, looked behind the mushroom anchors, among the chains, under the compressor unit and the windlass and behind the plastic models of periscope and guns. We found nothing. We even peered at the cleaning plates on the ballast tanks to see if any of those could have been unscrewed but there were no marks on them. And there was certainly no place where such a device could have been attached to the bulkheads themselves without being instantly detectable.

Smithy looked at me. It was difficult to say whether he was perplexed or, like me, increasingly and uncomfortably conscious of the fact that if such a time device did exist time might be swiftly running out. He looked towards the fore end of the hull and said: 'Or he might just have dropped it in one of those lockers. Easiest and quickest place to hide anything, after all.'

'Most unlikely,' I said, but I reached there before he did. I ran the beam of the torch over the paint locker and then the light steadied on a wooden batten close by the floor of the locker. I kept the light where it was and said to Smithy: 'You see it too?'

'A giveaway piece of fresh and unmelted snow. From a boot.' He reached for the lid of the locker. 'Well, time's a-wasting. Better open the damn thing.'

224

'Better not.' I'd caught his arm. 'How do you know it's not booby-trapped?'

'There's that.' He'd snatched back his hand like a man seeing a tiger's jaws closing on it. 'It would save the cost of a time-fuse. How do we open it then?'

'Gradually. It's unlikely that he had the time to rig up anything so elaborate as an electrical trigger, but if he did there'll be contacts in the lid. More likely, if anything, a simple pull cord. In either event nothing can operate in the first two inches of lift for he must have left at least that space to withdraw his hand.'

So we gingerly opened the lid those two inches, examined the rim and what we could see of the interior of the locker and found nothing. I pushed the locker lid right back. There was no sign of any explosive. Nothing had been put inside. But something had been removed—two cans of the quick-dry paint and two brushes.

Smithy looked at me and shook his head. Neither of us said anything. The reasons for removing a couple of paint cans were so wholly inconceivable that, clearly, there was nothing that could be gainfully said. We closed the locker, climbed up the conning-tower and regained the pier. I said: 'It's very unlikely that he would have taken them back to the cabin with him. After all, they're large cans and not easy things to hide in a tiny cubicle, especially if any of your friends should chance to come calling.'

'He doesn't have to hide them there. As I said earlier, there are a thousand snowdrifts where you can hide practically anything.'

But if he'd hidden anything he hadn't hidden them in any of the snowdrifts between the jetty and the cabin, for his tracks led straight back to the latter without any deviation to either side. We followed the footprints right back close up to the cabin walls and there they were lost in the smudged line of tracks that led right round the cabin's perimeter. Smithy hooded his torch and examined the tracks for some seconds.

He said: 'I think that track's wider and deeper than it was before. I think that someone—and it doesn't have to be the same person—has been making another grand tour of the cabin.'

'I think you're right,' I said. I led the way back to the

window of our own cubicle and was about to pull it open when some instinct—or perhaps it was because I was now subconsciously looking for the suspicious or untoward in every possible situation—made me shine my torch on the window-frame. I turned to Smithy. 'Notice something?'

'I notice something. The wad of paper we left jammed between the window and frame—well, it's no longer jammed between window and frame.' He shone his torch on the ground, stopped and picked something up. 'Because it was lying down there. A caller or callers.'

'So it would seem.' We clambered inside, and while Smithy started screwing the window back in place I turned up the oil lamp and started to look around partly for some other evidence to show that an intruder had been there, but mainly to try to discover the reason for his being there. Inevitably, my first check was on the medical equipment, and my first check was my last, and very brief it was too.

'Well, well,' I said. 'Two birds with one stone. We're a brilliant pair.'

'We are?'

'The lad you saw with his face pressed against that window. Probably had it stuck against it for all of five minutes until he'd made sure he'd been seen. Then, to make certain you were really interested, he went and shone his torch into Judith Haynes's window. No two actions, he must have calculated, could have been designed to lure us out into the open more quickly.'

'He was right at that, wasn't he?' He looked at my opened medical kit and said carefully: 'I'm to take it, then, that there's something missing there?'

'You may so take it.' I showed him the velvet-lined gap in the tray where the something missing had been. 'A lethal dose of morphine.'

CHAPTER ELEVEN

'Four bells and all's well,' Smithy said, shaking my shoulder. Neither the call nor the shake was necessary. I was by this time, even in my sleep, in so keyed-up a state that his turning of the door-handle had been enough to have me instantly awake. 'Time to report to the bridge. We've made some fresh coffee.'

I followed him into the main cabin, said a greeting to Conrad who was bent over pots and cups at the oil stove, and went to the front door. To my surprise the wind, now fully round to the west, had dropped away to something of not more than the order of a Force 3, the snow had thinned to the extent that it promised to cease altogether pretty soon, and I even imagined I could see a few faint stars in a clear patch of sky to the south, beyond the entrance of the Sorhamna. But the cold, if anything, was even more intense than it had been earlier in the night. I closed the door quickly, turned to Smithy and spoke softly.

'You're very encouraging,' Smithy said. 'What makes you so sure that those five—' He broke off as Luke, yawning and stretching vastly, entered the main cabin. Luke was a thin, awkward, gangling creature, a tow-headed youth urgently in need of the restraining influences of either a barber or a ribbon.

I said: 'Do you see him as a gun for hire?'

'I could have him up for committing musical atrocities with a guitar, I should think. Otherwise—yes, I guess. Very little threat to life and limb. And, yes again, that would go for the other four too.' He watched as Conrad went into one of the passages, carrying a cup of coffee. 'I'd put my money on our leading man any day.'

'Where on earth is *he* off to?'

'Bearing sustenance for his lady-love, I should imagine. Miss Stuart spent much of our watch with us.'

I was on the point of observing that the alleged lady-love had a remarkable predilection for moving around in the darker watches of the night but thought better of it. That

Mary Stuart was involved in matters dark and devious—Heissman's being her uncle didn't even begin to account for the earlier oddity of her behaviour—I didn't for a moment doubt: that she was engaged in any murderous activities I couldn't for a moment believe.

Smithy went on: 'It's important that I reach Tunheim?'

'It hardly matters whether you do or not. With Heyter along, only the weather and the terrain can decide that. If you have to turn back, that's fine with me, I'd rather have you here: if you get to Tunheim, just stay there.'

'Stay there? How can I stay there? I'm going there for help, am I not? And Heyter will be shouting to come back.'

'I'm sure they'll understand if you explain that you're tired and need a rest. If Heyter makes a noise, have him locked up—I'll give you a letter to the Met. officer in charge.'

'You'll do that, will you? And what if the Met. officer point-blank refuses?'

'I think you'll find some people up there who'll be only too happy to oblige you.'

He looked at me without a great deal of enthusiasm. 'Friends of yours, of course?'

'There's a visiting meteorological team from Britain staying there briefly. Five of them. Only, they're not meteorologists.'

'Naturally not.' The lack of enthusiasm deteriorated into a coldness that was just short of outright hostility. 'You play your cards mighty close to the chest, don't you, Dr Marlowe?'

'Don't get angry with me. I'm not asking you that, I'm telling you. Policy—I obey orders, even if you don't. A secret shared is never a secret halved—even a peek at my cards and who knows who's kibitzing? I'll give you that letter early this morning.'

'OK.' Smithy was obviously restraining himself with no small difficulty. He went on morosely: 'I suppose I shouldn't be too surprised to find even the *Morning Rose* up there?'

'Let me put it this way,' I said. 'I wouldn't put it beyond the bounds of possibility.'

Smithy nodded, turned and walked to the oil stove where Conrad, now returned, was pouring coffee. We sat for ten minutes, drinking and talking about nothing much, then Smithy and Conrad left. The next hour or so passed without event except that after five minutes Luke fell sound asleep and stayed that way. I didn't bother to wake him up, it wasn't

228

necessary, I was in an almost hypernatural state of alertness: unlike Luke, I had things on my mind.

A door in a passage opened and Lonnie appeared. As Lonnie, by his own account, wasn't given to sleeping much and as he wasn't on my list of suspects anyway, this was hardly call for alarm. He came into the cabin and sat heavily in a chair by my side. He looked old and tired and grey and the usual note of badinage was lacking in his tone.

'Once again the kindly healer,' he said, 'and once again looking after his little flock. I have come, my boy, to share your midnight vigil.'

'It's twenty-five to four,' I said.

'A figure of speech.' He sighed. 'I have not slept well. In fact, I have not slept at all. You see before you, Doctor, a troubled old man.'

'I'm sorry to hear that, Lonnie.'

'No tears for Lonnie. For me, as for most of pitiful mankind, my troubles are of my own making. To be an old man is bad enough. To be a lonely old man, and I have been lonely for many years, makes a man sad for much of the time. But to be a lonely old man who can no longer live with his conscience—ah, that is not to be borne.' He sighed again. 'I am feeling uncommonly sorry for myself tonight.'

'What's your conscience doing now?'

'It's keeping me awake, that's what it's doing. Ah, my boy, my boy, to cease upon the midnight with no pain. What more could a man want when it's evening and time to be gone?'

'This wine-shop on the far shore?'

'Not even that.' He shook his head mournfully. 'No welcoming arms in paradise for the lost Lonnies of this world. Haven't the right entry qualifications, my boy.' He smiled and his eyes were sad. 'I'll pin my hopes on a small four-ale bar in purgatory.'

He lapsed into silence, his eyes closed and I thought he was drifting off into sleep. But he presently stirred, cleared his throat and said apparently apropos of nothing. 'It's always too late. Always.'

'What's always too late, Lonnie?'

'Compassion is, or understanding or forgiveness. I fear that Lonnie Gilbert has been less than he should have been. But it's always too late. Too late to say I like you or I love you or how nice you are or I forgive you. If only, if only, if only. It is difficult to make your peace with someone if you're looking at that person and he's lying there dead. My, my, my.' As if with an immense effort, he pushed himself to his feet. 'But there's still a little shred of something that can be saved. Lonnie Gilbert is now about to go and do something that he should have done many, many years ago. But first I must arm myself, some life in the ancient bones, some clarity in the faded mind, in short, prepare myself for what I'm ashamed to say I still regard as the ordeal that lies ahead. In brief, my dear fellow, where's the scotch?'

'I'm afraid Otto has taken it with him.'

'A kind fellow, Otto, none kinder, but he has his parsimonious side to him. But no matter, the main source of supply is less than a Sunday's march away.' He made for the outer door but I stopped him.

'One of those times, Lonnie, you're going to go out there, sit down there, go to sleep and not come back again because you'll be frozen to death. Besides, there's no need. There's some in my cubicle. Same source of supply, I assure you. I'll fetch it. Just keep your eye open in my absence, will you?'

It didn't matter very much whether he kept his eyes open or not for I was back inside twenty seconds. Smithy, clearly, was a heavier sleeper than I was for he didn't stir during my brief visit.

Lonnie helped himself copiously, drained his glass in a few gulps, gazed at the bottle longingly then set it firmly aside. 'Duty completed, I shall return and enjoy this at my leisure. Meantime, I am sufficiently fortified.'

'Where are you going?' It was difficult to imagine what pressing task he had on hand at that time of the night.

'I am in great debt to Miss Haynes. It is my wish—'

'To Judith Haynes?' I know I stared at him. 'It was my understanding that you could with but difficulty look at her.'

'In great debt,' he said firmly. 'It is my wish to discharge it, to clear the books, you might say. You understand?'

'No. What I do understand is that it's only three-forty-five. If this business has been outstanding, as you said, for so many years, surely it can wait just another few hours. Besides, Miss Haynes has been sick and shocked and she's under sedatives. As her doctor, and whether she likes it or not, I am her doctor, I can't permit it.'

'And as a doctor, my dear fellow, you should understand the necessity for immediacy. I have worked myself up to this, screwed myself, as it were, to the sticking-point. Another few hours, as you say, and it may be too late. The Lonnie Gilbert you see before you will almost certainly have reverted to the bad old, cowardly old, selfish old, clay-souled Lonnie of yore, the Lonnie we all know so well. And then it will always be too late.' He paused and switched his argument. 'Sedatives, you say. How long do the effects of those last?'

'Varies from person to person. Four hours, six hours, maybe as much as eight.'

'Well, there you are then. Poor girl's probably been lying awake for hours, just longing for some company, although not, in all likelihood, that of Lonnie Gilbert. Or has it escaped your attention that close on twelve hours have elapsed since you administered that sedative?'

It had. But what had not escaped my attention was that Lonnie's relationship vis-à-vis Judith Haynes had been intriguing me considerably for some time. It might, I thought, be very helpful and, with regard to a deeper penetration of the fog of mystery surrounding us, more than a little constructive if I could learn something of the burden of what Lonnie had in mind to say to Judith Haynes. I said: 'Let me go and see her. If she's awake and I think she's fit to talk, then OK.'

He nodded. I went to Judith Haynes's room and entered without knocking. The oil lamp was turned up and she was awake, stretched out under the covers with only her face showing. She looked ghastly, which was the way I had expected her to look, with the titian hair emphasizing the drawn pallor of her face. The usually striking green eyes were glazed and lack-lustre and her cheeks were smudged and streaked with tears. She looked at me indifferently as I pulled up a stool, then looked as indifferently away.

'I hope you slept well, Miss Haynes,' I said. 'How are you feeling?'

'Do you usually come calling on patients in the middle of the night?' Her voice was as dull as her eyes.

'I don't make a practice of it. But we're taking turns keeping watch tonight, and this happens to be my turn. Is there anything that you want?'

'No. Have you found out who killed my husband?' She was so preternaturally calm, under such seemingly iron control, that I suspected it to be the prelude to another uncontrollable hysterical outburst.

'No. Am I to take it from that, Miss Haynes, that you no longer think that young Allen did?'

'I don't think so. I've been lying here for hours, just thinking, and I don't think so.' From the lifeless voice and the lifeless face I was pretty sure she was still under the influence of the sedative. 'You will get him, won't you? The man who killed Michael. Michael wasn't as bad as people thought, Dr Marlowe, no, he really wasn't.' For the first time a trace of expression, just the weary suggestion of a smile. 'I don't say he was a kind man or a good one or a gentle one, for he wasn't: but he was the man for me.'

'I know,' I said, as if I understood, which I only partially did. 'I hope we get the man responsible. I think we will. Do you have any ideas that could help?'

'My ideas are not worth much, Doctor. My mind doesn't seem to be very clear.'

'Do you think you could talk for a bit, Miss Haynes? It wouldn't be too tiring?'

'I am talking.'

'Not to me. To Lonnie Gilbert. He seems terribly anxious to speak to you.'

'Speak to me?' Tired surprise but not outright rejection of the idea. 'Why should Lonnie Gilbert wish to speak to me?'

'I don't know. Lonnie doesn't believe in confiding in doctors. All I gather is that he feels that he's done you some great wrong and he wants to say "sorry". I think.'

'Lonnie say "sorry" to me!' Astonishment had driven the flat hopelessness from her voice. 'Apologize to *me*? No, not to me.' She was silent for a bit, then she said: 'Yes, I'd very much like to see him now.'

I concealed my own astonishment as best I could, went back to the main cabin, told an equally astonished Lonnie that Judith Haynes was more than prepared to meet him, and watched him as he went along the passage, entered her room and closed the door behind him. I glanced at Luke. He appeared, if anything, to be more soundly asleep than ever, absurdly young to be in this situation, a pleased smile on his face: he was probably dreaming of golden discs. I walked quietly along the passage to Judith Haynes's room: there was nothing in the Hippocratic oath against doctors listening at closed doors.

It was clear that I was going to have to listen very closely indeed for although the door was only made of bonded ply, the voices in the room were being kept low and I could hear little more than a confused murmur. I dropped to my knees and applied my ear to the keyhole. The audibility factor improved quite remarkably.

'You!' Judith Haynes said. There was a catch in her voice, I wouldn't have believed her capable of any of the more kindly emotions. 'You! To apologize to me! Of all people, you!'

'Me, my dear, me. All those years, all those years.' His voice fell away and I couldn't catch his next few words. Then he said: 'Despicable, despicable. For any man to go through life, nurturing the animosity, nay, my dear, the hatred—' He broke off and there was silence for some moments. He went on: 'No forgiveness, no forgiveness. I know he can't—I know he couldn't have been so bad, or even really bad at all, you loved him and no one can love a person who is bad all through, but even if his sins had been black as the midnight shades—'

'Lonnie!' The interruption was sharp, even forceful. 'I know I wasn't married to an angel, but I wasn't married to any devil either.'

'I know that, my dear, I know that. I was merely saying—'

'Will you listen! Lonnie, Michael wasn't in that car that night. Michael was never near that car.'

I strained for the answer but none came. Judith Haynes went on: 'Neither was I, Lonnie.'

There was a prolonged silence, then Lonnie said in a voice so low that it was a barely heard whisper: 'That's not what I was told.'

'I'm sure it wasn't, Lonnie. My car, yes. But I wasn't driving it. Michael wasn't driving it.'

'But—you won't deny that my daughters were—well, incapable, that night. And that you were too. And that you made them that way?'

'I'm not denying anything. We all had too much to drink

that night—that's why I've never drunk since, Lonnie. I don't know who was responsible. All I know is that Michael and I never left the house. Good God, do you think I *have* to tell you this—now that Michael is dead?'

'No. No, you don't. Then—then who was driving your car?'

'Two other people. Two men.'

'Two men. And you've been protecting them all those years?'

'Protecting? No, I wouldn't use the word "protecting". Except inadvertently. No, I didn't put that well, I mean—well, any protection given was just incidental to something else we really wanted. Our own selfish ends, I suppose you could call it. Everybody knows well enough that Michael and I—well, we were criminals but we always had an eye on the main chance.'

'Two men.' It was almost as if Lonnie hadn't been listening to a word she'd said. 'Two men. You must know them.'

Another silence, then she said quietly: 'Of course.'

Once more an infuriating silence, I even stopped breathing in case I were to miss the next few words. But I wasn't given the chance either to miss them or to hear them for a harsh and hostile voice behind me said: 'What in the devil do you think you are doing here, sir?'

I refrained from doing what I felt like doing, which was to let loose with a few choice and uninhibited phrases, turned and looked up to find Otto's massively pear-shaped bulk looming massively above me. His fists were clenched, his puce complexion had darkened dangerously, his eyes were glaring and his lips were clamped in a thin line that threatened to disappear at any moment.

'You look upset, Mr Gerran,' I said. 'In point of fact, I was eavesdropping.' I pushed myself to my feet, dusted off the knees of my trousers, straightened and dusted off my hands. 'I can explain everything.'

'I'm waiting for your explanation.' He was fractionally more livid than ever. 'It should be interesting, Dr Marlowe.'

'I only said I can explain everything. *Can*, Mr Gerran. That doesn't mean I've got any intention of explaining anything. Come to that, what are you doing here?'

'What am I—what am I—?' He spluttered into outraged speechlessness, the year's top candidate for an instant coronary.

'God damn your impudence, sir! I'm about to go on watch! What are you doing at my daughter's door? I'm surprised you're not looking through that keyhole, Marlowe, instead of listening at it!'

'I don't have to look through keyholes,' I said reasonably. 'Miss Haynes is my patient and I'm a doctor. If I want to see her I just open the door and walk in. Well, then, now that you're on watch, I'll be on my way. Bed. I'm tired.'

'Bed! Bed! By God, I swear this, Marlowe, you'll regret —who's in there with her?'

'Lonnie Gilbert.'

'Lonnie Gilbert! What in the name of hell—stand aside, sir! Let me pass!'

I barred his way—physically. It was like stopping a small tank upholstered in Dunlopillo, but I had the advantage of having my back to the wall and he brought up a foot short of the door. 'I wouldn't, if I were you. They're having a rather painful moment in there. Lost, one might say, in the far from sweet remembrance of things past.'

'What the devil do you mean? What are you trying to tell me, you—you eavesdropper?'

'I'm not trying to tell you anything. Maybe, though, you'd tell me something? Maybe you would like to tell me something about that car crash—I assume that it must have been in California—in which Lonnie Gilbert's wife and two children were killed a long long time ago?'

He stopped being livid. He even stopped being his normal puce. Colour drained from his face to leave it ugly and mottled and stained with grey. 'Car crash?' He'd a much better control over his voice than he had over his complexion. 'What do you mean, "car crash", sir?'

'I don't know what I mean. That's why I'm asking you. I heard Lonnie, just snippets, talking about his family's fatal car crash, and as your daughter seemed to know something about it I assumed you would too.'

'I don't know what he's talking about. Nor you.' Otto, who seemed suddenly to have lost all his inquisitorial predilections, wheeled and walked up the passage to the centre of the cabin. I followed and walked to the outer door. Smithy was in for a hike, I thought, no doubt about it now. Although the cold was as intense as ever, the snow had stopped, the west wind dropped away to no more than an icily gentle breeze—

the fact that we were now in the lee of the Antarcticfjell might have accounted for that—and there were quite large patches of star-studded sky all around. There was a curious lightness, a luminescence in the atmosphere, too much to be accounted for by the presence of stars alone. I walked out a few paces until I was clear of the main cabin, and low to the south I could see a three-quarter moon riding in an empty sky.

I went back inside and as I closed the door I saw Lonnie crossing the main living area, heading, I assumed, for his cubicle. He walked uncertainly, like a man not seeing too well, and as he went by close to me I could see that his eyes were masked in tears: I would have given a lot to know just what it was that had been responsible for those tears. It was a mark of Lonnie's emotional upset that he did not so much as glance at the still three-quarter-full bottle of scotch on the small table by which Otto was sitting. He didn't even so much as look at Otto: more extraordinarily still, Otto didn't even look up at Lonnie's passing. In the mood he'd been in when he'd accosted me outside his daughter's door I'd have expected him to question Lonnie pretty closely, probably with both hands around the old man's neck: but Otto's mood, clearly, had undergone a considerable sea-change.

I was walking towards Luke, bent on rousing the faithful watchdog from his slumbers, when Otto suddenly heaved his bulk upright and made his way down the passage towards his daughter's cubicle. I didn't even hesitate, in for a penny, in for a pound. I followed him and took up my by now accustomed station outside Judith Haynes's door, although this time I didn't have to have resource to the keyhole again as Otto, in what was presumably his agitation, had left the door considerably ajar. Otto was addressing his daughter in a low harsh voice that was noticeably lacking in filial affection.

'What have you been saying, you young she-devil? What have you been saying? Car crash? Car crash? What lies have you been telling Gilbert, you blackmailing little bitch?'

'Get out of here!' Judith Haynes had abandoned the use of her dull and expressionless voice, although probably involuntarily. 'Leave me, you horrible, evil, old man. Get out, get out, get out!'

I leaned more closely to the crack between door and jamb. It wasn't every day one had the opportunity to listen to those family tête-à-têtes.

'By God, and I'll not have my own daughter cross me.' Otto had forgotten the need to talk in a low voice. 'I've put up with more than enough from you and that other idle worthless bastard of a blackmailer. What you did—'

'You dare to talk of Michael like that?' Her voice had gone very quiet and I shivered involuntarily at the sound of it. 'You talk of him like that and he's lying dead. Murdered. My husband. Well, Father dear, can I tell you about something you *don't* know that *I* know he was blackmailing you with? Shall I, Father dear? And shall I tell it to Johann Heissman too?'

There was a silence, then Otto said: 'You venomous little bitch!' He sounded as if he was trying to choke himself.

'Venomous! Venomous!' She laughed, a cracked and chilling sound. 'Coming from you, that's rich. Come now, Daddy dear, surely you remember 1938—why, even *I* can remember it. Poor old Johann, he ran, and ran, and ran, and all the time he ran the wrong way. Poor Uncle Johann. That's what you taught me to call him then, wasn't it, Daddy dear? Uncle Johann.'

I left, not because I had heard all that I wanted to hear but because I thought that this was a conversation that was not going to last very long and I could foresee a degree of awkwardness arising if Otto caught me outside his daughter's door a second time. Besides—I checked the time—Jungbeck, Otto's watch-mate, was due to make his appearance just at that moment and I didn't want him to find me where I was and, very likely, lose no time in telling his boss about it. So I returned to Luke, decided that there was no point in awakening him only to tell him to go to sleep again, poured myself a sort of morning nightcap and was about to savour it when I heard a feminine voice scream 'Get out, get out, get out', and saw Otto emerging hurriedly from his daughter's cubicle and as hurriedly close the door behind him. He waddled swiftly into the middle of the cabin, seized the whisky bottle without as much as by-your-leave—true, it was his own, but he didn't know that—poured himself a brimming measure and downed half of it at a gulp, his shaking hand spilling a fair proportion of it on the way up to his mouth.

'That was very thoughtless of you, Mr Gerran,' I said reproachfully. 'Upsetting your daughter like that. She's really a very sick girl and what she needs is tender affection, a measure of loving care.'

'Tender affection!' He was on the second half of his glass now and he spluttered much of it over his shirt front. 'Loving care! Jesus!' He splashed some more scotch into his glass and gradually subsided a little. By and by he became calm, almost thoughtful: when he spoke no one would have thought that only a few minutes previously his greatest yearning in life would have seemed to be to disembowel me. 'Maybe I wasn't as thoughtful as I ought to have been. But a hysterical girl, very hysterical. This actress temperament, you know. I'm afraid your sedatives aren't very effective, Dr Marlowe.'

'People's reactions to sedatives vary greatly, Mr Gerran. And unpredictably.'

'I'm not blaming you, not blaming you,' he said irritatedly. 'Care and attention. Yes, yes. But some rest, a damned good sleep is more important, if you ask me. How about another sedative—a more effective one this time? No danger in that, is there?'

'No. No harm in it. She did sound a bit—what shall we say?—worked up. But she's rather a self-willed person. If she refuses—'

'Ha! Self-willed! Try, anyway.' He seemed to lose interest in the subject and gazed moodily at the floor. He looked up without any enthusiasm as Jungbeck made a sleepy entrance, turned and shook Luke roughly by the shoulder. 'Wake up, man.' Luke stirred and opened bleary eyes. 'Bloody fine guard you are. Your watch is over. Go to bed.' Luke mumbled some sort of apology, rose stiffly and moved off.

'You might have let him be,' I said. 'He'll have to get up for the day inside a few hours anyway.'

'Too late now. Besides,' Otto added inconsequentially, 'I'm going to have the lot of them up inside two hours. Weather's cleared, there's a moon to travel by, we can all be where we want to be and ready to shoot as soon as there's enough light in the sky.' He glanced along the corridor where his daughter's cubicle was. 'Well, aren't you going to try?'

I nodded and left. Ten minutes' time—in the right circumstances which in this case were the wrong ones—can bring about a change in a person's features which just lies within the bounds of credibility. The face that had looked merely drawn so very recently, now looked haggard: she looked her real age and then ten hard and bitter years after that. She wept in a sore and aching silence and the tears flowed steadily down her temples and past the earlobes, the damp marks spreading on the grey rough linen of her pillow. I would not have thought it possible that I could ever feel such deep pity for this person and wish to comfort her: but that was how it was. I said: 'I think you should sleep now.'

'Why?' Her hands were clenched so tightly that the ivory of the knuckles showed. 'What does it matter? I'll have to wake up, won't I?'

'Yes, I know.' It was the sort of situation where, no matter what I said, the words would sound banal. 'But the sleep would do you good, Miss Haynes.'

'Well, yes,' she said. It was hard for her to speak through the quiet tears. 'All right. Make it a long sleep.'

So, like a fool, I made it a long sleep. Like an even greater fool I went to my cubicle and lay down. And, like the greatest fool of all, I went to sleep myself.

I slept for over four hours and awoke to an almost deserted cabin. Otto had indeed been as good as his word and had had everyone up and around at what they must have regarded as the most unreasonable crack of dawn. Understandably enough, neither he nor anyone else had seen fit to wake me: I was one of the few who had no functions to perform that day.

Otto and Conrad were the only two people in the main quarter of the cabin. Both were drinking coffee, but as both were heavily muffled they were clearly on the point of departure. Conrad said a civil good morning. Otto didn't bother. He informed me that the Count, Neal Divine, Allen, Cecil and Mary Darling had taken off with the Sno-Cat and cameras along Lerner's Way and that he and Conrad were following immediately. Hendriks and the Three Apostles were abroad with their sound-recording equipment. Smithy and Heyter had left over an hour previously for Tunheim. Initially, I found this vaguely disturbing, I would have thought that Smithy would have at least woken and spoken to me before leaving. On reflection, however, I found this omission less than disturbing: it was a measure of Smithy's confidence in himself and, by implication, my unspoken confidence in himself, that he had not thought it necessary to seek either advice or reassurance before his departure. Finally, Otto told me, Heissman and his hand-held camera, along with Jungbeck, had taken off on his location reconnaissance in the sixteen-foot work-boat: they had been accompanied by Goin, who had volunteered to stand in for the now absent Heyter.

Otto stood up, drained his cup and said: 'About my daughter, Dr Marlowe.'

'She'll be all right.' She would never again be all right.

'I'd like to talk to her before I go.' I couldn't begin to imagine a reason why he should wish to talk to her or she to him, but I refrained from comment. He went on: 'You have no objections? Medical ones, I mean?'

'No. Just straightforward commonsense ones. She's under heavy sedation. You couldn't even shake her awake.'

'But surely—'

'Two or three hours at the very least. If you don't want my advice, Mr Gerran, why ask for it?'

'Fair enough, fair enough. Leave her be.' He headed towards the outer door. 'Your plans for the day, Dr Marlowe?'

'Who's left here?' I said. 'Apart from your daughter and myself?'

He looked at me, his brows levelled in a frown, then said: 'Mary Stuart. Then there's Lonnie, Eddie and Sandy. Why?'

'They're asleep?'

'As far as I know. Why?'

'Someone has to bury Stryker.'

'Ah, yes, of course. Stryker. I hadn't forgotten, you know, but—yes, of course. Yes, yes. You—?'

'Yes.'

'I am in your debt. A ghastly business, ghastly, ghastly, ghastly. Thank you again, Dr Marlowe.' He waddled purposefully towards the door. 'Come, Charles, we are overdue.'

They left. I poured myself some coffee but had nothing to eat for it wasn't a morning for eating, went outside into the equipment shed and found myself a spade. The frozen snow was not too deep, not much more than a foot, but the permafrost had set into the ground and it cost me over an hour and a half and, what is always dangerous in those high latitudes, the loss of much sweat before I'd done what had to be done. I returned the spade and went inside quickly to change:

it was a fine clear morning of bitter cold with the sun not yet in the sky, but no morning for an overheated man to linger.

Five minutes later, a pair of binoculars slung round my neck, I closed the front door softly behind me. Despite the fact that it was now close on ten o'clock, Eddie, Sandy, Lonnie and Mary Stuart had not as yet put in an appearance. The presence of the first three would have given me no cause for concern for all were notorious for their aversion to any form of physical activity and it was extremely unlikely that any would have suggested that they accompany me on my outing: Mary Stuart might well have done so, for any number of reasons: curiosity, the wish to explore, because she'd been told to keep an eye on me, even, maybe, because she would have felt safer with me than being left behind at the cabin. But whatever her reasons might have been I most definitely didn't want Mary Stuart keeping an eye on me when I was setting out to keep an eye on Heissman.

But to keep an eye on Heissman I had first of all to find him, and Heissman, inconveniently and most annoyingly, was nowhere to be seen. The intention, as I had understood it, was that he, with Jungbeck and Goin, should cruise the Sor-hamna in the sixteen-footer, in search of likely background material. But there was no trace of their boat anywhere in the Sor-hamna, and from where I stood in the vicinity of the cabin I could take in the whole sweep of the bay at one glance. Against the remote possibility that the boat might have temporarily moved in behind one of the tiny islands on the east side of the bay I kept the glasses on those for a few minutes. Nothing stirred. Heissman, I was sure, had left the Sor-hamna.

He could have moved out to the open sea to the east by way of the northern tip of the island of Makehl, but this seemed unlikely. The northerly seas were white-capped and confused, and apart from the fact that Heissman was as far removed from the popular concept of an intrepid seaman as it was possible to imagine it seemed unlikely that he would have forgotten Smithy's warning the previous day about the dangers inherent in taking an open-pooped boat out in such weather. Much more likely, I thought, he'd moved south out of the Sor-hamna into the sheltered waters of the next bay to the south, the Evjebukta.

I, too, made my way south. Initially, I moved in a south-westerly direction to give the low cliffs of the bay as wide a berth as possible, not from any vertiginous fear of heights but because Hendriks and the Three Apostles were down there somewhere recording, or hoping to record, the cries of the kittiwake gulls, the fulmars, the black guillemots which were reputed to haunt those parts: I had no reason to fear anything at their hands, I just didn't want to go around arousing too much curiosity.

The going, diagonally upwards across a deceptively easy-looking slope, proved very laborious indeed. Mountaineering ability was not called for, which in view of my lack of expertise or anything resembling specialized equipment, was just as well: what was required was some form of in-built radar to enable me to detect the presence of hidden fissures and sudden dips in the smooth expanse of white, and in this, unfortunately, I was equally lacking, with the result that I fell abruptly and at fairly regular intervals into drifts of newly-formed snow that at times reached as high as my shoulders. There was no physical danger in this, the cushioning effect of newly-driven snow is almost absolute, but the effort of almost continuously extricating myself from those miniature ravines and struggling back up to something resembling terra firma—which even then had seldom less than twelve or fifteen inches of soft snow—was very wearing indeed. If it were so difficult for me to make progress along such relatively simple ground I wondered how Smithy and Heyter must be faring in the so much more wildly rugged mountainous terrain to the north.

It took me just on an hour and a half to cover less than a mile and arrive at a vantage point of a height of about five hundred feet that enabled me to see into the next bay—the Evjebukta. This wide U-shaped bay, stretching from Kapp Malmgren in the north-east to Kap Kolthoff in the south-west, was just over a mile in length and perhaps half of that in width: the entire coastline of the bay consisted of vertical cliffs, a bleak, forbidding and repellent stretch of grey water and precipitous limestone that offered no haven to those in peril on the sea.

I stretched out gratefully on the snow and, when the thumping of my heart and the rasping of my breathing had quietened sufficiently for me to hold a pair of binoculars steady, I used them to quarter the Evjebukta. It was completely bereft of life. The sun was up now, low over the south-eastern horizon, but even although it was in my eyes, visibility was good enough and the resolution of the binoculars such that I could have picked up a sea-gull floating on the waters. There were some little islands to the north of the bay and, of course, there were the cliffs immediately below me that blocked off all view of what might be happening at their feet: but if the boat was concealed either behind an island or under the cliffs, it was most unlikely that Heissman would remain in such positions long for there would be nothing to detain him.

I looked south beyond the tip of Kapp Kolthoff and there, beyond the protection of the headland, the sun glinted off the broken tops of white water. I was as certain as one could be without absolute proof that they would not have ventured beyond the protection of the point: Heissman's unseamanlike qualities apart, Goin was far too prudent a man to step unheedingly into anything that would even smack of danger.

How long I lay there waiting for the boat to appear either from behind an island or out from under the concealment of the nearest cliffs I didn't know: what I did know was that I suddenly became aware of the fact that I was shaking with the cold and that both hands and feet were almost completely benumbed. And I became aware of something else. For several minutes now I'd had the binoculars trained not on the north end of the bay but at the foot of the cliffs to the south on a spot where, about three hundred yards north-west of the tip of Kapp Kolthoff, there was a peculiar indentation in the cliff walls. Partly because of the fact that it appeared to bear to the right and out of sight behind one of the cliff-faces guarding the entrance, and partly because, due to the height of the cliffs and the fact that the sun was almost directly behind, the shadows cast were very deep, I was unable to make out any details beyond this narrow entrance. But that it was an entrance to some cove beyond I didn't doubt. Of any place within the reach of my binoculars it was the only one where the boat could have lain concealed: why anyone should wish to lie there at all was another matter altogether, a reason for which I couldn't even guess at. One thing was for certain, a landward investigation from where I lay was out of the question: even if I didn't break my neck in the minimum of the two-hour journey it would take me to get there, nothing would be achieved by making such a trip anyway, for not only did the descent of those beetling black cliffs seem quite suicidal but, even if it were impossibly accomplished, what lay at the end of it removed any uncertainty about the permanency of the awaiting reception: for there was no foreshore whatever, just the precipitous plunge of those limestone walls into the dark and icy seas.

Stiffly, clumsily, I rose and headed back towards the cabin. The trip back was easier than the outwards one for it was downhill, and by following my own tracks I was able to avoid most of the involuntary descents into the sunken snow-drifts that had punctuated my climb. Even so, it was nearer one o'clock than noon when I approached the cabin.

I was only a few paces distant when the main door opened and Mary Stuart appeared. One look at her and my heart turned over and something cold and leaden seemed to settle in the pit of my stomach. Dishevelled hair, a white and shocked face, eyes wild and full of fear, I'd have had to be blind not to know that somewhere, close, death had walked by again.

'Thank God!' Her voice was husky and full of tears. 'Thank God you're here! Please come quickly. Something terrible has happened.'

I didn't waste time asking her what, clearly I'd find out soon enough, just followed her running footsteps into the cabin and along the passage to Judith Haynes's opened door. Something terrible had indeed happened, but there had been no need for haste. Judith Haynes had fallen from her cot and was lying sideways on the floor, half-covered by her blanket which she'd apparently dragged down along with her. On the bed lay an opened and three parts empty bottle of barbiturate tablets, a few scattered over the bed: on the floor, its neck still clutched in her hand, lay a bottle of gin, also three-parts empty. I stooped and touched the marble forehead: even allowing for the icy atmosphere in the cubicle, she must have been dead for hours. Make it a long sleep, she'd said to me: make it a long sleep.

'Is she—is she—?' The dead make people speak in whispers.

'Can't you tell a dead person when you see one?' It was brutal of me but I felt flooding into me that cold anger that was to remain with me until we'd left the island.

'I—I didn't touch her. I—'

244

'When did you find her?'

'A minute ago. Two. I'd just made some food and coffee and I came to see—'

'Where are the others? Lonnie, Sandy, Eddie?'

'Where are—I don't know. They left a little while ago—said they were going for a walk.'

A likely tale. There was only one reason that would make at least two of the three walk as far as the front door. I said: 'Get them. You'll find them in the provision shed.'

'Provision shed? Why would they be there?'

'Because that's where Otto keeps his scotch.'

She left. I put the gin bottle and barbiturate bottle to one side, then I lifted Judith Haynes on to the bed for no better reason than that it seemed cruel to leave her lying on the wooden floor. I looked quickly around the cubicle, but I could see nothing that could be regarded as untoward or amiss. The window was still screwed in its closed position, the few clothes that she had unpacked neatly folded on a small chair. My eye kept returning to the gin bottle. Stryker had told me and I'd overheard her telling Lonnie that she never drank, had not drunk alcohol for many years: an abstainer does not habitually carry around a bottle of gin just on the off-chance that he or she may just suddenly feel thirsty.

Lonnie, Eddie and Sandy came in, trailing with them the redolence of a Highland distillery, but that was the only evidence of their sojourn in the provision shed; whatever they'd been like when Mary had found them, they were shocked cold sober now. They just stood there, staring at the dead woman and saying nothing: understandably, I suppose, they thought there was nothing they could usefully say.

I said: 'Mr Gerran must be informed that his daughter is dead. He's gone north to the next bay. He'll be easy to find—you've only got to follow the Sno-Cat's tracks. I think you should go together.'

'God love us all.' Lonnie spoke in a hushed and anguished reverence. 'The poor girl. The poor, poor lassie. First her man—and now this. Where's it all going to end, Doctor?'

'I don't know, Lonnie. Life's not always so kind, is it? No need to kill yourselves looking for Mr Gerran. A heart attack on top of this we can do without.'

'Poor little Judith,' Lonnie said. 'And what do we tell

Otto she died of? Alcohol and sleeping tablets—it's a pretty lethal combination, isn't it?'

'Frequently.'

They looked at each other uncertainly, then turned and left. Mary Stuart said: 'What can I do?'

'Stay there.' The harshness in my voice surprised me almost as much as it clearly surprised her. 'I want to talk to you'.

I found a towel and a handkerchief, wrapped the gin bottle in the former and the barbiturate bottle in the latter. I had a glimpse of Mary watching me, wide-eyed, in what could have been wonder or fear or both, then crossed to examine the dead woman, to see whether there were any visible marks on her. There wasn't much to examine—although she'd been in bed with blankets over her, she'd been fully clothed in parka and some kind of fur trousers. I didn't have to look long. I beckoned Mary across and pointed to a tiny puncture exposed by pushing back the hair on Judith Haynes's neck. Mary ran the tip of her tongue across dry lips and looked at me with sick eyes.

'Yes,' I said. 'Murdered. How do you feel about that, Mary dear?' The term was affectionate, the tone not.

'Murdered!' she whispered. 'Murdered!' She looked at the wrapped bottles, licked her lips again, made as if to speak and seemingly couldn't.

'There may be some gin inside her,' I conceded. 'Possibly even some barbiturate. I'd doubt it though—it's very hard to make people swallow anything when they're unconscious. Maybe there are no other fingerprints on the bottles—they could have been wiped off. But if we find only her fore-finger and thumb round the neck—well, you don't drink three-quarters of a bottle of gin holding it by the finger and thumb.' She stared in fascinated horror at the pin-prick in the neck and then I let the hair fall back. 'I don't know, but I think an injection of an overdose of morphine killed her. How do you feel about it, Mary dear?'

She looked at me pitifully but I wasn't wasting my pity on the living. She said: 'That's the second time you said that. Why did you say that?'

'Because it's partly your fault—and it may be a very large part—that she's dead. Oh, and very cleverly dead, I assure you. I'm very good at finding those things out—when it's too damn late. Rigged for suicide—only, I knew she never drank. Well?'

'I didn't kill her! Oh, God, I didn't kill her! I didn't, I didn't, I didn't!'

'And I hope to God you're not responsible for killing Smithy too,' I said savagely. 'If he doesn't come back, you're first in line as accessory. After murder.'

'Mr Smith!' Her bewilderment was total and totally pathetic. And I was totally unmoved. She said: 'Before God, I don't know what you're talking about.'

'Of course not. And you won't know what I'm talking about when I ask you what's going on between Gerran and Heissman. How could you—a sweet and innocent child like you? Or you wouldn't know what's going on between you and your dear loveable Uncle Johann?'

She stared at me in a dumb animal-like misery and shook her head. I struck her. Even although I was aware that the anger that was in me was directed more against myself than at her, still it could not be contained and I struck her, and when she looked at me the way a favourite pet would look at a person who has shot it but not quite killed it, I lifted my hand again but this time when she closed her eyes and flinched away, turning her head to one side, I let my hand drop helplessly to my side, then did what I should have done in the first place, I put my arms around her and held her tight. She didn't try to fight or struggle, just stood quite still. She had nothing left to fight with any more.

'Poor Mary dear,' I said. 'You've got no place left to run to, have you?' She made no answer, her eyes were still closed. 'Uncle Johann is no more your uncle than I am. Your immigration papers state that your father and mother are dead. It is my belief that they are still alive and that Heissman is no more your mother's brother than he is your uncle. It is my belief that he is holding them as hostage for your good conduct and that he is holding you as hostage for theirs. I don't just think that Heissman is up to no good, I know he is, for I don't just think he's a criminal operating on an international scale, I know that too. I know that you're not Latvian but strictly of German ancestry. I know too that your father ranked very highly in the Berlin councils of war.' I didn't know that at all, but it had become an increasingly safe guess. 'And I know too that there's a great deal of money involved, not in hard cash but in negotiable securities. All this is true, is it not?'

There was a silence then she said dully. 'If you know so much, what's the good in pretending any more.' She pushed back a little and looked at me through defeated eyes. 'You're not a real doctor?'

'I'm real enough, but not in the ordinary way of things, for which any patients I might have had would probably feel very thankful as I haven't practised these past good few years. I'm just a civil servant working for the British Government, nothing glamorous or romantic like Intelligence or counter-Intelligence, just the Treasury, which is why I'm here because we've been interested in Heissman's shenanigans for quite some time. I didn't expect to run into this other bus-load of trouble though.'

'What do you mean?'

'Too long to explain, even if I could. I can't, yet. And I've things to do.'

'Mr Smith?' She hesitated. 'From the Treasury too?' I nodded and she went on: 'I've been thinking that.' She hesitated again. 'My father commanded submarine groups during the war. He was also a high Party official, very high, I think. Then he disappeared—'

'Where was his command?'

'For the last year, the north—Tromso, Trondheim, Narvik, places like that, I'm not sure.' I was, all of a sudden I was, I knew it had to be true.

I said: 'Then disappearance. A war criminal?' She nodded. 'And now an old man?' Another nod. 'And amnestied because of age?'

'Yes, just over two years ago. Then he came back to us—Mr Heissman brought us all together, I don't know how.'

I could have explained Heissman's special background qualifications for this very job, but it was hardly the moment. I said: 'Your father's not only a war criminal, he's also a civil criminal—probably an embezzler on a grand scale. Yet you do all this for him?'

'For my mother.'

'I'm sorry.'

'I'm sorry too. I'm sorry for all the trouble I've given you. Do you think my mother will be all right?'

248

'I think so,' I said, which, considering my recent disastrous record in keeping people alive, was a pretty rash statement on my part.

'But what can we *do*? What on earth can we do with all those terrible things happening?'

'It's not what *we* can do. I know what to do. It's what you are going to do.'

'I'll do anything. Anything you say. I promise.'

'Then do nothing. Behave exactly as you've been behaving. Especially towards Uncle Johann. But never a word of our talk to him, never a word to anyone.'

'Not even to Charles?'

'Conrad? Least of all to him.'

'But I thought you liked—'

'Sure I do. But not half as much as our Charles likes you. He'd just up and clobber Heissman on the spot. I haven't,' I said bitterly, 'been displaying very much cleverness or finesse to date. Give me this one last chance.' I thought a bit about being clever, then said: 'One thing you can do. Let me know if you see anyone returning here. I'm going to look around a bit.'

Otto had almost as many locks as I had keys. As befitted the chairman of Olympus Productions, the producer of the film and the *de facto* leader of the expedition he carried a great number of bits and pieces of equipment with him. Most of the belongings were personal and most of these clothes, for although Otto, because of his spherical shape, was automatically excluded from the list of the top ten best-dressed men, his sartorial aspirations were of the most soaring, and he carried at least a dozen suits with him although what he intended to do with them on Bear Island was a matter for conjecture. More interestingly, he had two small squat brown suitcases that served merely as cover for two metal deed-boxes.

Those were hasp-bound with imposing brass padlocks that a blind and palsied pick-lock could have opened in under a minute, and it didn't take me much longer. The first contained nothing of importance, that was, to anyone except Otto: they consisted of hundreds of press clippings, no doubt carefully selected for the laudatory nature of their contents, and going back for twenty-odd years, all of them unanimous in extolling Otto's cinematic genius: precisely the sort of ego-feeding nourishment that Otto would carry around with him. The second deed-box contained papers of a purely financial nature, recorded Otto's transactions, incomes and outgoes over a number of years, and would have proved, I felt certain, fascinating reading for any Inland Revenue Inspector or law-abiding accountant, if there were any such around, but my interest in them was minimal: what did interest me though, and powerfully, was a collection of cancelled cheque-books, and as I couldn't see that those were going to be of any use to Otto in the Arctic I pocketed them, checked that everything was as I had found it, and left.

Goin, as befitted the firm's accountant, was also much given to keeping things under lock and key, but because the total of his impediments didn't come to much more than a quarter of Otto's, the search took correspondingly less time. Again as befitted an accountant, Goin's main concern was clearly with matters financial, and as this coincided with my own current interest I took with me three items that I judged likely to be handsomely rewarding of more leisured study. Those were the Olympus Productions salary lists, Goin's splendidly-padded private bank-book and a morocco diary that was full of items in some sort of private code but was nonetheless clearly concerned with money, for Goin hadn't bothered to construct a code for the columns of pounds and pence. There was nothing necessarily sinister about this: concern for privacy, especially other people's privacy, could be an admirable trait in an accountant.

In the next half-hour I went through four cubicles. In Heissman's I found what I had expected to find, nothing. A man with his background and experience would have discovered many years ago that the only safe place to file his records was inside his head. But he did have some innocuous items—I supposed he had used them in the production of the Olympus manifesto for the film—which were of interest to me, several large-scale charts of Bear Island. One of those I took.

Neal Divine's private papers revealed little of interest except a large number of unpaid bills, IOUs and a number of letters, all of them menacing in varying degrees, from an assortment of different bankers—a form of correspondence that went well with Divine's nervous, apprehensive and gener-

ally down-trodded mien. At the bottom of an old-fashioned
Gladstone in the Count's room I found a small black automatic, loaded, but as an envelope beside it contained a
current London licence for a gun this discovery might or
might not have significance: the number of law-abiding people
in law-abiding Britain who for divers law-abiding reasons
consider it prudent to own a gun are, in their total, quite remarkable. In the cubicle shared by Jungbeck and Heyter
I found nothing incriminating. But I was intrigued by a small
brown paper packet, sealed, that I found in Jungbeck's case. I
took this into the main cabin where Mary Stuart was moving
from window to window—there were four of them—keeping
watch.

'Nothing?' I said. She shook her head. 'Put on a kettle,
will you.'

'There's coffee there. And some food.'

'I don't want coffee. A kettle—water—half an inch will
do.' I handed her the packet. 'Steam this open for me, will
you?'

'Steam—what's in it?'

'If I knew that I wouldn't ask you to open it.'

I went into Lonnie's cubicle but it held nothing but
Lonnie's dreams—an album full of faded photographs. With
few exceptions, they were of his family—clearly Lonnie had
taken them himself. The first few showed a dark attractive
girl with a wavy shoulder-length thirties hair-do holding two
babies who were obviously twins. Later photographs showed
that the two babies were girls. As the years had passed Lonnie's
wife, changing hairstyles apart, had changed remarkably
little while the girls had grown up from page to page, until
eventually they had become two rather beautiful youngsters
very closely resembling their mother. In the last photograph,
about two-thirds of the way through the album, all three
were shown in white summer dresses of an unconscionable
length leaning against a dark open roadster: the two girls
would then have been about eighteen. I closed the album with
that guilty and uncomfortable feeling you have when you
stumble, however inadvertently, across another man's private
dreams.

I was crossing the passage to Eddie's room when Mary
called me. She had the package open and was holding the
contents in a white handkerchief. I said: 'That's clever.'

251

'Two thousand pounds,' she said wonderingly. 'All in new five-pound notes.'

'That's a lot of money.' They were not only new, they were in consecutive serial number order. I noted down the first and last numbers, tracing would be automatic and immediate: somebody was being very stupid indeed or very confident indeed. This was one item of what might be useful evidence that I did not appropriate but locked up again, re-sealed, in Jungbeck's case. When a man has that much money around he's apt to check on its continued presence pretty frequently.

Neither Eddie's nor Hendriks's cubicles revealed any item of interest, while the only thing I learned from a brief glance at Sandy's room was that he was just that modicum less scrupulous in obtaining his illicit supplies than Lonnie: Sandy stocked up on Otto's scotch by the bottleful. The Three Apostles' quarters I passed up: a search in there would, I was convinced, yield nothing. It never occurred to me to check on Conrad.

It was just after three o'clock, with the light beginning to fade from the sky, when I returned to the main cabin. Lonnie and the other two should have contacted Otto and the others a long time ago, their return, I should have thought, was considerably overdue. Mary, who had eaten—or said she had—gave me steak and chips, both of the frozen and pre-cooked variety, and I could see that she was worried. Heaven knew she had enough reason to be worried about a great number of things, but I guessed that her present worry was due to one particular cause.

'Where on earth can they all be?' she said. 'I'm *sure* something must have happened to them.'

'He'll be all right. They probably just went farther than they intended, that's all.'

'I hope so. It's getting dark and the snow's starting—' She broke off and looked at me in embarrassed accusation. 'You're very clever, aren't you?'

'I wish to God I were,' I said, and meant it. I pushed my almost uneaten meal away and rose. 'Thank you. Sorry, and it's nothing to do with your cooking, but I'm not hungry. I'll be in my room.'

'It's getting dark,' she repeated inconsequentially.

'I won't be long.'

I lay on my cot and looked at my haul from the various

cabins. I didn't have to look long and I didn't have to be possessed of any outstanding deductive powers to realize the significance of what I had before me. The salary lists were very instructive but not half so enlightening as the correspondence between Otto's cheque-books and Goin's bank-book. But the map—more precisely the detailed inset of the Evjebukta—was perhaps the most interesting of all. I was gazing at the map and having long, long thoughts about Mary Stuart's father when Mary Stuart herself came into my room.

'There's someone coming.'

'Who?'

'I don't know. It's too dark and there's snow falling.'

'What direction?'

'That way.' She pointed south.

'That'll be Hendriks and the Three Apostles.' I wrapped the papers up into a small towel and handed them to her. 'Hide those in your room.' I turned my medical bag upside down, brought a small coach-screwdriver from my pocket and began to unscrew the four metal studs that served as floor-rests.

'Yes, yes, of course.' She hesitated. 'Do you mind telling me—'

'There are shameless people around who wouldn't think twice of searching through a man's private possessions. Especially mine. If I'm not here, that's to say.' I'd removed the base and now started working free the flat black metal box that had fitted so snugly into the bottom.

'You're going out.' She said it mechanically, like one who is beyond surprise. 'Where?'

'Well, I'm not dropping in at the local, and that's for sure.' I took out the black box and handed it to her. 'Careful. Heavy. Hide that too—and hide it well.'

'But what—'

'Hurry up. I hear them at the door.'

She hurried up. I screwed the base of the bag back in position and went into the main cabin. Hendriks and the Three Apostles were there and from the way they clapped their arms together to restore circulation and in between sipped the hot coffee that Mary had left on the stove, they seemed to be more than happy to be back. Their happiness vanished abruptly when I told them briefly of Judith Haynes's death, and although, like the rest of the company, none of them had any cause to cherish any tender feelings towards the dead woman, the simple fact of the death of a person they knew and that this fresh death, suicide though it had been, had come so cruelly swiftly after the preceding murders, had the immediate effect of reducing them to a state of speechless shock, a state from which they weren't even beginning to recover when the door opened and Otto lurched in. He was gasping for air and seemed close to exhaustion, although such symptoms of physical distress, where Otto was concerned, were not in themselves necessarily indicative of recent and violent exertion: even the minor labour of tying his shoelaces made Otto huff and puff in an alarming fashion. I looked at him with what I hoped was a proper concern.

'Now, now, Mr Gerran, you must take it easy,' I said solicitously. 'I know this has been a terrible shock to you—'

'Where is she?' he said hoarsely. 'Where's my daughter? How in God's name—'

'In her cubicle.' He made to brush by me but I barred his way. 'In a moment, Mr Gerran. But I must see first that—well, you understand?'

He stared at me under lowered brows, then nodded impatiently to show that he understood, which was more than I did, and said: 'Be quick, please.'

'Seconds only.' I looked at Mary Stuart. 'Some brandy for Mr Gerran.'

What I had to do in Judith Haynes's cubicle took only ten seconds. I didn't want Otto asking awkward questions about why I'd so lovingly wrapped up the gin and barbiturate bottles, so, holding them gingerly by the tops of the necks, I unwrapped them, placed them in reasonably conspicuous positions and summoned Otto. He hung around for a bit, looking suitably stricken and making desolate sounds, but offered no resistance when I took his arm, suggested that he was achieving nothing by remaining there and led him outside.

In the passage he said: 'Suicide, of course?'

'No doubt about that.'

He sighed. 'God, how I reproach myself for—'

'You've nothing to reproach yourself with, Mr Gerran. You saw how completely broken she was at the news of her, husband's death. Just plain, old-fashioned grief.'

'It's good to have a man like you around in times like these,' Otto murmured. I met this in modest silence, led him back to his brandy and said: 'Where are the others?'

'Just a few minutes behind. I ran on ahead.'

'How come Lonnie and the other two took so long to find you?'

'It was a marvellous day for shooting. All background. We just kept moving on, every shot better than the last one. And then, of course, we had this damned rescue job. My God, if ever a location unit has been plagued with such ill luck—'

'Rescue job?' I hoped I sounded puzzled, that my tone didn't reflect my sudden chill.

'Heyter. Hurt himself.' Otto lowered some brandy and shook his head to show the burden of woes he was carrying. 'He and Smith were climbing when he fell. Ankle sprained or broken, I don't know. They could see us coming along Lerner's Way, heading more or less the way they'd gone, though they were much higher, of course. Seems Heyter persuaded Smith to carry on, said he'd be all right, he'd attract our attention.' Otto shook his head and drained his brandy. 'Fool!'

'I don't understand,' I said. I could hear the engine of the approaching Sno-Cat.

'Instead of just lying there till we came within shouting distance he tried to hobble down the hill towards us. Of course his blasted ankle gave way—he fell into a gully and knocked himself about pretty badly. God knows how long he was lying there unconscious, it was early afternoon before we heard his shouts for help. A most damnable job getting him down that hill, just damnable. Is that the Sno-Cat out there?'

I nodded. Otto heaved himself to his feet and we went towards the front door together. I said: 'Smithy? Did you see him?'

'Smith?' Otto looked at me in faint surprise. 'No, of course not. I told you, he'd gone on ahead.'

'Of course,' I said. 'I'd forgotten.'

The door opened from the outside just as we reached it. Conrad and the Count entered, half-carrying a Heyter who could only hop on one leg. His head hung exhaustedly, his chin on his chest, and his pale face was heavily bruised on both the right cheek and temple.

We got him on to a couch and I eased off his right boot.

The ankle was swollen and badly discoloured and bleeding slightly where the skin had been broken in several places. While Mary Stuart was heating some water, I propped him up, gave him some brandy, smiled at him in my most encouraging physician's fashion, commiserated with him on his ill luck and marked him down for death.

CHAPTER TWELVE

Otto's stocks of liquid cheer were taking a severe beating. It is a medical commonplace that there are those who, under severe stress, resort to the consumption of large quantities of food. Olympus Productions Ltd harboured none of those. The demand for food was non-existent, but, in a correspondingly inverse proportion, alcoholic solace was being eagerly sought, and the atmosphere in the cabin was powerfully redolent of that of a Glasgow public house when a Scottish soccer team has resoundingly defeated its ancient enemies from across the border. The sixteen people scattered around the cabin—the injured Heyter apart—showed no desire to repair to their cubicles, there was an unacknowledged and wholly illogical tacit assumption that if Judith Haynes could die in her cubicle anyone could. Instead, they sat scattered around in twos and threes, drinking silently or conversing in murmurs, furtive eyes forever moving around the others present, all deepening a cheerless and doom-laden air which stemmed not from Judith Haynes's death but from what might or might not be yet another impending disaster: although it was close on seven now, with the darkness total and the snow falling steadily out of the north, Heissman, Goin and Jungbeck had not yet returned.

Otto, unusually, sat by himself, chewing on a cigar but not drinking: he gave the impression of a man who is wondering what fearsome blow fate now has in store for him. I had talked to him briefly some little time previously and he had given it as his morose and unshakable opinion that all three of them had been drowned: none of them, as he had pointed out, knew the first thing about handling a boat. Even if they managed to survive more than a few minutes in those icy waters, what hope lay for them if they did swim to shore? If they reached a cliff-face, their fingers would only scrabble uselessly against the smoothly vertical rock until their strength gave out and they slid under: if they managed to scramble ashore at some more accessible point, the icy air would reach through their soaked clothes to their soaked bodies and freeze them to death almost instantly. If they didn't turn up, he said, and now he was sure they wouldn't, he was going to abandon the entire venture and wait for Smithy to bring help, and if that didn't come soon he would propose that the entire company strike out for the safety of Tunheim.

The entire company had momentarily fallen silent and Otto, looking across the cabin to where I was standing, gave a painful smile and said, as if in a desperate attempt to lighten the atmosphere: 'Come, come, Dr Marlowe, I see you haven't got a glass.'

'No,' I said. 'I don't think it's wise.

Otto looked around the cabin. If he was being harrowed by the contemplation of his rapidly dwindling stocks he was concealing his grief well. 'The others seem to think it's wise.'

'The others don't have to take into account the danger of exposing opened pores to zero temperatures.'

'What?' He peered at me. 'What's that supposed to mean?'

'It means that if Heissman, Jungbeck and Goin aren't back here in a very few minutes I intend to take the fourteen-footer and go to look for them.'

'What!' This in a very different tone of voice. Otto hauled himself painfully to his feet as he always did when he was preparing to appear impressive. 'Go to look for them? Are you mad, sir? Look for them, indeed. On a night like this, pitch dark, can't see a hand in front of your nose. No, by God, I've already lost too many people, far too many. I absolutely forbid it.'

'Have you taken into account that their engine may have just failed? That they're just drifting helplessly around, freezing to death by the minute while we sit here doing nothing?'

'I have and I don't believe it possible. The boat engines were overhauled completely before our departure and I know that Jungbeck is a very competent mechanic. The matter is not to be contemplated.'

'I'm going anyway.'

'I would remind you that that boat is company property.'

'Who's going to stop me taking it?'

Otto spluttered ineffectually, then said: 'You realize—'

'I realize.' I was tired of Otto. 'I'm fired.'

'You'd better fire me too then,' Conrad said. We all turned to look at him. 'I'm going along with him.'

I'd have expected no less from Conrad, he, after all, had been the one to initiate the search for Smithy soon after our landing. I didn't try to argue with him. I could see Mary Stuart with her hand on his arm, looking at him in dismay: if she couldn't dissuade him, I wasn't going to bother to try.

'Charles!' Otto was bringing the full weight of his authority to bear. 'I would remind you that you have a contract—'

'—— the contract,' Conrad said.

Otto stared at him in disbelief, clamped his lips quite shut, wheeled and headed for his cubicle. With his departure everybody, it seemed, started to speak at the same time. I crossed to where the Count was moodily drinking the inevitable brandy. He looked up and gave me a cheerless smile.

'If you want a third suicidal volunteer, my dear boy—'

'How long have you known Otto Gerran?'

'What's that?' He seemed momentarily at a loss, then quaffed some more brandy. 'Thirty-odd years. It's no secret. I knew him well in pre-war Vienna. Why do you—'

'You were in the film business then?'

'Yes and no.' He smiled in an oddly quizzical fashion. 'Again it's on the record. In the halcyon days, my dear fellow, when Count Tadeusz Leszczynsky—that's me—was, if not exactly a name to be conjured with, at least a man of considerable means. I was Otto's angel, his first backer.' Again a smile, this time amused. 'Why do you think I'm a member of the board?'

'What do you know of the circumstances of Heissman's sudden disappearance from Vienna in 1938?'

The Count stopped being amused. I said: 'So that's not on the record.' I paused to see if he would say anything and when he didn't I went on: 'Watch your back, Count.'

'My—my back?'

'That part of the anatomy that's so subject to being pierced by sharp objects or rapidly moving blunt ones. Or has it not occurred to you that the board of Olympus are falling off their lofty perches like so many stricken birds? One lying dead outside, another lying dead inside, and two more at peril or perhaps even perished on the high seas. What makes you think you should be so lucky? Beware the slings and arrows, Tadeusz. And you might tell Neal Divine and Lonnie to beware of the same things, at least while I'm gone. Especially Lonnie—I'd be glad if you made sure he doesn't

259

step outside this cabin in my absence. Very vulnerable things, backs.'

The Count sat in silence for some moments, his face not giving anything away, then he said: 'I'm sure I don't know what you're talking about.'

'I never for a moment thought you would.' I tapped the bulky pocket of his anorack. 'That's where it should be, not lying about uselessly in your cabin.'

'What, for heaven's sake?'

'Your 9 mm Beretta automatic.'

I left the Count on this suitably enigmatic note and moved across to where Lonnie was making hay while the sun shone. The hand that held his glass shook with an almost constant tremor and his eyes were glassy but his speech was as intelligible and lucid as ever.

'And once again our medical Lochinvar or was it Launcelot gallops forth to the rescue,' Lonnie intoned. 'I can't tell you, my dear boy, how my heart fills with pride—'

'Stay inside when I'm gone, Lonnie. Don't go beyond that door. Not once. Please. For me.'

'Merciful heavens!' Lonnie hiccoughed on a grand scale. 'One would think I am in danger.'

'You are. Believe me, you are.'

'Me? Me?' He was genuinely baffled. 'And who would wish ill to poor old harmless Lonnie?'

'You'd be astonished at the people who would wish ill to poor old harmless Lonnie. Dispensing for the moment with your homilies about the innate kindness of human nature, will you promise me, really promise me, that you won't go out tonight?'

'This is so important to you, then, my boy?'

'It is.'

'Very well. With this gnarled hand on a vat of the choicest malt—'

I left him to get on with what promised to be a very lengthy promise indeed and approached Conrad and Mary Stuart who seemed to be engaged in an argument that was as low-pitched as it was intense. They broke off and Mary Stuart put a beseeching hand on my arm. She said: 'Please, Dr Marlowe. Please tell Charles not to go. He'll listen to you, I know he will.' She shivered. 'I just *know* that something awful is going to happen tonight.'

'You may well be right at that,' I said. 'Mr Conrad, you are not expendable.'

I could, I immediately realized, have lighted upon a more fortunate turn of phrase. Instead of looking at Conrad she kept looking at me and the implications of what I'd said dawned on me quite some time after they had clearly dawned on her. She put both hands on my arm, looked at me with dull and hopeless eyes, then turned and walked towards her cubicle.

'Go after her,' I said to Conrad. 'Tell her—'

'No point. I'm going. She knows it.'

'Go after her and tell her to open her window and put that black box I gave her on the snow outside. Then close her window.'

Conrad looked at me closely, made as if to speak, then left. He was nobody's fool, he hadn't even given a nod that could have been interpreted as acknowledgment.

He was back within a minute. We pulled on all the outer clothes we could and furnished ourselves with four of the largest torches. On the way to the door, Mary Darling rose from where she was sitting beside a still badly battered Allen. 'Dr Marlowe.'

I put my head to where I figured her ear lay behind the tangled platinum hair and whispered: 'I'm wonderful?'

She nodded solemnly, eyes sad behind the huge horn-rimmed glasses, and kissed me. I didn't know what the audience thought of this little vignette and didn't much care: probably a last tender farewell to the good doctor before he moved out forever into the outer darkness. As the door closed behind us, Conrad said complainingly: 'She might have kissed me too.'

'I think you've done pretty well already,' I said. He had the grace to keep silent. With our torches off we moved across to what shelter was offered from the now quite heavily falling snow by the provisions hut and remained there for two or three minutes until we were quite certain that no one had it in mind to follow us. Then we moved round the side of the main cabin and picked up the black box outside Mary Stuart's window. She was standing there and I'm quite sure she saw us but she made no gesture or any attempt to wave goodbye: it seemed as if the two Marys had but one thought in common.

261

We made our way through the snow and the darkness down to the jetty, stowed the black box securely under the stern-sheets, started up the outboard—5½ horsepower only, but enough for a fourteen-footer—and cast off. As we came round the northern arm of the jetty Conrad said: 'Christ, it's as black as the Earl of Hell's waistcoat. How do you propose to set about it?'

'Set about what?'

'Finding Heissman and company, of course.'

'I couldn't care if I never saw that lot again,' I said candidly. 'I've no intention of trying to find them. On the contrary, all our best efforts are going to be brought to bear to avoid them.' While Conrad was silently mulling over this volte-face, I took the boat, the motor throttle right back for prudence's sake, just over a hundred yards out until we were close into the northern shore of the Sor-hamna and cut the engine. As the boat drifted to a stop I went for'ard and eased anchor and rope over the side.

'According to the chart,' I said, 'there are three fathoms here. According to the experts, that should mean about fifty feet of rope to prevent us from drifting. So, fifty feet. And as we're against the land and so can't be silhouetted, that should make us practically invisible to anyone approaching from the south. No smoking, of course.'

'Very funny,' Conrad said. Then, after a pause, he went on carefully: 'Who are you expecting to approach from the south?'

'Snow White and the Seven Dwarfs.'

'All right, all right. So you don't think there's anything wrong with them?'

'I think there's a great deal wrong with them, but not in the sense you mean.'

'Ah!' There was a silence which I took to be a very thoughtful one on his part. 'Speaking of Snow White.'

'Yes?'

'How about whiling away the time by telling me a fairy story?'

So I told everything I knew or thought I knew and he listened in complete silence throughout. When I finished I waited for comment but none came, so I said: 'I have your promise that you won't clobber Heissman on sight?'

'Reluctantly given, reluctantly given.' He shivered. 'Jesus, it's cold.'

'It will be. Listen.'

At first faintly, intermittently, through the falling snow and against the northerly wind, came the sound of an engine, closing: within two minutes the exhaust beat was sharp and distinct. Conrad said: 'Well, would you believe it. They got their motor fixed.'

We remained quietly where we were, bobbing gently at anchor and shivering in the deepening cold, as Heissman's boat rounded the northern arm of the jetty and cut its engine. Heissman, Goin and Jungbeck didn't just tie up and go ashore immediately, they remained by the jetty for over ten minutes. It was impossible to see what they were doing, the darkness and the snow made it impossible to see even the most shadowy outlines of their forms, but several times we could see the flickering of torch beams behind the jetty arm, several times I heard distinctly metallic thuds and twice I imagined I heard the splash of something heavy entering the water. Finally, we saw three pin-points of light move along the main arm of the jetty and disappear in the direction of the cabin.

Conrad said: 'I suppose, at this stage, I should have some intelligent questions to ask.'

'And I should have some intelligent answers. I think we'll have them soon. Get that anchor in, will you?'

I started up the outboard again and, keeping it at its lowest revolutions, moved eastwards for another two hundred yards, then turned south until, calculating that the combination of distance and the northerly wind had taken us safely out of earshot of the cabin, I judged the moment had come to open the throttle to its maximum.

Navigating, if that was the word for it, was easier than I had thought it would be. We'd been out more than long enough now to achieve the maximum in night-sight and I had little difficulty in making out the coastline to my right: even on a darker night than this it would have been difficult not to distinguish the sharp demarcation line between the blackness of the cliffs and the snow-covered hills stretching away beyond them. Neither was the sea as rough as I had feared it might be: choppy, but no more than that, the wind could hardly have lain in a more favourable quarter than it did that night.

Kapp Malmgren came up close on the starboard hand and I turned the boat more to the south-west to move into the Evjebukta, but not too much, for although the cliffs were easily enough discernible, objects low in the water and lying against their black background were virtually undetectable and I had no wish to run the boat on to the islands that I had observed that morning in the northern part of the bay.

For the first time since we'd weighed anchor Conrad spoke. He was possessed of an exemplary patience. Clearing his throat, he said: 'Is one permitted to ask a question?'

'You're even permitted to receive an answer. Remember those extraordinary stacks and pinnacles close by the cliffs when we were rounding the south of the island in the *Morning Rose*?'

'Oh blessed memory,' Conrad said yearningly.

'No need for heartbreak,' I said encouragingly. 'You'll be seeing her again tonight.'

'What!'

'Yes, indeed.'

'The *Morning Rose*?'

'None other. That is to say, I hope. But later. Those stacks were caused by erosion, which in turn was caused by tidal streams, storm waves and frost—island used to be much bigger than it is now, bits of it are falling into the sea all the time. This same erosion also caused caves to form in the cliffs. But it formed something else—I knew nothing about it until this afternoon—which I think must be unique in the world. Two or three hundred yards in from the southern tip of this bay, a promontory called Kapp Kolthoff, is a tiny horseshoe-shaped harbour—I saw it through the binoculars this morning.'

'You did?'

'I was out for a walk. At the inner end of this harbour there is an opening, not just any opening, but a tunnel that goes clear through to the other side of Kapp Kolthoff. It must be at least two hundred yards in length. It's called Perleporten. You have to have a large-scale map of Bear Island to find it. I got my hands on a large-scale map this afternoon.'

'That length? Straight through? It must be man-made.'

'Who the hell would spend a fortune tunnelling through two hundred yards of rock from A to B, when you can sail from A to B in five minutes? I mean, in Bear Island?'

'It's not very likely,' Conrad said. 'And you think Heissman and his friends may have been here?'

'I don't know where else they could have been. I looked every place I could look this morning in the Sor-hamna and in this bay. Nothing.'

Conrad said nothing, which was one of the things I liked about a man whom I was beginning to like very much. He could have asked a dozen questions to which there were as yet no answers, but because he knew there were none he refrained from asking them. The *Evinrude* kept purring along with reassuring steadiness and in about ten minutes I could see the outline of the cliffs on the south of the Evjebukta looming up. To the left, the tip of Kapp Kolthoff was clearly to be seen. I imagined I could see white breakers beyond.

'There can't possibly be anyone to see us,' I said, 'and we don't need our night-sight any more. I know there are no islands in the vicinity. Headlamps would be handy.'

Conrad moved up into the bows and switched on two of our powerful torches. Within two minutes I could see the sheer of dripping black cliffs less than a hundred yards ahead. I turned to starboard and paralleled the cliffs to the north-west. One minute later we had it—the eastward facing entrance to a tiny circular inlet. I throttled the motor right back and moved gingerly inside and almost at once we had it—a small semi-circular opening at the base of the south cliff. It seemed impossibly small. We drifted towards it at less than one knot. Conrad looked back over his shoulder.

'I'm claustrophobic.'

'Me too.'

'If we get stuck?'

'The sixteen-footer is bigger than this one.'

'*If* it was here. Ah, well, in for a penny, in for a pound.'

I crossed my mental fingers that Conrad would have cause to remember those words and eased the boat into the tunnel. It was bigger than it looked but not all that bigger. The waves and waters of countless æons had worn the rock walls as smooth as alabaster. Although it held a remarkably true direction almost due south it was clear, because of the varying widths and the varying heights of the tunnel roof, that the hand of man had never been near the Perleporten; then, suddenly, when Conrad called out and pointed ahead and

265

to the right, that wasn't so clear any more.

The opening in the wall, no more, really, than an indentation hardly distinguishable from one or two already passed, was, at its deepest, no more than six feet, but it was bounded by an odd flat shelf that varied from two to five feet in width. It looked as if it had been man-made, but then, there were so many curiously shaped rock formations in those parts that it might just possibly have resulted from natural causes. But there was one thing about that place that absolutely was in no way due to natural causes: a pile of grey-painted metal bars, neatly stacked in criss-cross symmetry.

Neither of us spoke. Conrad switched on the other two torches, pivoted their heads until they were facing upwards, and placed them all on the shelf, flooding the tiny area with light. Not without some difficulty we scrambled on to the shelf and looped the painter round one of the bars. Still without speaking I took the boat-hook and probed the bottom: it was less than five feet below the surface, and a very odd kind of rock it felt too. I guddled around some more, let the hook strike something at once hard and yielding and hauled it up. It was a half-inch chain, corroded in places, but still sound. I hauled some more and the end of another rectangular bar, identical in size to those on the shelf and secured to the chain by an eye-bolt, came into sight. It was badly discoloured. I lowered chain and bar back to the bottom.

Still in this uncanny silence I took a knife from my pocket and tested the surface of one of the bars. The metal, almost certainly lead, was soft and yielding, but it was no more than a covering skin, there was something harder beneath. I dug the knifeblade in hard and scraped away an inch of the lead. Something yellow glittered in the lamp-light.

'Well, now,' Conrad said. 'Jackpot, I believe, is the technical term.'

'Something like that.'

'And look at this.' Conrad reached behind the pile of bars and brought up a can of paint. It was labelled 'Instant Grey'.

'It seems to be very good stuff,' I said. I touched one of the bars. 'Quite dry. And, you must admit, quite clever. You saw off the eye-bolt, paint the whole lot over, and what do you have?'

'A ballast bar identical in size and colour to the ballast bars in the mock-up sub.'

'Ten out of ten,' I said. I hefted one of the bars. 'Just right for easy handling. A forty-pound ingot.'

'How do you know?'

'It's my Treasury training. Current value—say thirty thousnd dollars. How many bars in that pile, would you say?'

'A hundred. More.'

'And that's just for starters. Bulk is almost certainly still under water. Paint-brushes there?'

'Yes.' Conrad reached behind the pile but I checked him.

'Please not,' I said. 'Think of all those lovely fingerprints.'

Conrad said slowly: 'My mind's just engaged gear again.' He looked at the pile and said incredulously: 'Three million dollars?'

'Give or take a few per cent.'

'I think we'd better leave,' Conrad said. 'I'm coming all over avaricious.'

We left. As we emerged into the little circular bay we both looked back at the dark and menacing little tunnel. Conrad said: 'Who discovered this?'

'I have no idea.'

'Perleporten. What does that mean?'

'The gates of Pearl.'

'They came pretty close at that.'

'It wasn't a bad try.' The journey back was a great deal more unpleasant than the outward one had been, the seas were against us, the icy wind and the equally icy snow were in our faces, and because of the same snow the visibility was drastically reduced. But we made it inside an hour. Almost literally frozen stiff but at the same time contradictorily shaking with the cold, we tied the boat up. Conrad clambered up on to the jetty. I passed him the black box, cut about thirty feet off the boat's anchor rope and followed. I built a rope cradle round the box, fumbled with a pair of catches and opened a hinged cover section which comprised a third of the top plate and two-thirds of a side plate. In the near total darkness switches and dials were less than half-seen blurs, but I didn't need light to operate this instrument, which was a basically very simple affair anyway. I pulled out a manually operated telescopic aerial to its fullest extent and turned two switches. A dim green light glowed and a faint hum, that couldn't have been heard a yard away, came from the box.

'I always think it's so satisfactory when those little toys work,' Conrad said. 'But won't the snow gum up the works?'

'This little toy costs just over a thousand pounds. You can immerse it in acid, you can boil it in water, you can drop it from a four-story building. It still works. It's got a little sister that can be fired from a naval gun. I don't think a little snow will harm, do you?'

'I wouldn't think so.' He watched in silence as I lowered the box, pilot light facing the stonework, over the south arm of the pier, secured the rope to a bollard, made it fast round its base and concealed it with a scattering of snow. 'What's the range?'

'Forty miles. It won't require a quarter of that tonight.'

'And it's transmitting now?'

'It's transmitting now.'

We moved back to the main arm of the pier, brushing footmarks away with our gloves. I said: 'I wouldn't think they would have heard us coming back, but no chances. A weather eye, if you please.'

I was down inside the hull of the mock-up sub and had rejoined Conrad inside two minutes. He said: 'No trouble?'

'None. The two paints don't quite match. But you'd never notice it unless you were looking for it.'

We were not greeted like returning heroes. It would not be true to say that our return, or our early return, was greeted with anything like disappointment, but there was definitely an anti-climactic air to it; maybe they had already expended all their sympathies on Heissman, Jungbeck and Goin, who had claimed, predictably enough, that their engine had broken down in the late afternoon. Heissman thanked us properly enough but there was a faint trace of amused condescension to his thanks that would normally have aroused a degree of antagonism in me were it not for the fact that my antagonism towards Heissman was already so total that any deepening of it would have been quite impossible. So Conrad and I contented ourselves with making a show of expressing our relief to find the three voyagers alive while not troubling very much to conceal our chagrin. Conrad especially, was splendid at this: clearly, he had a considerable future as an actor.

The atmosphere in the cabin was almost unbearably funereal. I would have thought that the safe return of five of their company might have been cause for some subdued degree of rejoicing, but it may well have been that the very fact of our being alive only heightened the collective awareness of the dead woman lying in her cubicle. Heissman tried to tell us about the marvellous backgrounds he had found that day and I couldn't help reflecting that he was going to have a most hellishly difficult job in setting up camera and sound crews within the extraordinarily restrictive confines of the Perleporten tunnel: Heissman desisted when it became clear that no one was listening to him. Otto made a half-hearted attempt to establish some kind of working relationship with me and even went to the length of pressing some scotch upon me, which I accepted without thanks but drank nevertheless. He tried to make some feebly jocular remark about open pores and it being obvious that I didn't intend venturing forth again that night, and I didn't tell him, not just yet, that I did indeed intend to venture forth again that night but that as my proposed walk would take me no farther than the jetty it was unlikely that all the open pores in the world would incapacitate me.

I looked at my watch. Another ten minutes, no more. Then we would all go for that little walk, the four directors of Olympus Productions, Lonnie and myself. Just the six of us, no more. The four directors were already there and, given the time Lonnie normally took to regain contact with reality after a prolonged session with the only company left in the world that gave him any solace, it was time that he was here also. I went down the passage and into his cabin.

It was bitterly cold in there because the window was wide open, and it was wide open because that was the way that Lonnie had elected to leave his cubicle, which was quite empty. I picked up a torch that was lying by the rumpled cot and peered out of the window. The snow was still falling and steadily but not so heavily as to obscure the tracks that led away from the window. There were two sets of tracks. Lonnie had been persuaded to leave: not that he would have required much persuasion.

I ignored the curious looks that came my way as I went quickly through the main cabin and headed for the provisions hut. Its door was open but Lonnie was not there either. The only sure sign that he had been there was a half-full bottle of scotch with its screw-top off. So much for Lonnie and his mighty oath taken with his hand on a vat of the choicest malt.

The tracks outside the hut were numerous and confused: it was clear that my chances of isolating and following any particular set of those was minimal. I returned to the cabin and there was no lack of immediate volunteers for the search: Lonnie had never made an unwitting enemy in his life.

It was the Count who found him, inside a minute, face down in a deep drift behind the generator shed. He was already shrouded in white, so he must have been lying there for some time. He was clad in only shirt, pullover, trousers and what appeared to be a pair of ancient carpet slippers. The snow beside his head was stained yellow where the contents—or part of the contents—of yet another bottle, still clutched in his right hand, had been spilt.

We turned him over. If ever a man looked like a dead man it was Lonnie. His skin was ice-cold to the touch, his face the colour of old ivory, his glazed unmoving eyes were open to the falling snow, and there was no rise and fall to his chest, but on the off-chance that there might just be some substance in the old saw that a special providence looks after little children and drunks, I put my ear to his chest and thought I detected a faint and far-off murmur.

We carried him inside and laid him out on his cot. While oil heaters, hot-water bags and heated blankets were being brought in or prepared—apart from the general esteem in which Lonnie was held, everyone seemed almost pathetically eager to contribute to something constructive—I used my stethoscope and established that he did indeed have a heart-beat if such a term could be applied to something as weak and as fluttering as the wings of a wounded captive bird. I thought briefly of a heart stimulant and brandy and dismissed both ideas, both, in his touch-and-go condition, were as likely to kill him off as to have any good effect. So we just concentrated on heating up the frozen and lifeless-seeming body as quickly as possible, while four people continuously massaged ominously white feet and hands to try to restore some measure of circulation.

Fifteen minutes after we'd first found him he was perceptibly breathing again, a shallow and gasping fight for air, but breathing nevertheless. He was now as warm as artificial aids could make him, so I thanked the others and told them they could go: I asked the two Marys to stay behind as nurses, because I couldn't stay myself: by my watch, I was already ten minutes late.

Lonnie's eyes moved. No other part of him did, but his eyes moved. After a few moments they focused blearily on me: he was as conscious as he was likely to be for a long time.

'You bloody old fool!' I said. It was no way to talk to a man with one foot still halfway through death's door, but it was the way I felt. 'Why did you do it?'

'Aha!' His voice was a far-off whisper.

'Who took you out of here? Who gave you the drink?' I was aware that the two Marys had at first stared at me, then at each other, but the time was gone when it mattered what anyone thought.

Lonnie's lips moved soundlessly a few times. Then his eyes flickered shiftily and he gave a drunken cackle, no more than a faint rasping sound deep in his throat. 'A kind man,' he whispered weakly. 'Very kind man.'

I would have shaken him except for the fact that I would certainly have shaken the life out of him. I restrained myself with a considerable effort and said: 'What kind man, Lonnie?'

'Kind man,' he muttered. 'Kind man.' He lifted one thin wrist and beckoned. I bent towards him. 'Know something?' His voice was a fading murmur.

'Tell me, Lonnie.'

'In the end—' His voice trailed away.

'Yes, Lonnie?'

He made a great effort. 'In the end—' there was a long pause, I had to put my ear to his mouth—'in the end, there's only kindness.' He lowered his waxen eyelids.

I swore and I kept on swearing until I realized that both girls were staring at me with shocked eyes, they must have thought that I was swearing at Lonnie. I said to Mary Stuart: 'Go to Conrad—Charles. Tell him to tell the Count to come to my cubicle. Now. Conrad will know how to do it.'

She left without a question. Mary Darling said to me:

'Will Lonnie live, Dr Marlowe?'

'I don't know, Mary.'

'But—but he's quite warm now—'

'It won't be exposure that will kill him, if that's what you mean.'

She looked at me, the eyes behind the hornrims at once earnest and scared. 'You mean—you mean he might go from alcoholic poisoning?'

'He might. I don't know.'

She said, with a flash of that almost touching asperity that could be so characteristic of her: 'You don't really care, do you, Dr Marlowe?'

'No, I don't.' She looked at me, the pinched face shocked, and I put my arm round the thin shoulders. 'I don't care, Mary, because he doesn't care. Lonnie's been dead a long time now.'

I went back to my cubicle, found the Count there and wasted no words. I said: 'Are you aware that that was a deliberate attempt on Lonnie's life?'

'No. But I wondered.' The Count's customary cloak of badinage had fallen away completely.

'Do you know that Judith Haynes was murdered?'

'Murdered!' The Count was badly shaken and there was no pretence about it either.

'Somebody injected her with a lethal dose of morphine. Just for good measure, it was my hypodermic, my morphine.' He said nothing. 'So your rather illegal bullion hunt has turned out to be something more than fun and games.'

'Indeed it has.'

'You know you have been consorting with murderers?'

'I know now.'

'You know now. You know what interpretation the law will put on that?'

'I know that too.'

'You have your gun?' He nodded. 'You can use it?'

'I am a Polish count, sir.' A touch of the old Tadeusz.

'And very impressive a Polish count should look in a witness-box too,' I said. 'You are aware, of course, that your only hope is to turn Queen's Evidence?'

'Yes,' he said. 'I know that too.'

CHAPTER THIRTEEN

'Mr Gerran,' I said, 'I'd be grateful if you, Mr Heissman, Mr Goin and Tadeusz here would step outside with me for a moment.'

'Step outside?' Otto looked at his watch, his three fellow directors, his watch again and me in that order. 'On a night like this and at an hour like this? Whatever for?'

'Please.' I looked at the others in the cabin. 'I'd also be grateful if the rest of you remained here, in this room, till I return. I hope I won't be too long. You don't have to do as I ask and I'm certainly in no position to enforce my request, but I suggest it would be in your own best interests to do so. I know now, I've known since this morning, who the killer amongst us is. But before I put a name to this man I think it is only fair and right that I should first discuss the matter with Mr Gerran and his fellow directors.'

This brief address was received, not unsurprisingly, in total silence. Otto, predictably, was the one to break the silence: he cleared his throat and said carefully: 'You claim to know this man's identity?'

'I do.'

'You can substantiate this claim?'

'Prove it, you mean?'

'Yes.'

'No, I can't.'

'Ah!' Otto said significantly. He looked around the company and said: 'You're taking rather much upon yourself, are you not?'

'In what way?'

'This rather dictatorial attitude you've been increasingly adopting. Good God, man, if you've found, or think you've found our man, for God's sake tell us and don't make this big production out of it. It ill becomes any man to play God, Dr Marlowe, I would remind you that you're but one of a group, an employee, if you like, of Olympus Productions, just like—'

'I am not an employee of Olympus Productions. I am an

273

employee of the British Treasury who has been sent to investigate certain aspects of Olympus Productions Ltd. Those investigations are now completed.'

Otto over-reacted to the extent that he let his jaw drop. Goin didn't react much but his smooth and habitually bland face took on a wary expression that was quite foreign to it. Heissman said incredulously: 'A Government agent! A secret service—'

'You've got your countries mixed up. Government agents work for the US Treasury, not the British one. I'm just a civil servant and I've never fired a pistol in my life, far less carried one. I have as much official power as a postman or a Whitehall clerk. No more. That's why I'm asking for co-operation.' I looked at Otto. 'That's why I'm offering you what I regard as the courtesy of a prior consultation.'

'Investigations?' Clearly, I'd lost Otto at least half a minute previously. 'What kind of investigations? And how does it come that a man hired as doctor—' Otto broke off, shaking his head in the classic manner of one baffled beyond all hope of illumination.

'How do you think it came that none of the seven other applicants for the post of medical officer turned up for an interview? They don't teach us much about manners in medical school but we're not as rude as that. Shall we go?'

Goin said calmly: 'I think, Otto, that we should hear what he has to say.'

'I think I'd like to hear what you have to say too,' Conrad said. He was one of the very few in the cabin who wasn't looking at me as if I were some creature from outer space.

'I'm sure you would. However, I'm afraid you'll have to remain. But I would like a private word with you, if I may.' I turned without waiting for an answer and made for my cubicle. Otto barred my way.

'There's nothing you can have to say to Charles that you can't say to all of us.'

'How do you know?' I brushed roughly by him and closed the door when Conrad entered the cubicle. I said: 'I don't want you to come for two reasons. If our friends arrive, they may miss me down at the jetty and come straight here—I'd like you in that case to tell them where I am. More importantly, I'd like you to keep an eye on

Jungbeck. If he tries to leave, try to reason with him. If he won't listen to reason, let him go—about three feet. If you can just kind of naturally happen to have a full bottle of scotch or suchlike in your hand at the time, then clobber him with all you have. Not on the head—that would kill him. On the shoulder, close in to the neck. You'll probably break the odd bone: in any event it will surely incapacitate him.'

Conrad didn't as much as raise an eyebrow. He said: 'I can see why you don't bother with guns.'

'Socially and otherwise,' I said, 'a bottle of scotch is a great leveller.'

I'd taken a Coleman storm lantern along with me and now hung it on a rung of the vertical iron ladder leading down from the conning-tower to the interior of the submarine mock-up: its harsh glare threw that icily dank metallic tomb into a weirdly heterogeneous mélange of dazzling white and inkily black geometrical patterns. While the others watched me in a far from friendly silence, I unscrewed one of the wooden floor battens, lifted and placed a ballast bar on top of the compressor and scraped at the surface with the blade of my knife.

'You will observe,' I said to Otto, 'that I am not making a production of this. Prologues dispensed with, we arrive at the point without waste of time.' I closed my knife and inspected the handiwork it had wrought. 'All that glitters is not gold. But does this look like toffee to you?'

I looked at them each in turn. Clearly, it didn't look like toffee to any of them.

'A total lack of reaction, a total lack of surprise.' I put my knife back in my pocket and smiled at the stiffening attitudes of three out of the four of them. 'Scout's honour, we civil servants never carry guns. And why should there be surprise even at the fact of my knowledge—all four of you have been perfectly well aware for some time that I am not what I was engaged to be. And why should any of you express surprise at the sight of this gold—after all, that was the only reason for your coming to Bear Island in the first place.'

They said nothing. Curiously enough, they weren't even looking at me, they were all looking at the gold ingot as if it were vastly more important than I was, which, from their point of view, was probably a perfectly understandable priority preference.

'Dear me, dear me,' I said. 'Where are all the instant denials, the holier-than-thou clutching of the hearts, the outraged cries of "What in God's name are you talking about?" I would think, wouldn't you, that the unbiased observer would find this negative reaction every bit as incriminating as a written confession?' I looked at them with what might have been interpreted as an encouraging expression, but again—apart from Heissman's apparently finding it necessary to lubricate his lower lip with the tip of his tongue—I elicited no response, so I went on: 'It was, as even your defending counsel will have to admit in court, a clever and well thought-out scheme. Would any of you care to tell me what the scheme was?'

'It is my opinion, Dr Marlowe,' Otto said magisterially, 'that the strain of the past few days has made you mentally unbalanced.'

'Not a bad reaction at all,' I said approvingly. 'Unfortunately, you're about two minutes too late in coming up with it. No volunteers to set the scene, then? Do we suffer from an excess of modesty or just a lack of co-operation? Wouldn't you, for instance, Mr Goin, care to say a few words? After all, you are in my debt. Without me, without our dramatic little confrontation, you'd have been dead before the week was out.'

'I think Mr Gerran is right,' Goin said in that measured voice he knew so well how to use. 'Me? About to die?' He shook his head. 'The strain for you must have been intolerable. Under such circumstances, as a medical man, you should know that a person's imagination can easily—'

'Imagination? Am I imagining this forty-pound gold ingot?' I pointed to the ballast bars below the battens. 'Am I imagining those other fifteen ingots there? Am I imagining the hundred-odd ingots piled on a rock shelf inside the Perleporten? Am I imagining the fact that your total lack of reaction to the word Perleporten demonstrates beyond question that you all know what Perleporten is, where it is and what its significance is? Am I imagining the scores of other lead-sheathed ingots still under water in the Perleporten? Let's stop playing silly little games for your own game is up. As I say, quite a clever little game while it lasted. What better cover for a bullion-recovery trip to the Arctic than a film unit—after all, film people are widely regarded as being eccentric to the extent of being lunatic so that even their most ludicrous behaviour is accepted as being normal within its own abnormal context? What better time to set out to achieve the recovery of this bullion than when there are only a few hours' daylight so that the recovery operation can be carried out through the long hours of darkness? What better way of bringing the bullion back to Britain than by switching it with this vessel's ballast so that it can be slipped into the country under the eyes of the Customs authorities?' I surveyed the ballast. 'Four tons, according to this splendid brochure that Mr Heissman wrote. I'd put it nearer five. Say ten million dollars. Justifies a trip to even an out-of-the-way resort like Bear Island, I'd say. Wouldn't you?'

They wouldn't say anything.

'By and by,' I went on, 'you'd probably have manufactured some excuse for towing this vessel down to Perleporten so as to make the trans-shipment of the gold all that easier. And then heigh-ho for Merry England and the just enjoyment of the fruits of your labours. Could I be wrong?'

'No.' Otto was very calm. 'You're right. But I think you'd find it very hard to make a criminal case out of this. What could we possibly be charged with? Theft? Ridiculous. Finders, keepers.'

'Finders, keepers? A few miserable tons of gold? Your ambitions are only paltry, you're only skimming the surface of the available loot. Isn't that so, Heissman?'

They all looked at Heissman. Heissman, in turn, didn't appear particularly anxious to look at anyone.

'Why do you silly people think I'm here?' I said. 'Why do you think that, in spite of the elaborate smoke-screen you set up, the British Government not only knew that you were going to Bear Island but also knew that your purpose in going there was not as advertised? Don't you know that, in certain matters, European governments co-operate very closely? Don't you know that most of them share a keen interest in the activities of Johann Heissman? For what you don't know is that most of them know a great deal more about Johann Heissman than you do. Perhaps, Heissman, you'd like to tell them yourself—starting, shall we say, with the thirty-odd years you've been working for the Soviet government?'

Otto stared at Heissman, his huge jowls seeming to fall apart. Goin's facial muscles tightened until the habitual smooth blandness had vanished from his face. The Count's expression didn't change, he just nodded slowly as if understanding at last the solution of a long-standing problem. Heissman looked acutely unhappy.

'Well,' I said, 'as Heissman doesn't appear to have any intention of telling anyone anything, I suppose that leaves it up to me. Heissman, here, is a remarkably gifted specialist in an extremely specialized field. He is, purely and simply, a treasure-hunter, and there's no one in the business who can hold a candle to him. But he doesn't just hunt for the type of treasure that you people think he does: I fear he may have been deceiving you on this point, as, indeed, he has been deceiving you on another. I refer to the fact that a pre-condition of his cutting you into a share of the loot was that his niece, Mary Stuart, be employed by Olympus Productions. Having the nasty and suspicious minds that you do, you probably and rapidly arrived at the conclusion that she wasn't his niece at all—which she isn't—and was along for some other purposes—which she is. But not for the purposes which your nasty and suspicious minds attributed to her. For Heissman, Miss Stuart was essential for the achievement of an entirely different purpose which he kind of forgot to tell you about.

'Miss Stuart's father, you have to understand, was just as unscrupulous and unprincipled a rogue as any of you. He held very senior positions in both the German Navy and the Nazi Party and, like others similarly placed, used his power to feather his own nest—just as Hermann Goering did—when the war was seen to be lost, although he was smarter than Goering and managed to get out from under before the war-criminal round-up. The gold, although this will probably never be proved, almost certainly came from the vaults of Norwegian banks, and a man with all the resources of the German Navy behind him would have had no trouble in choosing such a splendidly isolated spot as Perleporten in Bear Island and having the stuff transferred there. Probably by submarine. Not that it matters.

'But it wasn't just the gold that was transported to Perleporten, which is why Mary Stuart is here. Feathers weren't enough for Dad's nest, nothing less than swansdown would do. The swansdown almost certainly took the form of either bank bonds or securities, probably obtained—I wouldn't say purchased—in the late thirties. Such securities are perfectly redeemable even today. An attempt was recently made to sell £30 millions' worth of such securities through foreign exchange, but the West German Federal Bank wouldn't play ball because proper owner-identification was lacking. But there wouldn't be any problem about owner-identification this time, would there, Heissman?'

Heissman didn't say whether there would or there wouldn't.

'And where are they?' I said. 'Nicely welded up in a dummy steel ingot?' As he still wasn't being very forthcoming, I went on: 'No matter, we'll have them. And then you're never going to have the pleasure of seeing Mary Stuart's father put his signature and fingerprints on those documents and of checking that they match up.'

'You're sure of that?' Heissman said. He had recovered his normal degree of composure, which meant that he was very composed indeed.

'In a changing world like ours who can be sure of anything? But with that proviso, yes.'

'I think you've overlooked something.'

'I have?'

'Yes. We have Admiral Hanneman.'

'That's Miss Stuart's father's true name?'

'You didn't even know that?'

'No. It's of no relevance. And no, I haven't overlooked that fact. I shall attend to that matter shortly. After I have attended to your friends. Maybe that's the wrong word, maybe they're not your friends any more. I mean, they don't *look* particularly friendly, do they?'

'Monstrous!' Otto shouted. 'Absolutely monstrous. Unforgivable! Diabolical! Our own partner!' He spluttered into an outraged silence.

'Despicable,' Goin said coldly. 'Absolutely contemptible.'

'Isn't it?' I said. 'Tell me, does this moral indignation stem from this revelation of the depths of Heissman's perfidy or merely because he omitted to cut you in on the proceeds of the cashing of the securities? Don't bother answering that question, it's purely rhetorical, as villains you're dyed in the same inky black as Heissman. What I mean is, most of you spend a great deal of time and careful thought in concealing from the other members of the board of Olympus Productions just what the true natures of your activities are. Heissman is hardly alone in this respect.

'Take the Count here. Compared to the rest of you he was a vestal angel, but even he dabbled in some murky waters. For over thirty years now he's been a member of the board and has had a free meal ticket for life because he happened to be in Vienna when the *Anschluss* came, when Otto headed for the States and Heissman was spirited away. Heissman was spirited away because Otto had arranged for him to be so that he could take all the film company's capital out of the country: Otto was never a man to hesitate when it came to selling a friend down the river.

'What Otto didn't know but what the Count did but carefully refrained from telling him was that Heissman's disappearance had been entirely voluntary. Heissman had been a German secret agent for some time and his adopted country needed him. What his adopted country didn't know was that Russia had adopted him even before they had, but this isn't germane to the main point: that Otto believed he had betrayed a friend for gold and that the Count knew it. Unfortunately, it's going to be very hard to prove anything against the Count, and not being a grasping man by nature, never having asked for anything more than his salary, there's nothing to demonstrate blackmail which is why I've chosen him—and he's accepted—as the person to turn Queen's Evidence against his fellow directors on the board.'

Heissman now joined Otto and Goin in giving the Count the kind of look they had so lately given him.

'Or take Otto,' I went on. 'For years he'd been embezzling very large sums of money from the company, virtually bleeding it white.' It was now the turn of Heissman and the Count to stare at Otto. 'Or take Goin. He discovered about the embezzling and for two or three years he's been blackmailing Otto and bleeding *him* white. In sum, you constitute the most unpleasant, unprincipled and depraved bunch it's ever

280

been my misfortune to encounter. But I haven't even scratched the surface of your infamy, have I? Or the infamy of one of you. We haven't even discussed the person responsible for the violent deaths that have taken place. He is, of course, one of you. He is, of course, quite, quite mad and will end his days in Broadmoor: although I have to admit that there's been a certain far from crazy logic in his thinking and actions. But a prison for the insane—one regrets the abolition of the death penalty—is a certainty: it may well be, Otto, as well as being the best you can hope for, that you won't live long after you get there.' Otto said nothing, the expression on his face remained unchanged. I went on: 'For your hired killers, of course, Jungbeck and Heyter, there will be life sentences in maximum security jails.'

The temperature in that icily cold metallic tomb had fallen to many degrees below freezing point, but everyone appeared to be completely unaware of the fact: the classic example of mind over matter, and heaven knew that minds could rarely have been more exclusively and almost obsessively possessed than those of the men in those weird and alien surroundings.

'Otto Gerran is an evil man,' I said, 'and the enormity of his crimes scarcely comes within the bounds of comprehension. However, one has to admit that he has had the most singularly wretched luck in his choice of business associates, and those associates must be held partly to blame for the terrible events that happened, for their extraordinary cupidity and selfishness drove Otto into a corner from which he could escape only by resorting to the most desperate measures.

'We have already established that three of you here have been blackmailing Otto steadily over the years. His other two fellow directors, his daughter and Stryker, joined wholeheartedly in what had become by this time a very popular pastime. They, however, used a very different basis for their blackmail. This basis I cannot as yet prove but the facts, I believe, will be established in time. The facts are concerned with a car crash that took place in California over twenty years ago. There were two cars involved. One of those belonged to Lonnie Gilbert and had three women inside—

his wife and two daughters, all of whom appeared to be considerably the worse for drink at the time. The other car belonged to the Strykers—but the Strykers were not in their car. The two people who were had, like Lonnie's family, been at the same party in the Strykers' house and, like Lonnie's family, were in an advanced state of intoxication. They were Otto and Neal Divine. Isn't that so, Otto?'

'There's nothing of this rubbish that can be proved.'

'Not yet. Now, Otto was driving the car, but when Divine recovered from the effects of the crash he was convinced— no doubt by Otto—that he had been at the wheel. So for years now Divine has been under the impression that he owes his immunity from manslaughter charges purely to Otto's silence. The salary lists show—'

'Where did you get the salary lists from?' Goin asked.

'From your cubicle—where I also found this splendid bank-book of yours. The lists show that Divine has been receiving only a pittance in salary for years. How admirable is our Otto. He not only makes a man take the responsibility for deaths which he himself has caused but in the process re-duces that man to the level of a serf and a pauper. The blackmailed doing some blackmailing on his own account. Makes for a pretty picture all round, does it not?

'But the Strykers knew who had really caused the crash for Otto had been driving when they left the house. So *they* sold their silence in return for jobs on the board of Olympus Productions and vastly inflated salaries. You are a lovable, lovable lot, aren't you? Do you know that this fat monster here actually tried to have Lonnie murdered tonight? Why? Because Judith Haynes, very shortly before she died, had told Lonnie the truth of what had happened in the car crash: so, of course, Lonnie would have been a danger to Otto as long as he had lived.

'I don't know who suggested this film expedition as a cover for getting the bullion. Heissman, I suppose. Not that it matters. What matters is that Otto saw in this proposed trip a unique and probably never to be repeated opportunity to solve all his troubles at one stroke. The solution was simple—eliminate all his five partners, including his daughter whom he hated as much as she hated him. So he gets him-self two guns for hire, Heyter and Jungbeck—no question about the hire aspect, I found two thousand pounds in five-pound notes in Jungbeck's case this afternoon: two alleged actors of whom no one but Otto had ever heard.

'In effect, Otto would clear his board in one fell sweep. He'd get rid of the people he hated and who hated him. He'd buy enough time by their deaths to conceal his embezzlement. He'd collect very considerable insurance money and get back in the black with the help of accommodating accountants who can be as venal as the next lot. He would get all that lovely gold for himself. And, above all, he'd be for ever free of the continuous blackmail that had dominated his life and warped his mind until it drove him over the edge of insanity.' I looked at Goin. 'Do you understand now what I mean by saying that without me you'd have been dead by the end of the week?'

'Yes. Yes, I think so. I have no option other than to believe you are right.' He looked at Otto in a kind of wonder. 'But if he was only after the board of directors—'

'Why should others die? Ill luck, ill management, or someone just got in his way. The first intended victim was the Count, and this was where the ill luck came in. Not the Count's—Antonio's. Otto, as I think digging into his past will show, is a man of many parts. Among some of the more esoteric skills acquired were some relating to either chemistry or medicine: Otto is at home with poisons. He is also, as so many very fat men are, extremely gifted at palming articles. At the table on the night when Antonio died the food, as usual, was served from the side table at the top of the main table where Otto sat. Otto introduced some aconite—only a pinch was necessary—into the horseradish on the plate intended for the Count. Unfortunately for poor Antonio, the Count has a profound dislike of horseradish and passed his on to the vegetarian Antonio. And so Antonio died.

'He tried to poison Heissman at the same time. But Heissman wasn't feeling in the best of form that evening, were you, Heissman—you will recall that you left the table in a great hurry, your plate untouched. The economical Haggerty, instead of consigning this clearly untouched plate to the gash bucket, put it back in the casserole from which the two stewards, Scott and Moxen, were served later that night—and from which the Duke stole a few surreptitious mouthfuls. Three became very ill, two died—all through ill luck.'

'Aren't you overlooking the fact that Otto himself was poisoned?' the Count said.

'Sure he was. By his own hand. To obviate any suspicion that might fall on him. He didn't use aconite though—all that was required was some relatively harmless emetic and some acting. This, incidentally, was why Otto sent me off on a tour of the *Morning Rose*—not to check on sea-sickness but to see who else he might have poisoned by accident. His reaction when he heard of Antonio's death was unnaturally violent—though I didn't get the significance at the time.

'Matters took another tragic turn later that evening. Two people came to check my cabin in my absence—one was either Jungbeck or Heyter and the other was Halliday.' I looked at Heissman. 'He was your man, wasn't he?'

Heissman nodded silently.

'Heissman was suspicious of me. He wanted to check on my *bona fides* and examined my cases—had them examined, rather, by Halliday. Otto was suspicious and one of his hired men discovered that I'd been reading an article about aconite. One death more or less wasn't going to mean much to Otto now, so he planned to eliminate me, using his favourite eliminator—poison. In a bottle of scotch. Unfortunately for Halliday, who had come to see if he could lay hands on the medical case that I'd taken up to the saloon, he drank the night-cap intended for me.

'The other deaths are easy to explain. When the party was searching for Smithy, Jungbeck and Heyter clobbered Allen and killed Stryker in this clumsy attempt to frame Allen. And, during the night, Otto arranged for the execution of his own daughter. He was on watch with Jungbeck and the murder could only have occurred during that time.' I looked at Otto. 'You should have checked on your daughter's window—I'd screwed it shut so that it was impossible for anyone to have entered from the outside. I'd also found that a hypodermic and a phial of morphine had been stolen. You don't have to admit any of this—both Jungbeck and Heyter will sing like canaries.'

'I admit everything.' Otto spoke with a massive calm. 'You are correct in every detail. Not that I see that any of it is going to do you any good.' I'd said that he was an artist in palming things and he proceeded to prove it. The very unpleasant-looking little black automatic that he held in his hand just seemed to have materialized there.

'I don't see that that's going to do you any good either,' I said. 'After all, you've just admitted that you're guilty of everything I claimed you were.' I was standing directly under the conning-tower hatchway, where I'd deliberately and advisedly positioned myself as soon as we'd arrived, and I could see things that Otto couldn't. 'Where do you think the *Morning Rose* is now?'

'What was that?' I didn't much like the way his pudgy little hand tightened round the butt of his gun.

'She never went farther than Tunheim where there have been people up there waiting to hear from me. True, they couldn't hear by direct radio contact, because you'd had one of your hard men smash the trawler's receiver, hadn't you? But before the *Morning Rose* left here I'd left aboard a radio device that tunes into a radio homer. They had clear instructions as to what to do the moment that device was actuated by the homer transmitter. It's been transmitting for almost ninety minutes now. There are armed soldiers and police officers of both Norway and Britain aboard that trawler. Rather, they were. They're aboard this vessel now. Please take my word for it. Otherwise we have useless bloodshed.'

Otto didn't take my word for it. He stepped forward quickly, raising his gun as he peered up towards the conning-tower. Unfortunately for Otto, he was standing in a brightly-lit spot while peering up into the darkness. The sound of a shot, hurtful to the ears in that enclosed space, came at the same instant as his scream of pain, followed by a metallic clunk as the gun falling from his bloodied hand struck a bar of bullion.

'I'm sorry,' I said. 'You didn't give me time to tell you that they were specially picked soldiers.'

Four men descended into the body of the vessel. Two were in civilian clothes, two in Norwegian Army uniforms. One of the civilians said to me: 'Dr Marlowe?' I nodded, and he went on: 'Inspector Matthewson. This is Inspector Nielson. It looks as if we were on time?'

'Yes, thank you.' They weren't in time to save Antonio

285

and Halliday, the two stewards, Judith Haynes and her husband. But that was entirely my fault. 'You were very prompt indeed.'

'We've been here for some time. We actually saw you go below. We came ashore by rubber dinghy from the outside, north of Makehl. Captain Imrie didn't much fancy coming up the Sor-hamna at night. I don't think he sees too well.'

'But I do.' The harsh voice came from above. 'Drop that gun! Drop it or I'll kill you.' Heyter's voice carried utter conviction. There was only one person carrying a gun, the soldier who had shot Otto, and he dropped it without hesitation at a sharp word from the Norwegian inspector. Heyter climbed down into the hull, his eyes watchful, his gun moving in a slight arc.

'Well done, Heyter, well done.' Otto moaned from the pain of his shattered hand.

'Well done?' I said. 'You want to be responsible for another death? You want this to be the last thing Heyter ever does, well or not?'

'Too late for words.' Otto's puce face had turned grey, the blood was dripping steadily on to the gold. 'Too late.'

'Too late? You fool, I knew that Heyter was mobile. You'd forgotten I was a doctor, even if not much of a one. He'd a badly cut ankle inside a thick leather boot. That could only have been caused by a compound fracture. There was no such fracture. A sprained ankle doesn't cut the skin open. A self-inflicted injury. As in killing Stryker, so in killing Smith—a crude and total lack of imagination. You did kill him, didn't you, Heyter?'

'Yes.' He turned his gun on me. 'I like killing people.'

'Put that gun down or you're a dead man.'

He swore at me, viciously and in contempt, and was still swearing when the red rose bloomed in the centre of his forehead. The Count lowered his Beretta, dark smoke still wisping from its muzzle, and said apologetically, 'Well, I *was* a Polish count. But we do get out of practice, you know.'

'I can see that,' I said. 'A rotten shot but I guess it's worth a royal pardon at that.'

On the jetty, the police inspectors insisted on handcuffing Goin, Heissman and even the wounded Otto. I persuaded them that the Count was not a danger and further persuaded them to let me have a word with Heissman while they made their way up to the cabin. When we were alone I said: 'The water in the harbour there is below the normally accepted freezing point. With those heavy clothes and your wrists handcuffed behind your back you'll be dead in thirty seconds. That's the advantage of being a doctor, one can be fairly definite about those things.' I took him by the arm and pushed him towards the edge of the jetty.

He said in a high-strained voice: 'You had Heyter deliberately killed, didn't you?'

'Of course. Didn't you know—there's no death penalty in England now. Up here, there's no problem. Goodbye, Heissman.'

'I swear it! I swear it!' His voice was now close to a scream. 'I'll have Mary Stuart's parents released and safely reunited. I swear it! I swear it!'

'It's your life, Heissman.'

'Yes.' He shivered violently and it wasn't because of the bitter wind. 'Yes, I know that.'

The atmosphere in the cabin was extraordinarily quiet and subdued. It stemmed, I suppose, from that reaction which is the inevitable concomitant of profound and still as yet unbelieving relief. Matthewson, clearly, had been explaining things.

Jungbeck was lying on the floor, his right hand clutching his left shoulder and moaning as if in great pain. I looked at Conrad, who looked at the fallen man and then pointed to the broken shards of glass on the floor.

'I did as you asked,' he said. 'I'm afraid the bottle broke.'

'I'm sorry about that,' I said. 'The scotch, I mean.' I looked at Mary Darling, who was sobbing bitterly, and at Mary Stuart who was trying to comfort her and looked only fractionally less unhappy. I said reprovingly: 'Tears, idle tears, my two Marys. It's all over now.'

'Lonnie's dead.' Big blurred eyes staring miserably from behind huge glasses. 'Five minutes ago. He just died.'

'I'm sorry,' I said. 'But no tears for Lonnie. His words, not mine. "He hates him who would on the rack of this rough world stretch him out longer." '

She looked at me uncomprehendingly. 'Did he say that?'

'No. Chap called Kent.'

'He said something else,' Mary Stuart said. 'He said we were to tell the kindly healer—I suppose he meant you—to bring his penny to toss for the first round of drinks in some bar. I didn't understand. A four-ale bar.'

'It wouldn't have been in purgatory?'

'Purgatory? Oh, I don't know. It didn't make any sense to me.'

'It makes sense to me,' I said. 'I won't forget my penny.'

BOOK ONE

TALES OF THE CANADIAN NORTHLAND

" And the dingy, empty cabin was transformed, and took on again something of the glamour of its former days, and seemed once more an enchanted hall of dreams. So that it was no more an abandoned heap of logs and relics, but was once again . . . in all its former glory.

" And quite suddenly the place that had seemed to be so lonely and deserted was now no longer empty, but all at once was filled with living memories and ghosts from out the past."

LEGEND

The Narrator sits before a fire, smoking, musing, lost in meditation, as the Past lives again in the changing embers.

The little whorls of smoke move across the hollow space beneath the coals, like actors on a stage.

And then the Narrator speaks, slowly, quietly; and pauses often, seeming to give ear to some old echoes in his memory.

Comes a sound, a low, melancholy moaning that rises slowly in crescendo to a sobbing wail that carries the seeming burden of centuries of wrong, and then trails off in oft repeated, ever lessening echo, and so to Silence.

And as the lingering vibrations die, and cease at last, the voice of the Narrator again takes up the Tales of the Empty Cabin.

The fire flares up, then dies; shadows flicker, hesitantly, back and forth.

The Narrator speaks on . . .

I

The Empty Cabin

In a valley deep amongst the looming hills that sweep in heaving undulation Northward from the Height of Land, there lies a little hidden, nameless lake.

It is not beautiful, this narrow, shallow pond, for receding waters have left on the margin of its shores a waste of swamp and cat-tails, and protruding rocks that, once submerged, now stand out bleached and bleakly naked at every angle, like neglected headstones in some long forgotten graveyard.

From the foot of it there winds a portage trail on which no foot of man has trod in recent years, and cluttered with fallen timber, that leads on downstream to a landing on a larger lake which, in its turn, empties into a chain of waters, that ever increasing in size and volume with the tributaries that fall into them from off the Great Divide, eventually become a roaring, rushing river that pours its flood into the Arctic Sea.

At the outlet of this obscure and sunken source that once had been a lake of some account, is an old and long untended beaver dam, a monument to the energy and patience of its builders, its summit a full four feet above the present level of the sheet of water; and at the eroded centre of its arc a small stream trickles through, seeming to mutter drowsily as it goes. And the sound it makes is like a voice that speaks indistinctly in a dream, so that what it says is lost.

All around are works, very old, yet having about them a remarkable air of permanency and purposeful intention; though none of them are of man's construction or devising.

Inclining down towards the lake, from out the woods along the shore line, are disused runways, the hauling trails of a long-departed colony of beaver, well laid as to grade and opportunity and bearing, even after a lapse of many years, the hall-marks of the skill and labour expended on their making; and at the head of these highways, down which the expertly felled trees had been transported, are innumerable stumps, the very teeth marks of the workers still discernible upon them. Nearby there is a beaver house, its tenants long since gathered to their fathers, stranded high beyond the fallen water's edge, its secret entrance now exposed to prying eyes, and its once well plastered walls all overgrown with hay and willow saplings; yet staunch and strong for many years to come—a mute and melancholy lasting tribute to the perseverence of its builders.

Opposite the lodge is a grove of pine trees, looming huge and dark above the prospect; uncommon trees beyond the Great Divide, and on account of this rarity seeming to stand in grim exclusiveness, remote and unapproachable, above the common run of trees that hem them in. Among them are interspersed a scattering of pale birches, slim and tall-appearing, though their bright green tops, seeking the life-giving light of the sun, scarcely reach above the lower limbs of the towering conifers.

In the shelter of this glade, solitary evidence of man's sojourn here, is a small log cabin, tenantless and lonely, the moss chinking long since fallen from the gaps between the timbers, its door ajar, and its windows staring blankly out at the beholder. A humble habitation it had been, even at its best; yet much care had been bestowed on its construction, and rude but not inartistic ornaments, of which some still remain, had at one time decked its bare and plain simplicity. And Happiness had been there too, for within it, in a corner, there stands a little withered spruce, the strings that once had held some gifts still hanging from its brown and withered branches. Neglected and abandoned, now mouldering to slow decay, it once had been a place of life and movement, of hope, ambition and adventure. Living things had used it for a shelter and a home, and besides the relics of its one-time human occupants, there can be plainly seen, beneath the poles of what had been the bunk, a rampart of sticks and dried-out mud, bearing, in its solidity and style, the unmistakable sign manual of the race and kindred of the builders of the beaver lodge across the pond.

For in its way, this humble habitation had been a rather celebrated place in days gone by, and all manner of creatures had befriended those who dwelt there, and had sometimes entered in to find a home, and others had gathered around it to enjoy the sanctuary they found there, in little troops and bands and pairs and individuals, both small beasts and great ones, and birds and men. Here each had had his day, and for a little time had trod upon this unpretentious stage and said his piece and played his part, and added to the history of the place.

The grove had known them all and known them well. None the less, the great pines, ancient, lofty and aloof, their plumed heads remote in contemplation of the valley, could well have been unconscious of those puny, short-lived creatures that for so brief a time had had their being at the foot of them.

Although so long deserted, so silent and so still, the place seems yet to live, to reflect some strange influence, vague, shadowy and undefinable; as though it held an echo of what had gone before, or resounded, very softly, to some lingering chord of music that thrummed on and on, long after the player had gone and was forgotten. And as some passing breeze flutters the leaves of the tall and graceful birches, that like slim girls stand docilely modest and demure among the haughty, lordly pine trees, they seem to nod and whisper and to talk, their upward reaching limbs like arms that claim attention, as though they were so many Sheherazades who, fearing to be choked and utterly extinguished in the sunless grottos in which they stand, they seek to gain reprieve by the recital to their grim and over-bearing escort, of the tales of the empty cabin. The events that went to make some of those tales, had occurred in widely separated places, and of these, many had been told within the cabin, told to a woman by a man one lonely Winter long, long ago, as they sat before a fire and watched the embers glow and fade, while pictures and little forms and faces came and went within this fiery auditorium, and called to mind some old-time scene, or stirred some memory of earlier days; and all these reminiscences the birches heard and had, no doubt, remembered.

And much, besides, had happened here. And those, man and beast, who dwelt here and those who only stayed awhile and others who passed by, left each his mark of thought, or word, or deed; and none of it was lost. And all the joy, the sorrow, the comedy and the tragedy, the trial and tribulation, the labour and achievement that were here enacted or accomplished or related, are indelibly recorded in the timeless recollection of the brooding hills, in stories that are now but memories; but memories that cannot ever fade whilst yet the nodding birches whisper them, and the stern escarpments of the Height of Land stand watch and guard upon them all.

They are borne, these unforgotten chronicles, upon the winds that drift and hover in the tree-tops, and they sigh among the rushes in the fen-lands; they are mirrored on the surface of the pond, and are repeated in the faltering murmur of the tiny brook and by all the myriad voices of the Wild-lands that are never stilled.

And somehow the actors in these scenes, those with two feet, and those with four, and others that had wings, those who lived here and others from afar, will never quite be gone; and long after they that sojourned here and here-about, and what they did or told, has become but legend and tradition, their souls will linger on. The aura of their vanished presence has settled in the memory-haunted vale, and will ever invest the still lake, the broken dam, the deserted lodge and the ruined, empty cabin, and the environs about them, with something of their lives, and aims, and being.

So that a watcher who perchance should wait there quite alone at twilight may fancy that he sees, in the fast fading light, a dark object swimming at the head of a rippling, ever-widening V towards the ancient, empty beaver lodge, and maybe catch the echo of a long, low, plaintive call; or espy through the wispy mists from off the neighbouring marshes, the scarce distinguished, swift and soundless passage of a yellow bark canoe.

And as he sits so silently and still, he may even feel upon his shoulder a light and evanescent touch, as of some unseen presence that would speak with him; and suddenly the steady, ceaseless rumor of the little stream, rising and falling, now approaching, now receding, can be no longer heard, and in its place there comes, as from a distance, the sound of low voices in a tongue he does not understand. Or perhaps he may catch a fleeting glimpse, a momentary movement in the darkness of the grove behind him, and turning, find gathered there a company of pensive, gazing shadows. And these gentle shades will hold no terrors for the lonely traveller; and in a sighing that is soft as the rustling of the sedge-grass, light as the shifting of the birch leaves, will seem to try and hold communion with him, and to plead wistfully for understanding, with one whose sympathy has so awakened them from out the dim and misty, storied past.

And I know this to be true. For I myself have been there many times and listened so, in that hushed hour of twilight, and have heard them, like small voices from another world, subdued, like voices from afar. And at such times the air about me would seem to be strangely stirred and filled with a faint rustling and a crepitation as of tiny footsteps, my face fanned by soundless, unseen wings, as though a great invisible assemblage had gathered there, to keep me company in this enchanted grove, and to hear with me the stories that the birch trees recounted to the solemn, listening pines.

Perhaps you will say that this spectral band of my familiars is but a figment of my dreams, conjured up by loneliness and long hours spent in visualizing old familiar landmarks, of reaching out for hands that are vanished, or of listening vainly in the darkness for voices that are stilled. If you think this, then do not judge too harshly, for these are Memories, and sacred to days and beasts and men you'll never see. Some tales I cannot tell you, lest in the telling I forever lose the power to make my happy shades, my ghostly congregation, those well-beloved wraiths of yesterday come back to me.

Yet much there is that may be told, and so, my Friend, come sit with me amongst the spirits of the Past and listen, and so pass an hour away.

II

The Sons of Kee-way-keno

In these modern days when radio and fast steamships have brought the Dominion of Canada and the Old Country into such close connection that one may hear a speech across the ocean, and a journey from Liverpool to Halifax is of little more moment than a trip to the sea-side, it is hard to realize that back of this up-to-date and flourishing Canada there exists a region of apparently interminable, virgin wilderness. Yet such is the case; almost at civilization's back door is a territory that is in most respects in the same condition as it was when it left the hands of its Maker.

This hinterland, which constitutes the largest part of the Dominion, lies North of the Great Divide that, over the whole width of Canada, separates those waters which run South from those that empty into the Arctic Ocean. It is not generally known that so far (and fortunately, for the future of the country) only the Southern and, in point of area, lesser slope of the Height of Land has been brought under the sway of modernity, and not all of it, at that. To those who inhabit these fastnesses the whole territory is known as the Keewaydin, an Indian word signifying "The Place of the North Wind." Mostly it is simply called "The North," a name that carries all the implication of mystery and vastness that the name implies. The settled country to the South is, to the dwellers in this Wilderness, a world apart, and those leaving for a rare visit to the railroad, are said to be going "down into Canada," as though they were making an expedition into a foreign country. This is not to be wondered at, when it is considered that a traveller may leave London, and be in Winnipeg in the time that it takes some trappers to cover the vast reaches of lake and forest trail that lie between their hunting grounds and civilization. Yet so closely does this wilderness in places approach the confines of civilization that men have died strange deaths, alone, within measurable distance of a silver screen on which the image of an actor performed in mummery, similar heroisms before a large and interested audience.

The Indians that roam the endless forests of the Keewaydin live much as their forefathers did. Although they make use of most of the appliances supplied by the trading posts (indeed they can now no longer do without them), many of the aboriginal weapons and articles of equipment are still in use, and most of the arts of forest lore are practised as they have been from time immemorial.

In many districts the old-time teepee rears its smoke-dyed, conical top above the sands of the lake shores. Blankets of woven rabbit-skins are still the only covering that is impervious to intense cold, and the deerskin or moosehide moccasin is yet the only footwear that ensures the light, firm tread so necessary on the treacherous footing of the forest floor. The spear, the bow and arrow, the wooden trap and the old muzzle-loading " beaver " gun are often seen in operation on the hunt, and in remote districts, where renewal of clothing is a matter of some difficulty, buckskin, or its equivalent in moose or caribou hide, is commonly worn. Yet these people, hardly to be classed as civilized, are not by any means savages. Almost universally honest, simple, kindly, although evasive and retiring before strangers, hospitality is almost a religion with the Indian.

His vigorous nature permits no deviation from a course of action once decided on and although he acknowledges no master, a self-appointed task once commenced is carried on in the face of difficulties of all kinds that may arise, till either the journey or the project is completed, or the man dead or disabled.

As an example of this deathless determination, and for sheer dogged grit, few examples can beat the case of two young Indian boys, belonging to a band of Ojibways whose hunting grounds I shared, in a district known as Manitou-pee-pagee, or Place-where-the-Devil-laughs. Kee-way-keno, North-Wind Man, was the father of these boys. Amongst men of a race noted for feats of endurance, North-Wind Man was remarkable for his powerful physique. Tall, gracefully rather than heavily built, as is common amongst Indians, yet he was capable of carrying as high as six hundred pounds of dead weight over a portage, and his fame as a packer and hunter was a by-word throughout that region.

It was at the time of the Fall of the Leaf, when the Hunting Winds course through the empty aisles of the sombre spruce forests, and all the Indians had left the trading post, and were on their way into their hunting grounds with their Winter supplies. Enormous quantities of provisions had to be transported over lakes of all sizes and portages of all lengths, for as far as two hundred miles, for these bands would remain, each family in its own territory, until the last trace of Winter had gone, a matter of six or seven months in the high North. Most families made two trips by relays, with their immense loads, using the ordinary sixteen-foot canoes for the purpose. But Kee-way-keno scorned such methods and took everything in one trip in a huge freighting canoe, one that it took two good men to lift, carrying it alone over each portage. He had also a small birch-bark canoe, with a lesser load, of which the two boys took charge, and which was to be used for the Fall hunt.

Things progressed as they usually do on such expeditions, the party making five miles some days, twenty on others, according to the kind of going, until they eventually arrived on their winter stamping ground. The Winter camp was erected, fish netted and salted down, meat killed and brought in, and the country, which was new to them, quickly explored and trails laid. Soon the brown grass of the beaver meadows became coated with a rime which showed the passage of foxes and lynx, and ice began to form on the edges of the marshlands. Traps were set and the hunt was on.

Now Kee-way-keno was known far and wide as a mighty hunter and a skilled canoeman; but many and various are the snares and pitfalls which abound in the Wilderness and to which even those with many years of experience to their credit sometimes fall a victim. One morning having apparently overcharged his trade-gun, and the bark canoe being slippery with ice, on his firing at a duck the frail craft upset, and the father was swept over a sixty-foot falls. The two boys, engaged in breaking camp on shore, were horrified but helpless spectators of the catastrophe. They rushed to the foot of the chute, but saw no sign of canoe or man, and as the river runs at this point for miles in a succession of falls and heavy rapids, gave up any attempt to recover the body at that time.

Such is the training of these people that these youths of thirteen and fifteen years of age respectively, considering the recovery of their father's remains paramount, decided to return one hundred and twenty miles, over thirty-two portages, and report the occurrence to the post manager. This they would have to do by means of the big canoe which it took two able men to raise to their shoulders, and that at a time of year when, owing to ice conditions, travelling might at any day become impossible. They first had to return on foot to their main camp, having brought only the bark canoe along on the hunting trip, a two-days' journey by lake and portage. But in a region where there seems at times barely enough dry land to go around the water, this distance was doubled at least. This accomplished, they set out on the return trip. In view of the short time left them before the freeze-up, they went as light as possible, took no camping outfit save an axe, and for provision only a bag containing flour, grease and tea, some matches, a frying-pan and tea pail. Thus they hoped to make the portages in one trip, a saving of days.

What followed seems unbelievable. At this time of year, heavy winds prevailed, and the huge canoe with its light crew and no load, became at times unmanageable, and was on occasion driven miles off its course. Head winds baffled them, as their course lay south-west into the teeth of the prevailing wind of the region. Beating into this with their high-riding and empty hull often became impossible, necessitating much travelling at night, when it would be generally calm, and this in a district with which they were unfamiliar, and on a route of more than a hundred miles in length over which they had passed but once.

These conditions imposed a severe enough tax on the boys' strength and ability, but it was on the portages where the real difficulty existed. The two boys would double on each end of the canoe, lifting it onto convenient fallen timber or rocks, and getting in under, each at his end, would struggle to their feet, and stagger, stumble, and at times crawl across the carry. Most of these were mercifully short, but several were very long, one being over a mile. Day after day they continued this exhausting and heart-breaking labour, eating hastily made bannock soaked in hot grease and washed down with tea, and sleeping without blankets under the canoe. On the smaller lakes ice began to impede progress, and latterly a channel had to be broken with a pole in the hands of the bowsman, at the rate of a quarter of a mile an hour, if that. There came a heavy fall of wet snow, which whilst it enabled them to drag the canoe on the smoother portages, increased their difficulties on the rough ones, as well as keeping them soaking wet all day. So that the time that should have been occupied in sleeping was spent standing naked before an open fire, drying clothes.

These delays, and the physical exhaustion that began to overcome them, shortened their daily journey to barely four or five miles, and food began to run low. They rationed themselves, and the weakness of undernourished systems worked to the limit, reduced their progress yet the more. Eventually they ran out of food altogether. The big canoe, without which they could not move, now began to be a grim white elephant that rode them, a merciless taskmaster that was slowly grinding the life out of them. It seemed to their fevered imaginings almost like an evil creature bent on their destruction. Indians they were no doubt, and to the manner born, but just now they were only two young lads, alone in an endless empty waste without food or shelter, where the least mistake in seamanship on the windlashed surface of a big lake, or a slight error in casting the route, meant death either by drowning or from hunger and exposure. Yet in the face of these almost insuperable difficulties they lived up to the Creed of the Trail, where that which is undertaken must be finished, and where none may falter or evade the issue.

With staring eyes and hollow cheeks, minds wandering in the delirium of starvation and clouded by the black shadow of an awful tragedy, the sons of Kee-way-keno arrived at the Post after nineteen and a-half days of suffering such as few boys of any race have been called on to endure. Only the intensive training to which Indian youths are subjected, together with a spartan spirit of fortitude inculcated by a life of hardship, enabled these striplings to win through where many a grown man would have failed.

III

The Light that Failed

I HAVE never been lost. The fact that I am here at Beaver Lodge proves it; when a man is lost there is an end to it. Never have I used a compass or any other mechanical or scientific device in travelling known or unknown territory, and never will; yet I have never been lost—but I have been "turned around," lost my bearings for a time, had sometimes to do some pretty fast calculating. A man who says he never was "turned around," as we call this state of affairs in our manner of speech, is either a pre-varicator or else he never travelled very much in the woods.

My own record is not as clear as it might be in this respect, having on three or four occasions been guilty of negligence that landed me in trouble for an hour or so. It is hard to get a real, honest-to-god woodsman to admit that he ever was in this kind of difficulty, but it happens once in a while to all of them, and even Indians are known to occasionally set their foot inside that deadly circle in which a man may wander for hours and not be able to break away from, and where some have died.

The word "lost" is open to a good many different interpretations, and quite the best of these that I have heard, was the one given by an old bushwhacker, who for some inexplicable reason, became so twisted in his calcula-tions that it took ten men over a week to find him; he would not plead guilty to having been lost; no sir; he wasn't lost, not he; but he had been "right bewildered"—for eight days!

And now I'll tell one.

a

As my name indicates [1], I have a decided liking, and some aptitude, for travelling at night. Not that my eyes are particularly adapted for seeing in the dark, or are especially piercing or capable of projecting any gleaming rays of light into the gloom of a midnight forest. Not that at all. Simply this, that not ten per cent. of nights are really dark; and to one who is accustomed to night work, the darkness seems a few shades lighter than to the ordinary person. A man may cover a lot of territory, even strange territory, in the dark if he has a good, comprehensive knowledge of Wilderness travel in general, a reliable sense of direction, a sensitive pair of ears, and a kind of nervous alertness that apprises him of what is going on around him; moreover he must be able to " feel " the lay of the land, and above all, he must feel perfectly at home, and not allow the fact that he is alone in the dark, in a wild country, to get under his skin.

Aside from the above, the matter is quite simple. There's nothing to it. I have travelled through heavy forests in what would pass for complete darkness (but wasn't really), and only in very few instances have I been compelled to use birch-bark torches to accomplish this. I have paddled over long routes, entire nights at a time, including the crossing of numerous portages with canoe and load, at a pace little less than that attained in daylight hours, and have both run down and poled up rapids at night by the sound of them, assisted somewhat by the blurred gleam of the starlight on wet rocks and on the white-crested breakers.

All very clever, if not actually uncanny, thinks you; and in such subdued light, or absence of it, these feats may seem to be unusual. However, they are commonly performed without undue self-commendation, by men of my calling. Such exploits excite small comment, and are expected. But there is such a thing as having too much

---

[1] Wa-Sha-Quon-Asin is translated into English as " He Who Walks By Night." (Publishers' note.)

light, when it will create a confusion far greater than
could have been occasioned by any amount of darkness;
and to this odd predicament I once fell a facile and very
humiliated victim.

On a Winter night, far in the Wilderness of Northern
Quebec, my trapping partner, who had never been a soldier,
demanded some stories of the war. Like most of those
who saw active service on any front, my reminiscences ran
more to thoughts of vermin, mud and short rations than to
fighting. So vivid were my portrayals of the deprivations
endured, that I talked the two of us into a practically starving
condition. Having that morning killed a deer only a short
distance from the cabin, I decided to go out at once and get
some of the meat, while my partner said he would in the
meantime make a bannock. It was very dark, and as I
would have to skin the deer [1] I took along a lantern.

Never before had I travelled in the woods by means of
artificial light, save on a trail, there being none in this
case as a heavy snowstorm had obliterated whatever tracks
I had made on my way home from the deer; and there
befell me just what I had always heard would happen
to any man who attempted to find his way in the bush
with a light—I couldn't find my objective. The deer
was probably three hundred yards away, and I had started
in the right direction. But lanterns have a fashion of throwing their glare in circles, and I was surrounded by a narrow
ring of light, which had the effect of intensifying the encircling darkness, so that everything beyond a radius of a
dozen feet was black as the bottomless pit, and nothing
outside of it was visible.

After going on for some time without finding the deer,
I now discovered something else—a snowshoe track, going
my way. In the deep, loose snow, the outline of the shoe
was blurred and more or less shapeless, and I could not

[1] In the winter, carcases were always left in the hide for twenty-four
hours or more to improve the meat, being left covered with heaped-up
snow so as to not freeze.

identify it. Now there was supposed to be no one but ourselves in the country; my own previous tracks were snowed under, so this called for investigation, which I decided to make later. I turned off short towards the deer, and went a considerable distance without encountering it; but I *did* find another set of snowshoe prints, this time crossing mine. I didn't know what to think of this, but went on looking for my kill, feeling, rather ashamedly, that I had shown some very poor scout-craft in so over-shooting my mark. I swung off a little, only to run slap into, not one snowshoe trail, but two of them. Both of these veered off to my right, and crossing one another ran into a third, and within a short distance, yet a fourth set of impressions. And all at once I seemed to be surrounded by tracks, and try as I might, I could in no way get clear of this maze of snowshoe trails by which I seemed to be beleaguered. All were going the same way, to the right,—who the devil were these trespassers careering around in this senseless, circuitous steeplechase! I went after them at a round trot, but they crossed their own trails, again to the right, and eluded me. I stopped and listened; but everything was silent as the grave, enveloped in the padded hush that pervades the Winter Wilderness, especially at night. The whole thing began to be a trifle spooky.

I cantered on, leaping and bounding along in great style; this went on for some time, and then I found that the other fellows (there were now four of them) must have heard me, as they were also leaping and bounding along, as their marks plainly showed, in what now amounted to a whole drove of people. I was never so exasperated in my life, and continued the pursuit on my big snowshoes, the light of the lantern throwing my leaping shadow, huge and distorted, against the background of the snow-bound trees, like a gigantic hob-goblin who grotesquely pranced beside me and followed with fantastical fidelity my every action. I seemed, within the orbit of my circle of lantern light, to be confined in a deep, illuminated pit, that walled me round and moved with me as I went, and the adventure was not without an eerie aspect of unreality. Entertained by the fanciful notion that this might after all be only a dream, (and having had, for the last while back, certain well founded suspicions) I became a little inattentive, and fell headlong over a large snow mound. The lantern was saved from going out by some gymnastics that would have done credit to a professional acrobat, and by the light of it I saw, sticking out of the mound of snow, the hoof of some animal.

I had at last arrived at my deer; and looking around I observed that all the men I had been chasing had arrived there also. There were just two—my shadow and myself.

In the woods at night, an artificial light will fool you every time; every way you face is straight ahead, and no bearings can be taken, especially from above, where the outline of the tree-tops is nearly always discernible, and of great help; and so, enclosed above, below, and on all sides, in a globe of light as it were, one is apt to travel round and round in a very circumscribed area. This I had done, my own tracks increasing in number as I overtook myself, so to speak, the circles getting smaller and smaller, until I had about wound myself down to a point. Taking some meat, I then unwound myself back again to the cabin, feeling rather subdued, to find my partner asleep and the bannock cold. I awoke him, being by now determined to eat deer-meat on this night of our Lord if it killed the two of us. And as we ate, my partner was from time to time obliged to turn his back and emit gurgling and suppressed choking noises that were quite unnecessary, and annoyed me considerably.

And I leave it to you to decide whether it was the light that failed me, or I that failed the light.

IV

Nemesis

FOR some time past I had heard the man coming. The tock, tock of his pole as he tapped the ice had been audible from a distance of perhaps a mile, the sound magnified and carried far and wide, as is the way with a blow struck on glare ice.

This testing ice by sound is often necessary during the early part of Winter, the pole being swung naturally and easily in the stride, the end being allowed to drop with its full weight at every fourth step, much as a drum major wields his staff.

The timing of the strokes in this case was such that the traveller seemed to strike the ice at every other step; the steps of one who is unhurried, walking slowly, but steadily. And as he walked came the tap tap, of the pole, regular as the " tuck " of the drum of marching infantry. It was late Fall, and I knew the ice to be bad, especially at this place, a large shallow lake bottomed with a treacherous, gaseous slime, which spelt death for him who should break through and be sucked into the hungry maw of the shifting ooze. The lake itself was walled in by the towering black palisades of a gloomy spruce forest, into which no ray of sunlight ever penetrated, and was backed by miles of almost impassable swamps.

A desolate region, and one that I avoided as much as possible in my goings and comings on the trap lines.

Suddenly remembering my duties as probable host to a tired man, I stirred up the smouldering fire, put the cold tea on afresh and endeavoured to make some semblance of a meal out of the remains of the lunch I had just eaten.

As I so busied myself, I wondered a little what event could bring a stranger into my hunting ground, at a time when the Fall hunt was in full swing.

My temporary camping place was not visible from the lake but the smoke was plain to be seen, and I knew that the voyageur would not fail to turn in and stop awhile, as is the custom with those who travel in the Wilderness. So I sat by my fire and smoked, and anxiously awaited the newcomer's arrival, for something in the manner of his coming indicated (for a lifetime on the trail trains the faculties to a degree of perception in such matters), that he who had penetrated so far within my boundaries was no ordinary trapper. There seemed, for one thing, to be some peculiar quality in this man's method of feeling out the ice; in the first place there was his unusual action of striking at every third step as though marking time on a line of march, and then the additional resonance he produced by the unusually heavy blows he struck, as though he carried a weightier staff than was commonly used. And over and above that was the changeless, unbroken rhythm of the strokes, which were as measured and uniform as the ticking of some gigantic clock.

And his slow, unfaltering strides seemed to suggest a dogged persistence, as of a man with a mission to fulfill, and a man, moreover, not easily swerved from his purpose. Onward he marched, his every step timed by the steady, persistent tap of the pole, tock, tock, tock, until the regularity and monotony of the sounds exercised an almost hypnotic influence on my mind as I sat and waited. He seemed long in coming, walking slowly as he did, yet so persistently that he should have long ago arrived. And then quite suddenly I realized that the sound was now beyond the stopping place and that the wayfarer, whoever he might be, had ignored the presence of my camp, in spite of the smoke and the light sleigh in full view on the shore, and had passed on. An unusual, nay, an unheard of proceeding amongst bushmen, and unaccountable unless the man be blind, or an enemy.

There does not live the man of any character who has not made at least one enemy in his lifetime, and this last thought stuck in my mind.

I went out onto the ice, but the passerby was already out of sight beyond a point, for the lake was one of irregular shores and many deep bays and inlets, in which concealment for purposes of ambush would have been an easy matter. And I could still hear plainly the measured stroke of the pole, a sound which, from being merely eerie, had now become ominous, seeming to tap forth a challenge, or a threat.

I hastened out to the centre of the lake for a fuller view, and still saw no one, so I returned to my camp, extinguished my fire, and quickly arming myself, started in pursuit. I travelled at a dog-trot the usual gait on glare ice, taking, as I did so, full advantage of the excellent cover that the broken character of the shore line afforded, having as a guide to the line of march of my quarry, the steady, never ceasing rapping on the ice.

For an hour or more I followed the intruder. There being now no necessity for testing the ice where one had passed ahead of me, I lost no time, yet great as was my speed, and slow as his appeared to be, found that I could in no wise catch up to him.

In spite of his apparently leisurely progress he seemed to be able to keep his distance. The sound swung off to my right, and following it, I saw that the chase had taken me into a deep and apparently endless bay, of which, up to that time, I had had no knowledge. Down this I pursued the elusive, baffling tattoo for miles, always trotting, and the invisible stranger always walking with his measured steps.

Almost it was as though the man carried a huge metronome, or that the creature itself were not a human being but a robot. Grimly determined to get to the bottom of this mystery, I followed mile after mile, regardless of where this will-o'-the-wisp of sound was leading me; over wide expanses of lake, through narrow gorges, along winding forest-bordered streams, but always on ice, and ever to the accompaniment of that unvarying and monotonous rapping.

Eventually I found myself in a part of my hunting ground that I had never before set eyes on, a barren desolation of blowdown, burnt lands, and black impenetrable swamp. How this section had escaped my observation after some years of constant travelling in the district, I could in no way account for, and I was somewhat piqued to think that a stranger knew more of my own territory than I did myself. More than that, the nature of the whole proposition began to border on the uncanny; even the wild and inhospitable appearance of the landscape, with its grotesque and twisted piles of shattered trees, and dark reaches of brooding swamp, seemed to reflect the atmosphere of weird unreality of this adventure.

The chase was long and I began to tire, and no longer able to run, I now walked; and strangely, I was still able to keep that haunting sound within earshot, and at about the same distance as before. It appeared as if the stranger was cognisant of my fatigue, and was, by some means unknown to me, able to gauge accurately my speed, and thus keep his progress timed to mine, never allowing me to catch up, yet never drawing away from me. And there occurred to me with startling suddenness, the possibility that he did not want to outdistance me, that I had blindly followed where he had led me, and that I had been decoyed with devilish ingenuity many miles into a country of which I knew nothing; for what purpose I could only guess.

The sun had set, and there was no moon; night was coming on and I was alone in a trackless wilderness with an unknown and evidently competent enemy. I became conscious of a feeling of uneasiness, and halting in my tracks, formed and rejected a dozen swift plans of action. Co-incident with my stopping, the sound slewed off to the East beyond a fringe of timber, and I noticed with a feeling of distinct relief that it seemed to be going further away. This, and the fact that I had no provision, decided me to turn back, resolving to return with some supplies and solve this vexing problem on the morrow. Snow threatened, and in that event, the man of mystery must at least leave some tracks.

I squatted on the ice and mapped out as well as I could the tortuous itinerary over which this man-hunt had taken me, in order to devise a short-cut back to my main trail, but found the project hopeless. I was now faced with the necessity of covering the entire route, most of it in the dark.

So I started on the long journey back to my lunching place. Off to one side I could still hear that infernal tock-tock, and as I proceeded I seemed to be unable to get away from the now hateful sound; in fact it seemed to be coming closer. I stopped and listened. It was approaching without a doubt, outflanking me from behind the thin fringe of timber just mentioned, which now proved to be an island behind which it had passed; and a sudden turn in the route brought the sound dead ahead of me, blocking my trail, and coming my way! I could no longer disguise from myself the certainty that this thing, whatever it was, was intentionally heading me off, and mixed with my feeling of affront at the overt act, was more than a hint of fear.

Nearer it came, nearer and yet nearer, and still no one was visible; a slow measured advance, as immutable as the onward march of Time itself; tock, tock, tock; now no longer reminiscent of the strokes of the homely metronome, but more suggestive of the ticking of an infernal machine, stalking me, marking off the seconds till it should close with me and destroy me. In something of a panic I sheered off, and it followed like a nightmare; I doubled, and the Thing crept on behind me.

I ran and the sound kept its given distance; I slowed up

with a like result. I twisted, turned, and back-tracked; I tried every shift and subterfuge learnt in a calling where stratagem and expedient become second nature, but without avail. I could not shake off my fiendish familiar. And I now knew in cold reality the awful fear of one pursued by some hellish monster in a nightmare.

I was no longer the pursuer but the pursued, and I was being hunted by some person or thing that could see without being seen, and could accurately forestall my every move. Escape into the bush was impossible, as the whole country was covered by a fallen forest that had been blown down by some recent hurricane, and in places newly burnt. And always behind and to one side or the other, that sinister tapping herded me relentlessly and inexorably on my way, as a steer is herded by a skilful cowboy. For I dreaded now to meet the one I had so assiduously sought, and kept as much distance between him and myself as the shape of the waterways allowed, for I felt that even armed as I was, weapons would be of little use against a being who could apparently so flout the laws of nature. I burst into a clammy sweat.

The terrible hitherto unbelieved tales of the man-eating windego and the Loup Garou, the were-wolf of bush mythology, flashed across my mind, tales of trappers found dead in ghastly and unexplainable mutilation.

The horror of what I now knew to be the supernatural drained the last vestige of resolution from my being, and I abandoned all attempts at a considered or calculated retreat; I no longer hoped to outdistance this Thing, seeking only in my desperation to delay as long as possible the awful moment when it should catch up to me and work its will upon me.

I lost track of my direction, except to see that I was being driven deeper and deeper into a savage Wilderness, the like of which I had never before seen; yet the terror of that unknown presence behind me goaded me on and on, whither I no longer cared so that I kept beyond the reach of this invisible peril. I was fatigued beyond measure, and knew that I could not much longer continue my flight. I became obsessed by the idea that if I could only leave the ice I could outdistance my pursuer, but I seemed held from making the attempt by some diabolical power beyond my control.

I then made the alarming discovery that the body of water on which I travelled was coming to an end. Towering, impregnable cliffs walled it in on either hand, closing in on me as the waterway narrowed, and at its termination, no great distance ahead of me, was a bristling rampart of torn and broken tree-trunks, through which no man could make any headway. I now saw that the matter had been brought to an issue, and that be it man, beast, or devil that was hunting me down, I must at last stand and fight it.

My aim was now to reach the foot of the narrow sheet of ice, where I would have protection of a kind on three sides of me, the walls of rock to my flanks, and the masses of fallen timber in my rear. The phantom sound was almost upon me, and not daring to look back lest I lose this terrible race, I stumbled forward with feet that seemed suddenly turned to lead. With a last despairing burst of speed I gained my objective, when hope suddenly sprang to life within me as I descried, by the failing light, a narrow trail that had but lately been hewed through the tangled slash before which I had intended to make my stand. This, I thought, must undoubtedly lead to some human habitation, or failing that, would at least enable me to leave the ice, and so perhaps outdistance my pursuer, whose element it appeared to be, and I made for it with all possible speed. My relief at finding my feet on solid ground, where my pursuer would be no longer able to tap out his accursed measure, was indescribable. And then, too late I discovered that a frozen creek ran parallel to the trail, hidden from it by the wall of prostrate tree-trunks, so as to be only inter-

mittently visible. My faulty strategy had now given him
the advantage that he needed.

And as, almost at the point of exhaustion, my face streaming with perspiration, and gasping for breath at every step,
I staggered along the narrow pathway, the ceaseless tock, tock,
tock, tock, beat its threat of a nameless horror into my reeling
senses, as it marched alongside me on the ice of the stream,
an invisible, but ever present escort. I could now no longer
turn to right or left, and ever the Thing was beside me;
I felt as one who walks with Death.

And then, to my unutterable relief, I saw a clearance
ahead of me, and a cluster of log cabins. The stream was
now plainly visible, and on its bank a group of men were
gathered around some object on the ground, and them I
approached with the feelings of one who has escaped from
the very edge of the pit. The sound from which I fled
was now close at hand, and I lost no time in acquainting
those present with my predicament. To my surprise they
looked coldly on me, and my remarks passed unheeded.
No one spoke, and a strained silence, such as greets the
appearance of an unwelcome visitor at any gathering, fell
upon the assembly, until one man said, pointing at me:

" There he is now, that is the man; show him his
work."

At that the group opened up, and I saw stretched out
before me the dead body of a young man, terribly mutilated,
evidently murdered with the utmost brutality.

" Who has done this? " I asked, even as there was borne
upon me the frightful realization that these people, for some
reason, accounted me the guilty party. My question
remained unanswered, but all eyes were turned on me with
cold, staring hostility. These men were all rough pros-
pectors and trappers, strangers to me, every one of them,
members of a community that I had not known even existed,
and their deadly calm and purposeful demeanour showed
me that the situation was fraught with terrible possibilities.

I made some attempt to clear myself, telling them who I was, and where I had been this two months past, stumbling over my words and faltering in my speech, as an innocent man will, when confronted by the evidence of his supposed guilt.

My disjointed and incoherent protestations met with no response; the men ignored the fact that I was speaking, staring at me in stony silence, on their faces the set expression of an unalterable purpose. Finally the man who had accused me spoke again. " This thing must be finished before dark. Here comes the boy's father; let him decide what is to be done." And at that instant the persistent, unearthly rapping that had driven me to the scene of what was liable to be my doom, at length caught up to me and, almost at my elbow, abruptly ceased. Turning, I now for the first time saw my pursuer, an old, old man dressed in faded buckskin, and armed with a heavy, steel-shod hardwood pole. His frame was so attenuated, being almost fleshless, and his demeanour so strange and wild, that he had all the semblance of one risen from the grave, or of a being from another world. His hair was white and hung in snaky locks below his shoulders, and a full beard covered most of his face; and out of this his burning eyes glared into mine with an unwavering stare of such malevolence and hatred, that it chilled me to the bone; for I plainly saw what he would desire to be done.

Without speaking he advanced on me slowly, raising above his head as he did so the heavy staff that, having driven me to my place of execution, was now to be the instrument of his just but misdirected vengeance.

The first blow struck by the parent as his unalienable right, I would then, without a shadow of doubt, be literally shot to pieces. Stiff with horror, held by some awful fascination in the old man's insane stare, I was struck dumb, until at last:

" Wait, men, wait." I screeched rather than shouted

"I am not the man," fumbling meanwhile in my pockets with fingers that refused their office, for some identification. Two men leaped forward quickly, and held me full in the path of the descending shaft. In my dire extremity and with the strength of despair, I tore myself loose with a mighty effort. A great light flashed before my eyes, and I awoke to find the landlord of the little frontier hotel, where I was passing the night, shaking me violently with one hand, while he held a lamp before my face with the other.

And at the same moment there came to my ears the steady and resonant ticking of the large kitchen clock that was suspended on the wall over my bed.

V

A Day in a Hidden Town

" Heavy with the heat and silence
Grew the afternoon of Summer;
With a drowsy sound the forest
Whispered round the sultry wigwam,
With a sound of sleep the water
Rippled on the beach below it."

LONGFELLOW

MODERN influences have taken away much of the romance,
picturesque appearance and exotic atmosphere from Indian
camps, as seen on the reserves and more easily accessible
areas of the Wilderness. The exploitation and subsequent
degeneration of some bands has sapped their racial pride,
and, destitute and hopeless, they no longer have the
ambition to keep up the old methods and traditions, so that
home life is slipshod and wretched, and national integrity
is falling into decay. Attempts at living in a poor imitation
of the white man's way without the means and training,
have not resulted in gaining for the Indian a reputation
for cleanliness. Only those of them having a long experience and good opportunities have succeeded in conforming
themselves to the limitations of a wooden house, as the
ill-kept, not always cleanly establishments of the more or
less mendicant Indians near the rail-road, plainly indicate.
Yet in the cramped quarters of a tent or a teepee they are
able to conduct their household affairs with neatness and
system, where a white family used to living in a house
would speedily become involved in hopeless confusion.
Many of the shack-living type of Indians have lost the art
of camping as an all year round method of living, and the

D

traveller has to journey far beyond the regular lines of bush travel, to find a band of Indians living in the primitive but highly specialized manner that has been evolved by centuries of adaptation and elimination. This type of community breaks up into small movable semi-permanent villages for the Winter, the location decided by the fluctuations of the hunt. These hunting bands are not large, and consist generally of from one to four or five families, according to the possibilities of the district. Being movable all the equipment and materials are very light, and apparently quite inadequate to withstand the rigors of a Winter North of fifty-two degrees. A well-sheltered spot is chosen where wood, fish, and moose are plenty, and tents and teepees are reared on walls three or four logs high, rectangular in shape for the tents, and octagon for the teepees. The logs are well chinked with moss and later banked with snow. Small tin stoves, generally without an oven, supply the heat in the tents. The wigwams rely on open fires inside, placed not as those used by the plains tribes in the centre, but nearer one side which is nearly perpendicular.

During the day all blankets and other materials not in use are placed out of the way in the back of the tents, or rolled back neatly into the empty space in the angle between the lodge wall and the floor. Each member of the family keeps his accustomed place, and has his or her belongings at their back, while the indoor work, including eating, is done on a deep and generous carpet of balsam brush which covers the whole floor of the habitation, and is frequently changed. Household affairs, under these conditions, are of the simplest and are carried on with a minimum of disturbance and with few implements, thus avoiding confusion. The accumulation of carcases and waste matter from tanning, skinning and other activities incidental to a hunter's life over a period of seven or eight months, are thrown out to freeze on brush piles or recognized dumps, and lay harmless until Spring, by which time the inhabitants have gone. It is the presence of this rotting waste matter in disused Winter camp grounds that is responsible for a widespread impression that Indian camps are necessarily unclean. Outside the habitations, shelves are secured between suitable triangles of trees, and high racks are erected to keep meat, fish and other eatable goods, as well as many things not supposed to be eatable, out of the reach of the ever-hungry huskies. Narrow snowshoe trails, dug out after every storm, connect the dwellings, each with its row of snow-banked dog houses of brush. Within the camps all is surprisingly snug and comfortable while the stoves are going. In the lodges open fire is maintained all night without difficulty, but in the tents, when the stoves die, it is another matter.

In summer, after the Spring trade, a few of these communities repair to some chosen spot, generally situated in some little known region far off a main route. White visitors, or intruders of any kind, are not welcomed at these villages, some of the sites of which have been used from time immemorial. The approaches are often carefully masked, and often no indication of their presence is encountered until the chance wayfarer comes upon them unexpectedly. These camps are known to the Indians as " Oden-na-ka-inne-hekaj," literally " Hidden Towns." Such towns are no longer common, but some still exist, and in them many of the old traditions are observed, and ancient customs, long supposed to have been forgotten, are still perpetuated.

It has been my good fortune to be a not unwelcome guest at several of these self-contained, self-supporting concealed hamlets, and on one occasion I had the remarkable good fortune to obtain entry to a typical Hidden Town with a party whose genuine and friendly interest in their red brethren led me to make the attempt.

It so happened that we camped one night within a few miles of this village, the proximity of which was known to we guides. Although, so far, no white people had ever succeeded in gaining admittance beyond the canoe landing, the head of the party urged me to see what could be done. I knew the chances to be poor. No select gathering of aristocracy into whose presence you have blundered unknown and unannounced, can so completely, definitely, and absolutely give you the air as the semi-civilized inhabitants of a primitive Indian village in which you are not welcome. The Chief of the band in question, Big Otter, had a well-sustained reputation for exclusiveness, and although acquainted with him, I had never so far had any pressing invitation to exchange calls. I had, however, found on a portage that Summer a well-made paddle of Big Otter's make, tagged with a sign on birch bark representing my name. This was a present of some account in a country of rough rivers, and seemed a good omen, but I did not build on it.

The next day, after a short lecture on the procedure common to such occasions, all hands but the cook embarked and headed for Big Otter's village. An hour's paddle, including some pretty stiff poling up several rapids, brought us to a beautiful sheet of water several miles in extent, a lake almost round with sandy beaches and hemmed in by precipitous hills covered with virgin pine; a forest untouched by the hands of man. Across the lake we paddled for an hour into the eye of the sun, and down a narrow bay. Behind a high protecting point we came suddenly on a row of canoes pulled up or turned over on the shore, and from them wound a narrow trail, leading up a low grade to a grove of immense red pines. Here, on the level ground between the giant boles, were scattered a number of habitations. A blue haze of smoke hung in the air of the glade, and indistinct figures appeared momentarily between the lodges, to vanish suddenly again.

No one came down to meet us; the silence was deep and oppressive—one of those thick, heavy silences. Not attempting to land, I gave the customary call, the cry of an owl, and on the instant an indescribable tumult tore the silence to ribbons as a round dozen of dogs, of strongly wolfish appearance and great lung capacity, raced down to the water's edge, there to carry on a most alarming demonstration suggestive of an unappeased lust for blood. One of the party permitted himself to wonder if they could swim.

A tall slim figure with flying hair ran down the slope and plunged into the surging, leaping huskies, belabouring impartially on all sides with a burning brand, when the savage-looking body-guard retired reluctantly and ranged themselves in skirmishing order on the slope.

The figure, who could now be recognized as the chief himself, advanced to the sandy margin and stood there.

He raised no hand in welcome, and gave no salutation of any kind. The setting was wild enough. The immense columns of the age-old trees, the conical teepees dimly seen in the shadows beneath them, the swift furtive movements of uncertain, half-seen shapes shifting among the smoke-wreathes, the tall, motionless, forbidding figure on the lake-shore, and behind him the herd of savage huskies. Something had to be said, so I opened negotiations. "How! Quay, quay, Kitche Negik!—Greeting, Big Otter! I have found the paddle, and must thank you. My friends wish also to make presents to the little ones." This last offer has softened the paternal heart of many an obdurate chieftain; but this one made no friendly sign, and even at that distance he exhaled a passive but very evident visitor-resistance. "Anoatch! Anoatch!" he cried. "This is not well done; who are all these people? Are they Kitche Mokoman?" (The Long Knives, Americans).

The situation called for no little tact and diplomacy, and I used what small amount of them I am blessed with.

I told him how far these people had come, their genuine interest, and sincerity in their desire to pay a friendly visit, and elaborated on their fortitude in the face of the hard-

ships of so long and difficult a journey from the rail-road
(a matter of ninety miles or more). The diplomatic
evasions, the carefully worded compliments, the guarded
statements and the discussions entered into, much resembled
those " conversations " held between the ambassadors of
two countries on the brink of war, and are beyond my
power to recollect. Suffice it that in time, having cross-
questioned me with no little skill, and adding unfortunately
as a proviso that no photographs were to be taken, he
pronounced himself satisfied : " Undush, kibaan : All right,
come ashore ; we will talk together."

I surveyed the wolf-pack in the rear. " There are women ;
perhaps you could tie your dogs," I suggested, in English.
An audible sigh of relief went up, and not all from the
ladies either. Big Otter turned and intoned a few words,
and soon an old woman and some children went fearlessly
in amongst these potential man-eaters and drove some and
dragged others away, to which treatment they tamely submitted.

At the landing the chief met us, gravely shook hands
with each one of the party, and his face crinkled into a
rare smile, his white even teeth in startling contrast to his
weathered countenance.

He led the way up to the camp. The dogs, although
out of sight, voiced their disapproval and commenced to
growl. One or two dark heads peered out at us blankly
from canvas door-flaps ; several children retreated some
distance, to turn and stare curiously at us. Two or three
men were present, but they regarded us not at all. No
women were to be seen. The situation was decidedly
strained, and there was a tendency on the part of our folk
to talk in whispers. Between them and these people there
seemed to exist a wall of reserve, intangible but very real ;
not to be seen but plainly felt. Then Big Otter spoke a
few words in smooth-flowing sibilants and gutturals, and
soon a man slipped noiselessly up to us on silent moccasined

feet and shook hands all around. He was young, and his handsome face was flushed with embarrassment. Other men appeared, of various ages, all with the same level gaze and soundless tread, and also shook hands, impressively, but without emotion and without speech. Women now came out from lodges and other places of concealment and performed the hand-shaking ceremony; these last addressed me as interpreter, bidding the women of the party welcome.

A buxom old lady dressed completely in Highland plaid and wearing a brilliant head shawl, and carrying a large butcher's knife in her left hand, declaimed loudly, passing apt but not unfriendly comment on the personnel of the entire party. Changing hands with the knife, she resumed her labour of removing the hair from a green [1] moosehide.

She and the other squaws relapsed into the state of self-abnegation and indifference common to Indian women, resuming their various tasks apparently laid down on our appearance.

Then came the children; shy, smiling faces with bright, shoe-button eyes alive with curiosity. Small boys stepped up manfully and shook hands with dignity. Little girls in head shawls and voluminous plaid skirts sidled up within measurable distance and whispered together in wonder; "Shaganash! Kitche Mokoman!"—White people! Americans! The simple presents were distributed, busy women-folk looked up from their work with frank approval, and the atmosphere of distrust and suspicion melted away like snow before the Summer sun. All was now well. Yet there could be sensed an attitude of watchfulness. The disposal of the dogs gave evidence of this; a belt of at least a hundred feet in width on the rear and sides of the village had been denuded of its timber and allowed to grow up in a tangled mass of undergrowth through which no creature of any size could pass without noise. Through this natural fortification, and radiating from the town, lanes had been

[1] Raw.

cut, and in these approaches the dogs were tied on long leashes that gave them control of the full width of the paths, and from whence on close approach they glared out at us in open hostility, their feral eyes red with hate.

This was the twentieth century, yet in a few minutes we no longer remembered it. Time, and the influence of modern civilization fell away from us like a discarded garment.

All around an ancient forest of trees that were old when Wolfe stormed Quebec; birch bark teepees, old ones grey with smoke-stained tops, new ones a bright yellow, scattered beneath the dark green limbs. In the foreground a scaffold hung with split-open fish and long strips of moose-meat, under which smouldered a slow and smoky fire. Women cooking at an open fire, others working ceaselessly at half-tanned hides. Farther off near the lake shore, surrounded by a litter of shavings, two men and a woman worked on a half-finished bark canoe. Rich-looking Hudson Bay blankets, red, green, or white hung out to air on high racks, adding a barbaric note of colour. The acrid smell of smoke, and the low hum of intermittent converse in an old, old tongue. An Indian village of the old regime; in just such another town Pontiac dreamed his dreams of conquest. We had slipped back down the pages of history a hundred years in as many seconds. The sportsmen in their outing clothes had suddenly become an incongruity, their speech anomalous. They had actually become an anachronism in this aboriginal setting. In spite of the official reception we had been accorded, one felt instinctively that there was a limit beyond which we dare not venture, inhibiting familiarity, and one became conscious of an air of secrecy and reserve that held more than a hint of savagery. Out in civilization these people might be awkward, ill at ease, negligible and nondescript. Here, far in the wilderness, in their own domain, they were supreme. Self-reliant and efficient, they proudly maintained their rights as Citizens of the Kingdom of the Wild.

And I tried to remember that I knew these men this many years. Big Otter himself had often made me gifts of meat; who could fear the wise and humorous Pad-way-way-donc—Here-he-comes-shouting—the teller of tales, who because he has lumbago will paint red and blue triangles at the corners of his eyes, play the turtle-shell rattle all night, and jump into the river through new ice in the Fall; old Sah-Sabik—Yellow Rock—who travelled alone, spoke only rarely and then in parables; Jimmy Twenty who always moved at a dog-trot and was seldom seen walking; Mato-gense—Little Child—he is a conjuror of no mean ability, and is reputed to be able to tell the weather two weeks ahead. Although he habitually chants to the tune of his wolf-skin drum, he is a pleasant old gentleman in conversation. Pad-way-way-donc has a daughter, a wonderfully built young woman with a wealth of long hair which she wears loose. She has not been near us, but stands apart, staring at us with the eyes of a wild thing.

Big Otter presently pointed to a large teepee and said " Go in and rest, the women have prepared food." This was a welcome diversion, and on entering we found ready a savoury if substantial repast of bannock, fried moose-meat, fried fish, and piping hot tea. The interior of the wigwam was scrupulously clean, and from the poles hung bunches of herbs and roots that gave out an aromatic and not unpleasant odour. Two young women were in attendance, and all the party squatted on the soft carpet of freshly gathered boughs, and ate off shining tin dishes, with modern implements, and drank tea out of porcelain cups.

To some of the party the affair was novel to a degree, and the experience of eating Indian-cooked wild meat on the floor of a smoke-stained birch bark teepee, within the precincts of a jealously guarded secret village, was, to one of the sportsmen with us, the fulfilment of a life-long ambition.

The ladies suggested that one of the women should tell

something about herself. She agreed after some persuasion, and it transpired that she had never seen a town or a train, nor did she care if she ever did. And forthwith arose a conversation in which I became the go-between. The questions on either side concerning mostly subjects beyond the knowledge of the object of them, I found myself saddled with the somewhat delicate task of steering the talk clear of shoals. I was obliged to extemporize considerably, thereby endangering my chances in the hereafter, in order that both parties should get the answers that pleased them, and so have everybody satisfied.

In the drowsy heat and silence of the wigwam, several of the visitors, fatigued with the journey, had fallen asleep. Others sat back to trees on the red-brown pine needles, or on logs near the central fire, and smoked contentedly. A young boy, armed with a cedar bow, drifted in. He had three partridges tied to his belt. These he skinned and cleaned deftly and hung above the lazy fire to smoke.

The day drew on and the heat waned. Two squirrels raced madly through the camp and up a tree, circling round and round the trunk in mimic chase with shrill profanities. A whisky-jack floated soundlessly here and there, lighting where he would, and no hand was raised to molest him.

Calm, repose, and an ineffable peace settled over the camp. A coolness and the damp of evening commenced to fall, and the shadows crept from behind the trees and from out the dark aisles of the forest. The day was drawing swiftly to a close, and we must now travel by moonlight. Sleepers were aroused and we embarked. No good-byes were said, but the chief followed us down to the landing. I raised my hand in a farewell gesture, when he spoke; "Ki sakitone na ki do mokoman—do you value your knife very much?" he asked; I was wearing an ordinary hunting-knife of good quality at the time. I replied that I valued it very much, so much so that I did not care to part with it. " But," I added, " as you are my brother, I will give it to you; " which I did, belt, sheath and all.

Once away from shore we paused with one accord, held by the wild beauty of the scene. The red sun was already half hidden behind the black rampart of the western forests. Rank on rank, file on file stood the dark legions of the pine trees, reaching in mass formation into the shadows of the already darkening hills.

A pair of loons, their white breasts flashing, swam lazily on water so calm that it seemed a void, in which they floated as on air. Slowly the thin columns of smoke ascended from the clustered teepees, to lay in a white pall above the town. Soon the moon rose, pale and very close, and against its broad and luminous expanse a single pine stood blackly out in silhouette. Somewhere an owl hooted once.

* * * * * *

We moved off silently from the Hidden Town with its mystery, its customs of a bygone day, and its aloof, silent inhabitants, inscrutable and unfathomable as the sombre forest that had bred them. And as we entered the narrow defile at the outlet, came the long drawn-out sobbing wail of the wolf-dogs as they saluted the full of the moon, even as their wilder kindred have done for untold ages.

And late that night there was faintly borne on the still air a sound, persistent, insistent and monotonous; the steady rhythmic throbbing of an Indian Drum.

VI

Red Landreville

A Tribute

"He the marvellous story teller,
Told his tales of strange adventure,
That the time might pass more gaily,
And the guests be more contented."

LONGFELLOW

IF you read this book faithfully, starting at the beginning and going on through to the bitter end, as every true and dauntless reader should, you will come to know about Red Landreville and his exploits on the Mississauga river. A canoeman in no sense of the word, no kind of a bush-man whatsoever, he none the less was one of the most valuable members of a canoe brigade that I once took down the Mississauga. Under the severe conditions imposed by Wilderness travel of several months duration, circumstances sometimes arise that will test the endurance and the patience of a man to the limit; days when everything seems to go wrong, when the mosquitoes are bad, the portages extra long and toilsome, when the canoes get punctured and the cooking gets burned, and there occurs a series of those exasperating incidents, trivial in themselves, but which seem to have been devised with fiendish ingenuity by some super-demon to try the temper of tired and hungry workers, so that men are civil to one another only by a superhuman effort of restraint, and the usually happy, carefree atmosphere of the camp is surcharged with the perilous potentialities of an unexploded powder-mine. This particular trip was full of incident; and that is where Red Landreville came in.

For Red had a sense of humour above the ordinary, exceptional even among a type of men noted for their dry, caustic wit and careless ribaldries which were, aside from the stern joy of battling with Nature in the raw, the only entertainment that they ever had.

And many a dangerous situation has been saved, and many a dejected, exhausted group of men who have begun to feel that life is just one damned thing after another, have been jarred into forgetfulness of their immediate troubles by some well-timed joke, and those who a few minutes before were sunk in the depths of a despair from which there seemed to be no escape, would be shouting with mirth and beating one another on the back, or head, or whatever part was handiest, over some perhaps not so decorous funny story, or be laughing themselves sick over the old one about the two Irishmen.

But Red dealt in no such banalities; his stories were clean, with the added virtue of being all new; and I think he must have made them up as he went along, on the spur of the moment. He was an artist. His sense of humour was unquenchable, though he seldom smiled, and he could be crushed by no misfortune whatsoever. Anything but an expert packer, he once fell on a portage, face down, with his load on top of him. I was behind him, and dropping my own load I helped him out from under. I asked him how he felt. His face was cut and his teeth were full of sand and pine needles, but he spat them out and replied that he had never felt better in his life and that if he did, he would be inclined to think the world was framing on him.

I first noticed Red sitting among a group of Rangers outside the headquarters cabin at Bisco, the starting point for those who would penetrate the vast wilderness areas that lay spread out for hundreds of miles in all directions. The travelling was by canoe and portage only, and sufficiently arduous for even well-experienced bushmen, and I saw, with certain misgivings, that several of those present, including Landreville, were going to be more ornamental than useful. Though certainly Landreville was no ornament. Tall and thin, with a homely, freckled face surmounted by a shock of violently red hair, he was talking with a kind of sarcastic twist to his lips that caused me to think that he was fomenting trouble among the men. So I stopped and listened. He waved me courteously to a seat on the bare ground, and said " Look, Chief, these guys won't believe me; isn't that true about the rabbits ? You know." Not wanting to spoil a story I replied, on general principles, " Sure it's true; what is it ? " " Well," he answered, " the way the Indians catch them, with pepper. You know." I didn't know, but it was all right with me. He asked me to explain the method to the group, knowing very well that I had not the faintest idea of what he was getting at; but I had not the time, I claimed, being busy, and suggested he do so. " You tell it " I said.

So he did. And then I completely forgot all about my pretence of business, and sat there and listened to Red Landreville.

I gathered that one of the group, an athletically built university man (who had been foisted upon us by the political patronage system then in vogue), had been asking innumerable questions concerning the coming voyage. However brilliant as a student he was utterly out of place in these surroundings, and green as grass—as I too would have been in college halls. In this he was forgivable except that he had made the rather bad mistake of boasting that he didn't really need the job, and that he had got himself enrolled so he could have a holiday in the woods and at the same time be paid for it. He turned out to be a dead loss, and considering that he would be only a drawback and was filling the place of some working man who needed the money to live, this remark had grated rather on the sensibilities of those present who earned their living by the sweat

of their brow. This gentleman, whom we shall refer to as
C——, in his thirst for knowledge asked numerous and rather
dumb questions instead of trying to profit by what he saw,
and had enquired among many other things how it was
possible to get fresh meat in the woods. On being told
that white people were not allowed to kill anything but fish
and rabbits in the Summer, he had asked how one caught the
rabbits. Red had at once volunteered the information.
The method, he said, was a secret known only to the Indians
and himself, and he begged those present not to divulge it
lest the Indians take revenge on him for betraying the
secret.

" You see how easy it is," he commenced. " Rabbits have
a way of sitting around at night in circles, like we are,"
he indicated his listeners, " and they sit there thumping their
hind feet on the ground—don't they? " he referred to me,
and I had to admit that this was true. Having very adroitly
made me an accessory, he continued: " Well they always go
to the same place to hold their *fiestas*, and where they sit
gets kinda worn, in a circle. Well, you go around through
the bush until you find a place like that, and then you put
stones inside the ring, one in front of where you think each
rabbit is going to sit; some stones will be right and some
won't, but that's all right, because you don't want to kill
'em all. All you got to do is to sprinkle some red pepper
on the rocks and go away. You see, when the rabbits bang
their hind feet on the ground, they kinda bob their heads
down; did I get that right? " he looked at me. Being now
hopelessly involved, I agreed with him again. He gave me
a friendly nod, as from one craftsman to another. He
resumed: " Well, when they bang their feet they bob their
heads, see, and when they bob their heads they get the pepper
that's on the stone in their noses and then they commence to
sneeze, and sneeze *and* sneeze, banging their heads until
they knock their fool brains out on the stones. All you do
is go round in the morning and collect. Nothin' to it! "

I was afraid he was going to ask me to corroborate this statement too, but he was too much of an artist to overdo things, merely remarking, " A man don't need much pepper for a Summer . . . four, five pounds, something like that."

None of this was lost on C——, who listened closely, but didn't quite know how to take it, as the others all carefully refrained from laughing. Nobody expected him to credit the unbelievable tale, of course—all Red was doing was to answer one of his foolish questions with an equally ridiculous reply, in order to chasten him for his tactlessness.

On the way in to the forest reserve C——, in spite of his muscular development—I have seldom seen a man so smoothly and evenly developed—had to have a great many things done for him to enable him to keep up with the party. Some newcomers are able to hustle around and grasp the essentials of an unfamiliar environment and so make some kind of a showing, often becoming good, useful men, but C—— never seemed to learn. This did not prevent him from being just the least bit too sure of himself, and about the third day of the trip he undertook to carry his canoe through the bush to the next lake, instead of using the portage—a foolish stunt if ever there was one. Half way there he became lost, and put down the canoe to find his way. He found his way to the lake, only to discover that he had now lost the canoe, and it then took all hands nearly half a day to find it.

One night he left his provisions out in a downpour of rain, and everything that could not hold out water was completely soaked. Red Landreville, ever ready to assist in an emergency, helped him sort out the water-soaked provisions. And in among them was a five-pound box of red pepper!

I don't think I'll forget the look of withering scorn which Red Landreville, standing with the pepper held up to view, turned on C——, while he gave utterance to the following :

" Hopeless "—he had named him Hopeless for obvious reasons—" Hopeless, you're dumb as ten men up a tree— Catch rabbits, would yuh! Someone should hang you up in the bush somewhere and sprinkle you with red pepper, so a moose could come and sneeze out his brains all over you; for I'm here to tell you that it's the only way you'll ever have any."

There is a story about this graceless prevaricator which, while I cannot vouch for it, is sufficiently typical of him, and is more than likely to be true. It seems that later on, after he became more or less expert, he came to like the wild, free life of the professional woodsman, which suited his own reckless nature to perfection.

A party he travelled with was in charge of a chief who was of a very irascible disposition, and whom, in order to get this story right, I must describe to you rather fully. A great stickler for efficiency, he drove his outfits at high speed and berated his men for the least delay. He went so far as to forbid the use of candles, allowing no one to carry any, claiming that a man stayed up till all hours by the light of them, talking when he should be sleeping, causing him to be abed in the morning. However, one day a Ranger's pack-sack burst open and the contents spilled, disclosing a large package of candles. At once the chief leaped at the offender and cried, "Ha! candles! candles! what have you got all those candles for, what for?" There was a silence while the two men measured each other. Then, " To get up in the morning by," calmly answered the Ranger. It is characteristic of this fire-eating speed worshipper, that his eyes crinkled a little at the corners as he nodded in appreciation of the witty answer. " You win! " he said.

Another time a canoe, manned by a pair of indifferent canoemen, capsized. Nearly all the load was lost and the men were only rescued with difficulty, the chief, beside himself with vexation, meanwhile bellowing instructions to the rescuers from the shore. And when the poor fellows

E

were safely landed, having narrowly escaped with their lives, he rushed at them and roared out, " What in the name of God did you do that for ! "

Red, who was rather a leisurely individual, got a trifle fed up on this kind of thing, and decided that he would put over a fast one on the chief, the first chance he got, " just to tone him down a few." His opportunity occurred when another one of those incompetents that were constantly inflicted on the forest ranging crews of those days by political chicanery, tumbled off a bridge of poles, load and all, into a creek. This individual, against advice, had made himself prisoner to the hundred-pound sack of flour that he was carrying, by tying himself securely to it with a tump line. He fell in the creek head first, and was held there by the sack of flour, from which he could not extricate himself, head down and with only his feet protruding. He was quickly hauled out of there of course. But Red Landreville, who had been hoping for something like this for a long time, did not wait to see whether he was still alive or not, but rushed immediately across the portage where the chief was, past the long line of packers, shouting as he went that a man was drowning, and creating a great commotion. At the other end of the trail the chief was declaiming loudly on the benefits of efficiency, and how it was already seven in the morning and they'd only made twenty miles and what was wrong with you today, you condemned . . . (stultified) . . . apes of doubtful ancestry, when Red dashed up with his hat in his hand and his hair all flared up on end, and the following conversation ensued :

" Hey, Chief, so and so's fallen in the crik."

" Why, what for ? "

" I don't know why, but he's there load and all."

" Cripes, did they save the load ? "

" No, they're both in there. He'll likely drown."

" Howling catfish ! hain't they got him out of there yet , . . how far is he in ? "

" Oh, up to the ankles."

" Ha! so you're a smart guy eh, up to the ankles, drowning! . . . darn your hide, you'll sweat for this . . . in up to the ankles, is he! . . .Yah!! . . ."

" Yeah," agreed Red, " up to the ankles; but, Chief, you don't know the half of it . . . he's in head first! "

For a long time Red Landreville had been going to tell us a ghost story about a hen. He never actually did, and I am inclined to suspect that there was no such story; ghosts and hens don't seem to belong in the same category, somehow. But he *did* tell us a tale about a bear.

As I recall it, he was walking along beside a stream when he met a bear. It was a big bear. The bear was running, so to be sociable he ran too, in the same direction of course, a little ahead of the bear. The bear, for some reason, had its mouth open; it had nearly fifty teeth in each jaw, with holes punched in its gums for more, and was making loud, uncouth noises. (Red made the noises.) Soon he came to a tree; the creek was on one side of him and the bear was on the other, so, not wishing to be in the way at all, Red climbed the tree. (He made hurried climbing motions, looking down over his back; we had all the action and the sound effects.) Landreville stayed up the tree, and the bear, having thought of something, remained at the foot of it. Presently the bear went away, and Red commenced to climb down, when the animal returned, bringing with him another larger, and probably more experienced bear. They sat at the foot of the tree, looked up at him, and then commenced to mutter and mumble together, evidently talking the thing over. Red now made a noise like two bears would make if they made that kind of a noise. He looked at me and asked if the noise had been correctly rendered; with a slight shudder I said it had. He had developed a practice of referring to me for support in any small point of natural history that came up in his stories, and I had been involved in several rather difficult situations. Well, after a lengthy conference the more talented bear went away, returning shortly with a beaver; (at this point I think that many of those present began not to believe the story). He set the beaver at the foot of the tree, but the beaver was not willing and the bears had to cuff him a couple of times before he would start to work; the bears were a lot bigger than he was, and there wasn't much he could do about it. So the beaver commenced to cut, on the side furthest from the creek, under the supervision of the bears. It was a very big tree; by the time the beaver had got to the centre of it nothing but the tip of his tail was visible. He came out of there, and prompted by his captors went to the other side, nearest the creek. There was no room for the bears between the tree and the stream, so the beaver had it to himself, Red noticed. Out of sight, he looked up at Red. The beaver winked at him. " So I knew it was going to be O.K.," said Red, " beavers are no fools. So, the beaver cut away at the tree, and pretty soon all I could see was the tip of his tail again, and knowed something was going to happen. The tree started to go; there was nowhere to fall but off, if you get what I mean, so I stayed with the tree. And then I saw why the beaver had winked. The tree fell square across the creek and I landed on the other bank. The beaver jumped in the creek, and the two bears were left there looking foolish as a bag of cats."

After the comments of respectful admiration had died down, Red said he had a good recipe for putting insolent bears in their place. " It's quite easy to keep a bear from chasing you," he asserted. " I mind one time I was in a country where bears was bad, real bad. I was pickin' berries at the time, and I seen a bear comin'. He was getting pretty close and I seen he meant business. So I took some berry juice and painted a face on the bottom of the pail, and when the bear got real close I put the pail backwards on my head, so the face was looking behind me, and started to run away. The bear saw the face and thought

I was runnin' backwards, so he decided I was crazy and ran the other way as fast as he could go."

Well, Red, if you should ever read this, give a thought to the old days on the River. And here's hoping that wherever you go, you may carry with you that priceless gift, the power to make men laugh when things go wrong.

VII

The Sage of Pelican Lake

THE time was that of the Fall Hunt. Domiciled as I am in
a National Park, to get my winter's meat it is necessary that I
travel beyond the Park boundaries, a matter of perhaps
twenty miles.

The country was new to me, and the short December day
had been dull and stormy, with heavy going; consequently
darkness found me still some miles from my objective, and
not a little tired, with camp still to be made. In the
darkness I had become mired in a field of slush and my snowshoes were now heavy with ice. So it was with some relief
that I caught the scent of smoke, faint but unmistakable,
borne to me on the light offshore breeze. I turned West and
followed it up. This was an area of original timber, and in
the murk the wall of spruce stood blackly opaque, like a low
dark precipice, and from it there showed no sparkle of a fire,
or gleam of a lighted window. The odour of smoke was not
acrid, but had that peculiar flatness which indicated a fire that
had been suffered to burn low; my prospective hosts might be
sleeping, and I none too welcome. The snow was deep
enough to smother the rattle of the icy snowshoe frames one
on the other and the wind, as mentioned, was toward me, so
that my approach was unnoticed until I started up the hard
trail that led to the hidden habitation. Instantly a herd of
dogs came to life and swooped down on me, and by their
uproar and actions seemed to be clamoring for my blood.
Surrounded by this howling mob I passed between the close
set boles of the spruce, and, directed by a square of illumination, came upon the camp. The door stood open, and a

voice in Cree called on me to enter. I slipped out of the
bridles, and as I did so a boy stepped forward, picked up the
snowshoes and threw them up on the roof; a friendly act
but viewed, no doubt, with disfavor by the dogs, who had
already begun to smell at them and who would, after the
fashion of all huskies, have liked to sample the rawhide
filling. Entering, I found myself in a dimly lighted log
cabin, floored with brush, and without fixtures, excepting
two stoves.

Two small families occupied part of the floor space near
two of the walls. By one stove, making fresh fire, knelt an
old man. He placed a tea-pail on it, and rising took my
hand in welcome. He relieved me of my pack, and taking
my rifle from the corner where I had stood it, set it outside.
This struck me as a strange proceeding, but I was too happy
at having escaped the inconvenience of making camp in the
dark, to care much what he did; though the reason I was to
learn before I left. My host wore a pair of blanket-cloth
leggings and his feet were bare; he had the straight back and
the quick, light movements of a much younger man, but it
was apparent that he was very old. Seldom have I seen a
face so seamed and weatherbeaten. The wrinkles that
furrowed his rugged features were bitten deeply in, and
from this mass of corrugation there looked out at me eyes of
a deep and brooding melancholy. Yet in his calm and level,
comprehending gaze, I somehow sensed a world of kindly
tolerance and understanding; evidently a man well mel-
lowed by the storms of life, and one to whom it would be
quite useless to lie.

He spread a caribou hide, and with simple courtesy bade
me be seated. He proffered his pouch which contained not
tobacco, but the dried and crumbled leaves of Kinni-kinnik,
and we smoked awhile. Although no apparent notice had
been taken of my arrival by the other occupants of the place,
I knew I was closely observed, and felt rather than saw swift
veiled glances turned my way. There was a little whispering,

and a young woman commenced to cut slices from a quarter of deer that lay on the wood-pile to thaw. I recounted, with proper deliberation, the circumstances of my trip, as was expected of me, using the language of the Ojibways, in which the old man had first addressed me. It is a far cry from the Height of Land Country of Algoma or Abitibi to the waters of the Upper Saskatchewan, and I found it remarkable that he was conversant with that tongue, or even knew I spoke it.

" You wear Ojibway snowshoes," he answered to my comment, " so I knew it was no use talking to you in Sioux, Plains Cree, or Swampy."

He informed me that he had been raised amongst the Ojibways, and knew about where I came from by my accent, and explained :

" In the days when you could tell where a man belonged, and what his tribe was, by the way he wore his hair or by the shape of his canoe, it was not hard to size up a stranger and know how to talk to him. I hunted west of Kitche-Gaming (Lake Superior) about sixty-five years ago. There was no rail-road then."

He outclassed me in my adopted tongue, besides making use of local dialect, and some of what he said was lost to me. But I gathered that he had moved from Minnesota to the great Plains around 1868, trapping as he went, and living with the Indians. He mentioned these happenings in quite a matter of fact way, as though they were quite recent, and not remarkable.

To hear the most interesting period of our history discussed by one of the few remaining participants in it, is a privilege accorded to the few; and to avoid any loss of detail I asked if he would speak in English. He showed a familiarity with it that I little expected, until he stated that he was a white man, a circumstance that had been none too evident at first. He admitted to four Indian languages and some dialects, also English and French. He preferred to talk in Indian, and it was noticeable that he was not nearly so expressive in English as in Ojibway.

He was by no means voluble and appeared to have given me this information more as a matter of introduction than as conversation, so I refrained from heedless questions. The aged live much in retrospect, and resent unwarrantable intrusion into their thoughts, and when the old man fell to silence I decided, and wisely, to hold my peace, and addressed myself to the meal which one of the women now placed before me. It finished, the Kinni-kinnik was passed, and we smoked in quiet contentment. The aromatic white smoke of the Indian tobacco floated up in whorls and wisps, and little clouds floated idly before us, drifted to the stove and eddied upwards to the roof-tree.

A sleeping infant stirred uneasily and whimpered, and the father reached up, half-conscious, and swayed the sling in which it was suspended. Outside a dog howled thinly; I commenced to feel drowsy. Soon my host suggested that we turn in, and handed me one blanket of the two he had, to supplement my bedroll which had been arranged with a view of lightness rather than warmth. Northern hospitality demands that you divide your blankets with a visitor or give up your bed to him, that each may sleep alone, in comfort. In this case however, I had company. At my side were three coyotes, dead and frozen stiff. These strange bed-fellows were more than welcome towards morning, as the camp was not any too warm, and I was glad to get my back against them for whatever warmth there was in their thick fur.

The old man was up and around at break of day kindling the fires, and soon the women commenced making bannock and cooking meat. At breakfast each group sat, squatted or reclined around its own particular spread. My ancient host waited on me, filling my dish with meat when it fell empty, and saw that my cup was always full of hot tea, which was of such a potency that I believe a nail would have sunk in it with difficulty. His solicitous attention to my welfare during my entire stay of four days, was such as we are led to expect only from those of a higher social plane. He dispensed the limited resources at his command in such a way that somehow each of these frugal repasts became a small event, and the plain boiled meat and bannock were more tasty, the tea more refreshing, and the home-made tobacco was the sweeter for his kindly ministrations. At his word my wants were all attended to with that tactful anticipation of need that puts a man at ease in any company, and I had not to stir a hand or foot on my behalf; nor did I attempt to do so, as insincere protestations have no part in the rigid creed of backwoods hospitality. That morning, having accepted an invitation to use this camp as a headquarters for my hunt, I equipped myself for the day's journey and went about my business.

During the evening we talked intermittently, the old man and I, on those subjects which are of interest to woodsmen, such as the lay of the land, the price of fur, prohibition and so forth, but no more history was forthcoming and only my appreciation of the old man's quiet and patriarchal dignity kept my vulgar curiosity from getting the better of me. It was the third night before I had an opportunity to re-open the subject. After about four smokes, during which no word was spoken, he unearthed an old magazine from the head of his bed, and asked me if I would explain the meaning of the pictures in it. It so happened that the book contained amongst other features, an article on Indian life, fancifully illustrated by the author's conception of different Indian activities, including that of the Sun Dance. I craftily refrained from discoursing on this topic until the old fellow's interest in the other subjects was beginning to wane, when I introduced it as a final ruse de guerre, coup de grace, or piece de resistance, or whatever. I asked him if the Sun Dance was properly depicted. "It certainly is not," he replied with emphasis. "How could it be? They do not put up a scaffold like that; and where are the thirst dancers?"

He expressed himself as outraged at the misrepresentation of an old and honoured custom. I enquired as to where the description was in error.

" Did you ever see the Sun Dance? " he asked.

Although I had been a witness to some of the tame and de-natured rites that are allowed in the revival of this bloody ceremony, I replied that I had not, and closed my mouth.

" That," he said, pointing at the picture, " is not the real thing. There's a lot more to it than that. They used to build pens like this," he illustrated in miniature with small sticks and brush. " One for each man. They'd make a lot of them, maybe a dozen, according to the number that wanted to go through the test. One man would go in each and dance there naked, right out in the sun, with no shade. They danced and sang without food or water and never stopped to rest at nights. They never quit singing. They were supposed to bring the rain. No water was allowed to touch them inside or out till rain fell on them; guards were stationed to see that nobody cheated. If a man couldn't stand the gaff, and quit, he was disqualified and disgraced; he was sent back with the women. That was the Blackfoot style; they called it the Thirst Dance."

I wanted to know if they ever had any difficulty in bringing the rain. He replied that they overcame that by dancing till it did rain. The medicine men arranged the time for the Dance and they were pretty good weather prophets. Sometimes, though, they calculated wrong, and some of the entries died.

I questioned him about the voluntary torture some of them submitted to.

" Men were different those days," he asserted. " A man had to be brave, or he didn't go into it at all. They would lop a poplar tree, limb it and bring it into camp and set it up. They left a limb about twenty feet above the ground, and hung from it by rawhide thongs skewered into their breasts, dancing. The thongs were wet, and shrunk as they dried, and the men danced at last on tiptoe till the flesh tore out."

Others, it appeared, cut loops in the skin of their backs, tied thongs to them, by this means dragging as they danced, heavy objects along the ground, such as the head of a steer or a small buffalo, or a dead dog. Yet others, craving more action, attached themselves in the same way to live dogs, whilst onlookers chivvied and beat the animals into a frenzy so that they jerked and ran about and strained on this ghastly leash until they tore it loose.

Drumming and chanting continued without intermission during these exercises, and horsemen galloped around the dancers shouting encouragement, thereby greatly increasing the travail of those who were at the mercy of the excited dogs.

"Those sure were great tests," declared the old man. "It took a warrior to go through with them. They don't allow it any more," he added wistfully. "Just the same it always meant trouble, and sometimes I'm not so sorry it's over." I asked if he would like to see the old days back again. "No," he answered emphatically, "I wouldn't. The plains were full of warriors, and we had to go round in large parties." No one was safe, save those the Indians favored. He spoke of unthinkable cruelties of which not only savages but also white men were the perpetrators.

He dissipated the ameliorating mists of time with a few vivid anecdotes, and with significant gestures he drew back the graceful veil of Romance from across the stage of the old Western frontier, and exposed it in all its stark and shuddering brutality. And by the wavering illumination of the tallow-dip the shadows moved strangely, and flickered and leaped grotesquely in and out, and made an eerie setting for his grisly tales. He peopled the ill-lighted cabin with dim shapes, shades that stalked grim and ghastly through the smoke wreathes, bent on errands of nameless and unnamable horror—with naked demons that lurked in darkened corners or danced the horrid bacchanal of death.

A young girl brought us tea, and I eyed her two long braids and tried to imagine how they would look as a scalp, stretched on a hoop, like a beaver skin. Many years ago I had listened with youthful eagerness to the related exploits of certain hoary murderers of ancient vintage, and had come to think that those stirring days were not quite so enthralling as some would have them be.

My old companion recounted many tales that had, I think, not often passed his lips before. This opening up of the floodgates of his memory was not on account of any alchemy of mine, or charm I put upon him with my presence, or open sesame that I pronounced, but was perhaps vouchsafed because he sensed in me an audience whose interest was genuine, and because he found a melancholy pleasure in the telling. He used none of the artful devices of the story-teller, stating plain facts without adornment, but with a wealth of detail. He garnished his tales with apt and homely comment on the characters in them so that they were very real, and despite the fact that he could read nothing save the phonetic signs of Indian writing [1] his accounts tallied with all I had ever read or heard. He betrayed too, a shrewdness of intellect and a keen insight into the ways of men, that is more often the result of observation and experience than it is of education. He appeared to have no idea of the historical significance of the scenes he had witnessed, seeming to think of them only as commonplace occurrences that no longer took place. I had thought to interest him in tales of my own travels, but decided to forbear from recounting any of my insignificant experiences.

On a day that was warm with soft Chinook, he sat awhile beneath a mighty spruce that stood beside the cabin, looking out across the wide expanse of lake in tranquil contemplation of the distant hills.

" This is my own tree," he told me. " The boys wanted

[1] This writing is a species of shorthand introduced among the Indians by missionaries, and is universally used amongst the tribes.

to cut it down, but it is getting old, like me, and I saved it."

Assisted by information as to the lay of the land and movements of game provided me by the two younger men to whom the trapping ground belonged, I had succeeded in killing a caribou and also a red deer. These were sufficient for my needs, and I now considered returning to my own territory. But in response to my host's insistence I stayed another night, and counted the time well lost, as I sat in silence and listened to the words that fell from lips that must soon be sealed forever.

Mindful of my duties as a favored guest, I took my turn and spun my yarns, folk tales of Apache and Ojibway. Foolish tales they were, of things that never did happen, myths and fables of an imaginative and superstitious people attempting to account for the phenomena of their environment, tales I had half-believed myself in younger and less sceptical days. And whilst I talked, these silent people listened gravely, yet with intense attention, listened politely, and never interrupted by voice or action, nor said the story was an old one, or unbelievable.

Stirred by the demands of this auspicious occasion, other members of the little company contributed their share of entertainment, and told legends of the Cree, the Saulteaux, and the Blackfeet, tales of wisemen and monsters, stories of devils and of prophets; allegories from the whispering forests and the wide rolling prairie, chronicles of old beginnings. Tea drinking and smoking followed.

Later and easier years have weaned me somewhat away from the diet of the trap trail, and I can no longer subsist on a diet of straight meat, bannock and tea, three times a day. My aged host, however, ate large quantities of meat and little else, caring nothing for the small delicacies the others allowed themselves. I suspected a little that he felt himself a burden on this younger brood, from whom he seemed, and indeed was, a being apart. Perceiving this, I could not without shame have eaten what he denied himself, and made a brave face but a shy stomach at the inevitable and monotonous boiled caribou steaks and ribs, and went often hungry. The patriarch, who by the way, had all his teeth, stated that he could live indefinitely on a straight meat diet, and asked nothing better than a good bone to chew on in moments of stress. In the early 70's he had lived amongst the Sioux, or Dakotah as they call themselves, and meat, especially buffalo, had been their only diet, save what plant foods and berries were gathered or traded for and saved for winter consumption. In Minnesota there had been acorn flour and wild rice; and later, coffee without milk or sugar had come into universal use.

His narratives were punctuated by long, thoughtful silences during which we smoked, seated on the caribou hide, whilst the women moved quietly and unobtrusively about their household tasks. On this last night of my stay, after the children had been suspended in hammock-like slings or laced into moss-bag cradles to sleep, and the floor was strewn with blanket covered forms and there were no longer any sounds save those of slumber, the old man mused and talked the whole night through, living again whole chapters from his long experience. Tales of privation and hunger he told, of fighting and feasting, of endless trails whose only limit was the skyline, of customs long discontinued and forgotten; and made them seem as though they had been but yesterday. By the light of the flickering tallow-dip he weaved before my eyes the fabric of a story that would have made an epic, had I sufficient skill to write it.

He had left the American plains, he stated, shortly before the Custer fight, and crossed to the Canadian side. He knew Sitting Bull, or Bull-Getting-Up, to use the literal translation of the name, who was a half-breed whom he believed to have been born near Fort Garry, now Winnipeg. He was in the Cypress Hill country when the victorious warriors from the battle of Little Bighorn crossed the border at that point to obtain sanctuary in this country, and he had circulated freely amongst them as an old acquaintance. They wore no panoply of battle, being on a peace mission, and the spectacular war-bonnets and other trappings had been laid carefully away. Most of the warriors wore only one or two feathers, and those always at an angle, never upright, so that their decorations and insignia carried no record of their prowess in the late wars, and nothing in their appearance could be construed as warlike. Many, however, carried tomahawks and war-hawks (egg-shaped stones set onto long slim, sometimes flexible handles) tucked into the crook of their elbows; the older men carried long pipes, and nearly all wore blankets. He found them very friendly, and in jubilant mood, and whilst they came over as a matter of expediency, apprehensive of the atrocities the soldiers often inflicted on the women and children, they seemed to have no fear of the bluecoats. Their account of the battle varied greatly from the popular conception of it. Asked if he saw any of the scalps that were taken, he replied no, that the Indians were ashamed of them and would not show them because the hair on them was short. There were several pure white men with the Indian forces, who had also taken part in the fight. Their defection, in his estimation, was no more reprehensible than that of the renegade Indians who at times had helped the white men against their own race. I agreed with him on that point, having long been of the opinion that certain Indians who have gone down in history as noble friends of the white man, were in reality nothing more or less than traitors to their own people, astute opportunists who saw on which side their bread was going to be buttered. They once chased the Mounted Police, one of whom threw himself, or fell, off his horse, and was rescued by an Indian girl whom he married.

He spoke of the North-West rebellion, and had been in the Prince Albert district during hostilities, refusing to serve as a scout against his adopted race. Neither would he carry weapons against his own colour, so took no part at all save as an onlooker. He used to watch the target practice with the gatling guns, of which he said that the cartridges were poured into the gun through a kind of funnel, like rocks dumped into a stonecrusher, while a gunner turned a handle and ground away at the target.

Whilst they feared and respected the trappers, scouts and other irregular frontier fighters, according to him the Indians did not take their uniformed enemies, on either side of the line, very seriously; and he further stated that the warriors had often been able to hold their own against the best troops and police when adequately armed. He knew of one half-breed who claimed to have killed thirty-one soldiers at the battle of Batoche, which was admittedly an overwhelming defeat for the soldiery, and who had furthermore asserted that the falling of darkness alone saved the troops from annihilation. The soldiers, inexperienced in prairie warfare, had been unable to take or use cover to advantage, and being often partly lost or bewildered had fired at times on their own men. History tells us that in old Indian wars in the Eastern forests, and later in the Boer War and other Wilderness campaigns, this same situation frequently arose in conflicts between rigidly trained soldiery and the more adept guerrilla fighters.

He showed me an arrow wound in his leg, quite as though arrow wounds had not been long out of date. It was an unsightly scar, as it had been a war arrow with fluked shoulders, having had to be cut out with a knife in the heat of battle. This was during a stand-off staged by his party against raiding Pawnees. He had been young at the time and not able to fight, and whilst the attack was in progress had passed his time playing with a pile of moulded bullets along with some other youngsters under a wagon.

Besides differences in hairdressing, styles of beadwork and moccasins, the mental and physical characteristics of Indians had varied greatly with the different tribes, he said. The

F

Stoneys, the Blackfeet, and the Pawnees were, he claimed, the most warlike, courageous and cultured in the Indian arts; the Saulteaux, Bush Cree and Ojibways were the most peaceable. The Blackfeet were very wild, and good fighters, but less aggressive and more level-headed than the central prairie tribes. They were also more temperate.

Some of his narratives were not without their lighter side, although he had rather unusual ideas of what constituted an amusing story. As an example of such bizarre comedy there was the anecdote concerning his first trip with a veteran of many Indian wars. One evening, being far from shelter and the weather stormy, they were glad to come upon a cabin which, whilst showing signs of having been lately inhabited, now appeared to be deserted. They found it, however, to be occupied. On entering, one of the travellers stumbled over what proved to be a dead man. Near him lay another. Closer inspection revealed three more, one of them having been careless enough to get himself killed in bed. It was raining hard, so there was nothing to do but get the bodies out and make the best of it.

" My, ain't we lucky," exclaimed the veteran, cheerfully, whilst the younger man commenced moving the bodies. " But hold on, just a minute; we have got to do this job up right," and with further remarks of appreciation for the good fortune that had befallen them, he proceeded to scalp all five of the corpses before finally dragging them outside. All good clean fun, so to speak. To a young man alone with a stranger possessed of such droll mannerisms, the humour of the situation must have been at once apparent. Personally I prefer the one about old Star Blanket, the well-known Cree Chief. Some white friends of his once took him East for a treat, or an object lesson, or for some such purpose, and lodged him in one of the biggest hotels in the city. The old fellow was well taken care of, and had been all dressed up in civilian clothes for the occasion. On his native heath, however, he had been in the habit of wearing little but a breech-clout and moccasins and the old feather, and one morning in a moment of forgetfulness, he sauntered down to breakfast attired only in his underclothes, thinking himself fully dressed.

Human nature seems not to have changed a great deal between the early aboriginal days of evolution and now. The Indian of that day was just emerging from what was virtually the Stone Age, yet he had his profiteers and racketeers, though small-time ones according to our more improved standards. Outside of a few copper weapons made by one or two tribes, they had no metal except gold and very little of that; and it had no value save for ornamental purposes. As for this supposedly very modern evil of countries conspiring together to foment war, and then selling deadly weapons and ammunition to each other to kill their own soldiers with, we learn that the best scalping knives were made in Sheffield and Connecticut and sold to the Indians by white men, to scalp white men with. And my host told me about an arrow maker who made such excellent arrows that his wares were in great demand. Not being satisfied with legitimate profits he decided to boost the trade a little, and went around, during his spare time, promoting trouble between his own and neighbouring tribes, and when war broke out, with a nice regard for symmetry, he sold arrows to both sides, meanwhile sitting by and enjoying the fun and, incidentally, raking in the profits. A pastime which we all know to be not entirely confined to arrow makers. And there is a certain grim humour in the story he told me of the occasion when a settler, in the early days, woke up at some sounds he heard coming from outside his window. He looked out and saw a party of Indians stirring something in a copper kettle that he valued very highly. " Hey, what are you fellows mixing in that kettle? " he demanded. " Paint " answered one of the Indians, shortly. " What for? " asked the settler. " The war path " said the Indian, looking pretty straight. " Oh "—the settler considered for a moment—" All right, all right, boys, go ahead. It's quite all right." " You're darn right it's all right," said the Indian. " It has to be."

The old trapper's experiences seem to have been more peaceful on the Canadian side of the line, as there was no organized attempt being made there to dispossess the Indians. Perhaps this was on account of their being less numerous, and possibly because, owing to the more vigorous climate, they spent much of their Summer getting ready for the Winter, and much of the Winter trying to keep warm, and so had little time for hostile activities. They did, however, make sporadic forays on each other, and there was lasting enmity between the Crees and the Blackfeet. Some of these raids were conducted on a grand scale, and as the Blackfeet came out the winners with rather monotonous regularity, they were feared and hated pretty thoroughly by their opponents.

While travelling in the Belly River country, the old man had occasion to spend a night with a band of Crees that had lately been badly whipped by their hereditary enemies. In this instance the defeat had been ascribed to the weakness of the brand of spiritual assistance supplied by the tribal Medicine Man, and he had fallen into disfavour. On the night in question there was a Medicine Dance being held in a large teepee set up for the purpose, and organized by a rival conjuror. Disgruntled, the deposed magician refused to attend, and was sleeping out near where one of his horses was picketed. Restless, he wandered around a little, and returning from a short excursion he was thunderstruck, and not a little alarmed, to see a strange Indian, whom he was able to distinguish as a Blackfoot, in the act of untying the animal, which was his very best horse. Not observing him, the thief started away, leading the horse. The owner, overcoming his natural timidity in the presence of a member of the invincible Blackfoot nation, and filled with righteous indignation, quickly drew the stake from the ground, crept up behind his enemy and knocked him cold. He then made a crude but thorough job with the stake, and took the scalp. He could scarcely credit his good fortune. One minute he has been a discredited charlatan, the next, here he was a proven warrior with a scalp to his credit. Here was a coup indeed . . . a man killed with a hand weapon, standing, and the weapon nothing but a stake! That rated two feathers, upright, no less. This exploit would certainly reinstate him in the good graces of his congregation, and to this end he tied the body by the neck to his horse's tail and trailed it into camp, making a triumphal entry on horseback into the big lodge where the dance was in progress. The ceremonies ceased forthwith while he sang his story and recounted his coup. Immediately pandemonium broke loose. Here was one of the hated race on whom the vengeance of the entire band might be visited! The fact that he was dead made no difference whatever. A fire was quickly built outside, and the victor rode round and round this, chanting his songs and incantations to the time of drums and rattles, while the entire personnel of the camp not engaged in producing the music surrounded the body, beating it with sticks, hacking at it with knives, and cutting pieces from it. Meanwhile the women screamed epithets and reminded the corpse of the harm it had done them in life.

" It is a long time we have waited for you."

" It is a long time you have angered us," they chanted as they plied stick, knife and tomahawk. Eventually the body was dismembered and pretty well divided up, and the pieces were held high whilst the dancers yelled and postured and sang in ever increasing frenzy.

At this point, the narrator relates that he tactfully withdrew. He had many worthwhile friends amongst the Indians who deplored these practices. Some of the old chiefs were good, upstanding, and intelligent men who only fought, as the leaders of any other nation would have done, in self-preservation. Polygamy was occasionally practised, though their family life was, in most tribes, above reproach. Women were generally chaste, excepting a few recognized cases in each band, who solved for each community a problem that their " betters " have yet found no other solution for. They loved their children devotedly, were good husbands and faithful wives, and until they began to be herded on reservations were as a rule, a clean, healthy people.

Some of the looser characters among the scouts and guides were more vicious than the savages, and committed depredations against peaceful Indians that were a fruitful cause of unrest and reprisal, and often precipitated war. That it was possible, even in those days, to avoid trouble and still carry on effectively, was evidenced by the fact that hundreds of men passed through that entire period without firing a shot in anger.

*   *   *   *   *

Few of the old man's habits reflect the influence of those violent times. For him they are over, and seemingly, unless he is reminded of them by others, they lie forgotten in the recesses of the past. But one thing I noticed that may have some bearing on the customs of a by-gone day; he will allow no gun to be brought into his camp, save by his immediate kin. I am constrained to wonder what he thinks of this modern day, what thoughts he has when he sees an aeroplane or hears a radio, if he ever does, and what is his opinion of the careless, noisy, happy groups of tourists who invade this Pelican Lake, his sanctuary for nearly forty years. I would much like to know what he thinks of me, descendant of a fighting race, living in ease that must seem to him unearned, whilst he, a lone survivor of that devoted band of pioneers of which the world will never see the like again, finds in plain meat, tea, a little flour, a few dried herbs and a blanket, the complete fulfilment of all his earthly needs.

But these things and many others I will never know. He keeps his secrets well—this courteous, gentle sage, this ancient warrior, as he sits nodding over his pipe, sits beneath his spruce tree that like himself is getting too old, dreaming who knows what dreams of dim and distant days, waiting patiently for the end that cannot now be far away, waiting at the gate of the Last Frontier.[1]

[1] This old warrior, whose name was Louis Levallé, died in 1935, soon after this account was written.

VIII

Cry Wolves!

TWENTY-FIVE miles from my main cabin, a hundred miles
north of the rail-road, an empty stomach, and darkness
coming on. Nothing for it but to make camp.

It was a good lynx country and tracks were thick as hair
on a dog's tail, and when a guy is busy setting traps in a
country like that, time slips by, and a fellow hates to stop.
A good heavy carpet of balsam boughs, half a dozen light
poles stuck upright in a semi-circle, with a sheet of canvas
stretched across them teepee fashion to reflect the heat of the
fire, and camp was made. And Oh yes, plenty of wood;
I forgot that.

The day had been long, and I was most hungry enough
to swallow the left hind leg of a caribou—hair, hoof, bones
and all. But on the trap-trail wood comes before food,
for away up north of 51 it sure knows how to freeze; so I
cinched up the old belt a couple, and swung an axe among the
dry timber for two solid hours, and when there was a pile of
wood two short men couldn't shake hands over, I made a
fire.

The iron of this country sure enters into a man's system at
such times; I was now dog-tired, and began to care little
whether I ate or not, but decided to do so in self-defence.
So I got myself on the outside of about two pounds of moose
steak, half a bannock, and somewhere around a quart of
hot tea, and got the old smokestack going.

That made quite a difference, and with my pipe drawing
just right I leaned back and watched the smoke billowing
up and spreading in a white canopy above, like a roof over

my head, and listened to the cheerful crackling of the fire, contented as could be. I commenced to think of some of the poor hungry people in the cities who didn't have as much to eat in a week as I had at a meal; things were not so bad with me, for all that I was alone with my little spot of fire in that endless white solitude.

A ring of giant spruces stood round brooding and solemn, just within the circle of light, and the shadows from the flames danced in and out at the foot of them; beyond that, blackness. And all the little imps and gnomes and Puck-wajees that the Indians believe in seemed to peer and look in at you from the darkness. Sometimes a white snowshoe rabbit came out from the shadows, and sat looking, looking, with never a sound, and then was gone like a puff of smoke. Out under the stars the whole world seemed to be standing still, listening, waiting for something that never happens. That sounds queer but it gets you that way, this Northland. You would know what I mean if ever you were alone on the edge of the world, with endless distances on all sides and above, all smothered in a glittering silence that weighs down on your soul.

After a while the sound of the fire died away, and I had lost track of things until I suddenly awoke chilled clear through, to find the fire low, and the echo of some sound dying away across the empty hills.

I listened for a while, and almost dozed again, when the sound was repeated; long, drawn out, and distant, mournful as the cry of a lost soul. The echoes didn't have time to fade away before it was answered from some place on the lake, right close to camp. Wolves!

I fixed the fire, took another smoke and rolled into my half blanket. Wolves were nothing new in that country, and all I hoped was that they wouldn't keep me awake. I had no more than closed my eyes when the wolf out on the lake let out another whoop and shot my sleep high, west, and sideways. This happened a couple of times and I got mad.

I dressed my feet and took off some clothes (for a fellow dresses up to go to bed when he sleeps out in forty below zero), slipped into my snowshoe bridles, and took a sashay down onto the lake. The Northern Lights were shimmering and swinging back and forth, almost low enough to touch, making a light a man could read a newspaper by. I almost seemed to hear them rustling as they moved.

I didn't feel nearly as ambitious about a wolf-hunt out on the lake as I had thought I would. Everything seemed weird and ghostly by the flare of the Aurora, and all the tall snow-covered trees along the shore seemed to stare down on me kind of dour and grim, like I had butted in where I wasn't wanted. And man! she was cold.

I had no rifle that trip, just a shot-gun, which was foolishness on my part, and goes to show how far some folks have to travel before they get to know anything. Anyway I piked off up the lake and saw a wolf alright enough, out of shot, and screeching blue murder. I sneaked up onto a point and saw the rest of the lake and say, it looked to be just covered with wolves. I counted nine that were close. It was a small lake and the wolves were very, very big; probably the biggest wolves in North America. They sure occupied a lot of room on that ice, to my notion. One fellow was prancing and gyrating around in front of the others, showing his stuff; doing the Wolf-Trot, I guess. I called the lake Dancing Wolf later, but at the time it looked too much like a war-dance for me to worry about names. Then they raised their long noses into the air, and one by one they started to howl. Noise! I'd never heard a noise till then.

The racket would make a fellow's blood stand on end. They had Bill Cody's Indians backed off the map for screeching. The nearest wolf was almost a hundred yards away, and me with a shot-gun! I'd have made some clean-up with a rifle. I was that mad I began to shiver, and decided to go back to camp whilst the going was good. I didn't attempt to scare the wolves any. I said to myself " Let the poor little creatures enjoy themselves while they may; they won't have long to live, once I get after them!"

They all seemed to be in pretty good shape, not sick or anything, and I figured they'd be quite all right out there on the ice.

The dancer, he seemed to have got a jag of some kind, and I was afraid he'd spot me any minute and get self-conscious and spoil the fun, which I wouldn't have had happen on any account. I didn't want to see anybody hurt, so I slid off, with my shot-gun, which began to look quite a lot like a pea-shooter.

I noticed it was a little pale around the gills, and I said "Quit rattlin' and shakin', you mutt gun; first thing you know they'll hear you and all go away, and then we'll be lonesome."

I set traps all the next day and that night I got back late to the sahaagan,[1] having to pass through a muskeg about a mile long that was just plastered with wolf-tracks, and no trees on it over six feet high to climb. The minute I hit the ice of my lake, the war whoop goes up from all around. I never saw a wolf, it being pretty dark, but I minded my own business and kept shoving one snowshoe ahead of the other in the usual way. My ears were sticking out some six or seven inches each way, listening to see if the wolves were warm and comfortable. I hoped they weren't hungry either. I always was kind to animals, and I like to see everybody contented.

I got back to camp where the trees were big and tall, and felt better; I figured they might come in handy, and if a fellow had any objection to freezing to death up a tree, why he could always come down and play around with the wolves, and keep warm that way. We passed the night in a kind of a way, me and my gun, the wolves making war medicine all night. The next day we moved away from that place.

---

[1] Canvas shelter.

About a week later I was crossing a long narrow lake at a spot where two streams came in on opposite shores. This formed a current where it never froze up till away late in the Winter, and even then the ice was always weak at this point. It was ten o'clock at night or thereabouts, and the moon had set. As I stepped out of the bush onto the ice I made out in the semi-darkness what looked to be a string of animals passing and re-passing a point of rock not fifty yards away. I knew that a neighbouring trapper intended to pass through my ground about that time, so I shouted to him to hold his dogs, on account of the bad ice. I got no answer and shouted again, and there was no reply. I felt kind of queer then, and stepped towards the dogs, when one of them made a sharp shrill yapping, seven times repeated, something like a dog, but more savage, shriller and wilder. My dogs were wolves! I got a whiff of the strong musky smell these animals make when they mean business, and I saw right away I was up against it; no fooling this time. The wolves came towards me, spreading out, and commenced to snap and snarl and worry at the air, for all the world like a bunch of dogs baiting a cow. I was right out on the weak spot, and as they crept up on me, the ice commenced to groan and crack with the extra weight, and I could see myself being soon measured for a harp and a pair of wings unless things took a change. This time I had the thirty-two special, and felt right at home. I didn't stop to do any figuring, but let go a few with the old artillery. The light was poor, and although I pass for being pretty handy with the hardware, I saw only two of the lobos fall. The rest backed off into the dark and commenced to howl, but it wasn't long before they came back for more. They fanned out like troops under fire, and came closer and closer, slowly, but most surely. I opened up on them some more, and they backed up again, but not so far this time. I began to think of my snug log cabin; it was only a short mile away across the portage, but I'll tell you boys, a mile can be a gosh-darned long piece on some occasions. The enemy came on again, bolder now; and then I learned something about wolves. They seemed to stop always a certain distance from me, held back by something that ringed me around, same as a horsehair lariat around your bed is supposed to (but doesn't) keep out a rattler. That something was the fear of man.

My ammunition began to be low, and I held my fire until they made their halt, and occasionally got a wolf.

Each time this occurred they took a walk into the dark and hollered for reinforcements, which same might arrive any minute. I am not an inhuman man by nature, and on one of these occasions, to avoid further bloodshed, I decided to go home. I moved off, in as dignified a manner as a man well can walking backwards on snowshoes (try it yourself sometime). I did this so there would be no misunderstanding as to my reasons for going.

Once on the portage where there were plenty of trees my hair lay down so my cap could cover my ears again, and I commenced picking them up and putting them down right smartly (my feet I mean, not my ears), so much so that I nearly broke a leg on a fallen tree. I would have liked awful well to have run, but public opinion is against that kind of thing.

All the way across I imagined I could hear the wolves behind me, and being too bull-headed to look back and find out, I could feel them climbing my backbone every inch of that portage. Believe me, that was a long mile, and the camp never looked so safe and sane to me before or since, as it did that night.

Pride forbids me to say how few wolves I killed that night, considering the amount of ammunition I used, but at forty dollars each as the bounty then was, I was able to buy me some long needed renewals in my outfit, and have some left over.

At this distance I get quite a laugh out of that fracas, and as I nearly froze my ears in the excitement, I often feel that I should have, for wolf-hunts, a specially designed cap with extra long earlaps, so that no matter how high my hair stood up on occasion, the laps would still reach down and cover up my ears.

The Mission of Hiawatha

" He prayeth well who loveth well
All things both great and small."

IT has become a pose of modern ultra-sophistication to scoff at those works of Fennimore Cooper and Longfellow that portray the life of the North American Indian. Those who do so are, not infrequently, equipped with little or no knowledge of the subject. On reading these works they realize at once that they could never have stood the racket, and assume this affectation of disbelief, attempting to discredit the words of men who knew very well what they were talking about. As if, because I prefer to have at least one foot on the ground and don't like aeroplanes, that I should refuse to believe that Lindbergh flew across the Atlantic.

The utter helplessness of civilized man as a whole when in the woods, even under the safe condition now obtaining, can be seen at outings and such like, that call for no more knowledge of the exigencies of bush life than is required at a picnic; and under the drastic conditions obtaining in those earlier days he would likely not have lived above a week. Not that there is anything disgraceful in this lack of enlightment regarding the other fellow's job—you should see me behind the steering-wheel of an automobile (which no one has ever done, and I am perfectly convinced, never will).

It has ever been the custom among the less generous, when confronted with conditions of which they have no experience, or see someone perform a feat of which they are incapable, to throw out a smoke screen of flippant disparagement of the whole business, and portrayals of Indian life, however authentic, have ever been a target for inexpert criticism. Unqualified scepticism is not the answer.

These writers, and some others, lived a great deal closer to the days and affairs that they described than we do, and it is reasonable to suppose that they had access to sources of information (much of it at first hand) that are closed to us. They were not, of course, unfailingly precise, and it must be admitted that in some of his technical details of woodcraft, Cooper, for one, made a few rather egregious errors, and idealized his characters in rather an exaggerated manner. Also he was a little heavy handed in spots; it is to be noticed, in *The Last of the Mohicans*, for instance, that none of his characters ever cracked a smile throughout the book, with the single exception of the white guide, Hawkeye, and even he laughed only at rare intervals, and that silently. Yet this author's description of the North American forests in the great hardwood belt of that latitude are very accurate, and he has described very vividly and with great fidelity the brutalities, and a good deal of the art, of warfare in a wilderness. And, above all, he seems to have been very well versed in the subtlety, the evasiveness, the stubbornness, the self-denying fortitude, and the inexplicable inconsistencies of Indian character.

Cooper's people were all extraordinarily clever, but under the rather trying condition that existed, a man had to be extraordinarily clever to live until the next meal (perhaps that is the reason why his characters are never recorded as carrying any provisions), because in that country, and during that period, it was no uncommon thing for a man to awaken in the morning to find that his face had slipped down during the night, because the scalp that formerly held it up had been removed; and it is safe to assume that there were strange faces in hell for breakfast most any morning of the week.

Longfellow, in his story of Hiawatha, depicted an entirely opposite side of Indian life. His poem opens with the abolition of all war and describes the warriors throwing away their weapons, washing off their war-paint, and the opposing tribes fraternizing together under the benign influence of the Peace Pipe that the Great Spirit offered them. Much of this description is liberally graced by poetic license, but a parallel situation, quite as well embellished, may be found in the Old Testament. Much of the poem is allegorical and much is legend; yet the allegories can, in nearly every instance, be applied to conditions of modern life, and the legends, if barbaric, are often beautiful, and truly told. And for that matter, modern history books contain as fine a collection of fairy tales, as is to be found anywhere.

With the exception of one or two mispronunciations, done intentionally in order to preserve the metre, all the Ojibway words have been correctly rendered, and in some cases translated. So authentic is the treatment that the whole thing could have been written by an Indian had there been one skilled enough to do it. The peculiar wording used, the declamatory style, the imagery, the reiteration of a thought successively in different ways, and the smooth-flowing, almost monotonous rhythm, make the work seem less like a poem than a chant, and reminds me of nothing so much as the intoning of some wise and aged Indian orator who, standing before some great assemblage of his people, recites, in well-selected phrase and measured utterance, the history of some great event of former days.

One of the best examples of the poet's style of annunciation is contained in the beautiful lines describing the passing of the spirit of Chibiabos, the singer, gentle Chibiabos:

> " From the village of his childhood,
> From the homes of those who knew him,
> Passing silent through the forest,
> Like a smoke-wreath wafted sideways,
> Slowly vanished Chibiabos!

Where he passed, the branches moved not;
Where he trod the grasses bent not,
And the fallen leaves of last year
Made no sound beneath his footsteps."

And as a contrast I once read a story by an author supposed to be an authority on Frontier history, who chose as a setting for his tale a Sioux encampment—and every Indian word he used was Ojibway, and very bad Ojibway at that; the point being that the Ojibway and the Sioux are two entirely different people with languages as dissimilar as Chinese and Hindustani (I hope I am right; I do not know a single word in either Hindustani or Chinese).

The personification of animals and natural objects is typically Indian. Each is identified by some exceptional and appropriate characteristic for which it is noted. The pine trees are said to sing, and whoever has heard the wind humming in their plumage, will understand. The Spirit of Winter wears a white blanket; the owls " laughing, hooting in the forest"; the whip-poor-will complains and the gulls are " noble scratchers "; the bull-frog " sobbed and sank beneath the surface "; the squirrel is called " tail-in-the-air," another way of translating the Ojibway word " Ajidomo," which means " head-down," given on account of the squirrel's preference for that position when clinging to a tree trunk.

The poet's account of life in an Indian village of the period is probably as nearly correct as any that comes down to us from the chronicles of early travellers, judging by what I myself have gathered from my own residence among semi-primitive tribal encampments in the North. Though these were never so gay as Hiawatha's village sometimes was; perhaps these unfortunate people have little enough to be gay about these days. And one has only to visit the periodical gatherings of the Blackfeet, the Sioux, the Stoneys and the Crees in the Western part of Canada, to see many of the identical scenes, ceremonies, dances and regalia described by Longfellow—even to the gambling, which is just as real and quite as serious as the rest of the proceedings.[1]

Longfellow has brought out points of Indian temperament that the latter has not usually been given credit for. He portrays him as emotional, shy and hospitable, and though relentless in warfare, a loving father and husband, and withal a dreamer and a philosopher. All of which is true, especially with regard to the strong family ties and the rigid adherence to the demands of hospitality; though the series of unfortunate episodes of the last half century or so, have not resulted in a feeling that promotes any very effusive welcome to wandering strangers in an Indian country today.

There is nothing far-fetched in the story, aside from the folk-lore and legends, which every race of people has; and it must be remembered that to the Indian of that time, and to not a few of the nomadic tribesmen of today, the twilight forest is peopled with gnomes and fairies and all manner of strange mythological beings. Yet the story of Hiawatha's people is very human, very simple, and very real, and runs the full gamut of human emotion. The delineations of Indian character are remarkably true to life, and these same folk who speak, and sing and dance their way across the Vale of Tawasentha, through the groves of singing pine-trees, and whom we cannot help but love as we come to know them, can be found—though modified perhaps—in every Indian village, and their counterparts in nearly any community, anywhere. Every village, however small, in every part of the world, has its Pau-puk-keewis—its idle, gay and likeable ne'er-do-well, a clever dancer and the life of any party but at times a trouble maker

[1] The Algonquin Indians of the Garden River Reserve near Desbarats, Ontario, in the Mississauga River country, claim that Longfellow lived among them for some time gathering the material for the poem. For many years they commemorated his visit by an annual performance of the story of Hiawatha, staged on the waters of Lake Huron and in the neighbouring woods. This was continued until quite recently, and I believe can still be seen there on occasion.

and no great shakes among the menfolk; its Iagoo, who lives in the past and tells brave tales about it; its Nokomis,[1] the practical, efficient homebody who mothers the whole community, but insists that Hiawatha bring no " useless woman " for a wife. We find that Kwasind [2] given to brawn and feats of strength, is not so strong in the head. Chibiabos, the sweet singer, gentle and retiring, has the soul of an artist. Hiawatha, though the hero, himself has many faults. Aside from his more saintly qualities, he seems to have been headstrong and passionate, and rather ruthless on occasion.

Hiawatha, or Hayowentha, as he should be called, was never a god to the Indians. Nor was he a prophet, in the true sense of the word. He was not even a medicine man, for we find that he enlisted the help of the tribal magicians when in trouble. But he had a lot of new, advanced ideas for the improvement of his people, and felt that he had a mission, which he tried very hard to fulfil. As is usually the fortune of far-seeing individuals who strive for the betterment of mankind, he encountered much opposition, and his fellow tribesmen paid him little heed, though they might have been a good deal better off today if they had listened to his advice. Subsequently, long after he had passed from among them, they found they had lost a great man. The Indians, unlike most other races, did not deify or translate their great teachers, but were very alive to their frailties and kept them down to earth where they belonged. So Hiawatha died in the usual manner and was buried, some say under Thunder Cape on the shores of Lake Superior, but all do not agree as to the actual spot. And no sooner was he dead than a host of tradition and legend sprang up around him and all kinds of utterly impossible accomplishments and feats were attributed to him. These made very pretty legends,

---

[1] Kokomis is the correct rendering.
[2] Mush-ka-wasind.

as did, and do, the achievements of many a theological or historical figure claimed by other imaginative peoples.

It is notorious that a man's true worth is not usually recognized until he is dead, and the longer he remains dead the more famous he becomes. Yet examination into the private lives of mighty personages of history has been often disappointing. I think, too, that the prowess and physique of the heroes of long-gone generations, who are popularly supposed to have been giants, have been vastly over-rated. On a late visit to the Tower of London, I discovered, much to my disillusionment, that the iron suits worn by the warriors of old, show them to have been far smaller physically than we are today. The accoutrements of the Black Prince would fit quite well on a fifteen-year-old boy; and when in England I obtained an authentic account of how it took four fully-armed ruffians (the gentle knights of the period) a matter of twenty minutes or so to murder a defenceless priest, these expert swordsmen missing him repeatedly with their wild swings, dulling their weapons against the surrounding stonework in the process.

I pick up a volume of Shakespeare. His life history is attached, and I cannot swallow quite all of it, because his intensely partisan biographers will not admit him, cannot possibly allow him, to have any human failings whatsoever. Yet, genius that he was, his constant coarse allusions to marriage are not pleasing, and Falstaff's eulogy of sack, as a beverage, would indicate that the immortal bard's acquaintance with the effects of alcohol was not altogether academic. In fact, if he had been even half as inhumanly holy as some of his commentators would have us believe, it is likely that he would not have had the deep insight into human nature that his plays reveal, and his dramas would have been lacking in their universal appeal.

We might do well to disabuse our minds of the fetish of super-men of days long past, and love our heroes, ancient and modern, for their very humanness. Hence, Hiawatha was no miracle-worker, no super-man at all, but appears to have been a lonely, rather melancholy figure, who was not so very successful at propagating his creed. Did he live today it is likely that he would be quite an ordinary man in most respects and probably be addicted to speeding, or crooning, or some other reprehensible practice; or perhaps would keep the neighbours awake playing the radio out of hours; they don't come perfect, no matter where they come from. Maybe he'd have written a book, and let it go at that. Human nature has not changed much since Adam discovered that he had a taste for apples. In my feeble way, I have done a little propaganding on behalf of my own Little Brethren myself, and have not, in some quarters, been received with quite the effusion I expected, my most steadfast opponents being most of the half-breeds I have met. Among the whites my experiences have been of the happiest, save in the sole instance, that was not without a touch of humour, when I was requested to leave a private hotel—the inhabitants of which were there for some kind of an imaginary rest cure—for wearing feathers and a knife, on the complaint of the addicts, or habituees, or clients of the place, the humour consisting on this, that I gave the land-lady a dignified and solemn dissertation on the ethics in-volved, which created quite an impression, and turning then to go, with my head and all its flaunting feathers held high in righteous indignation, quite spoilt my exit by tripping over the door-step as I left. As to being put out of a small hotel, for that matter I have been thrown out of whole towns, in my younger days, on account of certain perverted and rather unusual ideas on entertainment I possessed. But all is forgiven, and it will be all the same to all of us a hundred years from now.

The whites have dubbed this great aboriginal thinker an Indian God or Saint, which like many another accorded the same honour, he never was, nor ever wanted to be.

While some tribes of Indians have honoured Hiawatha

for what he was, others have made of him a sorcerer, and could he ever know how badly his intentions have been misunderstood and misinterpreted he would, like some other famous idealists, such as Buddha, Confucius, and Mahomet, did they return to earth, be bitterly disappointed. However, his inspirations and ideals have not so far been commercialized, which is lucky, and quite unusual.

What tribe this man belonged to has never been definitely established. The Iroquois claim him, and so do the Ojibways, the Malecites, the Micmacs and several other Indian nations. That he existed is certain, and enough stories of his work and aims have been handed down, which, shorn of their accumulation of aboriginal inexactitudes, give us some idea of his missionary efforts.

Hiawatha was a pagan; yet loved all things, both great and small; and though without a Church, he none the less prayed well. Although uncivilized, and having, no doubt, the deficiencies natural to his state, he was no avatar, nor a thing appalling as some accounts would have him be, but a gentle spirit and benevolent. Far ahead of his time, he worked hard for the betterment of his people, and on the advent of the white man, which took place during his lifetime, he tried, as did Tecumseh and Pontiac, to keep his people knit together, tried to have the tribes agree. He wanted to make a nation of them, and evolved new arts that should take the place of war, which he abhorred. But to them (how does history repeat itself, and the world continue to be small!) he was a disturber and a disputant— he was as a messenger who bursts without ceremony into a select and self-satisfied clique, come to shock them out of their comfortable complacency with unwelcome and disturbing news. He was called a dreamer and a visionary, like many another great man who saw a little further ahead than most. He showed them the writing on the wall, and strangely, nearly all of what he foretold has come to pass.

But where he failed with humans, he seems to have

succeeded with the animals, and he became the champion of these inarticulate and humble creatures, who appear to have been strangely attracted to him, and whom he called Little Brothers. He is credited with having been able to call them at will in the Wilderness, beaver particularly, whose language he is said to have learned, and with my own lesser experience with these remarkable animals I can well believe it.[1]

To the Indian of that time, and to not a few of them today, everything in the Wilderness had life and a soul. Rather a beautiful conception, even if it does clash with the more mature conceptions of a higher stage of culture. Individual trees were greeted as old friends, and mountains were addressed in the first person. And Hiawatha, from what we know of him, revered all life. So it is small wonder that, disillusioned and embittered by the attitude of the people he was trying to save, he left them and went to live apart among the guileless and friendly animals that gave to him the friendship that his own kind would not.

And now myth and legend enter in. Fearful of the fate that awaited his race, which, in spite of his teachings they would take no means to avert, Hiawatha decided to make one more appeal to them. So he called a great feast, passing among the tribes, inviting everyone; and he also included all the beasts of the forest. There on the shore of Lake Superior he made great preparations, but when the day came not a single human being appeared and only the animals came.

And the feast was not a merry one, but was eaten in silence; for all the creatures gathered there knew it must be a farewell repast. Hiawatha, realizing at last that his mission had failed, could no longer stay. Before he left he made a speech to the beasts, and thanked them for

[1] The inflections of a beaver's voice resemble greatly those of a human being; they have a wide range of sounds and can convey most of their emotions by means of them, in a manner that is remarkably intelligible.

coming to his banquet, and told them that as a reward for their courtesy, they would later on be well taken care of by the white new-comers, and would survive long after the Indians had disappeared—another prophecy that is also on a fair way to being fulfilled.

And so, embarking in his stone canoe alone, he set out towards the West, singing a song of farewell as he went. And the animals sat crowded in a sorrowful group, watching his lonely figure as it became smaller and smaller, until it vanished into the burning brilliance of the setting sun.

And the animals, a bewildered, unhappy crowd upon the shore, cried after him and found that all their voices had changed, that they no longer spoke the same language as heretofore, and not one could understand the other. So they waited in silence, but vainly, for his return. And when it fell dark they dispersed. Ever since then the wolves, remembering, have howled at intervals, moaning in their sorrow, and the loons wail like lost souls on the lakes at night. The owls and most of the other creatures have mournful voices, and some became dumb. All the face of Nature mourned his passing; and the forest often sighs for Hiawatha.

Long, long after, his song seemed to linger there behind him, and the birds learned it before it was quite gone and still sing it; though the words are lost.

And so passed the Man the Beasts Loved, a man that went around doing good without hope of reward, looking for no praise, and repudiated by his own people; a very Messiah of the Wilderness. Realizing at last what all the creatures of the Forest had always known, the Indians adopted all his precepts and his teachings and improvements; and the people were the better for his coming. But it was too late, and they were destroyed, as he had said they would be.

And the beasts that were his friends and called him Brother will always wait for his return.

The forest still sighs for Hiawatha. The wolves still mourn for him, the shouting brooks call out his name, and the eagles, high up in the sky, cry "Hiawatha!" And the beavers pause and listen in their building, cease their working, sniffing, watching, listening for their Brother, Hiawatha.

> " I beheld our nations scattered,
> All forgetful of my counsels,
> Weakened, warring with each other,
> Saw the remnants of our people
> Sweeping Westward, wild and woful,
> Like the cloud-reck of a tempest,
> Like the withered leaves of Autumn."
>
> LONGFELLOW

X

A Letter

This epistle was written by a North American Indian, an ex-sniper in the Canadian Expeditionary Force in France during 1915-17. It was addressed to a nurse in an English hospital where the Indian had lain recovering from his wounds, previous to being sent back to Canada for discharge. It is interesting to note the contrast, amounting almost to a conflict, between his original style and spelling, and that resulting from his attempts at self-education. The newly acquired erudition stands out rather incongruously in spots and was, happily, beyond the power of the writer to maintain throughout.

February 3rd, 1918.

DEAR MISS NURSE:

Nearly four months now the Canada geese flew south and the snow is very deep. It is long timesince I wrot to you, but I have gone a long ways and folled some hard trails since that time. The little wee sorryful animals I tol you about sit around me tonight, and so they dont get tired and go away I write to you now. I guess they like to see me workin. I seen my old old trees and the rocks that I know and the forest that is to me what your house is to you, I have been in it agen and am going back there in three days more, till Spring and the rivers run open agen and then I come out in canoe about last of April. I wisht youd ben here to see when I got back. The Injuns was camped and had their tents at the Head of the lake. I went up. They come out and looked at me and the chief took me by the hand and said How, and they all come one at a time and shake hans and say How. They ast me nothin about the War but said they would dance the Morning Wind dance, as I just came from East and that is the early morning wind on the lakes. Then they dance next night the Neebiche, meanin the leaves that are blown and drift before the wind in the empty forest. The white people, they got wise to it and come up, but a lot of them beat it away. The woman that teaches the white schol she fainted, which was comecal as we didnt mean nothin, ony they heard the yellin and drums and come up to see and they seen it in good shape. I kill 43 beaver now, 1 otter, 7 fisher, and a few wolves, and some moose and deer, have now meat for all winter, buckskin clothes and got my wound fixed so I can snowshoe as good as ever and wear moccassins. Comin out yestdy we made the last 18 miles in 5 hours in deep snow. Gee Im lucky to be able to travel the big woods agen. To us peple the woods and the big hills and the Northen lights and the sunsets are all alive and we live with these things and live in the spirit of the woods like no white person can do. The big lakes we travel on the little lonely lakes we set our beaver traps on with a ring of big black pines standin in rows lookin always north, like they was watchin for somethin that never comes, same as an Injun, they are real to us and when we are alone we speak to them and are not lonesome. only thinkin always of the long ago days and the old men. So we live in the past and the rest of the world keeps goin by. For all their moden inventons they cant live the way we do and they die if they try becase they cant read the sunset and hear the old men talk in the wind. A wolf is fierce, but he is our brother he lives the old way, but the Saganash is some-time a pup and he dies when the wind blows on him, becase he sees only trees and rocks and water only the out side of the book and cant read. We are two hundred years behind the times and dont change very much. . . . I have took a lot of pictures and will send you some. One is my friend (he is an Injun though, you mind the time you seen his letter). I am hunting at a place called Place-where-the-water-runs-in-the-middle becase the water runs in at the centre of the lake. I will send picture of it. I will show you the Talking Hill in a picture so long as the old

timers dont see me takin it. I wonder if all this means
anything to you I hope you wont laugh at it anyway. It
is now Seegwun when the snow is all melt of the ice and it
thaw in the daytime and freeze at night, making a crust
so the moose breaks through and cant run. This is the days
when we have hardship and our snowshoes break through
the crust and get wet an heavy an our feet is wet everyday
all the time wet. The crows have come back. Between
now and the break up is pleasant weather in the settlements
but it is hell in the woods. White men dont travel not at all
now and I dont blame him. March 20th/18 Well I lay
up today all day in my camp and it is a soft moon, which
is bad beleive me, so I write some more to your letter. I
travel all day yestdy on the lakes in water and slush half
way to my knees on top the ice. It will be an early spring.
My wound is kinda gone on the blink, to hard goin. . . .
Well the spring birds waken me up in the morning, but they
eat my meat hanging outside too, but they are welcom to
it, a long time I didnt see them and I am too glad too be
back wher I can get meat and be wher they is birds to eat
it I can get some more when thats done. They have sent
a runner in twice for me to go onto that Govt. job fire ranger,
but I am happy here and I want to be free. Thats a way
better than money an I guess I go ranging this summer.
I caught a squirrell in a trap by accident I had set for a
fisher (ojig).[1] He was dead and I felt sorry. I made my
dinner in the snow right there an sat an think an smoke
an think about it and everything until the wind changed
an blow the smoke in my face an I went away then. An I
wondered if the tall black trees standing all aroun an the
Gweegweechee [2] in the trees and the old men that still
travel the woods thats dead long long ago I wondered if
they knowed what I was thinking about, Me, I kinda
forgotten anyhow. Theys a bunch of red birds outside

[1] Indian name for fisher.
[2] Indian name for whiskey-jacks, or camp birds.

feeding. I guess youd find them pretty, red with stripes on their wings. Well Miss Nurse this is somewheres around the last of March. Half of the snow is went now and the lakes are solid ice about 4 or 3 ft thick. That all has to go in about one month. The sun is getting warm. . . . Did I ever tell you about my throwin knife I had, well I got it back it lays along side of me as I write, the edge all gapped from choppin moose bones with. I would sure like to show you this country with its big waters and black forests an little lonely lakes with a wall of trees all around them, quiet, never move but just look on an on an you know as you go by them trees was there ahead of you an will be there after you are dead. It makes a person feel small, ony with us, that is our life to be among them things. I kill that lynx today and somehow I wisht I hadnt. His skin is only worth $10 and he didnt act cross an the way he looked at me I cant get that out of my mind. I dont think I will sell that skin no. . . . I was on a side hill facing south and in spots it was bare of snow and the leaves were dry under my feet an I thought of what I tol you onct, about bein sick. Once I walked amongst flowers in the spring sun and now I stand on dry leaves an the wind blows cold through the bare tree tops. I think it tells me that wind that pretty soon no one cannot ever hear me. That must be so becase I cannot see my own trail ahead of me. a cloud hangs over it. Away ahead not so awful far the trail goes into the cloud, the sun dies behind the hills, there are no more trees ony the cloud. I had a freind he is dead now. I wonder if he is lonesome. I am now. They wanted to send me to a Sanatoriom before I was discharged, but I said No sir, nothin doin. I would be dead in about a week. A man has a good chance here. I knowd a guy with punk lungs come up here expectin to celebrate his funeral an he didnt die for seven years. Say, you poor people over there gettin no meat. Dont think me mean to tell you, but we have 300lb of meat on hand now.

Injuns can kill all they want for their own use. I wisht I could send you some. Hows the wee garden and the nieces coming along. Write and tellme all about them. My ears are open. . . . I will lisen to the song of a bird for a little while. Now the curtain is pulled down across the sun and my heart is black. A singing bird comes and sings an says I do this an I do that an things are so with me an I will lisen an forget there is no sun, until the bird goes, then I will sit and think an smoke for hours an say to myself, thats good, I am ony an Injun and that bird sang for me. When the morning wind rises and the morning star hangs of the edge of the black swamp to the east, tomorrow, I will be on my snowshoe trail. Goodbye.

ANA-QUON-ESI.

XI

On Comfort

IN recounting a bunch of unrelated stories the writer (I am not dodging the first pronoun, personal; any writer is meant) is very often apt to wander, especially if the narratives are drawn from the narrator's own experience and are more or less reminiscent in character. This deviatory style is very common among woodsmen of the old school, who are great sticklers for detail, the storyteller going off at a tangent in search of each contributory embellishment, the presentation of which, being a story all by itself, leads to another line of thought requiring more details, with further details of the details, each of which has littler details yet, so that the original story is in grave danger of becoming lost.

I had a friend, an old trapper, who was an acknowledged expert at this method; he once started off on a story about a pet frog and ended up with a vivid description of a man being chased by elephants in the heart of Africa.

This man was a great talker, as men who live much alone often are when they get the chance. His special line was the telling of yarns, of which he had an apparently unlimited supply, and it is remembered of him that on one occasion when in the morning some passing trappers were leaving after a night of his entertainment, he being in one of his more communicative moods, kept his visitors standing outside, fully loaded and accoutred for the trail, as he himself was, while he told one of those stories of his that covered, in all its ramifications, about one third of the known world. He was supposed to be bidding them goodbye, but presently his guests became fatigued, and taking off their loads, sat down. Whereupon he did the same, the visitors waiting with the greatest politeness until he should be done, meanwhile no doubt wishing him in Hades. Each had far to go, and eventually it became too late to make a start, and he had talked the entire party, including himself, out of going away that day at all. He has since passed to his long account, and if on the way he has met anyone who will listen to him, certainly neither of them will have yet arrived at the Pearly Gates, and there is a good chance that they never will—at least, not for some time.

I think that I have now wandered far enough away from my original subject, as indicated by the title, to let you see that I am bitten with the same bug, and I must now get down to it.

It has always been my contention that " comfort " is a comparative term, and in order to properly illustrate my point it will be necessary for me to follow something of my late friend's delivery, and pass from one story to another, though incapable of the easy, smooth-flowing style that he was master of.

Standards of comfort, or contentment, or satisfaction, call it what you will, may differ rather widely. As for instance, I was once seated at a gathering of exceedingly clever people, and towards the close of the repast, when brandy and fruit were served, one of the most brilliant of those present, a man whose conversation had held me more or less enthralled, suddenly ejaculated, " I have it! I have it! wonderful—indescribably marvellous—definitely, I have it! " or some such similar words. The entire company, their attention arrested, sat without a sound, expectantly, while he continued his exclamations. What it might be that he had discovered I, at least, could not imagine; but as he was either an artistic or literary man, I have forgotten which, I supposed he had suddenly come upon the solution to some troublesome problem connected with his profession, or else had been struck with some illuminating inspiration, or a great idea. " I have it now," he repeated in his creative ecstacy, " listen—brandy and figs!" (or cheese, I forget).

A new savoury, a new titillation of the sensory nerves! His discovery!

I was conscious of a keen sense of disappointment, almost of contempt, when it occurred to me that this very brilliant man might have his own standard as to what constituted creature comforts, which were as inexplicable to me as mine would be to him.

Long training in hunger-lore, which is a very necessary subject in the curriculum of a bush education, had ingrained in me a feeling that deliberate cultivation of any appetite was unmanly, and that the best condiment for any food was plain hunger, without which there was no excuse for eating. Well do I recollect the gruff old timber-cruiser who, on my turning up my youthful nose at some rather frugal fare, asked me " See here, young fellow, did you ever miss three meals hand running?" and on replying no, he said " Well, you've never really enjoyed a meal yet."

Whilst semi-starvation may not be essential as a preparation for the enjoyment of a good meal, it nevertheless has a wonderfully chastening effect on a finicky taste, as was forcibly illustrated to me on more than one starvation trip. There recurs to me, at the moment, a journey on which another young man, full-blooded Indian, and myself were obliged, after a four-day fast, to eat the rancid marrow from the bones of a long-dead moose. But far more bearable, and from all points of view in much better taste, was the adventure that was brought about by my becoming sleepy after travelling all night on very bad Spring ice, which was only held together by the nightly frosts. I had intended going right through to my destination in one long heat, travelling the whole night and as much of the early morning as would be necessary to accomplish the full journey. Thus

I expected to get there before the sun took the stiffening out of the badly rotted ice, rendering it dangerous.

I had gone thirty-six hours without sleep in my endeavours to beat the ice, and whilst passing a small, smooth rock island, I decided to lie down and rest until night, hoping it would then freeze again. The signs all spoke for rain, but such was my drowsiness that I decided to take a chance. A man who takes anything for granted in the bush is a fool; but sleep can become imperative, especially in youth; and I might add here that adventures of nearly every kind are almost always the outcome of either bad judgement or inexperience, or both; seasoned travellers just don't have any.

So, I slept—all the rest of that day and the whole of the following night, suddenly awakening in a downpour of rain to find the ice impassable, but not yet far enough gone to permit the use of the canoe that was on my sleigh. I was well marooned and it would be a matter of days; quite a number of days, it turned out to be.

There was not one stick of wood on the island. It was the only one for miles. My entire outfit consisted of a small square of canvas, a fine, large trout (uncooked), a tea pail and some tea. An interesting situation from any angle.

The canvas, stretched across the overturned canoe and held in place by stones, made a shelter of a kind, and I ate raw fish and made tea by soaking handfuls of tea-leaves in ice-cold water and straining the mixture through my neck-handkerchief. This went on for six or seven days, until the break-up of the ice released me.

To say merely that this diet began to pall on me, doesn't at all convey the idea. I can't even begin to express how it doesn't, and *my* great gastronomic satisfaction from then on, for quite some time, was the eating of a meal, any meal, in which fish, in any form, did *not* occur.

Whilst in civilization, during a late visit abroad, the peculiarities of the epicures were a constant source of interest to me, and I could never quite grasp the significance of the trivialities by which they apparently were governed. A great many of the recreations and thrills enjoyed by those who could afford them seemed somehow to be intensely artificial, and in this matter of food it appeared, to my inexperienced judgement, that life had become, for them, so safe and dull that this trifling form of stimulation was all they had left.

Retaining to a large extent my nocturnal habits, I slept little at nights and often sat up and pondered over what had been going on around me. In some big hotel or other, bored with lonesomeness, I went down to the lounge one night, and getting into conversation with the night waiter I learned a good deal about his profession, including the fact that a waiter can also be a perfect gentleman. This substantiated what I had for a long time suspected, that quite often the only difference between a waiter and the well (and almost identically) dressed patron that he served, was the slight difference in the length of the coat-tail, and the way his trousers acted around the ankles.

This man had a very good working knowledge of human nature, and among other tales, he told me of a celebrated gourmet who wanted a grouse, or some such bird, to be " hung " rather longer than was usual before it was to be served to him, and he stipulated that it be brought to table with the intestines still inside it. On the appointed day the bird was set before him, but when he opened it he refused to eat it, and was in a great rage. His complaint was that a new, fresh set of entrails from a similar bird should have been placed inside the body.

I was silent for a while, as I reflectively sipped at the hot cocoa this man had kindly brought me (" This is my treat," he said), and called to mind a happening of twenty years before when, staggering and weak from prolonged hunger I had found where an owl had killed a partridge. As the owl is rather a cleanly and careful eater, only the

feet, the feathers and the insides of the partridge remained.
I had been glad to salvage the latter, thaw them out, clean,
toast and eat them—man, the highest of creatures, playing
scavenger to an owl! And while I cannot claim to have
eaten these remains with any particular relish, they certainly
added greatly to my comfort for the time being.

And I wondered how this super-gourmet the night
waiter had described, who couldn't eat his bird without
properly selected intestines, would have liked to have eaten
the intestines without the bird.

I remember another adventure with a waiter, one that
made each of us in turn extremely uncomfortable, though
one of us achieved what must have been a very satisfying
feeling of triumph from the encounter. In England, it
seems that butter is not a regular part of some of the meals,
and when it does appear it is removed at a certain stage of
the repast. Now I like to have butter, or some kind of
grease, with each meal and all during the meal, and sometimes missed it badly over there. At one particular dinner,
having that day given three lectures and done considerable
travelling besides, I was exceedingly hungry. There were
a large number of people present, and under cover of their
numbers and conversation I managed, during the course
at which they were served, to spread butter on several pieces
of bread, which at once became highly valuable, so that I
kept them away from the oppressive ministrations of the
waiter (a man used to feeding himself does not take very
easily to these services). The generous hospitality and
kindness of the English people to the stranger within their
gates, is something to be remembered, let me tell you,
but sometimes a person longs for something he has been
used to, some foolish, trivial thing he dare not ask for,
and this night I wanted bannock and grease, or the nearest
approach to it, which was bread and butter. The other
people had by now lost theirs, but I secured mine. I could
see that the waiter intended to confiscate my hoard at the

first opportunity, and I was equally determined that he should not. This made it bad for both of us, because we both wanted it, and there was by now only one piece left, so I could not pacify him by offering to share up with him. He made several attempts to get my booty, and as I knew him to be in the right, I began to have the guilty feeling of one in possession of stolen goods. His professional instincts outraged, he became like a hound on the scent. He appeared and disappeared behind me like an apparition, hovering over me, and swooping down at unexpected moments on my unfortunate bread and butter. I shifted it, as unobtrusively as possible, from one point of attack to another, back and forth across my main plate. I had heard of the expression " taking the bread out of a man's mouth " but had never before seen it put into practice, and the situation developed into a battle of wits over the possession of this lonely piece of bread, which was the sole representative of the staff of life left upon the entire table. The manœuvres of this man—he was Italian and had very expressive movements—were highly edifying, and he was extraordinarily resourceful and not a little witty, murmuring confidentially in my ear " I beg your pardon, sir " every time he missed his stroke. In fact I no longer wished to eat this debatable tit-bit, we were both having too much fun out of it.

Once, when my opponent, in one of his thrusts, brushed his arm against the feathers I was wearing, our glances met as he whispered his usual apology and we smiled genially, though there was a glint in the eye of each that showed that we were foemen worthy of one another's steel, and that this was to be a battle to the death. And so it proved. The lady on my right engaged me in conversation, and the bread and butter, having made one of its periodic flights across my plate was on my left and momentarily unguarded —a stealthy approach, a quick dive, and the thing was done. I turned sharply, but it was all over; the waiter and the bread were both gone. And thus ended what might have been a great friendship. I like men of determination.

Well, reader, just put that one down in your list of digressions. You'll find plenty more too. This volume is full of them; and after all it *is* a book of stories, isn't it? And in a way, the inclusion of this inconsequential tale under the title is justifiable, as I am sure my friend the waiter must have experienced a deep feeling of comfort over his success, because he surely earned it.

It is impossible, I think, to experience a sense of refreshment and utter relief equal to that which pervades the soul and body of a man when, after hauling a toboggan loaded with perhaps a hundred pounds over a stretch of fifteen miles or so on snowshoes in deep, soft snow, he stops and sits upon the load to rest. The feeling of luxurious ease that then comes over him, can be gained only by long hours of submission to heart-breaking toil such as this, when a few minutes' rest means a momentary surcease from the steady, ceaseless, grinding pull of the tump-line against aching hands and shoulders, a short respite from the drag of heavy snowshoes, and from the unremitting strain of balancing precariously on a snow-drifted, hidden trail, to step off which on either hand would mean becoming mired in a deadly sea of slush.

And so, if you are that man, you sit upon your load for five minutes, say, regardless of the fact that you will find it very hard to start again, and that the under-side, or drawing surface, of your toboggan is becoming frosted, causing it to draw so much the heavier, and you relax utterly, absolutely and completely, sitting in a beatitude of complete inanition and an exquisite sense of well-being surges over you like a flood, while the whistling North wind, bitter and inimical enough at all other times, but now only soothing and refreshing as an iced drink in the Summertime, laves your heated body in its cool embrace until—there comes a little shiver, a sudden unwonted stiffness, a warning

—you may not linger longer here, lest you stay on forever. Reluctantly, you move, if you are wise, and find yourself strangely lethargic, and the North wind moans by and around you temptingly, compellingly, inviting you to rest some more; and almost you are prevailed upon to do so— to stop again, to rest, to fall asleep. But you urge your stiffened limbs and burdened feet to greater speed, strain strongly against the searing tump-line, feel with aching feet for an invisible trail.

It was a risk you took; but it was worth it. For never till that moment when you stopped, you are sure, did you ever really know repose, comfort or contentment.

On a night in mid-winter, eleven years ago, I stood on my snowshoes with my back to a small tree in a raging blizzard, and ate what was left of a small cache I had expected to find. The birds had stolen the most of it, and there remained only two tiny pieces of salt port and a chunk of bannock.[1] These were all frozen solid, and when knocked together gave out a clinking sound, like stones. It was about thirty degrees below zero and, snowing at such an unusually low temperature, the volleying snowflakes lashed my face like white-hot sand as they whirled around and past the not overly large tree, which covered little more than the centre of my back.

I had travelled hard, in five feet of snow all day. There had been nothing to eat since breakfast, and it was now well after midnight. I had twenty miles or so to go. In such circumstances, and with the terrific drain on the physical resources that such conditions imposed, all this meant something—might mean anything before morning. Making fire in such a tempest, in a country so exposed as this was, would be utterly out of the question, and later, having got fairly on my way, I would not care to stop— would not dare to, perhaps. So I thawed the pork by putting it in my mouth for a spell. At first it froze lightly to my

[1] Indian bread.

lips, but the warmth of my breath soon thawed it loose, and presently a gooey coating formed on the outside of it. This I scraped off with my teeth, and the resulting product burnt its icy way down my famished gullet like molten lead. The bannock was more obstinate, and responded to treatment only when it had been industriously whittled into chips with an axe on the edge of a snowshoe frame. Sounds simple, but it isn't—not in the dark, in a blizzard, and a man numb, exhausted and spent with hunger. It all took a very long time. The fires of vitality can burn very low at such times. And some of the bannock chips were lost; I would as soon have thrown away a bucket of diamonds.

Eventually the bannock and pork were thawed and munched and stowed away where the birds couldn't get at them any more. After this grotesque and unspeakable meal I left there feeling a good deal better, not at all uncomfortable, and in excellent spirits, arriving at my main camp in very fair condition, considering.

So perhaps comfort can after all be found in nearly anything, provided we need it badly enough at the time.

XII

On Hardship

As has been said before somewhere in these pages, untoward adventures are about always the outcome of a lack of knowledge, or of bad judgement on the part of the adventurer. And no matter how brave a tale it may make in the telling, most always there is some piece of utter foolishness, which at the time it was committed seemed inconsequential, and that would account for it. And I have been guilty of a number of these, several of which were like to have cost me my life.

While comfort, to those who travel in waste places, may often mean nothing more than alleviation from an intolerable situation, hardship can be simply an intolerable situation without the alleviation, and from which there is no present escape. Some of these episodes are attributable to sheer bad luck or misadventure, but not many of them; and most of mine have occurred in my younger and more careless days, or on well remembered occasions when I refused to listen to the still, small voice of discretion.

A good example of the former took place in Northern Quebec, a good many years ago.

The trapping was finished for the Winter, but prices had been low, and after all debts had been paid the exchequer was pretty slim, and stood badly in need of replenishment. So I decided on a Spring hunt in the same area in which I had spent the Winter.

There was still three feet or so of snow, and loading up the toboggan with fresh supplies I started in alone as usual.

The ice was on its last legs and the snow soft and mushy, making hard going, and about ten miles from camp I was obliged to cache everything, and taking only a few traps and a light axe, high-banked [1] it around the lake shores, getting in not long before dawn after some very precarious bouts with bad ice. The cabin intended only for Winter occupation had been built in a low spot, and I arrived at the camp-site to find the entire area flooded, the recent heavy thaws having caused the adjacent river to overflow its banks. The cabin floor was submerged under a foot or so of water and with it what was left of my Winter's supplies. These I had counted on to keep me going until the cache could be lifted by canoe, but they had lain in the water for perhaps a week and were thoroughly soaked and use-less. This was one, and perhaps the only instance when I had neglected the time-honoured custom of leaving a few provisions properly safeguarded for the benefit of possible travellers, and I was now to be the first victim of this breach of bush etiquette. And in no very good humour I muttered that that was always the way in the bush—you slipped up just one time and immediately got it in the neck. Actually, it had been just a piece of criminal care-lessness on my part, and it was going to extract the usual pound of flesh.

However there was a tent, some blankets, dishes and a stove that I had intended coming back for, besides of course the canoe, so the camp being uninhabitable I pitched the tent on a tiny knoll, and setting up the stove in it and spreading my blankets on a good layer of brush, made ready to sleep. The knoll was entirely surrounded by water, and I sat up there in state, as in some baronial castle encircled by a moat, but being in no mood to sample the watersoaked food, went to sleep pretty hungry.

I awoke late in the day to find that an old shrapnel

[1] High-bank. Expression meaning to follow the shores or banks of lakes or rivers; a very tedious operation.

wound, from being submerged in slush and ice water for a day and the better part of a night, was now so swollen as to make walking impossible, and it was as much as I could do to straighten my leg. Fortunately there was a good deal of last Winter's supply of wood floating around, which I fished for successfully and which, not being split, was dry enough to burn in the stove. But the food problem was not so easy. I knew by experience that I was going to be off my feet for several days, and must depend on the water-soaked leavings in the camp to keep me going.

The situation was quite devoid of those romantic features generally supposed to be associated with adventure.

By means of an improvised crutch to keep the trouble-some foot clear of the icy water, I waded back to the cabin, and salvaged some oatmeal, sugar, tobacco and flour. Some tea, baking powder and salt, and a box of matches, being on a shelf, were dry, also there was a can of milk. I eventually got all these things over to the castle on the island, bringing along a single-barrelled shot-gun, of the take-down variety, and some shells; there was sufficient of a pond to maybe attract a few ducks.

So fixed, I began to feel pretty secure, and was even a little disappointed that I was now only a hero under false pretences, and that this affair would not make nearly so heroic a tale with which to stir my friends as I had at first supposed. In fact I was apparently in as little need of sympathy as was Mr. Robinson Crusoe, who had everything except a full rigged ship to see him through, even to several kegs of rum. These I lacked, though under the existing condition the appearance of some good bootlegger who should stick his head into the tent and crook his finger at me with a knowing wink, would not have been unwelcome.

I examined the foodstuffs. The tobacco was of course denatured, and when dried it smoked like so much moss. The flour and oatmeal were mostly dough, being in cotton bags, but I made shift to cook some of them.

The remains of two moose and a pile of smaller carcasses lay in the water in front of the cabin, as I originally had had no intention of living here after the thaw, and these remains had been safely frozen when I left. Now they were different, having been exposed to the hot May sun for two weeks, and the provisions were no doubt well impregnated by now. They could not be otherwise. Thinking of this I gagged at the food, and threw the doughy bannock out into the pool, where it hit with a sullen splash and sunk without a trace. I tried the oatmeal, but it had a strange unaccustomed odour, and it was also dumped. I held out another day, drinking tea, and smoking large quantities of my tasteless, highly inflammable tobacco, hoping some ducks would soon arrive. My swollen foot and ankle showed no signs of abating, and I was getting hungrier all the time. So on the following morning I cooked up some more bannock and oatmeal. A man must eat. I think I hear you say you would not have done so. Perhaps not; it is hard to say. But I have seen some of them do worse, when hungry. Have you ever been that way? Washed down with tea the taste was not as bad as it sounds, and the used tea leaves, dried and mixed with the de-horned tobacco made not so bad a smoke. I ate two meals that day, and then sat back and waited for the effect: there was none. But some instinct of self-preservation made me save my one can of milk, which was a lucky break for me. There being no ill results I took courage and ate regularly and began to think of my delayed hunt. There was a family of beaver on a little lake not much over a mile away, which I should have been after long before this, as I intended to kill them out before the young were born, which would be any time now. My disabled foot being now on the mend, I decided to get a few traps out before going after my cache, which latter task might not be possible for another week.

One morning the waters being subsided somewhat, after

a hearty if unappetizing breakfast, I took my traps and a lunch and started out.

Here Fate, seeing me about to kick over the traces, decided that I was not going to get away with it, and proceeded to administer a slight corrective. I had gone no great distance before I was overcome by an attack of nausea, which passing off, I resumed my journey. Soon another similar spell followed, and yet another; and, thoroughly sick, I returned to camp and was glad to crawl into my blankets. Before night my face began to swell and by the next morning I was in a feverish condition and my throat and mouth were badly inflamed. Bethinking myself of the milk I drank a little, but had difficulty in swallowing it, and as time went on began to feel as if my throat was closing up. Soon breathing was a distinct effort. I thought of a number of what, at this distance, seem to be foolish expedients, but the very present fear that my breathing might be shut off, drove me to consider almost anything, however far-fetched. Respiration became more and more difficult, so that I breathed stertorously, gasping and choking, and was at times dangerously near suffocation. I thought that if only I had some kind of tube to force down my throat I could at least continue to breathe. I even, in my probable delirium, went so far as to detach the barrel from the take-down shot-gun and grease it in readiness for the attempt, though, sick as I was, I could not help thinking how absolutely absurd, not to say eccentric, it would look to be found dead with the empty barrel of a gun half way down my throat. The whole thing would look like a badly conducted suicide.

However, a life in the open makes a man pretty hard to kill. The milk exercised a soothing effect, though it was some days before I could make the journey to the cache; meanwhile I slowly recovered, nearly starving to death in the meantime.

Hardship is a comparative term, according to habit and

environment. I once was a guest in a house where something or other fused, and the electric lights went out. For those people it was a real hardship, perhaps the first that some of them had known, and very well I could appreciate this, as it was certainly highly inconvenient, if not in some degree dangerous. It was as though a person had gone suddenly blind, than which, aside from the thought of impending torture, I can think of nothing more terrifying. For I have been blind, out on a frozen lake at night, alone.

It was a matter of eight miles to the nearest human being, but eight miles is as good as a hundred if you are blind, out in the snow-bound Wilderness. Early that morning I had left from the last settlements. I was lucky enough to get a lift from some freighters who were going in with supplies for a party of surveyors. It was not at all cold, a state of affairs that made bad snowshoeing, but was very comfortable weather for enjoying a ride, something I didn't often have. That night the freighters made camp some miles from a cabin, where I intended to sleep, and I refused their invitation to stay with them, and slipping into my snowshoe bridles started off. There were signs of a possible storm and some of the men urged me to stay; but travelling at night, even in a storm, held no terrors for me, I supposed, and away I went. For a little time after leaving the warm, ruddy camp fire, with the congenial company gathered around it, the portage trail felt very lonely and dark and cheerless, and I almost turned back once or twice. However, with the concentrated attention to business that night travelling demands, I had little time for vain regrets and the feeling of lonesomeness soon passed. I then noticed that it was getting colder; all the better snowshoeing, thought I; which it was.

Arriving at the end of the portage, I discovered that the wind had changed to the North. Quite a stiff breeze was blowing, but there were no clouds. The waning moon, pale and on its back, the half averted face upon it pinched and sunken like the visage of one dead, gave out a pallid illumination that helped very little to distinguish the features of the landscape. The lake was about seven miles across, and on its far shore stood the cabin I was making for, and giving my snowshoe bridles a few twists to tighten them, I started across the wide expanse of lake.

The snow was badly drifted into hard irregular waves, and the sickly light of the recumbent moon was worse than none at all, constantly deceiving my eyes, so that I stubbed my snowshoes on the brittle crests of snow waves or else stepped out on to nothing, to land with a back-breaking jar in a trough. This was very tiring and I had to go slow at last, becoming so fatigued that I even considered going ashore, making fire and passing the night there. But the shores on either side were a couple of miles or so away, and I was now well over half way up the lake towards my destination. Moreover the wind had now freshened and was getting stronger every minute, and I had no idea of what it might portend before morning came. It presently increased to a steady gale that was neither blustering nor boisterous, but that blew with a ceaseless, changeless velocity that had the sweeping drive of a rushing wall of water and, in my tired condition, was nearly as irresistible. This wind was from the North and blew somehow dry and brassy, hard as sandpaper, and cut like a buzz-saw, even through my stout buckskins. Between the freezing, tearing wind and the continual stumbling over the snow-billows I was rapidly becoming exhausted. My eyes began to burn, and it seemed as if the wind was drying them, so that when I shut them and walked some distance with them closed, as I was now obliged to do from time to time, they felt as though filled with hot sand.

Presently I noticed that when looking straight ahead the shore on my right was, for some reason, getting dim. Now, I knew it to be only half a mile away as, hoping for a certain amount of shelter, I had been veering towards it for some time; while the shore on my left, at least three miles away, was plainly visible out of the tail of the other eye. Before long I found that unless I turned and looked at it directly the righthand shore showed only as a grey, shapeless wall. This struck me as strange, and not a little disturbing, and I hadn't gone very far when the other, more distant shore became dim, turned grey and disappeared entirely. I looked up, I couldn't see the moon. And then dawned upon me the realization that I was going blind! I could still see my snowshoes, and they were covered with new snow; I looked down at my buckskin shirt, it was white with snow—yet no snow was falling on my face; perhaps it was frost. I tried to brush it off; it wouldn't come. I turned up the shirt and looked inside; it was white too—that was it! my eyes were turning slowly white, everything else was turning white—eyes that could see only white—white blindness, the terrible White Death I'd heard the Indians talk about!

I stood still for a few moments and let this sink in. Then I made for the shore while I could still distinguish it. In my haste, unable to see the snow with my bleaching eyeballs, I tripped and staggered, and fell repeatedly. I wanted to get close enough so I could hear the gale roaring in the timber on the shore, otherwise if it too should disappear, I might not ever find it. I was surrounded by a wall of white save in this one direction. But I got there, just about in time, for as I approached it seemed to melt, dissolve away from either side, leaving in front of me only a narrow strip of grey, that stood upright before me. I remember thinking that it looked like a great grey bastion, and had the effect of being round as the sides fell away to where they were invisible; and this I watched as it too began to shrink, turned white and receded into nothingness. And I pawed the air to feel for it after it was gone, and I stumbled forward with outstretched hands to find it, this, my last link with the living world; and I ran a step

I

or two and crashed into a tree and fell upon my back there, in the snow.

And I knew then that I was blind. I knew all the stark horror, the awful helplessness, and the unutterable anguish of one stricken suddenly blind. I scrambled to my feet as the ghastly, inescapable FACT roared like thunder through my reeling intellect, that it had got me, that I was blind—white-blind! My snowshoes were off and hung around my ankles and as I stood I sank to the hips in the snow, and cried out, a terrible, animal sound, the agonized cry of some creature in a trap, my fists clenched above my head, staring out with my sightless eyes, trying to make them see. I must have been in a little bay, for there was no wind there, and that awful, demoniacal yell came back to me and I yelled again in answer to the echo, and while my face ran with perspiration I shouted " I am blind, blind, do you get it? I am BLIND!" And the echoes answered " I am blind—am blind—blind—blind." And a demon came and whispered " You are blind ", and beat at my brain with a downy, flocculent cudgel and the frenzy passed and my body became pleasantly numb and warm, and I sat down comfortably in the snow and my eyes didn't hurt any more; and I was very tired. And I thought this must be the end; the end. It seemed strange to go out in this way after having braved the Wilderness so long—so simple, and after all, so easy. And I remember thinking that if I was found, no one would ever know what it had been all about.

And then all at once I came out of my lethargy, and muttered to myself that I was not going to be found in the Spring spread out on the beach like a dead toad, but decently, with my weapons and my snowshoes beside me, kind of natural looking. What puerile things we think of in extremity! But I had lost my rifle and axe, and crawled around in the snow and felt for them, but could not find them. So I wallowed a little further inshore, my snowshoes dragging by the bridles, and ran into a large tree. With a snowshoe I dug a hole in the snow, at the foot of it, crawled in there, stood the snowshoes up beside it, then pulled as much of the snow in on top of me as I could. Thus I would sleep; and nothing else seemed to matter. The wind had now died down, and without it I could never find my way and would perhaps wander bewildered on the lake until I dropped from exhaustion. Better this, the cleaner way.

Reader, do not judge me, not until you have had a like experience. There was not the heat of battle, nor the heroic intoxication of some deed of valour or self-sacrifice. I had taken the field once too often against the power of Nature, had pitted my puny strength against the Wilderness; and this time I had lost. Just one more animal who must submit to the invincible decrees of the creed he lived by—the survival of the fittest. A small error in judgement had proven me unfit; I should never have started out from the freighters' camp. However, I was to get another chance.

Some hours later I awoke with a start, and stood up. At every move sharp daggers of pain shot through my muscles. I knew what that meant—I was beginning to freeze. I cursed myself for waking up. Now it had to be all gone through again. Water was streaming from my eyes and they felt as though on fire. I had tied my black silk neckerchief over them and this I now took off, and opened them.

It was with a distinct shock that I found that I could see; but that was about all. I could with difficulty make out shapes of tall grey spectres that stood about me, looking like huge columns wrapped in wool, enormously thick; these no doubt were trees. In one direction there was a faint glow, as of a candle light seen through a piece of flannel; this I supposed, was the moon. My snowshoes resembled twin tombstones and when I reached for them I missed them by a foot or so.

Well, if I was going to see, there was no use in dying. Everything was very dim and hazy and distorted, and every object appeared to be coated with wool, or of enormous size. But I could see—enough to make a fire, beside which I sat on a bed of balsam brush until my sight was sufficiently restored to move on. I worked on my eyes, opening and shutting the lids, massaging them, and mopping the stream of water that flowed from them. The balls felt rough, as if corrugated. Slowly, painfully, they resumed their office, even though imperfectly. All this took a long time to do, and I found myself weak and almost incapable. A little more and I would never have gotten away from there.

Owing to their fictitiously exaggerated size everything I reached for eluded me, and it would have looked strange to an onlooker to have seen me clawing away at things that were six or eight inches from my hands; under any other circumstances it would have been an interesting experience.

Towards morning I collected axe and rifle and after a rather severe ordeal arrived at the cabin.

The tips of all my fingers were frozen, and I didn't see very well for several days. But I had learned a very useful lesson, and had perhaps found out the reason why men of known skill and proficiency in Winter travelling, have been found, unaccountably, dead.

XIII

The Tree

The age of a tree can be accurately estimated by means of the concentric rings, one for each year.

Six hundred and fifty years ago or thereabouts, a squirrel picked up a jack-pine cone that he had dropped, amongst a score or so of others, from a tree-top on the neighbouring side-hill and carried it on its way for deposit in a cache of ripe, juicy cones that he had commenced, right in the centre of a pass in the Rocky Mountains. Arriving at his granary, he saw something that interested him, a little to the left, dropped the cone and went there, and forgot ever to come back.

There were probably a dozen cones laying there and the cache, not being completed was yet uncovered and the cones eventually became scattered some few feet apart by the action of the wind and rain. They passed the Winter successfully, and the following year took root, and most of them sprouted up as little jack-pines. Immediately the struggle for the survival of the fittest began. Each seedling tried to outgrow his neighbour in order to reach for the sun, on the light of which their tiny lives depended. Thus they all grew rapidly in a kind of a race, rather a grim one for things so tender and infinitesimal. And some were slower than others and payed the penalty; they were soon over-shadowed by their more precocious brethren, became sickly from lack of sunlight, were smothered and died. After five years there were seven or eight of them left, growing decorously apart, good healthy saplings.

On a day that Autumn a deer passed, and being on the

lookout for something tasty, ate the top, and the ends of all the shoots off one of them, and by Spring the tree was only a dried stick. During the Winter, rabbits being numerous they stripped the bark off some of the rest, girdling them very neatly up as high as they could reach, so that these also died. Four or five years later a bull moose, during late Summer, used one of them as a scraping post to remove the velvet from his antlers, breaking it down, along with several others, in the process.

At the end of two decades the survivors were sizeable young trees, and all had a fighting chance to live to a ripe old age, when a porcupine happened along, barked cleanly from top to bottom all but one of them and went on his way to richer fields of exploitation of the country's timber resources. Being alone, the one that remained attracted no further attention from potential enemies and grew undisturbed for a century or so, becoming a tree of noble proportions, though in its exposed position, standing high in the mountain pass at the brink of the prairies, it tended to be heavy of trunk and wide spread of limb, rather than tall; and its topmost branches were bent around and over, trained permanently by the prevailing South-east wind from the plains, and pointed, like great dark arms in a sweeping gesture, always towards the North.

The tree withstood the terrific winds, sometimes of tornado velocity, that blew constantly upon it from the prairies, far below; drought, rain and snowstorm, and all the elements, each with its own specialized form of destructiveness, tried to kill, uproot or blast it, or break it down. None the less it flourished, nay, appeared to thrive on such treatment, either becoming extraordinarily hardy on account of the resistance it was forced to put up, or else it lived because it was, in the first place, unusually sturdy. Either way, it increased to an immense girth, and after two centuries of life its limbs, themselves as big as small trees, gnarled, twisted and overhanging, made a wide, arched canopy under whose shade many a passing beast took shelter from the hot sun of Summer-time, or refuge from the storms of Winter.

Animals of various kinds had travelled this pass from time immemorial, and it being fairly even footing for most of its width, a matter of two hundred yards or so, they had passed wherever caprice or the pursuit of food might chance to take them. But now the presence of the tree began to attract them, to influence their line of march. Not only was its shade or shelter, according to conditions, grateful, but animals, like humans, travel on well defined routes from one prominent feature of the landscape to another; so that animal crossings are often to be found at spots such as an unusually large rock, through a particularly well-timbered gulley, across an extra large beaver dam or an especially convenient fording place, and well defined paths are worn between them. Because it was the last one of such a chain of links in the long and toilsome journey through the mountains, and it being, at the same time, the first of them on coming from the plains, the jack-pine became in time a kind of Mecca, towards which all the beasts who journeyed back and forth made each his intermittent pilgrimage to rest beneath it and then refreshed, or perhaps having enjoyed in some dim, dream-like way, a kind of temporary fellowship with the lonely tree, went on his way. There was, besides, the added attraction of a luxurious mountain meadow that like a green carpet lay spread out on all sides from the tree, where there were flowers for those that liked them and berries, in season, for everybody, and a little running stream in which were mountain trout.

The game trail that was at last worn smooth and hard and well-defined beside the tree, bore sometimes creatures that were notable, above the common run, and sometimes something noble. A great bull elk often led his herd in a long procession past it on the way to feeding grounds in the lower foothills. And every year when the first frosts turned the aspen leaves to bronze and gold, he took the meadow as his stamping ground, with the tree for its centre, and issued from there his ringing challenge to the world; until one Fall the herd had another leader and went by without him. A little band of wolves, rare animals at such an elevation, passed once, slant-eyed, grim and wary; they pattered up, moved restlessly about, and loping easily along as though on springs they pattered off again, to be no more seen—the corsairs of the Wild Lands.

Then there came a giant grizzly bear, who frequented the place from then on at regular and fairly frequent intervals. Huge and ponderous, yet good-natured, though swift and devastating when angered, king of the mountains he was, who gave place to no living thing in all that region. He was a silver-tip, and when he stood erect, the big horseshoe of silver hair upon his breast looked like some emblem of his royal degree. A gigantic beast, eight feet from nose to tail, four feet high at the shoulder his claws full five inches long, he could be a terrible engine of destruction if aroused. Yet, aside from necessary kills he made when hungry, he was not at all a quarrelsome fellow, but loved quietude and peace and sitting in the sun, living greatly on roots and berries, and on fish that he caught in the trout-stream that ran beside the meadow. Here he often fished, and having eaten lay beneath the tree and licked his paws and dozed, and maybe dreamed.

He had one great pastime, and that was to look long and steadily out across the vast expanse of prairie that stretched far below him on and on interminably, into infinity. Across these distant reaches there drifted from time to time in a dark flood, black bellowing masses that flowed over the rolling landscape like a moving carpet. And sometimes around the edge of these vast shifting waves of living creatures there rose clouds of dust, and there came u) to the pass, faintly, the distant howling of wolves and mingled with it a wilder, shriller sound and the throbbing of drums, a rhythmic uproar that was strangely exciting to the bear as he listened.

And these dark masses were the great buffalo herds, on whose outskirts there hung the gaunt, grey prairie wolves; and here whole tribes of tall, copper-coloured men gathered, and marching on foot, drove groups of buffalo into rude corralls, and shot them down with bows and arrows; for this was before the days when they had horses.

All this the bear saw and heard; and who can ever know what strange thoughts passed behind those small, sagacious eyes, or what unfulfilled longings surged through that mighty frame, as he gazed so steadily and so long out upon that, to him, undiscovered country with its far off vistas and its unknown inhabitants. But it was not his home, and he never went there. And the great jack-pine, giant of its kind and old, even as he was, became to him a kind of mile-post or a monument, and the companionship of the tree seemed to fill some want in his lonely life, and he began to feel, in his dim, uncouth way, that it lived and was, for all it seemed so quiet and never moved, a friend. And so he put his mark upon it with his teeth. And the tree, that had never been scored since the tiny cuts were made upon it by the rabbits' teeth, and was now covered by the concentric rings of four hundred years, felt a strange thrill go through all its fibres at this recognition, and knew then that it too, had life. And when the bear was no longer there, the ground around its foot felt bare and empty, and when the huge brown beast returned and took his accustomed place, the soul of the tree would thrill, and a kind of a tremor pass among its branches; and the bear would lie contentedly beneath it and gaze out over the wide plains that spread for ever on into the Unknown.

This strange companionship went on for nearly half a century. And the giant silver-tip began to be old, very old for a bear. And there came a Spring when he lay longer and longer at a time beneath the tree until, during late Summer, he never left it save on his short excursions to the berry patch and to the stream for water. For he was no longer able to capture the nimble mountain trout.

And now the leaves were turning, and the woods were painted with all the glory of Autumn; and the harsh outlines of the mountains were softened by the smoky haze of Indian Summer. And one day, just before the Falling of the Leaves, the bear lay in his old familiar place beside the tree, looking wistfully out over that mysterious, distant prairie that was, somehow, dimmer and more distant than it used to be, while he listened to the quiet humming of the wind in the branches of the pine. He had been very tired that day, but now a great peace came over him; and he gave himself over to his dreams. And the wide plains faded and were gone; and the voice of the tree became softer, fainter, further off, and soon died quite away. And the life of the bear passed on.

But the tree knew that his soul would be always there.

And the ancient, ancient jack-pine stood guard above his bones, and waited for another hundred years. And this was the fate of the tree, that all who loved it should die, while it lived on, and waited until the last of them was gone. And so it stood, alone, a dark, looming Sentinel at the gateway to the mountains.

Later two eagles nested in its top, two great war-eagles, king and queen of all the air who circled high above the mountains, ever upward, on and upward, floating without any effort, swinging wider, ever wider, pinions flashing in the sunlight. Every year several small eaglets appeared, and the nest in the summit of the tree, with its small, new inhabitants, became very important and a great care to the two royal birds; and the tree guarded them well, until after nearly a hundred years the nest was empty and the tree alone again. But other eagles came, and from then on there were always eagles nested there.

As the tree grew older its girth constantly increased.

The mark put upon it by the bear had partly healed, but still remained a scar, and always would. Its beautiful purple-red bark grew thicker and the mighty limbs became more massive, gnarled and widespread. With age it grew more solid on its roots, and every Summer morning, when the sky was clear, the rising sun shone redly on the stout, heavily furrowed bark and warmed the tree, after the cool mountain night, so that it felt the life within it stirring. And as the early morning breeze touched its needles, they hummed a deep, varying chord of thanksgiving to the Master of Life—the Sun.

The Indians of the plains below also adored the sun; for to them, the sun not only gave life, but caused it to endure, and drove away the Winter's. snows and made the grass to grow, and brought the flowers to brighten the monotony of the treeless prairie. This was the belief of the Blackfoot people, who often looked up at the great jack-pine that stood so boldly outlined, so dark and magnificent of aspect, against the snow-capped background of the mountains. And they marvelled that a jack-pine should grow to such a size, as could be distinguished even at that distance. And to the band whose ancestral camp grounds lay within the sight of it, the giant evergreen, that had been standing there at the threshold of the mountains so long that none had ever heard when first it grew there, became symbolical of their race. And so it had been, since times no longer now remembered, a landmark and a sacred spot and held inviolate, as all landmarks were in old Indian days,[1] and there was a tradition in this band that when it fell the Blackfeet would be driven from the plains into the mountains, and that if the Indians went first, then the tree too must fall. And the tree was looked up to with the greatest reverence.

Five hundred and eighty years from the time that a squirrel, in a moment of forgetfulness had planted it, the

---

[1] There is a parallel to this in the Christian Bible, which says " Cursed be he that removeth his neighbour's landmark."

tree for the first time gave shelter to a human being. A young man of the Blackfoot nation who was soon to be initiated as a warrior, made a vow to go and stay beside this venerated, venerable tree five days and nights without food, in order to purge his soul of evil, and have a vision, and then come down and tell his dream, which would be interpreted according to the wisdom of the magicians. And then, if he passed the tests, which were drastic, he would be made a warrior. Then, perhaps, a certain dark-eyed young woman would listen to his pleading and come to share with him his fine new tepee and share, too, the glory he was sure to earn in the coming war against a strange, pale race that was beginning to occupy the land.

So the young man went up and fasted five days and five nights at the foot of the sacred pine, who wondered why he did this, because the other creatures that came there always ate; and the tree was sorry for him and sheltered him with its wide branches and played, quietly, soft music in its foliage for him to hear. Five days the young man sat and meditated, and looked out over the wide expanse of plains where he could see, far below, the distant encampment of his people, and his keen eyes could pick out the teepee in which the maiden that he loved awaited anxiously his return; at least he hoped she did and could not be sure, so unfathomable are the ways of a maiden with a man. And when he slept, he used for a pillow the skull of a grizzly bear that he had found there. And while he slept, the creatures of the wild that lived nearby came close and watched him curiously, wondering what manner of beast he was, and what he did there; little mice with beady eyes who ran in and out of holes and sat erect and sniffed at him and sometimes ran across his feet; flying squirrels, like small, pale, flitting ghosts, in utter silence, soared and flickered from limb to limb above his head. A fox, with dainty, mincing steps, ears and nose delicately attuned to his surroundings, tripped lightly by, his tail streaming out behind him like a plume; and once a band of caribou, wraith-like in the moonlight, drifted soundlessly as phantoms through the meadow.

Now it was the custom among the Indians to seek a patron animal, that should appear in a vision during a vigil such as this young man had undertaken, who would henceforward be his crest, his ensign to be painted on his shield. But he dreamed of none of those that passed around him as he slept, but of a bear, a monstrous silver-tip that stood erect before him and made signs, and signalled to him with its forepaws, as sometimes is the fashion of a grizzly. And this was a lucky omen, and he decided then to take the bear for his patron beast, his totem; and moreover he found there, beneath the tree, two eagle feathers that had fallen from the nest in the wide-spread top, all ready for him to be made a warrior with. So in gratitude he made a mark upon the tree-trunk with his tomahawk, a long, narrow blaze, close beside the half-healed mark the bear had made so long ago. And he hung the bear skull on a short, dead limb, first placing in it an offering of tobacco, and carefully fastening the jaws in place with strings of spruce-root. This he did for a token, because the place had been lucky; and he thanked the tree, and spoke some friendly words to it before he left. And the tree quivered through every fibre when the Indian hung the bear's skull on the limb, and felt as though its old companion were nearer—quivered too, at the words of kindness that the youth had spoken, the first time it had ever heard a human voice, save the distant yelling of the buffalo hunters.

And the tree knew, after more than a century of waiting, that now it had found another friend.

After his initiation the young man, now a warrior, went to the home of the dark-eyed maiden; and she was pleased that he had passed his warrior's test so bravely, as the open wounds upon his breast so plainly showed,[1] and commended

---

[1] A reference to a part of the Sun-Dance, in which the candidate was suspended on rawhide thongs skewered through loops cut into the flesh

him for keeping his vigil so honestly and not having cheated by carrying little bits of dried meat on his person, as some had been known to do. And so she could no longer resist his wooing; and when he pressed her for an answer she gave to him the one he wanted but had scarcely dared to hope for; though she had known it all along. And she gave to him her hand and promise—but shyly, in a low, soft voice and with her face demurely hidden behind her head-shawl, as is the manner of an Indian maid. And she said she would like to see the place where he had spent his days of fasting, and which he had said was so very beautiful.

And so she said goodbye to her parents, quite as though she were going away into a far country, which she was not, and they journeyed together up to the pass to spend their honeymoon, to spend the sunny days of the Moon of Berries on the pleasant, flower-strewn meadow, under the great arms of the sheltering pine. And here between them they pitched the new lodge of buffalo hides that had been waiting for this event so long. And although the climb was steep they had brought many comforts with them on travois drawn by horses, for since several generations the Indians had found wild horses on the plains, offspring of those that had been abandoned by pale-faced explorers from the South. And after camp was made and the horses pastured the warrior brought his young wife some spotted trout from the stream, and berries from the meadow and sprays of flowers to deck the inside of their wigwam with, and fresh venison, and green, aromatic spruce fronds for a soft bed; he gathered cherry leaves and parched them a little before the fire to bring out the pleasant odour in them, and made of them a sweet-smelling pillow for her. And afterwards he made a fine blazing fire before the lodge, and put on his two black and white eagle feathers and his very best raiment, beaded, fringed and embroidered by the maid's own hands,

of his breast and throwing his weight on them, danced until the flesh tore out and released him. The entire ceremony, which was complicated, had also a religious significance.

secretly, this long time past, for this very occasion, which she had known full well would some day come to pass. And he took out from a gaily decorated bag a small, painted drum and sang songs to his sweetheart as they sat beside the fire beneath the mighty jack-pine, and with the high and sanguine hopefulness of youth, boasted in his chanting that some day he would be a chief. The maiden, now a wife, listened and was quite sure he would be a great man before very long; and being a woman, and practical, she dressed the hide of the deer he had killed for food, and smoked the meat and cooked the berries for their simple meals, and roasted trout before the open fire. And they were very happy there.

And the tree looked down with kindly sympathy upon them, and covered them with the protection of its widespread fan of limbs, and dropped light showers of pine-needles to make a carpet for them; and something like a sob came from the darkness among the branches far above. For the tree knew that, like all the other creatures it had known, they could not live for very long, that it must outlive them and be alone again.

For this was the Fate of the tree, to live on and on, while all others died. And it resolved to make them happy while it could.

One night the young warrior dreamed that outside the teepee there sat a great brown bear, with an ensign of silver on his breast, and so vivid was this dream that he arose and looked out, but found no bear and went to sleep again. The next morning he feared to tell his wife about this, lest he alarm her, but as soon as she awoke she told him that she had seen, in a dream, a huge bear with a great white mark upon its breast that was curved upward like a bow and shone like silver, who sat before the teepee in the moonlight, and made gestures to her with its forepaws. So her husband said that he too had dreamed of a bear, that it must be a vision, and that he must make propitiation to the spirit of the bear at once, as it was now his totem. And this he did, placing in the skull all the last of his tobacco and fastening to it, so it hung down like a banner, his finest beaded buckskin belt.

And at that the tree trembled with happiness in all its branches, and the soul of the bear rejoiced.

From then on he used the figure of a bear for his crest, and painted it on his shield and quiver, and his wife embroidered it in beadwork on his rich ceremonial garments; and on any set of apparel that he wore there could be always seen the likeness of a bear, not in brilliant colours, but in the bear's own natural shade of brown.

After that the warrior made a pilgrimage to the place every year and slept one night beneath the jack-pine; and always he dreamed about the bear, who sat each time, in his vision, before his sleeping place. And always the warrior left some offering or token to decorate the tree and to please the spirit of the silver-tip; and this he did once each Summer at the Time of Berries. And every year he renewed the blaze, and scraped away the accumulated gum from the scar the bear had put upon the tree, and renewed the offering of tobacco in the skull.

But one time he came attired differently to what he had ever been on any other visit. He was naked, save for a loin-cloth, a beaded belt that held a broad knife sheath, and his moccasins. His face and body were painted with strange devices in crimson, white and yellow, and on his head he wore an eagle-feather bonnet that spread wide, and stood out in a huge circle about his head. In his hand he carried a long pipe decorated with feathers and the quills of porcupines.

Full twenty years had passed since he first had visited this spot, and many times had he proved himself to be a brave and skilful warrior, and had fulfilled the confident prediction of his younger days, and had become a chief. And now he had come here, on this momentous occasion, to commune with the spirit of the tree, to ask for guidance from his patron, whom he called Brother, the grizzly bear. For the time was critical; tomorrow a great battle was to be fought with the pale people who were now coming in clamouring hordes to possess the land and drive the Indians out. On this battle might depend the fate of this band, of which he was now the chief.

Lighting his pipe he pointed the stem to the East, then the West, to the North and the South; then upward towards the Sun, whom he worshipped, and downward to the Earth, whom he called his Mother. Lastly he blew a puff of smoke up among the pine-limbs and another into the bear-skull; and stepping back he raised his arms in a gesture of supplication, and bowed his head, so that the eagle bonnet fell wide open, spreading out around his head and shoulders like an enormous crown.

And as he stood there, he cried aloud.

" O you, great Tree, Sentinel of the Mountains.

" O you Spirit of a Bear, my Brother.

" You are my patrons.

" Hear me.

" I want for myself, nothing; only this.

" Make me strong in battle.

" Help my knife and axe to fall heavily on the pale people, who would take away our homes.

" Make strong my arms to bend my bow and drive the arrows true.

" Help me to be brave on the field of battle.

" Not for myself I ask this.

" No longer do I fight for glory, but for my people, for my wife and children.

" The pale people are scattering the Indians like snowflakes before the wind.

" The Sun of the Indians is setting and the Sun of the pale ones is strong.

" Like the snowflakes of last year will we be consumed.

K

" Make me strong in battle.

" You are my patrons.

" O my Brothers.

" Hear me."

And the tree gave answer in the swaying and sighing of its foliage and whispered: " Be strong; we are with you." And the spirit of the bear breathed in the shadows " I will be beside you; mighty am I in battle."

After he had made his offerings the Chief went down to the plain to his people; and on the way he fancied that he heard, in the darkness there behind him, a sound of shuffling, a soft, yet heavy padding as of some huge beast that followed him, and he said, " It is my Brother; it is the bear who follows." And this gave him courage so that on his way he planned confidently for the fight that would take place on the morrow.

Dashing into the council lodge he cried, " Let the war-dance commence ! Make all your preparations quickly, for we will be victorious. Our medicine is very strong tonight. Let the young men paint themselves for the battle. Sound the war-drums, the rattles and the pipes of eagles wing-bones ! Shout the war-whoop ! Be strong ! To-morrow we will win." And cried again, " Be strong ! ", for that was the pass-word that his patrons on the mountain had given him.

But when the pale soldiers came with the early morning daylight, they proved to be better armed than the Blackfoot warriors; they had heavier horses too, and were in greater numbers. With cannon [1] and rifle, revolver and sword they spread death in the encampment, sparing none; women were shot down with babies on their backs, one bullet being sometimes enough for two. Young girls and boys, old people and children were sabred as they ran, by the blue-coated soldiers who laughed and cursed as they dealt out death unsparingly. Hard pressed, the Indians fled up the

---

[1] Gatling guns.

pass and here, in the mountains, the cannons could not be brought to bear, and the heavy military horses could not climb so well as the light Indian ponies.

The Indians loosed their horses and drove them up the pass to safety, remaining to fight among the rocks on foot, picking off the soldiers one by one with arrows at close range, catching whole parties in ambuscade, and shooting them down, capturing their arms and ammunition, and turning the soldiers' own rifles against them.

And on that mountain meadow, in which stood the mighty jack-pine, the fight was fought to a finish. The Indians rallied round their sacred tree; and now the tree was the centre of the conflict. And in the thickest of the fight the Chief felt beside him always the presence of the bear, no longer quiet and amicable, but swift and terrible and deadly, there beside him; and his arm was stronger because of it and he felt new strength at every stroke and none could stand before him—" Like a bear " his warriors said among themselves. And the tree and the surrounding walls of rock echoed with the terrific sound of battle, and threw it back and forth from one to another, flung the fearful uproar back and forth between them, so that it seemed as if they too joined in the combat, while the eagles manœuvred wildly and hovered screaming above the field of blood.

And high above the smoke and dust and din the pine stood calm and towering and collected, like some great general who overlooked the proceedings from an eminence, and laid the plan of battle and directed it.

And now the tide of battle turned. The Indians, their blood hot with the thought of their murdered families, fought fiercely, sparing no man; some were now using swords and cavalry pistols as well as rifles and fought man to man against the foe with desperate courage. The soldiers too were brave, but hampered by heavy boots and other military equipment, were slower and less active than the naked, agile Indians, and were slain almost to a man.

So the prediction of the Chief came true, and he told the assembled warriors of what help the power of the Tree had been, and how the spirit of the silver-tip had fought so valiantly beside him. And so each Indian that still remained alive laid a thank-offering at the foot of the pine, their now doubly sacred Tree around which they had made their desperate stand and won. And the bear-skull was festooned with beautifully beaded belts and feathered ornaments, and painted shields, fire-bags and other valuables were laid against the Tree trunk or hung from limbs, to show the gratitude of the owners.

For it had long ago been said by the wise men of the nation, that while the Tree stood, so they too would live, and when it fell, the Blackfeet would be driven from the plains; and the tradition further said that if the Indians should be first destroyed, or move away, the Tree would fall crashing to the ground. And now in its shadow they had triumphed.

But the heart of the Tree was troubled, and the soul of the bear was sad, and both stood apprehensive and appalled, because of what the warriors would find when they went down to count their dead. A warrior expects to die; but there amongst the torn-down teepees and smouldering remains of homes, women and children lay dead and mangled. And among them this Chief found his wife and two young sons. But the sorrow of all was so great that he said nothing of his own, and left the ruined encampment in the darkness and went up to the battle-ground, among the dead. And he stood beneath the tree in silence, there alone, his breath coming thickly in gasps of agony as he thought of the honeymoon that had been so happy, and of the gentle, dark-eyed maiden who had come so shyly, so timidly and yet so willingly to share his new teepee, here beneath the Tree; and his throat tightened at the memory—but this was weakness; with a stern, resolute gesture he saluted the bear-skull and the Tree, and thanked them for the victory—

the victory!—and throwing himself face down on the carpet
of pine-needles, in among the offerings and the tokens, he
pillowed his face on a huge, twisted root and wept. He was
no more a warrior but just a man.

And there was no one there to see. And the limbs of the
giant jack-pine bowed low about him, and the shade of the
bear sat by and never moved, and tried to speak but could
not, for sorrow.

And later, when the dew settled on the foliage of the pine
and gathered there and dripped down, it fell like slow, quiet
tear-drops down upon the man, and upon the still silent
field of a battle that had been a victory, and yet was lost,
on that mountain meadow, in the pass so long ago.

The whites, in too great a multitude to be overcome by
small, isolated reverses to their arms, slaughtered the Indians
without mercy. Where they could not prevail by honest
war or justice, then broken treaties, economic sanctions,
exile, whisky, entire destruction of the buffalo herds and
ruthless suppression of tribal life, customs, religion, language
and arts, eventually accomplished the desired results. The
tide of people from nearly every country in the world, pro-
lific as rabbits, domineering and land-hungry, swarmed
across the continent like locusts, and overran it; and what
they could not make use of or subdue, they destroyed. The
smoke of devastating forests and prairie fires darkened the sun
at noonday. Immense areas became little better than a
shambles, and whole reaches of the plains became almost
impassable owing to the stench arising from millions of
slaughtered buffalo, among which young calves, robbed of
their parents and useless to the hide-hunters, died by
thousands of starvation.

The few Indians who survived, now become outcasts in
their own country, were herded onto reservations, under the
supervision of Government agents who generally knew little
about Indians, and were dishonest as often as not. There

was bitter and useless fighting in which, to their shame be it said, numbers of "friendly" renegade Indians, with either a sheep-like submissiveness, a toadying subservience, or because knowing which side their bread was buttered on, according to temperament, helped the enemy against their own people; monuments have since been raised to some of these traitors, by the whites. Riff-raff of all kinds, often little better than hired assassins, engaged in the pastime of Indian-hunting with all the unnecessary brutality of those who know themselves to be in the wrong, and acted as scouts and guides to the troops, gaining thereby great historical reputations; some few of them were genuine frontiersmen, and respected by even those they fought against, but only too many were just plain killers having now a chance to indulge their natural propensities without getting hanged for it.

Both sides massacred indiscriminately, and terrible cruelties were perpetrated, on the one hand to gain, and on the other to keep, possession of the bloodstained soil. The original inhabitants of the country, both human and animal, became wary, elusive and unapproachable, and, not without some justification, frequently repaid broken faith with treachery.

In the mushroom border towns, the saloon and the jail were not unusually the principal buildings, and among the pale invaders there sprang up a race of gunmen and desperados who terrorized whole communities, and murdered and robbed and staged pitched battles against the forces of law and order.[1] Meanwhile the Indians sat by in helpless misery and watched, while the palefaces quarrelled and fought among themselves over the ownership of lands that belonged to none of them.

Civilization had come to the West, and *now* the West was

[1] At the time of writing, these conditions have not much improved, the chief difference being that the scene of these activities has moved further East, and the gunmen are of a lower order; some of the old time gun-fighters were really brave men.

wild—the great "Wild West" of romance, and song, and story was in its heyday.

And the Tree, who saw it all, made never a sign, just stood there very still, and dark, and silent.

Many years after the historic battle, now long forgotten, an old man came up the trail that led through the flower-carpeted meadow in the mountain pass. He walked very slowly, uncertainly, like one whose strength is far ebbed and whose span of life must be very near its close. When he came to the immense jack-pine that stood alone, over-looking the vast panorama of the plains below, he sat down on one of the massive roots and gazed long and thoughtfully down upon the prairie.

He saw there the habitations of men scattered everywhere, no longer teepees but the wooden dwelling of the white man, over a land partitioned off into squares in a chequer-board pattern of monotonous regularity. The dark moving masses that had been buffalo were no longer there, though their bones were piled in huge mounds and high, wide walls beside the rail-road, so as to be conveniently loaded and shipped away as fertilizer. This the old man knew to be true, for he had seen them there.

And he sat and mused and gazed in silence, out across the vast sweep of the plains.

What once had been a game trail in days gone by had now become a road. First had come the trapper, who nosed out all the secret places of the Wilderness and discovered or made routes to all kinds of supposedly inaccessible spots; then came the reputed "explorer," who was seldom in the vanguard, in most cases following the trappers lead, but getting the credit and often inflicting his name on portions of the scenery. Soon after came the missionary, good, self-denying and heroic, with the courage of his convictions, though perhaps, in the odd instance, at times a little misguided. There followed in quick succession the prospector, the whisky peddler, the cow-boy, the surveyor and the land agent. And none of them, except perhaps the trapper, even guessed that the trail on which they travelled had its being solely on account of the presence of the great, lone pine that overshadowed them as they passed it by.

The transition from game path to pack-trail and then to road, had been accomplished in less than twenty years. Each of the questing, acquisitive, adventurous spirits who passed by the big pine, had filched as much as he could carry away of the Indian regalia and accoutrements that, for some reason unknown to them, had been left piled around it. All except the missionaries who, although they forbade further tree or sun "worship" among the savages, and frowned on the belief the aborigines held concerning the "souls" of dumb brutes, were nearly always honest, though they had been not unknown, upon occasion, to use the spiritual ascendancy they had gained over the red-men, to the furtherance of the grasping tactics of the invaders. The bear-skull, by some caprice, or because it was of no value (for bears could be had for the shooting), was left to hang where it was; though the little mountain stream had long ago been denuded of its trout, and a large patch of timber that had stood upon its banks had been burnt, and in consequence the brook was nearly dry. The eagles had either been killed or had left the country long ago and their nest had been blown away piecemeal by the storms of half a hundred Winters.

After the first thin scattering of adventurers, the rank and file of Progress had marched into and over everything, and the cohorts of the civilization of the period, land-hungry, arrogant and avaricious, swept in and took possession—a miscellaneous host, to whom nothing was sacred save their own particular, personal gods, seeing nothing but the soil—

" land "—or gold, hating Nature for the most part, looking on it and the institutions of the original dwellers in the region, as something to be stamped out as soon as possible to make room for the great god wheat—the god that was later, like the embarrassingly profitable touch of Midas, to choke and starve them.

For even the old man seated beneath the tree that had stood firm through all these quick and violent changes, could not, with all his accumulated experience, have foreseen the day when people would go hungry in a land where wheat accumulated faster than it could be used, and where men still kept on growing only wheat because it was the thing to do, and prated of bumper crops when the land was choked with wheat and last year's yield lay undisposed of in the bins. Nor would he ever have understood why greed and mismanagement should have changed so much of the fertile prairies into dust-choked deserts where even cactus and rattlesnakes could no longer live.

Steadily the old man looked out over this now, to him, forbidden land. He was no longer welcome there. He was an Indian.

Dressed in patched, ill-fitting trousers, a coat too small for him, a pair of nondescript, rundown shoes, and a drooping, wide-brimmed hat through a hole in the crown of which some short bristles of white hair protruded, he who once had been a Chief was now a tramp, begging his food from those who had dispossessed him and wearing the cast-off clothing that they gave him. He wore no underclothes or socks, and round his neck, by a string, was hung a cheap medallion on which was pictured a theological personage of some sect or other of the many that these new people had, and about whose authority they seemed never to be able to agree.

Yet, from far above the bigotry and strife, the sad, gentle eyes in the face depicted on the medal must surely have looked down, and wept in pity.

The old Indian's bearing was bowed and abject. Only his face retained an expression of dignity, enhanced by the keenness of his eyes; but apart from his steady, penetrating glance that must have daunted many a beholder in his younger days, his dark unmoving features were composed into a settled calm that was exceeded only by the graven immobility of the eternal mountains themselves. He fingered the tin medallion absently until, as though becoming suddenly conscious of it, he looked down at it. With a sharp tug he snapped the cord that held it and flung it from him. The trinket struck a rock with a little tinkle, a fantastically trivial sound in the sublime majesty of the surroundings. The old man rose to his feet, staggering a little, and the old eyes flashed and his face set in lines of startling ferocity as, with a gesture of contempt, he kicked aside the unspeakable shoes, tore off the cheap coat and flung away his hat. Naked to the waist, it could be seen that his brown wasted torso and withered frame must once have been of magnificent proportions, and as he stood he achieved a certain wild nobility of bearing. He passed his hand over two abrasions on the mighty trunk, one that had been a blaze and one a scar of some sort, both now nearly covered by ingrowing bark and discernible only as narrow clefts. He tottered weakly, and his hands found the bear skull, of which the binding strings had long since rotted apart and the lower jaws fallen to the ground; and leaning heavily on the skull he raised his head, white with the passage of nearly ninety years, and looking up into the heavy canopy of massed and interwoven branches that, like a deep, wide-spreading transept, arched high above him, he began to speak.

" O Tree, my patron; you and I have lived very long, each after his kind.

" Too long have we lived.

" Too long.

" The Past has fallen and lays about our feet like an old, discarded garment.

" Let it lay, lest when we pick it up, it fall to pieces and be forever lost.

" Of those who knew this great Past only you and I remain.

" Only you and I are left to remember.

" Not for long now will our hearts be obliged to carry this burden, so great a load of memories to be borne by only two:

" Our people are gone and the pale ones have taken everything.

" Now our work is done, yours and mine.

" Before your limbs are white with Winter's snows and the Ghost Birds of the North whistle on white wings through the forest, I will meet her who was the mother of my sons.

" I will see the great bear whose spirit fought beside me here against the soldiers.

" Soon you will join us, for now the Indians are gone you too must go.

" The wise men of olden times, who knew you when you were young, have told it.

" It will be as they have said; the tradition must be fulfilled.

" And when you come to us in the Great Mystery of the Hereafter, once more will we sit beneath your branches, and rest, and talk about the past.

" And the great bear who is my Brother, will be there to listen.

" For we have been this long time kin together, you and I, and he.

" The Great Spirit is good and will not part us.

" No man, however wise, may say that only he shall live in the Kingdom of Hereafter.

" Till then, be strong, O my friend of many days.

" O Tree, O great bear, my Patrons, hear me.

" We will be waiting."

And then he ceased to speak, and fumbled in a pocket for

awhile, and pulling out a tiny wad of plug tobacco, pushed it into the brain-pan of the skull for an offering; though very carefully because the bone crumbled a little and pieces came away in his hands.

And the old chief sat down, his back against the Tree, that supported him but could not give him life; nor would have if it could. He remained very still, gazing out over the plains, listening to the Voice of the Tree, as the wind played among its top-most boughs, humming a deep, sustained and wavering note of unearthly beauty, as though picked from some wild, barbaric symphony; a chord that must have got its echo in Eternity.

Presently, as the aged man sat so quietly, the prairie lands grew dim and far away, so passed at last from his sight. And the Voice of the Tree was stilled. And the life of the old, old Indian passed on, as had that of the ancient silver tip, two centuries ago, in this the chosen place of both of them.

And the Tree knew that the very last of its friends was gone, and that now it too must follow them. For this was the Fate of the Tree that those that loved it should die, while it lived on until none of them was left.

That night there came a storm, crashing down from the mountains; and in the tempest the lonely Tree moaned and wailed, and shook wildly on its foundations, and silhouetted against the white glare of the lightning it seemed to writhe, and to be contorted into shapes of agony.

The next day a party of horsemen went by, discovered the body and buried it in a shallow, nameless grave beside the road. In an access of good spirits one of them took down the skull and threw it in the creek, among the tomato cans and other refuse that had gathered there.

Later it was decided to build a highway. Came engineers, hard practical men, skilled in their calling, who saw beauty in straight lines and rigid outlines and could view with complacency the fettering of primal forces that had run free for half a million years before man appeared at all, and who found romance in converting the face of Nature to man's needs. The old Sentinel at the gateway to the mountains, stood in the line of least resistance and was marked for destruction.

And the tree that had lived too long, stood patiently and waited for the end. The first axe struck. The Tree gave no sign, but stood in all its grand composure and nobility to the last—and then swayed a little, and started on its journey to the ground. With a moaning, screaming cry, as its fibres ripped apart and its sweeping superstructure tore downwards through the air, the mighty conifer crashed to earth, down among the berries and the wild-flowers, prostrate on the pleasant mountain meadow where it first had sprung to life nearly seven hundred years before. And so the Fate of the Tree was finally accomplished, and the ancient tradition of the Blackfeet had been fulfilled at last.

And the mountains looked on in stony calmness; for they knew that trees must die and so must men, but that they live on forever.

And as the final stroke was given and the life of the Tree, was severed for all time, the figure of a naked Indian, crowned with a spreading eagle bonnet, stood for a fleeting instant high upon a ridge—and then was gone.

And beside him there had been the shaggy, monstrous shape of a gigantic grizzly bear.

An automobile, the finest that mechanical skill could make it, and with a full complement of those more or less useful gadgets so clever and expediently designed to render the latest models quickly obsolete, stimulating trade, was racing along the new highway through the mountains. It carried two passengers. The driver had sensitive, almost delicate hands and the quiet steady glance of the habitual observer. His companion, who sat beside him, was a gross man with heavy pouches under his eyes and a pendulous jowl. He had bulbous lips and his fingers supported a superfluity of rings. A cigar was cocked at a high angle in one corner of his mouth.

As the car sped on, it entered a mountain pass from the summit of which, looking back, there could be had a very fine view of the prairie farm lands. The driver brought the car to a stop, and looked about him with evident appreciation of the surroundings. "Gosh!" he exclaimed. "Take a look at those mountains! Great stuff, eh?"

The other chewed on his cigar and looked out speculatively at the looming peaks.

"Can't use them in my business," he asserted, adding, "Poor lookin' country to me."

Beside the highway was an enormous jack-pine stump. The fat man removed his cigar and spat, forcefully and accurately, spattering the stump.

The car passed on.

A red squirrel raced across the highway with a pine-cone in his mouth, planted it somewhere in the meadow, and straightway forgot about it.

XIV

Canadiana

A VISITOR to this great Land of Canada of ours could be forgiven for supposing that, among the nations, we Canadians
alone do not honour our traditions. We have a lot of them,
and they're not bad, either. Yet let some writer as much as
hint that Canada is a pioneer country, when he will be
assailed by flocks of letters reminding him that the buffalo
were all killed off in 1880, that the Indians are all corralled
on reservations (as though these two facts were something
to be proud of), that what few cowboys there are left are
attired like farm-hands, and that pioneers are a thing of the
past. Perhaps this is all so, in some parts. But I'm proud
to tell you that Canada has, thanks to a branch of the
Dominion Government known as National Parks of Canada,
an immense herd of buffalo numbering over five thousand
head out there on the prairie, exclusive of an absolutely
wild herd, or herds, of these animals that the hide-hunters
and other vandals didn't get, and who roam the Wilderness
country in the unexplored North-West—that in Prince
Albert, Saskatchewan, I lately saw a band of cowboys
wearing chaps, high-heeled riding boots and ten-gallon
hats; not drug-store cowboys off a dude ranch but real,
honest-to-god range riders—and that about two thirds of
Canada consists of about the finest and most valuable
Wilderness area in the world. Settlers still go unbelievable
distances into the backwoods to hew out, if possible their
fortune, or failing that, a living, where they fight, not
Indians, perhaps, but forest fires and in many instances
wolves that menace their stock. And about a week from
today I, along with thousands of other interested sightseers,

will witness one of the biggest Indian conventions ever held
in this part of the country, where bows and arrows, peace
pipes, long braided hair, buckskin, beads and feathers and
ancient ceremonial will play a very prominent part.

Whatever is there to be so diffident about in all this?
Collectively, these things represent the most interesting
period of Canadian history. They will be quickly enough
gone without us having to so strenuously deny their
presence while we still, luckily, have them with us. And
not until they have disappeared will we learn to place a
proper value on them; and then, vainly, we will try with
both hands to bring them back again.

Our cities are getting more like London and New York
every day, granted. But every worthwhile country has
such places, and we must, naturally, keep up and be as
good as the rest. These things are in the hands of our
executives, and are well taken care of. But there will be
nothing distinctive about that; everybody is doing it. But
we have right here, at our back door so to speak, something
else that is our very own, that is of Canada, Canadian—our
North. And Canada's history and the typical Canadian
scene are unique among the nations. Let's be proud of
them. Canada's economic life is being built on a very firm
foundation, and this country ranks well to the fore com-
mercially, and with the advent of better times will, without
any doubt, make further and greater strides in the field of
national achievement. But this seems, to me, to be no
reason why we should sink our individuality as a very fine
specimen of a pioneer country.

I have heard it stated that Canada's comparatively
small population is one of her great advantages. This
gives a greater proportion per capita of the natural-resource-
wealth, and I am inclined to agree with this opinion. At
this period in its history the natural increase in the population would appear to be sufficient to carry on with. At the
present time countries having a heavy population are all in

trouble, the accumulation within their borders seeking an outlet in any direction, and finding themselves surrounded by others in a like predicament are all dressed up and have nowhere to go. We, on the other hand, are very lucky, in that we have all kinds of places to go within our own boundaries. Most of the troubles which today seem to threaten the structure of civilization itself come as the result of an over-population problem. It has been said that we need more consumers here and more producers too; but what object is served by having producers produce more than they can possibly dispose of, or of having an over-plus of consumers who cannot pay for what they consume.

There seems to be a disposition to hide that part of our light that emanates from the North, under a bushel, though it may yet prove to be the brightest ray of our national illumination. Numbers of people, whose knowledge of their own country is not as complete as it might be (a state of affairs for which there is no excuse), are unduly sensitive about the word " North ", apparently intimidated by a word because of its sometime connection with Arctic exploration. It would be just as logical to eliminate the word " South " from our vocabulary because it might signify drought or grasshoppers. I have experienced temperatures and climatic conditions in our North that, for a good part of the year, approximated those said to prevail in the South of France. And we *have* a North, far the largest proportion of the Dominion, possessing untold, inestimable possibilities, and with a climate consisting of a short Spring, a warm but bracing, sunshiny Summer, a very wonderful Autumn such as I think few other countries in the world are favoured with, and a bright, clear, cold, snappy, invigorating and healthful Winter. So why deny the facts, seek to hide them under a camouflage of ambiguities, damn with faint praise, when these facts can be turned so greatly to our own advantage?

Canadians that I have met abroad, do not talk of our

L

forests, our lakes and rivers, our rich mineral belts, our mountains or our mighty trees, but of a skyscraper on Yonge street or an advance in the price of hogs. Skyscrapers and hogs may rise and fall, but that Northland of ours is one of our best possessions and should be heard from.

I often wonder why, when naming a spot of exceptional loveliness, we should so frequently have recourse to foreign nomenclature, putting the place into quotation marks as it were, as though we apologized for its existence and sought to gain something for it by means of a borrowed appellation. Just try calling the Pyrenees the European Rockies, or refer to Geneva as the Swiss Lake Superior, and see how unpopular you are over there, as you should be. From time to time we hear of expressive, apt, and euphonious place-names changed to weakly pretentious pseudonyms or smug commonplaces by groups who, with a kind of snobbery, would sooner bend the knee to mediocrity than be reminded of their pioneer ancestry even by a name. Beautiful and romantic spots, prospects of sublime grandeur that typify so much of our Canadian scenery, have inflicted on them the names of those who made a lot of money but never did a thing worth while in all their lives. We read of new mining camps, far from civilization, where bridge and knitting seem to be the principal recreations, and where no good prospector would think of going to bed without undressing his feet, for fear he should pass away in the night and so be said to have died with his boots on, giving the place a bad reputation. Thus is the good old frontier spirit quenched, squelched, and withered by those who revel in the commonplace, liking to be thought "matter of fact," and who would take all the colour out of our sufficiently humdrum life, if we let them. And if modern mining camps have been ground down to such a condition of invertebrate desuetude as we are led to suppose, then someone ought to keep quiet about it. I have been in one or two of the "roughest" mining rushes we have had in Canada, and saw plenty of

" frontier " life in them; but I saw no murders, gun battles, bridge or knitting. Things were neither as wild as some would suppose, nor as deadly boring as some others would like to have it. There was plenty of hard work, and fun, and goodfellowship, and all the free and easy atmosphere common to such conditions. Frontiersmen don't as a rule have either the time or the inclination for homicide, however well conducted; but they have plenty of animal spirits just the same, and don't need any backhanded compliments from moralists as to how " well behaved " they are, and they belong usually to a type, of which the wild, free country that produced them has no need to be ashamed. And in those " lawless " days I speak of, a man could leave equipment and other valuable property in plain sight on portages and in caches that were visible to all passers-by, and be sure of finding it there when he went back for it. There are those who would like us to think that this kind of thing has been done away with; well, to a certain extent it may have been— for certainly the police quota appointed to some of the present-day camps seems to be far greater than that required in such a place as the Cobalt of 1905—but let's hope it hasn't, for it was on such stuff that Canada was built.

We know that this frontier is moving further North all the time, as it must. Commercialism comes in, inevitably, from which the country as a whole will reap (or should reap) the benefit. But let us beware lest we become a nation of hard, sharp-appearing bargain makers. Our souls need something too. One almost forgives a dictator on learning that he plants trees, preserves plots of natural scenery intact, and fosters the arts. I understand that Canadian authors, painters, actors and other artists are obliged to go to England and the United States in order to make a livelihood at their profession. And I am not speaking for myself, as I am not a professional writer, and have no intention of becoming one; I am only engaged in getting down, while I can, a record in word-pictures of this Wilderness, its creatures and its people, among whom my life has been passed and to whom I so irrevocably belong.[1]

While it may provide for a necessity, an ability for clever bargaining in wheat never, alone, made any nation great. The money-changers among the nations have failed signally to perpetuate their dreams of empire. If we are to become a people of some account in future history, we must think of something else besides the dollar sign. The sole representative Canadian arts that I, with the limited facilities at my disposal, have so far been able to discover, are the few products of the French-Canadians and the Indians. And not until the average Canadian ceases subconsciously to calculate the number of feet of board measure in every great tree that he passes, will we be able to produce an important Canadian art. At present we seem to be, to a greater extent than is good for us, like the farmer in the Oriental legend, who was so intent upon the soil from which he hoped to reap a fortune, that he forgot ever to look up, and so never saw the sky, never guessed the beauty of the heavens—which he could have done without in the least detracting from his work. I think that the souls of many of us who have had to hustle our way along and help build up this new, vigorous young country, are a little undernourished in some directions. We need an enrichment other than material prosperity, and to gain it we have only to look around (and we don't have to stop to do it) at what our own country has to offer, "see Canada first", to use a platitude; for, as I repeat, we have something here that no other country has. Every individual human being, every people as a whole, needs an æsthetic release; it is a part of the business of living, and

---

[1] *Neither am I a naturalist, as is so often stated. I conduct no researches into the technicalities of the biology, classification, or other purely scientific data of any of these creatures who share with me my environment. My interest lies more in investigation of their mental processes, disposition and lesser-known characteristics, and in those intimate details of their life history, habits and work that are sometimes outside the scope of ordinary scientific observation. To a true naturalist each animal, of its species, represents a given group. With me, each animal is an individual.*

aside from the arts, of which we have apparently so few, we will find it in the lakes and streams and woodlands of our North as nowhere else. Can you think of anything that has the majestic quietude, the reposeful calm, the slumbering restfulness of a forest of great trees?—or of anything to so stir the imagination as the leap and roar of mighty rivers—of anything quite so quelling to unworthy thinking as the stern magnificence of the snow-capped mountains—or of anything half as adventurous as following the far-flung half-hidden trails of Indian or trapper, by canoe, cow pony, or on snowshoes? Go see all these things, or only one of them, you who are sometimes tired of the hurly-burly, the conniving, the conspiring, and contriving that so wearies you, and you will come back twice the man or woman that you went.

Is not at least some of this great Northern heritage worth saving *in its original, unspoiled state*, for such a worthy purpose?

It is inconceivable that this entire Northern domain should be put to the axe. Too much of it is more valuable to the nation in other ways. Much of it is required to support the lumbering industry, and could, and should be cropped and replanted by those who are to profit from it. But they do not need it all. In the Eastern provinces, forest reserves have been long ago established, each containing fine examples of the zone forest conditions of their respective areas, and are of immense value, even if only potentially, as in some cases, to the people as playgrounds and recreational spots. Some of the most beautiful of these, places such as the Mississauga and the Algonquin Park, have been allowed to become little better than lumber reservoirs, and are being slowly demolished. Even these comparatively small districts, representing some of the finest forests left in that part of Canada, cannot be spared, and when they are gone will be an irreparable loss.

It is not as though we would have to take a loss if we set aside, for the good of our souls, good-sized areas of the original Canadian scene with the intention of keeping them inviolate for all time. A few private interests might be obliged to shift the field of their operations and so suffer some small inconvenience, or even loss, but it seems more important that some part of our heritage should be preserved for the people at large, and for posterity. And as I just said, we do not stand to lose, not in the long run. There's a pay streak in it, and a heavy one. Did you know that Canada's wild life, *alive*, and her natural scenery (and I mean *natural*, real forests of big trees, not burnt-over areas or lumberman's leavings) have made the tourist traffic one of Canada's foremost industries? But the wild life and scenery *must* be here for these guests of ours to see, or they won't stay long and won't come back, won't leave their dollars here any more. And forests, to fill the requirements, are not spindling second-growth, and wild life is not something in a cage.

The National Parks Service of the Dominion Government, alive to the importance of safeguarding some portion of our incalculably valuable birthright before it is too late, has apportioned out in some of the Provinces immense stretches of wilderness as national playgrounds. These National Parks, as they are called, vary in size all the way from a few acres enclosing some historical sites, to regions of wilderness, much of it virgin, up to four thousand square miles in extent. Owing to their comparative accessibility these regions have provided joy to many thousands; and they are also sanctuaries where no timber may be cut and where all forms of wild life are to be preserved in perpetuity. Animals common to those parts of North America exist there in probably the same profusion that they did at the time that Columbus discovered this continent (if he did—there seems to be some difference of opinion), and the Parks have been created so as to include within their boundaries the headwaters of numerous streams and rivers; thus the preservation of natural forest not only provides for the requirements of a rich variety of animal life, but its moisture-retaining cover has an important bearing on water supply for all the surrounding country, besides offering opportunities for Summer Wilderness travel in regions of unparalleled beauty that would otherwise have been long ago destroyed. But to keep these places beautiful so all may enjoy them, to keep the wild places wild, calls for the co-operation of the people to whom the country belongs, who will take steps, through legislation and personal conduct, to protect from fire, vandalism and crass carelessness these nation-properties that, once defaced or destroyed, can never be brought back again. In several of the Provinces no definite steps have so far been taken to preserve any such monuments of the original Canadian scene, and at the rate their forests are disappearing from all causes, they had better do something about it while there is yet something to do it about.

The Canadian Government has shown, also, a sympathetic attitude towards the development of native Indian art, something intrinsically Canadian and very well worth while, that had hitherto been neglected, if not actually suppressed. But much remains to be done in all directions, that can only be effected when the people of Canada come to a realization of the fact that their birthright, and with it the inheritance of future generations, is dwindling very, very fast, that it is being squandered and frittered away before it is even due to be collected.

And now the vexed question of our Winter. I could never quite grasp the point of view of those who think it is bad for business to speak above a whisper when the subject of our Winter is discussed. So many there are who attempt to minimize, or at least to hide, the fact that Canada has a Winter. I know little or nothing about the extreme Southern portion, or of British Columbia, but all the rest of Canada has a good, wintery Winter. And to attempt to deny it is fantastic. If the idea is to attract emigrants to these shores by misleading them, it is safe to say that those who do not like, and do not expect to encounter quantities of snow and

ice during part of the year, will quickly learn to hate us for
the deception, and will never be any good to the country.
Once their transportation fares are paid, nobody benefits
much from their being here.   These denials do no one any
good, and remind me very much of what I have noted, with
regret, regarding not a few of my own kind, who are part
Indian and part White, and because the Indian appearance
is not so obvious in them (and in many cases where it *is* quite
obvious), will deny their blood and call themselves Irish,
Scotch, French, Ukranian or anything else but what they
are—Indian.   Should they be, are they ashamed of it, and
if so why?   And are we, too, ashamed of our Winter?

Winter in Canada is in many ways the best time of the
year, and we have no reason to deny it, though I once heard
a man go us one better, and try.   He tried to deny an earthquake!   This was a very creditable feat of inverted exaggeration; I'll tell you about it.   This was by no means the
only earthquake that had taken place in those parts, and it
happened some three years ago.   I forget how many were
killed; thousands were injured and the property damage
ran into millions of dollars.   I listened to an all-night broadcast, and heard of the heroism and self-sacrifice with which
the inhabitants of the stricken city met the disaster.   I heard
about relief trains rushed half-way across a continent,
listened to messages of condolence from many distant
countries.   And then, a few nights later, this able prevaricator,
probably a community booster or maybe the owner of some
hotels he wanted to get filled up, or of real estate he wanted
to sell in the district, spoke over the radio to the effect that
what we had heard about the earthquake was all wrong.
It appeared, from what he told us, that all reports had been
grossly exaggerated, that there had been nothing to make
such a fuss about, and they never had earthquakes in that
part of the country anyway.   Everybody (including the
sufferers, I suppose) had been altogether too earthquake-
conscious, and indeed, he was hard put to it not to try and

make us believe that there hadn't been any earthquake at all!

Now our Winter season is no catastrophe, and we sure need it in many of our industries. Yet we try to make of it a lurking skeleton in the cupboard, which is pretty hard to do because everybody knows about it and it just won't be ignored, and who wants to ignore such a glorious season as we have for a Winter anyway? We seem to thrive on it remarkably well, and from what I see on the bathing beaches at Waskesieu, I'm pretty sure that young Canadian manhood and womanhood compare very favourably indeed with any of the recognized examples of physical perfection we see in the illustrated papers from abroad; and certainly they have more snap, and vim, and energy, and spirit than is common to those races that reside in the enervating regions of perpetual Summer.

To a good many Canadians the Winter is a sore point, as is the fact that so much of our land is unoccupied and unsuitable for agriculture. But as a climate such as ours breeds a virile, vigorous, healthy people, and agriculture seems, at present, to have been a little overdone, perhaps we should be thankful rather than otherwise. Decidedly our unpopulated North has a potential value far exceeding that of any amount of wheat, which is rather a drug on the market just now; and I have never heard of a timber surplus. And to open that North country up, at this present stage of our development, to the tender mercies of a teeming population of not-so-badly-wanted-settlers for them to make a Roman Holiday of, would be the poorest kind of economy. And as to the Winter, we have no more need to apologize for it than I had for my nationality, when a lady, whose husband had passed some thoughtless remark about it, said, with the best of intentions, "But, my dear, he didn't ask to be made a half-breed—it's not his fault!" And moreover, as a Winter sports country, I am of opinion that with its superior climatic conditions, Canada has Switzerland backed off the map. Perhaps, with the possibility of the Olympic Winter Games being held in this country at a future date, it may be that our so long reviled Winter will at last come into its own.

I'm advertising, you say. Well, perhaps I am; but I am not trying to sell you anything (except maybe the book, which would likely sell a lot better without this essay). And what I tell you is true. I don't give three hurrahs in Honolulu whether you come to our country or not; that's up to you and I won't coax you. But, brother, if you do, we will bid you very welcome here; and I want, and every good Canadian wants, there to be something here we'll be proud to show you.

Canada is a land of contrasts, where the Old and the New meet on common ground and equal terms. Canada is a land of Enterprise, of Industry, of picturesque Romance. Here Commerce, Beauty, and Art may move forward hand in hand to greatness. We have the goods; the rest is up to us.

BOOK TWO

MISSISSAUGA

And always I hear the stir of men dipping
Down to the Chaudiere, their thin blades dripping,
Catch the long low wraith of a bark canoe
And hear the wild sweet chansons of a phantom crew."

LLOYD ROBERTS

1

Requiem

I HAVE traversed the black swamps and the vast, reeking muskegs of the Abitibi, gone hungry in the bleak sterility of the distant, unknown North, and hacked my way through the impenetrable cedar jungles of far-off Temiscouata. I once spent a season in the great high oasis of Riding Mountain, with its poplar forest and rolling downs carpeted with myriad flowers, that stands like an immense island of green above the hot, dry sameness of the wheat-stricken Manitoba prairie that surrounds it. And now my home lies among the lakes that throng the spruce-clad lowlands of the upper Saskatchewan.

Each of these districts has its special claim on the imagination, and every one of them is imbued with the fantastic lure of the unknown that, like some all-powerful enchantment or magic spell, pervades the unpeopled places of the earth's surface. But they all, to me, lack the austere magnificence and the rugged grandeur of the highlands of North Ontario, with their bold, romantic scenery, uncounted and uncountable deep-water lakes and wild rushing rivers. And though happy here with my work and busy with my fast accumulating responsibilities and ever wider-reaching interests, even so, old memories linger on, memories of the old, wild, carefree days when I roamed at will through the rock-bound Ontario wilderness, all my worldly goods loaded into one small, swift, well-beloved canoe or, in Winter, contained within the four walls of a none too spacious log cabin, hastily erected on the shores of some frozen, or soon to be frozen lake.

I had not, at that time, written yet a line nor even thought of it, yet even then, so long ago, I felt that all this Wilderness would change and that some day we ourselves would soon be gone, that this was the last stand, and we perhaps the last of our kind. And often when alone, I used to wish I could record it just as it then existed, while it yet was there—though fortunately most of the country remains untouched. This urge came very strongly and insistently upon me when once I sat high up on a mountain [1] that stands beside the long portage to Washegaming,[2] a turquoise jewel set back in the forest on the crest of a lofty ridge. From my lookout there fell away in rapidly descending waves the immense billowing undulations of the Western watershed, clothed in a black forest of virgin pine, veterans of the last grand army of the Wildlands, paraded in massed and resolute array. The surroundings were steeped in an ineffable calm, and were bathed in a shimmering, lazy haze that, like a sporific, seemed to lull the tranquil landscape into peaceful somnolence, so that it appeared to sleep; and the outlines of the rolling, distant hills were softened and looked like deep green, far-sweeping carpets of moss, with here and there the white splash, like quicksilver, of a lake.

At the foot I could plainly see, drawn up on the gravelly beach, the canoe brigade [3] of my fellow-travellers, and for a long time I watched the river, there below me, racing madly on, singing, shouting in glee, rushing onward all unconscious of what lay before it, to its doom, onward to that grave of all lost rivers, the Ocean—fresh and furious in the Spring-time, tired and lazy in the Autumn, going on for ever, ever down to eventual oblivion.

And I wondered, once it got there and realised it never could come back, did it sometimes have a longing for the mountains, or did it ever miss the trees, or be lonesome for

---

[1] The high, rocky, precipitous hills of the region, varying from a few hundred to a thousand feet or so, are known as mountains.

[2] Pronounced Wah-*sheg*-aming, meaning Clear Lake.

[3] A brigade consisted of four canoes and upwards; loosely applied to all sizes of parties.

the joyous, carefree days it had spent in the far-off Silent
Places.

—But the flotilla awaits without—without me!

" Hey, you goin' to stay there all your life? C'mon you
damned redskin——" thus the affectionate urging of my
companions, chafing at the bit. The moment has passed;
I went down. After all we were on a journey, there was far
to go, I had a reputation to keep up with this brigade, and
to have a reputation at all with such men, is like receiving a
decoration on the field of battle—I mean the competition is pretty stiff—and this was not to be jeopardised
by any foolish day-dreaming. And although good fortune
has since wished on me a wider reputation in another and
perhaps more useful line of endeavour, it can never mean as
much to me, can never quite thrill me or make me quite so
happy as when I once overheard a remark I wasn't supposed
to hear, referring to myself, ". . . one of the best canoemen
in the country . . ." They'd never *tell* me that.

Is this boasting? Maybe it is; but perhaps you do not
know the burning ambition, the fierce pride of profession of
the riverman, that and his ability on snowshoes, perhaps the
only things in all my life I feel a pride in. And many hard
and toilsome years, many a hard battle with the river, and
with other distant rivers, was won, and I had to prove myself
worthy time and time again before this tribute was paid to
me behind my back. So I forgot all about making a record
of my thoughts and returned to my first love, the canoe,
and for many years gave the idea no more consideration.

Once a nomad, with a paddle, a canoe-pole or a pair of
snowshoes ever within reach, my hands now hold a pen;
instead of the pleasant gurgling of water as it caresses the
side of my canoe, or the stirring symphony of a snowstorm,
I hear the irritating, staccato clicking of a typewriter, the
usefulness of which arouses in me very little enthusiasm.
The rollicking chorus of the canoe brigades is replaced by
the pulings, over the radio, of pale emasculates with " soul-

ful " voices whining their lugubrious dirges, of which unfulfilled desire and self-pity seem to be the main themes in
which they bewail, in a helpless way that would turn any
healthy, modern girl sick to the marrow, their lost and
unattainable loves (thank God, for the betterment of the race,
these effeminates seem to be uniformly unsuccessful in their
amours), dishonouring with their cheap and trashy senti-
mentality and trashier music, the noble sentiment they bleat
about. Through all the history of mankind the sheik-
gigolo-lounge-lizard type, with his sticky eroticisms, fawning
insincerities and womanish ways, has been held in contempt.
But today he has come into his own and is suffered gladly,
as is often the privilege of fools, perhaps because he is an
exponent of the " easiest way " and panders to weak pleasures
that come as a relief to a war-weary generation, but temporarily, as a harassed man will sometimes go on a debauch.
This would appear to be the age of superlatives at a hasty
glance. A crooner sings that his love is lost, that he is
frantic and that because of it " the panic is on." A manu-
facturer invents some small improvements in his commodity
and calls it " dramatic "; attempts are made to hypnotize
us by the constant repetition of such words as marvellous,
stupendous, gigantic and so forth. I often wonder, if anything real ever happened to these hyperbolists, whatever in
the world would they do for adjectives. Yet the impressions
of futility and shallowness that these things give to one not
hitherto acquainted with them, is after all erroneous, for
beneath it there must run the strong current of sane virile
human existence.

I read an elevating story, taken from life, of a group of
financiers who (I am expected to admire their acumen), on
a deal in stocks, get together in a pack like timber wolves, to
crush, break and utterly destroy a fellow-man whose wife
and children will do most of the suffering, because he has
been unfortunate enough, or enterprising enough, to infringe
on their monopoly—though it can be said for the wolves

that they do not eat one another alive. Huge concerns will stoop to petty practices such as cutting the price of their product, accepting a loss that the little fellow, who is trying to make a living, cannot stand, underselling him and thousands like him until they go to the wall. Then I read somewhere of a child actor whose relations, like benevolent vultures, divide up his income among them as though it were a carcase.

I look with something of resentment at my skin these days, getting bleached and lifeless-looking from lack of honest hardship; it's getting so the mosquitoes bite through the palms of my hands, and my hide don't keep out the rain any more. Often, when I think back to more strenuous times, I view with small esteem the soft usages that civilization would have me now adopt. Specious advertisements urge me to indulge in stimulants to the limit, suggesting that they are good for me, and asserting naïvely that theirs is the *very* best kind and hasn't a kick in a crateful. I am asked to give way to excesses of all sorts (being sure to use *our* particular brand made especially for *you*), because self-indulgence is so much easier than self-control. I am menaced on all sides by B.O., B.B. ("bad breath"), athlete's ankles, red toothbrush, cosmetic complexion and complete social ostracism, and will very probably end up in a dishonoured grave that will be neglected by my friends if I do not obey the behests of those steely-eyed medical gentlemen who stare so fiercely out at me, some pointing at me with accusing forefinger, from the advertising pages of the magazines, insisting that I eat plenty of yeast or it will be the worse for me.

Thus Big Business, utterly humourless, taking itself very seriously indeed, carries on in its cult of due solemnity, daring me to be whimsical, or independent, or to see how terribly funny are some of its devices for making me purchase things I have no need of. It has been said that an ability to make money out of almost anything is a special gift of doubtful moral value. And when some brilliant mind, rating the mentality of the public on a level with that of a twelve-year-

M

old child or particularly backward savage, offers as an inducement to buy, some quaint gadget whereby the user of a perfume does not have to go to the labour of lifting the bottle to sprinkle the contents on his person, I am reminded of my old companions of the river, hard, lusty men, salt of the earth, to whom B.O. was just plain, honest sweat, to be readily washed off in good lake water, and who lifted their own bottles—being heedful to sprinkle *none* of the contents on their persons but with a good aim and true, carefully down their throats. Some of it makes me laugh, and more of it makes me wonder, whether the old ways were so greatly different, or if things were always that way and that I am just waking up. The well-known business deal that Jacob put over on Esau still works as well as ever, it would seem. And then I remember that this is not the substance of civilization, but is only the froth, and has as little effect on the mighty structure of man's real achievements, as the insignificant frivolities of a squirrel have on the serious operations of a beaver.

And as I sit before my door of evenings and ponder these imponderable things, my mind turns sometimes to reminiscence, as some little thing, a bird-note, a falling leaf, a fleeting, distant sound or a momentary scent upon the air, brings recollection of some well-beloved landscape; and I wander then in retrospect, back down the avenues of long-departed years. And memories crowd about me, and I long once more for the open trail, and the muted swish of snowshoes, and I watch in vain for the clean-cut lines of a fast canoe, coming round the bend. And I smell again the smoke of long-dead fires and see the images of faces and of figures that have forever vanished, seem to catch once more the sound of voices I'll never hear again. Familiar hands, rough, kind and friendly, paddle-calloused and strong, seem to reach towards me from out the past. A host of small, companionable creatures, bright-eyed, curious and pathetic, tiny guests at a thousand camp grounds, come rustling through the dry leaves with a welcome, as I commence my march back down the avenues of Time—an invisible escort that forms in column of route and marches with me, no longer backward but onward, to the River, the wild, romantic, spirit-haunted Mississauga River; where some few men have wrested, by skill and daring and endurance, some small laurels of achievement from its crashing, roaring rapids and where others have had to give the River best, admit themselves defeated; and where some have died.

For this is no ordinary stream, but a very King among the rivers, or perhaps it could be better likened to some turbulent Oriental chieftain who sends his savage hordes streaming across whole continents; for so does the Mississauga, the Grand Discharge of Waters of the Indians,[1] pour its furious way between its rock-bound shores, sweeping a path for twice a hundred miles through the forest lands, levying tribute, in all its branches, from four thousand square miles of territory, untamed, defiant and relentless, arrogantly imposing its name on all the surrounding country; so that a man may travel many a day by canoe and portage through an intricate network of stream and lake and forest, among a rich and infinite variety of scenery and still be within Mississauga's far-flung principality. And the man does not live who knows the whole of it, and I think that there are holes and crannies, and nooks and little ponds and lakes and streams no one has ever seen, not even the Indians, and there are hundreds of miles of virgin timber that have never felt the tread of human foot.

And the River has its moods, like any living thing, and no one stretch of it is like to any other. In some of its reaches a dark sullen flood, powerful and deep, flowing swiftly and smoothly with a high, forbidding precipice on either side,

[1] Pronounced *Miss*-iss-*awg*-y, though the correct Indian pronunciation has the last syllable " -ing " instead of " y " or " a ". The ending " ing " or " ming " or " aming " or " gaming ", indicates a name as being that of some body of water. The meaning in this case is Great or Grand Discharge.

running the grim gauntlet of the mountains, on emerging will spring to sudden fury and become a raging, irresistible torrent, tearing madly at the banks that hem it in, to break quite suddenly into a rabble of chattering wavelets, clattering amongst the gravel of a shallows. Often it runs docilely along, carefree and singing, or murmuring and sleepy, more and more placid as it goes, until its current is quite gone and it broadens peacefully out into tranquil, island-studded lakes with deep bays and inlets and picturesque, bold rocky promontories, all black with pine.

There are swift spots in between these lakes that are quiet and playful; but not all its rapids are so tame. In narrow gorges, constricted and compressed by walls of solid rock, the rush of water is compressed to half perhaps, or less its natural width, and on a sudden incline leaps madly over clustered rocks or sweeps between them at terrific speed and with devastating force. And these are the true rapids, the genuine "white water," the River's standing challenge to the canoeman, where the timorous (or perhaps the wise) take the portage trail and the practised voyageur stakes his life against the might of Mississauga. Some of these rapids are short, steep and vicious, difficult and dangerous. Others of lesser fury may be a hundred yards in length, or a mile, or three miles; and a famous one is seven leagues long, rapid succeeding rapid with tiny lake expansions for breathing spaces in between—seven leagues of speed, and turmoil, and dangerous excitement—the Twenty Mile.[1]

---

[1] With a good guide, Indian or White, this river can be safely travelled by tourists and others, so that the magnificent scenery, the excellent fishing and the adventure that go to make this voyage one of the finest canoe trips in North America, are accessible to those who prefer the more rough and ready kind of outing. A month should be allowed to complete the trip, though it can be done in two weeks. It is strictly a canoe trip, but is neither difficult nor dangerous when taken under the care of competent guides. It is no unusual thing for parties to include women and children, and I have taken several such down the river without hardship. The starting-point is from Biscotasing, a small town, more of a trading post, on the Canadian Pacific railroad. Much of the country is virgin, and is little frequented, the sole inhabitants being the nomadic Ojibway Indians.

Some there be that no man, however skilled, can ever run, and here and there along its course are cataracts, and thundering waterfalls that plunge down stupendous chasms into deep churning pools where sometimes great fish are to be taken.

The River's shores are lined with forests that stretch back without interruption, save for their innumerable waterways, a hundred miles and more to the Eastward, and Westward clear to the shores of Lake Superior. There is every variety of timber common to that zone, and an ever-changing panorama unfolds itself along the River's course; the poplar woods, with their bright trunks, restless fluttering leaves and lightly shifting shadows; the tangled brakes of willows, ash or alders; the hard metallic green of birch and maple; rich, grassy meadows and purple fen-lands; the cloistered, brooding calm of towering pines; each kind takes its turn and passes in review on either bank.

In places vast mountainous upheavals of granite and Keewaydin [1] stand high above the River, and on the face of them lone dwarfed and twisted trees cling precariously to ledges. There are sheer escarpments with queer images chiselled on them by the rain and frost of centuries, and sardonically featured gargoyles carved in stone, some sitting, others standing, others leaning outward from their eyries, all graven there immovably, looking forever down upon the hurrying, ceaseless procession of the River. And at length, as though wearied with the unending spectacle, the mountain turns about abruptly and bears off into the interior, standing like a forbidding, massive rampart, far into the distance; and at its flank deep, mysterious gullies lead back to undiscovered territories, ravines into which no ray of sunlight ever penetrated, and in which no human foot has ever trod.

Piled against the sky, huge cavernous clouds and rolling thunder-heads sometimes gather unaccountably, and hang

[1] Keewaydin is the oldest known rock, and is named after the Indian word, meaning North Wind, or the North.

ominously in heavy curdled masses above the crags that stand beside the Twenty Mile.

And back from the River, far away from the clamour of the River, there lies the Land-Where-Nothing-Ever-Happens, where the Eternal Silence is marked off in divisions of a thousand years by the colossal sweep of the pendulum of Time.

River of a Hundred Ghosts, you and I knew the River-men. Hard fighting, hard swearing and hard drinking, hard driving and hard driven, tough, enduring and efficient, their god was speed and their motto, " Get there, no matter how, but *get* there."

River, sublime in your arrogance, strong with the might of the Wilderness, even yet must you be haunted by wraiths that bend and sway to the rhythm of the paddles, and strain under phantom loads, who still thread their soundless ways through the shadowy naves of the pine forests, and in swift ghost-canoes sweep down the swirling white water in a mad *chasse galerie* with whoops and yells that are heard by no human ear.

Almost I can glimpse these flitting shades, and on the portages can almost hear, faintly, the lisping rustle of for-gotten footsteps, coming back to me like whispers from a dream that is no longer remembered, but cannot die.

There comes the song of a white-throat, high in the trees, above me. I hear the roaring of the River, the endless, noisy march-past of the River; and the distant rumour of the rapids sounds like the conversation of the Dead.

The plaintive, unfinished melody of the little bird trailing off into utter silence, burdened with all the sadness, all the heart-throb, all the glory of the North, and infinitely beautiful, sounds the Requiem of the Lost Brigade—singing, singing in far-away cadence, farther and farther—fainter—fainter——

2

Rivermen

BISCOTASING, Ontario—Bisco, we used to call it, do call it;
for we are there, you and I. I don't seem ever to have been
away; or have I been away? I don't get this. Everything
seems a little confused; and these people—I know them all,
knew them twenty years ago, when I left here; or did I
leave here? They greet me very casually for one so long
gone from their midst.

Have I dreamed the last twenty years, or imagined them,
and they never really happened? Maybe I was out with
the boys last night; I don't seem to remember. But everything seems natural, and this is real enough, and you, my
friend, are with me and you look real enough. Do you see
Bisco? You do? Well then, we are here. And we are
going on a trip; it seems to have been all arranged. How
do I know? Ask me another; but I can tell you that we're
going down the Mississauga tomorrow, with McDougal's
brigade — listen to that white-throat sing! " O-O-O-
Can-ada — Can-ada — Can-ada — Can——" He doesn't
finish it, never does. Canada birds, we used to call them.
All the Rivermen love the white-throats; I always think
of the River when I hear them. There were always
lots of them on the Mississauga—were? Are; this is
today—and it's twenty years ago!

And this is Bisco, the jumping-off place for the Mississauga
River. Well, seeing that you and I are going to be shipmates on this trip, I'll show you the town. My town. It
doesn't belong to me, no; I belong to it. Not much of a
place, you say; are you telling me? I know it very well,

this little burgh; it was my home-town for many years, and always will be, though I only saw it twice a year for a week or so. Let me introduce you.

Biscotasing, or Bisco, is a collection of small wooden houses gathered, or scattered rather, around the rocky hillsides that enclose a sheltered bay of Biscotasing lake. In Summer the twinkling camp-fires of the Indians are visible at the edge of the forest that surrounds the clearance on three sides. The fourth side is bordered by the lake, and in all directions from the edge of the clearing the forest stretches as far as the eye can reach; and this is no idle metaphor, for this is the Big Woods country that reaches nearly to the Great Lakes to the Southward and, with little interruption, clear to the Arctic Ocean, hundreds of miles to the North.

About thirty houses, perched among the rocks, complete the toll of habitations, with two churches a short rifle-shot apart to care for the spiritual needs of a population that spends ninety per cent. of its time in the bush. In my younger days (and perhaps today, for all I know), the visiting divines of the opposite denominations came infrequently, and seldom both together, so that the adherents to the sect that had not, at the time, any Divine Service, often went to the church of the one that had. And no matter who went, or which belief it was that they belonged to, it was all taken quite for granted as a matter of social etiquette and neigh-bourliness, and the minister or priest, as the case might be, always addressed a few friendly words of welcome to the visitors. It was that kind of a town. And perhaps these people, in their simple, straightforward open-mindedness, felt that even if the fashions of worship did differ a little, these plain wooden structures in which, turn about, they sat, were after all, each of them a House of God. And when, by chance, both priest and minister were there together they stayed at the same boarding-house, ate sociably at the same table, and discussed the affairs of each other's ministry, and traded tobacco and presided at dances, and were the life of any party that they went to.

And the God of both of them, who was after all the same God, must have been very happy indeed to see, in even so small a place, so many of His people gathered under one roof to do Him honour. And I think that one of the finest sermons that either of these good churchmen preached, was in the example they set of tolerance, of harmony, and good taste.

Biscoe has no roads whatever, and not a solitary yard of sidewalk. Here folks have supper instead of tea, dinner is at noon, and lunch is something you beg from the cook between meals or, failing that, take when he isn't looking; and all the breakfast in bed you'll ever get will be the extreme unction brought to you in the morning by the land-lady, if you have met with an accident and are expected to be dead before dinner-time. The waitress who, having served supper, asks the patrons, " Have you folks got all you want?—I have to fix my dress for the dance " (same being held in your honour, perhaps, as a distinguished guest), will very likely turn out to be the belle of the ball, and you are uncommonly lucky if you ever get her for a partner.

Thus the time-honoured custom of older Canada; and the sleepy, sensuous, languishing dances of 1936 would find scant favour there, in towns like Bisco, but there are snappy square dances and rollicking quadrilles, and sometimes some pretty clever stepping, and there was the odd lively fox-trot for those that like them—stuff with plenty of life and laughter in it. And always there were the " callers ", who chanted the tunes as they directed the figures of the dance. And no one ever fell asleep on the wooden benches that lined the bare walls of the hall, for things were far too lively.

In this little town there are not many left to dance. Once a place of some repute, a boom town in C.P.R. construction days, Bisco is settling into that reposeful calm that so often

enriches the close of an eventful life, and lives on memories
—memories of the days when it was an important supply
station for the Company's [1] inland Posts for many a hundred
miles around, when richly laden argosies came in from
mysterious, unknown places, manned by Crees, Algonquins
and Ojibways bringing produce of the forest, when it had
been a meeting-place for the canoe brigades from Old Green
Lake, Mozaboang, Flying Post and Fort Mattawgami.
On a main route to the salt water, far to the North, and at
the same time one of the principal gateways to the Great
Lakes to the South, trappers, rivermen and forest rangers
from the Spanish, the Ground-hog and the Mississauga made
merry here, and pitched their encampments beside the lake,
along the shore-line before the Post, and held their cele-
brations and their feasts while the night air resounded with
the shouts of merriment of those who stepped a measure in
the intricacies of the Duck Dance or the Rabbit Dance, or
flung their flying feet in wild abandon to the weird, minor
syncopations of the Mississauga Reel, and so woke the old
town up. And sometimes, too, were heard a strange, barbaric
chanting and the eerie, rhythmic throbbing of wolf-skin
drums, as the Indians postured and crouched through the
mystic ceremonial of the Wabeno.

But the old-time canoemen are very few today. They
are not needed any more; and the War got a lot of them.
Some have just disappeared. And the happy, careless
voyageurs, gay caballeros of the White Water who whooped
and laughed and shouted their way down or up unmapped
rivers, and thought their day would last for ever, have gone,
vanished like the snows of last year, their long-dead fires all
overgrown with moss and their footsteps hidden by the fallen
leaves of many an Autumn. And Bisco, its contribution to
the history of the Frontier nearly closed, lost in recollection,
sits musing on those ancient granite hillsides, waiting quietly,
and perhaps a little sadly, for the inevitable.

[1] Hudson's Bay Company.

But this is not what I brought you here for. Forgive me; my mind has wandered far down the long, winding corridors of reminiscence. For I too was once a Riverman, the canoe my trade, such men my boon companions. How I loved them, with their trousers baggy at the knees from long hours, and days, and months of kneeling—no, not in prayer, but in a canoe; even on land the posture was very much the same; we seldom sat anywhere but on the ground and only stood erect to walk. How I loved them for their sharp-barbed, gritty humour, their unparalleled skill in profanity, their easy-going generosity. For these were no kitchen-garden woodsmen or carpet knights, but hard-bitten bush-whackers, nurtured in hardship, who lived precariously by first principles, and who at no time called a shovel an agricultural implement. Though strangely perhaps, to those seeing them for the first time, they had, as a rule, none of the rough appearance or tough, characteristic mannerisms that one expects from reading of Frontiersmen, but were for the most part slim, light and wiry, with thin, almost ascetic faces, set sometimes a little sternly in lines of determination. Quiet on their feet, moderate of movement and of speech, on occasion demanding it any one of them could launch suddenly into a tornado of activity with either; though even the most exhausting feats of endurance and the highest flights of vituperation, however bitter, were liberally spiced with pungent humour.

White man, red-skin and half-breed, they belonged to that fraternity of freemen of the earth whose creed it is that all men are born equal, and that it is up to a man to stay that way. For in this society the manner of a man's speech, where he comes from, his religion, or even his name are matters of small moment and are nobody's business but his own. It is required of him only that he be able to cook his own meals, keep a canoe right side up in any kind of water, carry a man's load, make good camp under any circumstances, get around without becoming lost, and otherwise

show that he can take care of himself and so not become a
charge on the community or the object of a search party, or
turn up drowned or frozen to death. His personal history
can be pretty punk but his geography must be good. He
must be prepared to share his supplies, and his shirt if
necessary, with some brother in distress, and must unfailingly pay his debts. This is the type of man you'll have to
travel with; and I suppose you've been noticing that group
sitting on the steps of the Hudson's Bay store—well, that's
a bunch of them, right there. They are having a big laugh
among themselves at some huge joke or other. But don't
be squeamish; they'll respect your sensibilities, seeing you're
a stranger, but they might pull the odd fast one on you once
they get to know you—if they like you. Some of these boys
you'll be trailing with, so let's go over and get acquainted.
They're not very dark for frontiersmen, you say? Well,
no; excepting the coppery Indians, they have the faded
leathery skin of the true outdoorsman, and are a good many
shades lighter than the townsman out on a holiday; they
havn't much time to take sunbaths, and half their days are
spent in the shadows of the forest.

Here you are, brother, meet the gang. This is Augustus—
Augustus, this is a friend; "Gladdameetcha" says Gus,
taking off his hat—don't let him see you wince; he thinks
he's shaking hands gently because you are my friend—you
might hurt his feelings. It is fitting that Gus should head
the line because he is, in a way, our treasurer, a kind of
financial expert. He borrows money on all sides, and lends
just as freely. He says that a man who lends may also borrow
when he needs it; it is a kind of insurance. It doesn't
really matter, he will tell you, because somebody always has
it anyway. This works out very well for him because he
always has it.

Then—why, look who's here—rather an assorted company, I fear! But all good men and true, every one of
them—here's Mister Musho; he is an old Indian with long

hair, who speaks practically no English, but he is never called anything but Mister. Once, when a little the better for rather too much liquor, he left town on his dog-team, his hair decorated with feathers plucked from a dead owl, yelling, and proceeding at a speed of about twenty miles an hour. He had thirty miles to go. Halfway to his destination he fell off the sleigh, and being fatigued, slept a while on a warm-looking snowbank. The dogs continued the journey, taking with them his snowshoes, which were tied to the sleigh; this left him without any means of transportation. On awakening he took note of his predicament and was taken suddenly sober. He then walked fifteen miles without snowshoes in three feet of snow. This feat gained for him the title of Walking Man among his people.

This huge fellow is Zepherin—misnamed; he is no zephyr, but a kind of human cyclone. He has one of those room-filling personalities, has a fog-horn voice, and a smile that would, if measured, cover about a quarter of an acre. No, I wouldn't shake hands in this case, just bow from the waist; you'll recover quicker. When Zepherin first appeared in the country (from no particular place), he was asked his qualifications, and in reply he boomed, " I'll tell yuh! I'm the best man to curse on the North Shore of Lake Superior "; and when in his cups he was wont to announce, with terrible imprecations, that he was " the best man in the world," and then straightway fall to laughter, in which those present were glad to join. Rather an individualist. A very Pistol of a man, though with something more than a suspicion of Falstaffian predilections.

Here's Baldy; fifty years ago the Indians wouldn't have been interested in his hair; he hasn't any. He is a small man with a complex; he is convinced that the world was made for nothing but big men, and he carries enormous loads on every portage to prove that he is as good as any of them, even if he is below standard size. He is a born pessimist. Men are not what they were, he says; but he is resigned. Zepherin calls him "Half-pint," but admits that, after all, he talks good English for a small man; he says that Baldy has never been the same since the mouse kicked him. A great affection exists between these two opposites.

This quiet man with the aquiline features and level, considering gaze is Nikolas, soft-footed, efficient and tireless. His brevity of discourse is proverbial. He has the reputation of never speaking unless he has something to say; rather a good trait in the woods. He travels very lightly equipped. It was he who, on being asked what extras he would need for a particularly arduous trip of indeterminate duration, made the classic remark, "Nothing."

Now Matogense; Indian. A conjuror, or medicine man, who is reputed to have once put out a forest fire by means of some incantations which included chanting and the use of a drum. His wife, it is said, made their eldest daughter swallow a live fish, so she could " swim good."

Boyd Mathewson; that steady appraising look he gives you means something; he is sizeing you up. He has been Chief of our brigades for many years. We all worked for him one time or another, and had a wholesome respect for his dry, sly, caustic humour. He is always up at daylight (this comes at three o'clock during May and June in these latitudes), and thinks eighteen hours of furious travelling is a day's work. He has one blind eye, but that does no one any good because he sees more with the other than you do with both of yours. He worked his men hard, but they liked him the better for it; and he worked himself as hard as any of them. "Blood-for-Breakfast" we used to call him, though he will only know it when, and if, he reads this book.

How'ya Boyd! wherever you are.

This vigorous-looking individual, who sits leaning forward with arms akimbo, elbows out, and a hand on each knee looking as if about to leap into the air at any moment, is Charlie Dougal, Chief of the brigade we are going with, a go-getter and a devil for speed, burning holes in the scenery with fiery invective as he drives his brigade with speed and more speed, for miles and more miles a day. (We like to be driven that way; everybody is out to beat last year's record.) Fiercely resentful of weakness of any kind in any man, he is reputed never to rest save when rolled in his blankets, and he eats his meals walking up and down, claiming that rest only softened a man and lowered his efficiency, gaining the apt title of Quick-Lunch Dougal. A fire-eater who could take as much as he gave, he could eat his own fire and like it. This trip is going to be fun, isn't it?

This gentleman with the slightly bored expression, freckled face and a mop of hair that is rather more than auburn, is—you guessed it the first time, Mister, it's Red Landreville. If you've never met Red you've missed something, I'll say. He is not an A. No 1. canoeman, as canoemen go in this territory, but he supplies the light humour in any situation, and will tell funny stories on his death-bed, if conscious. I once heard him tell one when neck-deep in water, because upsetting out of a canoe reminded him of the one about the cat and the crocodile, or the ant and the alligator, or something. He has an inexhaustible stock of these, which you can believe at your own risk. They have this virtue, that you will not have heard them before. In their earlier stages they invariably ring quite true, but that is the artist in the man, and doesn't mean a thing. Don't let him get you.

Now I'll introduce you to Jimmy L'Espagnol, wiry, well-knit and hardy, supple as an eel, and having an unconquerable, dogged singleness of purpose that takes him far in a day. He'll get there, or be found dead on the way. Jimmy and I ate often out of the same dish, and we call each other brother—which is as it should be; he is the son of my best friend, Aleck, a veteran guide, full-blooded Indian, quiet, composed and humorous. Once when a cheap witticism, levelled at his dark complexion, was passed by someone, he blew out the light, plunging the room into darkness, and remarked good-humouredly that " we are all the same colour now." Unruffled in the face of any emergency, wise in forest lore, he is a steadying influence in any party. His is the Voice of Experience. Jimmy and I once paddled seventy-five measured miles, including sixteen portages of lengths varying from a hundred yards to half a mile, between six in the morning and eleven-forty-five the same night. Taking out two hours for eating several meals, the actual travelling time was around sixteen hours; average speed, a little less than five miles an hour. We didn't do much the next day.[1]

That fellow with the little wrinkles round his eyes and mouth is Billy Mitchell. His face has a mischievous, almost elfin look, made more pronounced by his bright bird-like eyes, thin nose and pointed chin. He seems to be laughing inaudibly, and invisibly, at something. See that so engaging smile, now? Beware of it; watch he doesn't spring something on you with that infectious grin of his! As a practical joker Billy is a genius. He plays the fiddle for all the dances, and he also tells stories. Those he means to be true, are true; those he means not to be true—well, that's up to you. His escapades are without number and exceedingly odd; and sober, reputable citizens get up in the night to laugh at them. I mind one time he was at a rather select birthday party where the drinks were a little slow in coming round. " Hold on," he whispered to me, " I'll fix it." He rose to

[1] These figures are not in the least exaggerated, and probably do not even constitute a record. With Alphonse Tessier as bowsman I tried one Summer for a record. We covered, in five months, three thousand two hundred (reputed) miles of distance by canoe and port-age trail, covering our allotted area six times in the course of the Summer. Some days we made fifty miles, very frequently forty, and once seventy; though there were many days when, owing to storms or rough going, or when poling up swift water, we were lucky to make five or ten miles. I afterwards found that this record was beaten by both Wishard Miller and Nikolas. All the characters are real in this line-up, and well known to me, though two or three names have been altered. Sah-Sabik, the old Indian, was an historic figure, but has since passed on.

N

his feet and announced that he would tell a story. Having engaged the attention of the entire gathering, he told one about a certain King, who was the King of North Carolina. This King, it appeared, was in the habit of visiting his neighbour, the King of South Carolina. Now this first-named King liked his drinks rather well, and liked them often; but at one of the banquets that his brother King was giving him, the cellar must have run dry, for after the first few cups of cheer, no more were forthcoming.

Everybody was listening very politely and attentively. Said Billy, continuing, " Well, the King of the North got tired waiting, and said something to the other king. Now then: the question is, what did the King of North Carolina say to the King of South Carolina—anybody know?" Nobody knew. "All right," finished Billy, "I'll tell you; he said, ' It's a hell of a long time between drinks! ' "

And now, last of all, you meet Pierre Jean Joseph Champoux. Because the letter x is silent in " Champoux," Pierre Jean Joseph is called " Shampoo " by the boys; it sounds about the same. Peter John speaks with a strong French accent, and makes the best moonshine whisky in the entire region. He once had aspirations to quit the woods and go into the bootlegging trade. But rapidly becoming his own best customer, he found that his supplies were too much for him and had to go out of business. He is back in the woods again, and is going down the River till " things blow over." He still makes the odd bottle.

The judicial and social welfare of this irregular and unconventional band of prominent citizens was very adequately cared for. We had among us a representative, long retired, of those red-coated riders of the Western plains, the North-West Mounted Police. He was one of the originals, and while he no longer belonged to the Force, he represented the law in this neck of the woods, and though he acted in an entirely unofficial capacity, we knew, understood and respected him, and were better pleased to have him around than a uniformed constable; for your real, dyed-in-the-wool, free woodsman is intensely individualistic, and has an instinctive dislike of a uniform—he may have accepted one for the duration of the War, but only as a means to an end. This ex-Mountie, even if he had at one time worn regimentals, was one of our own kind and we didn't hold it against him; in fact his past history (actually he had been more of a scout than a policeman) seemed rather glamorous to us, and with the rigour and severe discipline of the early days of service still upon him, was something of a martinet, and was a very hard nut to crack. And while he could enjoy a celebration with the best of them, he was always on the lookout for prospective clients and threw a professional eye on the wrists of new-comers to town, to see if they'd fit any handcuffs that he had. In the event of an arrest being necessary he would swear out the information, and serve the warrant with the utmost consideration, but with an extremely business-like look in his steel-blue eyes. He would go the prisoner's bail, feed him, house him, take a drink with him and generally provide what was probably the most efficient, all-round police service to be found anywhere in North America. The Compleat Police Officer, no less. A parental advisor to those in trouble—he had helped many a repentant transgressor over the lump—a stern disciplinarian of the conspicuously erring, he concealed under a bluff exterior and an habitual expression of suppressed ferocity, a heart as big as a barrel. This last infirmity he kept resolutely hidden, like it was some besetting sin. It was his one big failing, his own particular skeleton in the cupboard. But we all knew about it.

All honour to you, old friend. Very well I knew you, better than perhaps you ever thought. And in the old days, whether we met over a glass of the best, or maybe to discuss some small point of personal conduct concerning which we could not, for the moment, see eye to eye, there was a mutual respect, and an ungrudging appreciation of the other man's qualities. And besides it was all in the Game—the good old, sporting Game that is now so nearly played.

*　　*　　*　　*　　*　　*

And now if you are staunch of heart and strong in small adversities, and can face the sun and wind; if you would like to try sleeping in a tent on a bed of fragrant balsam brush, and sitting on the ground to eat, and if, above all, you have an abounding sense of humour, we'll take a voyage down this so impetuously autocratic River, you and I.

But if you love soft comfort and have a taste for tea-fights, or cannot share when stuff gets short nor laugh when things go wrong, you had better speak up now, or forever hold your peace.

3

The Lost Brigade

THAT night we sleep in the tent alloted to us, and just after we have got nicely to sleep, someone slaps smartly on the canvas door and shouts in a loud, unsympathetic voice, "Shake a leg there! Daylight in the swamp!" A muffled grumbling from one of the other occupants of the tent asks, "What the heck time is it?" "What do you care what time it is?" comes back this inexorable voice. "It's away after three o'clock. Going to stay in bed all your life? Get after your canoes"—Boyd Mathewson, brigade chief, at his best. Red Landreville, who is in our tent, suggests that the canoes must be awful wild when a person can't wait for daylight to catch them but has to creep up on them under cover of the darkness. And certainly the daylight *does* look a little thin.

Those hard-driving, pitiless chiefs! How we hated them, loved them, thumbed our noses at them (metaphorically speaking, or if otherwise, most discreetly from well-selected cover), and broke our backs to fulfil, and sometimes exceed, their orders. How we bragged of having worked for them and boasted over our "miles a day" and "pounds a trip"[1] on a portage.

But we are not here to boast; there's a two hundred and fifty mile journey to be made after breakfast, and we are going to see some speed. No, brother, we are not going to do it all today, nor even this week. This is more or less of a pleasure trip, thirty miles a day, or forty at the most—

[1] Loads of two hundred and fifty pounds and over were usual, and some men carried four hundred pounds on occasion.

what'll we do the rest of the day? says you. Say, you're quite a humorist too, ain't you—you'll get along, I guess.

Breakfast is soon over, and canoes are loaded and trimmed. There is the minimum of bustle, and no confusion whatsoever, as loads have been assembled and lashed the night before and there is nothing to do but pack the grub-boxes, one for each canoe, two men to a canoe. The only fanfare that heralds the starting out of one of these expeditions, some of which last six months, is the laconic " Well boys, let's go " of the chief.

And go we do. Paddles dip in unison, backs bend and sway, canoes leap forward at the rate of four miles to the hour. The great sun rises, goes on up, getting smaller but hotter as it goes, and becomes a burning red ball that beats down on unprotected heads and hands and faces. As the day advances the air becomes more torrid; the lakes lie vitreous, like seas of molten glass, and the palpitating landscape is immersed in a screeching, scorching glare. High overhead in a metallic sky the sun, like a burnished copper gong, beats a fierce tattoo to which the whole face of Nature quivers, and to whose tune the rows of jack-pines topping the distant ridges writhe, and swing, and sway in the steps of a fantastic sun-dance, reeling drunkenly in the shimmering waves of a merciless, breathless heat. But we don't let a little warm weather bother us; this is August, and the hot weather is about over in this North-country. The odd hot day gives the boys a break—sweats some of the infernal laziness out of their hides, says Charlie Dougal—resting softens a man——!

So, speed, speed, speed, grip the canoe ribs with your knees, drive those paddles deep, throw your weight onto them, click them on those gunnels twenty-five strokes to the minute; spurn that water in gurgling eddies behind you, bend those backs, and drive! Sternsmen, keep your eyes on the far objective, far off in the blue distance, and take your proper allowance for a side-wind, don't make leeway like a greenhorn! Thus, eyes fixed ahead, watchful of everything, breath coming deeply, evenly, backs swinging freely from the hips, paddles dipping and flashing, we drive her—fifty miles a day or bust. Some have busted, but not this outfit. You thought you heard me say thirty miles a day? Perhaps you did, but Dougal is running this brigade, not me. We are to make the first hundred miles in two days, he says, which is sense; we want to get out of the lake country while we have a fair wind to help us; the Indians say the wind is going to change, and so slow us up.

So drive her! We're on our way to Mississauga!

A duck flies in before the canoes, and taking the water, flaps along in front of us as though hurt. She has young ones hidden somewhere and is trying to decoy us away from them by this offer of easy capture, keeping just far enough ahead to be out of reach. Her ruse succeeds quite well, because we don't want her brood in the first place, and we are not going their way anyhow. She continues this pretence of disability until we nearly catch up to her, when she suddenly recovers, flies a short piece ahead, and commences the performance all over again. She does this time and time again, with a maddening persistence and an unnecessary expenditure of energy that, in this heat, makes us burst out into renewed streams of perspiration just to look at her—and all for nothing. We are just beginning to regard her with the greatest repugnance when, having lured us, as she supposes, to a safe distance, she flies back home, pursued by the objurgations of the entire brigade; except the Indians, who show no emotion whatsoever and pass no comment, though they watch the duck's every move intently, as they do everything else that is seen.

On the portages the leaves hang limp and listless, and the still air is acrid with the resinous odour of boiling spruce gum. Here men sweat under enormous burdens; earlier in the Summer, clouds of mosquitoes and black-flies would

envelop them in biting swarms. But it is August, and the
fly season is over, and those that are left are too weak
to do any damage, and sit balefully regarding us from nearby
limbs of trees. Pattering of moccasined feet on the narrow
trail, as men trot with the canoes, one to a man, or step easily
along under their loads; and in a miraculously short space
of time everything is over to the far side. Canoes are
re-loaded expertly, and we are away again. But out on
the lake there is a change. A welcome breeze fans us,
cooling us off, while it dries the sweat—also our throats.
Someone commences to sing in a high, thin tenor, this
seeming to be just the right note for a dessicated throat;
the refrain is, aptly enough " How dry I am——". We
all laugh and join in the chorus. We begin to enjoy ourselves, to rejoice in the fluid rhythm of the canoes, to feel
the ecstacy of this wild, free, vigorous life that seems all
at once to be the only life worth living. The free wind
of the open has by now blown away a thousand petty
thoughts of profit, or of desire to prevail over someone,
or of device or stratagem whereby to gain preferment.
For this is not a life of dodge and subterfuge, save only
where necessary to gain, not what another may have possession of, but only what Nature offers for the means to live,
to carry on.

And we carry on; there is no let-up. Any faltering will
draw meaning looks, and perhaps meaninger remarks
from our decidedly humorous, but quite remorseless and
entirely inflexible chiefs—Blood-for-Breakfast and Quick-
Lunch Dougal and their piratical crew are headed for the
River, men obsessed by the purpose of covering Distance,
disciples of speed, knight-errants of the canoe, devotees
of the Trail. And we must needs follow; you must stay
with it, my friend. Here is where the rich man's riches
buy him nothing, and where a parading of his business
acumen will only get him in wrong with his guides. A
repertoire of snappy come-backs, or the repetition of a

memorized " lino " or list of wise-cracks, will have a
negligible audience-appeal. And it is no use audibly
admiring the scenery (not unless you are doing your share,
however little it may be), because you can't curry favour
with the landscape. This, Mister, is the real thing, and no
moving-picture set. You are asking me why all the hurry,
and where *is* this so-famous Mississauga River? Well,
it is just seventy-five miles in from town, including sixteen
portages. No sir, we are not trying to do it all in one day,
though it has been done. This is to be an easy trip, on
account of our guest, that's you, and we will consume all
of a day and a half. You decide that further speech seems
unnecessary, futile, in face of the facts. This is the real
thing, and is no moving-picture set.

And so, in a continous alternation of lake and portage,
dazzling sea of glare and oven-like, leafy tunnel, we go on.
When do we eat? thinks you—or do we eat? You begin
to wonder. But, sooner or later, it comes noon and we
prepare a much needed meal. The cooking is not complicated. There is only one precept to abide by, so Augustus,
the financer, informs us, and that is to put salt into everything except tea and jam; that way, he says, you can't go
wrong. But we soon find that in spite of his pecuniary
predilections, this Gus fellow is also something of a humorist,
because there is no jam, and nobody ever puts salt in tea.
So the matter becomes quite simple. On talking the matter
over with this financial expert, we are told that it is not good
economy to carry stuff you don't need; it doesn't pay.
But he has a great nose for his own advantage, and being
German, is well provided with urbswurst, and with it he
makes a very palatable soup, which he shares around.

Gus's pleasantry concerning the non-existent jam, brings
up the subject of provisions. Limited to a canoe-load of
supplies for each two men for five months—the duration
of some of these trips—and with no trading posts, in this
area, at which to replenish, the provision list is shorn of all

luxuries and frills. And although this is more or less of a light trip, the dictates of established custom are adhered to, so we have not only no jam (because it has an uncomfortable fashion of coming open and mixing with the soap and matches), but also no potatoes, eggs, caviare, nor canned lobster. The last two items are entirely legendary in character so far as we are concerned, and we do not miss them. But we have flour, salt and baking powder with which to make bannock, a kind of large scone cooked over hot coals; this delicacy is of Scotch origin, having been introduced by the Hudson Bay people who were largely Scotsmen. It is also known as Indian loaf. It is going to be your principle article of diet, so take a good look at one—yes, you are right, it makes no attempt to float out of your hand; but don't drop it on your foot; it doesn't bounce. It stays right with you. We have long ago exploded the theory that ordinary bread is the staff of life. We almost never eat it, and have managed to thrive to quite a size without it.[1] No one wants to kill a large animal like a deer or moose, and have the meat spoil; we have no time to spend drying and smoking it as the Indians do. Instead we bring along several sides of very salt pork which have to be parboiled, in slices, before it can be fried and eaten; it comes in large, corpse-like slabs that go under the various titles of sow-belly, long clear, and rattlesnake pork. The flavour indicates the last name as being the most applicable. We have also tea, sugar, white beans,[2] which latter have a very high nutriment value, a few dried apples, and soap, matches and tobacco. This frugal but stimulating fare is eked out with fresh fish, of which we have the very best and lots of it, and also berries in season. The idea, of course,

---

[1] White bread is found, under the severe conditions imposed by constant bush travelling, to be almost useless as an article of diet except as a vehicle for butter, which we did not use, as it melted in Summer. The bannock was eaten fresh and dipped in hot lard or pork-grease. For over thirty years I never tasted bread save at very rare intervals in town, and during the war.

[2] Like small haricot beans; a staple article of food over all North America; *vide* Boston baked beans.

is to get as much solid eating material for as little weight and bulk as possible; hence the elimination of potatoes and canned goods.

This list seems rather limited, you think. Well don't say it aloud. These men, used to self-denial and hardship of all kinds, would think you were complaining. Remember, reader, you are away back in the days of the pork and bannock regime, when a man who brought along milk or breakfast bacon was deemed to be lowering the standard of manhood. Butter was taboo, not only because we never even thought of it, but also because its unlucky owner caused delay and friction as he fussed around in his futile attempts to preserve it and keep it from turning to oil in temperatures of ninety or a hundred in the shade. A man who was found to be in clandestine possession of butter, was considered to be lacking in force of character, and it was suspected that his morals were rancid. Goods labelled " Canned roast beef " and " Tinned dinner " were contemptuously referred to as " Horse," and the libertine who was caught eating them was said to be digging his grave with his teeth. And this was not all mere caprice, as such things were heavy for their size, didn't last long, and took up a lot of room in a canoe that could have been put to better use, and when after a few weeks these whimsies had been consumed, the culprit had perforce to beg donations from the meagre supplies of his fellow travellers, so that one having these luxurious tastes was something in the nature of a menace to society, or a public enemy. Today it would be impossible for me to live that way, and I fear, too, that my speed limit has been much reduced.

Eating, under ordinary circumstances, is merely a means of sustaining life, at least in our severely simple and unpolished social state. Yet after a long, hard siege at the paddle, the pole, or the tump-line,[1] a meal can become

---

[1] A tump-line consists of two ten-foot leather thongs attached to a leather headpiece about three inches wide, used for carrying loads on a portage. Ten-foot poles are used in canoes for climbing rapids, and are fitted with an iron socket. The poler stands erect in the canoe.

the sum total of the recreation, the relaxation and the entertainment of the day, and be an event of some importance; assuming, under these circumstances, a dignity and significance out of all proportion to the short time spent in cooking it, or the fifteen minutes enjoyment that it gives. There are no aperitives, no jaded appetites to prick into activity, and no condiments to grace the repast—though it is sometimes well flavoured with drops of sweat. And then the cool, lazy smoke in the shade afterwards; that is even better. Stretched out beneath an umbrella-topped jack-pine, his pipe going, contented, with that feeling of satisfaction that comes of labour successfully accomplished and the thought of congenial labour yet to do, quietly glorying in his strength and fitness and proficiency, as much a part of his environment as the tree he leans against, your true voyageur would trade places with no king. There are different ideas of comfort; to some it consists in a feather bed, or in the personal service given, for pay, by " lesser " men; to us it means getting outside of a full meal, or having our feet dry, or in fly season, having an hour's surcease from the mosquitoes; or, greatest of all, in experiencing the unutterable sense of relief, the feeling of luxurious ease that possesses a man's soul when he puts down a burden after carrying it, maybe, up three hills, or for a long distance on the uncertain footing provided by a lot of loosely-fitting boulders that move and wobble at every step. There's nothing just like it.

The dinner hour doesn't last long; it isn't even an hour before we are ready to go again. Fires are carefully put out, for the menace of forest fire hangs constantly over us, an ever-present threat. Quickly we resume our paddles and are away again. In the interim the sun has moved and, having been well burned on one side, we are now to be nicely browned on the other. This is no relief of course, but is at least a change; and after all there is something to be said for symmetry. We pass over a series of small, still lakes, where the arabesque tracery of the foliage is reflected as in a looking-glass. We pass historic places, thick with legend and tradition; the remains of an ancient Hudson's Bay post, relict of an older, wilder day. It's timbers can still be seen, and on the knoll behind it is a primitive Indian grave-yard; we pass the Place-of-Crying-Mink, where sometimes is heard the desolate, awful wailing of a phantom mink; to the South lies Woman Portage where a woman long dead walks at the full of the moon. There is a camping ground shunned by the Indians, because a ghost beaver who lived nearby once stole a hunter's paddles, and with very unghostly perspicacity cut them up and thoughtfully hid the pieces. This left the hunter stranded until he had made new paddles, upon which he immediately left the country. A steep bank is pointed out, where the May-May-Gwense, Indian elves, slide up and down in the moonlight for amusement. Some claim to have watched them and if you don't believe it, there is the little trail, plain to be seen. Back in the hills hereabouts, there is known to have been found, by an Indian named The Cat, an enormous footprint of a man. It is said to have been that of an Iroquois, one of those warriors who ravaged this country about a century ago, and are remembered by one or two still living; he is still supposed to be lurking in the vicinity.

In a narrow strait that joins two lakes, we meet an old prospector; he has an Indian guide, because he is not a water dog, as a canoeman is termed, but a desert rat from Nevada, and therefore has no knowledge of water travel. The Indian says that this desert man carries a water-flask everywhere he goes—in a country that is more than half water—and fills all available vessels with water before going to bed at night. Conversation reveals that he knows his rocks very well indeed; but everything else here is new to him. One of our canoes is marked H.B.C.; he has never heard of the Hudson's Bay Company and thinks it means

Here Before Christ, and he asks whimsically if we have really been here that long. He has noted our speed, and does not approve. He is never in a hurry, he tells us. His theory is, that life is short and we'll be a hell of a long time dead; So what's all the fury about? We smile gently and tolerantly at this inexplicable foible of an old man, and wishing him lucky prospecting, with a wild halloo, which he answers with a Piute war-whoop for a send-off, we race forward on our way. We pass Indian camps where dogs that are more than half wolf, bark at us menacingly, and high featured, tawny faces framed in lank black hair, peer out at us with eyes that are veiled, inscrutable, yet strangely penetrating.

On the next portage we have our first mishap. Baldy is carrying, defiantly, against expressed public opinion, one of his outsize loads when the tump-line, an old one, breaks. The sudden release throws the little fellow forward on his face, and his nose is bleeding. Self-conscious as usual, he sets out to explain. " My tump-line was no good; they don't make 'em that way any more. A good man can't get the stuff to work with any more." He goes on to say, with the blood dripping from his chin, that the world in general is hell-bound; even the mosquitoes are not what they were. Charlie (Quick-lunch) Dougal agrees, with heavy sarcasm, that the fly crop was a black failure this year; Red Landreville says yes, it's only too true, even gangsters don't use machine-guns these days—they are reduced to carrying concealed razor blades; it's a tough world. Zepherin, arriving on the scene, is in one of his Pistolian moods, and affecting to misunderstand the state of affairs, roars at the gore-stained Baldy, "Ha! Me blood-stained bucko! Fightin', eh?, and you with the best man in the world at your heels—you vampire! you ravaging scorpion, you!—you hideous monster, to be consortin' with decent men——" while Baldy stands in the silent dignity of for-bearance and asserts, very obviously, that he is no monster, hasn't fought and doesn't want to fight, and only needs a new tump-line. This is forthcoming, with advice not to let it (the tump-line) get him down, and not to carry *all* the load at once as there is another day tomorrow, reminding him that there is too much rock here to bury a man decently, and that a corpse won't keep in this weather, and so forth.

Soon after this, at an improvised landing of logs, someone, picking up a canoe by the centre (the proper way) knocks Matogense, usually so sure-footed, over into the quaking bog the timbers are supposed to bridge, out of which he presently scrambles, covered with an evil-smelling coating of slime. Everybody at once remembers, inconveniently for Matogense, the story of his daughter who was fed the live fish to help her learn to swim, and it is suggested that he be given a bull-frog to eat so that he will be able to get around better in the mud. It is characteristic that his load, which he has fallen in with, is salvaged first while he is left to shift for himself, the argument being that he can crawl out and the provisions can not; and it is the concensus of opinion that a man has to be dragged in the mud a couple of times before he is worth a damn, anyway. But these are two mishaps too many. Men are getting tired; their movements are not so sure. Things are slowing up, and it is getting late. So it is to our intense relief that Aleck L'Espagnol, with a glance at the rapidly darkening sky and the now rising mists, sagely suggests that we call it a day and make camp. Surprisingly, that devastating speed-fiend, Dougal, and the terse-spoken, adamantine Mathewson both agree; and in this they show the best of judgement, for Aleck is held in general esteem for his wisdom.

Camp is quickly made within an encircling grove of giant red-pines, whose crenelated columns, all ruddy in the fire-light, stand about the place like huge pillars that support a roof so high above us as to be invisible, reaching up to unknown heights into the blackness, giving us the feeling that we are encamped in some old, deserted temple. While all around us is the interminable, unfathomable forest, whose denizens live in impenetrable privacy, and in the dark recesses of which a thousand shadows lie in ambush all the day, awaiting only the coming of night to creep out and slowly, silently invest the whole world of trees, and rocks, and water, and the sleeping camp. But the camp is not sleeping yet; bannock has to be made for the next day's consumption, and other preparations completed for the morrow's journey. Everything is quickly disposed in its proper place, the whole camp a standing model of neatness and well-contrived arrangement.

And then comes that hour of rest and quiet contentment, when there is no sound save the light crackle of burning wood and the odd murmur of a voice, when all the face of Nature is immersed in that brooding calm that comes down like an invisible curtain with the falling of night. Besides the central fire most every one has settled down to sit and smoke, or sit and talk, or just to sit.

Suddenly an owl hoots overhead in a pitch unusual to his kind, and this attracts some attention. But he belongs apparently to that variety known as the laughing owl, who is liable to make any kind of a noise; and investigation is impossible as he is way up out of sight. He hoots again, going through all the gamut of chuckling and guffawing of which this uncouth bird is capable, when our casual interest is drawn away from him by something that rivets the attention of the whole camp. Just within the shadows, and dimly seen by the flickering light of the fire, is an enormous creature the like of which no one present has ever seen before. It advances with a steady, measured step, and a swaying, sidling motion, and as it slowly approaches it is seen to be quite hairless, and it has, horridly, hideously, gruesomely—no head! It appears to have a shell of some kind, like a monstrous turtle. There have been reports from some parts, of prehistoric creatures seen at large of late, and this phenomenon is viewed in dead silence and with something approaching consternation—except by the owl who, perched in safety up a tree, breaks out into peal after peal of inhuman, or nearly human laughter. And then the monster walks out boldly into the circle of light, and resolves itself into nothing more alarming than Billy Mitchell, walking on all fours, his body enveloped in a long roll of birch-bark, from under which only his arms and legs are visible. And then, with a final peal of ribald and unseemly mirth, unmistakably human this time, the owl comes scrambling down from its perch, and turns out to be Pierre John Joseph, who had failed so signally at the liquor business. But he had not failed to bring along on the trip a small bottle of his product which, obviously, he had shared with his accomplice; and evidently it had not been such a heck of a long time between drinks as on the occasion of Billy's famous story.

This rather elaborate hoax, of course, puts everybody in an exceedingly good humour, which in turn gives Red Landreville an excellent opportunity to tell one more of his unspeakable and unutterable falsehoods, an art in which he excels, far beyond the power of any common man to emulate. This particular story starts out well, as all his stories do. It appears that Red had a brother in Russia. It's the first time we've heard of him, but let it go! He was a newspaper man, and his skill and ability at this profession so attracted the notice of the authorities, that he found himself, one bright morning, blindfolded, with his back to the wall along with five other victims, facing a firing squad.

Here Red paused, emotion getting a little the better of him. "You know how it is," he says. Yes, we know how it is. However, it seems that Red's brother had been a close friend of the sergeant who had charge of the firing party. We had always thought that an officer conducted these affairs, but Red is sure that in this case it had been a sergeant—his brother, being a newspaper man, was

o

very particular about details. Sorry to contradict youse guys, he apologises urbanely. You know how a fella hates to be right. Yes, we know that too. Anyway they were buddies; smoked the same tobacco or courted the same girl or something. So the brother, who was nobody's fool, had been clever enough to make a bargain with his friend the sergeant (for a matter of a thousand roubles, or kopecks, or whatever the Russians used for money) to the effect that the soldiers who faced him would be the ones having the blank cartridges. " Of course," the narrator explains, " some of the firing party always has blanks; the sergeant loads the rifles, and nobody but him knows who actually bumps the boys off, see?" We had always heard this, naturally; the tale seems to be not so far-fetched; after all everything in it was possible, so far. It might even be true. We are, in fact, a little disappointed, but don't like to say the wrong thing when a man is describing the death of a long-lost brother—anyway, the volley crashed. The sergeant had been true to his contract, and the news-paper man, who was also something of an actor, gave a life-like imitation of a man being cut off in the prime of life, and fell down with the rest of them. The firing squad was marched off, and after a decent interval Red's brother, with the feelings of one literally snatched from the jaws of death, raised his head cautiously and looked around. The five others were also looking around, and all apparently in the best of health. This was rather ridiculous, to say the least, so feeling a little out of place they all got up, dusted off their clothes and moved away from there. They had all made the same deal with the sergeant.

Silence; the silent tribute of admiration paid to a master of his art, broken only by the gritty voice of Mathewson. " I shouldn't wonder," he observed softly, with one of those grim, one-eyed looks he was famous for, " if some day that man will tell a deliberate lie." Billy Mitchell, no mean raconteur himself, hands Landreville

a half-baked bannock; it's not a cake, but it will do—
" Here, take this " says Billy. " You earned it." Of course
it was a lie—an unblushing, stupendous, gorgeous lie;
but give the man credit—it was a good one.

This starts the ball rolling, and Zepherin decides to tell
one. This, he avers, is a true one. He always tries to
get himself believed, and is very hurt when you doubt him.
He goes on to describe the home-coming of a Sioux Indian
who, after many years spent in a white man's college,
returned to his people. He came home attired in the very
latest fashion and wearing a fine overcoat. He found his
people still living in teepees, dressed in buckskin and wrapped
in blankets. He found these, and other customs of his
compatriots, very distressing; their table manners were
bad and altogether in his new-found sophistication he was a
little disdainful of them. He was particularly offended
by their religious beliefs, which he himself had outgrown.
Now, a man had lately died in camp, and in pursuance of an
ancient custom the coffin, with the corpse in it, was left
beside the grave for one night. No one dare go near the
coffin during that one night before burial as, it was said,
if anyone approached the casket, the offended corpse would
reach out and hold them there till daylight. The college
Indian cast ridicule on this superstition, and in order to
show his people how wrong they were, he declared that he
would not only approach the coffin, but would sit right on
it. He was rather bombastic about this; no dead man
could hold him, he assured them, and he would return
unscathed to prove it to them. No one would go with
him to assist in this piece of sacrilege, and his fellow tribesmen would require proof, and to this end he was given a
hammer and a nail, with instructions to drive the nail in
the coffin, part way, leaving it there as proof that he had
been as good as his word. With a superior smile and the odd
jibe, and the overcoat, he took the hammer and the nail
and went to keep his tryst with the dead. Some small

vestige of his hereditary beliefs remained, and alone, in the darkness, with a corpse, some of his super-confidence began to ooze away. However, he had to make good, so he sat on the coffin and drove the nail firmly in for half its length, according to schedule. Much relieved, for the chill and eerie atmosphere of the grave yard was little to his liking, he rose, rather hurriedly, to go. Immediately he was pulled back on to the coffin. That was according to schedule too, most appallingly so, and he jumped to his feet with a bleat of fright only to be jerked back on to the coffin again with greater force than before. Beside himself with terror he made a frantic leap into the air, and was thrown back on the casket with a resounding thump—the corpse had got him! In a frenzy of fear he shouted for help, but alas, his friends were far off and wouldn't have dared come anyway. So, too terrified to make any further attempt to escape, lest his grisly host should reach out and embrace him, he sat there shivering with fright the whole night through, and when his relations, anxious, but not without a certain relish, found him there at daylight, he was in a gibbering condition. An investigation, which he himself had been too far gone to make, revealed the fact that he had, in the darkness, driven the nail through his fashionable overcoat and had spiked himself to the coffin.

There is a pause after this one, and then Aleck L'Espagnol, who is a little diffident in relating his experiences, is persuaded to contribute something. So he relates a gruesome yarn about a tenderfoot who once killed a moose during cold weather, and worked so late skinning and cleaning the carcase that it fell dark before he was through. His hands were now too numb to make camp, and not being very well versed in woodcraft, he bethought himself of rolling up, head and all, in the warm moose-hide to sleep. The skin froze hard during the night, and the unfortunate man was imprisoned as though in a case of iron; and as it continued to freeze he perished there, having to be thawed out of the skin before he could be decently buried.

The mood for story-telling passes, and talk turns to earlier days, and of men, great men, and mighty men, and men who were remarkable, in times gone by—and these are often different, for great men need not be mighty, and mighty men are not always great; and men who are remarkable may well be neither. Any conversation among a bunch of woodsmen will inevitably work its way round to these biographical anecdotes, which invariably take the form of reminiscences commencing with such introductions as " I mind one time——", or " In the early days——", or " 'Way back in '05, I think it was——", and are given with a great wealth of detail. And it is to be noticed that these are all tributes; the mean, the trifling, and the base have been forgotten, and at any ill-advised mention of them, a sudden silence is apt to fall upon the group. We hear of Joe McLean, the Indian, who in a storm at night, the canoe swamped and no longer able to hold two men, shouted goodbye to the tourist he was guiding, and letting go of the canoe, disappeared into the darkness and was never seen again alive. Many are the tales of Billy Friday who, on a bet, carried six bags of flour, one hundred pounds in each, from the wharf on Temagami lake up to the station, a distance of a hundred yards, part of it up hill. We are told, too, of the famous Larry Frost, another Indian, who fought on one occasion with nine men at once, and trimmed them all.

Then there was Joe Seidcrquist, the white trapper, who did everything in a big way, and undertook a friendly wrestling match with a half-tame bear. Towards the close of the second bout he bit the bear so badly that they had to be separated. "He was," stated the narrator, "a hearty man; you should have heard him eat!" Joe, we are informed, borrowed a dog team from Dan O'Connor, who was the Big Shot at Temagami in those days; he was known as the King of Temagami.[1] Joe kept the dogs all Winter, and brought them back safe and sound. But when the dogs arrived back in town Dan didn't recognise them, not having had the dogs very long in the first place. So Joe, for a joke, told Dan that he had lost the original team through the ice, paid for them, and sold Dan's own team back to him at a nice profit. This same Dan O'Connor was a man of rare ability, and performed prodigies of pioneering in that North country in the face of almost insuperable difficulties, all of which he overcame. He owned some hotels at the tourist resort that sprang up by the lake after the railroad came through, and would employ almost any means by which to boost his beloved town of Temagami. His resourcefulness was proverbial, and if there was any possible way of getting a thing done, he would do it; as for instance, when an important railroad magnate wished to examine into the game possibilities of the region, with a view to establishing a tourist traffic. This would be valuable, and Dan wanted it. But this official required duck shooting for his patrons, and he was coming at the one time of year when there were no ducks, in the middle of Summer. Dan decided to supply the ducks. This wouldn't be cheating, as there were always plenty of them in the proper season. So Dan had a crate of ducks sent up from the distant city. On their arrival Dan had an Indian take them over behind an island opposite the hotel. The magnate also arrived in due course, and sitting with O'Connor on the veranda after supper, began to ask about ducks. About that time the Indian sauntered up, and held a desultory conversation with O'Connor in Indian. This was according to plan. The

---

[1] Not Timagami, as it is now so often spelled. The word is Ojibway Indian, derived from "Temea," meaning deep, and "Gaming," meaning "the Lake" in particular, not "a lake" in the general sense. "Temea-agaming," meaning "deep-at-the-shore," is probably the original word, slurred by the Indians themselves to "Tem*a*gaming." The water at the shores and islands of Lake Temagami is generally very deep, often a hundred feet or so, and is so clear that the bottom can be seen at a depth of forty feet.

Indian had a gun, and presently moved off with it and was seen paddling over to the island. "Where's he going?" asked the magnate. "Duck hunting," replied O'Connor. "Do you suppose he will get any?" enquired the interested railroad man. "Sure he will," asserted the invincible Dan. Presently there was a fusillade behind the island. Shortly afterwards the same Indian paddled across to the landing before the Hotel, and as he walked slowly by, this astonished official was treated, in a wilderness removed a hundred and fifty miles from any farm, to the astounding spectacle of a round dozen of common barnyard ducks, tastefully arranged upon a pole.

Dan was wont to boast that he had brought "steamships to Temagami on snowshoes!" This was almost a statement of fact, as he had taken some Indians and broken a trail through the snow-bound bush and over frozen lakes forty miles to Ville Marie in the dead of Winter, on snowshoes of course, leading on his return journey a procession of teams, each bearing a component part of the first wood-burning steamboat that ever sailed on Lake Temagami. He it was who, greeting Lord Charles Beresford on the occasion of his visit to that country, remarked that it was a momentuous occasion, the Lord of the British Navy meeting the Lord of Temagami—two Lords so to speak—"So he'd feel at home," said Dan afterwards.

This man had done some extraordinary things in his time, which brings the talk round to the rather unusual exploit, in a very different connection, of a certain fur-trader, who shall be nameless. This affair had occurred at New Year's when, having accepted rather more than he could stand of the hospitality of his friends, he had had to be put to bed. He reappeared, however, almost at once, at a quiet social gathering in the neighbourhood, attired in his nightshirt, his wife's cape, and carrying an open umbrella; he was in his bare feet and on his head was a visored cotton cap, of the kind given away with somebody's baking powder, and having printed across the front of it in large letters, the words " Thanks for the buggy ride." Here, after paying his respects to the company, he executed, with the umbrella still unfurled, a dance that has gone down in the history of the entire region. His wife, unfortunately, returned home from another party earlier than was expected, and proved unappreciative. He walked home with her, still in uniform. Since this rather depressing incident he had been leading a somewhat subdued life, in retirement. And as the speaker concludes, Baldy is heard to mutter " Them was the days— men knew how to live——". To which statement there was concerted and unanimous consent. And a last name is brought up, one without which no roster from a Wilderness Hall of Fame is complete; that of Nu-tachuwan-ae-sin— Man-that-plays-in-the-Rapids, the best canoeman of them all.

And now the talk becomes desultory, dies down. The men retire, and soon all sound ceases. And the fire begins to burn low, and from it a thin, white, wavering column of smoke ascends, up into the pine tops, far above. The night-mist from off the water hangs in wisps and mingles with the smoke; until the fire dies at last, and the waiting shadows take final and complete possession, once and for all.

And the North, silent, eerie and primordial, filled with magic, peopled with gnomes, and spirits, and things mentioned only in a legend, now comes into its own, and swallows up the little camp, immersing it in the loneliness of a thousand leagues of Wilderness, engulfing it in the vastness of immeasurable and unimaginable Distance.

From some distant lake there comes, faintly, the wailing cry of a loon; the long-drawn cry of a wolf, deep, wild and melancholy, trails away behind the hills in diminuendo. Whilst on the parade ground of the Dead, the pale battalions of the Northern Lights change guard, and troop their rainbow colours, and swing and throb to the fantastic rhythms of the Dance of the Ghost-Men of the Indians.

*   *   *   *   *   *

There are many white-throats on the River. I hear them every day.

Yet strangely, on all this trip, there has always been one whose melody comes only in the night, as from some great distance, like a memory, or the last, fading notes of some half-forgotten Requiem.

Is it the song of a ghost-bird? I cannot tell.

Faint it is, but very, very plain. Do you hear it too?— There it is again, somewhere in the darkness; sweet and clear, and yet so distant.

It has some meaning, something I reach for and can nearly grasp—yet it eludes me——

The River

MORNING comes early with Boyd Mathewson, and once he is up, it is quite impossible for anyone else to sleep. Men stagger stiffly from their tents, and we all have a touch of that stale dryness, that washed-out feeling that comes on the morning after a forced march of any kind. And there is to be another one today, lasting to noon when, if there are no accidents or adverse winds, we will have arrived at the Mississauga river. Dougal, having already had a quick and very sketchy breakfast, is stepping around, bright as a new dollar and as smart as a particularly aggressive cricket. To the others he is, of course, nothing but an infestation and is earning, by his disturbing activities, some black looks and very pointed and uncomplimentary comment, none of which he heeds. Beside the fire squats Boyd, glowering in caustic silence at the leisurely movements of the men; by the process of raising one eyebrow while heavily depressing the other, and holding a fork at a kind of expectant angle over a suggestively empty frying-pan, he has managed to achieve an appearance of almost malignant preparedness. The men, meanwhile, pretend an elaborate and maddening indifference to all this and continue, speedily enough, with the work of breaking camp, chuckling among themselves. Red Landreville expresses himself, under his breath, as being by no means in love with these blood for breakfast ideas; but Zepherin, in a loud voice intended to be overheard, allows that for his part, he is glad somebody woke him up, as he had slept so hard he nearly broke his neck, that three in the morning is as good a time as any to get up, as it gave a man time to have an appetite for dinner, and that he liked long days because he could do more work. In fact, he liked work so well, he stated, that he could easily lay down and sleep beside it. A cold silence from the direction of the fire greeted these well-chosen remarks.

However, after a short time these minor and half-jocular irritations pass off, and everybody is soon busy around the fire with their cooking apparatus, one tea-pail and a frying-pan to every two men. Billy Mitchell, who is a pretty good cook and quite justly proud of it, has prepared what he calls " community pancakes " for the entire crowd. This is by way of asking the whole bunch out to dinner, so to speak, and it is much appreciated, and as Billy sets them out, he says, "These pancakes look pretty good, by gosh," which brings an immediate chorus of dissent—" They don't look any too good to me "; and " What's so good about them, the colour? They don't taste any hell "; and " Whatcha mak'em with, a shovel? " and " Their looks won't help them; better take a good look at them, you're seein' them for the last time! " But very soon they are all gone, which is about the best compliment they could have got.

Tents are folded, canoes are loaded, and we are away again. Paddles dip and swing (no, they don't flash—there is no sun, and won't be for another two hours) and canoes shoot ahead. You seem to ache in every joint, stiff from yesterday's gruelling drive, and muscles feel like rusty springs; but soon you burst into a profuse perspiration, which cleanses and lubricates the machinery and releases the hidden forces of energy for the day. It is fine weather today again. We are lucky; and the wind is with us, too. There are few cabins back in here; everyone (we haven't met anyone yet) lives in tents, and a log camp is only a place to keep a cache of provisions, or a good place to go into out of the rain; and as these shelters are very far apart, it sometimes rains between cabins.

What do we do then? Well, we can't do a thing about it,

so we let it rain. An ordinary shower stops nobody, but
there are often days when sheets of driving rain, the dull
skies, the dripping trees, soggy moss and streaming rocks
blend in a monotonous monochrome of grey; when it is
wise to stop and put up tents where there is plenty of wood,
light a huge fire and make as merry as possible under the circumstances, drying off before the cheerful blaze beneath
a canopy of tarpaulins. Sometimes a sudden storm, which
you saw coming, but took a gambler's chance that it would
pass a few miles to the Westward, catches you unprepared,
and under the scant shelter of a hastily overturned canoe,
its one end reared above the ground to give you room,
you sit for hours and shiver yourself warm until the rain
stops. You don't as a rule take these chances when on the
Trail, but you do when you are with Mathewson or Dougal.
Let's hope it doesn't rain, says you. And you're right.
The infrequent camps we encounter are, you notice, open
and generally contain supplies; nothing is hidden. In
this country, a man who conceals his cache or locks his camp
is considered to be an outlander, and is looked on with
suspicion as one who would steal—it seems to follow; and
not till easy transportation brings in a few of the wrong kind
of people, is this unwritten law ever broken.

As we approach the head of the River, the lakes become
smaller and, because you can see most of every part of them
at a glance, seem to be sort of intimate and friendly.
In such places we occasionally see moose, huge beasts,
upwards of six feet at the shoulder, who stand and stare at
us curiously as we pass, perhaps the first humans they have
ever seen. Mostly they are in the shallows near the shore,
digging up water-lily roots, and often having their heads
completely submerged, presently come up for air with a
mighty splurge, and seeing us, stand a moment to watch,
the water pouring in small cataracts from the pans of their
wide antlers. Invariably deciding that we are not to be
trusted, they spin on their heels with surprising agility

for so large an animal and lurch away at a springy, pacing trot that is a deal faster than it looks; and the noise of their going, once they hit the bush, is something like that of a locomotive running loose in the underbrush.

At noon we arrive at the Ranger's Headquarters on Bark Lake. This is a large body of water, beautiful with its islands, inlets and broken, heavily-timbered shores. At various points a number of streams enter the lake, and to follow the shore-line and discover all of them would take a week or more. Numerous routes, navigable by the methods we are using, lead off in all directions, and this lake is the gateway to an immense, little-known territory. From its outlet there flows the Mississauga river, small as yet— but don't worry; you'll find it big enough later on. So we got here, you see; we have made seventy-five miles in a day and a half. Not bad, admits Dougal, but if we'd have been getting up in decent time these last two mornings, we'd have been a lot further. It's been fun, hasn't it. And now the serious work is about to start. After dinner we run, in quick succession, a number of small rapids. There is not much to them. This is only the beginning; the River is as yet young. At the foot of one of these fast places we meet a crew of Fire Rangers. You, my friend, who expected to see dyed-in-the-wool bush-whackers, are disappointed. Well, they are not exactly woodsmen, at that, mostly college chaps, good-looking, well-built and athletic, most of them, all with their soft skins deeply tanned or burnt to a brick red, and wearing unnecessarily heavy boots that reach to the knee—all right for prospecting, but not the thing for canoe work. They cannot wear moccasins, and from this inability on the part of newcomers to the woods, has arisen the term " tender-foot." But this does not apply to all of them; there are experienced men among them, easily spotted, though they could all be counted on the fingers of one hand. Obviously they are not at home, and knowing little or nothing of practical bush-work should not be here. They get their jobs through political influence rather than any ability they may or may not possess. They are making the best of it, and are plucky enough to tackle the job, but one wonders just what protection they would be to the country in case of a forest fire, or how they could even find one if it were far off a well-travelled route. However, they have no intention of learning to be woodsmen, but are trying to make enough money to put themselves through college, which last idea is rather worthy. They are good lads for the most part, though some of them haven't shaved in quite a while, almost a sure mark of the townsman. But we don't lose sight of their courage, no matter if they are, all unwittingly perhaps, depriving some of us of employment, right in our own country. We have only one thing against them—*they use butter*!!! [1]

We pass several small lake expansions, and that night we camp beside swiftly running water, on the banks of the River proper. And all night, whenever we awaken, we can hear, in the distance, a dull, steady, ceaseless roar. Our first real white water, with all its unknown possibilities, lies just ahead of us. The next morning we arrive at the head of this. Part of the load is disembarked at the portage, as we will run with half loads, taking only stuff that can stand a wetting. For this is a tough spot, and we will ship water, inevitably. We go to centre of the stream again, set the canoes at the proper angle for the take-off. The canoes seem to leap suddenly ahead, and one after another, with a wild, howling hurrah, we are into the thick of it. Huge combers, any one of which would swamp a canoe, stand reared and birling terrifically beside us, close enough to touch. The backlash from one of these smashes against the bows and we are slashed in the face by what seems to be a ton of water; we are soaked to the skin, blinded by spray—on one side is a solid wall of water, there is a thunderous roar which envelopes us like it was a tunnel, a last flying

---

[1] Fire protection is carried out more effectually these later days.

leap and we are in the still pool below, safe, wet, and thrilled to the bone. It was a short, wicked pitch, and we have taken much water, in which we are now kneeling, but we have saved two loads on the portage, so it paid us well to run; and for you, I think, the experience was worth the wetting. We go ashore, unload and empty out, carry the remaining stuff over the portage, load up and are away again—happy, with a great, new-found sense of self-reliance, and looking for more thrills. There are plenty.

The current has much increased in volume and power. Rapid succeeds rapid in quick succession. Most of them we run, some full loaded, others with half loads, saving a lot of work on portages. A few are more in the nature of low waterfalls, or else too filled with stones, and are impossible. There is a marvellously picturesque cataract, running through a chasm in a series of chutes and sudden drops, that is worth the trouble of going off the portage to see. This spot is known as Hell's Gate. The old rapid is too dangerous to run with any load, and the canoes go down empty. No useful purpose is served in attempting these places, it being done only for the excitement to be got out of it. In such spots, brother, we leave you on the shore, and I think that the skill and daredeviltry, the utter disregard for personal danger with which a good canoeman flings (there is no other word) a good canoe from place to place through a piece of water in which it seems impossible that anything could live, will furnish you with a spectacle that you will be a long time forgetting. And you may sometimes, too, remember the narrow plot that is a grave, surrounded by a picket fence, at one of them. A man was drowned here a few years ago, an old, experienced trapper, who made perhaps this only one mistake in all his life. Some rivers have their private graveyards, to which they add from time to time. But Mississauga is not considered dangerous; there are portages round all bad places. We are only running them for the fun of it. We get wet quite often, and occasionally we have to step ankle-deep in water to make a landing. But things like that begin not to matter to you; it's all part of the game. You are by now becoming so used to these small hardships that to be too comfortable gives you an uneasy feeling of guilt. You say you have a sinking feeling at the pit of the stomach at the head of every piece of bad water; but I notice that you shout as loudly as the rest of them in the middle of it. Between rapids the river runs sometimes smooth and deep, at other places widens out into noisy shallow reaches, with scarcely depth enough to allow the passage of a loaded canoe; in such stretches the men get out and lead the canoes like horses. Frequently, a rapid stops abruptly to quieten down in a pool, deep and still and flecked with foam, where the River seems to pause awhile to reflect and lay new plans for the next wild and turbulent course.

We see no more moose but plenty of deer, and more than once we see a number of them together, standing ahead of us in a shallows, craning their necks, and weaving back and forth with very human curiosity, to get a better view. Sometimes they wait until the canoes are almost upon them before bounding through the shallow water with prodigious leaps and a great clattering and splashing, as they make for the safety of the tall timbers. One, a half-grown fawn, was encountered crouching in a pool, evidently in distress, and a wolf was seen hovering in the underbrush on shore. A stop was made and the wolf routed, while the exhausted fawn was tied by all its feet, and transported to a safer neighbourhood and turned loose again. Wolves, having chased a deer down to a river, not infrequently separate, and one of them having crossed over at another point, is there to meet the deer when the latter swims across. Twice we see wolves; one of them is swimming, and a frantic but unsuccessful attempt is made to catch him before he lands, but he has too much lead on us. We come suddenly on another whilst he is drinking, and before he goes have time to note that he does not lap the water, as does his kinsman the dog, but drinks like a horse, by suction. He makes stupendous bounds, far exceeding those of a deer in length, for a deer leaps up and down, and a wolf leaps ahead—which is one reason why a wolf can catch deer; persistence and a rather high order of intelligence, as well as an aptitude for learning by experience, being the other contributing factors. In all this he much resembles a dog—what's that? You object to this comparison; you say all wolves are poltroons, cowards? Don't let the boys hear you; they don't feel that way about it. I'll tell you: to them a wolf is just another hunter, like they themselves are. Only those who know nothing about wolves, or have a fear complex, can hate them so very much. And as for cowardice, did you ever hear a badly scared man tell how he was chased by wolves? when all he heard was one wolf, so spent a night in a tree and arrived home swearing to God that he ran eight miles with a dozen wolves after him before he climbed a tree to save his life. The wolf is no fool, and plays safe; but so does the man who goes into the woods armed to the teeth and shoots an animal that has no chance against his high-power rifle, and if the animal turns on him in self-defence, the beast is called ferocious, and the man clamours for his immediate extermination because his own hide has been endangered—he is ready to hand it out, but can't take it! Yes, I agree wolves kill lots of deer, but then so do the sportsmen; I kill them myself, who am no sportsman, but a hunter, though there is this to be said for the wolves and myself, we may not bring home the head, but we *do* eat the meat. And those who do most of the hollering about the wolves destroying these " beautiful creatures " (which they certainly are), are those who don't like to see the wolves killing something they want to kill themselves. I read where they shot seventy thousand of these " beautiful creatures " in one season, for sport. The wolf does do

P

harm in small restricted Wilderness areas, and to farmer's stock; so kill him if you like, or can—but don't revile him behind his back. He has his place in the scheme of things, like everything else here. Did it ever strike you that when the White man first struck this country, both deer and wolves were in an exceedingly flourishing condition? Everything fluctuated in those days, and the balance was kept perfect. Yes, I know, we have to kill lots of wolves; I've killed my share. But the wolf is no more to be denounced for following his natural instincts than is a beaver for cutting down a tree, or the whale for eating up the sardine crop (if that's what they eat). Man need find no fault with Nature's methods while he continues to turn whole territories into howling deserts by improper agricultural methods, or burns yearly millions upon millions of the finest and most valuable forests in North America for no good purpose, but just on account of damned carelessness. And now what? You don't believe that the dog and the wolf are so closely related? Did you know that the celebrated police dog, very nearly the most intelligent of his kind, is pretty close to being a domesticated European wolf? Sure, we may kill the next wolf we see, as a matter of expediency, but he is not the contemptible creature you think he is. Don't be prejudiced, my learned friend; fair play and justice are better for the health.[1] Of course I've got to give you this, as you say, this chasing and tearing down of a defenceless animal is brutally cruel; but while I won't defend it, you must know that Nature is sometimes as cruel as sin. And we have a parallel in the highest civilization, where people chase a fox with the assistance of a round dozen of dogs, and get the greatest satisfaction out of seeing the unhappy creature torn to pieces before their eyes. So what!

[1] A tame moose, a frequent visitor to my cabin, and very highly valued, has been badly lacerated by wolves. While I would, if possible, certainly destroy the wolves, it would be with no feeling of contempt, as they were only attempting what I myself often did, which was to kill a mo ose in order to get something to eat.

Well, we had our first argument, you and me, and I suppose we both learned something. Oh, that's nothing unusual. Sometimes everybody gets interested and the whole brigade stops and argues like nobody's business, about something that not one of them knows anything whatever about. Just to be different. Anyhow, we made two or three miles in the meantime—and say, there's a couple of bears, no, three of them, an old lady and two cubs; get out your camera. They won't do us any harm, naturally. (You'd best get that bug-a-boo of " wild " animals out of your head; they're just being themselves, same as us.) The little fellows are all alive with curiosity to find out what we are, but their mother isn't even interested. Clowns of the woods, these black, woolly boys, with a thoughtless, rollicking, good-natured disposition, though it must be admitted that they are often thoughtless enough to go rollicking through someone's provision cache; but their heart's in the right place—it's just a way they have. No, I wouldn't get out of the canoe and pet the cubs if I were you; the old woman is probably not a mind reader, and she'd likely think you were going to hurt her youngsters and slap you down. Good way to start a bear story, but it will do you no good. Bears are quite a common sight here, swimming, or walking along on sandy beaches.

There are incidents. At a stop, where we are to make tea, Shorty, always unfortunate, sticks the tea-pail pole into a hornets' nest. The mosquitoes may not be what they were, but the hornets prove to be as good as ever, and we move away from that place. One of the canoes has its canvas badly cut on a sharp stone. The leak is a bad one, and the crew hustle their craft ashore, where the puncture is mended, temporarily, with soap. Gus, the financier, explains that this is the real reason why we carry soap; but don't listen to him—remember how he caught you on the jam question? But the outstanding presentation is the one provided by Zepherin when, carrying a canoe up a steep bank, he begins to slide backwards, canoe and all, towards the river again. He struggles futilely to regain traction, and being an active man he puts on quite a show, and goes through the most extraordinary gyrations to regain his footing. All hands are gathered at the landing, and the exhibition is watched with the greatest interest. Zepherin is a heavy man, the place is steep and slimy, he has a good start, and we all know that he hasn't the chance of a snowball in Egypt. He has a canoe with him, so if he falls into the river it will be quite all right with us. Zepherin, red in the face, feeling as ridiculous as a car-load of circus clowns, and still sliding, gasps out in desperation "Simmering Cimmerean centipedes! None of you guys goin' to help me? see a fella' slide into this jee-hovally crik!"[1] and goes on sliding, until near the edge he throws the canoe from him with a terrific imprecation and shouts "I'll not go in! I won't go in!" and still he keeps on sliding, waving his fist at the scenery and bellowing "You can't put me in! You can't pu——" and slides, with an uncommonly good display of footwork, over the brink and into about three feet of water. Spluttering like a walrus, he scrambles to his feet immediately, and standing submerged to the waist he shakes his two fists above his head and roars in a terrible voice, "Put me in, did yuh?—but you can't keep me there, by cripes!— and I'll get out when I'm dam good and ready, so I will! Try and stop me!!" and with a blood-curdling whoop he surges ashore. By this time we all began to feel the least bit uneasy as to how he is going to take this, like small boys who have only too successfully defied the authority of a policeman. But Zeph has never actually killed a man— yet, and it is with some relief that we see him sit down upon a stone, as he enquires in his fog-horn voice, "Why didn't some of you mugs push me in so I could get it over with?" And then he laughs and laughs until he can laugh no more. So we laugh too, if you know what I mean—

[1] Creek.

keeps him from feeling self-conscious, don't you see? Dougal, who enjoys, among the more superstitious, the doubtful reputation of having once been seen at both ends of a portage at the one time, now puts in an appearance, just when he isn't wanted, and has observed the latter part of our little true-life drama. Ever a man who could ill brook delay or accident, he shoulders his way up to Zeph and asks him what in the name of all that is blind, black, and holy, was he fooling around in the water for. Zepherin looks at him for a moment in stunned silence, his cavernous mouth agape. "What was I fooling in the water for?" he repeats in a voice weak with astonishment, and then louder, "What for, you say?" and then in a roar, "Foolin' in the water, me! Why, you pollusive, reptilian rapscallion —g'wan, you runt yuh, or I'll make a pile of dog meat out of yuh, that two short men couldn't shake hands over, so I will"; and addressing the surroundings, one hand raised in a supplicating gesture toward high heaven, he asks, "Did yuh hear that one, did yuh?" and calls on all the powers to bear witness that he is an innocent man. Whereat Dougal, unable to remain serious any longer in the face of such an absurd situation, bursts into laughter with the rest of us. Such is our discipline, the kind that will, with the right men, move mountains.

And so, day succeeding day, we go forward. And as we penetrate deeper and ever deeper into this enchanted land, the River marches with us. More and more to us a living thing, it sometimes seems as if it were watching us, like some huge half-sleeping serpent that observes us dreamily, lying there secure in his consciousness of power while we, like Lilliputians, play perilously upon his back. Until, to our sudden consternation he awakens, as though some austere, immovable landmark that you had passed a thousand times before, should rise one day and look you in the face and ask you what you did there; so does this serpent, that is the River, turn on us unexpectedly, and writhe and hiss and tear, and lash out at us in fierce resentment at our audacity.

Here and there along its course are mighty waterfalls, some with rainbows at the foot of them; and one of these thunders down a deep chasm, down two hundred feet into a dark swirling eddy, seemingly bottomless, that heaves and boils below the beetling overhang as though some unimaginably monstrous creature moved beneath its surface. And in the vortex of this boiling cauldron there stands a pinnacle of rock on which no creature ever stood, crowned with a single tree, forever wet with the rainbow-tinted spray that in a mist hangs over it, while the echoing, red walls of the gorge and the crest of the looming pines that overtop them, and the all-surrounding amphitheatre of the hills, throw back and forth in thunderous repetition the awe-inspiring reverberations of the mighty cataract. And as we stand and watch it, it is borne home to us what a really little figure a man cuts in this great Wilderness. Even Landreville has no story to fit the occasion.

Long stretches there are of smooth, slow-flowing water where everything is quiet. Here the shores are level and in wide spots there are low alluvial islands covered with tall, yellow, waving grasses, with blue irises standing in amongst them, showing brilliantly against the darker, gloomy back-drop of the heavy timber. The River winds and twists much in such places. The bends are not far apart and the curve of the banks shuts off the view before and behind at no great distance, so that we are constantly walled around by trees and move inside a circle that never really opens up but goes with us, as if we were passing through a series of high-walled, tree-lined pools in some old, forgotten moat, that looked every one the same, save only for the ever-changing character of the timber that enclosed them. We pass the cavernous, high-vaulted forests of the hardwoods, full of long, shadowy vistas that seem, in their pale, green dimness to be peopled with uncouth and formless shapes, and that stretch vaguely off in all directions in an unending labyrinth of counterfeit roads that lead on to nowhere; then, the sepulchral gloom of spruce woods, muted corridors that, beyond a short distance from the River, had resounded to no sound of human voice; and more pleasant, the poplar ridges with golden pools of sunlight on their floor, and interspersed with huge individual pine trees, austere, towering and magnificent.

On the shores of the shallow, grassy lake we find the remnants of an ancient Indian town. A once proud flagpole had fallen in the midst of it and lay rotted beside the mouldering timbers, and good-sized trees grow within the moss-grown rectangle of what once had been Old Green Lake Post. On a low hillside, facing West, there is a graveyard and on one grave there stands a willow wand, and tied to it there is a tiny offering wrapped in yellow buckskin. It looks to have been quite recently placed there and arouses speculation; but we lay no finger on it and leave it quietly swaying there above its dead. And this evidence of remembrance and simple faith subdues even the rougher element among us. We wander round a little, and wonder who it was that lived here in those distant days, what trails they laid, and how the hunting was, how many of them there were who called this place their home. And the answers all lie buried in the graveyard, below the grasses on the sunny hillside, their secrets, and the swinging, beaded token, guarded by a regiment of pines.

Not far from here we meet a lone-fire Indian. He comes ashore as we are eating and drifts on soundless, moccasined feet over to our fireplace and stands there for a moment, very still. " I am Sah-Sabik," he says. " The white men call me Yellow Rock." He is ancient, and says that he had known the Post when it was young. Kebsh-kong he calls it, Place-Walled-in-by-Rushes; which it was. We had never seen him before but he knows us all each by name and reputation, by means of that old and very efficient line of communication, the moccasin telegraph. We suspect that the offering on the grave is his, but do not ask. He has no English, but some among us know his language; but he tells us little. He talks not so much to us but to himself, and speaks not of the present but of the past, the very distant past, and of the men beside whose graves we had so lately stood. So we give him some tobacco for a present, and in return he offers some strips of dried moose meat in a clean, white linen bag, which we accept. He allows us to give him some tea too, and some flour, provided, he says, that it is a very little. He doesn't want to get a taste for it, because he has no means of getting any more. He lives the old way, asserting that the modern Indians eat too many soft foods (does this sound familiar?), have strayed from the way of their fathers, have become unmanly and have not guts. Hearing him, we wonder do all nations, tribes and generations of men so lament the ineptitude of the generation that follows them. His own meagre resources suffice him, for your true Indian uses sustenance merely as an engine uses fuel. For Northern wild life, waters and the Wilderness are his existence and aside from his few human relationships, the phenomena and inhabitants of the wild lands are his only interests, his perpetual occupation in which his physical appetites are almost entirely sublimated, and their satisfaction, at intervals, only a means to an end, quickly accomplished and soon forgotten. His kind is rarely met today. A shadow amongst the shadows in this Shadowland the Indian recedes, as silently and as mysteriously, and as incalculably as he came, and will soon be gone. And so we leave the old man to his musing and his lonely recollections.

Tonight, the travelling being easy down a steady, uninterrupted current, we journey far and take our supper late, and travel on by moonlight. And now the forest that borders all the River becomes an eerie place of indeterminate outlines and looming, unfamiliar objects

that come and go, and rear themselves up before us only
to disappear on close approach. In the darker spots the
canoes become invisible and can be only placed by the soft
swish of the paddles; but where the moonlight filters
through the trees there are pale shafts of illumination
through which they pass like ghost-craft, or things impalpable,
seen only for a moment, to disappear again. The spruce
trees look like witches with tall, pointed bonnets and sable
cloaks, and the white birches that flicker here and there
among them as we pass, shine whitely out like slim, attenuated
skeletons and in the shifting, garish moonbeams seem gruesomely to dance. In these shrouded catacombs the fire-
flies glow on and off with pallid phosphorescence, little
lambent eyes that wink and blink at us like lights on dead
men's graves; while ever beside us loom the crowded
legions of the trees, and there is that feeling that we pass
before an endless concourse of motionless onlookers, unmoving and unmoved, shadowy spectators who watch
with a profound and changeless apathy from the tall
pavilions of the pine trees. And the brigade seems to move
in a world of phantasma and unreality, as though the River
were some strange, unearthly highway in another world
where tall, dark beings, shrouded and without faces, gaze
featurelessly from the river-banks upon us and stare and
stare, or loom over us with ghostly whispering while some,
to all appearance, beckon with impish, claw-like hands to
stay us, with a hideous suggestion of blind-men reaching
for us in the dark; while behind them lies a vast Kingdom
of Gloom of which they are the dark inhabitants, and
in whose shadowy thoroughfares untoward events lie
crowded, imminently, ready to happen.

And we pitch camp in a moonlit glade and make a
bonfire, which drives away the wraiths and goblins and
brings us back to commonplace reality, and we discover
then that we are tired. So we go to bed and sleep till noon
next day. The afternoon is spent overhauling canoes,

putting an edge on paddles, so they will cut sharply and without splashing or resistance in a heavy current. Dry spruce poles are cut ten feet long, are trimmed and smoothed and driven into short sockets known as poling irons that give weight to the pole and will grip a rock, and are used both in descending and in climbing rapids, in water where a paddle is of no avail.

These preparations are suggestive and a little ominous, though you would not think so to hear the crowd roaring with laughter as Red Landreville tells the one about the calf that was born with a wooden leg. But I don't hear you laughing, brother; you say you feel that something is about to happen? Well, you are right, something is— the smooth, uneventful stretch is over. Tomorrow we hit Seven League Rapids, the Twenty Mile. What's that? You say it needn't have come on quite so sudden, but that's what you came for, isn't it? And you can't go back, so you've got to go ahead. And besides, this is the high-light of the whole trip, and you'll enjoy it—and if you don't, you'd better not admit it. And besides, you don't expect to live forever, do you? and it's as good a place to die as any that I know of. That makes you cheerful? I kinda thought it would—but I was only joking, it's not as bad as all that; there hasn't been a man drowned there in years. I knew that would please you, and I bet you four dollars you'll want to come back and do it all over again. You can't hear it yet, but it's there, as you'll find.

Before second smoke the following morning, its deep voice is carried back to us by the South wind. The time of day is right, and the sun is in a good position for running; everyone is expectant, and iron-shod poles and extra paddles are placed firmly in position where they will not be jarred overboard, but can be snatched up at a moment's notice. For it will be fast work at times, in some spots a matter of split seconds.

Many a tall ship has foundered in the Twenty Mile, so

put your best men on the quarter deck, my bullies! And, a word to you who read—if you don't know your stuff, don't run the first half mile. People who believed they were canoe men are huddled in hell by the hundred. The portage is on the left. Take it; you may need it. We won't, but don't let that bother you. You only live once.

The distant mutter of the rapids, as we draw on it, swiftly becomes a growl, grows louder, and increases in volume by the minute, moving swiftly towards us, rising in diatonic progression up the scale of sound until it becomes a thunderous uproar. A hundred yards ahead the River suddenly drops abruptly out of sight, breaking off in a black, horizontal line from which white manes and spouts of foaming water leap up from time to time; below that—nothing, apparently, and the tree-lined banks fall away at what, from that distance, looks to be a most alarming angle. But now we feel the tug and pull of the tow. No more talk.

The current, smooth as oil, deep and swift, carries us in its irresistible suction towards the dark V of deep water that marks the channel, and the canoes, driven a little faster than the current to gain steerage-way, are worked almost broadside on into this and at railroad speed, one after another, are flung like chips into this raging inferno of water—God! Are we going down sideways on this dangerous curve in these light flimsy craft at twenty miles an hour! Crossways, into this seething vortex!! Yes, yes, we must, to fight the current, to escape it and catch an eddy, for just ahead is a standing rock against which the full force of the River hurls itself in ungovernable fury, striking with terrific impact; and towards this the canoes are dragged by the deadly pull of the undertow, inevitably, inexorably. Crossways in the current, canoes headed towards the opposite bank, the crews dig deep with heavy, powerful strokes, faces set, eyes intent on some object they are using for a marker, using all the skill they know and straining every muscle to tear loose from the grip of the current that is dragging them, inescapably it seems, towards destruction. Inch by inch we are gaining the necessary leeway—comes a sudden, sharp crack, faintly heard above the racket—a broken paddle! A canoe, out of control, whirls toward the rock—swiftly the man, (he is alone), grabs another paddle. His life depends on how quickly he moves—now his bow is furthest out, still sideways, and going fast—Look at that! he throws himself forward into it thus gaining a canoe's length, lifting the stern out of the current as his weight drives deep the bow—the canoe swings completely around and out, hurtling by the death-trap with only inches to spare. And then with a wild halloo the other canoes swing into line, head on, right to the edge of the current, and with whoops and yells of exultation the paddlers drive home into the thundering white water. A drumming sound passes swiftly, now it is far behind us— the rock—we have no time—confusion—an outrageous, dizzying medley of sound and furious action—snarling waves with teeth of stones, sheets of flying water, back-lash and hissing spume, the hoarse shouts of the white men and the high-pitched ululations of the Indians piercing the rolling drum-fire of the rapids. Men twist and heave and jab, and thrust with good maple paddles, throwing the canoes bodily, almost, from one strategic point to another, prying prow or stern aside from sure destruction. For this is Men against the River and all must run successfully. To fail means death. The bowsmen throw themselves forward, sideways, backward, the sternsmen sometimes standing, sometimes crouching in the bottom, reaching forward or behind, the paddles of both cutting the water like knives, their blades beneath the surface for half-a-dozen strokes. Each man senses his team-mate's every move, and each responds with lightning speed and the lithe quickness of a cat, as the canoes careen and plunge and pitch and the scenery goes reeling by, the trees an endless palisade on either side resounding, echoing and re-echoing with the roaring of the waters, a mighty close-packed concourse of immovable spectators, onlookers to the wild pageant of the River that races on between them in triumphant progress, decked with banners of white water and flashing crests of spray, and leaping waves like warriors, barbaric, plumed and shouting—this is the Twenty Mile.

And down its mad course go the Rivermen, carefree and debonair, wild, reckless, and fancy-free, gay caballeros riding the hurricane deck, rocketing down the tossing foaming River; a gallant, rollicking, colourful array, my trail companions; Men of the Mississauga.

But I am dropping behind—I cannot catch up, I cannot follow—What is this?—they are leaving me!

And now suddenly the canoes slip silently, swiftly away on the dark bosom of the River; the figures of the paddlers dwindle, become dim and disappear, and the sound of their singing is gone. The sound of the waters recedes, fades away——

Silence.

An old poling-iron and a faded photograph are on the table before me. In my hand is not a paddle, but a pen. I am alone.

The stove is cold and pale Dawn creeps in through the window. Faintly, from somewhere outside, there comes the clear, poignantly beautiful carolling of a white-throat. Ah, I remember now, the bird I heard so often in the night-time; the Requiem.

I have spent a night with the Lost Brigade.

BOOK THREE

AJAWAAN

". . . There is not a creature
On whom the infinite heaven hath not smiled
Wildly and tenderly; no thing impure,
Monstrous, deformed and hideous but he holds
The immensity of the starlight in his eyes."

BLUNT

I

Beaver Lodge

BEAVER LODGE is not an ordinary camp. It was intended
to be so in the first place, but the original plan has been
greatly changed and it has been put to strange, unusual
purposes, by the enterprise and queer adroitness of the
Beaver People.

Half of a good sized beaver house stands within it, the
other half without, both halves of a perfect lodge with the
wall of the cabin in between. All this may sound a little
odd and unbelievable, but the camera has provided an
incontestable record of its actuality. The outside half has
been erected on what was to have been a kind of a water-
front parade ground for myself. But on this plot, so
debonairly taken, there is an interwoven mesh of sticks and
mud, on which beaver from one to sixty pounds in weight,
work nightly with passionate and unconquerable fervour;
while spread out for thirty feet or more, there floats attached
to it a raft of logs and tree limbs, some six feet or so in
thickness, collected for provision for the Winter.

And inside this earthen fortress, in the night, there can be
heard the low murmuring of child-like voices, as the engineers
who live there confer on new improvements, and carry on
their sage deliberations.

*   *   *   *   *   *

My snowshoes hang unused upon a peg. My rifle, shot-
gun and revolver, oiled and very clean, are in their place
of honour on the wall, the place they had in every other
camp. I use them now to frighten bears away. Old and
well stretched tump-lines hang neatly coiled around a
wooden pin. The skinning knives cut only bread and bacon
Q

now, and graining tools for tanning, smooth and sharp, lie idle and forgotten on a shelf, and in a box, bedecked with simple decorations, are small relics, my old-time souvenirs. My old and faded suits of buckskin, worn and honourably scarred by years of honest travel, droop lifelessly, suspended in a row, their gay fringes all listless and dejected—all waiting for a day which for them, as for me, will never come again. For they are pensioned off, except the tump-lines, for which a thousand uses can still be found. And the tale of them, the hunts and explorations that they made, the far-off undiscovered countries they have been to, when we all worked together, always travelling, ever seeking what lay beyond the distant hills, ever following the lure of the Incalculable, would make a history worthy of the telling.

And when I am stuck for a story, or at a loss, or recollection fails me, I chew my pen and look at them. And in their utter immobility and silence they seem to gaze, these old companions of the trail, reproachfully upon me, that I should so forget the glamorous past which they helped to make, and of which they are, each one, so much a part.

And they seem to speak and say to me that it was here, or there, we went—or that this was the way of it; and don't I remember the time we caught the black fisher-weasel on the Spanish river, and the place where the Indian told us the story of the Magic Forest—how we camped out, the first of anyone, beside an undiscovered lake without a name, and how we all starved for days at Hungry Hall?

Among these old mementos is a long, narrow-bladed knife, its razor edge hidden in a tattered leather sheath that does not fit. And it never seems to speak, as do the others. This knife was found, with a grotesquely long, muzzle-loading trade-gun, at low water in a rapids not a rifle-shot from my door. The old rifle was only rusted steel and iron, and the haft of the knife was nearly gone, so I bound a rawhide handle on this effective-looking weapon, and from then on, carried it always on my belt, in a sheath that didn't belong to it, for use and for a kind of talisman, hoping that some of the wisdom of its erstwhile owner might fall to me.

And until the corroded gun, the mute and ancient knife, or the dark funereal jack-pines that guard the place shall speak, there will yet remain one tale that never can be told.

And now Beaver Lodge is open; come with me.

II

Lone Bull

ERNEST THOMPSON SETON once wrote to the effect that an animal is able to divine instantly man's intentions toward him. While an animal may not jump to a conclusion so speedily on all occasions, my own experiences with the creatures native to our forest lands leads me to believe that on the whole his statement is correct. While they may not be able to grasp his actual purpose, members of the brute creation seem to be gifted with some form of intuition whereby they can undoubtedly sense a man's attitude toward them and become suspicious or indifferent according to their findings. They are, however, by no means infallible, frequently making mistakes, but it is noticeable that the errors are all made on the safe side. Old experienced animals take nothing for granted, an axiom which not only beasts but humans as well may learn to profit by, through long years of wilderness travel.

This is no new idea and is so much a foregone conclusion amongst Indians and others who lay claim to any skill in the hunt, that deeming the deadlier purpose to be the more portentous, they will not, on close approach to their game, gaze too intently upon an individual, nor permit their minds to dwell too earnestly on the proposed kill, lest the animal become apprised of their intention.

In areas where man is still an uncommon sight, he is, to the creatures that encounter him, only an object of curiosity. Under these conditions wild animals of most species will sometimes stand in full view for an appreciable length of time, gazing at him in wonder; and on the man's actions on that occasion will depend the animals' estimation of him as either a harmless co-dweller of the Wilderness, or as a natural enemy. Not for long does a man reside in a virgin territory before a few overt acts will alienate for all time the furred and feathered inhabitants of the entire district. Conversely, a more tolerant, or an actively benevolent attitude will soon have the effect of attracting the interest of these same creatures, some of whom will, after a few experimental sorties, begin to frequent the habitat of that queer, two-legged, awkward looking creature that has come amongst them, is able to mind his own business and is not such a bad fellow after all.

Of the fauna now existent upon the North American continent, there have remained over to us from prehistoric times the moose, the beaver and the buffalo. They alone seem to have been able to adapt themselves to the drastic changes in climate that annihilated such mighty creatures as the dinosaur and the elephant. With the buffalo my experience has been nil, except in respect of some fifty-year-old pemmican partaken of on certain momentous occasions. However, I am led to believe that animals having the herding instinct have less ability for conscious mental effort than have those that fend for themselves in family groups or as individuals. The two former creatures mentioned seem, however, to be possessed of a modicum of that wisdom which antiquity is said to bestow. We expect something a little out of the ordinary from a beaver, as his manner of living demands exceptional powers both mental and physical, but we look for little in a moose save a natural keenness of scent and hearing and a certain amount of native cunning developed by the requirements of self-preservation. Yet I have come in contact, not long since, with a specimen of the latter animal to whom must be given credit, in spite of any preconceived notions to the contrary, for the ability to do at least a little light figuring on his own account.

Animals as a whole are apparently devoid of imagination,

which is fortunate for them as it enables them to meet the hardships they have to undergo with greater equanimity than can a man, and without any effort of will; but I have none the less been long convinced that, in many species, they are capable, to a more or less limited degree, of the power of thought. Even those of us having the most dim and distorted views on animal mentalities must concede something to the ape, the elephant and the beaver, and in many cases to the dog and the horse, but a long experience has hitherto failed to reveal to me any evidence of reasoning powers in any branch or individual of the deer family coming under my notice. The moose would seem to be a creature of slow mental processes, but that he is capable of using and does, on occasion, use his head, over and above his accustomed, almost automatic reactions, has been amply demonstrated to me and to others who have seen him, by an eight-year-old bull who has been a constant, if irregular visitor here for nearly five years.

At the time of writing he is lying alongside my canoe placidly chewing the cud with occasional grunts of satisfaction. The canoe, behind which he is ensconced, offers him a certain amount of shelter from the Easterly wind that is blowing, though he could get better protection from it in the rear of the cabin, where he occasionally bedded down last year. But this new position perhaps has more intriguing possibilities, as he can see all that is going on, including my own small affairs in which he seems to take a lively interest. In his present situation he is an object of curiosity and some resentment to the numbers of squirrels and whiskey-jacks that frequent this spot, and he is apparently quite undisturbed by the erratic movements of these small but rather violently active creatures.

Although I knew of the presence of this bull in the district on first taking up my abode here, and often had fleeting glimpses of him, I made no attempt at any friendly overtures and adopted a policy of quiet withdrawal on sighting him.

That Summer it became necessary to fell a number of poplar trees to provide light for photographic work, and he made furtive nocturnal visits to the fallen trees for the purpose of eating the leaves. These visits to the free lunch counter thus provided, continued as long as the leaves lasted, a matter of nearly two weeks, and during that period I made it a practice to be unobtrusively present at his feeding time. From then on, at intervals, he could be seen passing at no great distance from the cabin, and on occasion stood gazing down at it from some point of vantage. Often I observed him hovering on the hill-tops no great distance away, as I came and went on my constant patrol of the beaver works. He even ventured beyond the last fringe of the forest that borders the tiny clearance on every hand, and watched me cutting wood, silent and motionless as the trees themselves. I did not press the matter, nor did I abate my labours, but carried on as though unaware of his presence, as evidently his interest was already sufficiently aroused. It was noticeable that the movements of the beaver seemed particularly to engage his attention, and one evening he came boldly down and stood observing them. The beaver speedily collected in a body and treated him to a salvo of tail splashing and stirred the water to a great commotion. All this had no effect on the moose whatsoever, except to cause him to step a little closer to see what it was all about.

Now a bull moose weighs something short of half a ton and is altogether rather a staggering proposition to have around at such close quarters and could, if he chose, become the least bit unmanageable; so becoming a little dubious as to the outcome of this rather alarming intimacy I stepped out of the cabin, having so far watched the performance through a window. With no hesitation the moose spun around on his heel and fled up the hill, and I commenced calling to the beaver in my usual manner to calm them. And now occurred the most remarkable feature of this whole business. At the first sound of my voice the moose slacked down, slowed to a walk and stopped, and as I continued calling the beaver he slowly returned, coming most of the way back, and commenced feeding on a clump of alders that was handy to him. Unbelievably, the words and inflections I used to pacify the beaver, seemed to exert the same influence on the moose. On being further alarmed by my rapid movements the moose withdrew once more, but he did not go so far as before and was reassured by the same sounds, so that he again commenced to feed where he stood and spent upwards of an hour browsing unconcernedly around before he finally moved off. This, to me, unprecedented behaviour on the part of a wild animal with whom I had hardly even a bowing acquaintance, seemed very marvellous at the time and unless we are to admit that he figured the situation out for himself, an adequate explanation is hard to come by. I can claim little credit in the conduct of this affair, as the moose seems to have formed his own decisions and acted on them. I pondered long and deeply on the subject, and not yet satisfied, experimented time and again during the now frequent visits of this strangely complaisant beast and on most occasions with the same result, scaring him by a sudden appearance and easily recalling him. And each rehearsal was a further confirmation of what I scarcely could believe myself was true, that without any attempt at training or the exertion of any influence on my part this astonishing and unfathomable creature, wild, free and beholden to me for nothing, would respond willingly to my voice, and place himself in my power at a word. Fortunately this has occurred on different occasions before a number of witnesses, otherwise I would have some diffidence in committing the matter to paper, and an unusual aspect of animal psychology would go unrecorded.

Many of those who have not had the advantage of first-hand experience with wild animals accept as commonplace some of the really extraordinary manifestations of animal intelligence, and on that account it may appear to some that

I stress unduly the peculiarity of this particular case. But those who have hunted moose or who reside in districts where they are common will appreciate my point of view.

Many ridiculous stories have been circulated, some of them in print, relative to the sagacity of moose and other beasts, and while recorded truth is sometimes humdrum and uninteresting, cool and accurate observation will often disclose facts or incidents that transcend the wildest flights of fiction.

There is little doubt in my mind that this bull had a pretty fair idea of my attitude toward him from the outset, and it is highly probable that he had taken careful and lengthy observations of the situation and had listened long and intently to all the sounds emanating from this place long before I was aware of it. He had thus become accustomed to the sound of my voice, formed his own conclusions as to its significance, and without any artifice of mine, had come to share in the sense of security it was intended to convey.

Most animals are equipped with some means of identification so that they may be readily recognized by others of their own species. This exists sometimes in the voice, as with beavers, muskrats, porcupines, as well as birds. Some are marked by a patch radically different in hue from their general colour scheme, such as the white hind legs of a moose,: he orange rump of the elk, the stripes of the skunk, the white flag of the Virginia deer. I, too, have made use of yet one more device from the Economics of the Wilderness and have likewise established my own method of identification by means of one word uttered at a certain pitch and tone which all the creatures that frequent here are quick to recognize. This I did all unconsciously at first, falling into the prevailing custom from long association with it and not realizing how potent a spell it was until seeing its effect on an animal as extremely mobile and suspicious as is a moose. On my unexpected appearance, or on the occurrence of some unusual sound, any and all animals present, be they squirrels, muskrats, beaver or the moose, will freeze to instant immobility, appearing like stone images of various shapes and sizes and will momentarily remain in this position of suspended animation until at the sound of the well-known word, utterly foreign sound though it is, they spring instantly to life and resume their interrupted occupations.

During the past Summer and Fall the bull spent a good deal of his time within the camp environs strolling around complacently amongst my arrangements, the woodpile, store tent and canoes, etc. He sometimes stood outside the cabin door for long periods, close enough that some visitors were not unreasonably afraid that he might try to enter. I was not too sure myself as to what lengths this enterprising animal would go, as he had already got, at the one time, all four of his feet into a small canoe and smashed it beyond any possibility of repair. A canoe is a light rig of ribs and canvas, and a moose weighs in the neighbourhood of half a ton, if you get the idea. I actually had to drive him away from the door one night as his presence there, standing engaged in some ponderous cogitations, was obstructing the passage of the beaver in and out of the cabin with their building materials. By this time they no longer feared him, but were probably like myself, a little uncertain as to what his next move might be, and refused to pass him.

Every animal has its special fear, both as a species and as an individual. In the case of this particular moose, his pet antipathy was to have anyone pass between himself and a lighted window, throwing thereby a quick flitting shadow across him. This would cause him to break away at a run, and although he could invariably be called back, he would retire hurriedly on the offence being repeated, nor did he ever become accustomed to it.

Until the beaver began at last to accept this huge visitor as a regular feature, I always received fair warning of his approach at some distance by tail signals given out by the beaver. He has now become to them, I imagine, something of a necessary evil, to be tolerated even if not to be over-effusively welcomed, and he has become so ordinary that his presence is taken as a matter of course, and warnings are no longer given. And stepping out from the cabin into the night and almost falling, as I once did, over a beast the size of a horse, is a severe trial to the nervous system of any man, however bold.

While the weather was warmer, he had a habit of standing in the water at the landing, and whilst there, was evidently something of a spectacle to the young beavers, who would swim completely round him, slapping their tails on the water and creating a great uproar, all of which he would view with a lofty unconcern.

At times the behaviour of this strange beast led me to wonder if he was not lonesome, and that having at last found company that combined the advantages of being safe and at the same time interesting, he had attached himself to the place on that account. For animals of all kinds love entertainment, and become very excited and playful on the introduction of something unusual into the monotony of their everyday lives, and they seem to get much pleasure from the contemplation of something new and strange, always of course provided that it is first proven to be safe. This theory of a desire for social intercourse on the part of a dumb brute, I have long held to be as tenable as the better known and well attested one, that in some instances individuals of the brute creation will go to the opposite extreme, and become so unsociable as to be dangerous to their own kind.

This community of interest has no whit abated the native alertness and vigilance of this animal, as on my coming upon him once unannounced from behind a knoll he rushed immediately round to the far side of the little eminence and, using it for cover, beat a precipitate retreat. I cannot believe that animals under ordinary circumstances when running from danger do so in an excess of panic and blind terror.

For scared as he certainly was, he must have retained an admirable presence of mind, as on my running to the top of the knoll and calling out loudly the pass-word, he stopped within a hundred yards and eventually permitted me to approach him; but being far from camp and in a section where he was not accustomed to encountering me, I did not put his confidence to too great a test. This is by no means the only evidence I have that animals, even when in full flight and apparently panic-stricken, have all their mental faculties working one hundred per cent., and I am positive that only when dominated by the mating instinct, or driven to extremes by hunger, or on finding themselves in some utterly unnatural situation, such as unwanted confinement, do they ever completely lose control of themselves.

At the earliest view I had of him, about five years ago, this now proud bull was little more than a spike-horn. He had only two V shaped protuberances, each about a foot long, on his adolescent brow, which, as an abbreviated moustache sometimes does to an otherwise manly face, detracted from rather than added to his appearance of virility. The next year, however, he blossomed forth with a real set of antlers, his first, provided with a good-sized pan and several assorted spikes. In the mating season he strutted around with these in some style, putting on considerable dog and issuing loud vocal challenges that I am sure he was quite incapable of backing up. Although he had been, at other times, a model of propriety and decorum, acting always the natural gentleman, with the coming of the first sharp frosts he was transformed overnight into something resembling a dangerous lunatic. He strode into view one afternoon with a demeanour greatly changed from his usual quiet and dignified bearing. He had about him all the appearance of one looking for trouble. With some idea of testing his courage, I brought out a birch-bark horn, an instrument shaped like a small megaphone and used for calling moose at this season, and gave a couple of short challenging coughs. The effect was instantaneous. With no preliminaries at all he opened hostilities on everything within reach. He tore at willows and alders, emitting hideous grunts, gouged and gored helpless prostrate trees, made wicked passes at inoffensive saplings that stood in the path of his progress, entered into a spirited conflict with an upturned stump, threw a canoe off its rack and had a delirious, whirlwind skirmish with a large pile of empty boxes. The clash and clatter of this last encounter worked him up to a high pitch of enthusiasm, and he gave a demonstration of foot-work and agility hardly to be expected from so large an animal. All this had a very depressing effect on the spectators, who consisted of several of my furred and feathered retainers besides myself—about the same effect that a crazed gunman running loose on a city street would have on the pedestrians. I tactfully withdrew with the horn, which I carefully put away. Having, after a time, pretty well subdued all visible enemies, except the store-tent which he had fortunately over-looked, this bold knight moved off to fresh fields of glory, and from the way he surged through the scenery I judged it would not be very long before he got himself into serious trouble.

I viewed this exhibition with much the same feelings that would be mine were I to see a highly respected and respect-able acquaintance suddenly commence to throw handsprings in a public place, or to roll a hoop along the street, shouting. There was also a certain feeling of pity for the temporarily aberrated mind that one feels in the presence of an inebriate, with more than a little of the same uncertainty.

For a week or more he failed to show up at the camp and I began to fear that he had met his Waterloo, but one evening on returning by canoe from a trip to my supply cache, I saw in the dusk the familiar dark, ungainly form reclining at ease before my cabin. My canoe was heavily loaded and the water was shallow, so I was entirely at his mercy, but he allowed me to land and unload without any argument, merely get-ting to his feet and feeding on the surrounding underbrush.

He does not come so often now and stays but a short time, an hour perhaps. By his actions, I think that he has succeeded in finding himself a partner. I cannot conceive by what system of chiselling he was able to obtain her in a district so populated by big experienced bulls. He has no doubt all the optimism and enthusiasm of youth on his side, and perhaps he has met a cow who is, like himself, young enough to see romance and gallantry in the mock battles which this handsome young fellow no doubt staged before her, and to experience maidenly thrills to see him vanquish make-believe antagonists. And if he has made the same use of his brains in the selection of a mate that he did in his manner of adopting my domicile for refuge, he has no doubt picked himself a good one.

As he sits without, before the window, I see that he is gazing anxiously, wistfully back into the dark recesses of the woods. Ever and anon his head turns in this one direction, ears pointing, nostrils sniffing the air. And I know that back there his cow is lurking, afraid to come down into the open and brave the terrors of the unknown.

Soon he will follow the law of all nature and follow where his consort calls; and as he stalks majestically away, he will march as to the sound of drums and martial music, with regal pride and with the bearing of a king. For he has attained to his majority, has proved himself before the eyes of all the world. He is now a finished product from the vast repository of the Wild, a magnificent masterpiece of Nature's craft, scion of a race whose origin is lost in the mists of un-numbered ages, the most noble beast that treads these Northern forests.

And I cannot altogether subdue a little, sneaking feeling of satisfaction, when I realize that without subjugation, training or confinement, and on account of no consideration of food or safety, but just because he is contented here, happy and above all—free, he will leave for a time his chosen mate, to rest in my door-yard for an hour.

III

Little Pilgrims

CHAPTER ONE

SIX years ago, the Canadian Government took over my beaver colony, and we were all enrolled on the personnel of the National Parks of Canada. Thus there came to an end any further worry as to the welfare of my small fellow-pilgrims. We were to be shipped to one of the great National Parks in the West, and together we made a journey of some thousand miles, the beaver in a huge, specially constructed tank, and myself in the baggage car beside them. We arrived at our destination, Riding Mountain, after nearly a week of travelling. It had been a trying ordeal, but we all arrived at the end of our pilgrimage (though it, too, turned out to be a temporary stop) a little grubby, but none the worse for wear, and in the best of spirits.

Once on their new location the beaver made no attempt to wander away for other waters, though the first night they seemed a little bewildered and ran in and out of the tent a hundred times as though to see if I was still there. Their first step in establishing themselves was to clean out a landing at the tent; they then picked out a spot across the lake and built themselves an enormous house, taking only a month to complete it, although they worked at it all summer, desisting only when they had an erection eight feet high and upwards of sixteen feet across. Here Jelly had her first little family. The taming of these was a problem of no mean proportions; they were quite beyond my reach until they were well advanced, and they were as wild as hawks.

Every night I spent the time from dusk till break of day, sitting motionless on a kind of stationary raft on the floating muskeg, plagued by hordes of mosquitos, and unable to fight them vigorously for fear of alarming any emissaries who might approach from the beaver house. Here I waited for hours and nights until some wandering adolescent should come to my carefully chosen stand. They passed me at intervals, sometimes eyeing me knowingly, at others disregarding me entirely, until they became so used to my presence there that they at last began a practice of giving me a small note of greeting as they went sailing by. Eventually, intrigued perhaps by the appearance of this strange-looking creature who seemed to have become a fixture on their limited horizon, they commenced to land at the raft, and climbing on it would look at me intently for perhaps a full minute and slip silently away to think it over. They were absolutely beyond my control and in no way obliged to come near me, but I found that by careful manœuvring I could at length lay hands on them, but that the slightest untoward movement drove them away so that they avoided me for the remainder of the night. However, I received some timely assistance from Jelly Roll, who would sometimes bring all four of them over to my stand and there play with them, rolling round and round in the water with a kitten held tight in her hands, spinning them around in all directions with violent movements of her body, and engaging in hilarious wrestling matches with two or three of them at once, which she, by the way, always allowed them to win; and a lively scene it was, during which I was often splashed from head to foot. The advantage this gave me is easily seen, and I made every use of it, inserting my hands into the tumbling squirming mêlée, so that in their excitement, and urged on no doubt by their mother's example, they would actually seize my fingers, and, soon accustomed to the strange man-scent, would romp with me as they did with her. The rest was easy. At the end of a month they were well in hand and would follow me around, answer my calls and, with assistance, sometimes climb into the canoe. Here the Boss's oldtime jealous streak appeared again. Once when I had succeeded, after great trouble and patience, in coaxing all four of the kittens into the canoe, Jelly came steaming over, climbed aboard, and put every one of them out. The protective instinct of the father, Rawhide by name, was very strong, due to his having been captured from the wild state, and was a great handicap in the earlier stages. Sometimes when I had persuaded the kittens, by means of all the wiles that I was able to invent, to gather around me, he would come dashing amongst them scattering them in all directions and then drive them away individually, afterwards climbing ashore beside me himself. However I made no attempt to break this habit, it being his own particular method of protecting and educating his babies.

Several thousand feet of film were obtained here, and Rawhide played a heroic part, opposite the Queen's more unconventional rôle, although she had by now developed a temperament that compared well with other and perhaps less talented stars.

The water facilities in this area unfortunately proved to be inadequate for the prospective increase. A flying trip to Prince Albert National Park in Saskatchewan revealed a situation more suitable to the requirements. As it would be late fall when the beaver arrived there, they would have no time to do their own work, so it was necessary to provide artificial means whereby they would be able to winter successfully. It was essential that these arrangements should approximate as closely as possible those of their own devising. So I planned a camp that should stand at the water's edge, to have an artificial plunge-hole in the floor, leading, by a submerged tunnel, under one wall out into deep water. Thus the beaver would have temporary accommodation in the cabin itself, until the Spring thaw set them free to build for themselves. A temporary dam

R

was to be constructed at the outlet, and it is worthy of note that the following Summer, the beaver built another and slightly higher dam below it in a better place, and flooded out the man-made creation completely. On investigation it was found that this latter dam was built at the exact location of one that had existed there at least half a century ago, as the activities of these beaver exposed portions of the old work and the remains of a pre-historic looking lodge, covered with a good layer of soil on which a group of fair-sized trees were growing. That they should thus recognize the facilities of this particular place, and estimate so accurately the possibilities for distribution of pressure, obtainable at no other available location, seems to argue something more than a highly specialized instinct.

Word was soon received that the cabin and other arrangements had been completed. I wired for Anahareo—who was at her parents' home in Ontario—as there were now six animals to look after, and no one else knew enough about these particular beaver to be of much assistance. She curtailed her holiday and came at once. It was her first view of the youngsters, and both she and they had a great time on the trip. Jelly, Rawhide and myself carried on in the usual way, being by now seasoned travellers, and we were very bored, or blasé, or nonchalant, or whatever it is that seasoned travellers suffer from. This journey was not so monotonous, as our itinerary did not lie through the dreary arid-looking deserts of wheat that had before had such a depressing effect on us.

A whole flotilla of gasoline boats was needed to transport our community and its belongings the thirty miles to the first portage, and from there to Ajawaan Lake, our present abode, we packed everything across the half-mile canoe trail, beaver and all, finishing the journey by relays with a canoe.

The rear portion of the building, an area six feet across and the full width of the camp, had been railed off and an opening left for the passage of the beaver. This part of the structure was not floored, and had extending from it a covered tunnel which at the point of egress lay in about seven feet of water. This was all arranged as I had previously planned. It became necessary however to close the partition until freeze-up, as beaver that have been transplanted from a domicile where their work has been completed, will as a rule immediately go in search of their old surroundings, the urge to do so being especially strong in this case, as all the Winter's feed had been collected there. In searching for their old home the beaver will swim long distances up and down streams, and run around in a manner directly contrary to their usual habits. These particular specimens would not actually leave me, as had been repeatedly proved, yet, it being near the freeze-up, they might in their wanderings be frozen out far away from home, and be killed by wolves or perish miserably in other ways. We experimented with Jelly Roll as being the most trustworthy of the family, and even she became lost for three hours in the bush, returning to the camp *by a land route*, with her tail beginning to freeze and in a great state of despair.

The beaver well realized the presence of the plunge-hole, and spent all their waking hours endeavouring to reach it. They gouged up the floor in places and started to gnaw down the partition, so that it was necessary to protect it with blocks of timber. These they cut to pieces and removed, but we promptly renewed them. In this connection occurred a demonstration of feeling on the part of one of the young beavers, which illustrated the affection these animals have for one another. In their attempts to arrive at the plunge-hole, Rawhide, the aboriginal, was the most persistent. I once drew him away a little roughly by the tail in order to impress him, and immediately one of the kittens, a little male that had always been his favourite, of which he always has one in every litter, scurried over to him with little whimpering sounds, and clutched hold of him, and squeezed up tight to him nose to nose and made a little scene about it, as though in sympathy, so that I was the least bit ashamed of my impatience and felt rebuked. This affection is very strong although not always manifest until some incident or situation brings it into play. It is, however, eventually supplanted, if not overdone, by the inescapable and unappeasable urge to wander that later seizes them at maturity, as is often enough the case with beings a good deal higher in the scale of life.

We had installed in the cabin, for their convenience, a fair-sized tank in which they spent a good deal of their time. In their discontent they failed to dry themselves off as they usually do under normal circumstances, and the floor speedily became covered with water. The heat of the stove partially dried this up, but the steam condensed against the roof so that the walls ran with moisture. Everything became damp and some of the provisions were spoiled. Sleep was impossible for us except in the forenoon, when the beaver slept. Their continued clamouring to be taken up into the bunk was so appealing, that as a surcease to their state of unhappiness we put them into it and allowed them, wet as they were, to remain there as long as they wished. This contented them and enabled us to cook and eat—occasionally.

Jelly Roll, who had spent one Winter in camp two years before, accepted the situation philosophically and allowed nothing to upset her equanimity; of course she was a Queen and had an appearance to sustain, and was possessed of all the well-bred composure commonly supposed to be the attribute of queens. To us humans, however, the wailing, the crying, the gnawing, and the constant splashing, the unceasing efforts to build scaffolds with a view to climbing over the partition, the necessity for enduring vigilance to avoid the entire destruction of the camp fixtures, in fact the whole proceedings, were in the nature of a nerve-racking ordeal.

The situation, in spite of these troubles, had its humorous side. The mirth-provoking antics of the younger beavers trying to accommodate themselves to an unfamiliar environment, considerably lightened the cares of this tempestuous interlude. One of them did nearly all of his walking erect, staggering around like a decrepit old man. Occasionally the others, surging around the camp in a compact mass behind their mother and father would barge into him. He would fall, recover, and take his place in the ceaseless noisy procession, only to break away and resume his erect position. He strolled around in this attitude, continually peering here and there with his little shoe-button eyes, as if he were looking for something that he had misplaced.

The beavers seemed to depend on Jelly Roll to see them through, as though they sensed her calm and cheerful acceptance of the situation, or predicament, as it no doubt appeared to them. Wherever she went they followed. If I moved around the camp she, as always, dogged my heels, while behind her streamed her followers, a string of waddling gnomes, hopping and shuffling along on short legs, their voices seldom still. At times becoming tired, one would mount on her large flat tail which, dragging behind her like a toboggan, offered plenty of room for a free ride. In this manner, standing erect and clutching on to a handful of his mother's fur he would be taxied round and round the camp floor with every evidence of enjoyment, whilst his less enterprising companions trailed behind or scrambled alongside. They all eventually discovered the advantages of this mode of transportation, sometimes crowding on this novel vehicle two or three at a time. If there were not sufficient space for all of the big webbed hind feet on the tail at one time the passengers would stand on it on one leg only, and with the other mark time on the floor as they proceeded. Meanwhile Jelly Roll forged along unhurried, unworried, seemingly unconscious of her load. I think we would all be considerably better off if we could emulate the poise, unconcern, and dignified composure that permitted her to retain her peace of mind while the rest of us, beaver included, were becoming a little the worse for wear from the performance.

One night, mercifully, it froze up, and we opened up the aperture in the partition, hitherto barricaded with tin boxes and other forms of hardware. There was a concerted rush for the opening. Entering, the whole family commenced a tour of inspection of their new abode. They were a little suspicious of the plunge-hole at first, but soon began to take to the water. They did not immediately bring in the feed I had in the meantime placed in the usual raft formation out in the lake, but most methodically and with very laudable economy, collected and drew into the improvised den that had been constructed for them, all the poplar brought in by me and piled by them under the bunk. Nor did they touch the raft until this was all used up and the peeled sticks taken out and discarded.

They were now perfectly happy and contented; all the complaints ceased and they wrestled, played, quarrelled and ate as of yore, and for a few days the kittens paid no further attention to our end of the camp.

Not so with Jelly Roll. With her usual untiring and devastating zeal and energy, this practical-minded matron decided that now was the time to fix the door of the cabin, which leaked an infinitesimal quantity of air. She appeared from out the plunge-hole at intervals with large quantities of mud held against her breast, and with which she staggered along erect until she arrived at the flooring where, knowing from previous experience that various articles could be made to glide nicely on camp floors, she dumped the whole oozy, sticky mass on the newly scrubbed boards and proceeded to push it over to the door, leaving behind a trail at least a foot wide. The offending crack below the door was deftly but messily plastered up, and the finishing work continued far into the night, she making about eight trips an hour.

In the morning it was impossible to open the door without the assistance of a shovel. The sounds of labour aroused Jelly Roll from sleep and she came out to see what was going forward, and on discovering that her work had been demolished she screeched and scolded, and shaking herself impatiently went down the plunge-hole and soon returned with another load of mud. By evening things were much as they had been before, and on the completion of her work to her satisfaction—having patted everything down very solidly—she stood on her hind legs and twisted her head and the upper half of her body in the grotesque gyrations which, with a beaver, indicate a whole-hearted appreciation of any situation.

To us this war dance was fraught with sinister import. We knew that from now on, with opposition supplying the incentive, nothing short of sudden death would thwart Jelly Roll in the accomplishment of a task which she had found could be brought to a successful conclusion. So contrary are beavers that should it be desirable to have them enter an opening, often the only way to accomplish your purpose is to introduce them to the aperture, and then try to push them away from it. Opposition merely puts them on their mettle and the habits of a lifetime spent in overcoming difficulties are invoked, sometimes with rather spectacular results. In this particular case, the further removal of the earth work did not help a great deal as it was promptly renewed, she working with passionate fervour to beat us out, which she finally did. This went on for several nights until at last we decided to cut the door in two, crossways, thus making it possible to step over the obstruction and the lower part of the door at the same time.

Eventually Jelly ceased her repair activities and both she and Rawhide commenced bringing in from somewhere under the ice, large quantities of material for some construction work which they had commenced at the plunge-hole. As this erection began to take form we, thinking they were merely amusing themselves, agreed jokingly that they were building a house, and certainly, judging by their state of contentment, the matter-of-fact way in which they had taken complete possession of the camp, and considering the preparations they were making, it did not seem beyond the bounds of possibility. With soil, moss, and sticks collected under the ice from the shores of the lake, these two constructed a kind of lean-to over their exit, which provided room for sleeping quarters for all hands, besides the usual drying-off area. They left an aperture in the side of this erection through which they entered our living quarters, which they all now commenced again to frequent. This hole was completely plugged with mud when they retired to sleep and opened again when they awoke to the day's business. Observations made with the aid of a flash-light found the interior arrangements to be very neat and clean, and included a wet bath-mat section near the water, dry beds of long clean shavings taken from spare boards and torn-up magazines stolen from the camp.

The raft of feed I had provided being insufficient for the entire Winter, and it having been, as stated, too late on our arrival here for the beaver to get their own food supply, it was necessary to cut a hole in the ice and haul down to it a large number of poplar tops, and alder and willow saplings. Rawhide immediately realized my intentions, and disposed of these offerings by dissecting them and cacheing them under the ice. The larger portions I chopped in pieces to save time, and piled alongside the hole. These he quickly removed and getting ahead of my work patiently waited at the edge of the ice till I had some more ready for him. All this time Jelly was in the cabin with Anahareo. She is by no means lazy (Jelly, I mean), but her consort evidently thought so as, becoming tired of working alone, he went inside and routed her out to do her bit, which she did willingly enough.

And so all Winter, at all hours of the night and day these

six energetic, restless, loquacious creatures fetched and carried, begged and stole, fought, danced, and played on the floor of our habitation, until with the coming of Spring they were released to the more normal activities of a beaver's ordinary life.

CHAPTER TWO

A TRUE Canadian loves the Winter, revels in it, especially in the North. I often think that instead of belittling our Winter, as some do even to the extent of indulging in prevarications that sometimes amount to deliberate falsehoods in their endeavours to impress Europeans with the idea that Canada has not a " severe " Winter, we should boast that four feet of snow and from ten to thirty degrees below zero during three and a half months of the year, place Canada in the forefront of the Winter sporting countries of the world. After the exquisitely beautiful season of the Fall of the Leaf is over, and Winter is on, the air becomes like rich wine that strengthens and invigorates; pure, crisp and health-giving. Colds are almost unknown, and all of the population that can spare the time enjoy, in such places as the Gatineau hills, the Highland of Ontario, and the Rocky Mountains, such healthful and exciting pastimes as snow-shoeing, ski-ing, and tobogganing. In Montreal and Quebec and Banff huge Winter Carnivals are held. Those who have not travelled in the vast, snowbound lake country of the North, or tramped on snowshoes in the Winter forest, where the brilliant sun, shining out of a sky that is pure, clear blue, turns the frost-crystals that adorn every bough and branch of every pine and spruce into brilliant scintillating diamonds that glitter like the bright many-coloured ornaments on a Christmas Tree; those who have never witnessed the wild, majestic spectacle of a swiftly marching snowstorm—To them I will say that no matter what they may have seen and done, life still holds something for them that they should not miss. Not every country has these things and I, for one, say we are fortunate.

Have we a Winter here in Canada? I'll say we have—and how!

But the Spring is something else again. The beauty of the Canadian climate consists in its variety; not the monotonous cold of the Arctic, nor the equally monotonous heat of the tropics, or semi-tropical countries, but four distinct, definite seasons; and each season has its special joy.

And the joy of the Spring is in the sound of running water and the smell of new-blown flowers; it comes in the resounding, military tattoo of a woodpecker on a dry limb, the measured, muffled drumming of a ruffled grouse, in the sound of countless song-birds at the time of Dawn, in the shrill chattering of gulls wheeling whitely overhead, and the weird and wailing, half-human laughter of the loons. Something, too, of the freedom and the wanderlust of Springtime, surges through the blood of one who watches the spectacle of the migration of the geese, the flying phalanxes and legions of the wild-geese honking their way in broad V's and long, wavering lines towards the North—often a mile above the earth, yet the rushing beat of the mighty pinions is plainly audible.

And to me the Spring means one thing more; or perhaps I should say many things more—numbers of beaver who, liberated after six months of imprisonment, sealed hermetically in by ice, now go completely mad and race in and out of the cabin on frequent and apparently objectless visits and engage themselves in projects that create a great deal of noise, quite oblivious of the fact that I am trying to write a book. And between the picking up of what they pull down, the taking down of things they push up, the righting of chairs, the rescuing of stolen stove-wood, the responding to clamorous outcries for attention, and the handing out of bribes and peace offerings in the way of apples and other treats, I will try to tell you what the Spring is like at Beaver Lodge.

The time is just one year ago.

SPRING came. The snow and ice had slowly disappeared. For two weeks the adult beaver had been alone, as the half-grown youngsters of last Spring moved off to take up land, or rather water, on their own account. The splashings, the wrestlings and the ceaseless commotion incident to their residence here had given place to a deadly quiet, and the cries and calls of voices that had kept up an incessant din nightly since the advent of open water, were no longer to be heard. No longer did busy earnest beings with their hair on end and eyes almost bursting from their sockets with expectancy, rush into the cabin at all hours, to search with feverish anxiety in every corner for something that was not there—never had been there—or to bring in two or three useless sticks and leave them just inside the door for some kind of a token, and then to dash out on some important undertaking. The beaver pond seemed pretty empty and lonesome, as I listened from force of habit for some noisy demonstration, or for the echo of a welcoming call pitched in a childish treble as some home-coming wanderer signalled his return.

But the silence was unbroken, save for the quiet murmur of the running water at the outlet, and I grieved that my little friends had left me, felt lost without them, and almost wished that I too could join the merry company on its high adventure. But this is the immutable law of Nature, that the young of any living creature must, on attaining their majority, fare forth and carry on the Great Plan and so fulfil their destiny. Besides, the pond could not long support a constantly increasing colony; yet knowing they must go I wished it otherwise. The beavers seemed to miss them too, Rawhide, especially, mooning around in utter silence save for an occasional plaintive call, but eventually he appeared to accept the inevitable with the equanimity and composure with which he habitually meets the vicissitudes of a beaver's life.

One day soon after the emigrants had departed, as I was seated at the supper table, I heard a heavy, regular, thudding sound outside, which approached the door and then ceased. Always on the alert for strange sounds, I opened the door, to find Rawhide waiting patiently to be let in. He was standing upright and had in his arms a load of mud, and keeping this position he stepped over the door-sill, walked on his hind legs the full length of the cabin, and dumped his load on top of the lean-to he had, during the Winter, erected over the plunge-hole. He turned to go, and evidently well pleased with himself gave a few skips and hops, went to the door and scratched again to be let out—a most astonishing performance. But that was not all. He soon returned, not once, but time and again, and kept it up all night, carrying on each entry heavy burdens of sticks, mud, and stones, which he carried in his arms beneath his chin, whilst he travelled the forty or so feet from the water's edge to the pile inside the cabin. Larger sticks and small logs were trailed in as he progressed on all fours, but he transported by far the greater part of his material in an erect position, walking almost as upright as a human being, though with some suggestion that if delayed he might fall forward, yet never hesitating nor resting, marching steadily ahead with a swift, well-balanced gait.

My hope that perhaps the beaver might take up their permanent residence in the cabin was no longer a joke, but a stern, and rather messy reality.

He was building a beaver house in the parlour, right before my eyes.

Meanwhile Jelly was away on a little job of her own, namely, the commencement of a new dam intended to supersede the man-made erection. It is characteristic of her that on its completion at a later date, in order to avoid the trouble of climbing over the protruding upper works of the discarded structure on her journeys back and forth, she punched a hole in it for a doorway, and let it go at that. This was later in the Summer; for the present the building of a lodge occupied the full attention of them both; and all night, every night, and for the latter half of each day there was a steady sound of tramping and hauling, and plugging, and there were squashy sounds, and thuds, and stertorous breathing as the materials came in and were applied. Mud was pounded down and sticks were forced into the interstices by very efficient hands, and then cut off where they projected. The severed portion was in turn shoved in, and any projecting part again cut off and likewise embedded, and so on until sticks six feet in length completely disappeared into the mesh of the cunningly woven rampart.

They worked with the utmost diligence and perseverance, collecting their material from the lake shore or, grasping a stick crossways in their hands as a kind of shovel, dug on the bottom for mud, and swimming carefully to avoid any loss of their load, landed with it in front of the camp, rearing up on their hind legs immediately they touched bottom with their feet. They laboured steadily and unremittingly, about twelve trips to the hour, marching along sometimes separately, or in solemn procession one behind the other with that resolute, purposeful, unfaltering step of theirs that is suggestive of the march of Time itself.

Jelly made no bones about opening the door, throwing it wide open with the self-assertive sweeping gesture to be expected from her, and Rawhide soon learned to do the same, though in a fashion infinitely more suited to his quiet retiring manner. In time the Boss learned, of her own accord, to open it from the inside also, and I attached a leather loop as a handle for her which she invariably used; but Rawhide would have nothing to do with such new-fangled notions. He always waited patiently for the door to be opened for his exit, although as a matter of fact I subsequently found it a good deal more convenient to leave the door open and be done with it, in spite of the clouds of mosquitoes that poured in.

Eight years have passed since McGinnis and McGinty, the first of all our Beaver People, swam on to their death, since that fatal night when we, Anahareo and I, stood on the shore of a tiny nameless pond and answered to that last, long, plaintive farewell call, and watched the small rippling waves that spread out from them as they went; little waves that made no sound, little waves that said no word, but would have told us of their passing, had we had the ears to understand.

And as I watched all this going on, and observed the satisfaction, if not downright exultation, with which these two applied themselves to their job, I could not but give a passing thought to the pitiful barricade that those poor little creatures had built with so little material in the cabin on far-away Birch Lake, and it struck me how happy they would have been here. Yet had they been present, neither Jelly nor Rawhide would have ever been found, and so I was forced back into the admission that the things that are— are, and cannot be altered, and that if suddenly faced with the necessity of deciding which between the two pairs should be alive, I would have been incapable of choosing. We cannot change the course of events; but we may remember.

Jelly at this time became possessed of a new notion; she conceived the idea of digging up the earth in front of the cabin, as making for shorter hauls and less work, scratching the land, if not to put in a crop, at least to provide for the future. This she had to be dissuaded from doing, after much argument, as she was undermining the cabin. But she none the less succeeded in making a number of sly occasions to persist in this, so that one day on arising from sleep, I stumbled out of the door into a yawning hole which had been dug by the Agricultural Department during the night. Besides this easy-first practice she also adopted the labour saving device of dumping her loads inside the door and pushing them across the floor, so that every morning the resultant mess had to be cleaned out with a shovel and a hoe.

This construction work went on apace, and inside of two

weeks there was a beaver house of pretty fair proportions occupying one end of our residence, and at this time I deemed myself justified in recommending to the National Parks Office that the time was propitious to make these activities a matter of photographic record. In response to my communication, the same operator who had taken the film at Riding Mountain now came in, bringing several men. It was found necessary to tear the roof off the cabin to obtain photographic light, but the work of removing and replacing it was well repaid. Close on two thousand feet of first-class material was obtained, so that quite aside from the records of their more normal occupations, Jelly and Rawhide have immortalized themselves in a number of quaint performances greatly suggestive of the exploits of one, Mickey Mouse.

They were very obliging all during the week of photographic work, though Jelly, with the ebullience of disposition for which she is famous, or notorious, made things at times a little uncomfortable for those present, and she often found herself alone in complete possession of the set, on which she performed her funny war dance.

The camera man had, besides his big machine, a battery of still cameras and other hand machines held in readiness by helpers posted in strategic positions, and he passed from one to another of these, as opportunity offered, snapping, clicking, and winding. The tenseness of the atmosphere occasioned by all this excited the beaver, so that they were at times very erratic, and Jelly on occasion became disgusted with the whole proceedings, absented herself from the set and remained A.W.O.L. for long periods. Only Rawhide seemed to retain his composure, and so I circulated amongst them speaking to them soothingly and giving quietly and often the, to them, well known signal, " A-a-a-ll-r-i-i-i-ght Jelly," — " A-a-a-a-ll-ri-i-i-ght Rawhide," — "A-a-a-a-ll-r-i-i-i-ght Mah-wee." And this monotonous cry so worked on the nerves of the camera man, who being an expert and an artist, was nearly as temperamental as the Queen herself, that he at last took up the cry himself, and presently was heard to pass among his men, muttering, " A-a-a-a-a-ll r-i-i-ght Tommy,"—" A-a-a-a-ll r-i-i-i-ght Jimmy,"—and nobody dared to laugh, either.

I was none too cool myself during some of the proceedings, and sometimes we had the authentic studio atmosphere.

The house was now serviceable, and apparently complete, although the beaver still continued to work on it every Summer, so that at this date of writing it occupies easily a third of the cabin floor space; and this lodge surpasses in stability any of those built by the Three Little Pigs, and is a solid structure into which no wolf, however bad or bold, could ever force his way.

And now the reasons for all this labour were becoming more and more apparent every day. There began to be a change in the demeanor of the beaver.

A great event was soon expected, the greatest event of the year.

Jelly Roll began to be listless and to lay off work, and took to spending longer and longer periods of her time with me, often laying with her head on my knee and would sometimes fall asleep there. She would also creep between my knees as I knelt in the canoe, a position she had adopted in her younger days when lonesome or in trouble. She seemed to need the solace of my sympathy in her condition, and a few kind words or a little petting would cause her to push and squeeze further ahead with subdued sounds of contentment. This was highly uncomfortable at times as she now weighed all of fifty pounds, and when flattened out in the manner of a beaver resting, was about fifteen inches across.

There began to be considerable coming and going, a fetching and carrying, taking place during the night season. The expectant mother spent much of her time digging around the shore line, coming home with small collections of spruce and other roots, whilst Rawhide made numbers of mysterious

s

trips back into the woods, on nights when the wind was right, and in his anxiety, on some nights when it was not, returning each time with a few roots and herbs that he had dug up. None of these were eaten, but were taken into the lodge and stored there. The walls of this lodge, which must have been by now at least four feet thick, allowed for the cutting out of a larger interior accommodation, a process plainly audible.

The beaver had left an opening in one side of their house which gave them entry to the living quarters of their human associates, and the household arrangements were plainly visible. The inner chamber had been raised so that the beds would remain dry and well drained, and no member of the family would take his place there without first having thoroughly squeezed, combed, and scrubbed, in the depression provided for the purpose, all the water from his or her coat. The new dam had been adjusted to heighten the water in the plunge-hole to a level so nearly even with the floor of the lodge, so that should feeble tottering footsteps find the water during the first aimless infant wanderings, the helpless delicate mites could climb out easily, and not perish miserably in the unaccustomed element during their mother's absence in search of food.

A large mat or raft of sticks and brush had been secured outside so as to float over the deep-water entrance to their home. This would serve later as a nucleus to the Winter's feed, which would be held in position by it. Its immediate use, however, was to provide a shelter under which the kittens could dodge if attacked by predatory birds, being unable to dive until three weeks or more of age. Supplementing this were emergency entrances, dug out to afford ready avenues of escape in the event of the main tunnel being commanded by an amphibious enemy, such as an otter or even a hungry pike. Some weeks earlier an Indian had visited me, leaving behind him on his departure a quantity of hay remaining over from his horse's feed. Rawhide had several times been up and inspected this hay, and one night he commenced to remove it. He took it away in good-sized loads, carrying it in his arms and walking erect with it a distance of about a hundred and thirty feet in the water, and that down-hill—no easy task, for not only did his immense bundles prevent him from seeing where he was going, but he was at a further disadvantage owing to the fact that a beaver's frame is constructed for progression on the level or uphill in this attitude, not down. This gathering of bedding, and the fact that Jelly had not showed up lately, apprised me that the looked-for event was about to take place, and one evening near the full of the moon in May, the Month of Flowers, there came issuing from the aperture in the thick walls of the lodge, a thin wailing, startlingly like the cry of a very tiny baby. Another and yet another voice added its weak and quavering contribution to the feeble chorus, mingled with the rather hoarse crooning, mooing and blowing sounds with which beaver of both sexes endeavour to sooth their young. To me this clamor was anything but reassuring, and I felt that it must be rather terrifying than otherwise to the little creatures, to have these deep bass voices well-nigh roaring in their ears. Perhaps after all, the happy father and mother were only telling one another how beautiful their babies were, as is the fashion with fond parents in any walk of life.

Very carefully I peered through the door of this nursery, and became the sole witness to a little domestic drama that could not but arouse the sympathy of any looker-on. Four fuzzy, reddish-brown, perfectly formed little beavers about four inches long, with round black eyes and short rubbery-looking tails, lay helplessly whilst the work-roughened, hand-like forepaws of the mother ministered to their immediate wants. And as she performed her delicate task with soft muttering, there could be already traced in the cries and wails of her offspring, the almost human note of protest which is the first to be developed, and the most familiar, of the many inflections by which a beaver expresses his emotions.

There was indisputable evidence that the father assisted, if not actually at the birth, at least immediately afterwards. Later he crept over to the plunge-hole and effaced himself, sinking beneath the surface so quietly and smoothly that, in the shadowed exit, the exact moment of his disappearance was a matter of doubt. Once outside, his behaviour changed. With loud cries he disported himself, lashing the water with his tail, birling and rolling in the water in an apparent accession of ecstacy, or perhaps relief. He then started on a tour of the lake, and on this journey I accompanied him in a canoe, alone. To one who witnessed his performance there was no doubt but that it was the direct result of the recent happy event within the lodge. And the trip began to take on much the appearance of a watery march of triumph as the excited beast called loudly at intervals, climbed often into the escorting canoe, and rushed precipitately on and off landings, seemingly at a loss sometimes to adequately express his feelings. And as I knelt in the canoe and spoke gently the words and phrases with which two years of close association had made him familiar, I pondered much, and reflected sadly that there were those who would, given the opportunity, deprive him of his life partner and his new-born babies, and heartlessly destroy his entire works and defences on their behalf, built with such assiduous labour. And I pitied the poor, dumb, devoted brute that was my friend, and somehow wished that my joys could be as simple as his, and as unclouded by any concern for the future.

All that night and for many nights after, Rawhide was as busy as the proverbial beaver, collecting and carrying bedding and doing other odd jobs. He even tended the kittens, crooning to them as the mother did, withal somewhat terrifically, whilst she took her opportunities to go abroad and seek necessary nourishment. Even if she did not return for a lengthy period, he would not leave the house during her absence, and when on such occasions the kittens became querulous or restless, his attempts to quiet them caused him to make some remarkable sounds. At times his unselfish submission to the claims of fatherhood was a little touching and was quite one of the most singular developments of this affair.

And once, as we sat and watched and listened, I remembered an incident that had taken place many years ago, when on a trapping expedition in the Abitibi district, before that country was opened up. One night after camp had been made, one of the party had laid in wait for and shot a large female beaver. This was in the Spring of the year, but none of us gave a thought to the helpless little creatures dependent on her, that must now starve. My own reaction, I recall, was a feeling of chagrin that I had not gone out and got the beaver myself. And all that night I had heard at intervals, from the direction of the nearby pond, a sound that I had never before heard, one long wailing note, as of some stringed instrument, oft repeated, searching, insistent. I had asked one of the older men what animal was responsible for it, and he had replied, rather gruffly as I remember, that it was an owl. This I knew not to be true. And in the early morning as we moved out, this peculiar cry still could be heard. I know now what that sound was—the call of a beaver searching for his mate; and I think I know too the reason for the roughly spoken reply given to my question by the old experienced hunter who no doubt knew, as I do today, its true significance. I have seen the care and affection that Rawhide, for all he is a male, lavishes on his young ones, and have been a witness and an assistant to his frantic searching and heard his outcries, when Jelly once was too long overdue. And that haunting sound that I now hear so often, sometimes brings back to me the thought of that night of nearly thirty years ago, when a bewildered lonely creature searched wildly for a mate that he would never see again— calling, calling to ears that never heard him and, when she did not return, did his poor best to tend his helpless little ones, and watched them slowly die.

A period of heavy rains and raw, searching winds caused the father to close the observation hole, both from within and without, so that the new family was not to be seen again for three weeks at least, a period during which they seldom if ever ventured beyond the plunge-hole. In accordance with a policy of non-interference which we very strictly adhere to, we made no attempt to re-open the aperture, and although some valuable data had been obtained, this precaution put a period on my observation of that part of beaver family life hitherto a closed book, and it also added greatly to the difficulties of my task of taming these erratic, capricious, and self-willed little creatures.

CHAPTER THREE

Towards the end of the second week in June, one morning before daylight, I heard the shrill treble cry of a young beaver coming from the direction of the lake. An inspection of the protecting raft revealed three kittens swimming aimlessly around, and herded by their mother into an angle formed by projecting portions of the floating brush pile. I was able to attract them by imitating their cries: The mother made no move to interfere, but reposing in her long-tried human friends a trust seldom yielded by a wild animal, she played with them beside me in the water, rolling over and over on her back with them, holding them out of harm's way as she did so. I picked them up and handled them each in turn, which their parents did not resent. After a short period of playing she manœuvred one of them into a position across her cradled arms, and getting a gentle but firm grip of its fur with her teeth, dived with it. Shortly she reappeared and disposed of another in like manner. Again returning, she nosed the one remaining which I held, experimentally, away from the water. In no wise disturbed she expressed her approbation in the usual beaver manner by shaking her head and body back and forth, and with a few friendly sounds retired, leaving me in possession. It was not long before this became a nightly performance.

Her confidence, however, whilst gratifying, was carried to the point where she once either completely forgot an infant that she had committed to my care in this manner, or else considered him safe until next feeding time. I waited in vain for well over an hour, turning him loose in the water to get warm and hoping that he would go home. But he returned almost immediately and seemed to look to me for protection, bleating contentedly when I picked him up, and it was soon noticeable that when placed in the water, he was unable to submerge sufficiently below the surface to gain the entrance. At length I was obliged to carry the now shivering mite into the camp to be warmed up. He sat contentedly on the blankets performing a miniature and very inexpert toilet, and on again being taken outside he set up a pitiful wailing. This had not long continued before the father appeared, and reaching for the disconsolate little creature, with a low note of recognition grasped him in the manner described and dived into the entrance with him. This occurred on a number of occasions, in each case he appearing soon after the cries commenced and taking his progeny home with him.

Soon the kittens commenced to appear nightly, provided it was calm, and becoming more or less expert were no longer in need of this assistance. Should, however, any of them wander too far and become lonesome or lost, which they frequently did in the early stages, they would send out strident calls for help, and before long one or the other of the adults would appear, from nowhere apparently, and herd the youngsters home. Never at any time during the first month were both parents absent from home at the same time; always one remaining in the lodge to tend the constantly vociferating brood of budding engineers. At the slightest unfamiliar sound, he or she emerged to ascertain the cause of it, inspecting the environs of the cabin and swimming in questing circles with nose held high, searching the wind for strange scents. On being reassured by the phrases and inflections I used for that purpose, they would retire. Loons, ducks, and muskrats, the latter having, up till now, used the alley-way out of the beaver house for the purpose of entering the camp for apples, were chased away in a most determined manner, and learned to give the colony, for the time being, a wide berth. Any visitors who came by canoe were met and the canoe circled, and its occupants treated to a salvo of tail-splashings.

These two devoted souls, besides attending to these important domestic duties, continued their labours on the house, dam, and bank dens, and carried on the work of cleaning out runways and clearing the usual playgrounds, of which they now had several. Often they seemed to be very tired, yet, once the young were weaned and able to eat solid food, no matter how fatigued or hungry the adults were, on receiving the treats we habitually gave them, they would retire into the house with them, and often the sounds of strife over the tidbits of apple or brown bread waxed loud, long, and vigorous. The old people would then come out and take from me their own share of dainties and eat them at the water's edge. Rawhide seemed to take turns with the mother in keeping watch over the kittens, and during the first two weeks of their appearance outside the house one or the other was in constant attendance on them. By the lakeside, a short distance from the lodge, this solicitous parent built a kind of bower of branches, protected on the side and top, but open to the water, and here they would gather, making short sorties from it into the great outside world, rushing back into its shelter on the slightest alarm; and any undue outcry caused one of their elders to put in an appearance at once.

And this solicitude is not always confined to the parents. Any and all beaver domiciled in the lodge (or as in this and many other cases, set of lodges) do their part in the care, feeding and protection of the young, carrying in sprays of leaves for them, playing with them, crooning to them precisely as the mother and father do, and answering distress signals, keeping a watchful eye on them at all times. They will go to all kinds of trouble to avoid injuring them in the midst of their rather vigorous employments, exhibiting a tolerance and a consideration for these sometimes exceedingly provoking little creatures, that might serve as an object lesson in forbearance to more than one impatient human parent that I know; and all this whether they are actually related to the kittens or not.

A case in point is that of the wild beaver who, coming from some distance (the nearest native "aboriginal" colony is at least ten miles from here) to visit us, decided that he liked the place and stayed with us. He has been accepted by the Beaver People, has been with us now two years, is thoroughly tame and an accredited citizen of the place. His initiation took the whole of the first Summer, and at first he would approach no closer than a distance of at least fifty yards. I was plenty bad medicine to him, no matter where I stood; for he is Argus-eyed and misses nothing. Yet when he saw Jelly's brood gathered around me he would overcome, by what must have been a supreme effort of determination, or will power, or whatever you have a mind to call it, his natural inborn deep-rooted, instinctive fear of the Unknown (myself), and dash over from the safety of his outpost and scatter the youngsters, and approaching me within a few feet, threaten me with voice and action, and splash me from head to foot in his endeavours to oust me from the landing. That he was risking his life must have been to him a certainty, but he took that chance to safeguard the lives of these small creatures to whom he was under no obligation to do so whatsoever; and to hear him crooning to them in the softest voice he is capable of, nosing them, or guiding them gently homewards if they strayed too far, would have touched the heart of even the most callous observer. This behaviour, as well as the way he has conquered all his inhibitions and adapted himself to conditions here, as well as his astuteness and his dignity of bearing, and a kind of pride he seems to have, by which he seems to regard me as an equal and no more—all this causes me to look on him with the greatest respect, and I am very careful and punctilious in my dealings with him; for he is above all things, the most sensitive creature in all the world. The young travelling beaver that brought him here has since wandered off, whether to return or not I do not know; but the stranger stays on and seems now to be a fixture.

In order that she might not have to forage far, and so to minimize any danger she might get into in her eager search for the wherewithal to support four other lives besides her own, I made a practice of feeding Jelly in the cabin, giving her boiled rice. She has this portion of rice every day all Summer, but during the nursing period I add a good strong mixture of milk to it. On her first visit after the arrival of her babies, she being unexpected, and in no very patient frame of mind, in my hurry I could not find the milk. After smelling the rice, which she habitually eats plain, she refused it, and followed me around on her hind legs chattering, pulling at my leggings and getting between my feet, all of which did not greatly assist me in my search for the missing can of milk. No sooner did I discover the can than she immediately knew what it was and tried to take it from me, unopened as it was. And when I poured some milk on to her food, having now got what she craved, she commenced picking it up in both hands, wolfing it down ravenously,— quite contrary to her normal delicate and refined manner of eating with one paw. This I considered a pretty fair feat of memory and association of events for an animal, as she evidently expected some addition to her usual diet, although it had been a year since she had had it, under the same circumstances, and for a limited time only.

She does a lot of bustling around as becomes a mother with six new-born babies on her hands, and keeps the trail pretty warm between the entrance to her domicile and the door of mine. The beaver, as I have told you, have constructed a well-built house inside my cabin, entered from the lake by a plunge-hole under the wall nearest the lake, coming out in six feet of water. Thus any sound emanating from this lodge can be plainly heard in any part of the building (*my* building I mean), and as she eats she stops and listens at frequent intervals; and if things do not sound just right, she will rush out precipitately, going right home to investigate, returning, when satisfied, to finish her meal. Rawhide is also very watchful, but he is cooler and more calculating, listening longer and more intently, and not leaving unless pretty well assured that his presence is required. Should he, however, decide to investigate, it is for some very good reason, and when he goes he stay there. He too is much occupied these days, finding tidbits for the mother of his family, collecting bedding, and scouting around. He is very methodical and efficient, and carries his responsibilities with all seriousness.

The difference in character and disposition of these two animals is very marked. Except in his attitude towards me and his self-acquired familiarity with the house, canoe and other of my equipment and arrangements, Rawhide has not changed his aboriginal habits one iota. His diligent pursuance of any course of action he undertakes could be emulated with profit by not a few humans, and his quiet insistence in the carrying out of his intentions would suggest that there is a definite policy behind nearly everything he does. His is the unassuming forcefulness of real power; of them all he is, undoubtedly, the supreme ruler here, and I think that the control of affairs at Beaver Lodge could not be in much better hands. Jelly is more temperamental and erratic, though just as industrious as her spouse. She is at times very demonstrative, and will often leave her work to mingle with any company that may be around. While extremely capable, I have seen her at some slight disadvantage in situations where Rawhide was perfectly at home. This is only another instance of the many that have come to my notice in this work, that too close or prolonged a contact with man impairs, to a certain extent, the natural attributes of any wild animal whose intelligence is of a high enough order to be greatly influenced by it. Some animals may, of course, be trained to suit man's purpose, a project I am not engaged in, but not as a rule without some impairment of the animal's more delicate instincts. Whether this is desirable or lamentable depends on the point of view. In this particular instance the discrepancy is in one direction only, and not so good; for whilst Rawhide can be depended on to take care of himself, Jelly is often too bold and stands in need of protection. Her ability to recognize danger became sadly deranged during the carefree existence she led with me in earlier years, and this protective instinct has largely given way to a very militant curiosity, so that she is now as liable to tackle a bear as she is to run from a mouse—of which infinitesimal beast she has a wholesome and ludicrous fear; and this lack of judgment could easily be the cause of her demise some day.

When returning from her expeditions in search of feed she, ordinarily so leisurely in her movements, can be seen coming in at great speed, hull down, flags flying (I hope these nautical terms are correct), and leaving a wake suggestive of a small launch. Instead of coming direct to me and indulging in some aquatic pastimes or desultory conversation, she now sails by with a perfunctory " ump " and dives into the house as if she had been greased and fired out of a gun. Immediately on entering, with a preliminary shake to dry off her coat, she turns loose her whole vocabulary, and the entire brood seems to spring to attention at the sound of it with loud and shrill vociferations of welcome, or perhaps more likely of famine.

At times, after she has ministered to their wants and is maybe weary, and trying to rest, but is unable to do so owing to the activities of this squirming, squealing pack of little parasites, she scolds, and even whimpers, like some tired and peevish child; and then she seems no longer the grown-up mother of today, but is once again the small wee Jelly Roll of long ago, who has been teased too long by small companions, and would be alone. And then she comes to me, for the solace that has never failed to comfort her in her small troubles since the day when she was very, very small.

Now that the critical period is over, and things are pretty well squared away within the thick-walled lodge that now occupies such a generous portion of the cabin, the grown-ups are able to indulge a little of that spirit of light-hearted gaiety which is in such contrast to their more serious and sedate behaviour, and which is so pronounced a feature of their make-up. They seem to have quite forgotten the other little band so lately gone (which I have not), and nearly every morning, if the weather be fair, just before the sun rises, they stage a little show of diving, wrestling, back flips, and other sports. Perhaps it is for my benefit, as I am the only spectator at that early hour, and often they come ashore and gambol clumsily and rush at me with apparent evil intent, throwing themselves on their backs before me with queer outcries. And so I feel that I am invited to share in this carnival of fun; but as I lack the proper equipment, such as a tail and a few other minor physical details, this is of course impossible. And if I am thus denied a part in this hilarity, I have at least the consolation of knowing, by their invitation, that this brand-new family has not entirely relegated me to the background.

Although slow-growing, the kittens develop quickly and soon learn to follow one or other of their parents on trips for building material, and often on returning from the bush with a load of sticks the latter will find the kittens gathered in compact formation at the foot of the runway, and it is indeed remarkable to observe the extreme care that is taken to avoid injuring them, even to the extent of luring them out into the lake under false pretences, and then going back for the load put down for that purpose.

One evening a fifth kitten, seemingly hitherto overlooked, appeared on the scene. He was identical to the others, and seemed as familiar as they with my presence on runways and playgrounds, and in the canoe. On being called they would come to me, singly or in pairs, sometimes the whole band of them, unless their erratic and capricious mentalities were otherwise engaged and often they would leave the water and scramble around me.

The methods of training used to bring them to this state of domesticity, were similar to those practised on their fore-runners at Riding Mountain, but their accessibility made the work easier and they had become most familiar, actually seeking my company at nearly regular intervals. The wel-coming note which they emitted on these occasions was, in contrast to their usual noisy clamour, so fine a sound as to be almost inaudible, and was made tentatively, at some distance, until a reassuring call was given to encourage them. They would then rush up in breathless haste with arms outstretched to grasp the proffered hand, or run up the board attached to the canoe for their convenience. When the whole family approached together, as occasionally happened, this approach became more or less a race, and was so pre-cipitate that those first up the board often fell in a heap into the canoe, pushed by those behind. The ensuing scramble to disembark stirred up a good deal of excitement, and as they righted themselves after falling back into the water, they engaged in their favourite amusement—that of wrestling. This they did by pairs, floating erect, cheek to cheek and embracing tightly, whilst each strove by desperate use of webbed hind feet and dexterous skulling with flexible tail to overcome his opponent, and all apparently in great good humour. At length one would prevail and the loser, squealing as though in great agony, but really not in the least hurt, would duck his antagonist's hold and dive with a prodigious commotion, which seemed to be the signal for all hands to disappear with loud splashes. The water would subside, and for a short time silence would prevail and not a beaver was to be seen, until a cautious head would appear beneath a broad lily-pad, and raising it, peer slyly out from under it with watchful eyes. One by one heads would appear and the surface of the water become streaked by small v's; squeaks, bleats and whistles of recognition would be exchanged and soon the performance would recommence, and another alarm be given and recovered from, and so on until thoroughly tired and hungry, they would eat quantities of green leaves and go home to rest.

Lately a sixth youngster has been added to this mysteriously increasing gang. He, also, appears to be thoroughly at home under all the strange conditions occasioned by my presence. It is rarely that the entire family is collected together at one spot, and as the youngsters are at present indistinguishable one from another, it is reasonable to suppose that each has, in his turn, been as constant a visitor as the others, and has probably been stealing a march on me this two months past.

They have ceased from making any loud outcry when out in the open, or during their short forays up and down the lake, but when safely inside they throw off all restraint and become very garrulous. The complainings, the acclamations, the pleadings for food, the cries of distress at some fancied wrong and, most touching of all, though not so frequent, the little soft whimperings of affection, can be plainly heard from within the lodge, and are easily distinguished by even those who have had little experience with these child-like creatures. The disciplining of the peevish or greedy ones, the scoldings, and the more soothing tones of the adults, and the shriller and immature but equally expressive voices of their babies, so closely resemble the inflections of the adolescent human, as to somewhat pique the curiosity of those who hitherto believed that it is the prerogative of only man to express the emotions intelligibly through the medium of the voice.

In this efficiently organized and well-ordered miniature household, and in the expertly conducted activities of the working parties, these playful youngsters will receive the training and the education that will fit them to become useful citizens of the Kingdom of the Wild. Until, after a Summer of work and play and training, and a Winter of well-fed safety, they will be fully equipped to strike out for some, to them, far distant land of promise, there to carry on the work for which Nature intended them, and for which she has so well endowed them. When the sun of Spring-time has melted the ice from around the lake shores, and unshackled the forest streams to run deep and free, I will lose my small friends. And, although I will always have my old companions, I will be lonesome. For these talkative, carefree, whimsical and affectionate little beasts will be missed when, swelling with ambition, lured on by promise of adventure, they swim gaily away on the Spring flood. For there will be no familiar crowd to welcome the canoe, no small brown bodies gamboling on the runways; the lake will seem a little empty for a while. Yet they must, in obedience to an unchangeable law by which they are governed, sally forth into the unknown world about them, to carry on the purpose for which they were created.

And each year when the Medicine Winds of Spring have awakened the trees to life and growth, and the forest puts on again its mantle of green leaves, near the full of the moon in the Month of Flowers, there will come another band of little pilgrims to stay a while with me, later to pass on like the winds of yesterday, trooping on in ever-increasing numbers, into the Unknown.

T

IV

The Bears of Waskesieu

WASKESIEU is a tent city situated on the shores of a lake of the same name, a lake the far end of which is invisible to you as you stand on the broad expanse of sandy beach, some hundreds of yards in length, that stretches before this town of tents. The furthest you can see is at a point where the shores taper down from the bold, spruce-clad hills on either side, and nearly meet, forming a narrows only a bow-shot across, and even this point, in the middle distance, is visible only as a long, low line that shimmers in the sunlight of a Summer day. And far off as you may consider this, when you get there you are still only half way up the lake.

Standing on the beach at Waskesieu, you begin to have a faint idea of the real meaning of the word Distance. Thirty miles from the camps, and beyond the distant narrows, accessible only by water, is Ajawaan Lake, where my Beaver People and I have our home in one of Canada's greatest Wilderness playgrounds, Prince Albert National Park.

Far enough away to gain seclusion, yet within reach of those whose genuine interest prompts them to make the trip, Beaver Lodge extends a welcome to you if your heart is right; for the sight of a canoe approaching from the direction of the portage, or the appearance of some unexpected visitors on the mile-long trail that winds through the forest from larger and more navigable waters, all coming to bid the time of day to Jelly Roll and Rawhide and their band of workers, is to me an event of consuming interest. Save for my animal friends I live here quite alone, and human contacts, when I get them, mean a lot, and are important.

The whole region is one vast Wilderness of lake and forest, and you may pass beyond the boundaries of the Park (if twenty-three hundred square miles of country is not enough for you) and never know the difference, and you can go East and West for unthinkable distances, and North as far as the Arctic circle, with little interruption save that provided by the trading posts.

Every Spring the tent dwellers move into Waskesieu, and every Fall move out again, leaving this vast, unpeopled territory to the Mounted Police, the Park wardens, the teeming wild life population and myself. And perhaps the most interesting of all these Summer visitors are the bears. Waskesieu has bears of all kinds—excepting grizzlies—from little fellows of a hundred pounds or so, just youngsters starting out in life, to others that will go six hundred pounds— by no means the largest—just good, comfortable-sized bears, if you get what I mean. There are black ones with red muzzles, black ones without red muzzles, reddish brown, dark brown, and just plain brown bears, and I have seen some that were a rich bronze colour. They are inoffensive, good-natured fellows, who pay not the slightest attention to anybody, and it is no uncommon thing to meet a bear or so walking peacefully along the highway. The streets of the tent city are lighted up at night, but the lights are some distance apart, and it has been suggested that more lights be provided so the bears can see their way around and not get scared stiff by having people bump into them in the dark. They forgather around the various cook-shacks in groups of half a dozen or more, nosing around among the scraps that the cooks throw out for them, acting towards each other with an unfailing courtesy which it is very elevating to observe, and politely ignoring the sightseers, who are getting the thrill of their lives and who, at a distance of about twenty feet, get all the bear pictures they could ever wish for. Some of these bears, the bigger ones, are regular visitors every year, and must be nearly worn to the bone from being photographed.

There is a seventy-mile highway between Prince Albert and the tent city of Waskesieu, that runs bang through the bush for the last forty miles of its length, and there is a spot, near the resort, where a she-bear and her cubs (one of those ferocious she-bears we hear so much about) will wait for cars, and if you stop for them the entire family will come over and beg for tidbits in the most barefaced fashion. This, of course, rather discredits a lot of good old-fashioned traditions concerning bears, but the occupants of the car get quite a kick out of it, and can truthfully say thereafter that they are able to look a bear in the face.

Some of the younger set, among the newer bears, before they become thoroughly acquainted with the regulations, indulge in some rather ill-considered pranks, such as entering unoccupied tents and falling asleep there or getting their heads in garbage cans and having to be extricated, and a lady of my acquaintance entered her camp to find in it what she thought was a large black dog, who was making himself very much at home, and who regarded her entrance with supreme indifference. Somewhat nettled by this cavalier behaviour, the lady administered a severe drubbing to the intruder first with the flat of her hands and then with the broom, only to discover of a sudden that it was no dog at all, but a middle-sized bear, who behaved with admirable restraint, and allowed himself to, so to speak, be swept out of the house.

Yet another had, during his wanderings, been unchivalrous enough to annex a pair of ladies' shorts. He played with them awhile, but there was no kick in them, and quickly tiring of the pastime he moved off to fresh adventures. However, his claws had become entangled in the material and he could not detach it, and every so often he would stop and try to shake it loose, sometimes standing erect to do so, waving the offending piece of apparel at arm's length above his head, like a flag. He went through the most extraordinary contortions to rid himself of his encumbrance, and his evident embarrassment at his inability to remove it was highly diverting to onlookers. Eventually the garment flew high in the air and landed on the branch of a tree, and the bear, greatly relieved, looked at it fixedly for a moment and kept on going.

Then there is the one who is said to have attached himself to the hotel, and every day, at a certain hour, he would walk most unconcernedly into the kitchen. He being rather a large bear, the staff would walk just as unconcernedly out. Arrangements were always made for his accommodation, the odd pie and so forth being left out for him to eat, in order that he would not burglarize the premises. Having eaten he would walk out in a state of the greatest gratification, and the staff would then walk in, also with a good deal of satisfaction, and not without some feelings of relief. So everybody was quite cheerful about the whole business.

Sometimes a store-house gets broken into, but this is generally by the lower, and less educated type of bear. No real harm is intended of course, it being really the fault of the night watchman who omitted to leave the door open. However, no bear who knows his onions, or has at least a grain of self-respect, will do this, it being more ethical, and also a deal less labour, to beg his meals at the cookery.

There is a report comes from one Summer resort (not Waskesieu!) that certain bears, wrongly accused of wilful damage and being victims of misunderstanding by the grown-ups, have been caught playing clandestinely with the children. How far these misunderstood bears would go in their endeavours to make themselves better appreciated is problematical, but probably no further than to take whole parties of youngsters on their backs for rides into the country.

Your bear is really a good fellow, and will eat most anything that you give him, or that you may inadvertently leave lying around, just to show you that his heart is in the right place. He has a humorous outlook on life, and a few minor depredations should not be allowed to detract from his character. He expects you to be very broad-minded; and why not? That bears sometimes break open provision caches and take out bags of flour, scattering the flour all over about a half an acre of land and rolling in it, proves nothing except that bears are playful in disposition and like to roll in flour. I will admit that a bear who behaves in this manner should be severely reprimanded, but a judicious display of several quarters of beef, or choice hams, or a few jars of honey tastefully arranged so as to catch the eye (leave the jars closed, the bear will open them himself quite easily), will divert the bear's attention and prevent this sort of thing, for the time being at least.

Seriously, these bears give rather an atmosphere to the place, and are considered by most of those who see them, to be one of the chief attractions there. Some few timorous souls might not perhaps relish the idea of meeting a whole troop of bears on a main street, but for every one who doesn't, there are twenty that do. The bear is the clown of the woods, clumsy, and often a thief, but he is amiable enough if not abused; and it says a good deal in his favour that with bears in some numbers constantly present around the resort at Waskesieu, apart from certain ludicrous and quite harmless incidents, there has never been an accident.

Animals are very quick to appreciate a sanctuary when they find one, and will become very tame in a short time, minding their own business so long as the human being minds his. They seem to enjoy the novel and interesting entertainments that the place affords them. There are several foxes, very beautifully coloured in black and silver-grey and red, who have adopted this Summer camp ground for a head-quarters. Although naturally great travellers and given to ranging far and wide over large areas, these enterprising creatures spend most of their time at the resort, and once I was treated to the sight of a fine silver-grey mother fox and her four half-grown puppies, all black as your hat, who stood beside the road and watched me pass them. In the Winter they make regular visits to the cabin of the interpreter and guide attached to the Mounted Police, one Wally Laird, where they find food and a welcome and above all, a little kindly understanding when they feel the need of it—and it would be just too bad for the man who would try to do them harm.

My visits to Waskesieu are infrequent, and I know little of what takes place there from year to year, so it was with some surprise that I saw, walking quietly among those gathered there to see them, a little drove of deer. There were five of them stepping daintily and gracefully along in Indian file, seeming to pick each step, springy and effortless of gait, wary and alert, wild, free creatures of the Wilderness, swift envoys from the Silent Places, emissaries from the far-flung Kingdom of the Wild. A man said " They are the real thing."

And he was right; they were.

Some time before this there had been a tame deer who practically lived at Waskesieu. He has since passed on, some say from an overdose of tobacco. No, he didn't smoke it, but some animals are very fond of it and eat it, and this one was, so I am told, something of an addict. One evening when he saw a lady going for a walk along the beach, he thought it might be a good idea to go too. So he accompanied her. Being acquainted with this particular deer she raised no objection, and they walked along together, on the beach. Presently the lady, becoming tired, sat down. So did the deer. Rested, the lady decided to return home and rose to her feet. But the deer, apparently, was not yet ready to go, and pushed her down again, more or less gently, and lay down beside her. After a decent interval the lady attempted to rise once more, only to be again forced to a sitting position by her escort. This happened a number of times until, fearing to anger the animal, the woman remained where she was, with the deer beside her. As long as she remained sitting down everything was all right; this deer was not going to allow any lady to walk out on *him*. And she didn't, not until a party of her friends arrived, when the deer surrendered her quite amicably, and walked back to Waskesieu along with the rest of the folks.

These deserters from the rank and file of the furtive folk who dwell in the Wilderness that surrounds Waskesieu on every side, must be something of a pain in the neck to the regular troops who, following the old traditions, remain back in the hills, no doubt viewing this defection from accepted custom with the sternest disapproval. But they do nothing about it, and the number of recruits to the ranks of these mutineers increases year by year, and there is a not so remote possibility that eventually they will have to be included in the census.

V

All Things Both Great and Small

THE sun has set on Ajawaan. The moon shines palely down upon the still surface of the water, and in the lonely forest the shadows of the great trees fall big and dark.

And all around is Silence, the Silence of ten thousand years of waiting, the mighty Hush of a timeless, changeless Purpose.

Ajawaan; a small, deep lake that, like a splash of quicksilver, lies gleaming in its setting of the wooded hills that stretch in long, heaving undulations into the North, to the Arctic Sea. Its waters day by day reflect its countless moods, and the ever-changing colours of the sky; to-day a perfect shadowgraph of the surrounding woods, unruffled, lucent and jade green; to-night, silver in a flood of moonlight, and at the end of every day, crimson with the glory of the sunset.

At its edge there stands a small log cabin, Beaver Lodge, my home. An unpretentious place, built just as I designed it, to be more or less a replica of the House of McGinnis, that faraway Winter camp in Temiscouata which was the beginning of all things, the Empty Cabin of the Tales I lately told you. This Beaver Lodge is not only my home; it is the home, too, of my Beaver People and is the gathering place of many other creatures, denizens of the forest that encircles it on every side. They are of all shapes and sizes, these shy, elusive Dwellers among the Leaves who have broken the rules of all the furtive folk, and have come from out the dark circle of the woods to stay with me, some permanently and others from time to time. They range all the way from the small, black, woolly beaver-mouse who goes hopefully around wondering when I am going to leave the lid off the butter-dish, to the great moose, as big as a horse and having, in the proper season, antlers three feet and a half across,[1] who, an intermittent but fairly regular visitor, does some of his heavier thinking while standing outside my window.

Though living quite alone, and far from the haunts of my fellow-men, I am seldom lonely; for I have but to step outside, and it is not long before some little beast, bedight with gay caparison of flaunting tail, or smart display of tuft or coloured stripe, goes racing by and seeing me, or hearing my low call, comes to see what I may have for him. For it has not taken them very long, these smaller fry, to discover where I live, and to find that no one ever leaves here empty-handed. The bigger beasts are not much influenced by offerings of food, as theirs is usually abundant and easily come by, but pay their visits more, apparently, for the companionship they find here; as does a woodsman who goes occasionally to town to share in the small excitements of the place.

But some of the bird population are more practical, being swayed by considerations of an economic nature; and they make no bones about it either, especially the whiskey-jacks, those companionable, impertinent grey brigands who appear, soundlessly like ghosts from nowhere, at the first stroke of an axe or first wisp of smoke from a camp fire. Chiselers and gold-diggers of the first water, they contrive to make themselves welcome by an ingratiating amiability that may, or may not, be counterfeit. Their antics are amusing and they provide considerable light entertainment at times that might otherwise be dull. A man feels that their companionship at a lonely camp fire is worth a few scraps of bannock or meat, until he discovers that they want, not part of his lunch, but all of it. But these lads are pertinacious to a degree that is unbelievable, and if they do not get as much as they expected they will sit around on branches

[1] This is the moose described in these pages, in the story entitled "Lone Bull."

with a kind of sad, reproachful, half-starved look about them that causes the inexperienced traveller to make further and handsome contributions for very shame.

The two original whiskey-jacks who were attached to this spot when first I came here, have called in off the endless, empty streets of the forest, all of their kin who resided within a reasonable distance, say about five miles, judging by the number of them. This assembly of mendicants follows me around closely on my frequent tours of inspection, wholly, I fear, on account of what there is in it for them, and my exit from the cabin with something in my hands, supposing it is only an axe or an empty pot, anything at all, is the signal for piercing outcries from watchful sentinels who have been waiting patiently for hours for my appearance, they calling loudly to their fellows the bird-equivalent of " Here he is, boys! " When I stop they gather on branches on all sides, regarding me alertly, solemnly, or wheedlingly, according to the disposition of the individual, whispering meanwhile confidentially among themselves. And as they sit in mock decorum, dispersed among their various vantage points, a direct and steady glance nearly always discomposes them, causing some to turn their heads away—whether as a disclaimer of any ulterior motive (they would steal the eyes out of a brass monkey), or from a hypocritical desire to appear not too eager, I cannot attempt to divine. Perhaps they have the grace to simulate some slight feeling of shame at the means, little short of bare-faced robbery, that they are adopting to satisfy an insatiable and very undis-criminating appetite; in which case this assumed diffidence does not prevent them from keeping a keen weather-eye on every move I make, and they readily observe morsels thrown to the ground behind them, or otherwise supposedly out of sight, and are able to detect a single crumb that would be invisible to the eyes of more honest folk. Most of them have learned to alight on my extended hands, and will sit there picking daintily at their portions, while others will dive at me like attacking planes and seize their share in passing. Gourmands and thieves they undoubtedly are, but they are cheerful, good-natured pirates and good company withal, and these engaging rascals have a pleasant, plaintive little ditty that they sing, as if to please the hearer, but which I gravely suspect is but a siren song used only to charm contributions from reluctant prospects.

They will go to almost any lengths to gain their ends, and I once saw one of them, dislodged from a frozen meat-bone by a woodpecker (a far stronger bird), waiting with commendable patience until the red-head should be through. However, the woodpecker was far from expert, and using the same tactics on the bone that he would have employed on a tree, he pecked away with great gusto, throwing little chips of meat in all directions, thinking them to be wood, only to find, when he got to the heart of the matter, that he was the possesser of a clean, well-burnished, uneatable bone. This pleased the whiskey-jack mightily, for at once appreciating his opportunities, he hopped around among the flying scraps of meat and had a very good lunch, while the unfortunate woodpecker, who had done all the work, got nothing.

Birds of bright plumage are not common in the North, and the woodpecker, with his bold, chequered patterns and crimson-tufted head, provides a welcome note of brilliance on his short, darting flights from tree to tree. And he dearly loves a noise. To keep the beaver from cutting down some of the best trees near the cabin, I have been obliged to put high, tin collars around the bases of them, and these are a godsend to the woodpeckers from all over the country, who amuse themselves by rapping out tinny concerts on them with their beaks. It has long been my custom to be up and around all night, going to bed at daylight, but no sooner am I settled when, at the screech of dawn, the woodpeckers commence a rattling tattoo on the tin. The result is a clangorous uproar to which salvos of machine-gun fire would

be a welcome surcease, and in the midst of this unholy
pandemonium I am expected to sleep—sometimes succeeding, and sometimes not. This diabolical racket takes me
somewhat back to my earlier trapping days, when I had no
clock, and in order to ensure my early rising, I used to freeze
a piece of meat solidly into a tin dish and set it on the low
roof of the shack, directly above my head. At the first
streak of daylight the whiskey-jacks would hammer on the
frozen meat, creating a clatter in the tin dish that would wake
the dead. I believe I can claim to be the sole inventor of
this very serviceable alarum; and it had one great advantage
not shared by alarm clocks in general, that when the weather
was bad it remained quiet, as the birds didn't show up, or if
it was snowing heavily the sound was deadened, and I knew
then that I didn't have to get up.

Near the cabin there lives a mama woodpecker. In a
hollow tree she has a nest, with young ones in it, who keep up
a continual monotonous chattering which is going on just
as stridently when I get up as it was when I went to bed, and
I think never ceases. They have very penetrating voices
which never seem to tire, and if at any time there is a public
demand for bird voices that are guaranteed never to wear
out, they would have an excellent future on the radio. The
jetty black-birds, very black indeed, with bright carmine
patches on their wings, give another note of colour, but the
most resplendent of all my bird guests is a humming bird.
He is a tiny, lustrous little creature, and his feathers are so
very miniature that they seem like tiny scales, and in his
tightly-fitting, iridescent sheath of opal, emerald and ruby
red, he seems more like some priceless, delicate work of
Chinese artistry, than a living thing. For a short time only
he stays, hovering among the wild rose bushes, his wings
winnowing at an incredible speed, so as to be a nearly
invisible blurr until he darts away with almost bullet-like
velocity, a brilliant streak of fabulous coloration.

For several years now a brood of partridges has appeared

here in the Spring. The owls get a few, but most of them survive, greatly owing to the militant defence tactics of their mother. Ducks and snipes and other waterfowl and even singing birds with nests upon the ground, will feign disability, and retreat as though badly injured, and so appear an easy prey, hoping, with pathetic optimism, to draw an intruder away from young or nest. The partridge (or if you want to be meticulous, the ruffed grouse) will do this too, but far more frequently will attack even a man with reckless bravery, flying in his face with shrill battle-cries or rushing at him with outspread wings, hissing like a snake—truly, an exhibition of determined courage that should win the little bird a meed of admiration from even the most callous. In the Winter, her brood long gone to parts unknown, she stays around, sleeping warmly in a tunnel in the snow at night, and in the daytime, if it is not too cold, stepping daintily about the yard. If the weather is cool, she alternately puffs out and flattens down her feathers, so that she looks to be inflating and deflating as she walks, appearing to be first a bird, all sleek and smooth, and then a feathered football going forward on spindling, inadequate legs. She had a habit of feeding up in a good-sized poplar near the house, year after year eating the buds from it all Winter. She always picked on the same tree, until at last the tree gave up, and now is dead.

Today an eagle swept majestically above the camp, flying very low, the beat of his great wings loud and portentous in the still air. He checked a little in his flight as though minded to stay awhile; but he changed his mind and kept going on his way. I had not seen him for two years, though his nest is not over a mile from here. An eagle is the only bird that I have so far noticed who turns his head from side to side and looks around him as he flies, and this one looked back and gave me a look of keen appraisement as he passed.

And now, of a sudden, I hear behind me a light, but furious trampling, and a squirrel hurls himself through the

air and lands on my back, and clambering to my shoulder he
snatches from my fingers the pea-nut I always have for him.
Precipitating himself onto a shelf arranged for his accommodation on the wall of the cabin, he expertly shells his pea-nut
and there eats it. He sometimes does this for a visitor, if in
the mood, and whilst on his shelf keeps one very bright eye
keenly on the donor. Most of his kin that visit me are
content to hull the nuts, but he is more fastidious, and skins
them too. Like all his kind he lives at the rate of about a
hundred miles an hour, and when seen is always in a state of
delirious activity. This is Shapawee, The Jumper. Vastly
different in disposition and unusually sedate, is my little
friend Subconscious, so named because, when quite young,
he would enter the camp and roam around without apparent
object, like one in a dream, or under the influence of his
subconscious mind, meandering aimlessly around. He was
the only squirrel I have ever met who walked, most all
of the others moving at nothing less than a round gallop.
Subconscious is more leisurely, and very gentle in his ways,
one of the very few who have permitted me to handle them.
He used to spend most of his day around my feet, monopolizing my time, and when I cut wood he stuck around
and different times narrowly escaped being chopped or cut in
two. He was on a fair way to becoming a nuisance, when
one day he ran across the top of a hot stove. Then he came
no more. I mourned him for dead, and missed my merry
little companion who had become almost like a familiar
spirit. The yard looked a little empty without him, and his
familiar trails and vantage points became snowed under,
or were used by other and less interesting specimens of his
kind. But this Summer he has returned, and is as gentle and
friendly as ever, though he has evidently learned something
of the ways of the world during his wanderings, as the
appearance of another squirrel, regardless of sex or size,
transforms him immediately into a little termagant.

During the absence of Subsconscious, I undertook to tame

another of these flying acrobats and succeeded up to a certain point. Then a third offered himself voluntarily as a candidate (with reservations), so that I now find my footsteps dogged by three of the, to each other, most unsociable, irascible and pugnacious bundles of dynamic energy ever forgathered together in any one place—three minds with but a single thought—to do unto others as they would be done by, but to do it first! Each considers the environs of the camp as his personal property and will fight at the drop of the hat, or less, any of his breed who dare set foot on, or even breathe, in his chosen territory. The squirrel is not a gregarious beast, and these territorial rights are pretty generally respected. But I am afraid that I have somewhat upset the regular balance of things by my well-meant attempts to arrange that a good time is had by all. This difficulty I have endeavoured to adjust by feeding each one in his own small district, but have failed signally. Most of what they get is not eaten, but is hidden away in tree tops, crotches of limbs and such places, and on each cache being made the owner issues a long, quivering screech of defiance to all the world. This challenge, instead of driving away possible robbers, under present circumstances only serves as an advertisement, and attracts the attention of the other two of this militant triumvirate, who both know what it is all about. Their appearance on the scene precipitates immediate battle, the aggrieved party being always the aggressor and launching himself at his opponent as though to annihilate him on the spot. But the prospective victim is not there when his assailant lands, being already well on his way, and a lively chase ensues, carried on with shrill skirrings and chatterings of rage, and at a devastating speed. The intruder, however big, seems to feel the weakness of his case, always giving way before the onslaught of the proprietor, irrespective of size. I notice that the pursuer is always careful not to run any faster than the fleeing enemy, so that they keep always the same distance apart, and the duel is never brought to an issue; showing that they possess not only valour, but also the discretion that is said to be the better part of it.

One day Shapawee and Subconscious appeared simultaneously, one on each side of me. With some misgivings I gave them a pea-nut apiece, keeping them as far apart as possible—but they saw one another! Each at once assumed a most ferocious aspect and glared at the other with manifest evil intent. And of a sudden both turned and ran in opposite directions as fast as they possibly could, each thinking the other was behind him. It is all very harmless and entertaining; no blood is spilled and it is doubtless good exercise. And meanwhile the remaining squirrel, the whiskey-jacks, and other non-combatants, make a Roman Holiday with the caches that are being so valiantly defended. Whilst not gifted to the extent that some other creatures are, squirrels are by no means unintelligent. They have good memories too, recognizing me immediately among strangers, even after an absence of a year. It is to be noticed, too, that they will test all cones dropped by themselves from the tree tops, to see if they are good, before laying them away for Winter provision, and will bury the duds separately, out of the way, to avoid mistakes. Their strength is quite disproportionate to their size; I have seen a squirrel with half of a large apple in his mouth, jump without noticeable effort up and onto a root projecting out from a fallen tree, twenty inches above his head—equivalent to a man leaping ten feet into the air with a bushel of potatoes in his arms.

Once a family of muskrats lived under the flooring in one corner of the camp, having reproduced an almost perfect replica in miniature, of the domestic arrangements of the beaver. They were docile little fellows, and they learned to come to my call precisely as the beaver did, and frequented the cabin with the same freedom and lack of fear, save that they were not strong enough to open the door themselves. However, they would pull at a loose board until it rattled

U

loudly, and stand chittering outside, with the greatest impatience, until admitted. One of them, when I fed the beaver tidbits, would sit humbly by waiting for his share until the bigger folk were done, and whenever I called the Mah-wees (young beaver), he thought he was Mah-wee too, and would come helter-skelter through the water along with them. Unlike his fellows he associated with the beaver, except with Jelly Roll, who was jealous of him, and if noticed by her, he would make himself, if not invisible, at least as inconspicuous as possible; though when the young musk-rats first appeared out in the open, and were sometimes abroad under the guardianship of this one (as with beaver, muskrats of both sexes help take care of the young), Jelly Roll would swim beside them, exhibiting great interest, and make no hostile demonstration towards him. But if he was alone she would chivvy him around as often as not. These interesting and intelligent little rodents should not be called " muskrats," as they are not rats at all, but are first cousin to the beaver, whom they much resemble in appear-ance, habits and disposition. I had good company with them for several years, but much to my sorrow, a periodical epidemic which they, like the rabbits in the woods are subject to, killed every one of them. And I often wonder if their little ghosts do not sometimes swim on Ajawaan, and haunt the small, well-kept home they had, where they had been so happy while they lived.

There was a wood-chuck, a special chum of mine, who year after year made her home under the upper cabin, where she had every Spring a brood of wood-chucklets, or whatever they are called. She was an amiable old lady, who used often to watch me at my work and allowed me a number of privileges, including the rare one of handling her young ones. But if a stranger came, she would spread her-self out so as to quite fill the entrance to her domicile, to keep the youngsters in, and when the stranger left she would emit shrill whistling sounds at his retreating back, very sure that she had frightened him away. She too has gone, her time fulfilled, and another has taken over her old home; a well-built, very trim young matron who stands up straight and very soldierly before her doorway, and tries to look in windows.

I must meet these losses with what equanimity I can muster, without vain regrets. Yet I miss these old-time friends of so long-time standing, each a small, humble presence that has entered, for a little time, my life and then passed on.

People having the dim, distorted ideas that are held by so many concerning animals, can gain very little insight into their true natures. Each animal has his separate personality, easily distinguishable to one who knows him. Among the more highly intelligent species no two individuals seem to be alike, each having an individuality all his own. Their ways are often so extraordinarily human, and this is especially true of the rodents. They seem at times so rational, their movements are often so much to the purpose, and their actions, and their manner of expressing their emotions sometimes so childlike—the little side-glances, the quaint and aimless gestures, their petulance if unduly annoyed, their artlessness and lack of guile, their distress when in some small trouble, their so-evident affection for each other—I have never ceased to regret the thousands of them I destroyed in earlier days. Even then I never enjoyed killing them, preferring to find them dead, refusing to visualize the hopeless struggle, the agony, the long hours of awful misery. And today I feel that however great the inconvenience they may put me to, it can never pay the half of what I owe them. Only those who have suffered similar tortures can have any conception of what trapping by present methods really means to the animal population of the woods.

Perhaps you, whom I am trying to entertain, find these thoughts a little serious. But this life I lead lends itself not only to watchfulness, but also to heedful observation and deep thinking. Remember, reader, that those who live within the portals of the Temple of Nature, see far into things that are outside the scope of ordinary existence. There is a kind of sanctity in these forests of great trees that makes me think of dim cloisters in old, vast cathedrals in England, and causes the ceremonious pomp and the sonorous insincerities of not a few theosophies to seem cheap and tawdry in comparison.

Owing greatly to the ignorance, thoughtlessness or intolerance of many who come in contact with them, some really harmless creatures have been saddled with a reputation for evil that they do not deserve, and are penalized accordingly. All that most of them need is a little sympathy, and most of all to be let alone to mind their own business. Though I must admit that sometimes this " business " is a little ill-judged, as in the case of the skunk who took refuge in my store-tent, sleeping there regularly, and who repaid my hospitality by having, in amongst my provisions, a family of kittens, or pups, or skunklings—or is it skunklets? This was no doubt an oversight and no harm was intended, I am sure, and everything turned out all right, and no one was a bit the worse off for it. The skunk is really a natural gentleman (or lady), but unfortunately is not a mind reader, so he cannot always gauge with accuracy your intentions towards him when you bump into him suddenly in the dark. Usually they (your intentions) are hostile, and he acts accordingly, but he is slow to anger and of monumental patience; and his feelings must be badly outraged before he will turn his battery on you. Meeting him in the moonlight is sometimes startling, for then his long, white horizontal markings and white cap are accentuated and, the rest of his coat being black, are all that can be seen; so that as he turns quickly this way and that with supple movements, he looks at first like some darting white snake with a venomous head. But he is an inoffensive, happy-go-lucky beast with a fixed idea that human beings like to find him in tents, camps, and out-

houses, and under the flooring of summer cottages. Even
so, finding a skunk in the store-house is not nearly as inconvenient as discovering a moose in a canoe; and I once
had this interesting experience, although I hasten to add that
I was *not* in the canoe at the time. It was on shore, drawn
up, awaiting my early departure that day for Waskesieu,
thirty miles away and all by water. As I was making my
preparations I heard, outside, a sort of light crackling,
crushing sound, and looking through the window saw my
friend the moose (previously mentioned) walking slowly,
steadily, and very thoroughly, through and along my canoe.
I rushed out of the cabin at him, shouting, and this seemed to
remind him of something, so he extricated his feet from the
various holes, where they must have felt most uncomfortable,
and stood aside, surveying the wreckage with an air of rather
thoughtful detachment. Now this was nothing but rank
carelessness on his part, and I remember having a distinct
feeling of annoyance about it. Granted that he was a
youngish moose, and perhaps didn't know much, the fact
still remains that a canoe is a very handy thing to have
when you have a thirty mile trip to make, entirely by water.
A moose is rather a terrific object to have around, being
about the size of an overgrown horse, and it is as well, if
your visiting list includes one, not to leave any breakables
around where he can walk on them. So in all fairness I
must take some of the blame for this affair, for not having
carried the canoe up a tree in the first place and secured it
there. So, forgiving the moose, I placed the injured craft
up on a rack, intending to mend it, where, in this unusual
position, it became an object of intense interest to the beaver.
One night these enterprising animals, with the high intelligence for which they are celebrated, carefully felled a large
tree across the long-suffering canoe, reducing it to the very
best of matchwood.

None of these guests of mine stand in any need of gifts from
me. With the exception of the beaver, who came with me,

they fended for themselves before I arrived on the scene and if I were to suddenly disappear, though they might disperse, no one would be a whit the worse; though I like to think that some of them would miss me. But it makes me happy to put out treats for them, and to take note of the so very different way in which each one takes his daily portion from my hand; to observe his manner of approach, and his reactions afterwards. It is great fun in the morning (or at noon in my case) to wake up and find everything gone, and to know that small forest people—and sometimes big ones—have been busy whilst I slept, running back and forth with all they can possibly carry with them of my bounty. It pleases me immensely to hear some hungry worker who has been absent for hours on a working party, mumbling his satisfaction as he eats a well-earned meal of dry bread, or an apple, or steps into a dish of rice with both hands at about a mile a minute; and in Winter I view with the deepest satisfaction a hole in the snow beneath an old root, maybe, with a tell-tale ring of rime around its rim, revealing the home of some happy little beast who has a full belly and is fast asleep.

Every one of these so-busy dwellers in the Wild Lands presents intriguing possibilities, and has a life history well worth a little patience in the studying. Even those that live in the water, or on it, and are therefore more difficult to cultivate, have an interest that is easily discovered by a little investigation; all the way from the water beetles, that leave their natural element and climb on rocks to sun themselves, to the proud, white-throated loons, greatest and most accomplished of all the diving birds, who run races round and round the lake with the most inordinate splashing and other uproar, and play a kind of water-leapfrog, driving the beaver to distraction with their weird, half-human laughter. These royal birds, however, cannot walk, but are strong fliers and real artists in the water. When they take their young ones out for exercise—there are usually only one or two—the wee, jet black chicks sit upon their mother's back,

getting a free ride while they look around in the most com-
placent manner at the scenery. Though they receive
visitors, and I have seen as many as eight of them swimming
before the cabin together, these stay only a short time, and
each lake, unless a large one, provides a home for only two.
And here they play and fish all Summer, winging South in
early Autumn and returning every year for a period of their
lives, which some say to be a hundred years. It seems
probable that, like eagles and wild geese, they mate for life,
and in support of this supposition is the fact that the same
pair has lived on this lake every Summer since I came here,
and I do not know how long before. These two know me
very well, though the female is not so intimate with me as the
male, who always visits near the cabin very punctually,
soon after daylight every morning, and holds a conversation
with me at a distance of a hundred feet or so, very noisy on
his part, and quite unintelligible to me, and he hails me with
a not unmusical fanfare of recognition when he sees me pass
in the canoe. He is a splendid bird, and besides being highly
ornamental he is very useful too, giving out a loud, unusual
call should anything uncommon, or a stranger, appear upon
the lake or in the timber near the shore.

Every one of these creatures has his proper function, and
each, however apparently useless, serves well the purpose for
which he was created. Even diminutive birds, negligible
appearing denizens of these wide solitudes, have their own
appointed place to fill. Seemingly quite superfluous in the
vastness of the mighty scheme about them, yet as they hop
happily in little groups among the fallen leaves, seeking the
wherewithal to maintain their tiny lives, competent, wise,
and bright-eyed and very much at home, who that watches
them will question their right to be, or doubt but what they
also do their part?

Animals quickly know a sanctuary when they find one.
How, I cannot tell; something in the atmosphere of the
place perhaps, or some kind of telepathic divination all wild

creatures seem to be possessed of, may account for this; nor is this sixth faculty of sensing the presence or absence of danger confined to animals alone. While some need time in which to figure out the situation, others will respond almost immediately to my advances, depending on the disposition or intelligence of the individual. Take an instance of the latter case; the time is evening, on a day in Autumn, two years ago. I look out of my window and see a deer feeding in the glade upon a knoll beside the camp. I open the door without sound, unhurriedly; with quiet, easy movements I step out, smoothly, but without any suggestion of stealth. The deer tenses in every muscle, raises his head and stares at me—almost an unseeing stare, you would think. But a squirrel passes swiftly, and inaudibly because the leaves are wet, and with a sudden shift of his eyes (but not his ears) the deer acknowledges the slight, momentary flicker of the tiny beast's passage—he is watching all right; he sees very well indeed. He swings his eyes back into line with his ears, to me. I speak softly, soothingly. Now he flicks his tail—that is the sign; his mind is made up—either he will bound with high, rocking leaps out of sight, or he has decided to accept the situation and stay—which? I speak again, advance a little towards him, talking to him. Then, he relaxes; the stare becomes a gaze and, supreme gesture of confidence, he turns his back on me. He reaches down for some jack-pine shoots a squirrel has obligingly dropped there from the tree-tops, and nibbles at them, looking at me casually from time to time. He is satisfied. I have made another friend.

Seldom am I without one or another of my dependents, even though they are not always visible. The crash of a new-fallen tree, or a shrill outcry of adolescent beaver voices from the lake, may disturb the sleeping echoes. The door is thrown open and a load of mud and sticks comes in, borne in furry arms and intended as materials for the earthen lodge that stands inside my cabin; then a light pitter-patter across the floor, as a muskrat calls in for his nightly apple; comes the rattle of antlers among the willows—these sounds, familiar to me as are street noises to a town-dweller, tell me that I am not, after all, alone.

This region, like any other Wilderness, has its population of predatory animals, and I must be for ever on the watch to safeguard my fellow-citizens from harm. Wolves, coyotes, bears, owls and mink and weasels are all potential and very active enemies; nocturnal creatures who can operate in the daytime with the same facility that they do at night, furtive, sly and ever-hungry, could slip silently in to deal out death in a moment of time, and be quickly gone. So I have not spent a night in bed in years, and during all the hours of darkness I travel back and forth through the velvet blackness of the sombre, whispering forest. And as I traverse these imponderable halls of Silence, there comes not a sound that is even faintly audible, but my ears will register it. For these are all the sounds there are to hear. Each has its meaning, which I must determine swiftly and with unerring accuracy; for on the acuteness of my senses and the precision of my findings, may depend the lives of those who look to me; for as I heed their danger signals, so do they mine.

So that my life has become something like that of a scout of ancient days of forest warfare, and even if asleep, any unusual sound from the surrounding woods, an unwonted commotion in the beaver house, or even the abrupt cessation of some familiar noise, brings instant wakefulness. Danger lies hidden in the lurking shadows, waiting for the day when the high-tuned senses of my retainers, or my less perfect ones shall be at fault; yet not without due warning can it ever strike. The wood-chuck who haunts my wood-pile, and who should be sleeping, whistles sharply, for no apparent reason, into the night; comes the discordant warning cry of a whiskey-jack, the sudden alarmed scurry and subsequent shrill defiance from a safe retreat of a squirrel—then, softly, the muffled hoot of an owl who, in his downy, sanctimonious robe of white, like the robber-priest of some false religion fattening on the community about him, broods rapaciously above them like an evil spirit—or, a breath of sound, a flicker that is quick as a flame, the sinuous, reptilian slither of a weasel, small but deadly, swift, lithe and ruthless— gangster and cut-throat par excellence of all the Wilderness. Either one I must destroy at once; there will be no second opportunity.

Later, perhaps, as I listen, the precise, dainty stepping of a deer ceases for a moment, to break into a series of startling leaps; a nearby moose, visible to me by the light of the moon, pauses suddenly in his browsing to catch some seemingly non-existent sound, or to sniff a warning from a vagrant current of air; from the lake the cry of a loon, pitched at an uncommon note, off-key a little, weird and alarming, strikes a jarring note of discord. And then, most portentous of all, shattering the night like a rifle shot, there crashes out the appalling detonation of a beaver's tail-slap on the water— and then falls silence, ominous and nerve-racking, surcharged with menace, as every living creature within earshot stops motionless in its tracks, crouched, or in an attitude of suddenly arrested motion, its senses keyed to an excruciating pitch of sensitivity, waiting for someone to make the first move. And then I see shifting, wavering like a disembodied spirit through the shadows, unsubstantial as a phantom, the ghoul of all the forest lands—a wolf!

And then, if the moon is right and I line my sights quickly enough, and above all, if my calculations are cool and accurate, the smashing report of my rifle will end the incident and save many a day of anxious uncertainty.

And all these things that may be seen and heard, and other things that may not be even heard, but are a kind of feeling, advise me more positively than the spoken word, are as clear to me as lines of print, telling me how it fares with my Little People, and the big ones too, reminding me, sleeping and waking, of my responsibilities towards all things both great and small that within, without, and all about, dwell here under my protection.

VI

At Dawn

EVER greyer and more grey grew the landscape as I sat motionless beneath a venerable jack-pine at the water's edge, awaiting what a new-born day might bring.

He who would probe deeply and intimately into the secrets of that hour and mystery that, like a half-world, hangs just within the realm of unreality, will not gain his ends by early rising. Better by far that he sleep not at all; for let him step his sprightliest, his faculties, numbed a little and dulled by slumber, will lack something of keen alertness and sensitive perception.

During that dim hour between the passing of night and the coming of daylight, all of the Wild that has the power of locomotion is abroad. Creatures whose gift it is to pursue their labours during the hours of darkness have not yet retired to rest, and those whose conscious life is spent in the more generous effulgence of the sun have awakened to a new activity. Sounds have more penetration and are audible at greater distances than at other times, scents and odours are more pungent and hang heavy in the early morning air, proclaiming with certainty the presence of an enemy, or food. Birds and beasts that are seldom to be seen or heard at any other time, now carry on their appointed tasks and indulge in play and pastimes with a feeling of security that either the brilliance of full sunlight or the obscurity of night fails to give them.

This is an hour of mystery, of strange sights and unaccustomed sounds, when the eye and ear are tuned to their highest efficiency. No impression, however fleeting, escapes the perception of senses keyed to a hair-trigger delicacy by the tonic properties of this magic hour. There are no shadows, and on the flat perspective of the middle distance, objects that would melt vaguely into the lights and shades of noon-day now stand out in sharp and definite outline. The faint echo of a broken twig in the dry brule,[1] the swiftly changing contour on the side-hill that is a deer, the soundless flight of a pair of whiskey-jacks, spectral in the half-light, are recorded instantly and without conscious mental effort.

And so I sat silent, motionless beneath the fan-topped jack-pine, and waited.

The Aurora had long since ceased its danse macabre, and across the face of the paling sky there moved in slow and stately procession lines of clouds, battleship-grey.

Behind me was an enchanted world of twilight forest, where the portentous silence was broken by no sound, save the occasional drip of dew from the leaves. On its floor one would have moved in a kind of pale translucence, as in some dim ocean cavern, where common objects loomed crouching, indistinct and shapeless, and the fronds of scattered clumps of undergrowth hung like queer aquatic-looking plants, in this green and liquid pool of murky light.

Above my head, somewhere in the jack-pine, a white-throat commenced his carolling. The first few plaintive notes stole out into the silence tentatively, as though seeking a response, and, being answered, broke forth courageously into a full volume of song. Ever increasing in numbers, the feathered choir joined in the litany of joy and praise for the gift of a new day, until all around the air seemed full of harmony.

As the light increased a fog rose above the water, and lay thinly in folds and layers with openings in between. Out from this I saw, swimming towards me along the shore-line, a creature that had all semblance of some dark

---

[1] Burnt-over country, with new growth. Of French origin.

amphibious reptile, with a large head and a long sinuous body. Its back was ornamented with a row of excrescences such as are seen on a floating crocodile, and was divided into small, close-fitting segments, giving it the appearance of a jointed wooden snake.

Now being the hour of spells and witchery, I regarded this apparition with some interest. On its approaching within range of my unobstructed vision, it resolved itself into nothing more dangerous than a mud-hen leading a parade of ten tiny black chicks, who swam behind her in file, following faithfully the weaving course of their parent with serpentine exactitude. Almost immediately there came the sudden heavy thudding slap of a beaver's tail on the water, and the entire family disappeared abruptly beneath the overhanging alders; nor did any sound or ripple from then on betray their further presence.

At the warning sound a kitten beaver, that, tired with a night of small explorations, had fallen asleep in the warmth of my two hands, scrambled hastily down to the water and also disappeared. The last lingering echoes of the tocsin of alarm had barely died away before the originator of it himself appeared, and with a deep prolonged mumble of greeting climbed ashore and performed an unconcerned and very elaborate toilet.

The weird and ghoulish cachinnation of the grey owls, they of the Shining Beak,[1] had not yet ceased, and at intervals broke forth into an indescribable tumult, an unearthly sound, suggestive of the unholy laughter of a crew of demons, or the obscene revels of a band of monsters. This discordant clamour disturbed the beaver not a whit, but the sharp " chuck," as a flying squirrel, not yet abed, landed expertly on the bare trunk of the pine behind my back, caused him to take the water with one movement, in a neat, clean dive. The direction of his line of flight was marked

[1] So called by the Indians on account of his white shiny beak. This bird laughs hideously in certain seasons.

by a row of tell-tale bubbles, evidence that he had not been seriously alarmed, as in cases of real emergency these animals are able to so arrange their manner of retreat that the air is not allowed to escape from the fur. By what means this is accomplished I have yet to determine, but it is probably connected in some way with the manner of using the tail, as it is only from a spot just above this appendage that these bubbles rise. The little grey rodent still clung flatly to the bark of the jack-pine, his gliding apparatus still spread out, so that he looked to be about six inches square; and as he stared out of his big round night-eyes, I doubt if he even saw me. He had volplaned from the top of a lofty tree about forty feet away, and I had noticed that the last twenty feet or so of his flight had been flat, with a distinct upward trend towards the end of it. The sound he made had been slight, but the beavers had become unusually wary of late, and with good cause. Not many days ago a she-bear with two cubs had dug up several bees' nests within a stone's throw of the cabin; and only the morning before a lone coyote had shown himself, cantering effortlessly along just within the border of the woods lining the far shore of the lake; a grey, lean, furtive beast, slipping unobtrusively along, flickering wraith-like between the tree trunks.

The cabin was visible from my point of vantage, and at the door I had placed a piece of apple, my usual early morning offering to a red squirrel that lived near by. He had not yet appeared, and presently a muskrat, ears, eyes and nostrils alert, with many backward runs and false alarms, trotted up to the door, seized on the booty and scurried away with it, no doubt considering himself well rewarded for his perilous sortie. Presently the squirrel for whom the offering was intended would come for his accustomed tidbit, and finding it gone would scold shrilly and rush madly about, breathing anathema and searching for imaginary enemies.

Within the near-by beaver lodge the murmur of voices

and other strangely domestic sounds had died down, and
the feeble infantile wailing that had commenced at feeding
time, for the juveniles, had also subsided. Above the water
a flock of terns performed their evolutions with swift swooping and shrill cries, and a pair of loons swam by on their
regular morning round, so close that their red eyes were
plainly visible. The male gave vent at intervals to a low
plaintive note, not unmusical, and not to be heard at any
great distance. Noble birds they were, with their white
breasts and alert, independent bearing. They saw me and
checked momentarily, watching me curiously, and I had a
good look at them. The female had a young one with her,
jet black and not much bigger than a chick partridge, that
sat upon her back and viewed from there the scenery with
great self-composure. The light mist that for some time
had hung over the water, had by now disappeared; and the
surface of the little lake, before so smooth and glassy as
to be scarcely distinguishable from the void above it, now
became blurred in streaks as some finger of a breeze touched
its face, and the leafy crowns of some tall white poplars,
pink with the first high-flung shafts of the coming sunrise,
fell into an iridescent fluttering. The slim and limber,
graceful aspens that stood out upon a little point, commenced
to bow and nod and gently bend and sway, as the song of the
morning wind whispered in their foliage. Beneath the
sombre arches of the forest of evergreens, lights and shadows
formed and fell apart, and as the bright places became
brighter, so the shadows were the darker; whilst far above
the heavy canopy of fan-like limbs, the towering spires of the
spruce, tipped with carmine, stabbed the sky like crimson-
headed lances.

Down from the North, headed for the big lakes, a company of pelicans, blood-red in the glow, winged their
unhurried way just clear of the tree-tops. They moved in
echelon, and held their course in precise and orderly array.
These birds seem to have evolved a great economy of labour

in their method of progression by flying and gliding alternately, so that they rest half of the time and must be able to go on indefinitely. This change in the manner of using their wings occurs at regular intervals, and is accomplished without the slightest change in speed or formation, and with no loss of elevation during the gliding process. The leader sets the stroke followed by the next in line, and each picks up the " step " successively from the one ahead of him, just fly, then glide: fly and glide. This disciplined conduct is marvellous to behold, and, like most of the expedients which Nature has devised to promote the safety or efficiency of its children, is the result of countless ages of evolution and strict adherence to the gospel of the line of least resistance. Purposeful, undeviating and tireless, they pursued their chosen route and soon were gone.

Abruptly the sun, that had been smouldering behind the rampart of the hills, blazed up in flaming brilliance.

The sudden tap and rattle of a woodpecker drummed a startling reveille.

The Wilderness was awake and about its business.

x

VII

The Keepers of the Lodge

FOR the past two months I have been trying to write a book.
Whether it is a good book or not I leave you to judge. But
if it isn't, I can give you a number of very good reasons why.

About the best of these is a bumping, banging, thudding
noise, accompanied by wailing, screeching and chattering
in what sounds like a foreign tongue from some obscure
corner of the earth's surface. This is caused by a number of
beaver of assorted ages from one to seven years, expostulating with each other over the ownership of a pile of stove-
wood that I have, in a weak moment, left before the door of
Beaver Lodge. The wood is mine of course, but this in no
way lessens its suitability for material to be added to the
already impregnable defences of the beaver house that has
lately been built a short distance down the shore. The only
real difficulty seems to be that of deciding who is to have the
honour of removing it. There are sounds of strife, sounds of
anguish, sounds of outraged sensibilities, and sounds of
supplication. When a beaver wishes to be heard, he is not
without the means. Up to three years, the age of maturity,
each generation has an intonation all its own, and every
individual has a different voice. As a tribe, or race (or
whatever division they come under), they step heavily, pound
violently, haul, push and heave vigorously, and are fanatically
determined in the carrying out of any project they have
decided, at all costs, to complete. Hence the noise, which
is unspeakable, unthinkable, indescribable and unsupport-
able. These are good words; I got them out of a book.
But there were not enough of them; they do not begin to
tell it.

I try to concentrate, to marshal my ideas for your approval. There is a fresh sound, a loud clattering as of a tin dish being thrown with monotonous and devilish persistence against a stone. I am trying to write about beaver, but begin to feel a good deal more like writing something vivid about a bull-fight. So, I put down my pen and go outside. I see at a glance that I am a little late; the wood is nearly gone. It appears that while the second and third generations have been squabbling over who is going to have all the wood (the fourth is too young to do much but squall), the first, or largest generation has been quietly getting away with most of it. They are moving up and down, one coming and one going, with that clockwork regularity that makes two beaver engaged in transportation work look like an endless chain. I like my food cooked, but not at this price; it will be cheaper to eat it raw. So I push the remainder of the stove-wood into the lake, so that there will be no further discussion. This makes a difference, the difference being that the fun will now take place inside the cabin. Three of the yearlings, finding themselves temporarily unoccupied now that the wood is satisfactorily disposed of, come bustling in through the door, bringing their potentialities for mischief along with them. They wander around for a while, peering into every-thing, fairly dripping with curiosity and exuding wilfulness from every pore, eventually entering into a spirited contest over the remains of a box of apples, with the usual sound-effects. Having pacified these highbinders and bribed them, with an apple apiece, to go away, I pick up my pen and resume my work, although I have not yet been able to deter-mine the cause of that exasperating tinny clattering; the only tin dish outside is the one used to hold the beavers' rice, and it is still in its place, full and intact.

I have just got nicely started when, in the middle of a word, there comes another sound, a kind of a rich, satisfying sound, as of some keen-edged tool of tempered steel cutting into very good timber; it also sounds not unlike a beaver's teeth going into a canoe. I put down my pen, go out and investigate. It is, indeed, a beaver's teeth going into a canoe. You see, an overturned canoe looks a little like part of a tree, and offers the same excellent opportunities for idle teeth; the canvas looks something like bark, is the same colour and comes off as easily, with the nice, interesting sound mentioned above. Of course, even if you are a beaver, you can't eat green paint and canvas, but it's great fun and you can always spit out the paint. After a short altercation I put the canoe on the rack out of reach, soothe injured feelings with an apple, and go in again. I pick up my pen and complete the unfinished word.

I write uninterruptedly for perhaps fifteen minutes. Then commences that infernal clattering again, as though someone were dropping a tin plate repeatedly on the hard ground. It is now broad daylight, so I take my observations through the window, and am enlightened. A beaver of the third generation, old enough to be effectively mischievous, is alternately lifting and dropping on the ground the tin dish of rice. Those of the younger beaver who haven't yet learned to eat out of a receptacle, are content to dump the rice out on the ground; they can get at the rice easier that way. They then throw the dish in the lake, to join a number of other articles, besides dishes, that they have consigned to a watery grave. But this fellow has another notion, apparently. I watch the process interestedly. He picks up the dish with his teeth, keeping it right side up, and tries to walk away with it; he wants, for some reason best known to himself, to take the whole works home with him. The container is large, and he is not a very big beaver, and as soon as he stands upright it overbalances and falls. He picks it up and tries again, and it falls again, and so on, so many times to the minute. I begin to count them. The clang of the now empty pan seems to amuse him, and he keeps experimenting, until at last he discovers the way. He finds the point of balance, stands erect with the dish in his mouth, and placing both his hands under it to support it, starts to march down the incline to the lake. Seeing my dish about to be sacrificed I rush out, whereupon the young scallawag slides down the slippery approach and throws himself, dish and all, into the water. The pan rocks for a moment or two and sinks. The beaver birls round and round in the water, in celebration of his success, and also disappears, and I am left in complete possession of the empty landing.

This is a pretty fair example of the perseverance of these animals, who will try every possible means to accomplish their ends, until they have either succeeded, or proven the project to be impossible.

And I think you will agree that any man who will attempt to write a book whilst surrounded by a number of these exceedingly active and industrious creatures, can claim to have learned from them at least the virtue of patience. And this is no idle alibi, for at the moment, even as I write, a full-grown beaver has just burst open the door and entered, bringing in, as an addition to the beaver house that stands here beside the table, a stick six or seven feet in length. And it is no unusual thing for beavers, walking erect with loads of mud supported in their arms, to pass around my chair on their way to further plaster this house within a house, and not infrequently I am obliged to cease my work, lift the chair out of their way, and stand aside until their job is done.

* * * * *

Of all the natural laws that govern this Universe, or that part of it with which we are acquainted, there is one that, although it may not at times seem to be very rigidly enforced, is in the long run inescapable—the Law of Compensation. It has caught up with me here, and is exacting the usual penalties. Having, against Nature's express decree, succeeded in partly eliminating from the mentality of a number of wild animals the natural fear that is their only safeguard, I must now afford them that protection myself. So that I no longer spend my nights in sleeping, but unceasingly patrol

the scene of their activities all the hours of darkness, resting
only in the forenoon. And as it is not unlikely that the
beaver will live as long as I do, it seems highly probable
that I will spend the term of my natural life doing penance
for my meddling, in this topsy-turvy fashion.

The beaver, in their immunity, have become over bold,
and instead of disappearing from view at the first unusual
sound, and abolishing themselves from the landscape as
though they had never even existed, they now stand waiting
curiously to see what they are to run away from, long after
their less cultured brethren would have been in the lake,
sunk and out of danger. The cuttings are often far from
water, and ever I must haunt the beaver works, armed
against possible and very probable marauders such as bears,
wolves, coyotes, and even great horned owls that might try
for a straggling kitten. And as the mediaeval watchman
passed along the streets of cities calling, "All's well,—All's
well," so, as I go, I take up my own monotonous cry, "A-a-a-
all r-i-i-ight,—A-a-a-all r-i-i-ight." This is my signal and
identification, and well known to them, and without such
utterance I never venture forth, so they may know that
any unannounced approach is not I, and therefore dangerous.

One night, on checking up, as I do almost hourly, after
an intensive and widespread search I could find neither hide
nor hair of Jelly Roll. Bears are numerous here, and tragedy
lurks always threatening in the shadows. Unable by any
means to find her, I decided to remain at my original stand,
and commenced to send out certain searching calls such as she
only would respond to. Patiently, but with growing uneasiness, I sent out my S.O.S. at intervals, casting the beams of
a powerful electric torch in all directions. I kept this up for
some considerable time and was beginning to feel the least
bit anxious, when all at once I felt a tug at my leg, and turned
the light downward to see standing at my feet, erect and
looking up at me, the missing Jelly Roll. She was bone dry,
and beginning to be impatient, and must have been there all

the time. I didn't blame her for being out of patience, in a way. No doubt she and Rawhide, figuring that they own me, talk me over between themselves, and I had a feeling that this fresh stupidity of mine was, to her way of thinking, only one more example of my lack of culture and training; and I sometimes imagine that they both must be at times a little disappointed in me, after all the trouble they have been to, getting me into shape.

I have sat beside her on guard whilst she, confident in my protection, tired and weary with her working, slept in the moonlight that flooded the mouth of a runway. This often happens, and as she lies there with her head on my knee as in the old days, making soft murmuring noises in her dozing, she is no more Queen of the Beaver People, but is just Jelly the old-timer—the Tub. If I move she will clutch at my clothing to keep me there, and make sounds I hear from her at no other time. And then her voice is like a muted keyboard that runs the gamut of her emotions, recording every slightest variation; or like some delicately balanced instrument on which impressions come and go, swiftly wavering back and forth, even as her rich, dark fur mirrors the gossamer touch of every imperceptible, tiny breeze that stirs it ever and anon. And when I look down at the ugly body, unlovely till you see the eyes, I cannot but think that beauty may not be all in form, but may rest in strength, in grace of motion, in symmetry and rhythm, and in fidelity, and in a harmonious conformation to an environment.

Despite her affection and the disarming innocence of her softer moments, Jelly Roll is the most self-willed creature in all the world. She knows what is forbidden, and constantly attempts to outwit me; but on being caught red-handed, as she nearly always is (she is the most guileless, transparent old bungler imaginable when it comes to artifice), she flops down and flounders around in an apparent agony of fear, though she must know that she has nothing to fear but my disapproval and reproach, to which she is very sensitive indeed. On being comforted (a little later, of course), she will jump up at once and start to frolic; yet the lesson is not forgotten—not that day, anyway. This edifying performance has by now become perfunctory, and through long practice is now more or less automatic, and she assumes her abject pose immediately I appear on the scene of her misdoings, as though to have the unpleasantness over with as soon as possible. A scolding from me puts her in the greatest misery, but a peremptory word or two, or an overt act, from another, causes instant and sometimes very active hostility. She has a strong instinct for protection towards her young, as has her partner. This is a trait possessed by most animals but, like some dogs, she goes further and without training of any kind, stands with threatening attitude and voice between a stranger and myself, should I happen to be lying down. However, if I am standing up, I can darned well take care of myself. She herself has no fear whatsoever of strangers, and will face any crowd, and go among them, inspecting them and taking charge with the most unshakeable aplomb.

She still polices the estate, as before, and should someone unknown to her be in the canoe she quickly gets to know about it, and knowing that I will not allow her to approach the canoe too closely when someone else is with me, she will play sly and swim beneath the surface, bobbing up suddenly alongside from nowhere at all with a deep, explosive grunt, not always of welcome. She cannot climb into this high-sided canoe unless her diving board is attached, but she will stick pertinaciously to the canoe, swimming underneath it, getting in the way of the paddle and doing everything possible to retard our progress; failing this she will escort the canoe ashore in the hopes of getting a chance to investigate the newcomer. This intention I must of course frustrate, as my guest will have only my word for it that she does not mean business, or that taking a leg off him is not her idea of good clean fun. Her perception of what is going on about her is very keen; she undoubtedly knows what it is all about, and takes a lively interest in many things not supposed to be of interest to animals. So also does Rawhide, though in a less obvious manner; yet on occasion arising he shows a matter-of-fact familiarity with many things about him, that his indifferent and sphinx-like demeanour would seemingly have left him unconscious of; evidently a keen observer in a quiet way. His self-possession, steadiness of mien, and unchanging equanimity of bearing are in direct contrast to the varying moods of his temperamental consort. At times genial, almost affable, withal somewhat of a busy-body and stuck into everything, there are occasions when Jelly Roll carries about her something the same air of disapproval one detects in the presence of a landlady with whom one is a little behind with the rent.

On his visits to the cabin Rawhide acts exactly as if he could not hear the radio, even closing his purse-like ears, as beaver are able to do in order to exclude water, shutting them tight against any programme of which he does not approve. But Jelly takes in this machine the almost feverish interest she has in anything new, standing sometimes stock-still, listening, with hands and fingers making queer aimless little movements, a stiff, brown column of intense attention. During one broadcast she was present at, the characters in a play became engaged in a fight and one of them was killed. The sounds of battle had a strong effect upon her. Her eyes began to stare, her hair became erect and she commenced to blow loudly. On the woman of the cast falling unconscious, the resulting uproar had such a strange effect on her, and she stood so stiffly and unnaturally, and showed, in the unmistakable way she has, such a strong disapproval of the whole business, as to be rather alarming. She began to weave and totter back and forth, and I wondered if she too were not about to faint—though actually she had more than half a mind to join in the conflict. So to save the radio from being wrecked I gave her an apple and broke the spell. She is still a paper addict, and I keep in the cabin for her special convenience a bag full of nice crackling papers, the very sound of which drives her frantic with joy, and this she always looks for in its accustomed place on her visits. These occur, in fine weather, almost hourly, and whilst on deck she likes to stir things up; she weighs all of sixty pounds, and can stir up very effectively when so minded, and her entry into any gathering that may be assembled here, injects into the proceedings all that feeling of delightful uncertainty that one has in the presence of a large fire-cracker that is liable to explode at any moment.

She has often stolen papers of some value to me, and gets all the envelopes from my correspondence, which is considerable. She has a preference for periodicals, as the advertising pages are on stiffer paper than is the reading matter, and they can be induced to make a more deliciously exciting noise, and when she gets hold of one of these she is beside herself with happiness, shaking her head back and forth as she walks out of the door with it, her whole person emanating triumphant satisfaction. Once, at the request of an onlooker who thought that her patriotism should be tested, I placed before her three separate magazines, Canadian, English, and American. After giving each one a searching examination, she chose the Canadian periodical and walked out with it. The visitor was rather taken aback, and still believes that I made some secret sign to her that she acted on. Pure accident, naturally, but the effect was quite good. Sometimes the sober Rawhide joined in these escapades, a few of which were positively uncanny, had they not been so utterly ridiculous. Here's one that would have knocked Baron Munchausen for a loop. (A loop, reader-across-the-sea, is a circle, a cipher or a nought). Beaver like to have dry cedar on which to exercise their teeth, it being nice and crunchy. As there were no cedars in that particular area, I took a bundle of shingles that had been left over from the roofing of my new cabin, and left them down on the shore for the beavers' use. Next morning

I found that the fastenings had been cut off and neatly laid
to one side, and the whole of the shingles removed. I
wondered what was the purpose of this wholesale delivery,
until, the next afternoon a man came to see me, who wanted
very much to see the beaver at work. It was a few minutes'
walk to the beaver house, and as we drew near to it I noticed
that it had a strange appearance, and arriving there we, this
man and I, stood perfectly still and stared, and stared, and
stared—one side of the beaver house was partly roofed with shingles!
At length my visitor asked in a hushed voice, "Do you see
what I see?" I replied that I did. "Exactly!" he agreed.
"We're both crazy. Let's get out of here." We retired,
I remember, in awe-struck silence, went to the cabin and
drank quantities of very strong tea. I asked him if he didn't
care to wait and see the beaver themselves, and he shook
his head. "No," he answered, "I don't believe I do. I'm
not long out of the hospital and just couldn't stand it, not
today. Some other time——" and went out of there
muttering to himself. The explanation is of course quite
simple. Beaver will seize on any easily handled material
they find, and make use of it for building purposes (this
includes fire-wood, paddles, dish-pans, clothing, &c.), and
seized on the shingles at once, and being unable to push the
shingles, owing to their oblong shape, into the mesh of the
structure, had just let them lay there on the sides of the house.
But the star performance, in its implication of the burlesque,
was one of Jelly's very own. One afternoon, shortly after
the affair of the shingles, I heard a woman's scream, long
and piercing, from the direction of the beaver dam. Beside
the dam ran the trail that led to my cabin. Now Jelly is a
real watch-dog when I am not around, and at that time,
in her younger and less judgematical days would lay in
ambush, waiting for people so she could chase them (a
practice since abandoned), and thinking she had caught
somebody in her ambuscade and was scaring them to death,
I hustled down to the dam to see about it. I found there a

woman, evidently badly frightened, who exclaimed: "Do you know what I have just seen?—a beaver going by with a paint brush!" "A who going by with a what?" I demanded. "A *beaver* going by with a *paint brush*!" she affirmed. "Oh, I know you won't believe me, but that's what I saw." Accustomed though I was to the hair-brained exploits of these versatile playmates of mine, this rather floored me, so I simply said, "Oh!", and led the woman to the cabin. I left her there and went to the stump on which the man who had been painting the new roof had left his paint brush. Sure enough, it was gone, removed by busy fingers whose owner was always on the watch for something new. So I told this to the lady, and the matter was explained. But it never was explained to me why, later in the evening, I should find laying at the foot of the stump, with the fresh imprint of four very sharp incisor teeth upon it, the missing paint brush. Why was it returned? Your guess is as good as mine.

And reader, believe it or not, all during the latter part of this last paragraph, a beaver of the third, or inexperienced generation, finding that his efforts to open the door have been persistently disregarded, has been trying to get in through the window. It will I think, be cheaper, in the long run, to open the door. I have opened the door, and there are three beaver; I'll be seeing you later, reader.

To resume. Today there were a large number of visitors here. The moose, a great bull with his antlers half developed, but for all that wide and formidable-looking enough, obligingly stalked down within a distance of a few yards and had a look at the crowd. They also, with mingled feelings, had a look at him. But Jelly Roll, after all the complimentary things I have written about her, let me down rather badly. Having demolished a chocolate bar offered her by a lady, she turned her back on the entire assemblage, took a branch I proffered, smelled it, threw it to one side, launched herself into the lake, and was no more seen. This behaviour is not usual with her. In fact, at times she is rather difficult to get away from, and is one of those ladies who do *not* take " No " for an answer. She is very self-assertive, and has no intention of being overlooked when there is any company around or anything especially good to eat to be had. At these times she is very much to the fore, assuming a bustling and extremely proprietory manner, and whether excited by the presence of strangers or on account of the reward she has come to know that she will get, or from sheer devilment, I cannot pretend to say, but she will very often stage a little act. She first inspects, one by one, the visitors who, by the way, are seated well out of the way in the bunk—she thoroughly enjoys a taste of good shoe leather—and if pleased, which she generally is, she commences her show. This consists in trundling back and forth the bag of papers, the removal perhaps of the contents of the bag, with resultant rumpus and mess, the replacing of sticks removed by me from the beaver house for that purpose, and various other absolutely unnecessary evolutions. And all this with such an air of earnestness and in such breathless excitement, and with such manifest interest in the audience and such running to and fro to them between the scenes, that those present could be excused for supposing it to be all for their especial benefit. We have, of course, a slight suspicion that the anticipated reward may have some bearing on this excessive display of histrionic ability. But a good time is had by every one present, and that is all that really matters. Speaking to her conversationally attracts her instant, if casual attention, and often elicits a response. She has come to understand the meaning of a good deal of what I say to her; but this faculty is not confined by any means to her alone. The beaver is an animal that holds communication by means of the voice, using a great variety of inflections, very human in character, and the expression and tone indicate quite clearly to human ears what emotions they are undergoing; and this resemblance makes it fairly easy for them to understand a few simple words and expressions. I have made no attempt to train them in this, or in anything else; everything they do is done of their own free will, and it has all been very free and easy and casual. I do not expect them to knuckle down to me, and I would think very little of them if they did; nor do I let them dominate me. We are all free together, do as we like, and get along exceedingly well together. Rawhide I know, for one, would not tolerate for a moment any attempt to curtail his freedom or to curb his independent spirit. He is rather a solemn individual, and he ignores nearly everything that is not directly connected with his work and family. Yet even he has his times to play, and carries always about him an undefinable air of " howdy folks and hope everything's all right and it's a great world." The obstinacy of a beaver when opposed by any difficulty, also applies if you try to get him to do anything against his will, but personal affection has a great influence on their actions, and given sufficient encouragement and a free hand they will learn, of themselves, to do a number of very remarkable things quite foreign to their ordinary habits. Rawhide, for instance, has learned to kick open the door when walking erect with a load in his arms. He built his house inside mine, and will climb into a canoe and enjoy a ride, as does his life partner. Jelly Roll is able to open the camp door with ease from either side, pushing it open widely to come in, and making use of a handle I have affixed to the bottom of the door to get out again. And as the door swings shut of itself, she has succeeded in creating the impression that she always closes the door behind her, which is all to the good. Though he rarely answers me as Jelly does, Rawhide listens closely, with apparent understanding, when I talk to him, and dearly loves to be noticed, often rushing up to me when I meet him by chance on a runway, and clasping my fingers very firmly in his little hands. But his old, wild instincts are very strong in him, nor do I try to break them; and he has not bothered to learn very many of Jelly's tricks, being, it would seem, quite above such monkey work. But he will come at my call, when disposed to do so, and can be summoned from his house upon occasion, he selecting the occasion.

In the more serious matters, however, Rawhide plays a more notable part, being direct in all his actions, and rather forceful in his quiet way, and in family matters is something of a martinet. For instance, he took a strong objection to Jelly Roll sleeping in my bed, at a time when they lived together with me in the cabin. She had been always used to sharing my bed and no doubt expected to keep it up all her life. But when he would awaken and find her absent from his couch, he would emit loud wailing noises, and come over and drive her away into their cubby-hole. To see him pushing her ahead of him, she expostulating in a shrill treble of outraged sensibilities, was about as ludicrous an exhibition as I have ever seen, and when with childish squeals she would break away and rush to me for protection from this unwelcome discipline, her wonted dignity all gone, she would stick her head in under my arm and lie there like the big tub she is, imagining herself safe but leaving her broad rear end exposed to his buffeting. And this ostrich-like expedient availed her very little, for Rawhide is about the most determined creature I ever knew, and always gained his point. And from then on, not wishing to be the cause of further family discord I discontinued my habit of sleeping on the floor.

But don't get the impression that Jelly only plays and never works. She does both with equal enthusiasm, and can be a play-girl and a builder-upper at the same time—one of those dual personalities we hear about. Jelly, when on labour bent, fairly exudes determination. She will arrive at a runway under a great head of steam, and on striking shore there is no perceptible pause for changing gears; she just keeps on, out, and up, changing from swimming to walking without losing way. Her progress on land is not so much a

walk as it is the resolute and purposeful forward march of a
militant crusader, bent on the achievement of some important
enterprise. Her mind made up, without further ado she
proceeds immediately to the point of attack, and by an
obstinate and vigorous onslaught will complete in a remarkably short space of time, an undertaking out of all proportion to her size. She accepts my occasional co-operation
right cheerfully, but being, as she is, an opportunist of the
first water, instead of making a fair division of labour she
sees her chance to get that much more work done, and
attempts to haul sticks of timber or move loads that are more
than enough for the two of us, attacking the project with an
impetuous violence that I am supposed, apparently, to
emulate. Her independence of spirit is superb, and her
bland disregard of my attempts to set right any small
mistakes I think she has made (a practice I have long ago
desisted from) show her to be the possessor of no mean
superiority-complex. She is pretty shrewd and misses no
bets, and belongs to that rare type of worker who finds the
day all too short for his purpose.

For a resting-place she has a little, low pavilion backed by
a large fallen tree and roofed with spreading spruce limbs.
This bower looks out upon the lake, and in her spare time
here she lies and gazes out across the water, and heaves
long sighs of pure contentment. I have often caught her
talking to herself in a low, throaty little voice, which on my
approach would drop to the deep-toned sound of welcome.
Beaver are the most articulate of any beasts I know of and
perhaps I can best describe the sounds they make as being
very nearly those I imagine a child of three would utter, if
he had never learned to talk in any language; and Jelly
Roll's attempts to make herself intelligible to me are often
quaint and childlike, and not a little pathetic. Rawhide is
not nearly so talkative as some, and is much given to working
apart from the others, and this self-abnegation is characteristic of most heads of beaver families. Although he takes

kindly to the circumstances of his new surroundings and has, in his own quiet and unassuming way, adapted himself very thoroughly to camp life, he retains nearly all the characteristics of a wild beaver in so far as his work is concerned. He looks with a jaundiced eye on my attempts at assistance, and is expert beyond the power of even Jelly to attain to; whether as a result of his early training, or because the female is naturally more care-free, does not appear. On the rare occasions when he rests, he will sometimes share with Jelly her piazza, and with both of them my approach to this retreat is always acknowledged by some small sound of greeting, and is often the excuse for a frolic or even one of those rare sentimental spells, absurd but touching evidence of an affection that seems so firmly rooted yet is so deeply submerged, save at infrequent intervals, by the demands of a vigorous life. Though not very demonstrative, Rawhide has his softer moments too, and in a way that seems so very humble, as though he knew that Jelly had some method of expression that he can never have but does the best he can. But this is only when everything is properly squared away and he has time on his hands. For he is methodical in this as in all his ways. And if he does permit himself a little space for play, it is not for long, and becoming suddenly serious, as though he felt that he had committed himself in a moment of weakness he walks or swims very soberly away. He has a fine regard for the niceties too, and never interferes in conversation or speaks out of his turn, as Jelly often does. A visitor once said that Rawhide reminded him of some old man who had worked too hard when very young, and never had his childhood.

This methodical beast is something of an unsung hero; not that he does actually a great deal more than Jelly, but he is less spectacular and attracts less notice. Yet most of the undertakings that have been completed here, bear the stamp of his peculiar methods and devising. His studious attention to what he deems to be his duty, his quiet com-

Y

petence, and his unruffled and unconquerable poise, are on a different plane to Jelly's violently aggressive, but none the less effective programme. So repressed are his emotions and so hidden his reactions, and he carries on so unobtrusively, that he is something of an enigma, and I have not been able to, and perhaps never will, quite gauge the full measure of his sagacity. And as he sits sometimes so motionless, regarding me so steadily with his cool and watchful eye, I often wonder what he thinks of me.

> Jelly Roll, jovial, wayward and full of whims.
> Rawhide, calm, silent and inscrutable.
> These two; King and Queen of All the Beaver People,
> These are the Keepers of the Lodge.

VIII

Tolerance

" The brute tamer stands by the brutes, by a head's breadth only above
  them!
  A head's breadth, ay, but therein is hell's depth and the height up to
  Heaven."

PADRIAC COLUM

THUS says the poet. But with all due regard for his meaning,
if I understand him aright, I am inclined to disagree with
him. There is not so wide a difference between man and
beast as all that. Often I think that the term " brute " as
applied to a dissolute fellow is somewhat of a misnomer.
Brutes are rarely depraved, and at least with animals you
do not have to watch for symptoms of an overdeveloped
business instinct, nor is it necessary to guard against the
double dealings of self-interest. There is nothing much to
fear save a little wilful mischief and the odd misunderstanding. These cerebral shortcomings may perhaps be
the result of a lack of imagination, but it is very refreshing
to be confronted by constant evidences of sincerity, even if
they are at times a little vigorous. Few forms of affection
are more genuine than the guileless and intense devotion
that is given only by children and some animals.

As a man lives longer and longer in the woods, so he enter-
tains, if he be of an entertaining nature, an ever-increasing
respect and love for Wild Life in all its varied forms. He
hesitates at last to kill, and even when necessity demands
that he take life he does so with feelings of apology, even of
regret for the act. So natural and compelling is this
instinct for reparation that old Indians, not yet made self-
conscious of their pagan customs (many of which, by the

way, are rather beautiful and worth perpetuating), have a ritual fitting for such occasions in respect of the more highly esteemed creatures. Years ago I came to this attitude, and it enveloped me so slowly, and yet so surely, that it seemed at last to be the natural outcome of a life spent over-much in destroying rather than in building. I cannot believe that I am alone in this, but have pretty good evidence that of those whose experience has been such as to cause them to consider the matter at all, only the ignorant or un-thinking or the arrogant, or those governed by selfishness are not so affected, at least to some degree.

A man will always lack something of being a really good woodsman, in the finer sense, until he is so steeped in the atmosphere of the Wild and has become so possessed, by long association with it, of a feeling of close kinship and responsibility to it, that he may even unconsciously avoid tramping on too many flowers on his passage through the forest. Then, and then only, can he become truly receptive to the delicate nuances of a culture that may elude those who are not so tuned in on their surroundings. Many instances have I seen of men who, half-ashamed by the presence of spectators, yet had the courage to save the lives of ants, toads, snakes and other lowly creatures in the face of ridicule. And these were virile, hard-looking " he-men," to whom such abject forms of life should supposedly have been of small consideration. And speaking of toads and harmless types of snakes, and other ill-appearing but inoffensive and often beneficial beasts, their persecution is generally the outcome of fanatical hatred, springing from an unreasoning fear of them on the part of those who know nothing whatever about them.

There are many who walk through the woods like blind men. They see nothing but so many feet of board measure in the most magnificent tree that ever stood, and calculate only so many dollars to each beaver house. (With all due respect for economic necessities, there is, I believe, even a certain amount of sentiment present in some slaughter-houses.) For such the beauties of Nature do not exist, and their reactions to the scenic splendours that surround them are similar to that of a man I once accompanied to the top of an eminence, to view a wide-spread panorama of virgin pine forest that stretched from our feet into the blue distance. He looked at the scene before him—such a one as few men are privileged to see—and I thought him rapt with appreciation, when he presently remarked, "Gosh, wouldn't that look good all piled on skidways!"

The function of the forest is *not* exclusively that of providing lumber, though judicious and *properly controlled* garnering of a reasonable forest crop is essential to industry. There are many reasons, æsthetic, economic and patriotic, for the perpetuation of large tracts of unspoiled, *original* timber—exclusive of re-forestation. This last scheme should be carried on intensively, and commercial concerns should be obliged (and many of them do, to their credit) to plant six or a dozen trees for every one they cut, thus putting in their own crop, and so be made to keep their acquisitive eyes off some of Canada's remaining beauty spots, which will be irretrievably ruined if commerce has its way with them. There is plenty for all purposes, if patronage does not outdo honesty.

It is said that all creatures are put here for our exclusive use, to be our servants. Perhaps they are. Yet the abuse of servants is no longer popular; and no one will say that the deer are put in the woods expressly for the wolves to eat, or the spruce cones especially for the squirrels. And once in the woods we are apt to be not much greater than the wolves and squirrels, and are often less. Human beings, as a whole, deny to animals any credit for the power of thought, preferring not to hear about it and ascribing everything they do to instinct. Yet most species of animals can reason, and all men have instinct. Man is the highest of living creatures, but it does not follow as a corollary that Nature belongs to him, as he so fondly imagines. He belongs to it. That he should take his share of the gifts she has so bountifully provided for her children, is only right and proper; but he cannot reasonably deny the other creatures a certain portion. They have to live too. And he should at least use some discretion about it and not take the whole works. Proper use should without doubt be made of our natural resources, whether animal or of any other kind, but it could be done more in the spirit of one who, let us say, is walking in a lovely garden where he may gather, by invitation, choice blossoms sufficient for his needs. But only too often we (I say " we " because I too have not been altogether guiltless in the past) have acted like irresponsible children who, not satisfied with the bounty that should suffice them, must needs tramp down what they cannot carry away.

Man's unfair treatment of the brute creation is too well realized to need a great deal of comment. It varies all the way from neglect, and a callous disregard of any claims the animal may have on his (the man's) sense of fair play, to active cruelty. There are those who are able to indulge a craving for a sense of power, only by exercising it over others who cannot retaliate. This is weakness, not strength such as real power bestows, and from it springs the proverbial cruelty of the coward. The bravest men are generally the kindest, as I saw very often proven during the war; and when, on returning from active service, I heard and saw demonstrations of bitter and implacable animosity, I learned that only the weakling or the non-combatant can hate with such terrible intensity. You have to meet the enemy to appreciate him; and the frank hostility that is sometimes seen to exist between some of those belonging to different social strata, could be much ameliorated did each have a chance to cultivate the other. I have met the great, the near great, and the not great. Some say that the higher you go, the simpler and more unassuming they are. I will go further and say that wherever you go, be it up or down, they are quite usually—just people, real folks. Kindness, hospitality and consideration are not the prerogative of any class, and a difference in accent is no indication of any great difference in heart. I have met traffic policemen who were natural born gentlemen, and one of the kindest and most courteous hosts I ever had was an ex-bartender who was also an ex-pugilist; and I have dined with a patrician whose conversation missed on every cylinder. But he was an individual.

Titles can be convenient appendages whereby those who have them may be sufficiently bedeviled by those who have not; though I observe that few refuse them. Certainly, the great ones among us, title or no, once they know that you wish only to talk with them as one human to another, with mutual respect, as we should meet all men—when they find, to their relief, that you do not propose to cross swords with them in a crackling duel of splintery, two-edged trivialities, they can be as simple, kindly and unaffected as any son of the soil. And they have so genuine an interest in what you have to tell them and have, moreover, such very well-considered things to say, and they have, altogether, brought to so fine an art that priceless ability to put at his ease the stranger within their gate, that it is at once ascertained that therein lies the real secret of their greatness. And in this they seem to me to be very close in spirit to those great trees that stand so nobly, and yet so proudly tranquil, who never will offend, and who bring grace and elegance to the landscape that they dominate.

If this tolerant attitude is so desirable, nay essential, in our dealings with our fellow humans of whatever class, race or creed, all of whom can, when put to it, ask our aid if need be, would it not seem to be at least fair, a little like good sportsmanship, to permit ourselves just a little sympathy, to exercise some small amount of thought, in our dealings with those creatures who sometimes stand so badly in need of the consideration for which they cannot ask?

That chivalry towards the weaker in which man so prides himself, does not appear to any large extent, if at all, in his attitude towards dumb animals that are unable to upbraid him, or to contribute verbally to public opinion and so damn him. Man's general reactions to his contacts with the animal world (here I speak only of that unfortunately rather large class to whom these remarks apply) are contempt or condescension towards the smaller and more harmless species, and a rather unreasonable fear of those more able to protect themselves. There are many men who inspire our respect by their love for their horses, dogs and other animal companions; yet we still have the bull fight, which I once saw described as a game in which the whole effort of the human players, they having the odds all on their side, was to commit a series of fouls and expect applause for them. I am given to understand that in at least one country whose people regard with disgust this brutal " sport," certain dealers carry on a trade in old, worn-out horses who, as a reward for their long years of service, are shipped away to be tortured in the bull ring for the satisfaction of audiences whose ancestors for hundreds of years blackened the pages of history with the most fiendish cruelties, and annihilated a whole race of Indian people in the name of God. Dogs are still beaten to death in the harness by their owners, and so-called sportsmen, willing to take a chance which only the animal will have to pay for, take flying shots at distant or moving game, and frequently their only reaction to the knowledge that the beast has escaped to die a lingering death, is one of irritation at losing a trophy or some meat.

I had a hunting partner who in attempting such snap shooting, smashed the bottom jaw of a deer. Some days later we found it dead, on which he looked at the carcase and said " Well, you . . ., I got you anyway." Nor is this an extreme case. All through the woods, in hunting season, careless hunters allow maimed animals to escape them to either die in the throes of suffering, or to slowly starve to death owing to their inability to take care of themselves in a crippled condition. Whole species of valuable and intelligent animals have been exterminated for temporary gain, and useful varieties of birds have been destroyed to the point of annihilation (and in one case completely) to tickle the palates of gourmets.

Kindness to animals is the hall-mark of human advancement; when it appears, nearly everything else can be taken for granted. It comes about last on the list of improvements as a rule, so that by the time animal care has been allowed to assume a place of real importance in the curriculum of human activities, it will generally be found that most other social advancements have already been brought to a high degree of refinement, and it is perhaps not too much to say that, using animal welfare among a people as the lowest level in the gauge of their accomplishments, the degree of culture that they have attained to may be indicated by it.

Much of the cruelty perpetrated to provide fashionable adornment is not realized, or even suspected, by the wearers who, somewhat unjustly, get most of the blame. Few perhaps, if any, of those who wear one type of lamb's wool coat, know that the excellence of texture they demand, and which is merely ornamental, is obtained by beating the pregnant mother with sticks until she, in her terror and pain, gives premature birth to her young, who provide the skins, and I have heard that ranches or sheep farms are maintained to cater to this horrible industry. Not much comment is needed on this except, on my part, that the much played-up ferocity of the North American Indian supplies nothing quite like it, and that I would like very much to believe that the general public, including those who wear the coats, did they know of this most inhuman practice, would no longer countenance it.

It would seem as though the making of money would excuse almost anything, and that nearly any undertaking, however unethical, can be termed " business " and so get itself excused, provided it is successful and does not muscle in on some big-shot monopoly. Sheep, I know, are often skinned alive, and I hear that certain kinds of fish are cut in pieces from the tail to the head, so they will remain alive to the last, in order that jaded appetites may be stimulated by the crimped appearance of the flesh that is thus obtained. Is the mere shape of the food, then, of such consequence? Can anyone really be so childish? And perhaps fish do not feel; I cannot know, but I am pretty sure, from what I have seen, that those to whom these puerilities are of such consuming importance, number such unprofitable speculations among the least of their worries. However, I think we can agree that birds are capable of feeling, and I am given to understand that live ducks are crushed in a press for some outlandish dish designed for connoisseurs of food, and that larks and other song-birds are killed by thousands in some countries, and cooked to feed the delicate sensualism of epicures. I cannot believe that these little songsters were put on earth to feed gross appetites, but to give joy to mankind in another way, and even this gift of song is perverted by the bird-catchers, who have been known to blind the tiny eyes with needles, so the helpless little creatures should sing unceasingly, and then to put them in the nets as bait.

Vivisection may be necessary, lamentably, and medical men of the utmost honesty and sincerity may be working by this means for the good of humanity, and are perhaps as merciful as circumstances allow. We understand that important results are sometimes obtained. Yet the importance of the findings provides little surcease from suffering for the poor dumb brutes that are subjected for hours, even days, to excruciating agonies on our behalf. And many a cold-blooded torturer of sadistic inclinations performs, in the name of research, as has been proved, terrible experiments that are of little or no benefit to the human race. And benefit or no, I think the price is too great for any living creature to be called upon to pay, far greater than we have any right to ask.

Personally, I could not ever feel at ease if I knew that I had prolonged my not so important life by the infliction of long-drawn-out and agonizing pain on perhaps hundreds of helpless and inoffensive creatures, tortured until they died in misery that I might live, who some day must die in any case.

Every living creature is parasitical to some degree, in one way or another, on some other form of life, in order to live; but man extracts tribute from everything, even including the less fortunate of his own kind. Almost always he extorts far beyond his needs, destroying without thought for the future—the parasite supreme of all the earth. And in spite of the high position he has gained, he has still much to learn of tolerance, moderation and forbearance towards not only the lesser of created things, but towards his fellow-man.

And now I have discovered, in my slow way, that it is actually necessary in this day and age of our civilization, to enact legislation forbidding the exploitation of children in industry, and that in one year thousands of young people were injured, and not a few killed at their work, whilst profiteers waxed rich on the proceeds of their cheap labour. It is more than a little saddening to find that even children fall a prey to the predatory instincts of a mercenary ogre, and when I first heard of it, I found some difficulty in believing that it could be true and still cannot quite grasp why a *law* should be necessary to put a stop to it.

And now, have I offended you, my readers? It has not been my intention. But if in my ignorance and little knowledge I have erred, it is because in my late travels in the centres of civilization I have seen and heard much that was unexpected, some of it not easy to grasp and leaving me at times a little bewildered. We who live in the woods have different standards—not all of them good.

* * * * * *

I am still a hunter, in a little different way. The camera is my weapon today. It is, after all, more fun, and if sport is the object, a lot harder. Yet hunting calls into play many manly attributes and I would not, if I could, lay a hand to the suppression of this most noble sport (I do not refer here to either fox, stag, or otter hunting with hounds, all of which are, to my way of thinking, grossly unfair and exceedingly unsportsmanlike)—noble, that is, if carried on with at least a reasonable consideration for those creatures that are giving, not for your necessity, Mr. Sportsman, but for your amusement, all they have to give—their lives. I go so far as to say that in most cases, the circumstances of the hunt mean more to the average hunter—if he is a sportsman—than the actual kill itself. The healthful, invigorating exercise, the beauties of the scenic Wilderness, the zest of such achievements as are necessary in order to get around in a rough country, the tonic properties of the pure, fresh air, the association with his guides, the hearty meals over crackling camp fires, the romance and the adventure—all these things go to make a hunt worth while. And if you are lucky, a good, clean, merciful kill is excusable, provided the animal is put to proper use and not killed for the sake of its eye-teeth or a pair of horns, while several hundred pounds of the very best of meat are allowed to lie in the woods to rot. And hunting has this to recommend it, that everything you get you work for.

Me, I kill no more, unless in case of absolute necessity, having had perhaps my share and over. Some prefer to have a den full of trophies; others a hunting-lodge decorated with skins, maybe. Each to his own taste; I like mine alive.

I make no false claims that I am out especially to try and do the public good, or that I have some " message " for the world. I am only trying to do what little is within my power for those creatures amongst whom my life has been passed. And if by so doing I can also be of some little service to my fellow-man, the opportunity becomes a twofold privilege. I do not expect to accomplish much in the short span that is left to me, but hope to assist, even if only in a minor rôle, in laying a foundation on which abler hands and better heads may later build. In this way I may perhaps be instrumental, at least to some extent, in the work of saving from entire destruction some of those interesting and useful dwellers in our waste places, in whom lie unexpected possibilities that await but a little kindness and understanding to develop—the rank and file of that vast, inarticulate army of living creatures from whom we can never hear.

Quite the most interesting of the developments that have arisen from this self-imposed task of mine, has been the opportunity given me of coming into contact with people from every walk of life. I have been privileged to make many friends, and expect to make some more. These experiences are valuable to me, and apart from their educational angle and the broadening effect they have on my views in general, I enjoy them.

One of my most absorbing tasks is that of answering the letters I receive from schools. Some are written in a childish scrawl, some are smudged, others extremely neat with the lettering all erect and very soldierly; but every one is so carefully inscribed, and all bear the signs of the labour that has been put into them by their intensely sincere and hopeful writers—labours of love if ever there were any. And in this, above all things, am I greatly honoured. I try to answer them all, either collectively, or through their teachers, or, if the case should call for it, individually; for this is a responsibility I may not shirk.

This is to me my most important correspondence, for I feel that by this means it is given to me to build, even if only a very little, and to implant in fertile minds, anxious for knowledge, seeds that perhaps will blossom into deeds after the planter has been long forgotten.

EPILOGUE

And now the moon has risen here, on Ajawaan. It shines through a window and touches the peak of the beaver house that stands within.

I sit alone. And all the Voices of the Night are all around me, and swift rustlings, soft whisperings and almost noiseless noises encompass me about.

And the moon throws eerie shadows down along the aisles between the trees, where strange shapes and formless objects stand like waiting apparitions, where moonbeams lie in glimmering pools, and spots of light like eyes peer out from darksome ambuscade.

On the shore, in a little group, some tiny beavers sit, and sniff, and look, and whisper low, like children seeing goblins in a graveyard.

*　　　*　　　*　　　*　　　*　　　*

And now my Tales are done.

And as I wrote, I wonder if the actors in them did not come back from out the Past, and live again, and play their parts once more. And as I told of them and what they thought, and what they said or did, who can say but that they gathered there, around the Empty Cabin and listened, in that silent and enchanted grove of pine trees?

Perhaps the grove was no more silent, but was filled with all the voices of those whose tales were told here, long ago. And maybe the Cabin was not empty, but was filled again with movement, while its door stood wide in welcome and its window glowed with light, and its fire was burning brightly and it woke from all its dreaming, when those who once had lived here, lived again.

And the Cabin won't be empty any more, nor the grove again so silent and deserted, while yet remains a solitary reader whose sympathy and kindly understanding brings Life to that memory-haunted valley in the hills, and awakens those others, who have dreamed and waited there so long.

THE END